The Door Into Fire

"*The Door Into Fire* expands the limits of the sword and sorcery genre. Exciting, magical, intelligent."—*Publishers Weekly*

"Duane is a writer to pay attention to."—*F&SF Magazine*

"Arousing trumpet voluntary for Diane Duane's *The Door Into Shadow*. A fine tale of daring, caring, and sharing, of self-revelation and self-sacrifice, with a superbly realized religion, integrated into a civilization at risk to the evil side of that religious ethos. The Duane dragon Hasai is a 'gentleman' to be reckoned with and of special interest to me!"—Anne McCaffrey

The Door Into Shadow

"The *Door Into Shadow* is a delight: smooth, clear, strong prose, memorable characters, adventurous fantasy." — Marion Zimmer Bradley

"This fantasy sequel of *The Door Into Fire* is energetic and features original twists, some good ideas and lots of excitement...different and above average."—*The Kirkus Review*

"To my way of reckoning, this is an even stronger story than the first...I found it absorbing—the kind of book one reads in gulps and cannot put down...Her talent is outstanding in a field in which there are so many excellent craftspeople. I found her heroine one I could feel with and for...She is to be highly complimented on the whole book—which I hope will at least bring her a Hugo. This is one of those volumes one can read over again and find new points of interest in every reading."—Andre Norton, author of the *Witchworld* series

Tale of the Five:
The Sword and the Dragon

∾

by
Diane Duane

This is a work of fiction. All the characters and events portrayed in this book are fictitious. Any resemblance to real people or events is purely coincidental.

Door into Fire by Diane Duane © 1979
Door into Fire—author's prefered edition by Diane Duane © 2002
Door into Shadow by Diane Duane © 1984
Door into Shadow—author's prefered edition by Diane Duane © 2002
Tale of the Five: The Sword and the Dragon by Diane Duane © 2002

All rights reserved by the publisher. This book may not be reproduced, in whole or in part, without the written permission of the publisher, except for the purpose of reviews.

TALE OF THE FIVE: THE SWORD AND THE DRAGON

Published by Meisha Merlin Publishing, Inc.
PO Box 7
Decatur, GA 30031

Editing by Stephen Pagel
Copyediting, proofreading & interior layout by Teddi Stransky
Cover art by Don Maitz
Cover design by Kevin Murphy

ISBN: Hard cover: 1-892065-50-9
        Soft cover   1-892065-51-7

http://www.MeishaMerlin.com

First MM Pubnlishing edition: May 2002

Printed in the United States of America
0 9 8 7 6 5 4 3 2 1

Tale of the Five:
The Sword and the Dragon

As before, so again:
for David

Book One:

Door into Fire

Aye, night commes and Hee risith from the Flame;
Lyoun and Eagle loudlie cry His name:
The Phoenix that schall spurn the shatter'd Spere.
Hys Fire shall fede upoun his darkest Fear:
But nott yntil the Starres fall owt the Skye,
Dawn coms up Blue, and our Daye be past by...

   —rede fragment, *Héalhregebócan,*
   IV, 6-12

 one

Smiths and sorcerers come both from the same nest.

Chronicle of the White Eagle, XII, 54

Herewiss sat cross-legged on the parquet floor, his back braced against the wall, his eyes closed, and concentrated. Part of the problem was that he couldn't stop thinking of the thing resting across his upturned hands as a sword; a noisy feeling of weaponness trickled through him from it. *It* knew that it was a sword—that was the problem. It was good Darthene steel, folded on itself in its forging the required sixty times, and sealed with the Mastersmith's hallmark down on the rough tang of the metal. It knew that it was destined to be a killing weapon, an elegant, finely polished thing, soft of back, hard of edge, with the Mastersmith's distinctive forging pattern embedded like waves in water within its silver blade. It knew what it was for: woundings and death, the abrupt soft parting of flesh beneath its stroke, the sudden crunch into cloven bone...the taste of pain, like wine. It lay there across his hands, waiting to be presented with slayings as a banqueter waits eagerly for the first course.

No, dammit, Herewiss said to himself, and pulled away from the perception. *Sometimes I wish I weren't so sensitive. How the Dark can something dead know so well what it's for?*

—This is ridiculous. I should be able to impose my will on a piece of steel, for Goddess's sake. Maybe this way.

He took a moment to clear his mind, and then concentrated on seeing the thing in his hands not as a sword, but as a great number of particles of metal that just happened to be arranged in the long, rough bar shape he held. If it was filed down, it would be just so much steel-dust. See it that way, he told himself. *A thousand thousand glittering points of steel, bound together only loosely—soft, porous enough for a sorcery to pass through them—*

It took him a while, but he achieved the perception.

The metal fought him, trying again and again to become a killing instrument. It knew what it was for, and Herewiss couldn't say as much; but he was alive and concentrating, and that gave him a slight edge. Finally the blank presented itself the way he wanted to see it, as countless tiny brilliances, sparkling metallically as they danced about one another, shining like dust in sunlight.

All right. Now, then—

Holding the image in mind, he began to construct the sorcery he had planned. It was an old formula, one of the very few sorceries that had any power over life at all—a binding used to temporarily prevent the dying soul from leaving the body. However, Herewiss had made certain changes in the formula, since the soul he planned to slip among the glittering points of metal was nowhere near death. The words of the spell were hard and dull like black iron in the back of his mind as he linked them one through another like chain mail, the stress on the last syllable of each word sealing each ring closed. He sang the poem softly over and over inside him, adding link to link, until the spell surrounded the bright bar of metal like a wide sheath.

Herewiss had some trouble finishing the spell, welding the two sides of it together—like most circular spells, it wanted only to go on and on, building itself back inward until it had trapped the sorcerer inside its own coils and choked the life out of him. But he prevailed, and sealed the spell shut, and pulled himself away from it, inspecting it for flaws and undone links. There were none.

Now for the interesting part, he thought.

Sorcerers and Rodmistresses had been speculating for as long as anyone could remember on the question of why the Science and the Art killed their practitioners so young. Many people believed that sorcery chipped away slowly at the soul, so that when the soul became too small to support the body, the body died; and the blue Flame, of course, since it had power over both the giving and taking of life, as mere sorcery did not, had the same effect but more quickly. Herewiss's mother had been a Rodmistress, and he could remember hearing her laugh about the idea some years before. "Your soul is as big as you can make it," she had said to him as she walked through the Woodward's chicken yard, scattering grain for the hens, "and the only thing that can diminish its size is your decision to do so. Belief's a powerful influence, too—it's quite possible to talk yourself into an early grave, and climb in when the time comes." She had died three years later, at the age of twenty-eight.

Herewiss felt around inside himself, looking for his soul. He found it where it usually was, an amorphous silvery mass tucked down just a bit below his breastbone, snuggled up against the spine. The blue Fire was threaded all through it, a faint half-seen tracery like the lines of veins beneath the skin, glowing a pale blue-white. *Hold on,* he told the Flame, affectionate; *hold on for a while longer. It won't be too long now. This should work.*

He reached out and teased loose a strand of his soul-stuff. It stretched easily outward as he pulled at it. A faint trace of Flame came with it, twisting around its length, graining the strand with spiraling light like a unicorn's horn. Gently, for he didn't want to break the thread until he was ready, he eased it on outward and toward the dancing sparks of steel, into them, through them, and out again, and back in—winding the soul-stuff through the structure, beckoning it in and around, luring it onward with promises of Power about to be achieved. The Flame followed after, hopeful. Herewiss tangled the bit of himself like a bright cord, weaving it through itself again and again, drawing it finer and finer, silver wire thinning out to silver web, and always followed by that faint blue flow of Fire. Finally the steeldust glitter could hardly be seen at all for the sorcerer's weave stranded through it.

Herewiss stood back, then cut the web's attachment to him with one sharp word.

It hurt. He had expected it to, but he had no time now to deal with the ache. The entangled soul would start undoing itself almost immediately if he didn't bind it. He spoke in his mind the word that would activate the binding sorcery, and it heard him and responded on the instant, the hard dark links of restraint drawing in close around the shining bar, snicking in cold and tight like a sudden scabbard, prisoning the soul-stuff within.

He stepped back to make sure that the sorcery would hold without his immediate supervision. It did. He poked at it once, experimentally; it resisted him.

Satisfied, he broke trance and opened his eyes.

Herewiss had to blink for a few moments, his eyes watering with the seeming brightness of the tower room. The place was full of smith's furnishings; the forge took up the middle of the room, a wide brick pit with a downhanging bellows, and a pedal-powered grindstone stood in one corner. Anvils, ingots, and scraps of metal were everywhere. A number of blanks of the Darthene steel were leaned up in a row against one wall, like so many barrel-staves.

The fire in the forge was out, and the tools were racked up on the walls. Halwerd, his son, was also sitting on the floor, over against the other paneled wall beside the window; he had taken off his apron, and was doing an elaborate cat's cradle with a piece of string. Herewiss never tired of the joys of having a smaller version of himself around, and spent a few minutes just watching the child.

Halwerd sat there in his greasy green tunic, all dark curly hair and fierce concentration. He flipped his hands, and the cat's cradle turned suddenly into a mess. "Dark!" he said.

"You're too young to be swearing," Herewiss said with affection.

"I'm nine," Halwerd said, as if that should have been enough. "Did it work?"

"Yes."

"It doesn't look any different." The boy gazed across the room, and Herewiss looked down at the piece of metal he held.

"No, it doesn't. Well, we'll see if it holds up tonight. It's Full Moon; this is a good day for it. Though I could wait for the Maiden's Day Moon. What do you think?"

Halwerd considered gravely. "Do it tonight."

"All right."

Herewiss got up, wobbling from the backlash of the sorcery. "Oh my," he said. "I must be getting better at this...the backlash is hitting me faster than it used to."

"How many is this now?" Halwerd asked, starting the cat's cradle over again.

"Swords? Twenty-three. No, twenty-four. Cheer up, Hal, maybe this'll be the last one." Herewiss tossed the sword blank clanging onto the worktable and looked around him as he stretched. He was a tall, slender man, lean and lithe and dark-haired, with a finely featured face and a mouth that smiled a great deal. His arms and shoulders were well muscled from much work at the forge, but not yet overly so. At first glance he gave an impression of spare, restrained power, the taut strength of youth. But his deep blue eyes were beginning to look weary, and his face was gradually acquiring frown lines. "Be nice to turn this back into a bedroom," he said, "and get all this mess out of here, Dark eat it—"

"Grampa would say," Halwerd said, "'you're not a good example. Watch your mouth.'"

"So he would. Listen, Hal—"

A pigeon landed on the windowsill with a clapping of wings. It strutted there, fluffing its gray-and-white feathers and looking confused. Herewiss looked at it, momentarily startled, and then unease began to trickle coldly down his back. It was one of the homing pigeons that he had given Freelorn for use in emergencies.

"Hold still, Hal." He walked smoothly around the forge to the window. In one quick motion he grabbed the pigeon before it had a chance to shy away. Stripping off the steel message-case, he threw the bird out the window, and fumbled at the little capsule with suddenly sweaty hands.

The stiff hinge cracked open, and the expected roll of parchment fell out on the floor. Herewiss picked it up, unrolling it, and the throbbing in his head quickened pace. The message said:

> AM HOLED UP IN OLD KEEP THREE LEAGUES SOUTH OF MADEIL. A FEW HUNDRED STELDENE REGULARS AND ABOUT SEVEN HUNDRED CONSCRIPTS BESIEGING ME AND THE GROUP. I NEED A COMPETENT SORCERER TO COME GET ME OUT OF THIS RABBIT-HOLE. HAVE ENOUGH FOOD TO LAST US A FEW WEEKS, BUT MUCH LONGER THAN THAT AND IT WILL BE BOOT-CHEWING TIME. GET ME THE DARK OUT OF HERE AND I'LL BE YOUR BEST FRIEND. THE GODDESS SMILE ON YOU. FREELORN AS'T'RAID ARLENI.

"'High Lord of all Lords of Arlen', my—! You know, I am a bad example, Hal. Listen, did you see where your grandfather was?"

"He was down in the writing room a while ago," Halwerd said. "What happened?"

"Your Uncle Freelorn may be back for a visit in a month or so," Herewiss said, heading for the door, "but I have to go and get him first. Forget it, Hal, go get yourself some lunch."

"All right."

Herewiss loped down the long paneled stairway that curled around the inner wall of the tower, and hit the bottom of the stairs running. He went down the south corridor at full speed, ignoring the surprised looks of household people and relatives, and ducked into the sixth room to his left. It was a bright, warm place, full of the rich carving work typical of the Woodward. The fireplace was framed in the wings of carven sphinxes, and two-bodied dogs guarded the corners where the moldings met. Over one closet was carven in slightly frantic figures the history of the sixteenth Lord of the Brightwood, who had married a mermaid. The sunlight gleamed from the woodwork, and from the great brassbound table that stood on eagle-claw feet in the middle of the room; but its surface was bare, and no one had been working there for some time.

I hope he didn't go out, Herewiss thought. *Damn!* He ran out of the room again, turned left and headed to the end of the south corridor. A stair led down from it to the central hall of the Woodward, where the Rooftree grew. He had no patience for the stairs, but hopped up onto the central banister, which had been polished smooth first by its craftsmen and then by the backsides of generations of the children of the Ward. At the bottom of the stairs he took a bare moment to nod courtesy to the Tree before he loped off across the tapestried hall, and out into the sunlight of the outer courtyard.

His father was there, kneeling in a newly dug flowerbed and setting in seedlings. Hearn Halmer's son was an average-looking man, a little on the lean side, dark-haired except for the places where he was going gray on the sides. He had the usual lazy, sleepy expression of the males of the Brightwood ruling line, the usual blue eyes, and the large hands that could be so very delicate. Those hands had been mighty in war, so that Hearn had led his people through two battles with the Reavers and one border skirmish with only a cut or two. This had prompted some to suggest that he had pacted with the Shadow, and had brought his relieved family to refer to him as "Old Ironass." Now, though, he no longer rode to the wars, and it was often hard for visitors to the Woodward to reconcile the conquering Lord of the Brightwood with the quiet, gentle man who could usually be found training ivy up the Ward's outer wall.

"Father," Herewiss yelled, "he's doing it again!"

Hearn sat back on his heels in the loose dirt, brushing off his hands, and looked over at his son.

"Who?"

"Here," said Herewiss, coming up and holding out the parchment, "read it!"

"My hands are dirty," Hearn said as Herewiss knelt down beside him. "Hold it for me."

"Dirty? It hardly matters if it gets dirty—" But Herewiss held it out. His father rested hands quietly on knees and read it through. After a moment he snorted. "As't'raid Arléni, my ass!"

"That's what I said."

"Not in front of Hal, I hope."

"Father, please."

"So," Hearn said, "you're surprised?"

Herewiss laughed, a short rueful sound. "No, not really."

"And so you're going riding off to get him out of whatever he's gotten himself into."

"May I?"

"You're asking me?"

"You're the Lord."

Hearn chuckled and took a seedling out of the cup of water beside him. Herewiss noted with amusement that it was one of the ceremonial cups for Opening Night, the rubies flaring in the sunlight and making bright dots of reflection in the mud. "Could I stop you? Could the Queen of Darthen stop you? Could our Father the Eagle stop you if He showed up? Go on. But when you see that idiot, tell him from me that he'd better not sign himself as King of Arlen unless he's willing to do something about it."

"I had that in mind."

"You'd never say it, though, you're too damn kind. You tell him I said it. Will you be needing men?"

"I'm sorcerer enough to handle this myself, I think. And the less people involved, the better. If Cillmod hears that Brightwood people were involved, it could be excuse enough for him to break the Oath again and move in on Darthen."

Hearn planted the seedling. "There speaks my wise son," he said.

"And besides—I don't want any Wood people getting killed because of this. And neither do you—but you'd never say it—because you're too damn kind."

Hearn laughed softly. "My wise son. But don't let it stop you from bringing him back here if he needs a place to stay. No one will hear about it from us."

Herewiss nodded and stood up.

"Take what you need," Hearn said. "Take Dapple, if you think he'd help. And Herewiss—"

Hearn turned back to his work, his strong hands moving the soil. "Be careful. I'm short of sons."

Herewiss stood there looking at his father's back for a moment, and then turned and headed back into the Woodward to start preparing for a journey.

The Brightwood is the most ancient and most honored of the principalities of Darthen. It was the first of the new settlements established after the Worldwinning, by people who came down out of the eastern Highpeaks and found the quiet woodlands to their liking after their long travels. It took them many years to free the Wood and its environs from the Fyrd that infested it, but while many other peoples were still living in caves in the mountains, the Brightwood people were already building the Woodward in the great clearing at its center.

Though the Woodward is held by outsiders to be at the Wood's heart, the Brightwood people know that its real heart—or hearts, for there are several—lie elsewhere, in the Silent Precincts, secret, holy places where few people not born in the Wood or trained to the usages of the Power have ever walked. There, upon the Forest Altars hidden within the Precincts, the Goddess was first worshipped again as She used to be before the Catastrophe—invoked in Her three forms as Maiden and Mother and Wise Woman. There too Her Lovers are worshipped, those parts of Herself which rise and fall in Her favor, eternally replacing one another as Her consorts. Even the Lovers' Shadow is worshipped there, though with cautious and propitiatory rites enacted at the dark of the Moon. Other places of the worship of the Pentad there may be, but there are none older or more revered except the Morrowfane, which is the Heart of the World and so takes precedence.

Night with its stars spread over the Wood, and the pure silver moonlight made vague and doubtful patterns on the grass as it shone through the branches. Spring was well underway; the night was full of the smell of growing things, and the chill wind laced itself through the new leaves with a hissing sound.

In the center of the little clearing, before the slab of moon-white marble set into the ground, Herewiss knelt shivering. An indefinite dappling of moonshine and shadow shifted and blurred on his bare body and gleamed dully from the sword he held before him. It was beaten flatter than it had been that morning, and had some pretense of an edge on it; but it was not finished yet. Herewiss had learned better than to waste time putting hilts and finishing on these swords before he tried them with this final test.

The dappled horse tethered at the edge of the clearing stamped and snorted softly, indignant over having to be up at this ridiculous hour. But right now Herewiss had no sympathy for him, and he shut the sound out as he prayed desperately. This had to work. It had to. He had done a good day's spelling, a good piece of work, though he had paid dear for it, both in backlash and in the pain cutting away part of his self had cost him. But it might work. No, it *had to*. This was the Great Altar, the Altar of the Flame, the one most amenable to what he was doing, the one with the most bound-up power. And this sword felt better than any of the others he had tried; more *alive*. Maybe he had managed to fool the steel into thinking it lived. And if he had fooled it, then it would conduct the Power. His focus, his focus at last—

O Three, he said within himself, for no word may be spoken in those places, *Virgin and Mother and Mistress of Power, oh let this be the last time. Goddess, You're never cruel without a reason. You wouldn't give me the seed of Fire and then let it die in bondage. Let the Power of this place enter into me and kindle the spark into full Flame. And let that Flame flow down through this my sword as it would through a Rod, were I a woman. Oh, please, my Goddess, my Mother, my Bride, please. Let it work. In Your name, who are our beginnings and our endings—*

He bowed his head, and then looked up again, shuddering with cold and anxiety, and also with weakness left over from that morning's sorcery. If only it would work. It would be marvelous to go riding off to Freelorn's rescue with a sword ablaze with the blue Fire. To strike the whole besieging army stiff and helpless with the Flame, and break the walls of the keep in the fullness of his Power, and bring Freelorn out of there. To strike terror into the army just by being what he was—the first man to bear Flame since the days of Lion and Eagle! And the look in Freelorn's eyes. It would be so—

Herewiss sighed. *I never learn, do I. Let's see what happens.*

Delicately, carefully, he set the sword's point on the white stone of the altar, and took hold of the rough hilt with both hands. Herewiss became aware of a change, a stirring; something in the air around him moved, waited expectantly. His underhearing, that inner sensitivity that anyone experienced in sorcery develops, whispered that the Power of the place was moving about him, surrounding him, watching. His own Power rose up in him, a cold restless burning all through his body, demanding to be let out.

Herewiss lifted the sword away from the stone, and held it straight up before him, point upward, watching moonlight and shadow tremble along the length of the blade with the trembling of his hands. And he reached down inside him, where the Flame was running hot now, molten, seething like silver in the crucible, and he channeled it up through his chest and down through his arms and out through his hands—

The sound was terrible, a thunderous silent shout of frustration and screaming anger as the blue Fire, the essence of life, smote against something that had never lived, had never even been fooled into thinking that it lived. *A silly idea*, Herewiss thought in the terribly attenuated moment between the awful unsound and the sword's destruction. *As if plain sorcery could ever mix successfully with the Flame. Stupid idea.*

And the sword blew apart. Fragments and flying splinters shot up and out with frightening force, gleamed sporadically as they flew through light and shadow, ripping leaves off branches, burying themselves in the grass. One of them struck itself into Herewiss's upper arm, and another into his leg just above the knee, though not too deeply. A third went by his ear like the whisper of death. He held in his cry of terror, remembering where he was, and dropped the hilt-end of the shattered sword in the grass.

He plucked the metal fragment out of his arm and threw it into the grass, grimacing. For a long while Herewiss knelt there, bent over, hugging himself as much against the bitter disappointment as against the cold. *I was so sure it would work this time. So sure.*

Finally he regained some of his composure, finished picking the splinters out of himself, and turned to make farewell obeisance to the Altar. It seemed to crouch there against the ground, cold white stone, ignoring him.

He forgot about the obeisance. He went straight over to Dapple and got dressed, and rode away from there.

It was several minutes before he passed the marker that indicated the end of the Silent Precincts. Just the other side of it he paused, looking up through the leaves at the starlit sky. "Dammit," he yelled at the top of his lungs, "what am I doing wrong? Why won't you tell me? *What am I doing wrong?*"

The stars looked down at him, cold-eyed and uncaring, and the wind laughed at him.

He kicked Dapple harder than necessary, and rode out of the Wood to Freelorn's rescue.

 *two*

If the cat who shares your house will not speak to you, remember first that cats, like the Goddess their Mother, never speak unless there is something worth saying, and someone who needs to hear it.

Darthene Homilies, Book 3, 581

They were called the Middle Kingdoms because they were in the middle of the world as men then knew it. To the north was the great Sea, of which little was known. Ships had gone out into it many times, seeking for the Isles of the North mentioned in tale and rumor, but if those Isles existed, no ship had found them and returned to tell the tale. To the west, beyond the far western border of Arlen, a great impassable range of mountains reared up. Legend said that the demons' country of Hreth lay beyond them, but no one particularly cared to brave the terrible snow-choked passes to find out. Southward lay more mountains, the Highpeaks or Southpeaks, depending on whether you were speaking Arlene or Darthene; no one had even ventured far enough into them to find out if they ever ended, though there were stories of the Five Meres hidden among them. Eastward, past the river Stel, the eastern border of Steldin and Darthen and civilized lands in general, the land stretched away into great empty desert wastes. Many had tried to cross them; most came back defeated, and the rest never came back at all. Those who did come back would occasionally speak of uncanny happenings, but most of the time they flatly refused to discuss the Waste. The Dragons might have known more about what went on there, or in the lands over the mountains—but Dragons would only talk to the human Marchwarders who are sometimes their companions, and the Marchwarders, when asked, would only smile and shake their heads.

The Kingdoms were four: Arlen, Darthen, Steldin, and North Arlen. Through them were scattered various small independent cities and principalities. The Brightwood was one of these, though like most of the smaller autonomies it had joined itself to a larger Kingdom, Darthen, for purposes of trade and protection. Arlen and Darthen were the two oldest Kingdoms, and the greatest; between them they stretched straight across all the known lands, from the mountains to the Waste Unclaimed, slightly more than three hundred leagues. The river Arlid, which flows from the Highpeaks to the Sea, south to north, a hundred leagues or so, defined the border between them. It was not a guarded border, for the two lands had been bound by oaths of peace and friendship for hundreds of years. That, however, might change shortly...

Herewiss rode along through the sparsely wooded, hilly country three days' journey south of the Brightwood, and thought about politics. It seemed that there was nothing in the world that could be depended upon. The Oath of Lion and Eagle had been sworn for the first time nearly twelve hundred years ago, and sworn again every time a king or queen came to the throne in either country—until now. When Freelorn's father King Ferrant had died on the throne six years past, Freelorn had been in Darthen; but it might not have been possible for Freelorn to claim the kingship even if he had been in Prydon city when it happened. Ferrant had not yet held the ceremony of affirmation in which the White Stave was passed on to his son, and Freelorn's status was therefore in question. Power had been seized shortly thereafter by a group of the king's former counselors, backed by mercenary forces hired by the former Chancellor of the Exchequer; and this lord, a man named Cillmod, had declared Freelorn outlawed.

These occurrences, though personally outrageous to Herewiss, were not beyond belief. Such things had happened before. But six months ago, armed forces, both mercenaries and Arlene regulars, had moved into Darthen and taken land on the east side of the Arlid. Though the Oath had not been sworn again by Arlen's new rulers, that did not make it any less binding on them. In all the years since its first swearing at the completion of the Great Road, neither country had ever attacked the other. Herewiss was nervous; he felt as if lightning were overdue to strike.

"Listen," his father had said to him, leaning on the doorpost of Herewiss's room three days before, "are you sure you don't want some people to take with you?"

"I'm sure." Herewiss had been packing; he stood before his bookshelf, choosing the grimoires he would take with him. "Notice would be taken—there would be reprisals later. The situation would only get worse. And even with the biggest force we could muster, we wouldn't have a third enough people to crack a siege that size. Besides, our people need to be here, putting in crops." Herewiss took down a thick leather-bound book, filled with notes and spells of illusion.

"That's so...have you got food?"

"Plenty." Herewiss dropped the book in his saddlebag, along with another that already lay on the bed. The ornate carving of bed and paneling and windows was lost in evening dark, and only an occasional warm highlight showed in the light of the single oil lamp on the bedside table. "I cleaned out the pantry. I have enough trail food to last me through four years of famine, and I ate a big dinner." He went over to a chest, lifted the lid and took out a white surcoat emblazoned with the arms of the Brightwood: golden Phoenix rising from red flame, the third-oldest arms in the Kingdoms. "Should I take this, do you think?"

"Is there some formal occasion out in the wilds that you're planning to attend?"

"No. But if I need to exert political pull, it might come in handy."

"You could take my signet."

"What if I lost it? That's almost the oldest thing in the Wood; I'd never forgive myself if something happened to it. No, hang on to it. The surcoat should be enough—the device could be counterfeited, but the gold in the embroidery's real." He folded up the surcoat, stowed it in the saddlebag.

"Do you want some mail?"

"No. I'm going to travel light so I can move fast. Besides, why bother giving anyone the idea that I might be worth robbing? I've got that damn turtle-shell of a leather corselet, and I have plenty of padding, and that nice light Masterforge knife you gave me last Opening Night. And the spear; and the cloak is good and thick—Anybody who gets past all that probably deserves to kill me...and if they do, it'll prove that you and Mard were wasting your talents on me these sixteen years." Herewiss stood up straight from checking his bags. "Besides, I inherited your iron britches. Don't worry so much."

Hearn looked with concern at his son. Clothed in dark tunic and breeches and riding boots, cloaked in brown, Herewiss seemed one more shadow of the many in the room. The lamplight reflected from his eyes, and from the metal fittings of the empty scabbard hanging from his belt. "Son," Hearn said, "I'm not too worried about you. But the pattern that's been forming bothers me. I worry about Freelorn. Not so much the fact that he's been running around the Kingdoms like a crazy person for the past six years, staying at petty kings' courts until someone finds out he's there and tries to poison him. He's pretty alert about such things, usually. Or the business of his running around with his little swordtail and stealing for a living. He seems to steal from people who need it. But lately he's been coming to grief a bit too often, just missing getting caught— and you've been having to go and get him out of these scrapes. And now this; here he is, stuck in this old keep with a thousand Steldenes waiting to starve him out—and *you're* going to go get him out of it. Alone. Herewiss, it's not really safe."

"I'll manage," Herewiss said. "What are you thinking, father?"

"This. What happens when he gets into something that you can't get him out of?"

"By then I hope I'll have my Power…"

"But you don't have it yet, and if you get killed for Freelorn's sake, you never will. Son of mine—" and Herewiss's underhearing brought him a sudden wash of his father's sorrow, a feeling like eyes filling with tears—"I've long since reconciled myself to the fact that you're going to die young—by use of the Flame, or more slowly by all this sorcery. Yet I want you to be what you can. Here you are, the first male in an age and a half to have even the small amount of Fire you have—the first sign that the Kingdoms are getting back to the way things were before the Catastrophe. But you have to *live* to be what you can. At least for a little longer. And Freelorn is endangering you."

"Father," Herewiss said very softly, "what good is the Power to me if Lorn dies? He's the only thing I need as much as the Flame. Life would be empty without him; the Fire would mean nothing to me. There *are* priorities."

"Is your life one of them?"

Herewiss reached out, took his father's hands in his. "Da, listen. I won't follow Lorn into any of his famous last stands or impossible charges. I'll try not to let him get *into* them. I'd like to see him king, yes—but I won't let him drag me into some crazy scheme that has a dead Dragon's chance against the Dark of succeeding. However, I also won't let him get killed if there's any way I can help it—and if my life is the price of his continuing, well, there it is. I can't help how I feel."

Hearn sighed softly. "You're a lot like your brother," he said, "and just as hard to reason with. I gave you the oak as your tree at your birth, my son, and sometimes I think your head is made of it…"

"It was a good choice," Herewiss said, smiling faintly. "Lightning strikes oak trees more than any other kind. And I have to be crazy sometimes: I have a reputation to uphold. 'The only thing sure about the Lords' line of the Wood—'"

"'—is that there's nothing sure about them,'" his father finished, smiling too. "Fool."

"They told Earn our Father that He was a fool at Bluepeak, and look what happened to Him."

"I would sooner be father to a live son," Hearn said, "than to a dead legend."

"I'll be careful," said Herewiss.

"Have a safe journey, then. And good hunting."

So Herewiss had taken his leave of his other relatives and friends in the Woodward, and had said good-bye to the Rooftree, and then had stopped in the stable to choose a horse. He had originally been of a mind to take Darrafed, his little thoroughbred Arlene mare, a present from Freelorn—or perhaps Shag, his father's curly-coated bay warhorse. But as he had walked down the aisle between the stalls, Dapple had put his head out over his stall's half-door and looked at Herewiss as if he knew something. Herewiss was not one to ignore a sign when it presented itself.

The horse moved comfortably through the low hill country. As long as he kept to a steady southward course, Herewiss let Dapple have his head. The horse was a wise one. About a hundred years before, a Rodmistress had put her deathword on one of Dapple's ancestors and had decreed that the horses of that line would always have a talent for being in the right place at the right time. The talent had seemed to do their riders good as well. One horse, the third generation down, had carried an unsuspecting lady to the arms of the lover who had searched the Middle Kingdoms for her for twelve years. Another had led its thirteen-year-old mistress to the place where the royal Darthene sword, Fórlennh BrokenBlade, had been hidden during the Reavers' invasion of Darthis City. Having Dapple along, Herewiss reasoned, would make his father worry less—and might incidentally ease his way as he worked on getting Freelorn out of that keep.

For three days he had been riding through empty land. It was not bare—Spring had run crazy through the fields, as if drunk on rose wine, flinging wildflowers and garlands of new greenery about with inebriated extravagance. The hills were ablaze with suncandle and Goddess's-delight, tall yellow Lovers'-cup lilies and heartheal. Butterwort and red and blue never-say-die clambered up the gullies toward the hillcrests, and white mooneyes covered the ground almost everywhere that grass did not. But there were no people, no homesteads. For one thing, the land was poor for farming. For another, that part of the country was full of Fyrd.

The Fyrd had always been in the Kingdoms. They were said to be children of the Shadow, sent by Him to spread death and misery in the Goddess's despite: or even creations of the Dark itself, changed things which had been made from normal animals when the Dark still covered the world. Whatever the case, most of North Darthen was still full of the major Fyrd species—horwolves, nadders, keplian, lathfliers, maws, and destreth. In Herewiss's time, the land around the Wood was free of them, kept that way by constant use of the Power and the cold-eyed accuracy of Brightwood archers. But outside the Wood's environs the Fyrd raided constantly, taking great numbers of livestock, and also men when they could get them. Sheep were pastured here in the hill country, but all the shepherds came up together after the Maiden's Day feasts. Both flocks and men stood a better chance in large numbers.

The hills were thinning out now, and farms were slowly beginning to appear. They became more frequent as Herewiss and Dapple descended into the lowlands, and one very large farm with stone markers at its boundaries indicated that Herewiss was close to the town he had been expecting to reach that evening. The farm was the holding of a prominent Darthene house, the Lords Arian. He could have stopped there and received excellent hospitality, being after all the next thing to a prince; but attention drawn to himself was the last thing he wanted at this point.

He rode on down from the hills, crossing a rude stone bridge over the Kearint, a minor tributary of the river Darst, and came to the forty-house town of Havering Slides just as dusk was falling. Most of the people who lived there were hands on the big Arian farm. Herewiss rode up to the gate in the wooden palisade around the town, identified himself and was admitted without question.

The inn was as he had remembered it from earlier visits, a motley-looking place with a disjointed feeling to it; new buildings ran headlong into old ones, and afterthought second storeys sagged on their supports over uneasy-looking bay windows. It seemed that some of the artisans who had done carving work in the Woodward had also passed this way. The gutterspouts were fashioned into panting hound-faces and singing frogs; crows stealing cheese in their wooden beaks leered down from the cupolas.

Herewiss rode up to the stable door and handed Dapple over to the girl in charge. As he strode toward the doorway of the inn, his saddlebags slung over his shoulder, he was greeted by the sudden and beautiful odor of roast beef. After three days of nourishing but tasteless journey rations, the prospect of real food seemed almost an embarrassment of luxury. He paused at the door just long enough to admire the carving over it, a cross-grain bas-relief of a local Rodmistress casting the Shadow out of a possessed cow.

Herewiss pushed open the door and went in. It took his eyes a few minutes to get used to the dim interior of the place, though there were oil lamps all around. He was standing in a fairly large common room crowded with tables and chairs and long trestled benches. The room was not too full, it still being early in the evening. Several patrons sat about a table, dicing for coppers, and off in one corner a hulking farmer was devouring a steak pie in great mouthfuls.

The steak pie particularly interested Herewiss. Bags in hand, he went to the kitchen door, which was carved with dancing poultry, and knocked.

The door opened, and the innkeeper looked out at him cordially. She was a tall slender woman, gray-haired but pretty, in a brown robe and a long stained apron. "Can I help you, sir?" she said, wiping her hands on a dirty gray towel.

"Madam," Herewiss said, bowing slightly, "food and lodging for the night for myself and my horse would do nicely."

"Half an eagle," the innkeeper said, looking at his clothes, which were in good repair.

"A quarter," said Herewiss, smiling his most charming smile at her. She smiled back at him. "A quarter eagle and threepence."

"Two."

The innkeeper smiled more broadly. "Two it is. Your horse is inside?"

"He is, madam."

"Dinner?"

"Oh, *yes*," Herewiss said. The good smells coming out of the kitchen were making his stomach talk. "Some of what that gentleman is having, if there's another one…"

She nodded. "Anything to drink? We have wine, red and white and Delann yellow; brown and black ale; and my husband made a fresh barrel of Knight's Downfall yesterday."

"Ale sounds good: the black. Which room should I take?"

"Up the stairs, turn right, third door to your left." The innkeeper disappeared back into the kitchen's steam.

Herewiss hurried up the creaking stairs and found the room in question. It was predictably musty, and the floor groaned under him. The shutters screeched in protest when he levered them open to let the sunset in, but he was so glad to have a hot meal in the offing that the place looked as good as any king's castle to him. He dropped his bag in the corner, under the window, and changed into another clean dark tunic; then headed for the door. Halfway through the doorway, an afterthought struck him. He raised his hands to draw the appropriate gestures in the air, and since no one was near, spoke aloud the words of a very minor binding, erecting a lockshield around his bags. Then down the stairs he went.

Herewiss sat down at an empty table in a corner and spent a few moments admiring the window nearest him, which was a crazy amalgam of bottle-glass panes and stained vignettes. One of them, done in vivid shades of rose, cobalt, and emerald, showed the end of the old story about the man who fooled the Goddess into lifting her skirts by confronting Her with an illusion-river. There he lay under the trees at Harvest festival, inextricably stuck to and into an illusionary lover, while the Goddess and the harvesters stood around and laughed themselves weak. The man looked understandably mortified, and very chastened. He had been very lucky that he'd played his trick on the Mother aspect of the Goddess; had She been manifesting as the Maiden at the time, She might not have been so kind. The Mother tends to be forgiving of Her children's pranks, but the Maiden can be fatally jealous of Her modesty.

Someone blocked the light, and Herewiss looked up. Before him stood a girl of perhaps eighteen years, pretty in a bland sort of way, with a droopy halo of frizzing black hair. She bent in front of Herewiss, putting his steak pie and ale on the old scarred table. Herewiss took brief disinterested notice of the view down her blouse, but much more of his attention was on the steak pie.

"Nice," he said. "A fork, please?"

"Hmm?" She in her turn was being very interested in Herewiss.

"A fork?"

"Oh. Yes, certainly—" She reached into her pocket and brought one out for him. Herewiss took it, wiped it off, and hurriedly dug into the pie.

"Ahh, listen," she said, bending down again, and Herewiss began an intensive study of a piece of potato, "are you busy this evening?"

Herewiss did his best to look up at her with profound sorrow. She really wasn't his type, and there was a mercenary look in her eye that sent him hurriedly to the excuse box in the back of his head. "If you're thinking what I think you are," he said, "I'm sorry, but I'm under vows of chastity."

"You don't look like you're in an Order," she said.

"Perpetual chastity," Herewiss said. "Or until the Lion comes back. Sorry."

The girl stood up. "Well," she said, "if you change your mind, ask the lady in the kitchen where I am. I'm her daughter."

Herewiss nodded, and she went away into the kitchen. He sagged slightly as the door closed behind her, and settled back against the wall.

That was a bit panicky of me, Herewiss thought as he began to eat. *I wonder what it is about her that bothers me so—*

He put the thought aside and concentrated on the hot-spiced food and the heavy ale. The common room began slowly to fill up while Herewiss ate, as the local clientele came in from the fields and houses to enjoy each other's company. Soon the big table nearest him was occupied by a noisy, cheerful group of farmers from the Arian landholdings, nine or ten brawny men and lithe ladies, all deeply tanned and smelling strongly of honest work. They called loudly for food and drink, and hailed Herewiss like a brother when they spotted him in his corner. He smiled back at them, and before long they were exchanging crude jokes and bad puns, and laughing like a lot of fools.

When their table and Herewiss's were being cleared of emptied plates, and tankards were being refilled, the inn's cat came strolling by. It was greeted politely by the farmers, and offered little pieces of leftover meat or game. The cat accepted some of these, declined others graciously and in silence, and went on by, making its rounds. As it passed it looked hard at Herewiss, as if it recognized him. He nodded at it; the cat looked away as if unconcerned, and moved on.

As the ale flowed and the evening flowered, the storytelling and singing began in earnest. Most of the stories were ones already known to everyone there, but no one seemed to care much about that—Kingdoms people have a love of stories, as long as the story wears a different face each time. Someone began with the old one about what Ealor the Prince of Darthen had done with the fireplace poker, which was later named Sarsweng and had its haft encrusted with diamonds. Then someone else got up and told about something more recent, news only a hundred and five years old, how the lady Faran Fersca's daughter had gone out with her twelve ships to look for the Isles of the North, and how only one ship had come back after a year, and what tale its captain told. The story was related in an unusual fashion, sung to an antique rhyme-form by a little old lady with a surprisingly strong soprano. There was a great deal of stamping and cheering and applause when she finished; and several people, judging correctly that the lady was quite young inside, whatever her apparent age, propositioned her immediately. She said yes to one of the propositions, and she and the gentleman went upstairs immediately to more applause.

In the commotion, the lute was passed around to the farmers' table and one of them started to sing the song about the Brindle Cat of Aes Arädh, how it carried away the chief bard of a Steldene king on its back because of an insulting song he had sung before the Four Hundred of Arlen, and what the bard saw in the Otherworld to which the cat took him. Herewiss joined in on the choruses, and one of the ladies at the farmers' table noticed the quality of his voice and called to him, "You're next!" He shook his head, but when the man with the lute was finished, it was passed back to him. He looked at it with resignation, and then smiled at a sudden memory.

"All right," he said, pushed his chair back, and perched himself on the edge of the farmers' table, pausing a moment to tune one of the strings that had gone a quarter-tone flat. The room quieted down; he strummed a chord and began to sing.

Of the many stories concerning the usage of the blue Fire, probably the most tragic is that of Queen Béaneth of Darthen and her lover Astrin. Astrin was taken by the Shadow's Hunting one Opening Night, and Béaneth went to her rescue. That rescue seemed a certain thing, for Béaneth was a Rodmistress, one of the great powers of her time. But the price demanded of her for Astrin's release was that Béaneth must mate with the Shadow, and take into herself whatever evil He would choose for her to bear. Béaneth, knowing that the evil to grow within her would warp her Power to its own use, lay down with the Shadow indeed, but killed herself at the climax of the act, thereby keeping her bargain and obtaining her loved's release.

Her little daughter Béorgan was five years old when all this happened. Béorgan made the decision early to avenge her mother, and determined that she would meet the Shadow on His own ground and destroy Him. She trained, and grew great in Power—and also in obsession—waiting and preparing for Nineteen-Years' Night, that night when it is both Opening Night and Full Moon. All the Kingdoms know how the story ends—how Béorgan went down to the Morrowfane on that night, being then twenty-four years of age, and opened the Morrowfane Gate beneath the waters of Lake Rilthor, and passed through into the Otherworlds. There she met the Shadow, and there she slew Him, on one of the only nights this may be done, when the Goddess's power conjoins with the returning Sun past midnight. Béorgan's triumph was short-lived, though, and so was she. She had never planned her life past that night, and in a short time wasted away and died. Even her victory was hollow, for however bright the Lover may be, still he casts the Shadow: seven years after He died, He was back again, leading the Hunting as always.

Freelorn had always loved the story, and some years back had composed a verse form of it, and a musical setting that Herewiss had liked. At the time, though, Freelorn's voice had been changing, and Herewiss had had to restrain himself from laughing as his loved sang that greatest of tragedies in a voice that cracked crazily every verse or so. He had even refrained from singing it himself for the longest while, for the sound of his pure, clear, already-changed tenor had made Freelorn twice as self-conscious as he usually was.

He sang the setting now, letting his voice go as he would have liked to all those years ago, pausing between verses to insert the last dialogue between Béaneth and Astrin, and later the farewell of Béorgan to her husband Ánmod, who later became King of both

Arlen and Darthen because of her death. Herewiss forgot about the hot, smoky room, forgot about time and pain and the systematic destruction of swords, and just sang, feeling very young again for the first time in ever so long.

At the end of it he received tremendous applause, and he bowed shyly and handed the lute to someone else, going back to his table and his ale. There Herewiss sat for a few minutes, recovering. Someone began singing something else almost immediately, but the farmers started talking quietly among themselves. The contrast between the sung verses of terrible tragedy beyond the boundaries of the world and the homely talk of the farmers was abrupt, but pleasant; they had slow, musical voices, and Herewiss dawdled over his ale, listening alternately to the words and the sound of them. One of the farmers started telling a long, drawn-out story of a loved of his who had gone traveling. "All the way to Dra'Mincarrath she went," he said in a drawl, "aye, all that way south, and then east again into the Waste she went, not knowing where she was going. North she went, but 'twas the wrong way; no way out of the Waste Unclaimed from there. And she came in sight of that hold in the Waste, indeed, and—"

"Ssh!" said several of the other farmers, looking upset. "She came out again," said one of them, seemingly the eldest. "Count her lucky; that place is bad to talk of, even here. Leave it for now. Where did she go afterwards?"

Herewiss sat nursing his ale, curious at the sudden and vehement response. Hold in the Waste—? What could that be? No one lives out there—

His thought was broken by the underheard feeling that someone was looking at him with unkindly intent. He glanced up and saw the innkeeper's daughter. She was across the room, serving someone else, but he could feel her eyes on him. Herewiss looked down at his ale again quickly, not particularly wanting to see her bend over again.

There was a sudden motion to his right. He looked, and saw the cat, a big gray tabby with blue eyes, balancing itself on the table edge after its leap. It lay down, tucking its forepaws beneath its chest so that it looked like a broody hen, and half-closed its eyes.

"Well, hello," Herewiss said, putting down his mug to scratch under the cat's chin. It squeezed its eyes shut altogether and stretched its neck out all the way, purring like a gray-furred thunderstorm.

Herewiss went back to the contemplation of his ale, rubbing under the cat's chin automatically for a few minutes. Then suddenly the cat opened up its round blue eyes. "Prince," it said in its soft raspy voice, "mind the innkeeper's daughter."

He laughed under his breath. "No one keeps a secret from a cat," he quoted. "May I ask what you're called?"

"M'ssssai," it said. "That's my inner Name, prince; the outer doesn't matter."

Herewiss blinked in surprise. "I'll keep your secret," he said in ritual response. "But I fear I have none to give you in return. I don't know mine yet."

"Well enough. Time will come, and then you can come back and tell me."

"Forgive me," Herewiss said, "but how did you know who I am?"

"I've been in your saddlebag."

"It had a binding on it."

The cat smiled, and after a moment Herewiss smiled back at it. Cats, the legend said, had been created second after men, and had a Flame of their own, one which they had never lost.

"The very fact of a binding," M'ssssai said, "made me slightly suspicious. I could smell it from down here, and know you for its author. And the contents of the bags settled the matter. Only two men alive wear that surcoat, and you're too young to be one of them, so you must be the other."

"Granted."

"What are you doing with those grimoires in your bags?"

Herewiss made a face. "Isn't it said of my line that there's no accounting for us? I'm a part-time sorcerer, out seeing the world."

M'ssssai half-closed his eyes again. "Sorcerers usually stay home unless they have something in hand. And you're more than just a sorcerer, prince. I know the smell of Flame."

"I have no focus," Herewiss said, very softly, "and no control. I can't use a Rod."

"The innkeeper's daughter," said the cat, "is a dabbler; she has just enough Flame to be able to smell it herself, though she has no control or focus either. But she's looking for a way to free her Power, and I dare say she's noticed at least part of what you are. If I were you, I'd keep the shields up around your bags tonight, or else sleep lightly. She's a brewer of semi-effective love potions, and she throws her curses crooked. She has a most undisciplined mind. Not to mention that she'd probably try to drain you—"

"A vampire?"

"Only between the bed sheets; unfortunately she's acquired a taste for it. I see too many people going out of here looking lost and drained in the morning."

"M'ssssai, I thank you." Herewiss scratched behind the cat's ears. "But why are you telling me all this?"

The cat put its whiskers forward, amused. "You have good hands."

M'ssssai stood up, stretched, arching his back, his tail straight up in the air. "Mind her, now," he said, and jumped down from the table, vanishing into the forest of trestles and benches.

Herewiss looked up cautiously. The innkeeper's daughter had just come down from upstairs, and was going through the kitchen door. He took his opportunity and eased out from behind the table, heading hurriedly for the protection of the shadows of the stairway. He took the stairs two at a time, sloshing ale in all directions, pausing at the top of the stairs to get his bearings; it was dark up there. Then Herewiss headed softly down the hall, trying to keep the floor from creaking under him, his breath going up before him like pale smoke in the chill air.

His room door was ajar. He listened at it, but heard nothing. A swift cold draft was whispering through the crack. Gently he put his weight against the door; it opened with a low tired groan. There was no one inside.

He went in, still moving carefully, and bent down by the window to check his bags. The surcoat was ever so slightly mussed, unfolded just enough to clearly show the Phoenix charged on it; and the lockshield around the bags was parted cleanly in one place, an invisible incision right through the spell, big enough for a cat to put a paw through.

Herewiss laughed and got up. With flint and steel he lit the room's one candle, a stub of tallow in a smoky, cracked glass by the big four-poster bed. Even in the glass, the flame bent and bobbled wildly until Herewiss closed the shutters at the window. For a few seconds he regarded the worm-holed old door.

"All right," he said softly. "Let her think I had a bit too much to drink." He crossed to the door and closed it without shooting the bolt, then flicked a word and a gesture back at the bags and dissolved the lockshield.

Herewiss pulled back the faded, patched coverlet and sat down on the bed. Immediately there was a sudden sharp feeling in the back of his head, a nagging feeling like a splinter, or the dull hurt of a burn.

He got up again hurriedly, stripping the covers all the way back and feeling about the sheets. When he lifted up the pillow, there it was—a small muslin bag, with runes of the Nhàiredi sorcerer's-speech crudely stitched on it, and a brown stain that was probably blood.

Herewiss took his knife from the sheath at his belt and lifted the little bag on its blade, carrying it over to the table where the candle sat. It took him a while to poke a large enough hole in it without touching it directly, but when he did, and shook out the contents, he nodded. Asafetida; crumbs of choke-pard and wyverns-tooth; a leaf of moonwort, the black-veined kind picked in Moon's decline; and also a small lump of something soft—a bit of potato from his plate at dinner. He scowled. Elements of sleep-charm and love-charm, mixed together—with the moonwort to befuddle the mind and bind the sleeper to someone else's wishes.

What does she think I am? She must not know I'm a sorcerer, or she wouldn't try something so ridiculously simple—Shaking his head, Herewiss laid the steel knife down on the little pile of herbs. "Ehrénie haladh seresh," he said, and spat on the blade. When he picked it up again, the moonwort had shriveled into a tight black ball, and the warning pain in the back of his head was gone.

He set the cloth bag afire with the candle flame, and carried it still burning to the window, opening the shutter and throwing the bag out along with the bits of herbs. Then he went back and stretched out on the bed, reaching for the mug. The ale was getting warm. Herewiss made a face, put the mug aside, and lay back against the headboard, crossing his arms and sighing. It was going to be a long wait.

At sometime past one in the morning Herewiss was listening wearily to the sound of some patron of the inn wobbling about in the courtyard, singing (if that was the word) the old song about the King of Darthen's lover. The inn's good ale seemed to have completely removed any fears the drunk had ever had of high notes, and he was squeaking and warbling through the choruses in a falsetto fit to give any listener a headache. Herewiss certainly had one.

The man had just gotten to the verse about the goats when Herewiss heard the door grunt softly, and saw it scrape inward a bit. He lay back quickly, peeking out from beneath lowered lids. There was another soft scraping sound, and in stepped the innkeeper's daughter, wrapped in a blanket against the cold. She looked long and hard at him, and it was all Herewiss could do to keep from grinning. After a few moments, satisfied that he was asleep, she smiled and crossed the room quietly to where his bags lay.

The one she peered into first was the one with the surcoat. Slowly and carefully she pulled it out and spread it wide to look at the device. There was no light in the room but the pale moonlight seeping in through one half-open shutter, and the dim glow of the torches down in the courtyard. It took her a while to make out the Phoenix in Flames, but when she did she bit her lip, then smiled again, and folded up the surcoat.

Deeper down in the bag she found the book bound in red leather, the unsealed one, and drew it out carefully. The innkeeper's daughter sat down on her heels and muttered something under her breath. A weak reddish light grew and glowed about her hands, clinging to the book's pages as she turned them. For a few minutes she went through the book, turning the leaves over in cautious silence. Then suddenly she stopped, and across the room Herewiss could hear her take in breath sharply. He watched her as she traced down one page with a finger, moving her lips slowly as she read.

That's a bad habit, Herewiss thought. *Let's see if I can't break you of it.*

The girl was holding the book closer to her eyes, and speaking softly. *"Neskháired ól jomëire kal stói, arvéya khad—"*

Herewiss breathed out in irritation. *I might have known. Doesn't she know it's all illusion-spells? She can't know much about what real sorcery is, or what it does. And Goddess knows she would pick that one. She needs a lot more to be beautiful on the inside than she does on the outside. It's not going to work, of course. She's not making the required gestures, and she's set up no framework inside her head. Dark! I'll teach her to mess with things she doesn't understand—*

Herewiss cleared his mind and began to think of another incantation, on another page. He had long since ceased to need to draw diagrams or make passes while conjuring. Constant practice had taught him to build viable spell-structures in his head, without external aids. He built one now, a fairly simple one that he'd used many times to entertain Halwerd, an illusion-spell that required minimal energy and provided surprisingly sophisticated results. It went up quickly, in large chunks, taking form and bulking huge and restless—it was one of those sorceries that has to be used quickly before it goes stale. He completed the structure, checking once to make sure that it was complete, and thought the word that set it free to work.

The girl, intent on her reading, did not notice the air behind her thickening and growing dark. Something darker and more tenacious than smoke curled and roiled within a huge man-shaped space in the air, until at last it stood complete behind her—tenuous at the edges, where its stuff wisped and drifted into the still air, but dark as starless midnight at its heart. The innkeeper's daughter finished reading the spell and raised one hand to feel at her face. In that moment the great dark shape put out a hand and lightly brushed the back of her neck.

She slapped absently at what she thought was an insect, and felt her hand go through something cold and damp. Her eyes went wide with startlement; she turned. She saw, and opened her mouth to scream. But Herewiss was ready. Since freeing the illusion, he had been readying another spell, and as she drew breath he said the word of control and struck her dumb and stiff. There she knelt, her mouth ridiculously open, head turned to look over her shoulder—probably a most uncomfortable position. Herewiss got up out of the bed, praying that the backlash would hold off for a few minutes.

"Do you always go through your guests' bags at one in the morning?" he said, bending down to take the book away from her and toss it onto the bed. "And do all the rooms come equipped with that charming little addition under the pillow?"

She couldn't even move her eyes to follow him as he went to open the window wide. "Would you excuse us?" he said to the smoke-creature. There had always been controversy over whether illusion-creatures were alive and thinking in any sense of the words, but Herewiss, being both cautious and courteous by nature, treated his illusions as if they were both. "And while you're out there, please take that man down there and bed him down in the stable or something. If I hear that part about the goats again, I may turn him into one."

The dark shape waded slowly through the air, trailing streams of black smoke behind it, and climbed over the windowsill into the night. It drifted down silently into the courtyard.

"Would you like to be a goat?" Herewiss said, going back to look at the girl from behind, so that she could see him. "Or an owl might be better—you seem to like being up in the middle of the night."

He was bluffing outrageously, for no mere sorcery could do such things. She seemed not to know that, though. She stared at Herewiss wide-eyed, the terror frozen in her face. Outside, a voice broke off its singing. "Boy, izh really *dark* out here," it said, woozily surprised.

"Or maybe you'd like to bed down with my friend out there," Herewiss said, adding another layer of bluff still more outrageous, "since you do seem to be so eager, with that love-charm and all. I should tell you, though, he is a bit cold—and you might have a baby afterwards, and I couldn't guarantee what it would look like."

He made a small adjustment in his mind and snapped his fingers, freeing her upper half but keeping her legs bound tight. She sagged and turned her face away from him quickly. "Tell me what you were after," Herewiss said.

"I—" She shuddered. "I don't want to share with *that*—"

"Then be quick and answer me."

She stared sullenly at the floor. "I smelled the Power," she said. "You have it. I want to know how. If a *man* can have it, then there has to be a way for me to bring *mine* out." She looked up, glared at him. "How did you do it?" she demanded, bitter. "Who did you pact with?"

"My my," Herewiss said. "You *are* a dabbler. Everyone has the Power, dear, didn't you know that? Men and women both, everyone born has the spark. But all too few have enough to do anything with. And Goddess knows there's more to it than just having enough Flame. What was the bag for, by the way?"

She scowled at the floor again, and would not answer him.

"A little draining to amuse yourself? The Bride doesn't look kindly on such things. Draining away your lovers' potency is likely to make you less of a woman, not more. And anyway, who taught you your Nhàired? Two of the words on the bag were misspelled, and there was too much asafetida. If you'd left that there much longer, it would have recoiled, and half the place would probably have tried to rape you. Try draining *that*."

She answered him not a word, and Herewiss sighed. "You're not being very open with me," he said. "I'm in a quandary as to what to do with you. Maybe you really *do* want to be a goat." He went over to the bag on the floor and took out the other book, the one with the seals on it. Softly he said the word to undo the seals, and the second word that spoke the pages apart, and then went through the book slowly, looking for the right page.

The innkeeper's daughter was beginning to worry now. "Please," she said, "please, no—I'll do anything—"

She squirmed her torso at him, and Herewiss shook his head in mild amazement. "I'm not interested in that kind of anything," he said. "I might consider information, though. Tonight at dinner some people were talking, and someone mentioned a place called the 'hold in the Waste,' and everyone else hushed them up. What is that? Why won't they talk about it?"

Fresh fear went across the girl's face like a shadow. "I don't know—"

Herewiss's underhearing jabbed him hard under one rib, like the pain one gets from running too hard, and he knew she was lying. "Then I guess I'll have to turn you into a goat," he said, wondering how in the world he was going to make the bluff good, and turned his attention to the page before him. *'Faslie anrástüw oi velien—"*

"No, no, wait!" She looked around fearfully. "It's unlucky even to talk about it—"

"Being a goat isn't unlucky?"

"Uh—well. Out in the Waste Unclaimed, about forty miles or so into the desert, there's an Old Place—they say it's the oldest of all the Old Places in the world." She gulped. "It's full of the ancient kind of wreaking, and ghosts and monsters walk there. Sometimes the desert around it—*changes* somehow, and becomes other places. I don't know how..."

"Go on."

"They say that the rocks roll uphill, and water flows sideways along the hills there, or up the sides of valleys—and it rains scorpions and stones instead of water. Even the Dragons won't go near it; they say it's too dangerous. There are doors into Otherwheres—"

"Doors?" Herewiss echoed.

"That's all I know," the girl said. "It's not lucky to talk about it. It's a cursed place."

"No," Herewiss said, "just Old, I would imagine. We don't know enough about the Old people's wreaking to know their curses from their blessings. Forty miles into the desert. Near where?"

"North of the pass above Dra'Mincarrath," she said, "about sixty miles or so, they say. But it really is cursed—"

Herewiss stood there silently for a long few moments, holding the backlash away while reading the spell in the book, readying it. "That'll do, I think," he said. "But one thing only."

She looked at him in fear. "I don't trust any promises you might make about your future behavior," he said. "So I'm going to give you a conscience of sorts."

He spoke the last word of the spell under his breath, and immediately the girl groaned and doubled over, clutching at her stomach. "The next time you sleep with a man or woman for whom you don't care, *that* will take you," Herewiss said. "Don't bother trying to rid yourself of it; if you meddle, you may find that particular avenue of pleasure permanently closed. And let me give you advice—don't play around with sorcery. It shortens the life."

He cut the air with one hand in a short quick motion, and the girl staggered to her feet and lurched without another word out the door.

Herewiss closed and sealed his book, fetched the other one from the bed, and put them back in his bag again. His head was aching violently, and his stomach churned, threatening to reject the steak pie.

Suddenly a dark shape loomed at the window. It was the smoke-creature, peering in curiously.

"Oh Dark, I forgot," Herewiss said. He gestured at the window, the same quick cutting motion. "Go free! And thank you."

The creature bent sideways in a passing breeze, and dissipated silently.

"Oh, my head," Herewiss groaned as he headed back to bed. "Shortens the life indeed. I wish I *were* dead."

He pulled the covers up around him again, and laid his throbbing head down on the lumpy pillow as tenderly as he could. The darkness was almost peaceful for a few moments—until the sound of a drunken countertenor began to float up from the stable, half a tone flat, singing of what the King of Darthen did with the shepherdess and her brother.

"Oh Goddess," Herewiss moaned, and buried his face in the pillow.

ॐ *three*

Opening Night is not so much a time of year as it is a state of mind. It can be invited, by no more difficult a measure than keeping one's eyes and heart open all the time. There are Rodmistresses who could not share in the Opening if they stood at the Heart of the World on Nineteen-Years' Night; and there are children, and the eager of heart, who can break the walls between the Worlds in broad day, and call the wonders through. Those who do not close their hearts to Possibility soon find their lives full of it.

    Reflections in the Silent Precincts, Leoth d'Elthed, ch.7

The next day was gray and overcast, threatening rain. Herewiss left early, having been awakened by the impending light of dawn though there was no sunrise to be seen. He didn't stop for breakfast—partly from a desire to hurry, and partly to avoid running into the innkeeper's daughter again. He felt guilty for laying as restrictive a spell on her as he had. But then again, she *had* been tampering with his private property—and her actions had hardly been intended in benevolence.

"Aah, the Dark with it," Herewiss said to himself as the inn receded behind him, and he headed south again over open country. Dapple was trotting along briskly, needing little encouragement to hurry, and Herewiss had leisure to ponder what he had learned. *Doors into Otherwheres...*

Such doors were legendary. They might open onto other times, like the Eorlhowe Door hidden in the mazes beneath the melted stones of the Howe in North Arlen; or other places, like the old

King's Door in the Black Palace in Darthis; or other worlds entirely, as does the Morrowfane Gate beneath the waters of Lake Rilthor in southern Darthen. There were not many permanent doors, and they tended to be difficult of access and dangerous to use, because of time limits or unpredictable behavior. One of the Queens of Darthen acquired the sobriquet One-Hand when she crossed through the King's Door and it closed unexpectedly.

Out in the Waste? Well, it would make sense to put them there, away from casual access, if they're time-gates. At least the Dragons would think so—they won't let anyone but Marchwarders near the Eorlhowe Door, and the human Marchwarders won't go near it themselves for fear of changing the past.

Herewiss sighed. From the time he first heard of the concept, he would have given almost anything to go through a time-door, or just look through one, to find out if things really happened as the histories said they had. Or to see the great days of the past happen again—to see Earn and Héalhra take the Power upon Themselves at Bluepeak, to see the terrible Gnorn come tottering over the mountains and go up in a blaze of the blue Fire as the Lion and Eagle gave Themselves for the destruction of that last menace. Or to see the founding of the Brightwood, or of Prydon city, or Darthis. To watch the last stone being set into the paving of the Great Road, and watch the Oath of Lion and Eagle being sworn for the first time by Earn's and Héalhra's grandchildren. Maybe even to see what no man had seen, the Worldwinning, as the Dragons dropped out of the darkness and the Messenger in Her glory drove the Dark away—

I'm getting carried away with this, he told himself severely.

And you're enjoying it, another part of him answered back.

Well, why not? Dreaming was free. Consider this: how about going back to the day Freelorn's father died, and finding out where old Hergótha had been hidden? That would certainly make Freelorn happy. True, Freelorn had Súthan now, and that was not exactly a sword without lineage—the princes of Arlen had been carrying it since the time that Ánmod had used it to kill the Coldwyrm lairing in the fords of Arlid. But it was just that, a prince's sword, and Freelorn was king, if not in name, at least by right. Herewiss didn't need his underhearing to detect Freelorn's dissatisfaction with Súthan. Lorn wanted Hergótha, which was the proper sword of the Arlene kings and queens; he lusted after it the way some people lust after others' bodies and desire to possess them.

Hergótha, though, had gone missing after Ferrant's death. He had not been wearing it on the day his heart stopped, and it had never been found in the palace. Perhaps he had taken the sword with him past the Door into Starlight, and walked the shore of the final Sea with it slung over his back, the kingliest of the shadows that dwelt there. Or perhaps the Lion had taken it back into His keeping again, possibly to return it to the rightful wielder one day, if one of the Line ever came back to claim the throne. Herewiss doubted that Freelorn would have the patience.

To find Hergótha, bring it back to Freelorn—

This is ridiculous, Herewiss thought. *I don't know for sure that this place has time-doors in it—or any doors, for that matter. And even if it does, there's no guarantee that I'll be able to get through them. Or even make them serve my purpose.*

Yet he sighed. It was still nice to think about. To look back in time. To see his mother. To see Herelaf—

Or to look forward in time, perhaps, and see how he would finally forge the sword that would work for him, then do it.

Yes. And if those doors looked out into other worlds, mightn't there be one world somewhere much like this one, except that both men and women had the Flame? Or maybe there would be a door into that long-past time before the Catastrophe, when everyone could use the Power—

Dapple stopped abruptly, and Herewiss looked up in confusion. About a hundred yards away, at the foot of a little hill that rose suddenly from the grassland, stood a small building.

It was built of logs stood up on end and bound together. The roof was thatched, and there was one door, and a window on the side that faced him. It wasn't a house—there was no sign of a garden, or even a cow. A shrine, perhaps?

His curiosity nudged him, and he pulled on Dapple's reins and rode up to the place. He dismounted before the open doorway. "Hello—?" he called. No one answered.

There was a wooden plaque fastened next to the door, and though it was weathered, the runes were deeply scratched and easy to read: OF OUR LADY OF LIBERATIONS—USE, CLEAN, BLESS, AND GO SAFELY.

Herewiss stepped in and looked around. The inner walls were plastered, and there were scenes painted on them in a primitive and vigorous style, the colors bright, the figures stylized, stark and clean.

In the middle of the room was a rough wooden offering table. Dead leaves and bits of grass were scattered about on the table and floor. Something twittered in irritation, and Herewiss looked up to see a sparrow's nest high in the corner, where the plaster had fallen away and left an opening to the outside.

He smiled at the appropriateness of the place, for there was one aspect of his personality sorely in need of liberation. The few minutes it would take to clean and reconsecrate the shrine wouldn't be wasted. Besides, if the Goddess were to come to his house when *he* wasn't there, and if it were full of leaves and such, *She* would certainly clean it up.

For a moment he grinned at the image of the Tripartite Lady busy in the Woodward with a broom. But the Goddess had never been known for standing on ceremony. On Her travels through the world She tended to leave home Her Cloak which is the night sky, and the Robe glorious as Moonlight, in favor of plainer and more utilitarian clothes. Even at that most sublime and beautiful of times, when She comes to share Herself in love—as She comes to every man and woman born—even then She rarely appears in any of the forms or manifestations attributed to Her by legend. Once in a lifetime, a person will know the joy of being held in the Goddess's arms. She comes as just another person, with human quirks and wrinkles; sometimes She comes in the form of someone you know— perhaps even your own loved, by way of an affectionate joke. But She never comes when or where you expect Her. As the proverb says, "The Goddess is as likely to come in the window as through the door."

Herewiss found a broom in one corner, not much more than a mildewed bunch of birch twigs, and did his best to sweep up the detritus on the floor. As he swept, he looked at the figures painted on the plaster. One wall depicted the Triad in its first form—Maiden, Mother and Wise Woman, Their hands joined to show that They were One: and then underneath that, the Maiden with Her hands full of stars, busy with creation. But her back was turned to the other Two, illustrating the Error. Behind the Three of Them hung the symbol for the great Death, the down-pointing Arrow, and only the Eldest of the Three saw it. Her hand was outstretched to Her younger self, but the Maiden ignored the Eldest and went on creating as if her works would last forever.

In the next panel the Maiden stood in Her sorrow, Her hands covering Her face, as She realized the nature of Her error. She had forgotten about Death...and now that She had spoken the final Word that set the Universe on its way, Death was trapped inside it. This whole Universe would have to run down and die itself before She could make it perfect. The Mother and the Wise Woman stood beside the Maiden, trying to console Her; but for some things there is no consolation.

The following panel showed the Maiden's solution for Her own grief and guilt. She knew Her other selves in the manner of woman with woman, and became with child. Now She sat on the birthing-stool, and was no more Maiden, but Mother. The children She bore were twin sons, and She suckled Them one at each breast with a smile of maternal joy. The panel below showed the Twins grown already, beautiful young men, Her Lovers, and She stood between Them and They all three embraced one another. Then came the New Love, and the Lovers knew Each Other and found yet another joy. In the painting, Their mouths touched with almost ritual solemnity, even as Their strong arms strained about each other and They strove to be one.

But then the great Death entered in, casting the Shadow over the Lovers, filling Them with jealousy, each desiring to alone know the other Lover to the Mother's exclusion. The Lovers' hands went about each other's throats, and They choked the lives out of each other. The Triad stood above them in sorrow, and together They lifted up the dead, and with Them entered into that Sea of which the Starlight is a faint intimation, therein to be renewed and reborn, to close the circle and make all things whole again.

The last panel, near the door, showed why the shrine had been built. There was a sorrowing mother with her four dead children in her arms, three little girls and a boy; and the inscription, *My Children. The Plague Came in the Night. Having Pronounced, She Sets Free. May I Meet Them on the Shore.*

Herewiss stopped there, leaning on the broom, saddened. He thought how it must have been for that poor mother, building this place with her own two hands, most likely, hard by that little hill which probably housed her children's bodies; painting those scenes, slowly and with care, and trying to find some sense in the deaths of her little ones. Possibly there wasn't any. But at least she had left something beautiful behind in their memory, and it may have been that having something to do had brought her at least partway through her grief.

He swept the last of the leaves out the door. The sparrow chittered faintly in its nest, and Herewiss looked at it with affection—another mother, and her children, safe and comfortable. The nameless lady who built this place would probably be pleased.

He went out to where Dapple stood grazing, and rummaged around in the left-hand saddlebag until he found what he wanted, his lovers'-cup. Herelaf had made it for him, long ago. It was of white oak, simply carved and stained, with a border of leaves running around the outside just under the lip, and Herewiss's name scratched under the foot. He remembered watching Herelaf carve it. "When it's finished," his brother had said, "take good care of it and it'll last you a long time—"

It certainly had. Fourteen years. Herelaf had been dead for twelve of them.

Herewiss took a water bag out of the pannier, and filled the cup with it. Carefully, so as not to spill any, he carried the old brown cup into the shrine, and set it on the altar.

"Mother of Days," he said softly, looking for the right words, "Mother of Stars—bless the lady who built this place, and her children, whether they're reborn or not—may she find love again, and may they too. Take care of the people who pass here; keep the Fyrd off them, and the terrors of night, and save them from loneliness. And take care of Freelorn for me, until I get there, and afterwards too." He paused, swallowed the lump that was filling his throat. The hurt was twelve years gone, it was silly to be still crying about it. "And take care of Herelaf—let him come out of the Sea and find joy—"

He picked up the cup, drank quickly. It was harder to cry with his head tilted back and his eyes squeezed shut. By the time he had drained the cup, he was back in control again.

"—and help me find my Power when I get back home," he said. "In Your name, Who are our beginnings and our endings—"

He went out of there in a hurry. Dapple had stopped grazing, and was looking at him inquisitively. It had begun to rain. "Let's go," Herewiss said. "Freelorn's waiting." He undid his rolled-up cloak from the back of his saddle and swung it around him. The rain began in earnest then, pelting down hard. Herewiss made as if to mount, and to his utter surprise Dapple reared up and danced away from him, whickering.

"*What?*" he said. "What's the matter?"

The horse's eyes were calm, but when Herewiss reached for the reins, Dapple backed away again. "What, then?" said Herewiss. "Am I supposed to stay here?"

Dapple took a step backward and gazed at him.

"Dammitall, when Dareth made your family smart, I wish she'd made you more verbal! All right, let's see what I can find—"

Herewiss pulled his cloak more tightly around him and slipped the hood over his head, then leaned up against the wall of the shrine and closed his eyes. He tried to put his underhearing out around him like a net. It was a fickle talent, one which often refused to manifest itself when it was needed, and for a moment or so he couldn't find it at all. He concentrated, and tried to listen—

—tried—

Warmth?

—he listened harder—

Very faint warmth. A banked fire. No, more like a fire being rained on, going out gradually. The first drops splattering into the flames, and the fire in panic, seeing its own destruction.

What in the world is that? *Not a human reading—no one I ever read felt anything like this. It feels so dry, and I can hear the heat—*

Fire in the rain. The fire in terror, the flames being beaten down, steam rising—

Somewhere over to the west—

—coming this way—

Herewiss opened his eyes and looked westward. The rain made it difficult to see clearly. It was coming down hard, a silver-white rushing wall, the typical spring cloudburst that seemed to beat the air right into the ground. If there was something out there, it would have to come a lot closer before he would be able to see it.

Fire, dwindling, dying out—Whatever it was, the source of the feeling was coming closer: the image had intruded on Herewiss's underhearing that time without his having to listen for it—

Herewiss pulled his hood further down over his face and took a few steps into the rain, following the feeling. It wavered, grew stronger. Possibly it was sensing him too. Herewiss squished along for several minutes, shivering as the rain soaked through his cloak.

A shadow loomed suddenly behind the gray rain curtain, and Herewiss slowed down. It was bigger than he was—

(—fire in the rain—)

He went closer to it.

A horse?

It staggered toward him. A horse indeed; but a miserable sickly-looking thing, wobbling along on spindly legs. Its mane and tail were plastered to it, skin scalloped deep between its ribs, drawn drum-tight over its sunken belly. The horse's eyes bulged out of their sockets, staring horribly. It looked as if it had been starved and abused by a whole town full of people, one after another. It looked ready to die.

Herewiss reached out with his underhearing again, to make certain. He got the same feeling: a fire, going out, almost too tired and weak now to be afraid any more. Steam rising, flames dying—and indeed there was steam wavering about the horse's hide, as if it had been ridden hard on a cold day.

He went over to the poor stumbling thing, took its head and stopped it. It regarded him dully from glazed eyes, taking a long time to realize what he was. And a feeling stirred in his head. The horse was bespeaking him.

(Help...) it said. (Dry...)

It collapsed to its knees.

Herewiss was utterly amazed. No one had ever bespoken him but his mother, who had had the talent as a result of her training in the Fire; they had used it so commonly between them while she was alive that some of his more remote relatives in the Ward used to accuse him of disliking her, since when together they rarely spoke aloud. But after her death he had hardly ever used the talent again. There were no others in the Wood who had it, not even Herelaf; and after numerous disagreements with the Wardresses of the Forest Altars, Herewiss had little to say to them.

But a *horse?*

Then again, something in a horse's shape could very well have the bespeaking ability. Rodmistresses sometimes took beast-shapes. If that was the case, though, why the distress—and why that strange underheard reading like none he had ever experienced?

(Dry!) the horse-thing said again, more weakly.

Herewiss bent over and grabbed the horse by the nose. Had it been in any better shape, it would certainly have bitten him. But now as he pulled at it the horse only moaned pitifully and struggled to its feet again. Herewiss pulled it, step by trembling step, back toward the shrine.

(It hurts,) the creature said, bespeaking him piteously. (It *hurts!*)

"I know. Come on."

This close to it, touching it, Herewiss's underhearing was coming much more fiercely alive. He could feel the creature's terror as if it were his own, and moreover he could feel its agony, for with every drop of rain that touched it the horse was seared as if by hot iron. Abruptly it collapsed in front of him, and then screamed, both out loud and within, trying to flinch away from the wet ground on which it had fallen.

Herewiss was shaken to the heart by the sound of its terror. *I can't carry it or drag it*—It screamed again, thrashing helplessly on the ground.

Oh, damn, damn, dammit to Darkness! Herewiss thought. He bent down, put his arms around the barrel of its ribs just behind the forelegs, and began to pull. It was terribly heavy, but nowhere near as heavy as a real horse would have been, even one as emaciated as this creature seemed to be. It was wheezing with pain as he got its forequarters just clear of the wet grass and dragged it along.

Herewiss wanted desperately to drop the horse, just for a moment's rest, but he was also deadly afraid of hearing that terrible lost scream again. He kept pulling, pulling, cast a look over his shoulder. The shrine was a dark shadow through the rain, not too far away. And another shadow was approaching with a sound of wet squishing footfalls. Dapple came up through the rain, looked at Herewiss, and then turned sideways to him, facing him with the saddlebag in which the rope was coiled.

"Thanks!" Herewiss said, reaching up with one arm to get the rope out. He uncoiled it, wound a bight around the strange horse's chest behind the legs, knotted it, and tied the other end to Dapple's saddlehorn. Dapple began backing steadily toward the shrine, and with Herewiss holding the horse partly clear of the ground, they got it to the door of the shrine quickly. There was a slight problem getting the horse through the door—Herewiss had to drop the poor creature on the floor halfway in and go around to push its hind legs inside. When he had managed that, he undid the rope, coiled it, stowed it, and went back into the shrine. He dropped to his knees beside the horse's head, gasping for breath and rubbing at his outraged abdominal muscles.

"Well," he said. "Now what?"

The horse lay there with its sides still heaving, its breath rasping in and out, harsh with pain, as if it had been ridden to the point of foundering. Herewiss looked at it through the odd detachment that sometimes accompanies great exertion. In color the horse was a brilliant bay, almost blood-color, and its stringy, wet mane and tail were pale enough to be golden when they were dry. Under the taut-drawn skin, it had a beautiful head, fine-boned like that of a racehorse.

But racehorses don't bespeak people, Herewiss thought. *And the way the rain was hurting it. Water...could this be a fire elemental, then? People meet them so rarely, the stories say. But the reading I got from it—*

Herewiss closed his eyes and listened again. A feeling like fire, still, but not being rained on any more. Gathering strength, burning hotter, growing—

He bespoke it, making the thoughts as clear as he could. (What happened?)

(Don't shout,) it answered faintly.

(Sorry. What happened?)

Its thought was weak, but had an ironic tone. (I didn't know enough to come in out of the rain. Get out of me for a little, will you?)

Herewiss did, and pushed himself over to where he could lean against the wall. The horse was still steaming slightly. He reached out a hand to touch one of its legs, and then jerked it away again, sucking in breath between his teeth. His fingers were scalded.

A fire elemental. I'm in trouble.

The legends were fairly explicit about elementals of any kind being capricious, dangerous, tricky. Some elementals were death just to see. Flame would be a protection, but a lot of good that did *him*. Sorcery wasn't supposed to be much use either. Herewiss's Great-great-great-great-aunt Ferrigan was supposed to have had dealings with some elementals, those of water and air mostly, and she had survived to tell about it, but no one was sure just how...

Herewiss looked at the horse with apprehension. Its breathing was slowing, and it looked less emaciated than it had before. Herewiss shrugged his cloak back, and then realized that the air in the shrine was getting much warmer. And the blood-bay "horse" seemed to be drying out as he watched. In fact, it was becoming better fleshed out, growing sleek, growing whole—

(What are you called?) Herewiss asked.

It bespoke its Name to him, and Herewiss reflexively started back and shielded his eyes. The elemental showed him a terrible blazing globe of fire—the Sun close up, it seemed to be saying—and out of that blinding disc a sudden immense fountain of flame leaped up, streamed outward like a burning veil blown in a fierce wind. Then it bent back on itself with an awful arching grace, and fell or was drawn back into the vast sphere of flame below. That single pillar of fire would have been sufficient to burn away all the forests of the world in a moment; but the creature bespoke the concept casually, as a small everyday kind of thing, not a terribly special Name. And—Herewiss shuddered—it made free with its inner Name as if it had nothing to fear from *anything*—

(Sunspark,) Herewiss said. (Would that be it?)

(That's fairly close.) It looked up at him from the floor. Its voice was sharp and bright, and currents of humor wafted around it as if the elemental balanced eternally on the edge of a joke. (What's your name?)

(I'm called Herewiss, Hearn's son.)

(That's not your Name,) it said, both amused and scornful. (That's just a calling, a use-name. What is your *Name?*)

(You mean my inner Name?) Herewiss said, shocked and terrified.

The elemental was confused by his fear. ("Inner?" How can a Name be "inner" or "outer?" You are what you are, and there's no concealing it. Don't you know what you are?)

(No....)

More confusion. (They *told* me this was a strange place! How can you be alive, and thinking, and able to talk to me, and *not* know?)

(How can you be so *sure?*) Herewiss said. (And if this is "here," where's "there?")

It showed him, and he had to hold his head in his hands for fear it would burst open from the immensities it suddenly contained. "There," it seemed, was the totality of existence. Not the little world he had always known, bounded by mountains and the Sea; but his world and all the others that were, all of them at once, a frightful complexity of being and emptiness, and other conditions that he could not classify.

Herewiss knew there were other planes of existence—everyone knew that—but he tended to think of them as being separated from the world of the Kingdoms by distance as well as by worldwalls, and accessible only by special doors such as the ones he was looking for. Sunspark, though, had more than an abstract conception. He had breached those walls under his own power, had made his own doors and walked among the worlds. Herewiss, seeing as if through Sunspark's mind, could actually perceive the way they were arranged.

The worlds all *overlapped* somehow, each of them coexisting in some impossible fashion with every other, a myriad of planes arranged on the apparent surface of a sphere that could not possibly be real, since all of its points were coterminous with all of the others. Still, all the countless places held distinct positions in relation to one another. Each of them was a thread in the pattern—a Pattern past his understanding, or anyone's, actually, though some few by much travel might get to know small parts of it, or might come to understand the spatial relationships on a limited scale. It could be traveled, but the order and position of the worlds within it changed constantly, from moment to moment. The important thing was to know what the Pattern was going to do next.

During the brief flickering moment when Herewiss tried to perceive the thought in its entirety, he knew with miserable certainty that he stood, or sat, right then, upon an uncountable number of locked doors. If he only had the key, he could step through and be anywhere, anywhen he could possibly imagine. Sunspark had the key.

The hope and jealousy that ran through Herewiss in that one bare moment were terrible, but they didn't last long; they dwindled and fragmented as the thought did when Sunspark finally pulled away from the contact.

Herewiss found himself left with a few pallid shreds of the original concept. *I'm not big enough of soul to hold so much at once…* (That's where you come from?) he said to Sunspark.

(Somewhere there. I've forgotten exactly where. I've been so many places.)

(Can you take other people into those—those places?)

(No. It's a skill each must learn for himself.)

(Oh…) Herewiss sighed, shook his head. (Well. You are a fire elemental, aren't you?)

(I am fire, certainly,) it said.

(How did it happen that you got caught out in the rain?)

(I was eating,) it said, and Herewiss thought of the distant brushfire he had seen. (I was careless, perhaps—I knew the storm was coming, but I thought I could elude it just before it started to rain. However, the rain came very suddenly, and very hard, so that the shock weakened me—and then it wouldn't let up. I thought I would go mad or mindless—we do that when too much water touches us. It is a terrible thing.)

Herewiss nodded.

(You saved me,) the elemental said, almost reluctantly, and there was something in its tone that made Herewiss regard it with sudden suspicion. (I—) It cut itself off. Herewiss's underhearing caught a faint overtone of concealment, fear, artifice. (—thank you,) it finished, a little lamely.

The hesitation told Herewiss what he needed to know. The old tales he'd unearthed in his studies claimed that elementals and creatures from other planes respected nothing in the worlds but their own ethic. That ethic, the "Pact," stated that travelers-between-worlds *must* help one another when need arose, and return favor for favor, lest the overwhelming strangenesses and dangers of the many worlds should wipe out the worldwall-breaching ability and all its practitioners forever. *But there are so many stories,* he thought. *Still—*

(Sunspark,) Herewiss said, doing his best to mask his slight uncertainty with a feeling of conviction. (You would have been left mad and in horrible pain if I hadn't helped you.)

It looked at him, no emotion showing in its eyes or its tone of thought. It moved its legs experimentally. (I think I could stand up now—)

(Sunspark. You owe me your well-being at this moment. Otherwise you would be out there still, in the rain.)

It shuddered all over, so that its nonchalance of thought did not quite convince him. (What of it?)

(A favor for a favor, Sunspark. Until the End.)

He held his breath, and held its eyes and mind with his, and waited to see whether the line that appeared again and again in Ferrigan's old tale would work.

Sunspark looked at him, its eyes distraught, his underhearing catching its consternation and unease, its desire to be out of there, away from this horrid narrow little creature who knew of the Pact but didn't even know what its own self was—

(Sunspark,) Herewiss said again, this time letting his thought show his disgust at the elemental's trying to slip out of an obligation by concealment. (A favor for a favor.)

It closed its eyes. (What do you want?)

(You know very well!)

It sighed inwardly. (A favor for a favor,) it said. (Until the End. What do you want of me?)

Herewiss paused for a long moment. (I'm not really sure yet. Get up, if you think you can, and we'll discuss it.)

Sunspark struggled a little and then heaved itself all at once to its feet. It stood there for a moment swaying uncertainly, like a new foal. (That's better,) it said. (You know, I am likely to be a lot of trouble to you—)

Herewiss stood up too. It was distinctly unnerving to have something the size of a horse looking down on you and talking to you, especially when it wasn't really a horse. (You're trying to frighten me,) Herewiss said. (The stories *are* true, it seems. If you refuse to aid me, you're forsworn, outside the Pact, outside the help of any of the other peoples who walk the worlds. No traveler survives long under such conditions. You owe me a favor, a large one, and you will repay it.)

The elemental looked at him with grudging respect. (I will. You understand, though, why I did not—)

(You weren't sure whether I lay within the Pact or not. And who wants to be bound when it's not necessary? But I'm within it, by intention at least...and if that's not enough, there's ancestry.)

(Oh?) It understood him, but there was some slight confusion about some of the nuances he had applied to the thought, and Herewiss didn't know which ones.

(Yes. I am descended from Ferrigan Halmer's daughter of the Brightwood Line; she walked between the worlds, or so our traditions say. My father is presently Lord of the Brightwood—)

Sunspark stared at Herewiss, and emitted a wave of total shock and incredulity. (Your progenitor is still *alive??*)

(Uh—yes. My mother is dead, though—)

(Well, of course. Why two different concepts for your progenitors, though?)

Herewiss was becoming more than slightly confused himself. (One of them is a man, and the other was a woman—)

There was a brief silence. (You are a hybrid? Well, such matings aren't unheard of in parts of the Pattern—)

(Uhh—no. "Man" and "woman" are different forms of the same creature.)

(Oh. Like larval and pupal?)

Herewiss was shaking his head in amazement. (Well, uh, not really—)

The elemental was bewildered, but still intrigued. (This is too hard for me,) it said finally. (I can't understand how your "father" is still extant after union. But there are patterns within the Pattern, and

no way to understand them all. No matter. Your "father" was a master of energies, you said—)
 (I did? Well, yes, you could say that, though how you mean it and how *I* mean it is—)
 (Later. What does his mastery have to do with you?)
 (Well, among other things, when he dies, I'll inherit the Wood—)
 (Well, of course. How can it be otherwise, but that progeny shall take their progenitors' energy unto them?)
 (Uh—right.)
 (I think I see. Are you seeking to bring your progenitor to his ending that you may have his energies?)
 Too puzzled to be angry, Herewiss said, (No. I am traveling to find a friend who is being held against his will, and to release him.) He kept the thought as simple as possible, feeling that this was no time to go into the political ramifications.
 Herewiss could feel Sunspark pondering the whole thought curiously, taking it apart. (Oh. This person is your mate?)
 (Uh—my loved, yes.)
 Sunspark looked with interest at the concept "loved." (Your mate. And you will unite and engender progeny? You seem young for it...)
 (It, ah, it doesn't quite work that way. You see, we are both men...)
 (Yes?) It waited politely for the explanation. Herewiss sagged against the wall, looking for the right words.
 (Well—see, Sunspark, in this world, "progeny" are—well, there are many ways to achieve union, but there is only one way to have a child. The women bear the children, always; and though men may know men in, uh, union, and women may lie with women, a child only happens if a man lies with a woman. There have been times when babies were supposed to have happened when women lay together—but it's hard to say, because men had been sleeping with the women too.) Herewiss, to his utter surprise, was becoming embarrassed. Even Halwerd at four years of age had not been as completely confused about sex as Sunspark obviously was. (My loved and I are both males and cannot have 'progeny' of our own.)
 Sunspark digested this. (Yours is not a fruitful union? Yet you pursue it? Such behavior is not survival-oriented for a species.)
  Herewiss laughed. (Perhaps it wouldn't be if the Goddess hadn't given our kind the Responsibility. When we come of age—)

(Oh. You come into heat too? Well, there's *one* similarity, anyway.)

(Uh, I'm not sure. But when we come of age, or soon after, we must have union in such a manner as to reproduce ourselves at least once—one union for a man, one bearing for a woman—though there are some who say it should be two. That's between each woman and the Mother, though. After that Responsibility's discharged, union is our own business, and we may love whom we please.)

The bay stallion stood there and mused over this. Sunspark was now fully recovered, and it looked magnificent as the mount of a king—its hide a true deep crimson, bright as blood, and its mane and tail glittering like wrought gold even in the subdued light from the door.

(How very strange,) it said. (Union again and again, it seems, without consummation. And even without progeny! —So your "loved" is in durance?)

(Yes.)

(And you are going to free it?)

(Him. Yes, and then go back to my work.)

(This is *definitely* too much for me,) Sunspark said. (You will go to your mate—and *not* unite—and then go do something else?)

(Well, we may, uh, unite, but—yes.)

(What else could you possibly want to *do?*)

Herewiss sighed. (I have, well, a certain kind of Fire within me—)

(Yes: that's why I was heading in this direction, as well as because the rain felt less over here. I could feel the fire, and I thought we might be related...though I didn't understand how the water could not distress you. I see that we aren't relatives, though, except in a rather superficial manner.)

(That's for sure,) Herewiss said. (At any rate, I have this Fire—but not control of it. With the Flame, one must have a tool, a focus with which to dissociate it from one's self, or it won't work. I'm looking for such a focus. It would be a shame to die of old age and never have had use of the Flame at *all*...)

(Excuse me. "Die?")

(Uh...cease to exist?) Herewiss said.

Sunspark actually shied at the thought. (That's an impossible concept.)

(...pass on? Go through the Door into Starlight?)

(Oh, you mean leave your present form,) Sunspark said. (I see. Why the time limit, though? Is it a game?)

Herewiss shook his head slowly, not knowing what to say. Sunspark sensed his bemusement, and fell silent.

(Where are you headed?) Herewiss asked.

(I have been roaming—like the rest of my kind, I am condemned to restlessness. But you've bound me to you by the Pact, and I must pay back your favor in kind.)

Herewiss thought for a moment. (Well enough, then. If you'll keep company with me until you have opportunity to save my life, I'll consider the favor paid. With the things I'm going to be doing, it shouldn't be too long...)

(Done, and done,) Sunspark said. (Shall we match off energies to bind the agreement?)

Herewiss raised his eyebrows, uncertain what to make of this. (It's in the nature of my kind to match off energies whenever possible,) Sunspark said. (The loser's energies are bound to the winner's, so that when the winners come to mate, their progeny are more powerful than the parents. I think you would probably consider it as something of a social exchange. Like—) it slipped further into his mind to find an analogue—(like clasping hands?)

(With a little knuckle-work,) Herewiss said, grinning. (I hear a certain air of permanence in the thought, Sunspark. Are you looking for a way to make an end of me accidentally, and so be free of our agreement?)

(Make an end? Oh, I see, force you to change form.) Sunspark chuckled softly, with innocent savagery. (I told you I was probably going to be trouble for you...)

(Yes,) Herewiss said, laughing himself. (Trouble indeed. Sunspark, I'm minded to try my strength with you. I'd like to engage in a social exchange with you, for I'd sooner have a friend than someone whom I could never trust, and that's what you'd most likely be without this—)

It looked askance at the concept "friend." (You want to *mate* with *me?*) it said, incredulous. (How perverse. And how very interesting—)

There was something about the sudden smile in its voice that made Herewiss wary. (I didn't say *that,*) he said. (Never mind it now, Spark. There seem to be differences in our ways of looking at things, and with luck we'll have leisure to discuss them later. How are these matches usually handled?)

(Best two fights out of three.)

(So be it. I have certain limitations that you haven't, though, and I'll ask that you take them into consideration so that the match will be a fair one.)

(Who ever said anything was fair?) said the elemental in surprise.

(True, but it behooves us to try to make it that way,) Herewiss said. (Will you agree not to burn me up, or otherwise kill me?)

("Kill?" Oh, form-change. My, you have a lot of ways to say it. What a shame, that's one of the best ways to win a match. Why should I refrain?)

(I don't want to leave this form yet.)

(Is it that comely? You can always get another, can't you?)

(Not just like this one, certainly; the process isn't under my control. And besides, I would no longer be able to reach my loved if I lost this body.)

(That would be tragic,) Sunspark said, (but then, all union is tragic, when you come right down to it. Oh, very well. There's something here that I don't understand, and since you keep insisting, it must be important. I won't 'kill' you. Shall we begin?)

(Right here??)

(Where better?) said Sunspark, and then the change came upon it, and Herewiss had no time to think about anything.

The creature that leaped at his throat had many of the worst characteristics of Fyrd—a nadder's coily, scaled body walking on the ugly hairy legs of a bellwether, and the knife-sharp legs of a keplian at the ends of those legs. Herewiss wrestled wildly with it, trying to get some kind of decent hold, but there were too many legs, and the thing seemed to weigh as much as he did. The fact that he was braced against the wall helped Herewiss somewhat, but Sunspark had perceived that. There were legs pushing at his own, trying to knock him off-balance.

Herewiss spread his legs wider, strove to feel the balance flowing through them, the upflowing power of the earth, as Mard his weapons instructor had taught him. After a few straining moments the power began to come. Sunspark, though, feeling the change in the tension of its opponent's muscles, shifted its attack toward Herewiss's head. Herewiss was confused, for the form Sunspark had taken seemed to have no real head, nothing which he in turn could attack—the top half ended in a blunt place where the serpent like body came to an end, and talons erupted from it in a clutching rosette like some malignant flower. They grabbed and slashed at him, and it was all Herewiss could do to hold the thing at a distance. For a long moment their respective positions did not change. Then Herewiss found a fraction more leverage than he'd thought he had, and slung the creature away from him, halfway across the room. The nadder-creature cracked into the offering table and lay still for a moment.

(First fall,) said Sunspark. (Not bad. Are you ready?)

He sucked in a few deep breaths. (Come ahead—)

It flashed a bright, edged feeling like a sharpened smile at him, and changed again. A sudden hot wind began to fill the room as its physical form dwindled away, and Herewiss suddenly had a hunch that it would be wiser not to breathe for the rest of this bout. He sucked in one last gulp of air before Sunspark had time to finish the change— and then found himself being pressed brutally from all sides, his muscles being painfully squeezed, his eyes smashed back in their sockets, his joints being broken open, his skull being crushed by something that clothed him all around like a stormwind turned in on itself. Herewiss held onto his lungful of air, but then it too was pressed out of him, and white lights danced behind his closed eyes as the awful pressure began crushing him down into unconsciousness...

He slapped the ground to which he had fallen, hoping that Sunspark would understand the gesture. Immediately the pressure let up, and he lay there for a few seconds, at least until the lights went away. He felt as if he had been run over by a cart.

(That one was mine, I think,) came the quiet voice. (Shall we take the third?)

(Go ahead,) Herewiss said. He dragged himself to his feet, and braced himself once more against the wall.

The air swirled, coalesced, and Sunspark stood before him in the red bay form again. But it did not move, just looked at Herewiss.

—and then it was inside Herewiss's head, and Herewiss began to understand the elemental's statement that it was fire. The quiet, familiar confines of Herewiss's mind went up in a terrible conflagration. His brain and body burned inside, thoughts and emotions threatening to drown in heat and pain. But Herewiss held on, held part of himself away from the burning, concentrated on survival, on the help that this creature could be to him if he could bind it. He was not as afraid of fire as most people might be; fire was his companion at work, his old familiar friend. He bore the marks of his acquaintance with it all over his arms, pink places where blisters had been. This fire, a fire of the mind, was no different, really. Herewiss withstood the flames for a long few moments, making sure of his control. Then, (Two can play at this,) he said—

—and thought of water: storms of it, deluges of it, cold and free-running; the shaded place in the Wood where the Darst runs through, widening out into the pool he and Lorn used to swim in during the summers. The leap out from the green bank, and the splash, first too cold, then just right, cool clear liquid softness covering all the body, sliding, surrounding—

He heard Sunspark scream.

—the Sea, the northern Darthene coast in late summer, waves crashing and spray flying cold and salty, a blue infinity of water that could swallow an elemental without even noticing—

The contact broke. Herewiss stood there, sweating and trembling, and saw that Sunspark was doing the same. It looked at him, pleased and irritated both.

(You have nothing to fear from me,) it said. (I am bound to your will until you see fit to release me. I should have let the Pact-oath be the term of our agreement—)

(Maybe you should have,) Herewiss said, (but I for one have no need to keep you past the time of the original agreement.)

(You can afford to be generous,) Sunspark said grumpily. (I've never lost a match before. Shows you what comes of being fair.)

(Sometimes,) Herewiss agreed. (Come on, Sunspark, let's go; the rain's stopped.)

They walked out of the shrine. Above them the clouds were moving eastward before a brisk wind. (One thing I will require of you,) Sunspark said, (and that is that you keep water off me.)

(That's easily done; there are spells enough to manage it.)

Dapple was grazing again; as Herewiss approached him he looked up placidly, as if to ask what would happen now.

(Hmm. Sunspark, will you mind if I ride you?)

(It's a binding of energies, is it not? It seems appropriate.)

He transferred his gear to Sunspark's back, piece by piece, and finally took the bridle off Dapple and rubbed the horse's nose. "It's a long way back home for you," he said, "but you can't help but find your way there. Though they might be confused to see you without me. Here—"

He put the bridle on Sunspark and then went to rummage in the saddlebag, finally finding the little steel message-capsule from Freelorn's pigeon, along with the scrap of parchment it had contained. Ink stick and brush were further down in the bag. Herewiss wet the brush from his mouth, scrabbled it against the ink stick, and paused for a, moment. *Should I—? Oh, why the Dark not, he loves riddles!*

"From Herewiss Hearn's son to his sire," he wrote,
"Your son's making good on his hire—
He sends you your horse
(and regards, Lord, of course)
and the news that the prince rides with Fire."

Then he enclosed the note in the capsule and tied it around Dapple's neck with some cord from the saddlebag.
"Have a safe trip home," he said. "And thanks."
Dapple nuzzled him in the chest, turned, and trotted off.
Herewiss swung up into the saddle, intrigued to feel Sunspark's heat seeping up through it, and hoping it wouldn't make the leather crack. (We're heading south,) he said. (The place where Freelorn is stuck is about five days' ride from here—)
(For a horse,) Sunspark said with an inward smile. (We'll go faster; I'm curious to see this 'loved' of yours. You'd better hold on tight.)
Several times that night and the next day, the country people of southern Darthen and northern Steldin pointed and wondered at the sudden meteor that blazed across their skies and did not strike the ground anywhere.

four

"Are you a sorcerer?" Ferrigan asked.
"Dear me, no!" the Pooka said, shocked. "Who wants to be a sorcerer? You spend five days of a week recovering from one day's spelling; and if you die in the middle of a spell, it takes three months before the headache goes away."

"Tale of Ferrigan and the Pooka,"
from *Tales of Northern Darthen*, ed. s'Hearn, ch. 8

The keep, a single round-tower built of fieldstone, was old enough to have been erected in the first wave of the Kingdoms' colonization. For outworks it had nothing more than an earthen dike, surrounded by a ditch that had once been full of sharpened stakes. They had long since rotted away, the place having been abandoned centuries before for some newer castle of hewn stone, more defensible, or built closer to the present habitations of men.

But the keep was still quite solid—thick-walled enough so that an earthquake could hardly have brought it down. There were no windows but arrow slits, the tower top was deeply crenellated, and the door was heavily bound in iron thick enough not to have rusted away in all the intervening years. Time had been relatively kind to the place. Its mortar had grown stronger with age, and only here or there was any stone shattered by frost. It was a redoubt worthy of the name, and it stood there at the center of the cuplike vale with stolid rocky patience, frowning at the surrounding hills, antique and indomitable.

Herewiss leaned wearily on Sunspark's crupper and frowned back at the keep from where they stood, about two miles away, atop one of the long bare surrounding ridges. The keep was surrounded by a fairly large force, disposed around it for a siege in the usual Steldene fashion. The troops were about half a mile or so from the walls, separated into four large camps, each oriented to one of the compass points. Herewiss agreed with Freelorn's estimate; there were about a thousand of them, and maybe more.

"For five people!" he said aloud, putting his head down on his folded arms. "Steldin must be awfully nervous."

Sunspark stood beside him in the red bay form, idly switching flies with its long glittering tail. It looked at the besieging army with supreme disdain, and snorted softly. (It hardly matters. Give me half an hour and I will bring the fire down on them and leave not a one alive.)

"Sunspark, I don't want to kill; there's no need. Restraint is considered a virtue in these parts."

The elemental snorted again, flicking its tail at a nonexistent fly and fetching Herewiss a stinging blow across the back.

"Behave yourself or I'll make it rain on you again."

(That's no mastery, there are rain clouds coming in anyway; it'll be pouring after nightfall. You keep me dry, now!)

"I keep my promises. You'll be fine. Look, it's getting on toward sundown—I want you to take a message to Freelorn for me."

(What am I—a pigeon?)

"Spark—"

(All right, all right.)

"Get in there any way you like, so long as it's unobtrusive. Say to Freelorn that I'm waiting for nightfall to make my move. Tell him that he should try not to be too bothered by what he sees—I'm going to try to go past the bounds of the battle-sorceries he's seen in the past. Tell him how to find this spot—or better still, after I'm finished, go and meet them and bring them here. There are times when Lorn needs a map to find his own head."

(Shall I tell him that too?)

"Don't bother; I've told him enough times myself. When you finish with that, get back here. This place is wild enough for there to be a few Fyrd still wandering around. I don't want to get eaten while I'm trying to concentrate on my spelling."

(Tell Freelorn this. And tell Freelorn that. There are five people in there, oh Master mine. What does he *look* like?)

Herewiss sighed. "Look for a small man, about a span short of my height, with longish dark hair and a long mustache, and a sense of humor like yours. Chances are that he'll have on a surcoat with the White Lion on it. Is that enough for you?"

(If there are only five people in there, then I think I can manage.)

"Then get going."

Sunspark's horse-shape wavered and turned molten, gathered itself together and swirled about with a blast of oven-heat, became a bright amorphous form that put out wings and rose against the sky, cooling and darkening. A moment later a red desert hawk spiraled up a thermal partly of its own making.

Herewiss sat down, making a face at the smell of scorched grass, and considered what he was going to do. It wasn't going to be easy to dispose of an army this large. There weren't too many of Steldene regulars among the forces; most of these were conscript peasantry, un-uniformed and hurriedly armed. That would be a help. But the regulars and their commanders would have seen real battle-sorcery before. They would be familiar with the tricks of the trade, and unafraid of illusion. Herewiss did have some advantages: a great deal of native power, and access to references and methods about which most sorcerers knew little or nothing. Also, the lack of any army attacking them in concert with the illusions would confuse the Steldenes somewhat. By the time any of them realized what was happening and tried to mobilize a force to stop him, it would be too late...he hoped.

Still...a thousand men. Herewiss shook his head. The King of Steldin must have been worried about the possibility of the Arlene countryside rising against his people when they brought Freelorn home—or the possibility of Freelorn getting away, and the Arlene army moving into Steldene lands in retaliation. If the Oath of Lion and Eagle wasn't protecting Darthen from Cillmod's incursions, the King of Steldin had good reason to worry.

Sighing, Herewiss looked at the thunderheads massing on the northern horizon. The storm would make a fine cover for their escape. He disliked the prospect of leaving over ground wet enough to hold their trail. But speed, and fear, and the direction in which he would lead his friends, would confound the pursuit. Now he had to concern himself with the sorceries he would need.

Herewiss spent at least half an hour leafing through the grimoires, making sure he had properly memorized a number of pertinent passages, and wishing he weren't so ethical. To frighten a thousand men into flight was more difficult than killing them. It would have been simplicity itself to turn Sunspark loose. The elemental's methods were swift and brutally efficient, and its conscience would be clean afterwards, for to Sunspark death was nothing more than a change from one form to another. Or else Herewiss could himself have laid warfetter on the lot of them, leaving the whole army deaf and blind and stripped of their other senses, fighting nothing but their own terror, and probably dying of it. But his conscience wasn't as accommodating as Sunspark's. The last time he had slain was one time too many, and even if that had not been the case, there was still sorcerer's backlash to consider. To lay warfetter on so many people was to open the way for a huge cumulative backlash to strike *him*, one which could leave him dead or insane.

So Herewiss chose illusions as his weaponry. He would have to alter the formulae to accommodate so many people, and the backlash would still hit him proportionately; he would be unconscious for a couple of days. As he went through the book, making his final choices in the fading light, Sunspark dropped out of the sky onto his shoulder.

"Loosen up with the talons, please," Herewiss said. "Did you find him?"

The hawk snapped its beak with impatience. (Of course. He's waiting for you.)

"Was there a message?"

(Your friend greets you by me,) Sunspark said, (and says, 'Get me the Dark out of here.' He also says that you should make your preparations for *six* people. Evidently he has picked up a stray somewhere.)

"That's Lorn. Sunspark, I'm going to need a good while to get ready for this. You'll have to stand guard while I meditate. Also I'll need your services during the sorcery."

(As you say.) Sunspark whirled and dissolved in heat again, reappearing in the blood-bay persona.

"You really do like that shape, don't you."

The elemental curved its neck, looked around to admire its shining self. (It has a certain elegance, I must admit—)

"You're vain, firechild, vain," said Herewiss, smiling. He walked off a short distance and unlaced his fly to relieve himself before the long sorcery; Sunspark followed, regarding the process with interest.

(You are *really* strange,) it said. (Why bother drinking water if you're just going to throw it away again? And what is this 'vain' business? I'm *gorgeous*, you've said so. I don't understand why you can tell me that I'm beautiful, but I can't tell myself—)

"Spark, shut up, please."

Sunspark strolled away a few paces and began cropping the grass in silence, leaving little scorched places where it had bitten through. Herewiss settled himself comfortably on the ground and began to compose himself for the evening's work.

Sorcery, like all the other arts, is primarily involved with the satisfaction of one's own needs. Though a sorcerer may mend a pot or raise a storm or set a king on his throne with someone else's benefit in mind, still he is first serving his own needs, his own joys or fears or sorrows. To work successful sorcery one must first know with great certainty what he wants, and why. Otherwise the dark secretive depths of his mind may take the unleashed forces and use them for something rather different than what he thinks he wants.

In addition, sorcery is affected by how completely the sorcerer's needs are filled before he begins—whether he's hungry or tired, secure in his place in life, whether he is loved or has someone to love. It's easy for a hungry sorcerer to find food by his art, since the need fuels his skill. But it's much harder for that same starving sorcerer to, say, open death's Door and sojourn in the places past it. And only the mightiest of sorcerers could manage to conjure powers or potentialities if he hadn't eaten for a week, or felt his life was in danger for some reason. Sorcery is ridiculously easy to sabotage. Beat your sorcerer, frighten him, deprive him of food, ruin his love life—destroy one of his fulfillments, and he'll be lucky to be able to dowse for water.

So Herewiss sat there in the grass, as the Sun went down and the thunderclouds rolled in, and strove to shut out all external things and evaluate his inner self. A brief flicker of thought went across his mind like lightning, a white line of discomfort and irritation: *If I had the Flame, I wouldn't need to go through this rigamarole. Will alone is enough to fuel the blue Fire, you think a thing and it's done.* But he put the thought aside. Freelorn was waiting for him.

Herewiss sounded himself. He was well fed, not thirsty or cold or tired. He was the Lord's son of the Brightwood, had a home and family and people that he could call his own. Love—there was his father, and Freelorn of course, and the knowledge of their feelings for him was a warm steady support at the back of his mind.

Then after a moment Herewiss reached out and took hold of the thought he would have liked to banish, the lack of Flame, the lack of completion. Oh, he was so empty in that one place inside of him. It should have been full of blue Fire and prowess and shouting joy. Instead it ached with emptiness, as parts of him sometimes did after lovemaking. It was a vast stony cavern that echoed coldly when he walked there. Nothing but a faint flicker illuminated it, a single tongue of blue.

Herewiss turned wholly inward, walked in the still, dry air of that place, listened to the sound of his passage as it bounced back from the walls, a distant, hollow step. He went toward the little blue tongue of Fire, crouched down beside it where it sprang from a crack in the bare rough rock. Though there was no wind passing through the darkness, the Flame trembled. It was a sad fire, afraid of dying before it was unleashed to burn through the rest of him, terrified of going out forever. Herewiss was surprised, and pierced with sorrow. He had never really pictured the Flame as anything but a possession of his, no more emotional than an arm or leg. Yet here it was, frightened of endings as he himself was, lonely in the dark.

He spent a little time there, trying to comfort it with his presence, and finally stood up again and gazed down at the tiny tongue of cold fire. If it would die some day, then that was the Goddess's will. It was better to have treasured the wonder this long than never to have had it in him at all.

Finally Herewiss got up, turned his back on the Flame, and went out of that dark place, looking for Freelorn's image inside him. Besides need, sorcery was also fueled by emotion. He would summon up his emotion as a smith might beat out iron, slowly, with care and skill and calculated brutality. Then he would turn it loose, take it in hand like the weapon it was and scatter an army with it.

He didn't have to walk far. The path to where Freelorn dwelt was a wide one, one that Herewiss traveled often when his friend was gone. It was a bright place. A lot of the memory looked like the halls of Kynall castle in Prydon, where they had lived together for a while, all white marble and sunlit colonnades—very different from the dark, carven walls of the Woodward. Some of it looked like Freelorn's old room in the castle, cream-colored walls veined in green, Freelorn's old teak four-poster bed with the hack-marks in it from Súthan, armor and clothes scattered around in adolescent disorder. They had had good times there together, lounging around and tossing off horns full of red Archantid as they talked about the things that the future might hold.

But there was a lot of the memory that looked like the Brightwood, too, and it was there that Herewiss finally found him. The image of a dead spring day was there, all sun on green leaves, and there was Lorn; newly arrived with his father King Ferrant on a visit of state. Herewiss, of course, was both within that memory and without it. From the outside he looked at Freelorn and marveled that he had ever really been that young. Lorn didn't even have a mustache yet, and he looked laughably unfinished without it. And he was little, so very small for his age.

Freelorn was as nervous as a new-manned hawk, trying to look in all directions at once. He hung onto the golden-hilted sword at his belt with one white-knuckled hand, and spurred his sorrel charger till it danced, meanwhile staring around him trying to see if any of the Wood people had clothes as grand as his, or such a sword, or such a father. From within the memory Herewiss, fourteen years old, looked with mixed disdain and jealousy at the newcomer. He was loud and flashy and arrogant, the way Herewiss had imagined a city princeling would probably be. He had disliked Freelorn immediately, and he saw himself frown and turn away from Hearn's side to stalk back into the Woodward, fuming quietly at this foreign invasion.

Then suddenly the scene changed, faded into darkness and stars seen through leaves and branches. The Moon sifted down through silvered limbs to pattern the smooth grass around one of the Forest Altars, and shone full and clear on the altarstone in the midst of the clearing. On the low slab of polished white marble Freelorn sat, huddled up with his head on his knees, shaking as if with cold. Beneath the trees at the edge of the clearing Herewiss stood very still, confused, wondering why the prince was crying. At the same time he was resisting the urge to laugh; the idea of the Prince of Arlen *sitting* on one of the Forest Altars and weeping was ludicrous. But disturbing—it wasn't right for a prince to be seen crying, and Herewiss wanted him to stop...

The scene shifted again, ever so slightly, and Herewiss was sitting next to his friend-to-be, trying to help, his arm around him; and Freelorn put his head against Herewiss and cried as if his world was ending. "No one likes me," Freelorn was saying, in choked sobs, "and I don't, don't know *why*—"

They began to see through each other that night. Herewiss had been playing cold and silent and mature, and Freelorn merry and uncaring and free; that night they began coming to the conclusion that there was at least one more person with whom the games and false faces were unnecessary. The next morning they looked at one another shyly, each studying the other's weak places as he himself knew he was being studied, and decided that there would be no attack. They spent the next month teaching each other things, and savoring that special joy that comes of having someone to listen, and care. Their friendship became a settled thing.

Herewiss gave the scene a nudge of adjustment. They were in rr'Virendir, the King's Archive in Prydon castle, sitting with their backs against one of the huge shelves filled with rune rolls and musty tomes. It was dark and cool, and the air was laced with the dry dusty smell of a great old library. The summer sun burned down outside, and in this weather the Archive was one of the few comfortable places to be. The assistant keeper was snoring softly in his little office down at one end of the long room; Freelorn, who due to a hereditary title was the Keeper of the Archive, was hunched up against the very last row of shelves with Herewiss.

"I don't want to learn all this stuff," he was saying. "I'll *never* learn it all. I'm a slow reader anyway; it would take me the rest of my life."

"Lorn, you've got to." Herewiss was fifteen now, and feeling terribly broadened by his travels; this was his first trip to Prydon, and the first time he had ever been more than ten miles from the Wood.

"I don't need it!" Freelorn said, scowling at a pile of parchments that lay on the ground next to him. "Look at all this stuff. Half of it is so rotted away I can hardly read it, and the rest of it is in some obscure dialect so full of thees and thous that I can't make sense of it."

"Lorn," Herewiss said with infinite patience, "that one on top there is a rede that's been copied over more times than either of us know, because no one knows what it means, and it's tied to the history of your Line somehow. It's Lion's business, Lorn. That makes it *your* business. This whole place is your business. That's why you're its Keeper."

"Dammit, Dusty, I love my family's history. Descent from the Lion is something to be proud of. But I don't want to sit around reading when I could be out doing great things!"

"What did you have in mind?"

"Are you making fun of me?" Freelorn made an irritated face. "I don't *know* what kind of great things. But they're there, waiting for me to get to them, I know it! I want to see the Kingdoms. I want to take ship for the Isles of the North, and talk to Dragons. I want to climb in the Highpeaks and see what the lands beyond the mountains look like. I want to go into Hreth and kill Fyrd. I want to find out what the Hildimarrin countries are like, I want to—oh, Dark, *everything!* And you know what I get to do?"

"You get to stay home and be prince for a while. Listen, Lorn, it's not that long ago you were in the Wood with me. That's not traveling? Almost two hundred leagues away? What about the mare's nest we saw on the way back? That's not adventure? You wanted the nightmare, maybe? She would have had you for breakfast. We saw three wind demons and a unicorn, and heard the Shadow's Hunting go overhead, and you want more? Goddess, Lorn, what's it take to make you happy?"

"Danger. Intrigue. Hopeless quests. Last stands. Heroism! Courage against all odds! Valor in defeat!"

"You remember when we used to play Lion and Eagle?"

"Yes, but—Dusty, what's that got to do with this?"

"How many times did we stage Bluepeak out behind the Ward?"

"Every day for a month at least, but—"

"Did you notice something interesting? We always got up again afterwards. Earn and Héalhra didn't."

"Yes, They did. They come back once every five hundred years—"

"—and the last two times no one recognized Them until they were dead, because They didn't come back as Lion and Eagle. That's not important here, though. Lorn, I'm not—oh, Dark." Herewiss reached over and took Freelorn's hand, slowly, shyly.

"My father," he went on, looking at his boots, "keeps saying, 'A king is made for fame and not for long life.' Which is all right as long as it's some other king—but Lorn, it's going to be *you* some day, and I'm not sure I want to see you die. No matter how damn heroic your last stand is." He closed his eyes. "I'm probably going to go the same way; Brightwood people never die in bed. They vanish, or get eaten by Fyrd, or get turned into rocks, or something weird like that. All the old ballads make my ancestors sound just wonderful, but they have to be divorcing the emotion from the reality in places. *I don't want to find out how it feels to vanish.*"

Freelorn nodded. "I don't really want to end up lying on a battlefield bleeding, either—but on the other hand, it'd be great to be a hero. Even a common robber baron, putting down oppressors and giving money to the common people. Or a wandering sorcerer, doing good deeds and slipping away unnoticed—"

Herewiss sighed, and a wild impulse compounded of both daring and humor rose up in him. "All right," he said. "Hopeless quests are what you want? Valiant absurdity? Something that the Goddess would approve of?"

"What the Dark are you talking about?"

"Lorn, *I'm* on a quest."

"What?"

Herewiss grinned at the sudden confusion in Freelorn's face. He considered and discarded several possible ways of explaining things, and finally simply held out his hands. Usually he had to close his eyes when he made the little tongue of external Flame that was all he could manage. But he strained twice as hard as usual this time for the sake of keeping his eyes open. He didn't want to miss the look on Freelorn's face.

It was an amazing thing. It was so amazing that Herewiss broke out laughing like a fool, and lost his concentration and the Flame both a moment later. He laughed so hard that he had to hold his stomach against the pain, and all the while Freelorn stared at him in utter amazement.

Finally Herewiss calmed down, caught his breath, wiped his eyes.

"You have it," Freelorn said softly. "You have it."

"It looks that way."

"You have it! *Dusty!!*"

"That's me."

"MY GODDESS, YOU HAVE IT!!!"

"Sssh, you'll wake up Berlic."

"But you have it!" Freelorn whispered.

"Yeah."

And then Freelorn looked at Herewiss, and the joy in his eyes dimmed and flickered low.

"But a focus—"

"I tried. Can't use a Rod."

There was a long, long silence.

"Lorn," Herewiss said. "This is my secret. And yours, now. My mother taught me a lot of sorcery when I was younger, but there was always something else I could feel in the background that I knew wasn't anything to do with that. I didn't know what it was until last year—I made Flame accidentally in the middle of a scrying spell. I thought it might have been a fluke, but it's not; it's there, and it's getting stronger. If I can channel it, I can use it. And the Goddess only knows what I'm going to use for a focus. Will this do for a hopeless quest?"

Freelorn was silent for a while. Then he looked at Herewiss again.

"I am the Keeper of the Archive," he said solemnly, as if he were summoning Powers to hear him. "There must be something in here that would help you. I'm going to start looking. And when I find it—"

Herewiss smiled. "When you find it," he said.

They hugged each other, stirring up dust.

The memories were making Herewiss feel warm inside. The analytical parts of him approved: he was heading in the right direction. The warmth was building, washing through him—He shifted the scene again, and it was night out in the eastern Darthene wastelands, a hundred miles or so from the Arlene border. They were on their way to Prydon again after a trip to the Wood, and the day's riding had left them exhausted; Freelorn was anxious to get home, and they had spared neither themselves nor the horses. It was cold, for Opening Night was approaching, and they lay close to their little fire and shivered. The stars were beginning to fall thickly, as they do at Midwinter when the Goddess is angriest—when She remembers Her own thoughtlessness at the Creation, and flings stars burning across the night in defiance of the great Death. Herewiss lay on his back gazing up at the sky, watching the distant firebrands trace their silent paths out of the heart of the Sword, the constellation that stands highest on those deep winter nights. Freelorn lay curled up in a tight bundle next to him, facing west.

"Dusty—"

Herewiss turned his head to him.

"You want to share?"

Within the memory, Herewiss, now sixteen, went both warm with surprise and pleasure, and cold with fear. It was a thought that had occurred to him more than once. But Freelorn was younger than he was inside, and easily frightened. He wouldn't want to scare Lorn, ever—

—yet no one in the world knew him as well as Lorn did, no one else cared as much about all the little things in Herewiss's life and how he felt about them. He could share things with Lorn that he would never dare say to anyone else, and never be afraid of the consequences. And Lorn mattered so much to him. His loved. Yes. And he was beautiful outside, too, small and strong and fine to look at—

I've paid off the Responsibility. I can love whom I please—

"You want to?" he said aloud.

"Yeah."

Herewiss felt at the knot of fear inside him, wondering what to do about it. If Lorn wanted to—

But—

"I had to think about it for a while before I could say it," Freelorn said quietly, from inside the blankets. "If you don't want to, it's all right."

"No, it's not that—"

Freelorn chuckled, so adult a sound coming out of him that it startled Herewiss. He identified it as one of Ferrant's laughs, which Freelorn had borrowed. "I should have asked," Freelorn said. "Your first time?"

"No!—I mean, yes. With a man."

They were quiet for a while. Freelorn turned over on his back and looked up at the sky, watching a particularly bright star blaze out of the Sword and clear across the night to the Moonsteed before it went out. "There's not much difference," he said, "except that, instead of being different, we're alike. Some things are easier—some are harder—"

The voice was still suspiciously adult, and Herewiss looked at Freelorn for a moment and then smiled. "Your first time too, huh?"

Freelorn's face went shocked, then irritated, and finally sheepishly smiling. "Yeah."

Herewiss laughed softly to himself, and reached out to hug Freelorn to him. "You twit!" he said, laughing into Freelorn's blankets until the tears came.

They held each other for a long time, and then drew closer. Outside the memory, Herewiss looked on with quiet amusement, and with reverence, feeling as if he was watching an enactment of some old legend being staged by well-meaning amateurs. In a way, of course, he was: the Goddess's Lovers always discover each other after being initiated by Her—one of the things which makes for the tragedy of Opening Night, when the Lovers, male or female as the avatar dictates, destroy one another in Their rivalry. But this was an enactment of the birth of that new relationship, and the freshness and innocence of it easily compensated for whatever ineptitude there may have been as well.

"Oops—"

"Huh? Did it hurt?"

"Yeah, a little."

"Well, let's try this instead—"

"Ohhh…"

"Hmmm?"

"No, no, don't stop. It feels so good."

Silence, and further joinings: warm hands, warm mouths, growing comfort, trust flowing. A slow climb on smooth wings, easing into the upper reaches, then gliding into the updraft, soaring, daring, higher, higher—

—sudden and not to be denied, the brilliance that is not light, the dissolution of barriers that cannot possibly break—

—a brief silence.

"Oh, Dark, I'm sorry. I hurried you."

"Oh, no, don't be. It was—it was—oh, my…"

"I saw your face." A warm arm reaches around to pillow Herewiss's head; gentle fingers stroke his jaw line, his lips, his closed eyes. "You looked—so happy. I was glad I could make you feel that way."

"I felt…so *cherished.*"

"It was something I always wished somebody would…do for me…"

"You mean you *haven't*—"

"Oh, my dear loved. —Can I call you that?"

"Why not? It's *true*—oh, *Dusty*—!"

"Lorn, you're crying—? Are you all right, did I say something wrong—"

"No, no—it's just—nobody ever called me their loved before—and it's—I always wanted—I'm *happy*—"

"Oh, Lorn! Come here. No, come on, if we're going to share ourselves with each other, that means the tears too. My loved, my Lorn, it's all right, you're happy—"

"But, but my face gets—gets funny when I cry—"

"So does mine. Who cares? You're beautiful. I love you, Lorn—"

"Oh, Goddess, Dusty, I love you too. I was just scared—I didn't see how someone as gorgeous as you could ever want to share with me—"

"Me? Gorgeous? Oh, Lorn—"

"But you are, you are, don't you see it? And inside, too." A chuckle through passing tears. "It's almost unfair that anyone should be so beautiful as you are inside. But it makes me so *happy*—Am I making sense?"

"Yes. Oh, Lorn, I want you to feel what I felt, I want to give you the joy—you deserve it so much…and it makes me so happy to make *you* happy…"

—and again the slow dance, stately circling on wings of light—

—and much later, the long drift down.

Silence, and falling stars.

Outside the memory, Herewiss wept.

Inside the memory, Freelorn held Herewiss, and Herewiss held Freelorn, and their hearts slowed.

"Again?"

"I don't know if I could…"

A chuckle. "Neither do I." Another silence.

"Hey, maybe we should get married some day."

"Are you thinking of us, or of marriage alliances?"

"It could be good both ways. Hasn't been an alliance between our two Houses since the days of Béorgan."

"And you know how *that* turned out. I don't want to be history, Lorn, I just want to be *me*."

"Yeah."

"So think about us, then, and leave politics out of it."

"Can we?"

Herewiss thought about it. "At least until our fathers leave us their lands. I'm tired, Lorn."

"Yeah. We've got a long ride tomorrow."

"Yeah."

They held each other against the cold, and fell asleep.

Herewiss dwelt on the scene for a while, and then reluctantly changed it again. Another night, another place out in the cold: the battlefield where they fought the Reaver incursion, far to the south of the Wood…the night after the battle, and Herewiss wounded in the shoulder with the blow that he took for the king's daughter of Darthen. Later on that blow had gotten him awarded the White Mantle. But at this point Herewiss lay huddled on the ground, wrapped in his own tattered campaigning cloak, innocent of honors and just trying to get some sleep. He was cold and tired, and in pain from the wound. The hurt of it kept waking him up every time he drifted off. During one hazy time of almost-sleep, a figure came softly toward him in the dark, and Herewiss didn't move, didn't particularly care who it was—

"Dusty?"

He tried to get up, and Freelorn was down beside him, helping him. "Quiet, quiet—do you know how long I've been looking for you?" His voice was frightened.

"No."

"I couldn't find you. I was beginning to think you were—"

"Well, I'm not. I heard you were all right and so I just found a spot out of the way where I could get some sleep."

"That's interesting," Freelorn hissed. "Because you're behind the lines. Do you mind coming with me now before they find out who we are and carve the blood-eagle on us?"

"Behind the lines?"

"The *Reaver* lines! It's obvious you're being saved for something besides dying in battle. If you haven't managed it by now—Oh, Dusty, come *on!!*"

"I lost a lot of blood. I think I need a horse. Oh, poor old Socks, he got killed right out from under me—"

"Blackmane is here, I brought him. Come on, for Goddess's sake—"

The next while was a nightmare, an interminable period of jouncing and wincing and nearly falling out of the saddle. The wound reopened, and Herewiss bit back his moans with great difficulty. Blackmane was stepping softly; he seemed to have something tied around his feet. Herewiss later found out they had been pieces of Freelorn's best clothes—his Lion surcoat, the one embroidered in silver and satin, that he had loved so well. But in the midst of the hurt and the fresh bleeding, as they passed back through the enemy lines and slipped softly past the guards, Herewiss heard himself thinking, like a chant to put distance between one and one's pain, *He really must care about me. He really must—*

The slow wave of love that had been building in Herewiss was coming to a crest. He let it grow, let it build power. He would need it. Holding himself still in the twilight inside him, he reached out a tendril of thought to Sunspark.

(What?) it said. Its voice seemed distant, and he could perceive no more of the elemental than a vague sensation of warmth.

(Warn away anything that approaches. Don't hurt it, just keep it away.)

(It would be easier to kill.)

(It would disturb the influences I'm working with. Take care of me, Spark. If I have to drop what I'm doing suddenly, the backlash may catch you as well.)

(Whatever.)

He returned fully to the awareness of his inner self, and watched with approval as his building emotion began to shade toward anger. He encouraged it. *This is my friend; my loved; a part of me: this is the one they want to take and kill! Will it happen? Will it?* Will it?

The answer was building like a thunderhead, piling threateningly high. He turned his attention away from the building storm of emotion and started to work on the sorcery proper. The spell had to be built, word by cautious word, each word placed delicately against another, stressed and counter stressed, pronunciations clean and careful, intentions plain. The words were sharp as knives, and could cut deeper than any sword if they were mishandled. A word set here, and another one against it there: this one placed with care atop two others, taking care always to keep the whole structure in mind—too much attention to one part could collapse others. Here a jagged word like cutting crystal, faceted, many-syllabled, with a history to it—don't pause too long to admire the glitter of it; the others will resent the partiality and turn on you. There a word fragile as a butterfly's wing—indeed, the word has lineal ties with the Steldene word for butterfly, but don't think of that now; this winged word has teeth too. Now the next—

Herewiss was doing what few sorcerers care to do—building a spell without reference to the actual words written in the grimoire. It requires a good memory, and considerable courage. The mind has a way of shaping words to its liking, and that can be fatal to a sorcery and the one who works it. But keeping himself conscious enough to actually read the words from his books would have meant a diversion of needed power, and Herewiss was worried enough to forgo the safer method. He was making no passes, drawing no diagrams to help him; those measures would have cost him energy too. The greatest sorceries are always those done without recourse to anything but the words themselves, and the effect they have on the minds of the user and the hearer. But Herewiss didn't think about that just now. It would have scared him too much.

He built with the words, making a structure both like and unlike the towering concentration of love and anger within him. The structure had to be big enough to let the emotions flow freely, strong enough to contain them—but it also had to be small enough not to scrape the barriers of Herewiss's self and damage him, and light enough for him to break easily if the sorcery got out of hand. It was a perilous balance to maintain, and once or twice he almost lost it as a word shifted under another's weight. Another one turned on the word next to it—they were too much alike—and savaged it before Herewiss could remove the offender and put another, less violent, but also less effective, in its place. He had to make up for the loss of power elsewhere, at the top of the structure He wasn't sure whether it would stand up to the strain or not, and the whole crystalline framework swayed uncertainly for a moment, chiming like frozen bells in the wind, like icy branches, brittle, metallic—

It held, and he surveyed it for a moment to be sure that nothing was left out. Satisfied, he took a long moment's rest.

(Sunspark?)

(Yes?)

(Almost ready.)

(It's getting ready to rain.)

(In here, too. Hang on.)

He composed himself and examined the structure one last time. It was ready; all it was missing was the tide of emotion that had to be imprisoned inside of it, and the last three words that were the keys, the starting-words. He had them ready to hand, and the emotion had built to the point that it rolled like a red-golden haze all about the insides of his self, looking for an outlet. He began to direct it into the structure. It was hard work; it wanted to expand, to dissipate, as is the way of most emotion. But he forced it in, packed it tighter. It billowed and churned within the caging words, blood-color, sun-color, alive with frustration. He took two of the words of control in his hands. One of them was simple, smooth and opaque, though of a shape that could not exist in the outer world without help. He tucked it into the structure at an appropriate point, and then placed the other near it, a yellow word with a confused etymology and a lot of legs.

The third one was in his hands, ready; the gold-and-red storm seethed, rumbling to be let out. Now all that remained was for him to become conscious enough to direct the course of the sorcery, while remaining unconscious enough to set it working. Herewiss shifted about in his mind, found the proper balance point. Then with one hand he took the last word and shoved it into the structure. With the other he grabbed hold of his outer self and pulled his mind behind his eyes again. He looked out.

The Othersight, the perception of the hidden aspects of things, is a side effect of most large sorceries, caused by the intense concentration involved. It was on Herewiss now; he looked out of himself and saw things transfigured. The old keep was made of the bones of the earth, and a sort of life throbbed in it still, a deep gray light like the glow behind closed eyelids on a cloudy day. All around it the men and women of the Steldene army shone, a myriad of colors from boredom to fear—mostly weighted toward the blues and greens, smoky shades of people who wished themselves somewhere else. Many of them also showed the furry outlines of those who are willing to let others do their thinking for them. Well, *army types,* after all, Herewiss thought. *Now for it.*

Behind him, in the back of his mind, the pressure was becoming alarming. He let it build just a little longer, the red haze beating within the glittering framework like a second heart, throbbing, pulsing—

Go free! he thought, and the sorcery flowed away and outward from him, sliding down the hill. He could see it now with the Othersight, instead of just sensing it as a construct inside him. Though it flowed like water, it still bore the marks of his structuring, faint traceries of words and phrases gleaming through it like stars through storm swept clouds. The sorcery rolled down and away, expanding, slipping slowly and silently over the besieging forces, over the hold and the surrounding land. Finally it slowed, finding the boundaries that Herewiss had set for it in the spell. It stopped and waited, moving restlessly. To Herewiss's eyes the whole valley was filled like a cauldron with slowly boiling mist, and the men and the hold shone faintly through it.

All right, he thought. *First, boundaries that they can see—*

In a wide ring around the keep, the air began to darken. Within a short time a wall of cloud half a league in diameter surrounded the hold and the Steldene forces, a threatening roiling cloud that walled away the last of the sunset, leaving the field illuminated only by the lurid choked light at the bases of the thunderheads. Herewiss looked down at the cloudwall, watched it pulse and curl in time with his heartbeat.

Tighter, he thought. The ring drew inward until it was about a mile across. The men and women within it looked around them and became very uneasy. Herewiss could see the drab greens and blues start to shade down through murky violet as they knew the cloud for something unnatural. There were dark-bright flickers as swords were unsheathed, the brutalized metal living ever so slightly where hands touched it and charged it with disquiet.

Good. Now just a few minutes more—

The last of the sunset light faded from the storm clouds. Now there were no stars, and no Moon, not even a horizon any more. Fear built in the camps below Herewiss until all the swirling mist was churning dusk-purple in his sight, and people were moving about in increasing agitation.

Good. Now for the real work.

He put forth his will, and shapes began to issue from the wall of cloud. They were vague at first, but as his control and concentration sharpened, so did they, gaining detail and the appearance of reality.

He started small. Fyrd began to slip out of the dark mist, moving down on the besiegers with slow malice. There were great gray-white horwolves snarling softly in their throats, and nadders coiling sinuously down toward the hold, spitting venom and shriveling the grass as they went. There were dark keplian, almost horse-shaped, but clawed and fanged like beasts of prey, and destreth dragging scalded bodies along the ground, and lathfliers beating heavily along on webbed wings, cawing like huge, misshapen battle-crows. Herewiss made sure that his creations were evenly distributed around the army. In a flicker of black humor he added a few beasts that had lurked in his bedroom shadows when he was young, turning them loose to creep down toward the campfires on all those many-jointed legs of theirs.

The temper of the army was shading swiftly darker, the deep purple turning into the black of panic in places. There were still spots, though, where the commanders stood and knew that this was illusion-sorcery. They showed pale against the darkness of their fellows, suspicious green or nervous murky blue as they tried to rally their people.

They're holding too well. Fyrd are too real maybe. Legends, then—

A gigantic ravaged figure came tottering through the cloud, a look of ugly rage fixed on his face. It was the Scorning Lover, of whom Arath's old poem sings. Attracted by his beauty and brilliance, the Goddess had come to him and offered what She always offers, Her Self, until the Rival comes to take the Lover's place. But this young man had had a calculating streak, and as price for sharing himself had asked eternal youth and eternal life. The Bride tried to warn him that not even She could completely defeat Death in this universe, and told him he was foolish to try. He would not listen, and She gave him the gifts he asked and left him, for the Goddess cannot love one who loves life more than Her. And indeed as the centuries passed, the Lover did not die—nor did he grow, frozen as he was in the throes of an eternal adolescence. Time and time again he tried to kill himself, but to no avail; immortality is just that. And over all that time, all thought and hope died in him, leaving him a demon, a terror of waste places, killing all who fell into his hands while bitterly envying their deaths. He stumbled toward the army now, raging with pain from the thousand self-inflicted wounds that can never heal, and never kill him, his clawing hands clutched full of gobbets of his own immortal flesh—

The forces on the eastern side, from which he approached, gave way hurriedly, consolidating with those to the north and south.

Herewiss smiled with grim satisfaction, and out of the cloud to the north summoned the seeming of the Coldwyrm of Arlid-ford, which doomed Béorgan had killed with the help of her husband Ánmod, Freelorn's ancestor. The thing crawled down the slope, an ugly unwinged caricature of the pure hot beauty of a Dragon. The Wyrm was scaled and plated, but in a thick fishbelly blue-white rather than any Dracon green or gold or red. A smell of cold corruption blew from it, like fetid marshes in the winter, and the ground froze with its stinking slime-ice where it crawled. The Wyrm's pale blue tongue flickered out, tasting the fear in the air, and the cold black chasms of its eyes dwelt on the huddling troops before it with malice and hungry pleasure.

The commanders were trying hard not to believe in what they saw. But the campfires were too faint to show whether any of the stalking shapes had shadows or not. The army was collecting into a frightened mass of men and women at the southeast side of the keep.

Just a little more pressure, Herewiss thought, *and they'll be ready for Sunspark. But first I need something that'll be sure to panic them all... Dark, I could—it's almost blasphemy, and no battle-sorcerer in his right mind would ever try it. That alone makes it worth trying. And, anyway, it is for Freelorn's sake, and I don't think his Father would mind the use of His seeming—*

Herewiss hesitated. *It's for love,* he decided. *I just hope Lorn's watching.*

From the south, as might have been expected, pacing slowly out of the cloud, came a great form that cast its own silver-white light about it. It was a Lion, one of the white Arlene breed, longer of mane and tail than the tan Darthene lions which run in prides. But this Lion was twenty times the size of any ordinary one; it towered as tall as the keep. And its eyes held what no earthly lion's ever had—intelligence, frightening power, towering wrath. It was Héalhra Whitemane, in the shape that He took upon himself at Bluepeak, where the Fyrd were broken and scattered...the Father of the Arlene kings, and one of the two males ever to have use of the Power.

Herewiss halted his other creations where they stood, banished the Fyrd altogether, and poured all his power into making this one illusion as real as it had been in his boyhood dreams. Earn Silverwing should have been there too, the White Eagle companioning the Lion as They had always been together in life. But Herewiss doubted he could handle it and do Them both justice. He poured himself out, and the Lion approached in His majesty, His growl rumbling softly in the air like the thunder waiting in the clouds above. He drew to a halt no more than three or four spear casts from the tightly clustered army, and looked down at them, towering over them—shining, silvery, His eyes grim and golden—

In the Othersight the army was a black blot of leashed panic, terror with nowhere to run. Now, while they couldn't move to prevent the damage—

Herewiss gave the sorcery an extra boost, a push of power to keep it alive while he turned his attention away from it. Then he turned to Sunspark, looking at him with the Othersight—

—and was amazed. Sunspark burned beside him, almost intolerable even to his altered vision, blazing as flaming-white as the pain at the bottom of a new wound. Its outline was that of a stallion still, but confined within that outline was the straining heart of a star, an inexpressible conflagration of consuming fires. Now Herewiss began for the first time to understand what an elemental *was*. This was one note of the song the Goddess sang at the beginning, when She was young and did not know about the great Death. One pure unbearable note of the song, a note to break the brain open through the ears and the burnt eyes—a chained potency looking for a place to happen, a spark of the Sun indeed, whose only purpose was to burn itself out, recklessly, gloriously. One more falling star, one more firebrand flung against the night by the Creatress in Her defiance—

Herewiss slipped warily into Sunspark's mind, confining himself to the narrow dark bridge that represented his control over it, a sword's-width of safety arching over unfathomed fires. (Sunspark. Go, take their tents, their wagons, everything, and burn them. I don't want us being followed.)

(And the men?) Its inward voice was no longer a thing of concepts, but of currents of heat and tangles of light.

(Don't kill!!)

It resisted him, testing, defying his control, and in his heart Herewiss shuddered. He had not really understood what a terror he had chosen to bind. Its fires ravened around him, barely constrained by its given word. Nothing more than its sense of honor kept him from being consumed, but at the same time it was not above trying to frighten him into releasing it. And it did not understand his scruples at all. (What is death?) it sang, its up-leaping fires dancing and weaving through the timbre of its thought. (Why do you fear? They would come back. So would you. The dance goes on forever, and the fire—)

(Maybe for you. But they have no such assurances, and as for me, you know my reasons. Go do what I told you!)

It laughed at him, mocking his uncertainty, and the flames of its self wreathed up around Herewiss, licking, testing, prying at the cracks in his mind. It was without malice, he realized; it was only trying to make him understand, trying to make him one with it, though that oneness would destroy him. He held his barriers steadfastly, though in some deep part of him there was a touch of longing to be part of that fire, lost in it, burning in nonambivalent brilliance for one bare second before he was no more. The greater part of him, though, respected death too much, and refused the urge.

(Go!) he said again, and withdrew himself. Sunspark gathered itself up, leaped, streamed across the sky like a meteor, a trail of fire crackling behind it and lighting the lowering clouds as if with a sudden disastrous dawn.

The men before the keep, frozen in their silent regard of the Lion, saw Sunspark coming and knew it for something perhaps more real than they were. The few minds still bright with disbelief bent awry and went dark as if blown out by a cold wind. Herewiss, though shaken, turned his thought back to his sorcery, and as Sunspark swept down among the tents of the soldiers, the Lion roared, a sound that seemed to shake the earth clear back to where Herewiss sat.

It was too much. The army broke, scattering this way and that in wild disorder, screaming. Sunspark flitted from place to place in the first camp, the one on the eastern side, leaving explosions of white fire behind it. The flames spread with unnatural speed, leaping from tent to wagon as if of their own volition. Herewiss opened a door in the encircling cloud, parting it to the northward, and people began to flee through it. Sunspark saw this and hurried the process. It dove into the southern camp like a meteor and ignited it all at once into a terrible pillar of flame, driving the stampeding army around the west side of the keep and toward the opening in the cloudwall. They fled, officers and men together, with their screaming horses. Sunspark came behind them, though not too closely, spitting gledes and rockets of fire with joyous abandon.

Herewiss sighed and dissolved his remaining illusions, the Lion last of all. The great white head turned to regard him solemnly for a moment. Herewiss gazed back at it, seeing his own weary satisfaction mirrored in the golden eyes, himself looking at himself through his sorcery; then he withdrew his power from it with a sad smile. The image went out like a blown candle, but Herewiss imagined that those eyes lingered on him for a moment even after they were gone…

He shook his head to clear it. The backlash was getting to him already.

(Sunspark?)

It paused and looked back at him, a tiny intense core of light far down in the field.

(Are they all out?)

(Nearly.)

(Good. Look, the keep door is opening—it's all fire there, go and part it for Lorn and his people and bring them through.)

(As you say.)

Slowly, hesitantly, six faintly glowing figures rode out of the keep and paused before the flaming eastern camp. The bright blaze that was Sunspark joined them there, and they all headed toward the fire, which ebbed suddenly.

The Othersight departed without warning, in the space of a breath. The sorcery dwindled and died away, the wall of cloud evaporated, emotion dissipating before the wind of relief. Herewiss sagged, feeling empty and drained. The fragile spell-structure swayed and fell and shattered inside him, the bright crystalline fragments littering the floor of his mind, sharp splinters of light hurting the backs of his eyes. *Backlash*...He put his hands behind him and braced himself against the ground, fighting the backlash off. There was one more thing he had to do.

The pain in his head was like hammers on anvils—Herewiss laughed at the thought, and found that it hurt to laugh, so he stopped—but he held himself awake and aware by main force, waiting. It was hard. Presently there were hands on him, helping him up. Herewiss opened his eyes and knew the face that bent over him, even in a night of impending storm and no stars.

"Lorn," he whispered, reaching out, clinging to him.

"Herewiss. Oh Goddess. Are you all right?" The voice was terrified.

"Yes. No. Get me up, Lorn, I have something to do. When I finish, tie me on Sunspark here—"

"Fine. Up, then, do it, you've got to rest."

"You're telling me. Where's Sunspark?"

"The horse, he means. Dritt, give me a hand. Segnbora, help us—"

"Right." *A new voice. Female. Where did she come from?*

Oh—the sixth one... Strong hands stood him up, guided him to Sunspark.

He put out his hands, braced himself against the stallion's shoulder. *"N'stai llan astrev—"* he began, spilling out the simple water-deflecting spell as fast as he could, for the darkness was reaching up to take him—

He finished it, and sagged back into the supporting arms. "East," he said, but his voice didn't seem to be working properly, and he had to push the words out again harder, "—straight east—"

Darkness deeper than the stormy night enfolded him, and as he drowned beneath the black sea roaring in his ears, he felt the rain begin.

five

*Silence is the door between Love and Fear,
and on Fear's side, there is no latch.*

Gnomics, 33

Sunset was glowing behind his back when Herewiss woke up. He opened his eyes on a wide barren vista of earth and scattered brush, streaked with crimson light and long shadows. He stretched, and found that he ached all over. It wasn't all backlash; some of it was the pain of having been tied in the saddle and taken a great distance at speed.

"Good evening," someone said to him.

He didn't recognize the voice, a deep, gentle one. Then as he turned his head, the memories snapped back into place. The new person, the woman. This must be her.

Looking up at her, Herewiss's first impression was of large, deep-set hazel eyes that lingered on him in leisurely appraisal, and didn't shift away when he returned the glance. And hands: long, strong-fingered hands, prominently veined, incongruously attached to little fragile bird-boned wrists and too-slender arms. She was very slim and long-limbed, wearing with faint unease a body that didn't seem to have finished adolescence yet. But her muscles looked taut and hard from assiduous training. She sat cross-legged on the ground by Herewiss's head, those strong hands resting quietly on her knees, seemingly relaxed. But his underhearing, hypersensitive from the large sorcery he had worked, gave him an immediate feeling of impatience, an impression that beneath the imposed external calm seethed something that *had* to be done and *couldn't*. Her dark hair was cut just above the shoulders; Herewiss looked at it and smiled. *She wants to make sure they know she's a woman,* he thought, *but she doesn't have the patience for braids...*

"Good evening to you," he said, propping himself up on one elbow and then frowning—he had forgotten how sore he was. "I'm sorry I missed your name when we were on the way out—"

"You were hardly in a condition to remember it if you'd heard it," she said, reaching out to touch hands with him. "Segnbora, Welcaen's daughter."

"Herewiss, Hearn's son," he said, touching her hand, and then flinching. No matter how fordone he might be, there was no mistaking the feel of Flame. And she was full of it, spilling over with it. It had sparked between their hands, faint blue like dry-lightning, as if trying to fill the empty place in him. Something very like envy whirled through Herewiss's mind, to be replaced immediately by confusion. With power like *that*, what was she doing *here?*

She was rubbing her hands together thoughtfully, and still looking at him, her curiosity more open. But at the same time she read the look in his eyes, and her expression was rueful. "You felt right," she said softly. "The funny thing is, I think I did too…"

For a few moments more they regarded each other. Then Segnbora dropped her eyes, reaching down with one hand to play with the peace-strings of her sword, sheathed on the ground beside her.

"That was some sorcery you worked," she said, and looked up again. Her face was all admiration, masking whatever else was in her mind. "You were out for two days."

"Where are we now?"

"About fifteen miles from the border of the Waste. We only have to cross the Stel. Freelorn will be glad you're awake. He was worried about you."

"Don't know why," Herewiss said, and sat himself up with an effort. "He knows I always take the backlash hard."

"I'm sure. But he never saw anything like *that* display before. Some of the effects were—"

"Unexpected."

"Yes. Especially that business with the fire."

"Where is he?" Herewiss said hurriedly.

"Out hunting. They left me here to watch you. This is safe country, too empty for Fyrd, I think. They'll be lucky to find anything. Dritt is here too."

He looked around and located Dritt sitting atop a boulder, a big stocky silhouette against the sunset. He was munching something, and Herewiss became immediately aware of the emptiness of his stomach.

Segnbora was rummaging in a pouch. "Here," she said, handing him an undistinguished-looking lump of something crumbly.

"Waybread?"

"Yes."

It looked terrible, like a lump of pale dirt with rocks in it. He bit into it, and almost broke a tooth.

"Goddess above," he said, after managing to get the first bite down, "this is *awful.*"

"And what waybread isn't?"

"Worse than most, I mean."

"It's also more sustaining than most."

"I think I'd rather eat sagebrush."

"You may, if they don't find anything out there. Eat up."

Segnbora took a piece too, and they sat for a few minutes in silence, passing her water skin back and forth at intervals.

"The fire," Segnbora said suddenly. "And your messengers—the hawk, that ball of flame that met us when we came out—those really interested me. Those were no illusions. Those were *real.*"

He studied her uneasily, not responding, trying to understand what she was up to. She was looking thoughtfully over his shoulder at something fairly close by. Herewiss put his mind out behind him and felt around. Sunspark was some yards behind him with the other horses, once again a vague blunt warmth wrapped in the stallion-form, grazing unconcernedly.

(Yes?) it said.

(Our friend here—) Herewiss indicated Segnbora.

(So?)

(I think she sees you for what you are.)

Sunspark waved its tail, making a feeling like a shrug. (That's well for her. I'm worth seeing...)

Herewiss returned his attention to Segnbora. She continued to gaze past him for a moment. Remotely he could sense Sunspark lifting its head, returning her look.

(Another relative,) it said. (This world seems to be full of my distant cousins.)

"An elemental?" Segnbora said, turning her eyes back to Herewiss.

"Yes. Why?"

She gestured at his empty scabbard. "You have no sword."

"I *beg* your pardon?" Herewiss said, shocked.

"I'm sorry—I didn't mean to change the subject. But I'd been meaning to ask you about that."

Herewiss felt outrage beginning to grow in him, and a voice spoke up in his memory: some Darthene regular, way back during the war. ("Spears and arrows are a *boy's* weapons! Afraid to get up close to a Reaver?...A man isn't a boar to be hunted with a lance. A *man* takes on another man blade to blade. Earn's blood must be running thin in the Wood—)

Oh, Dark, I thought I got over this a long time ago! Herewiss took a deep breath and pushed the anger down "It may be none of your business," he told Segnbora, as gently as he could

"Then why are you so obvious about it? You wouldn't be wearing that around if you didn't want to attract attention to it. Freelorn's people think it's something to do with a family feud, and they won't mention it for fear you'll take offense. But there's something else there—"

"Freelorn knows. And he doesn't speak of it either," Herewiss said, trying to frighten her away from the subject with a sudden knife-edge of anger in his voice.

"Maybe someone should," Segnbora said, so very softly that he sat back in confusion. "I saw how he looks at that scabbard. He looks at it, but he doesn't look at it—as if it was a maimed limb. He hurts so much for you. I didn't know why—but now—It's a matter of Flame, isn't it?"

"Listen," Herewiss said, "why should I discuss it with you? We've barely met."

Segnbora smiled at him, that dry, rueful smile again. "Fair enough," she said. "Let me tell you who I am, and perhaps you'll understand. I come of fey stock from a long way back—generations of Rodmistresses and sorcerers. The male line has descent from Gereth Dragonheart, who was Marchwarder with M'athwinn d'Dháriss when the Dragons were fighting for the Eorlhowe. The female line comes down from Enra the Queen's sister of Darthen. Two terribly eminent families...and I'm something of an embarrassment to both of them."

Segnbora began playing with her sword's peace-bindings again, smiling slightly. "We usually come into our Power early, if it's there. They took me to be tested when I was three years old, and they weren't disappointed. The Flame that was in me shattered all the rods and rings and broke the blocks that they gave me to hold, and the testers got really excited. They said to my mother and father, 'This one is a great power, or will be when she grows up—you should have her trained by the best people you can find. Anything less would be a terrible waste.' So they did. And I studied with Harandh, and Saris Elerik's daughter, and the people at the Nhàirëdi Institute in Darthis, and I did a year with Eilen—"

"That old prune?"

"You know her. Yes. And others too numerous to mention. I hardly spent more than a year or two in the same place."

"It's not very good policy to change teachers so often," Herewiss said. "I wouldn't think there would be time to build up a good relationship—"

"You're right, it's not, and there wasn't," Segnbora said. "There was this little problem, you see. I had too much Flame. I kept breaking the Rods they gave me to work with; they would just blow right up, boom—" She waved her hands in the air—"any time I tried to channel through them. And all my teachers said, 'It's all right, you'll grow out of it, it's just adolescent surge.' Or, 'Well, it's puberty, it'll be all right after your breasts grow.'" She chuckled. "Well, they grew all right, but that wasn't the problem. After a while I started wondering why every teacher seemed in such a hurry to refer me to another one, supposedly more experienced or more advanced. Once or twice I made so bold as to ask, and got long lectures on why I should let older and wiser heads decide what was best for me. Or else I got these short shamefaced speeches on how I needed more theory, but everything would be all right eventually."

Herewiss made a face.

"That's how I felt," Segnbora said. "Well, what could I do? I gave it a chance, stuffed myself with more theory than most Rodmistresses would ever have use for. It was better than facing the truth, I suppose. And eventually I got to be eighteen, and they took me to the Forest Altars in the Brightwood, and I spent a year there in really advanced study—or so they called it. You know the Altars?"

"I live in the Brightwood," Herewiss said dryly. *And a lot of good it did me!* "Go on."

"Yes. Well, when I turned nineteen, and Maiden's Day came around, I swore the Oath, and they took me into the Silent Precincts, and they brought out the Rod they had made for me. They were really proud of it, it came from Earn's Blackstave in the Grove of the Eagle, it'd been cut in the full of the Moon with the silver knife and left on the Flame Altar for a month. And they gave it to me and I channeled Flame through it—"

"—and you broke it."

"Splinters everywhere, the Chief Wardress ducked and turned around and took one right in the rear. Oh, such embarrassment you haven't seen anywhere. The Wardress claimed I did it on purpose—she and I had had a few minor disagreements on matters of theory—"

"Kerim is a disagreement looking for a place to happen."

"Yes," Segnbora said tiredly, "she is. Well. They went down the whole Dark-be-damned list of trees, and I broke oak Rods and ash and willow and blackthorn and rowan and you name it. Finally the Wardresses who were there said they'd never seen anything like it, but they couldn't help me. So here I am, so full of Power that sometimes it crawls out my skin at night and changes the ground where I lie—but I can't *control* so much of it as to heal a cut finger, or bring a drop of rain." She sighed. "A whole life wasted in the pursuit of the one art I can't master."

Herewiss sat there and felt an odd twisted kind of pleasure. *So I'm not the only one like this! Well, well*—But then he pushed it aside, ashamed of it.

"Precisely," Segnbora said, her voice tight, and Herewiss blushed fiercely. "Oh," she said, and smiled again, "they really push you at Nhàirëdi; my underhearing got awfully good."

"I'm sorry—"

"Don't be. I must confess feeling a moment's satisfaction when I realized what your problem was. I'm sorry, too."

Herewiss sighed. "You're a long way from the Forest Altars."

She shrugged. "How long can a person keep trying? I spent three more years in the Precincts, fasting and praying and trying to beat my body into submission—I thought I could tame the Power that way." She snorted. "Silly idea. I ended up half-wrecked, with the Fire almost dead in me from the abuse. I had to let it rest for a long time before it would come back. Then after a while I said, 'What the Dark!' and just went off to travel. The Power's going to wither up in me soon enough, but there's no reason to be bored while it does. I made Freelorn's acquaintance in Madeil; and traveling in company is more interesting than being alone. Especially with him." She chuckled.

"But you still have a lot going for you," Herewiss said, though the empty place in him realized how such a statement might feel to her. "You studied at Nhàirëdi, you certainly got enough sorcery from them to make yourself a living by it—"

Segnbora shrugged again. "True. But I have better things to do with my life than spell broken cartwheels back together or divine for well diggers or mix potions to make men potent. Or I thought I had. I was going to reach inside minds and really understand motivations—not just make do with the little blurred glimpses you get from underhearing, all content and no context. I was going to untwist the hurt places in people, and heal wounds with something better than herbs and waiting—to really *hear* what goes on in the world around, to talk to thunderstorms and soar in a bird's body and run down with some river to the Sea. I was going to move the forces of the world, to command the elements, and *be* them when I chose. To give life, to give Power back to the Mother. To sing the songs that the stars sing, and hear them sing back. And they told me I'd do all that, and I believed them. And it was all for nothing."

She looked out into nothing as she spoke, and her voice drifted remotely through the descending dusk as if she were telling a bedtime story to a drowsy child. From the quiet set of her face, it might have been a story laid in some past age, all the loves and strivings in it long since resolved. But the pain in her eyes was here-and-now, and Herewiss's underhearing caught the sound of a child, awake and alone in the darkness, crying softly.

He sat there and knew the sound too well; he'd heard it in himself, in the middles of more nights than he cared to count. "If you had it, you know," he said, trying to find a crumb of comfort for her, "you'd just die early."

He had tried to make a joke of it, an acknowledgment of shared pain. But she turned to him, and looked at him, and his heart sank. "Who cares if you die early," she said very quietly, "as long as you've *lived.*"

He dropped his eyes and nodded.

They sat and gazed at the sunset for a while.

"I'm sorry," Segnbora said eventually, pulling her knees up to her chest and wrapping her arms around them. "The problem is much with me these days; it's dying, you see. But it must be worse for you. At least for me there's hope—"

"There's hope," Herewiss said harshly, "just fewer people to believe in me. A lot fewer."

"That's what I meant," she said, and to his surprise, he believed her. "That jolt you gave me when we touched—you certainly have enough to use. If you live in the Brightwood, you must have tried the Altars too—"

"Yes."

"And?"

"They turned me away."

"They did *what?*"

"I couldn't use a Rod."

"Well, of *course* you couldn't! It's a woman's symbol, your undermind would interfere with it. What were they thinking of?"

She was all indignation now, and Herewiss, feeling it was genuine, warmed to her somewhat. "You're a *man;* what did they expect? And just because you couldn't use a Rod, they gave up on you?"

"Yes."

Segnbora frowned at Herewiss, and he leaned back, stricken by the angry intensity of the expression. "There are few enough women since the Catastrophe who have the Power," she said, "less than a tenth of us—and no men at all—Do they think there are enough people running around using Flame that they can afford to throw one *away?* A *male,* no less." She shook her head. "They must have been crazy."

"I thought so at the time."

"What did they say?"

Herewiss shrugged. "I asked for help in finding something else to use as a focus. I thought that, since the sword is very symbolic of the Power for me, that I might use one as focus. They said it was hopeless, that the Power was a thing of flesh and blood and the lightning that runs along the nerves, and that it could never flow through anything that hadn't been alive, like wood. Well, I said, how about a sword made of wood or ivory? Oh, no, they said to me, the sword in concept and design is an instrument of death, and unalterably opposed to the principles of the Power. They just wouldn't help me at all. I guess I didn't fit their image of how a male with the Power would act, when one finally showed up. So I left, and went my own ways to study."

Herewiss stretched, making an irritated face. "Well, for whichever of the reasons they gave me, they've been right so far. I tried using various sorceries to condition the metal of a sword to the conduction of Flame. That was silly—the Power and mundane sorceries are two entirely different disciplines. But I tried it. I tried swords of wood, and ivory, and horn, and bone, but those didn't work. I finally started forging my own swords and using my blood at various stages—melding it with the metal, tempering the sword with it, writing runes on the blade with it—"

"Nothing, though."

"Well, not quite. Once, the business with the runes, that began to feel as if it would work—almost. Not quite, though. There was a stirring—something was starting to happen—but the sword still felt wrong. They all do. It could be they're right about the dichotomy between swords and life."

"Maybe you need to know your Name," Segnbora said.

Herewiss went stiff for a moment, feeling threatened by the subject. The matter of Names wasn't usually mentioned in casual conversation, and certainly not between two people who had just met. But Segnbora's tone was noncommittal, and her expression reserved. She shifted her eyes away as he looked at her, and Herewiss relaxed.

"Maybe," he said, looking away himself, his fingers playing idly with the empty scabbard. "But I don't know how to find it. I mean, I'm not all that sure who I'm supposed to be. I have ideas—but it's like water in a sieve. I pour myself into them, into this role, or that identity, and they won't hold me. I'm a passable sorcerer—"

"A little more than passable."

"Yes, well—but that's not what I want to be. Sorcery is an imposition on the environment, a forcing, a rape. The Power is a meshing, a cooperation, like love. You don't *make* it rain; you *ask* it to, and usually it will, if you ask it nicely. You know that. I have no desire to be just a very talented rapist, when I have the potential to be a lover, even a clumsy one. So. I'm all right as a warrior, but I don't have a sword; and I don't want to kill anyone anyway. I'm a fair scholar—I know six dead Darthene dialects and four Arlene ones; I can read runes a thousand years old. But there's more to life than sitting around translating moldering manuscripts. I'm not much of a prince—"

Segnbora's eyebrows went up. "My Goddess. You're *that* Hearn's son? I didn't make the connection—that's a fairly common name up north."

Herewiss bowed slightly from the waist. "The same."

"And I thought *my* family was impressive. I'm sorry; please go on."

"There's not much more to say, really. I don't know—I'm so many people, and no one of them is all of me—"

Segnbora nodded. "I know the problem."

"There was a period when I gave the problem a lot of thought. I said to myself, 'Well, maybe the Power will follow if the Name is there.' So I tried all the ways I could think of to find out. Fasting—yes, you know how that is—and a lot of time spent in meditation. Too much. Once I sat down and turned everything inward, *everything,* and all that happened was that I got stuck inside and couldn't find my way out again. I rattled around in the dark and struck out at the walls, but they seemed to be mirrored—and I found myself thinking that if I hit the walls, I would hurt the inside of *me*—and there were voices in the dark, some of them seemed to belong to my parents, or to people I knew; some of them were kind, but some were ugly and twisted—" Herewiss shook his head. "I got out eventually, but I'll never go that way again. I might not be so lucky the next time."

Segnbora stretched her arms over her head and let them drop to encircle her knees again. "I heard it said once," she said, so softly that Herewiss had to strain to hear her, "—oh, a long time back—that to find your Name, you have to turn the mind and heart, not inward, but outward rather; that you have to pay no attention to the voices in the dark—or, rather, accept them for what they are, but take their advice only when it pleases you, and don't allow yourself to be driven by them. Look always forward and outward, not back and in."

"Now, I understand *that* not at all," Herewiss said. "How can you get to know yourself by looking out? Who besides yourself can tell you what you are, or what you're going to be?"

"I don't know. I haven't found my Name, either. Maybe I never will."

They sat there in depressed and companionable silence for a while. Then Herewiss looked up and grinned at Segnbora. "Well," he said. "Maybe I can't command wind and wave, but this much I *can* do—"

He cupped his hands before him, and beside him Segnbora leaned close to watch. Herewiss closed his eyes, reached down inside him, found the flicker of Flame within him, breathed softly on the little light, encouraged it, cherished it, and then willed—

It flowered there in his outstretched hands, a tiny wavering bloom of fire that grew and bent in the wind of his will: as vividly blue as a little child's eyes, with a hot white core like a new sprung star, but gently warm in his hands—

It went out, and he folded his hands together and strove to thank the Power in him, rather than cursing at it for being so feeble. He looked at Segnbora. "Can you?"

She gave him an amused sidelong look. "Watch," she said, and reached out before her as if to support something that Herewiss could not see, hanging in the air. It came before he was ready for it, sudden, brilliant, so bluely brilliant that it outraged his eyes and left dancing violet afterimages: a lightning flash, a starflower, a little sun, hanging in the air between her hands. For a moment an odd blue day lit the desert, and everything had two shadows, sharp short black ones laid over long dull streaks of red-purple light and darkness. Then the light went out, and Segnbora let her hands fall. "As you see," she said, "I can't maintain it. Maybe I can find work as a lighthouse beacon."

Herewiss looked up at Dritt, who still sat on his rock, unconcerned, eating; he had spared them no more than a curious look. "Do you do this often?" Herewiss said.

"Every now and then, in dark places. They've seen it before—they think it's an illusion-charm. None of them but Freelorn would know real wreaking from sorcery if it walked up and bit them; and Freelorn never says anything about it...And speak of the Shadow, here he comes."

They both stood up, and Herewiss wobbled for a moment, the world darkening in front of him and then brightening as the dizziness passed. He made a mental note to keep being careful of the backlash for the next couple of days. Four forms on horseback were approaching slowly, and the horse in the lead had a young desert deer slung over its withers.

Herewiss stood there, his hands on his hips, and watched the figure in the saddle of the lead horse. Their eyes met while the riders were still a ways off, and Herewiss watched the smile spread over Freelorn's face, and felt his own grow to match it. The horse ambled along toward the camp, and Freelorn made no attempt to hurry it. An old memory spoke up in Freelorn's voice. "I hate long good-byes," it said, looking over a cup of wine drained some years before, "but I love long hellos..."

(Are you going to do it now?) Sunspark asked, with interest.

(Do what?)

(Unite.)

(Spark, don't *ask* questions like that! It's not polite.)

The group drew rein and dismounted, and Herewiss glanced at them only briefly. They all looked about the same as they had when he had last seen them. Lang, a great golden bear of a man, slid down out of his saddle like a sack of meal, grinned and winked at Herewiss, and then went over to hug Segnbora; when the hug broke, the two of them got busy starting a fire in the lee of the boulder. Tall, skinny, cold-eyed Moris with his beaky nose swung down from his horse, nodded to Herewiss and spoke a word of greeting; but his eyes were mostly for big Dritt, still up on the rock, and for him Moris's eyes warmed as he climbed up to sit beside him. Harald, a short round sparse-bearded man, staggered past with the deer over his shoulder. He waved a hand at Herewiss and hurried past him, puffing.

And then Freelorn eased himself out of the saddle. Herewiss went slowly and calmly to meet his friend—

—and was hugging him hard before he knew what happened, his face crunched down against Freelorn's shoulder, and much to his own surprise, tears burning hot and sudden in his eyes as Freelorn hugged him back. *Five-in-Heaven, did I really miss him that much? I guess I did…*

(So where are the progeny?) said someone in the background.

(Sunspark, *what* within the walls of the world are you talking about?) Herewiss said, prolonging the hug.

(That wasn't union? I thought you'd changed your mind and decided to go ahead. You give off discharges like that just for *greeting* each other? Isn't that wasteful?)

(Sunspark, *later.*)

They held each other away, and Freelorn was laughing, and sniffling a little too. "Goddess Mother of us all, look at you!" he said. "You're bigger than you were. You *cheat,* dammit!"

"No, I don't. Lorn, your mustache is longer, you look like a Steldene."

"That was the idea, for a while. Look at the *arms* on you! That's what it is. What the Dark have you been doing?"

"I'm a swordsmith," Herewiss said. "I hammer a lot. If you want to look like this, you can, but it'll take you a year or so. That's how long I've been at it. Lorn, you twit, what's the use of trying to look like a Steldene if you're going to wear *that* around?" He nodded at Freelorn's black surcoat, charged with the Arlene arms, the white Lion *passant guardant* uplifting its great silver blade.

"Who's going to see it out here?"

"That's not the point. You were wearing it in Madeil, weren't you?"

"No—my other one got stolen out of my saddlebag. Let me tell you what happened—"

"I can imagine. For such an accomplished thief, you get stolen from awfully easily. How many times have I—oh, never mind, come on, sit down and tell me. Tell me everything. We haven't talked since—Goddess!—since not last Opening Night, but the one before. When you came to the Wood."

"Yeah." They sat down by a chair-sized boulder and put their backs to it. Herewiss slid an arm around Freelorn's shoulders. "Let's see, let's see—" Freelorn chewed his mustache a bit. "After we left the Wood, we went west a ways—stayed in the empty country north of Darthis until spring came. And then south. We made a big wide detour around Darthis, didn't even cross the Darst until Hiriden or so—"

"That *is* quite a detour. Any trouble?"

"No. That was the interesting thing, though. One Darthene patrol stopped us and I was *sure* they knew who I really was. I lied splendidly about everything, though, and they let us go. You wouldn't know anything about that, would you?"

Herewiss laughed softly. "Oddly enough, I would. My father has been exchanging letters with Eftgan recently, and the queen is not happy with Cillmod and his co-conspirators in Arlen. Not at all. She told Hearn in one letter that she considers the real Arlene government to be in exile. Right now she doesn't dare openly support or recognize you; she's too new to the throne, and the Four Hundred are still unsure of her. But because of the Oath of Lion and Eagle she feels obligated to do *something* for you. Those guards may or may not have known who you were—but if they did, they had orders to let you pass unhindered. You're safe in Darthen, so long as you don't make yourself so visible that they have no choice but to notice you."

"What about public opinion?"

"That may have influenced her. Most of Darthen is in outrage over Cillmod having the gall to break Oath. Especially the country around Hadremark, where a lot of people went homeless after the burning, and all the crops were ruined. But Eftgan's hands are tied. She can't really move against Arlen, or she'd be breaking Oath herself. She's strengthened the garrisons on the Arlid border, but there are ways to sneak past those. She even went so far as to ask the human Marchwarders in Darthen to talk to the Dragons, ask *their* help—but the answer is pretty likely to be the same as usual. The Dragons won't get involved."

"Granted."

"So in a way, you're her best hope. The story running in Darthen seems to be that you're alive and traveling around to raise force so that you can get Arlen back. The people seem to approve. They want the Lion's child back on the throne again, as much for their own welfare as for yours."

Freelorn nodded. "'Darthen's House and Arlen's Hall,'" he recited,

"'share their feast and share their fall—
Fórlennh's and Hergótha's blade
are of the same metal made,
and the Oath they sealed shall bind
both their dest'nies intertwined—'"

Herewiss finished,

"'Till the end of countries, when
Lion and Eagle come again.'

"You always did like that one."

"I recite it nightly," Freelorn said with a somewhat sour expression, "and hope that both our countries live through this interregnum."

"They'll manage, I think. But after you went south, what?"

"We went further west, nearly to the Arlene border—" Freelorn went on, telling of a close encounter with a large group of bandits, but Herewiss wasn't really listening. He nodded and mmm-hmmed in the appropriate places, but most of his mind was too full of the sight and nearness of Freelorn—the compactness of him, the quick brilliant eyes and fiery temperament, the bright sharp voice, the ability to care about a whole country as warmly as he could about one man.

Herewiss suddenly recalled one of those long golden afternoons in Prydon castle. He had been stretched out on Freelorn's bed, staring absently at the ceiling, and Freelorn sat by the window, picking at the strings of his lute and trying to get control of his newly changed voice. He was singing the Oath poem with a kind of quiet exultation, looking forward to the time when he would be king and help to keep it true; and the soft promising melody wound upward through the warm air. Herewiss, relaxed and drifting easily toward sleep, was deep in a daydream of his own—of a future day brightly lit by the blue sun of his own released Flame. Then suddenly he was startled awake again by a shudder of foreboding, a cold touch of prescience trailing down his spine. A brief flicker-vision of this moment, lit by a fading sunset instead of the brilliance of midafternoon. The same poem, but not sung; the same Freelorn, but not king; the same Herewiss, but not—

"—and left them in our dust—What's the matter? Getting cold?"

"No, Lorn, it was just a shudder. The Goddess spoke my Name, most likely."

"Yeah. So, anyway, we left the southeast and came back this way. Stopped at Madeil, and that's where my surcoat got stolen—"

"Your good one, I suppose."

"Yeah, I don't seem to have much luck with them, do I? They've probably sold it for the silver by now. But word of whose it was got out, and evidently the Steldenes have been feeling the weight of Cillmod's threats, since they sent all those people after us. I could hardly believe it when they came piling up outside that old keep. I said to myself then, 'Time to call in some help.' Which I did. Goddess, what a display that was."

"Thank you."

"Are you all right? I mean, that messenger, and the fireball, and the Lion—oh, the Lion! That was beautiful. Beautiful. Just the way He always looks to me."

"Oh. You see Him regularly?"

"Shut up! You know what I mean. But are you all right?"

"Just a touch wobbly—it'll pass in a couple of days. I never did anything on that scale before. In fact, I didn't know I had it in me. I guess I found out..."

Freelorn laughed softly. "I guess. But listen: what have you been doing?"

Herewiss shrugged, trying to think of some way to put a cheerful face on a year's worth of broken swords, wasted time, and pain. He couldn't, and anyway, Freelorn would only catch him at it.

"Forging swords," he said. "I got tired of breaking old ones. At one point Hearn offered me Fánderë—he thought that since the legend says that Earn forged it, it might be more amenable to the Power—but I just couldn't. That sword is older than the first Woodward, and I knew I would destroy it. It was just as dead to the touch as all the others. So finally I apprenticed myself to old Darg the blacksmith. You remember Darg—"

"I certainly do. The one-eyed gent with the lovely daughter. I think you had ulterior motives."

Herewiss laughed. "No, not really. Though Meren and I did come of age at the same time, and since we'd always been playmates, we decided to relieve one another of the Responsibility as soon as we could. She had twins—they'll be coming to the Ward for fostering soon, since Mother left no love-children behind her. Goddess, I miss them—they're nine now; though Halwerd never fails to remind me that he's a quarter-hour older than Holmaern. He helps me with the forging sometimes, working the bellows. I put a forge together up in the north tower, and he watches me working the metal, and asks a thousand questions about tensile strength and temper and edge. He has a blacksmith's heart, that one, and instead of apprenticing himself to Darg's son when Darg retires, he's going to have to be Lord of the Brightwood after me. I don't think Hal's entirely happy about it."

"The business with swords made of griffin-bone and ivory and such—I take it that didn't work."

"No. What use is a sword of ivory? It seems that it *has* to be a working sword. Yet a real sword is an instrument of death—and to make it carry life—"

"You'll find a way."

"I wish I had your faith in me."

Freelorn stretched, discomfort and concern flickering across his face. "Well, whatever—you'll keep trying. Where are you going now? Back home?"

"I'm heading east."

"From *here?*"

"From here."

"But Herewiss—listen, it was a brilliant idea to head this far east to start with—even if the Steldenes had their supplies intact, they wouldn't follow us this close to the Waste. But another fifteen miles or so will take you right up to the Stel itself—"

"I don't intend to stop there, Lorn. On the way down here I came by some interesting information—" Briefly he told of his encounter with the innkeeper's daughter, and what she had told him. Freelorn nodded.

"There's an Old Place like that down by Bluepeak in Arlen, just under the mountains," he said, "though it must not be as haunted, or whatever—the Dragons took it as a Marchward some years ago, and there are human Marchwarders there too. *This* place, though—if the Dragons won't go near it, I don't much like the idea of your going there. What do you want it for, anyway?"

"There are supposed to be doors, Lorn. It could be that I could use one of them to go across into a Middle Kingdom where males have Flame, and train there. Or if there's no door that goes there already, I might be able to *make* one of them do it—"

"How?" Freelorn said, all skepticism. "Worldgates are supposed to be a Flame-related manifestation, since they're partly alive, aren't they? I mean, you need wreaking to open them. When Béaneth went to Rilthor, even though it was Opening Night and a Full Moon, she still needed Fire for the Morrowfane Gate. And there's that story about the Hilarwit, and the other one about Raela Way-opener, and it's always Flame—"

Herewiss listened patiently. He had had this argument with himself more than once. "So?"

"So I don't think you can do it like that! You need control of Flame, and you haven't got it—"

"You could be right."

"And—what?"

"What you're saying is true, Lorn, for as far as we know. According to the old stories, which usually have truth in them. But each instance is different. And if you're going to quote examples, well, what about Béorgan? Despite her expertise and her power and all the information she had access to, she still couldn't have had all the facts. Why else would she have bothered trying to kill the Lover's Shadow, when He was just going to come back?"

"She was driven," Freelorn said, "by her desire for vengeance. It blinded her."

"Maybe. That's not the point. The *point* is that I have to try. There's no telling till I do. It may be that those doors are set to turn to the use of whatever mind or power comes along. And it may not. But it's a place of the Old wreaking, which was always Flame-based, and damned if I'm not going to try tapping it."

"Herewiss, you're not seeing what you're getting into—"

"Lorn, are you scared for me?"

Freelorn, who had been warming to the prospect of a good argument, opened his mouth, shut it, and scowled at Herewiss, a dark stabbing look from beneath his bushy eyebrows. "Yes, dammit," he said at last.

"Then why don't you just *say* so."

Freelorn made a face. "All right. But I spent a lot of time in the Archives, and I know more about Flame and its uses from my reading than most Rodmistresses do—"

"Reading about it and having it are two different things. No, Lorn, don't start getting mad. Do you think I don't appreciate all the research you did? But theory and practice are different, and I'm not a usual case. And look at us: half an hour together, after almost a year apart, and already we're fighting."

"Tension. I'm still nervous from two nights ago."

"Fear. You're afraid for me."

"Yes! You want to go poking around in some bloody pile of stones in the middle of nowhere and nothing, a place that was there since before the Dragons came, for Goddess's sake!—and which *they* won't go near because it's too dangerous. Damn right I'm afraid! How would you feel if our positions were reversed?"

Herewiss gave the thought its due, and did his best to put himself in Freelorn's place for a moment. "Scared, I guess."

"Petrified."

"And how would *you* feel if our positions were reversed?"

Freelorn sighed and let his hunched-up shoulders sag. "Scared too, I suppose."

"Yeah. But I have to go."

Freelorn nodded. "You *have* gotten a little too big to sit on."

The sudden bittersweet memory rose up in Herewiss: the day after Herelaf died, and Herewiss drowning in a dark sea of pain and self-hatred, wanting desperately to kill himself. Trying and trying to do it, first with the sword that had killed Herelaf, then with anything that came to hand—knives, open windows. Freelorn, filled to overflowing with exasperation, fear for Herewiss, and his own pain, finally knocked Herewiss down and sat on him until the tears broke loose in both of them and they wept to exhaustion, clutching each other.

"I have," Herewiss said, setting the memory aside with a sigh.

"Well, then, I'm coming with."

"Of course," Herewiss said.

Freelorn's eyebrows went up. "You sneaky bastard—"

Herewiss grinned. "It was a good way to make sure you realized what you were getting into before you said yes."

Freelorn grinned back. "I'm still coming with you."

"And the rest?"

"They're with me. We couldn't stop them from coming along. This is better—much better than you going alone."

"Yes, it is."

(And what am I, then?) Sunspark said indignantly.

(An elemental, Spark. But people need people.)

(I don't understand that. But if you say so...) It went back to its grazing.

"And besides," Herewiss added, "I can use someone else who's well-read in matters of Flame and such—you may see things about the place that I wouldn't."

"I don't want to see any 'things.'"

"Lorn, please."

"Did you talk to Segnbora?"

"Yes. Interesting person. She should be of great help to us too. How did she happen to join up with you? She didn't mention."

"Oh, it was in Madeil. It was how I found out that my surcoat had gone. We were in this inn, drinking quietly and minding our own business, when in come a bunch of king's guardsmen looking for me! Well, we ran out of there with the guards chasing us in five different directions. I went down a dead end, though, and the one who'd followed me cornered me there, and a moment later we were at crossed swords. I was pretty hard pressed—he was a lot bigger than I was, and a shade faster. And all of a sudden this shadow with a sword in its hand just melts out of the alley wall, and *fft!* the guy sprouts a hand's length of steel under the breastbone. It was her; she'd followed me from the inn. There she stands, and she bows about a quarter of a bow, and says, 'King's son of Arlen, well met, but if we don't hurry out of here you're shortly going to be neck-deep in dungeon, with King Dariw's torturer dancing on your head.' I thought she had a point."

"I could see where you might, yes."

"So off we go, back to the inn again. Up she goes, cool as you please, and gets our things from our rooms. The innkeeper sees her, and he says, 'Madam, if you please, where are you going with those?' and Segnbora smiles at him and says, 'Sir, if you want every skin of wine or tun of ale in your place to get the rot, ask on. Otherwise—' and out the door she goes, gets the horses from the stables and rides off. We met her a few streets away and got ourselves out of there in a hurry."

Herewiss raised his eyebrows, amused. "Why did she do it?"

"I asked her. Seems she's related to one of the Forty Noble Houses. She said, '*They* may not hold by the Oath, but *I* do, by Goddess—' I believe her."

"I get the feeling you can."

Freelorn smiled. "Well, this venture will be safer with all of us along. Damn, I hope you're right about the doors! Suppose there was one into another Arlen where I'm king—"

"You'd be there already. And how would you feel if you were king, and another Freelorn popped out of nowhere to contest your claim to the throne?"

"I'd—uhh."

"—kill the bastard? Very good. Better stay here and do what you can with *this* world."

Freelorn looked at Herewiss and smiled again, but this time his eyes were grave.

"Come on," he said, "let's give them a hand with dinner."

Stars shone on them again; this time the warm constellations of spring: Dolphin and Maiden and Flamesteed and Stave. The Lion stood near the zenith, the red star of its heart glittering softly through the still air.

They held one another close, and closer yet, and found to their delight that nothing seemed to have changed between them.

A soft chuckle in the darkness.

"Lorn, you remember that first time we shared at your place?"

"That was a long time ago."

"It seems that way."

"—and my father yelled up the stairs, 'What are you doooooooing?'

"—and you yelled back, 'We're fuckinnnnnnnnnnng!'"

"—and it was quiet for so long—"

"—and then he started laughing—"

"Yeah."

A silence.

"You know, he really loved you. He always wanted another son. He always used to say that now he had one…"

Silence.

"Lorn—one way or another, I'm going to see you on your throne."

"Get your Power first."

"Yeah. But then we get your throne back for you. I think I owe him that."

"Your Power first. He was concerned about that."

"Yes…he would have been. Well, we'll see."

A pause. A desert owl floated silently overhead and away, like a wandering ghost.

"Dusty?"

Herewiss started. No one had called him by that name since Herelaf's death.

"What?"

"After I'm king—what will you do?"

"I haven't the faintest idea."

"Really?"

"I haven't thought about it much. I don't let myself. Heal the sick, I guess, talk to Dragons—make it rain when it's dry—travel around, walk the Otherworlds—"

There was a sinking silence under the blankets; suddenly disappointment and fear flavored the air like smoke. Herewiss was confused by the perception. His underhearing sometimes manifested itself at odd moments, but never without reason.

"Dusty—Don't forget me."

"Forget you? Forget you! How do I forget my loved? Lorn, put it out of your mind. How could I forget you? If only fr—"

Herewiss cut himself off, shocked, hearing the thought complete itself inside his head: "*—from all the trouble you've caused me—*"

"From what?"

My Goddess. How can I think such things? What's the matter with me!! "—from all the distance I've had to travel to get into your bed…"

Freelorn made a small sound in his throat, a brief quiet sigh of acceptance. "I'm glad you did," he said.

"Again?"

"Why not? The night is young."

"And so are we."

 *six*

Whatever may be said of the Goddess, this much is certain: She enjoys a good joke. For proof of this, examine yourself or any other member of the human race closely—and then laugh along with Her.

Deeds of the Heroes, 18, vi

"I thought you said it was just another fifteen miles."

"Well, I thought it was..."

"Maybe the river changed its banks."

"The Stel? Unlikely. Maybe I got us lost."

"Likely."

The eight of them rode along through country that was becoming increasingly inhospitable. The gently rolling scrub country of southern Steldin had given way to near-desert terrain. It was afternoon, and hot. A steady, maddening east wind blew dust into their eyes, and into their horses' eyes, down their collars and up their sleeves, into their boots and even into their undertunics. Even the most casual movement would sand some part of the body raw.

Herewiss sighed. For the past two hours Freelorn had been straining his eyes toward the horizon, swearing at himself for having lost the river. He had been abusing himself so skillfully that Herewiss, in exasperation, had joined in and helped him for a few minutes. Now he was regretting it.

"Lorn, the Dark with it," he said. "You *can't* lose the Stel. If you just go east far enough, you're bound to run into it."

"It is possible," Freelorn said tightly, "to lose just about anything."

"Including your mind, if you work at it hard enough. Lorn, relax. Worse things could happen."

"Oh?"

"Certainly. A cohort of Fyrd could find us. Or the Dark Hunt. Or the Goddess could sneeze and forget to keep the world in place, and we'd all go out like candles. Don't be so grim, Lorn. It'll work out all right."

Freelorn's poor Blackmane, half-blind with the dust, sneezed mightily and then bumped sideways into Sunspark. Herewiss's mount didn't respond, but Blackmane danced away with a whicker of scorched surprise, nearly throwing Freelorn out of the saddle. He regained his balance and looked suspiciously at the stallion.

"None of our horses care much for that one of yours," he said. "What happened to Darrafed?"

"She's home."

"Dapple?"

"He was with me partway. I sent him back."

"Is that safe?"

Herewiss laughed. "Safe? Dapple? He'll probably rescue a princess on the way home."

"Where did this one come from, then?"

"I don't know," Herewiss said, which was certainly the truth. "I found him."

"I know that look," Freelorn said. "You've got a secret."

Herewiss said nothing, and tried to keep from smiling.

"Sorcerers," Freelorn said in good-natured disgust. "Well, have it your way. Where the Dark is the river?!"

"It'll be along. Lorn, you didn't tell me. What were you doing in Madeil?"

"Oh...I was meeting a man who was supposed to know a way into the Royal Treasury at Osta. He had been there as a guard some years back, but he moved to Steldin when my father died and everything was going crazy."

"Did you meet him?"

"Oh, yes. That was what we had been at the tavern for. It was about half an hour after he left that the guards came in."

"Why were you still there?"

Freelorn looked guilty. "Well...it had been so long since any of us had a chance to get really drunk."

"So you did it there in the middle of a city, with all those people around who you didn't know? Lorn, you know you get talky when you're drunk...What if you'd let something slip?"

Freelorn said nothing for a second, said it so forcefully that Herewiss went after the unspoken thought with his underhearing to try to catch it... *talk about being drunk,* it said in a wash of anger...*what about Herelaf?* And then it was smashed down by a hammer of Freelorn's guilt. *How can I think things like that? Wasn't his fault.*

Herewiss winced away. *Even Lorn,* he thought. And then, *Goddess, did I do that? If this is the kind of thing I'd be doing with the Power, maybe I'm better without it.*

"I'm sorry," he said aloud. "Lorn, really."

"No—you're right, I guess. But we did find out about the way into the Treasury—there's a passage off the river that no one knows about."

"What about the guards who are there?"

"There aren't many left who know about it—all the lower-level people have been replaced by mercenaries, and many of the higher levels left in a hurry when Cillmod had me outlawed. They could see the way things were going. At present that entrance isn't being guarded."

"What sort of things do they have there?"

"No treasure, no jewelry—just plain old money. My contact said that there are usually about fourteen thousand talents of silver there at any one time."

"What are you thinking of?"

"My Goddess, you have to ask?"

"No...not really. Lorn, do you think you have any chance to pull this off?"

Freelorn hesitated for a long moment. "Maybe."

Caution?! Herewiss thought. *He's being cautious? I'm in trouble.*

"Are you *sure* those are rocks?"

"Yes. Lorn, how many people do you think you're going to need to get into the place?"

"Oh...my own group will be enough."

Ten would be better, Herewiss thought glumly, *and twenty better still. More realistic, surely.* "Don't do it," he said out loud.

"Why not? It's the perfect chance to get enough money to finance the revolution—"

"Your father should be an example to you," Herewiss said tiredly, "that no one supports a dead king."

"A what?"

Herewiss sighed. "I'd like to see your plans before you go ahead and do it," he said. "Maybe I'll come with and help you. But Lorn!— I don't believe that six people are going to be enough."

"Seven—*There's* the damn river!"

"Seven," Herewiss said softly, watching Freelorn kick Blackmane into a gallop.

(Is he always so optimistic?) Sunspark asked.

(Usually more so.)

(Won't this additional foray keep you from getting back to the work you have to do?)

(Yes, it will—)

Herewiss thought about that for a moment. *The timing,* he thought, *until now I had always thought it was coincidental. But this timing's just a little too close—oh, Dark. What can I do?*

(What?)

(I was thinking to myself. Catch up with him, will you, Spark?)

(Certainly. That *is* the river ahead, by the way. I can feel the water. I hope there's a bridge there; I'm not going to ford it in what they would consider the normal fashion.)

(So jump it, Spark. They're already sure that you're not quite natural. A spectacular leap won't give much away at this point.)

They drew even with Freelorn again. "Look," he shouted over the noise of the horses' hooves, "there's a house up ahead—"

"Where?"

"To the left. See it?"

"Uh—I think so. The dust makes it hard. Who would live out here, Lorn? There's not a town or village for miles in any direction, and this is practically the Waste!"

"Maybe whoever lives there wants some peace and quiet."

"Quiet, maybe. Peace? With the Waste full of Fyrd?"

"Well, maybe it isn't, really. How would anyone know? If there's nothing much living in the Waste, there can't be Fyrd, either. Even Fyrd have to live on something."

"It makes sense. There *are* so many stories—Lorn, that's awfully big for just a house. It looks more like an inn to me."

The rest of Freelorn's people gradually closed with the two of them. "What's the hurry?" yelled Dritt.

Freelorn pointed ahead. "Hot food tonight, I think—" They slowed down somewhat as they approached the river. It was running high in its banks, for the thaw was still in progress in the Highpeaks to the south. Trees lined the watercourse for almost as far as they could see, from south to north. These were not the gnarled little scrub-trees of the desert country, but huge old oaks and maples and silver birches. Though they leaned backward a little on the western bank, their growth shaped by the relentless east wind of the Waste, they still gave an impression of striving hungrily for the water. Branches bright with flowers reached across the water to tangle with others just becoming green. Somewhere in the foliage a songbird, having recovered from the sudden advent of all these people, was trying out a few experimental notes.

"It *is* an inn," Freelorn said. "There's the sign—though I can't make out what's on it. Let's go."

"Lorn," Herewiss said, "how has your money been holding up?"

"I am so broke," Freelorn said cheerfully, "that—"

"Never mind, I think I have enough. Lorn, you're *always* broke, it seems."

"Makes life more interesting."

Usually for other people, Herewiss thought. *Oh Dark! I'm bad-tempered today.*

"—and besides, if I spend it as fast as I get it, then no one can steal it from me."

"That's a point."

Herewiss frowned with concentration as he did the math in his head. *Prices will probably be higher out here—say, three-quarters of an eagle or so—and there's seven of us...so that's...uhh...damn, I hate fractions!...Well, it can't be more than seven. Wonderful: all I have is five. Maybe the innkeeper'll let us do dishes...*

The inn was a tidy-looking place of fieldstone and mortar, with three sleeping wings jutting off in various directions from the large main building. A few of the many windows of diamond-paned glass stood open, as did the door of the stable, which was set off from the inn proper. A neat path of white stone led down from the dooryard of the inn, past the inn sign, a neatly painted board that said FERRY TAVERN, and down to the riverbank, where it met a small fishing pier. Just to the right of the pier was the ferry, a wooden platform attached to ropes and pulleys so that it could be pulled across from one side of the river to the other whether anyone was on it or not.

The place was marvelously pleasant after the long ride through the dry empty country. They dismounted and led their horses into the dooryard, savoring the shade and the cool fragrance of the air. The inn was surrounded by huge apple trees, all in flower. The only exception was the great tree that shaded the door-yard proper, a wide-crowned blackstave with its long trembling olive-and-silver leaves. Its flowers had already fallen, and carpeted the grass and gravel like an unseasonable snowfall.

"Goddess, what a lovely place," Freelorn said.

"I just hope we can afford it. Well, go knock on the door and find out—"

"You have the money, *you* do it."

"This is *your* bunch of people, Lorn—"

The door opened, and a lady walked out, and stood on the slate doorstep, drying her hands on her apron. "Good day to you!" she said, smiling. "Can I help you?"

They all stood there for a second or so, just appreciating her, before any of them began considering answers to the question. She was quite tall, taller even than Herewiss. The plain wide-sleeved shirt and breeches and boots she wore beneath the white apron did nothing to conceal her figure, splendidly proportioned. She was radiantly beautiful, with the delicate translucent complexion of a country girl and eyes as green as grass. What lines her face had seemed all from smiling, but her eyes spoke of gravity and formidable intelligence, and her bearing of quiet strength and power. She wore her coiled and braided hair like a dark crown.

"Ahem!" Freelorn said. "Uh, yes, maybe you can. We're interested in staying the night—"

"Just interested?" she asked, raising an eyebrow. "You're not sure? Is it a money problem?"

"Well, lady, not really," Herewiss began, still gazing at her with open admiration. *Oh my,* he was thinking, *I never gave much thought to having more than one loved at a time—but I might start thinking about it now. She's like a tree, she just radiates strength—but she's got flowers, too—*

She looked back at him, a measuring glance, a look of calm assessment, and then smiled again. It was like day breaking. "It's been a long time since anyone was here," she said. "Let's take it out in trade. If you're agreeable, let one of you share with me tonight, and we'll call it even. You're leaving tomorrow, I take it—"

They nodded assent.

"Then it's settled. Go on in, make yourselves comfortable. Two tub rooms on the ground floor if anyone wants a bath—I'll help with the water after I've taken care of your horses. Dinner's two hours before sunset. Go on, then!" she said, laughing, stepping down from the doorstep and shooing them like chickens. Bemused, Freelorn and his people started going inside.

Herewiss turned to lead Sunspark toward the stable. "No, no," said the lady innkeeper, coming up beside him and reaching across Herewiss to take the reins.

"Uh, he's a little—I'd better—" Herewiss started to say, watching in horror as Sunspark suddenly lifted a hoof to stomp on the lady's foot.

"It's quite all right," the lady said, and hit Sunspark a sharp blow on the nose with her left fist. The elemental danced back a step or so, its eyes wide with surprise.

The lady smiled brightly at Herewiss. "I love horses," she said, and led Sunspark away.

(Be nice!) Herewiss said.

(I think I'd better,) Sunspark replied, still surprised.

Herewiss followed the others inside and found them standing in a tight group in the middle of the cool dark common room, all talking at once. "All right, *all right!!*" Freelorn yelled over the din. "There is no *way* to arbitrate this; we'll have to choose up for the chance."

"How about a fast game of Blade-on-the-Table?" Dritt said.

"The *Dark* it would be fast—it would need six elimination hands, and I want my bath *now*. Besides, you cheat at cards. It'll—"

"I do not!"

"—have to be lots. Look, there's kindling over there, and some twigs; we'll draw sticks for it."

"Fine," Moris said darkly, "and who holds the sticks?"

"I'm the only one I trust not to gimmick the draw, so—"

This observation was greeted with hoots of skepticism. "What about me, Lorn?" Herewiss said. Freelorn looked at him with an expression close to dismay.

"You're right," he said. "Go ahead, give them to him—he's got an honest streak."

Herewiss received the twigs and spent a few moments snapping them to equal lengths, all but one, which he broke off shorter. He turned back to the others. "Here."

Freelorn chose first, and made an irritated face; his was long. "The river I didn't mind losing so much," he said, "but this—aagh!"

Dritt chose next, and came up long also, as did Moris and Lang after him. Then Segnbora chose.

"Dammit-to-Darkness," Freelorn said, with immense chagrin. "Well, give her our best."

Segnbora smiled, tossed the short stick over her shoulder for luck, picked up her saddlebags from the floor, and headed up the stairs to find herself a room. "See you at dinner," she said.

"That could have been *me*," said Harald softly. "If I'd just gone ahead of her..." He followed Segnbora up the stairs.

Moris and Dritt went away, muttering, to raid the kitchen.

Lang kicked a chair irritably and went outside. "I wish it had been me," Freelorn said quietly.

"You're not alone." Herewiss put an arm around him, hugging him. "But, Lorn—how long has it been since we had a bath together?"

Freelorn regarded Herewiss out of the corner of his eye. "Years," he said, smiling mischievously. "Though of course you remember what happened the last time."

"Goodness, I'm not sure, it was so *long* ago—"

"Come on," Freelorn said, "let's go refresh your memory."

Everyone who had good clothes to wear, or at least clean ones, wore them to dinner that night. They sat around the big oaken table down in the common room and admired one another openly in the candlelight. Herewiss wore the Phoenix surcoat, and Freelorn beside him wore a plain black one, still grumbling softly over the loss of his good Lion surcoat with the silver on it. Lang and Harald wore plain dark shirts with the White Eagle badge over the heart, for they had been queen's men at the Court in Darthis before taking up with Freelorn. Dritt wore a white peasant's shirt bright with embroidery around the sleeves and collar, a farmer's festival wear; while Moris beside him looked dark and noble in the deep brown surcoat of the North Arlene principality. Segnbora, down at the end of the table, was wearing a long black robe belted at the waist and emblazoned on one breast with a lion and upraised sword—the differenced arms of a cadet branch of one of the Forty Noble Houses of Darthen.

The food did justice to the festive dress. Dinner was cold eggs deviled with pepper and marigold leaves, roast goose in a sour sauce of lemons and sorrel, potatoes roasted in butter, and winter apples in thickened cream. Moris made a lot of noise about the eggs and the goose, claiming that the powerful spices and sours of Steldene cooking gave him heartburn; but this did not seem to affect the speed with which he ate. There also seemed to be an endless supply of wine, which the company didn't let go to waste.

Once the food was served, the innkeeper took off her apron, sat down at the head of the table, and ate with them. In some ways she seemed a rather private person; she still had not told them her name. This was common enough practice in the Kingdoms, and her guests respected her privacy. But when she spoke it became obvious that she was a fine conversationalist, possessed of a dry wit of which Herewiss found himself in envy.

She seemed most interested in hearing her guests talk, though, and was eager for news of the Kingdoms. One by one they gave her all the news they could remember: how the new queen was doing in Arlen, the border problem with Cillmod, the great convocation of Dragons and Marchwarders at the Eorlhowe in North Arlen, the postponement of the Opening Night feast in Britfell fields...

"Opening Night," the innkeeper said, sitting back in her chair with her winecup in hand. "Four months ago, that would have been. And the Queen would have held the feast all by herself, without any Arlene heir in attendance, as her father did while he was still alive?"

"Evidently," Freelorn said. Herewiss glanced at Lorn, watching him take a long, long swig of wine. There was nervousness in the gesture.

"Yet they say that the Lion's Child is still abroad somewhere," said the lady. "It's strange, surely, that he never came forward in all that time to partake of the Feast, even secretly. It's one of the most important parts of the royal bindings that keep the Shadow at bay, and the Two Lands from famine."

"I hear he did show up at the Feast once," Freelorn said. "Three years ago, I think. He just barely got away with his life."

Herewiss had all he could do to hold still. *So that's where he was that winter—! And that's where he got that sword cut that took so long to heal! 'Robbers,' indeed—*

"—Cillmod had slipped some spies in among the Darthene regulars that went south with the king," Freelorn was saying. "The king and the Lion's Child had just gotten to the part of the Feast where royal blood is shed, when they both almost had all their blood shed for them. The king's bodyguards killed the attackers—but Darthen was wounded, and as for Arlen—" Freelorn shrugged. "Once burned, twice shy. No one has seen him at a Feast since. Nor did the king ask again. Evidently, Goddess rest him, he wanted to live out the year or so left him in peace, without bringing Arlen's assassins down on his own head. What the new queen will do—" And Freelorn took another long drink.

"If she can't *find* the Lion's Child," said the innkeeper, "what she'll do is moot. Now that she's becoming secure on her throne, he might want to send her some certain word concerning his future participation in the Feast and the other bindings. Seven years is too long for the Two Lands to go without the royal magics being properly enacted. Disaster is just over the mountain, unless something's done."

"She can't do anything anyway," Lorn said disconsolately. "Any move on her part to support the Lion's Child could antagonize the conservative factions in the Forty Houses. Their people are in an uproar over the poor harvests lately, and all they want is to avoid war with Arlen, or anyone else. If the Queen of Darthen gives Arlen's heir asylum or supports him in any way, war is what she'll have. Then she'll go out into the Palace Square on Midsummer Morning next year, to hammer out her crown, and some hireling of the conservative Houses will put an arrow through her, and that'll be the end of it—"

"A queen, like a king, is made for fame, not for long living," the innkeeper said quietly.

Freelorn's head snapped up. The suspicion that had been growing in Herewiss for some minutes now flowered into fear. *She knows, she knows who he is! Oh, Lorn, why can't you keep your mouth shut—!*

"It's possible," Lorn said, so quietly that Herewiss could hardly hear him, "that the Lion's Child isn't too excited about dying in an ambush, or in someone's torture-chamber. He may be able to do more good alive, even if he's a long way from home."

"That's between him and the Goddess," the innkeeper said. "But as for the other, royalty is not about comfort or safety. Painful death, torture, many a king or queen of both the Lands have known them. It's not so many centuries since the days when any king's lifeblood might be poured out in the furrows any autumn, to make sure that a poor harvest wouldn't happen again, that the next year his people wouldn't starve. But that's the price one agrees to pay, if necessary, when one accepts kingship. Put off the choice, and the land and the people that are both part of the ruler suffer. Who knows what good might have been done for the Two Lands, and all the Kingdoms, if the Lion's Child had somehow found the courage to go through with that Feast three years ago, instead of panicking and fleeing when it was half-finished? He might not have died of the wound he took. He might be king now."

"Yes," Freelorn said, looking very thoughtful.

"And as for the queen," the innkeeper said, "it wouldn't matter if that was 'the end of it' for her, would it? Even if she died in the act of one of the royal magics, she has heirs who will carry on after her...heirs who know that the only reason for their royalty is to serve those bindings, and the people the bindings keep safe from the Shadow. But as to other heirs to Arlen, who knows where they may be? And who knows what the Lion's Child is thinking, or doing?"

"The Goddess, possibly," Lorn said.

"Men may change their minds," the innkeeper said, "and confound Her. I doubt it happens often enough. But I suspect She's usually delighted."

Freelorn nodded, looking bemused.

Herewiss looked over at the innkeeper. She gazed back at him, a considering look, and then turned to Segnbora and began gossiping lightly with her about one of her relatives in Darthen.

Freelorn once again became interested in the wine, and Herewiss sighed and did the same. It was real Brightwood white, of three years before, from the vineyards on the north side of the Wood. A current of unease, though, still stirred on the surface of his thoughts. *Where is she getting this stuff?* he wondered. *It's a long way south from the Wood, through dangerous country. And I've never heard mention of this place—which is odd—*

There was motion at the end of the table; the lady had risen. "It's been a pleasure having you," she said. "I could go on like this all night—but I have an assignation." She smiled, and Segnbora smiled back at her, and most of Freelorn's people chuckled. "If one or two of you will help me with the dishes—maybe you two," and she indicated Dritt and Moris, "since you obviously liked the looks of my kitchen earlier—"

Everyone got up and started to help clear the table—all but Herewiss, who hated doing dishes or table work of any kind. Out of guilt, or some other emotion perhaps, he did remove one object from the table—the carafe full of Brightwood white. He went up the stairs with it, into the deepening darkness of the second story, feeling happily wicked...and also feeling sure that someone saw him, and was smiling at his back.

Herewiss's room had a small hearth built of rounded riverstones and mortar. It also had something totally unexpected, a real treasure—two fat overstuffed chairs. Both of them were old and worn; they had been upholstered in red velvet once, but the velvet was worn pale and smooth from much use, and was unraveling itself in places. Herewiss didn't care; the chairs were both as good as kings' thrones to him. He had pulled one of them up close to the fire and was sitting there in happy half-drunken comfort, toasting his stocking feet. The red grimoire was open in his lap, but the light of the two candles on the table beside him wasn't really enough to read by, and he had stopped trying.

A steady presence of light at the far corner of his vision drew his attention. He looked up, and gazing across the bare fields saw the Full Moon rising over the jagged stony hills to the east. It looked at him, the dark shadows on the silver face peering over the hillcrests at him like half-lidded eyes, calm and incurious.

He stared back for a moment, and then slumped in the old chair and reached out for the wine cup.

There was a soft knock at the door.

So comfortable was Herewiss that he didn't bother to get up, much less reach for his knife. "Come in," he said. The door edged open, and there was the innkeeper, cloaked in black against the night chill.

At sight of her Herewiss started to get up, but she waved him back into his seat. "No, stay put," she said. Pulling the other chair over by the hearthside, she sat down, pushing aside her cloak and facing the fire squarely.

Herewiss let himself just look at her for a moment. Beauty, maybe, was the wrong word for the aura that hung about her, though she certainly was beautiful. Even as she sat there at her ease, she radiated a feeling of power, of assurance in herself. More than that—a feeling of certainty, of inevitability; as if she knew exactly what she was for in the world. It lent her an air of regality, as might be expected of someone who seemed to rule herself so completely. A queenly woman, enthroned on a worn velvet chair that leaked its stuffing from various wounds and rents. Herewiss smiled at his own fancy.

"Would you like some wine?" he said.

"Yes, please."

He reached for another cup and poured for her. As he handed her the cup their hands brushed, ever so briefly. A shock ran up Herewiss's arm, a start of surprise that ran like lightning up his arm and shoulder to strike against his breastbone. It was the shock that a sensitive feels on touching a body that houses a powerful personality, and Herewiss wasn't really surprised by it. But it was very strong—

And he was tired, and probably oversensitive. He lifted his cup and saluted the lady. "You keep a fine cellar," he said. "To you."

"To you, my guest," she said, and pledged him, and drank. He drank too, and watched her over the rim of the cup. The fire lit soft lights in her hair; unbound, it was longer than he had expected, flowing down dark and shimmering past her waist. Some of it lay in her lap, night-dark against the white linen of her shift and the green cord that belted it.

"This is lovely stuff," Herewiss said. "How are you getting it all the way down here from the Brightwood?"

The lady smiled. "I have my sources," she said. She lowered her cup and held it in her lap, staring into the fire. The wine was working strongly in Herewiss now, so that his mind wandered and he looked out the window. The Moon was all risen above the peaks now, and the two dark eyes were joined by a mouth making an "o" of astonishment. He wondered what the Moon saw that shocked her so.

"Herewiss," the lady said, and he turned back to look at her. The expression she wore was odd. Her face was sober, even sad, but her eyes were bright and testing, as if there was an answer she wanted from him.

"Madam?"

"Herewiss," she said, "how many swords have you broken now?"

Alarm ran through him, but it was dulled; by the wine, and by the look on her face—not threatening, not even curious, but only weary. It looked like Freelorn's face when he asked the same question, and the voice sounded like Freelorn's voice. Tired, pitying, maybe a bit impatient.

"Fifty-four," he said, "about thirty or thirty-five of my own forging. I broke the last one the day I left the Wood."

"And the Forest Altars were no help to you."

"None. I've also spoken with Rodmistresses who don't hold with the ways of the Forest Orders or the Wardresses of the Precincts, but there was nothing *they* could do for me either. But, madam, how do you know about this? No one knew except for my father, and Lorn—"

He looked at her in sudden horror. Had Lorn been so indiscreet as to mention the blue Fire—

She shook her head at Herewiss, smiling, and was silent. For a while she gazed into the fire, and then said, "And how old are you now?"

"Twenty-eight," he said, shortly, like an unhappy child.

The lady rubbed her nose and leaned back in her chair until her pose almost matched Herewiss's. "You feel your time growing short, I take it."

"Even if I had control of the Power right now," Herewiss said, "it would be starting to wane. I'd have, oh, ten years to use it if I didn't overextend myself. Which I would," he added, smiling at himself. "Oh, I would."

"How so?" She was looking at him again, a little intrigued, a little bemused.

Herewiss drained his cup and stared into the fire. "Really! If I came into my Power, there I'd be, the first male since Earn and Héalhra to bear Flame. That is, if the first use didn't kill me. Think of the fame! Think of the fortune!" He laughed. "And think of the wreaking," he said, more gently, his face softening, "think of the storms I could still, the lives I could save, the roads I could walk. The roads..."

He poured himself another cup of wine. "The roads in the sky, and past it," he said. "The roads the Dragons know. The ways between the Stars. Ten years would be too high an estimate. Better make it seven, or five. I'd burn myself out like a levin bolt." He drank deeply, and set the cup down again. "But what a way to go."

The lady watched him, her head propped on her hand, considering. "What price would you be willing to pay for your Power?" she asked.

The question sounded rhetorical, and Herewiss, dreamy with wine and warmth, treated it as such. "Price? The Moon on a silver platter! A necklace of stars! One of the Steeds of the Day—"

"No, I meant really."

"Really. Well, right now I'm paying all my waking hours, just about; or I was, before I had to get Freelorn out of the badger-hole he got himself stuck in. What more do I have to give?"

He looked at her, and was surprised to see her face serious again. Something else he noticed; there was an oddness about the inside of her cloak... He had thought it as black within as without, but it wasn't. As he strained his eyes in the firelight, there seemed to be some kind of light in its folds, some kind of motion, but faint, faint—He blinked, and didn't see it, and dismissed the notion; and then on his next look he saw it again. A faint light, glittering—

No...it must have been the wine. He rejected the image.

The lady's eyes were intent on him, and he noticed how very green they were, a warm green like sunlit summer fields. "Herewiss," she said, her voice going very low, "your Name, would you give *that* for your Power?"

Of all the strange things he had heard so far, *that* startled him badly, and the wine went out in him as if someone had poured water on the small fire it had lit. "Madam, I don't know my Name," he said, and wondered suddenly what he had gotten himself into, wondered what kind of woman kept an inn out here on the borders of human habitation, all alone—

He looked again at the cloak, with eyes grown wary. It was no different. In the black black depths of it something shone, tiny points of an intense silvery light, infinite in number as if the cloak had been strewn with jeweldust, or the faint innumerable stars of Héalhra's Road. *Stars*—?

She looked at him, earnest, sincere; but the testing look was also in her eyes, the look that awaited an answer, and the right one. A look that dared him to dare.

"If you knew it," she said, "would you pay that price for your Power?"

"My Name?" he said slowly. Certainly there was no higher price that he could pay. His inner Name, his own hard-won knowledge of himself, of all the things he could be—

But he didn't know it. And even if he had, the thought of giving his inner Name to another person was frightening. It was to give your whole self, totally, unreservedly; a surrender of life, breath and soul into other hands. To tell a friend your Name, that was one thing. Friends usually had a fairly good idea of what you were to begin with, and the fact that they didn't use it against you was earnest of their trustworthiness. But to *sell* your Name to a stranger—to pay it, as a price for something—the thought was awful. Once a person had your Name, they could do anything to you—bind you to their will, take that Name from you and leave you an empty thing, a shell in which blood flowed and breath moved, but no life was. Or bind you into some terrible place that was not of this world. Or, horrible thought, into another body that wasn't yours; man or beast or Fyrd or demon, it wouldn't much matter. Madness would follow shortly. The possibilities for the misuse of a Name were as extensive as the ingenuity of malice.

But—

—to have the Power.

To have that blue Fire flower full and bright through some kind of focus, *any* kind. To heal, and build, and travel about the Kingdoms being *needed*. To talk to the storm, and understand the thoughts of Dragons, and feel with the growing earth, and run down with the rivers to the Sea. To walk the roads between the Stars. To be trusted by all, and worthy of that trust. To be *whole*.

Even as he sat and thought, Herewiss could feel the Power down inside him; feeble, stunted, struggling in the empty cavern of his self like a pale tired bird of fire. It fluttered and beat itself vainly against the cage-bars of his ribs every time his heart beat. Soon it wouldn't even be able to do that; it would drop to the center of him and lie there dead, poor pallid unborn Otherlife. Whenever he looked into himself after that, he would see nothing but death and ashes and endings. And then soon enough he would probably make an end of himself as well—

"If I knew it," he said, and his voice sounded strange and thick to him, fear and hope fighting in it, "I would. I would pay it. But it's useless."

He looked at the innkeeper and was faintly pleased to see satisfaction in her eyes. "Well then," she said, pushing herself straighter in the chair, "I think I have a commodity that would interest you."

"What?" Herewiss was more interested in her cloak.

"Soulflight."

He stared at her, amazed, and forgot about the cloak. "How—where did you get it?"

"I have my sources," she said, with a tiny twist of smile. She was watching him intently, studying his reactions, and for the moment Herewiss didn't care whether she was seeing what she wanted to or not.

"Are you a seeress?" he asked.

She shrugged at him. "In a way. But I don't use the drug. It fell into my hands, and I've been looking for someone to whom I might responsibly give it."

For a bare second Herewiss's mind reeled and soared, dreaming of what he could do with a dose of the Soulflight drug. Walk the past and the future, pass through men's minds and understand their innermost thoughts, walk between worlds, command the Powers and Potentialities and speak to the dead—

But it was a dream, and though dreams are free, real things have their price. "How much do you have?"

"A little bottle, about half a pint."

Herewiss laughed at her. "I would have to sell you the Brightwood whole and entire with all its people for that much Soulflight," he said. "I'm only the Lord's son, not the Queen of Darthen, madam."

"I'm not asking for money," she said.

"What then? How many times do I have to sleep with you?"

She broke out laughing, and after a moment he joined her. "Now *that*," she said, "is a gallant idea, but unless you have the talisman of the prince who shared himself with the thousand virgins, I doubt you could manage it. Not to mention that *I'd* be furrowed like the fields in March, and I wouldn't be able to walk for a month. How would I run the place?"

Herewiss, smiling, looked again at her cloak. The fire had died down somewhat, and he could see the stars more clearly—countless brilliantly blazing fires, burning silver-cold. He also perceived more clearly that there was a tremendous depth to the cloak, endless reaches of cool darkness going back away from him forever, though the cloak plainly ended at the back of the chair where the lady leaned on it.

He looked at her—dark hair, green eyes like the shadowed places about the Forest Altars, wearing the night—and knew with certainty who she was. Awe stirred in him, and joy as well.

"What's the price, madam?" he said, opening himself to the surges building inside him.

"I'll give you the drug," she said, "if you will swear to me that, when you find out your inner Name, you'll tell it to me."

Herewiss considered the woman stretched out in the old tattered chair. "Why do you want to know it?"

She eased herself downward, looking into the fire again, and smiled. After a silence she said, "I guess you could call me a patroness of sorts. Wouldn't it be to my everlasting glory to have helped bring the first male in all these empty years into his Power? And as all good deeds come back to the doer eventually, sooner or later, I'd reap reward for it."

Herewiss laughed softly. "That's not all you're thinking of."

"No, it's not, I suppose," said the innkeeper. "Look, Herewiss: power, in all its forms, is a strange thing. Most of the power that exists is bound up, trapped, and though it tries to be free, usually it can't manage it by itself. The world is full of potential Power of all kinds, yes?"

He nodded.

"But at the same time, loss of power, the death of things, is a process that not even the Goddess can stop. Eventually even the worlds will die."

"So they say."

Her face was profoundly sorrowful, her eyes shadowed as if with guilt. "The death is inevitable. But we have one power, all men and beasts and creatures of other planes. We can slow down the Death, we can die hard, and help all the worlds die hard. To that purpose it behooves us to let loose all the power we can. To live with vigor, to love powerfully and without caring whether we're loved back, to let loose building and teaching and healing and all the arts that try to slow down the great Death. Especially joy, just joy itself. A joy flares bright and goes out like the stars that fall, but the little flare it makes slows down the great Death ever so slightly. That's a triumph, that it can be slowed down at all, and by such a simple thing."

"And you want to let me loose."

"Don't you want to be loose?"

"Of course! But, madam, forgive me, I still don't understand. What's in it for you?"

The lady smiled ruefully, as if she had been caught in an omission, but still admired Herewiss for catching her. "If I were the Goddess," she said, "and I am, for all of us are, whether we admit it to ourselves or not—if I were She, I would look at you as She looks at all men, who are all Her lovers at one time or another. And I would say to Myself, 'If I raise up that Power, free the Fire in him, then when the time comes at last that we share ourselves with one another, in life or after it, I will draw that strength of his into Me, and the Worlds and I will be the greater for it.' And certainly it would be a great thing to know the Name of the first male to come into his Power, lending power in turn to me, so that I would be so much the greater for it..."

Herewiss sat and looked for a moment at the remote white fires of the stars within the cloak. They seemed to gaze back at him, unblinking, uncompromising, as relentless themselves as the lady seemed to be.

"How do I know that you won't use my Name against me if I ever do find it out?" he said.

The lady smiled at him gently. "It's simple enough to guard against, Herewiss," she said. "You have only to use the drug to find out Mine."

The look of incalculable power and utter vulnerability that dwelt in her eyes in that moment struck straight through him, inflicting both amazement and pain upon him. Tears started suddenly to his eyes, and he blinked them back with great difficulty. Full of sorrow, he reached out and took her hand.

"None of us have any protection against that last Death, have we," he said.

"None of us," said the innkeeper. "Not even She. Her pain is greatest; She must survive it, and watch all Her creation die."

Herewiss held her hand in his, and shared the pain, and at last managed to smile through it.

"If I find my Name, I will tell you," he said. "I swear by the Altars, and by Earn my Father, and by my breath and life, I'll pay the price."

She smiled at him. "That's good," she said. "I'll give you the drug to take with you tomorrow morning."

A silence rested between them for a few minutes; they rested within it.

"And if I should in my travels come across *your* Name," Herewiss said, "well, it'll be my secret."

"I never doubted it," she said, still smiling. "Thank you."

For a while more they sat in silence, and both of them gazed into the fire, relaxed. Finally the lady stretched a bit, arching her back against the chair. The shimmer of starlight moved with her as she did so, endless silent volumes of stars shifting with her slight motion. She looked over at Herewiss with an expression that was speculative, and a little shy. He looked back at her, almost stealing the glance, feeling terribly young and adventurous, and nervous too.

"Let's pretend," he said, very softly, "that you're the Goddess—"

"—and you're My Lover—?"

"Why not?"

"Why not indeed? After all, You are—"

"—and You are—"

—and for a long time, They were.

Something awoke Herewiss in the middle night. He turned softly over on his side, reaching out an arm, and found only a warm place on the bed where She had been. Slowly and a little sadly he moved his face to where Hers had lain on the pillow, and breathed in the faint fragrance he found there. It was sweet and musky, woman-scent with a little sharpness to it; a subtle note of green things growing in some patterned place of running waters, sun-dappled beneath birdsong. He closed his eyes and savored the moment through his loneliness; felt the warmth beneath the covers, heard the soft pop of a cooling ember, breathed out a long tired sigh of surrender to the sweet exhaustion of having filled another with himself. And despite the empty place beneath his arm, that She in turn had filled so completely with Herself, still he smiled, and loved Her. With all the men and women in the world to love, both living and yet unborn, She could hardly spend much time in one place, or seem to.

He got up, then, moving slowly and carefully with half-closed eyes so as not to break the pleasant half-sleep, half-waking state he was experiencing Herewiss wrapped a sheet around himself, went out of the room and padded ghost-silent down the hall to listen at the next door down. Nothing. He pushed the door gently open, went in, closed it behind him. Lorn was snoring faintly beneath the covers.

Herewiss eased into the bed behind Freelorn, snuggled up against his back, slipped an arm around his chest; Freelorn roused slightly, just enough to hug Herewiss's arm to him, and then started snoring again.

Herewiss closed his eyes and sank very quickly into sleep, dreaming of the shadowed places in the Brightwood, and of serene eyes that watched eternally through the leaves.

When Herewiss came down to breakfast, Freelorn was there before him, putting away eggs and hot sugared apples and guzzling hot minted honey-water as if he had been up for hours. This was moderately unusual, since Freelorn almost never ate breakfast at all. More unusual, though, was the fact that he was up early, and looked cheerful—he was usually a late riser, and grumpy until lunchtime.

Herewiss sat down next to him, and Freelorn grunted by way of saying hello. "Nice day," he said a few seconds later, around a mouthful of food.

"It is that." Herewiss looked up to see Dritt and Moris come in together. Dritt was humming through his beard, though still out of tune, and Moris, usually so noisy in the mornings, went into the kitchen silently, with a look on his face that made Herewiss think of a cat with more cream in his bowl than he could possibly finish.

Herewiss reached over to steal Freelorn's mug, and a gulp's worth of honey-water. "Is she making more?"

Freelorn nodded. "Be out in a minute, she said."

Segnbora came down the stairs, pulled out the chair next to Herewiss, and sat down with a thump. She looked tired, but she smiled so radiantly at Herewiss that he decided not to ask her how it had been.

"Did you give her our best?" Freelorn asked, cleaning his plate.

"It was mutual, I think."

Freelorn chuckled. "I dare say. Where are Lang and Harald?"

"They'll be down—they were washing up a few minutes ago."

"Good. We should get an early start—if we're going to find this place of yours, I want to hurry up about it. And I would much rather see it in daylight."

"Lorn, I doubt it's any worse at night."

"*Everything* is worse at night. With one exception."

"Is that all you ever think about?"

"Well, there *is* something else, actually. But it's easier to make love than it is to make kings."

Lang came thumping down the stairs and sat down across from Segnbora. "How was it?"

"Oh *please!* It was fine."

"This hold," Lang said, "will we be seeing it tomorrow?"

"If the directions I got are right."

(They are,) Sunspark said from the stable. (Tomorrow easily. I can feel the place from here.)

"Before nightfall?"

"I think so."

"Good."

"I wish you people wouldn't worry so much," Herewiss said. "It's not haunted, as far as I can tell."

"—which can't be far. Nobody will go near the place! Morning, Harald."

"Morning." Harald sat down across from Herewiss. "How was she, then?"

Segnbora sighed at the ceiling. "She was *fine*. Twice more and I can stop repeating myself…"

"Can you blame us for being curious? I mean, a lady like that—" But as Lang said it, the smile on his face caught Herewiss's eye. A little reflective, that smile, and reminiscent, almost wistful.

The kitchen door swung open, and Dritt and Moris and the innkeeper came out laden with trays; more eggs, more steaming honey-water and hot apples, with a huge bowl of wheat porridge and a pile of steamed crabs from the river. They put the things down, and as the grabbing and passing commenced, Herewiss looked over the heads of Freelorn's people to catch the lady's eye.

She was back in her work-day garb, the plain home-spun shirt and breeches, the boots, the worn gray apron; her hair was braided again into a crown of coiled plaits. Though she was no less beautiful, she seemed to have doffed her power, and Herewiss began to wonder whether much of their night encounter mightn't have been a dream provoked by good wine. But she returned his glance, and smiled, winking at him and patting one of her pockets, which bulged conspicuously. Then back she went into the kitchen.

Herewiss reached for a mug of honey-water, and a plate to put eggs on.

"How was it?" Dritt said to Segnbora.

Segnbora smiled grimly and put a fried egg down his shirt.

When it was time to go, they gathered outside the door that faced the ferry, and the innkeeper brought out their horses. First Lang's and Dritt's, then Harald's and Moris's, and then Segnbora's and Freelorn's. Herewiss watched as the lady spoke a word or two in Segnbora's ear, and when Segnbora smiled back at her, shyly, with affection, Herewiss felt something odd run through him. A pang, a small pain under the breastbone. He laughed at himself, a breath of ruefulness and amusement. *Why am I feeling this way? Am so selfish that I can't stand the thought of someone else sharing Her the same night I did? What silliness. After last night, I'm full in places I didn't even know were empty. Such joy—to know that the Goddess Who made the world and everything in it is holding you and telling you that She loves you, all of you, even the parts that need changing—I should rejoice with Segnbora, for from the look on her face this morning, she's known the joy too…*

The lady brought out Sunspark last of all. To judge by the arch of his neck and the light grace of his walk, he was in remarkably good temper. When Herewiss took the reins, the lady bent her head close to his.

"It's in the saddlebag," she said. "Remember me."

"I will."

"I'll remember *you*. You understand me—somewhat better than most." And she smiled at him; reflective, that smile, reminiscent, even wistful.

Herewiss swung up onto Sunspark's back; the others were already ahorse, awaiting him.

"Good luck to you all," said the innkeeper, "and whatever your business is in the Waste, I hope you come back safe."

They bade her farewell in a ragged but enthusiastic chorus, and rode off to the ferry. There was not much talk among them until they crossed the river; though Sunspark bespoke Herewiss smugly as they waited for the second group to make the crossing.

(The lady is likely to lose her guests' horses, the way she keeps her stable,) it said.

(Oh?)

(She left my stall open. Did you know there are wild horses hereabouts?)

(It wouldn't surprise me.)

(And what horses! Look.)

Herewiss closed his eyes and slipped into Sunspark's mind. It was twilight there, and the plain to the west was softly limned and shadowed by the rising Moon. Standing atop a rise like a statue of ivory and silver, motionless but for the wind in the white mane and the softly glimmering tail, there was a horse. A mare.

(How beautiful,) Herewiss said. (So?)

(It was an interesting evening.)

(I thought you didn't understand that kind of union,) Herewiss said.

(The body has its own instincts, it would seem,) Sunspark answered, with a slow inward smile. (It will be interesting to try on a human body and see what happens...)

Herewiss withdrew, with just a faint touch of unease. He wasn't sure he wanted to be involved in the experiment that Sunspark was proposing.

(But there was something more to it all than that,) Sunspark went on, sounding pleased and puzzled both at once. (When first I saw...her...I thought she was of my own kind, for she was fire as well. And I was afraid, for I am not yet ready for that union which ends in glory, in the dissolution of selves and the emergence of progeny. Yet...there was union...in glory even surpassing that of which I have been told. And I am still one...)

(What happened to the mare?)

(Oh, she lived,) Sunspark said with a flick of its golden tail.

(By your standards or by mine?)

(Yours. Even had things not gone as they did, I would have been far too interested to have consumed her.)

(I'm glad to hear it...)

Herewiss opened his eyes to watch Segnbora, Dritt, and Freelorn approach, pulling on the ferry-rope. Dritt was facing back toward the opposite bank, looking at the lone figure that stood and watched them. Experimentally, Herewiss reached out with his underhearing. He caught a faint wash of sorrow from Dritt, overlaid and made bearable by an odd sheen of bright memory. Then the perception was gone.

Something was strange. When the group was assembled again and once more riding eastward into the rocky flats, Herewiss rode up to Freelorn's side and beckoned him apart.

"A personal question, Lorn—" he said softly.

"Yes, I did."

"Did *what?*"

"Sleep with her last night." He said it a little guiltily, shooting a glance at Segnbora out of the corner of his eye. "Before she did, I guess. And let me tell you, she was—"

"Please, Lorn."

"Listen, I didn't—I mean—"

"Lorn, how long has it been since something like that mattered with us? You love me. I know that. I have no fears."

"Yes, well..."

"Besides," Herewiss said, grinning wickedly, "so did I."

Freelorn laughed. "She gets around, doesn't she?"

"It looks that way."

"Just out of curiosity—what time was it when you—"

"About Moonrise—yes, I remember the Moon coming up. I had a lot of wine, but *that* much is—Lorn, what's wrong?"

Freelorn was shaking his head and frowning. "Couldn't have been."

"Couldn't have been *what?*"

"Moonrise. Because she was with *me* at Moonrise."

Herewiss sat there and felt it again—that odd hot thrill of excitement, of anticipation. But different, somehow sharper in the daylight than it had been in the twilight.

"Segnbora," he called.

She reined Steelsheen back and joined them. "What, then?"

"This is personal, granted—"

"And I didn't save any eggs. Oh, well."

"No, no. I was just wondering. What time was it when you and the lady were together?"

"Now it's funny you should mention that—"

"Oh?"

"—because I just overheard Dritt discussing that same subject with Harald. And he was saying that the lady had visited *him* about the time the Moon came up, and I was...thinking..."

She looked at them for a long few seconds, and Freelorn blushed suddenly and became very interested in Blackmane's withers. Herewiss watched Segnbora. She stared for a few seconds at the reins she held, and then looked over at him again.

"It *was* the Bride, then."

He nodded.

When she spoke again, the sound of her voice startled Herewiss. Her words went gentle with awe, and Herewiss had heard women take the Oath to the Queen of Silence with less reverence, less love. "You didn't ask," she said, "and I'll tell you. No sharing I have ever known was like last night. Oh, give as you will, there's only so much that can be shared in one evening, or one day, before the body gives out, gets sore, gets tired. There's always some one place left uncherished, some corner of the heart not touched, or not enough—and you shrug and say, 'Oh, well, next time.' And next time that one place may be caressed to satisfaction, but others are missed. You make your peace with it, eventually, and give all you can so that your own ignored places feel warmer for the giving. But last night—oh, last night. All, all of me, all the depths, the corners, the little fantasies I never dared to—the sheer delight, to open up and know that there's no harm in the sharing anywhere, only *love*—"

She turned her face away; Herewiss could feel her filling up with tears. "To have Her slide into bed behind me," Segnbora said quietly, "and put Her arms around me, and hold my breasts in Her warm hands, and then slip down and kiss the lonely place between my shoulder blades that always wanted a kiss, and never got one. And without asking..."

She smiled, and let the tears fall.

Freelorn looked up at Herewiss again, and he was smiling too. "It was like that," he said. "Funny, though, I wasn't expecting it so soon."

"She never comes to share Herself when you expect Her," Herewiss said. "That's half the joy right there."

Freelorn nodded.

"How She must love us," Herewiss said. "To share with us all, to give us so very much—I can't understand it. Just for my own part, even. What incredible thing have I done, or will I do, to earn— to deserve such, such blessing, so much love..."

"You're reason enough," Freelorn said, very quietly. "And, besides, She cherishes what's returned. What could we possibly give the Mother that She couldn't make better Herself, except love? She could make us love Her—but it wouldn't be the same."

Herewiss reached out and took Freelorn's hand. "I was thinking mostly in terms of you, Lorn."

Freelorn chuckled, squeezed Herewiss's hand hard. "And anyway," he added after a moment, "She can afford to be generous. They say that most of the time She drives a hard bargain."

Herewiss looked down at his front saddlebag, and at the slight bulge in it.

"That's what I hear," he said.

 seven

Memory is a mirror—but even the clearest memory reverses right to left.

Gnomics, 418

When frogs fell all around them out of the clear hot sky, smacking into the dust and sand with understandable grunts and squeaks, the party was surprised, but not too much so. When it hailed real stones, instead of ice, they covered their heads with helms or shields and made small jokes about the quality of the weather in this part of the Waste. When, while climbing a rise, they noticed that the rocks dislodged by their horses' hooves were rolling up the hill after them, they shrugged and kept on riding. They knew stranger things were to come.

"There it is," Herewiss said. He pointed through the blown dust clouds at a low gray shape on the horizon.
"Are you sure it's there?" Freelorn said. "Look how it wobbles."
"That's heat, and this damn dust. We'll be there in an hour or so, I would say."
"What are those?" Lang muttered, shielding his eyes. "Towers?"
"Hard to tell from here. We'll see when we get closer."
They cantered on across the desert. Herewiss was in high good spirits, expectant as a little boy at Opening Night waiting for the fireworks to start. To some extent the attitude was infectious. Most of Freelorn's people were joking and straining their eyes ahead in anticipation; Segnbora was rigidly upright in the saddle, her sword loose in its sheath. Sunspark was requiring constant reminders to maintain contact with the ground. But Freelorn was frowning, resolutely refusing to get excited.

"Well," he said, "we haven't been eaten alive yet. But I reserve judgment until we leave."

"We? Lorn, if the place is safe, I'm staying."

"Not for long, surely."

"For as long as I have to."

"You don't mean you're planning to *live* there for any length of time!"

"Uh-huh."

"You," Freelorn said with frank irritation, "are a crazy person."

"You know us Brightwood people," Herewiss said, "the only sure thing about us—"

"Is that insanity runs in the family," Freelorn said. "Let's see what the place is like before you make up your mind."

"Who's that?" Harald yelled. His eyesight was better than anyone else's, and for a moment they all squinted through the dust at the faint figure ahead of them.

"No horse," Segnbora said. "No tent, nothing—"

"No one lives out here!" Moris said.

"Not for long, anyway, without a horse or a water supply," Herewiss said. "Let's see who it is—could be they need help—"

(He's not there.)

Sunspark's thought was so sudden and shaken that Herewiss gulped involuntarily.

(He's not *there*. Or—he appears to be, but he's not an illusion; he's *real*. And yet he's not—)

(Make sense, Spark! Is this something you've encountered before?)

(No. It's as if he were not wholly present, somehow—his thoughts are bent on us, but his body isn't *here* enough for his soul to be—)

(Where's his soul, then?)

(Ahead—)

They rode closer. The figure stood there with its arms folded, watching them approach. It didn't move.

"He looks familiar," Moris said, rising up in the stirrups to stare ahead.

"Yeah." Freelorn squinted. "Damn this dust anyway—"

They approached the waiting man, came close enough to see his face—

Freelorn's mouth fell open. Herewiss was struck still as stone, and Sunspark danced backward a few paces in amazement. Segnbora spoke softly in Nhàired, drawing a sign in the air.

Dritt sat on his horse, his eyes wide, and looked at himself; the same elaborately tooled boots, the same dark tunic and light breeches, the same long silver-hilted sword, the same sandy hair—

Dritt stood there in the dust and looked at himself. He put out a hand to one side, as if to steady himself against something. "Sweet Goddess," he said, just loudly enough for them to hear, "oh *no!*"

And he turned away, and was gone, with a soft sharp sound like hands clapped together, and a swirl of stirred-up dust—

Dritt swayed a bit in the saddle, and Moris was beside him in a moment, putting a hand on his arm. "Take it easy," he said, "*you're* here, and that's what matters. No telling what kind of a sending that was—"

"That was *me*," Dritt said with conviction. "Not a sending. Not a premonition, or an illusion, or anything like that. *Me*. I could feel it."

Freelorn turned to Herewiss, almost in triumph. "*There*. You want to live in a place where things like *that* happen?"

"Lorn, we're not even there yet."

"I know. I know."

At last they sat on their horses in a tight little group before the place, and stared at it.

It was built all of shining gray stone that looked like granite, sparkling with deeply buried highlights. The outer wall, perfectly square and at least forty feet high, completely surrounded the inner buildings, an assortment of keeps and towers, some leaning at crazy angles as if half-toppled by an earthquake. Some seemed unfinished, having great gaps in them. Some were shorn off oddly at the top, as if sliced by giant knives. Nowhere were seams or jointures apparent at all; the place seemed to have been carved from single blocks of stone. And though there were windows in the inner buildings, there was no opening in the outer wall anywhere. It towered up before them, slick and unscalable as glass.

"Well," Freelorn said with scarcely disguised satisfaction, "*now* what?"

Herewiss made an irritated face, but Sunspark laughed privately, unconcerned. (I think,) the elemental said, (it's time to disabuse them of the idea that I am a horse.)

(What? You're going to jump it?)

(No, nothing like that. Just inside the wall I can sense a courtyard. I'll take part of the wall away.)

(Can you *do* that?)

(It'd be silly to suggest it if I couldn't,) Sunspark said, amused. (Get off and take everyone back a quarter of a mile or so. I'm going to have to exert myself somewhat, but the stretch will do me good.)

Herewiss dismounted. "Lorn," he said, "let me up behind you, will you? We're going to have to back off a ways."

"Uh, look," Freelorn said, sounding alarmed, "I don't want you to strain yourself—"

"Let's go."

Herewiss put his foot in Blackmane's stirrup and swung up behind Freelorn. He was aware of Segnbora regarding him with a small and secret smile; he winked at her. "Back the way we came," he said to Freelorn, "a quarter mile or so."

"But your horse—!"

"Sunspark is going to take part of the wall away," Herewiss said.

"*Sunspark* is—"

With Freelorn in the lead, shaking his head, the group rode back into the desert. After a while Herewiss stopped them.

"Far enough," he said. "Now then." (Are you ready, Spark?)

(Yes.)

(Will it be all right for us to look?)

(Mmm—yes, I'll damp the light. You'll probably feel the heat, though.)

"It's going to be hot," Herewiss said, "and bright. Be warned."

(Go ahead,) he told Sunspark.

For a few seconds there was nothing, only the sight of the high towers peering over the wall, and the small red-brown horse-shape standing before the stone. Then Sunspark reared.

—Searing brightness like a sunseed fallen to earth and exploding into flower! A hard stabbing brilliance like a knife through the eyes! And a crack of thunder like being hit in the face, followed by a wave of stinging hot wind—

By the time they got their horses back under control again, the light and the heat were gone. There was only the little red horse-shape, standing before a huge gap in the wall.

Freelorn turned to look over his shoulder at Herewiss. "You were *riding* that?"

Herewiss smiled at him. "Let's go see what the inside of the place looks like."

They rode back to the wall, and dismounted, looking at it in wonder. About a hundred feet of the wall's four-hundred-foot length was gone. The edges of the sudden opening were perfectly smooth, though slightly duller than the slick polished stone of the wall's outer surfaces; the seared stone was crackling as it cooled.

Sunspark walked over to Herewiss, its eyes glittering with pleasure. (That was fun.)

(The stone, Spark, where did it go?)

(I consumed it. Anything'll burn if you heat it enough. It made a nice meal.)

(But stone—?)

Sunspark smiled at Herewiss in its mind. (I have to eat *sometimes.*)

"Lorn?" Herewiss said.

"Yeah, what?" Freelorn was gazing in through the opening at the courtyard. It was paved in the same shining gray stone, and at the other side of it was a low, oblong structure like a great hall.

"Let's have a look."

"You first," Freelorn said.

"All right, me first—"

Herewiss walked cautiously through the opening. Immediately it was much quieter; the sound of the wind seemed muted and far away. There was no dust on the pavement at all, and like the walls, the paving stretched without a seam or crack from one side of the courtyard to the other. Sunspark's hooves clattered loudly on it as it followed him in.

Freelorn and his people came close behind Herewiss. No one spoke. Though the place was quieter than the surrounding desert, that was not what was oppressing them. The sheer stone walls and the crazily tilted towers rising above the central hall seemed to be *ignoring* them somehow—as if nothing human beings could do there would ever make a difference, as if the suddenly breached wall was a matter of no consequence. The place had an aura about it as of impassiveness and unconcern—as if it were alive itself, in some way, and did not recognize *them* as living things.

"This paving," Lang said softly, "it isn't level."

"Yes it is," Harald said, almost whispering. "You can see that it is—"

"It doesn't feel that way."

"No, it doesn't," Herewiss said, very loudly. "And why are we whispering?"

A ripple of nervous laughter went through the group.

"There's something about this place," Segnbora said. "Some of these towers, the—the *perspective* of them seems wrong somehow. They're *off*. That one over the big square building, it should look closer than the other one behind it, tilting off to the left—but it *doesn't*."

"Let's see what the inside is like." Herewiss headed toward the opening in the building before them, wide and dark.

They left the horses hobbled in the courtyard and followed him in. It wasn't as dark inside as they had expected. They stood at one side of a great square room, with a huge opening in the stone of the ceiling, like a skylight; it was positioned directly over what appeared to be a firepit raised some feet above the floor on a platform. Around the walls of the hall were doors opening onto vaguely lit passageways. Through one of these they could see a flight of stairs leading upward. The stairs were uneven, one broad one being staggered with two steep narrow ones as far up as they could see.

"Well," Herewiss said, "if this is the dining hall, I wonder what the bedrooms are like? Let's look."

The group went slowly across the hall, clustered together. "I keep expecting something to jump out of one of those doors," Freelorn said, as they started up the stairs.

"Well, I doubt it would be one of the original inhabitants," Herewiss answered. "The lack of furniture makes me think they moved out permanently—unless they have very severe tastes in decorating."

At the top of the stairs they all paused for a moment. Nothing was to be seen but a long, long corridor full of open doorways into dark empty rooms. One door, the fourth or fifth one down on the left, must have opened to a room with a window; sunlight poured out through it and onto the opposite wall.

"We could look at the view," Herewiss said, and started down the hall. He looked into the first door he passed—

—and halted in midstep. Freelorn bumped into him, and Lang into Freelorn, and Segnbora into Lang, and they all looked—

There was no room behind the door. The stone of the doorsill was there, hard and solid under their hands as they reached out to reassure themselves of it; but through the opening cut in the glittering gray they saw a mighty mountain promontory rearing upward from a sea the color of blood. Pink foam crashed upward from the breaking waves and fell on the rose-and-opal beaches; the wind, blowing in from the sea, stirred trees with leaves the color of wine, showing the leaves' flesh-colored undersides. The mountain was forested in deep purples and mauves, a cloud of morning mist lying about its shoulders.

Herewiss reached out, very slowly, and put his hand through the doorway. After a moment he withdrew it, rubbing his fingers together.

"It's cooler there," he said, "and damp. Lorn, this is *it*. Doors into Otherwheres—"

They moved on slowly to the next door.

It showed them sand, endless butter-colored sand carved by relentless winds into rippled dunes with crests like knives, stretching from one horizon to the other in perfect straight lines...a corrugated desert, showing not one sign of life, not the tiniest plant or creature. The sky was such a deep pure blue-violet as one sometimes sees in the depths of a lake at evening.

"If you cut our sky with a knife," Segnbora whispered, "it would bleed that color."

"Come on—"

The next doorway opened on a hallway of gray stone, crowded with seven people who looked through a doorway at a hallway of gray stone, crowded with seven people who looked through a doorway at a hallway—

"Dear Goddess!" Freelorn said, and spun to look behind him. There was nothing there but another doorway, this one showing a volcano erupting with terrible, silent violence against a night sky. A flying rock fell close to the door as he watched. He flinched back and Herewiss reached out to steady him.

"It's all right. Let's go on."

"What if that had come through?"

"I don't know if it can. Look at the sun coming out of this one—"

They gathered before the next door. "Suns, you mean," Dritt said. They looked down on a placid seashore. Out over the dark water, one small red sun was going down in a fury of crimson clouds; another one, larger and fiercely blue, shone higher in the sky.

"Two suns." Moris's voice, usually loud and abrasive, was hushed. "Two *suns*! What kind of place is that?"

"Goddess only knows. Look at this one—"

The group relaxed, broke slightly apart as each person went looking through a separate doorway, looking for a wonder of their own.

"—*blue* trees?"

"What the Dark is *this??*"

"Look, it's *our* country. Moris, isn't that the Eorlhowe? And the North Arlene peninsula—"

"This one is underwater—look, there goes a fish!"

"I didn't know the Goddess *made* birds that big."

"It's snowing here, I can't see a thing."

Herewiss was standing before a doorway that showed nothing— nothing at all, a vague blurry darkness. Not the darkness of night, but an absence, an absence of anything at all. He looked at it, and his heart was beating fast. An unused door? Maybe—

Freelorn came to him from further up the hall, took Herewiss's arm and began to pull him along. "What? *What?*" Herewiss said, but Lorn wouldn't answer him.

He pulled Herewiss in front of one door. "Look," he said.

The door showed them a view from a high place, looking down into a landscape afire with a sunset the color of new love. Below and before them stretched a fantastic growth of crystalline forms, islanded between two rivers; jutting upward against the extravagant sky like prisms of quartz or amethyst or polished amber, but scored and carved and patterned, stark in the sunset light. They grew in all sizes and shapes, a forest of gigantic gems, spears of opal and dark jade and towers of obsidian. They caught the light of day's end and reflected it back from a thousand different planes and angles, golden, red, orange, pink, smoky twilight blue; a barbaric and magnificent display of a god's crown-jewels, the diadem of Day set down between the crimson rivers as the Sun retired. One spire reached higher than all the others around it, a masterwork of crystal set in gray stone and topped with a spearing crown of silver steel. On the crown's peak a single ruby flared, pulsing like a Dragon's eye, and rays of light struck up from the circlet like pale swords against the deepening blue. In the silences of the upper sky, a crescent Moon smiled at the evening star that flowered beside it.

Beside Herewiss, Freelorn moved softly, as if afraid to break a dream. "What is it?" he whispered. "Is it real?"

"Somewhere it is."

"Is it really what it looks like, a city? How did they build it? Or did it grow? And is that all glass? How did they make it that way—?"

Herewiss shook his head, and out of the corner of his eye he caught sight of Segnbora moving slowly and silently toward the door, like one entranced. He reached out and caught her by the arm, and she pulled at him, wanting to be let go.

"No," he said. "Segnbora—look at the view. The door opens out onto somewhere very high. There may be ground under it, but there may not be. You could step out onto nothing. And it would be a short flight for someone who doesn't have wings."

She stared out the doorway with longing, the colors of the softening sunset catching in her eyes. "It might be worth it," she said.

"Come on—"

The next doorway was dark, but not as the one Herewiss had seen. In the endless depths of its darkness, stars were suspended. Not the remote cold stars of night in the desert, but great flaming swarms of them, hot and beautiful, cast carelessly across the boundless black reaches of eternity. And close, so close you could surely put your hand out and pluck one like an apple. They spun outward from a blazing common core, burning like the sudden fiery realization of joy—

Freelorn took a step toward the doorway. "This is the real Door," he said, very softly, "the last Door—"

Alarm stirred in Herewiss, drowning his appreciation of the beauty in sudden concern for Freelorn. "Not the Door into Starlight, no," he said. "You can't see that until you're dead, Lorn, or have the Flame—and you're in neither condition."

"But my father—"

"That's not where he is." Herewiss took Freelorn by his shoulders, as much from compassion as from fear that he might cast himself through. "Your father is *past* that other Door—down by that Sea of which the Starlight is a faint intimation. They're lovely, but these are just stars. Not the final Sea."

Freelorn turned away, but Herewiss was troubled: there had been no feeling of release, of giving up the vision, no feeling of Freelorn accepting what *was*. "Lorn—"

"Let me be." Freelorn walked away from him, walked down the stairs, oblivious to the wondering comments of his people as they peered through one door or another.

Herewiss stared after him, worrying. He was distracted after a moment by a touch on his arm; Segnbora looked up at him. There was concern in her eyes. "Are we staying the night?" she asked.

"I think so."

She turned to look through the starry door, and sighed. "That's been much on his mind lately," she said.

"It's *always* on his mind," Herewiss said sadly. "As you'll find when you've known him as long as I have."

Segnbora nodded and went off to look through another door. *Damn,* Herewiss thought, *there's going to be crying tonight...*

That night they camped in the great hall around the firepit. There was no need to gather firewood, for Sunspark decided to inhabit the deep-set hearth, and burned there the night long. Freelorn and his people made much of it, and Sunspark flamed in unlikely shapes and colors for quite a while, showing off. But Herewiss was vaguely uneasy about something, and found himself bothered by the occasional perception of bright eyes in the fire, watching him with an odd considering look.

They ate hugely that night, and went to sleep early. Dritt and Harald went off to investigate one or another of the doors before they slept. After being gone for not more than a few minutes Dritt came down the stairs again, looking slightly dazed.

Freelorn and Herewiss were sitting with their backs to the firepit, working at a skin of Brightwood that Freelorn had liberated from the Ferry Tavern; the lovers'-cup was halfway through its fifth refill, and both of them looked up at Dritt with slightly addled concern as he went by.

"It was me," he said. "May I?" He gestured at the cup.

"Sure," Freelorn said.

Dritt reached down and took a long, long drink. "This morning," he said, "that was me, just now. I went upstairs, and it was daytime in one of the doors, and there were people coming—the first people that any door showed—and I got excited and walked through it to have a look."

"What was it like," Herewiss said, "going through?"

"Like nothing. Like going through a door." Dritt put the cup down. "Thanks. So I waited there for a while—and of course, it was us. Of course. It shook me at the time, and I stepped back, and then I couldn't see me any more—"

"Which of you couldn't see you?"

"Hell," Dritt said, bemused, "I'm not feeling terribly picky about the details right now. I'm going to bed."

"G'night."

"Yeah, good night..."

Dritt wandered away toward Moris's bedroll, and Herewiss picked up the cup and finished it. "How much more of this is there?" he said.

"There's another skin."

"Lorn, you amaze me. What else did you take out of there that wasn't nailed down?"

"No, no, I was a good boy. Only took the wine. I knew you'd like it, and I don't think the lady minded."

"No," Herewiss said. He chuckled then. "Lorn, this has been some month for me…"

"How?"

"Just the strange things happening—and then seeing you again. It's good to have you close." He put an arm around Lorn, hugged him tight.

"Yeah, it's good to be with you too… Listen, what are you going to do now?"

"Stay here."

Freelorn was quiet for a long moment.

"Lorn, I have to. I need this place. You saw the doors, you know what they can do. I have to try to find one that'll do what I want it to." Herewiss put out his hand to the lovers'-cup and played with it, turning it around and around. *Please,* he was thinking. *Please, Lorn, don't start this—not now—*

"I wish you wouldn't stay," Freelorn said.

Herewiss didn't answer.

"If you cared," Freelorn said. "If you did care, about how I feel, the way you say you do, you wouldn't worry me by staying here. This place isn't natural—"

"Neither am I, Lorn." *Damn, I know that phrasing. We're both going to wind up in tears. And afterwards he'll get what he wants out of me, just like he always does—*

"But you'll be all alone here—"

"Sunspark will be here. You saw what it did to the outer wall. I don't have much to be afraid of with a watchdog like that."

"Herewiss. Listen to me." Freelorn looked at him, earnestly, his face full of pain and hard-held restraint and the need to make Herewiss understand. Herewiss's insides went *wrench* at the sound of the pain and fear in Freelorn's voice. "This place—there's too much *power* here for other forces not to have taken notice of it. What is it you told me once, that as soon as you came into your Power, or started to, that would be the time to watch out, because new Powers are always noticed? And as soon as they come into being, the old Powers come to challenge them, to test them and see where they fit into the overall pattern?"

"Yes, but—"

"—and here's this place, there must be *incredible* power bottled up in it to make it do the things it does. And you'll sit here, merrily forging swords, and getting stronger and stronger, and Sunspark staying with you, a Power in its own right certainly—you think you won't attract notice? Doors open both ways, you know. Things can come in those doors as well as go out. If you needed proof, Dritt just gave it to you. Suppose something comes in while your back is turned?"

"Lorn—" *Listen to him fighting for control. Oh, Goddess, how can I refuse him? I don't want to hurt him but I have to stay here—*

"—Listen, you could stay here a few days, a week, two maybe; we'd stay with you. And then you could come with us when we raid the Treasury at Osta, and get the money we need to hire mercenaries—"

"Lorn, the more I think about it, the more I feel that the whole Osta idea is a bad one. And I really don't think mercenaries are going to be the right way to handle this. If at all possible, I'd prefer to avoid shedding blood."

"You're awfully careful with other people's blood," Freelorn said, a touch of anger beginning to creep into his voice now. "And not enough with your own. But maybe that's it. Have you decided down deep that since Herelaf died by your sword, you should too? Something out of Goddess-knows-where should come up on you while you're busy working on the one sword that will redeem you, and kill you then? Atonement? Blood shed for blood shed? There is a certain poetic justice to it—"

"Lorn, stop it." *He's goading me on purpose, now. He must be so very afraid. But I never thought he would hurt me like this—Is he so afraid that he can't give in a little, let me have my own way? The danger isn't that great—*

"If you die under conditions like that," Freelorn said, his anger growing, "your death will mean *nothing*. Herelaf would shake his head at you, and he'd say, 'Dad was right, your head *is* made of wood, just like everything else in this place—'"

I won't yell at him. I won't. He's my loved— "Lorn, I never thought that you—"

"—but you're determined to die before you forge that sword and reach your Power, because success would mean giving up your guilt—and you haven't really worked on anything else since Herelaf died. It's sharper than any sword, by now. You stick it into yourself every chance you get, and bleed a little more of your life and your power away, so that every time there's a little less of you left to pursue the search, a little less chance that you'll succeed. Now, though, you're getting close to success, and so you have to risk your life even more wildly by messing with places like this alone—"

"Lorn, *shut up!* Who brought me on this journey, anyway? I would likely never have *heard* about this place if I hadn't been coming to get you out of that damn keep. And as for nursing guilts, how about you? Maybe it *is* easier to make love than to make kings, but it's also easier to talk about being a king than it is to *be* one! You've never forgiven yourself for being out of the country when your father died, instead of by his side to do the whole heroic last-stand thing that you always wanted; and you were too damn guilty about it to go back and try to take his throne, because you didn't think you deserved it! Idiot! Or coward! Which? You could have gone back and tried to make a stand, tried to take the Stave. Maybe you *would* have died! But is this life? Living in exile, mooching off poor Bort until he died? At least you had the sense to get out of Darthen until Eftgan's reign was settled, and she remembers the favor; she likes you as much as Bort did, it seems. Lucky for you—otherwise it'd have been all over with you by now. Lately you couldn't lie your way out of an open field—"

"Dammit, Herewiss—!"

He almost never calls me by name. Sweet Goddess, *he's mad. But so am I*—"Shut up, Lorn! And don't come mouthing to me about deathguilt, because yours has nothing on mine, and even if it did, it's fairly obvious that you wouldn't be handling it any better. At least I'm trying to deal with mine—"

Freelorn's mouth worked, and nothing came out. Herewiss stopped, his satisfaction at Freelorn's anger suddenly draining out of him. *This is a thing I never knew about us,* he thought in shock. *We resent each other. My Goddess. Can love and resentment like this live in the same person at the same time and not kill each other?*

"What are you going to do?" Freelorn said, his voice tight.

"I'm going to stay here." Herewiss made his voice noncommittal, unemotional. He was trembling.

"Then I'm going to Osta. And I'll see you when I see you. Good night." Freelorn got up and went to the corner where his bedroll was laid out; he wrapped himself up in his cloak and lay down with his face to the wall and his back to Herewiss.

Oh, Dark, Herewiss thought, *we've had fights before...* But he couldn't stop shaking, and something inside him told him that this had been no normal fight. *"Died by your sword,"* Freelorn's voice said, again and again, echoing like the cold howls of the Shadow's Hunting through midwinter skies. *He never said anything like that to me before.* Never—

He sat there a long time, unmoving, staring at Freelorn's turned back, or at the lovers'-cup, half-full of wine, sitting on the floor beside him. Sunspark burned low at his back, watching in silence.

(Spark—) he said.

(Do you do that often?) it said very softly.

(Uh—no. Not really.)

(It is a considerable discharge of energies.)

(It, ah, it is that.)

(Such random discharges,) the elemental said, (usually preclude the possibility of union—)

(Yes,) Herewiss said. (They do.)

(He is—no longer your mate?)

The elemental's thought made it plain that such an occurrence was quite nearly the end of the world; and Herewiss, beginning to sink downward into his pain, was inclined to agree. (I don't know,) he said. (Oh, I don't—No, I really don't know…)

He got up, went over to where Freelorn lay, reached down and touched him. "Lorn—"

Nothing. He might as well have touched the gray stone of the hold and asked it for an answer.

He lay down, wrapping himself up in his cloak too and stretching out beside Freelorn. But he did not need his underhearing to perceive the wall of hostility that lay between them like a sword thrown in the middle of the bedroll. There was a stranger on the other side of the wall, a stranger who wanted fiercely to be left alone, who would strike out if bothered—

It was like trying to lie still on hot coals. Herewiss got up and went away, back to the firepit. He sat on the edge of it and stared into the shifting flames. Bright eyes looked out at him.

(He doesn't want to talk to me. Maybe he will in the morning. Sleep heals a great many ills, including unfinished quarrels, sometimes—)

(I would not know. I don't sleep.)

(Tonight, I doubt if I will, either.) Herewiss sighed. (I'm going outside for a bit, Spark.)

It flickered acquiescence at him and cuddled down into the pit, pulling a sheet of fire over itself.

Herewiss paused, looking over his shoulder at Freelorn. His loved lay still unmoving, but Herewiss could feel the space around him prickling with anger and frustration.

Oh, hell, he told himself. *Let be. You know how Lorn is. He does a two-day sulk and then everything's all right again.*

But we never fought like this—

He walked to the front doorway of the hold and looked out. The gray walls of the courtyard were walls of shadow now, hardly to be seen at all except where their tops occluded the sky. Herewiss leaned against the doorsill, sighed again, folded his arms and gazed up at the stars. His brain was jangling like windchimes in a storm of fears and fragmented thoughts; it took him a long few moments to calm down and greet the blazing desert stars, the Mother's sky, as it deserved to be greeted. It took him a few minutes more to realize that the constellations with which he was familiar were nowhere to be seen.

Uhh—wait a moment—!

Very quietly, so as not to disturb Lorn or anyone else who might have been trying to sleep, Herewiss stepped across the courtyard, past the dozing horses, to the doorway which Sunspark had opened. As he passed through it, the sound of the solano, the relentless spring wind of the Waste, reasserted itself; somewhere to his left he heard the squeaks and chirrups of a colony of bounce-mice going about their nightly business. He looked up at the cold-burning sky. Dragon, Spearman, Maiden, Crown, all the constellations of spring shone unperturbed high in the clear air.

How about that, Herewiss thought. He went back into the courtyard, and looked up. Within the walls, the sky glittered again with alien stars, strange eyes looking down on him from a nameless night.

This is definitely where I need to be, he thought as he headed back toward the hall. He sighed again. Part of him was indulging itself in a delicious shivering excitement at the prospect of where he was. The rest of him was weighed down with the aching feeling of the angry, untouchable presence on the other side of the bedroll.

He slowed down. *I don't really want to go back in there—*

—oh, Goddess, yes, I do—

—but—

He stopped still in his indecision, and as he listened to the odd silence that prevailed within the walls, he heard something more. Someone was outside, playing a lute. The individual notes stitched through the quiet like needles through dark velvet, bright, precise; but the pattern they were embroidering was random. There was a pause as Herewiss listened; and then a chord strung itself in silvery lines across the still air, and another after it, gently mournful, though in a major key. When a voice joined the chords, singing in a light contralto, Herewiss was able to localize the sounds better. Whoever it was was somewhere to the left, around the corner of the building.

The tone of the singing, though he could not make out words, had touched Herewiss at the heart of his mood—night-ridden, melancholy. He went quietly over to the corner of the hall, leaned against the warm gray stone, peered around. Segnbora was there; sitting on the smooth paving with her back against the wall, her cloak folded behind her to lean on, a wineskin by her side. Her head was tilted back against the stone, relaxed, and the lute rested easily on her lap. If she noticed Herewiss, she gave no sign of it, but kept on serenading night and stars like a lover beneath some dark window.

"—and she fared on up that awful trail
and little of it made:
She stood laughing on the peak-snows
with the new Moon in her hair—"

Herewiss listened with interest. *With her deep voice, who'd suspect she had a high register? Needs work on her vibrato, but otherwise she sounds lovely—*

"Thank you!" said the deep voice, with laughter. The strumming continued as Segnbora looked over at him and smiled. "You going to stand there all night, or will you sit down and have a little wine?"

"Um," Herewiss said, as he went over to sit against the wall beside her. "I may have had more than I should already."

She raised an eyebrow at him, at the same time squeezing the lute's neck and wringing a tortured dissonant chord from it. "That bad, huh?"

"You underheard what went on in there?"

She shook her head. "There's something about these walls that makes them good insulators. But once you came outside, it felt like someone was trying to beat a dent out of a big pot with a sledgehammer. Noisy."

"Sorry," Herewiss said.

"For what? A lot of it was the walls, anyway; they make even a fourth-level ideation echo as if it were being shouted in a cave." She stroked the lute again, and it purred in minor sevenths. "I take it he doesn't approve of your staying here."

"No."

"I can't say that I would, either, if I were in his place—but you have to stay. There's too much possibility here—"

Herewiss looked at her. (You *would* understand,) he said, bespeaking her.

"I'd better. Please, prince, the mindtouch—let's not and say we did. With these walls all around, the echo is really bad."

"That's why you came outside?"

She nodded. "Partly. Every time someone subvocalized, my head felt like a gong being struck."

"I didn't feel much of anything. You have sensitivity problems?"

Segnbora chuckled. "Normally—if that's the word for it—I hear everything from fourth level up. Sometimes, if I'm drunk enough, or tired enough, I'll only pick up subvocals. But *this* place—" She sighed in exasperation, shook her head. "Or maybe it's because of my flowering: I'm just past it. Though usually I don't have that problem with the hormonal surge. But I was getting tired of hearing people's bladders yelling to be emptied, and stomachs complaining that they weren't full enough, and neural leakage rattling like gravel in a cup. All multiplied by six..."

"I used to wish I had that kind of sensitivity—"

"Don't. Unless you also wish to be able to turn it off. I can't, and it's awful. I'm tired of hearing Dritt's conscience chastising him about his weight problem, and Moris wondering if Dritt really loves him when he's so skinny, and Harald's arthritis crunching in his knee, and Lorn wanting Hergótha every night when he cleans Súthan, and Lang thinking...I'm just tired." She closed her eyes, rubbed the bridge of her nose as if a headache was coming on.

"I'm sorry," she said then lifting her head. "I hear good things, too: I don't mean to whine." She reached down for the wineskin.

—*But even the good things make me feel so lonely,* Herewiss underheard her finish the thought. He closed his eyes in pain.

Segnbora looked at him quickly; her eyes were worried, and then in a tick of time they went regretful. "I leak, too," she said sadly. "I should have mentioned. Wine?"

"What kind?"

"Blood wine."

"Which region?" Herewiss asked, interested. The grapes were only grown along the North Arlene coast, where a combination of capricious climate and daily beatings of the vines produced an odd wrinkled grape, and eventually a sweet red liqueur with a hint of salty aftertaste—hence the name.

"Peridëu. My family has a connection with the vintners—one of my great-aunts cured their vines of white rot, oh, years back. They keep sending us the stuff every year or so."

"I might have a sip of that."

Segnbora passed Herewiss the wineskin, and he drank a couple of swallows' worth and restoppered it. "I didn't know you were a lutenist," he said.

"I'm not, usually." She smiled in the dark, leaned her head back against the stone, looking up. "But it's a good excuse. No one goes outside just to look at the stars, you know. So I take the lute with me some times."

Herewiss chuckled, jerked a thumb at the sky. "You noticed."

"How not? But what do you think I'd do, run in and shout, 'Hey, look, everybody, the stars are all wrong'? Lorn would love *that*." She laughed too. "I was going to tell you before we left, in case you hadn't seen it already." She touched the lute strings again, tickling them into a brief bright spill of notes like laughter, a half-scale in the Hakrinian mode.

Herewiss settled back against the wall, and looked at the sky once more, regarding the bright eyes of the elsewhere night as they regarded him. "So what else aren't you," he said, "besides a lutenist?"

The scale modulated into the chords Herewiss had heard while peeking around the corner. "I'm not a poet," Segnbora said, "and not a singer, and not a dancer, and not a loremistress…" She laughed softly. "Better not to be too many things at once: it scares people. Besides, in the case of the dancing, better they shouldn't see. I love to dance, but I'm afraid I'll look funny—so I don't, unless I'm very drunk…and then in, the morning, I don't remember it anyway…"

She keeps laughing, Herewiss thought. *As if she has to convince herself it's funny. But it's not working…*Aloud he said, "So how's your dancing when you're drunk?"

"No one else remembers," she said. "They're all drunk too."

"Then it doesn't matter, does it?"

"No, I guess it doesn't." She smiled at him, a more relaxed look, almost a benediction. "You *do* understand."

"I'd better," he said. "I'm about singing the way you are about dancing. Goddess knows why—they tell me I have a good voice—but I'm just shy... What was that you were singing before? I didn't recognize it."

"Huh? Oh. 'Efmaer's Ride.' It's south Darthene, came north with my mother's side of the family. We were related to Efmaer, remotely." Again the chords, soft and sad for all that they were in a major key.

"Wasn't she the queen who disappeared?"

"Well, according to the song, she didn't just disappear. You know the stories about Sai Ebássren in the mountains, south of Barachael?"

"Sounds familiar. Maybe it has another name I know it by—"

"In Darthen they call it Méni Auärdhem."

"Glasscastle, yes. The place in the sky that appears every so often—"

"Not very often, really. There are Moon phases and lighting conditions involved, it's very complicated. But anyway, Efmaer's loved killed himself, and since suicides go to Glasscastle, Efmaer went to get her Name back from him. She took the sword Shadow with her—Skádhwë, it was called then—"

"How much of this is true?"

Segnbora shrugged. "It was a long time ago. But we know that Shadow existed, and the queen went missing. It's a nice song, anyway—"

"Does it have a happy ending?"

"It depends," Segnbora said. "See, here's the last verse—" The lute whispered the sorrowing chords, and Segnbora's voice was hardly louder—

"'She stood laughing on the peak-snows
with the new Moon in her hair,
and she smiled and set her foot upon
the Bridge that isn't There:

'She took the road right gladly
to the Castle in the sky,
and Darthen's sorrel steed came back,
but the Queen stayed there for aye...'"

"So," Segnbora said, modulating out of the last chord into a minor arpeggio, "who knows? No one came back to tell whether Efmaer found what she was looking for, or whether she was happy..."

"Glasscastle is where you go when you're tired of trying, isn't it? I remember hearing something like that." Herewiss sighed.

Segnbora looked at him sharply. "Don't you dare even think of it," she said. The anger in her voice caught Herewiss by surprise, and Segnbora too, after a moment. More gently she said, "You'll get where you're going, prince. They'll be singing about you for centuries."

"The question is, will they be happy songs? ...And besides, even when you're in the middle of a song, you don't always feel like singing. I don't right now..."

She reached out a hand and touched his where they lay folded in his lap. "He'll come through it," she said. "He's in love with you, that's all."

"Then why can't he see why I need to be here?!" Herewiss said, surprised again by anger, this time his own. More softly he added, "He knows how much the Fire means to me—"

"He's in love with *you*," Segnbora said again, almost too softly to be heard.

Herewiss held very still. Not even the lute broke the silence.

"Yes," he said. "I see what you mean."

"If I were you," Segnbora said, "I'd get some sleep."

Herewiss nodded, stood up, stretched. "Thanks for the wine," he said. He headed back toward the courtyard and the hall. Her voice stopped him.

"Brother—" she said.

Herewiss turned to look back at her. She was a shadowy shape, dark against the dark wall, surprisingly bright where starlight touched her—sword hilt, belt buckle, finger-ring, cloak clasp, and the half-seen eyes. In the stillness he felt the air go suddenly thick and sharp with power, mostly hers, partly his. She was having a surge, hormonal or not, and it had touched his own Fire, roused it—

—his precognition came alive, as it had once or twice before. The image was blurred and vague, and out of context, strange-feeling. Darkness, and cold; somewhere a bright light, but bound up, concealed; and over all, a looming shadow, eyed with silver fire—

She's hiding, something in him told him suddenly. *But why? From what?* The feeling ebbed, drained away, leaving the air just air again, and Segnbora was just a young woman sitting against a wall, not a numinous shadow-wrapt figure gazing at him through darkness and silence. She looked back and shuddered all over. Herewiss wondered what she had seen.

"It doesn't matter," she said. "I didn't see anything clearly. That wasn't what I was going to say. Prince, you *will* do it. I'll help any way I can."

She cares a little, he thought in quiet surprise. *More than a little.* Well, she would.

He bowed to her, the deep bow of greeting or farewell from one veteran of the Silent Precincts to another. "Sister," he said; and there was nothing else to say. He went around the corner and back inside.

Nothing had changed. Lorn's people were all asleep, and Lorn was still rolled up in his cloak, in a tight angry-looking ball. He was snoring.

Herewiss stopped by the firepit, sank down wearily into his chair. The flames flurried momentarily higher, and Sunspark was looking at him again.

(So how is the night?)

(Strange,) Herewiss said, (but then that could be expected.) He sat there for a while and avoided looking in Freelorn's direction.

(I'm never going to get to sleep by myself,) he said eventually. (Maybe I should take something—)

He stopped short. (The Soulflight drug—)

(?)

(The innkeeper at the Ferry Tavern gave it to me. If I took a little, I could probably drop right off into pleasant dreams—though with the smaller doses you sometimes don't remember what happens to you—)

(You could probably use some pleasant dreams tonight,) Sunspark said.

Herewiss went and got the little bottle out of his saddlebag, then sat down by the firepit again and regarded it. He unstoppered it and put his nose to the opening. There was a faint sweet odor, like honey. He stuck his finger in, took a little and licked it off.

The taste was extremely bitter; he choked as he put the stopper back in the bottle and set it aside. *Well,* he thought, *let's see what happens—* He leaned back and closed his eyes, and waited.

—an easy, drifting passage into—
CRASH!!

—and he looked around him, terribly shaken. All was still, nothing was wrong anywhere that he could see. It had been one of those falling-dreams that slams one suddenly into the wall between sleep and waking, and out the other side.

False alarm. One more time—

—drifting easily downward into empty lightless places, filled with uncaring as if with smoke; spiraling down, sailing on wings feathered with fear, and now suddenly the—

WHAT??! NO!!

Cold dusk, a gray evening, no sunset pouring crimson-gold through treetops and touching the Woodward with fire; torches quarreling weakly with the evening mist; and silence, deadly silence. No children running and playing, though even on chill evenings they would be out this late, resisting their mothers' attempts to get them back inside. Little sound, little movement. Walk quietly up to the great carven door, pass silently through it. Greet the Rooftree with reserve, and go by; up the stairway, left at the top of the stairs and down through the east gallery, but softly, softly. Someone is dying. Turn right into the north corridor, one of the more richly carven ones, and keep going. There on the walls is carved the story of Ferrigan, your ancestress, and the panels show her rebuilding the Woodward after its burning, with the help of creatures not wholly human. You always loved her story, that of a person who mastered her own powers and went her own way, disappearing into the Silent Precincts one day, never to be seen again. Herelaf liked that one too. But very shortly now Herelaf will be past liking anything at all, at least in *this* life. Walk softly, and go on in: last room on the right, the corner room, the room that is the heir's by tradition.

There is the bed, there is Herelaf, the sword out of him, now; your father standing there, not looking at either of you, not daring to. For fear that he will see one of you die, and the other of you live. Oh, he loves you well enough, that much is certain. But right now Hearn is finding it hard to love you at all, who were so stupid as to play with swords while drunk.

Herelaf is lying very still, looking very pale. How strange. He was always the darkest one in the family; you used to tease him about it sometimes, saying that there must be Steldene blood in him somewhere; and he would grin and say, "Mother never told us half of what she did while she was out Rodmistressing. You can sleep with some strange sorts in that business. Maybe something rubbed off." That was the way he always was: big, gentle, inoffensive, easygoing; no one had a bad word for him, not a single person anywhere, most especially not the many people he called loved. There were enough of them in the Wood, men and women both, and people used to marvel that he never took one loved with an eye to marriage. "I like to spread myself around," he would always say. "So far there's nobody that special that I'd want to give all of me to just them. But maybe…"

Forget *that*. He's going to die tonight, and all the chances close down forever. You did that to him. Yes you did. Don't try to deny it.

DAMMIT LET ME OUT OF HERE!!!

Hearn stands there, looking like he wishes he were anywhere else than this—facing down the Shadow Himself, *anywhere* but here. But he cannot desert either of you; he knows that you both need him now, both of you need him there desperately, and Hearn was always brave. Maybe not prudent; certainly if he were prudent he would go out of here. But brave.

Herelaf lies there, drained dry, waiting for the Mother to come for him. She can't be far; his body has a castoff look about it already—or maybe it is his closeness to the Door that is apparent, and the light from that Sea of which the Starlight is a faint intimation is shining through him, as if he were a doorway himself. The gray light makes everything in the room look unreal, except Herelaf—and he will be unreal soon enough.

You go over to him, kneel sidewise by the bed, take his hands in yours. They are chill, and this shakes you more terribly than anything else; his hands were always warm, even in wintertime when you always went clammy and stiff with the cold. Herelaf, now, with those big warm hands of his—big even for a Brightwood man—getting cold; getting dead. You did it. Oh yes.

NOT THIS AGAIN!! PLEASE, NO!!

Oh yes. "Dusty," he says, his beautiful soft deep voice gone all cracked and dry and shallow with pain. "Little brother mine. It wasn't your fault."

The words go into your head, but they make no particular sense. At least they didn't then. They do now, and it hurts at least twice as much, because you know it was your fault. Then, though, you bury your face in those cold hands, punishing yourself with the terror of what is going to happen. The Mother is kind, but inexorable; when She comes, there's no turning Her back. And you know She's coming.

"Dusty, are you listening to me? Look at me." He turns your face up to him, and you try to look away, but it's no good; even dying those hands have all their strength.

You look at him: dark curly hair like yours, big around the shoulders the way you got to be eventually; the droopy sleepy eyes, the smile that never comes off. Even dying, there's a ghost of it apparent, a slight curling-at-the-corners smile. He loves you. That's the worst part of it all, really.

"Don't do anything stupid," he says. "I expect you to stay right here and get things straight. You're going to be the heir now. You have a lot to learn. Don't run out on Da."

And you nod, the pain becoming even worse as you realize that this is a lie. There is *nothing* that will keep you here after Herelaf dies, not pleas nor threats nor even Hearn's need. You have a more imperative one—punishment of the deathguilt, and getting it attended to as quickly as possible, before the deed starts to rot and smell up the Wood. You know you'll try to go after Herelaf, to achieve whatever justice is meted out on that last Shore to those who murder their brothers.

Lying to your brother on his deathbed. You *are* worthless.

He flicks a tired, tired glance at the bandage around his middle, and at the stain spreading on it. "Wasn't your fault," he says wearily. How that voice used to sing in the evenings; now it can barely speak. Herelaf looks up at something, Someone on the other side of the bed. He smiles faintly. "Mother," he says.

And then is still.

And you get up, and wander away.

Into the gray places where nothing matters.

Here's a window. That's as good as anything else.

Someone is stopping you. It's Freelorn.

Damn him anyway.

You pull yourself gradually out of his grip and wander off into the gray places again. Where nothing matters.

You emerge occasionally to try to make an end of yourself. They stop you. You wander off into the gray again.

Nothing matters.

Nothing.

It's all gray.

Thank Goddess that's over. How do I get out of this?

Gray mist, cold. There are voices, remote, speaking words in other languages; other wanderers lost in the gray country. You ignore them.

And someone singing. Freelorn? Yes. The voice is changing, and cracks ludicrously every other verse.

"On the Lion's Day,
When the Moon was high,
then the queen went to the Fane
for her loved to die,

On that Night of dread,
opened up the deeps,
and she knew the Shadow there,
and in Rilthor forever she sleeps,

And her daughter wept,
vengeance in her heart,
and swore herself as vow
to take her mother's part,
bating love and breath
till the Shadow's death.

And she laid Him dead,
and herself she died,
never dreaming all the while
that in His death, He lied…"

You shake your head sadly. Freelorn's song, to be sure, redolent as usual of last stands and heroism past the confines of time and expectation. But all Béorgan's heroism couldn't change the fact that the Shadow was stronger than she, immortal, more permanent than death. What use is anything, anyhow—all hearts chill, and all loves die, and maybe the time has come for yours too—there in the mist, beckoning, waits the dark shape with the heart of iron and the eyes of ice, and all you have to do is despair, He'll do the rest—

(Oh, Mother. No.)

You summon your strength, and go away from there quickly, before the cold eyes see you and mark you for their own. Here, now, the mist is thick, and warmer. Faintly you can sense a body passing by, not far away—

"—to bring the lightning down,
one a shadow, one a fire,

one a sun and one a sire,
one who's dead—"

—a quiet voice, unfamiliar, singing a fragment of something to itself. It passes through the gray and is gone again. Follow it, if you can: it might show you the way out—

Suddenly in the grayness a tall form appears before you, vague through the fog. You press closer to it to ask for directions. Even if it can't tell you the way out, company would be welcome.

It's company, all right.

It's you.

Now you know how Dritt felt this morning. This is the you that you've seen in clear pools and mirrors, but changed. He's about three inches taller than you are, more regal of carriage. He moves with easy unthinking grace, whereas you just kind of bump along. He doesn't have those ten extraneous pounds on the front of his belly, where you have them; his eyes are bluer; his muscles are lithe under the smooth skin. He doesn't have any of your moles, and his face is unlined where your frown has long since indented itself; he doesn't have the little scar just above the right eye where Herelaf hit you with the fireplace poker when you were three and he was five. His face is serene, wise, joyous. You look at him with awe, reach out to him—and your hand goes through him. He's a dream Herewiss. You might have suspected as much. (*I never looked that good,*) you think.

He doesn't really see you; he is interacting with someone else who isn't there. Someone who is dreaming about you. Well, if you follow him, you may get back to the real world again.

He moves away through the mist, and you go along with him, feeling unnerved to be in the company of such perfection—even if he is you.

Eventually the fog begins to clear, and you find yourself back in the hold again. Your body is sitting over by the firepit. You glance at it and look away quickly. Two of you at once is a bit much, and three, especially when the third has all the imperfections, is almost more than you can bear. The dream-Herewiss is conversing with a dream-Freelorn over in the corner. Their eyes are warm as they look at one another, and their faces smile as they speak words of love. Freelorn is curled up in his usual ball again, snoring noisily. You might have known it was his dream of you—he never *could* see those little imperfections of yours, even when you pointed them out. Goddess love him.

You're tired, and sad, and you want to call it a night, so you ease yourself back over toward yourself and melt down into the body, pulling it up and around you like the familiar covers of your own bed—

He woke up with a terrible taste in his mouth, and a raging headache.

Freelorn was gone.

Freelorn's people were all in such a state of embarrassment that Herewiss found it difficult to be in the same room with them, and he went away into other parts of the hold, wandering around, until he heard their horses' hooves clatter out of the courtyard into the Waste. When he came downstairs, though, he found one of them still there. Segnbora was puttering around the hall, checking Herewiss's supplies to make sure he had enough of everything.

"He just left," she said from the other side of the hall, not stopping what she was doing. "Very early this morning, he got dressed, saddled Blackmane, and rode out. I don't think he even stopped to pee. His trail will be easy enough to follow."

Herewiss nodded.

Segnbora stood up, hands on hips, surveying the supplies. "That should do it. I should go after them, now; he'll miss me, and get mad—"

"I wouldn't want that to happen," Herewiss said.

Segnbora looked at him with deep compassion. "He'll get over it."

"I hope so."

She went out to the courtyard and spent a few silent minutes saddling Steelsheen. Herewiss followed her outside listlessly. When she was ready, she gave the saddle a final tug of adjustment, then went very quickly to Herewiss; she took his hands in hers, and squeezed them, and standing way up on tiptoe kissed him once lightly on the mouth. "I'll give it to him for you," she said. "He'll be all right; we'll take care of him. Good luck, Herewiss. And your Power to you—"

Then she was up in the saddle and away, pelting off after the others, leaving nothing behind but a small cloud of dust and a brief taste of warmth.

Herewiss watched her go, then turned back. The hold swallowed him like a mouth.

eight

It is perhaps one of life's more interesting ironies that, of the many who beseech the Goddess to send them love, so few will accept it when it comes, because it has come in what they consider the wrong shape, or the wrong size, or at the wrong time. Against our prejudices, even the Goddess strives in vain.

Hamartics, s'Berenh, ch. 6

"Sunspark?"
(?)
"What do you make of this?"
(Just a moment.)

Herewiss sat cross-legged before one of the doors, making notes with a stylus on a tablet of wax. Visible through the door was an unbroken vista of golden-green hills, reaching away into unguessable distances and met at the mist-veiled horizon by a violet sky. The brilliant sun hanging over the landscape etched Herewiss's shadow sharply behind him, and struck gray glitters from the wall against which he leaned.

Sunspark padded over to him in the shape of a golden North Arlene hunting cat, the kind kept to course wild pig and the smaller Fyrd varieties on the moor. It peered through the door, its tail twitching. (Grass. So?)

"That's not the point. I've been by this door five times today, and that sun hasn't moved."

(It could be a slow one. You remember that one yesterday that went by so fast, three or four times an hour. There's no reason this one couldn't be slow.)

"Yes, but there's something else wrong. That grass is bent as if there's wind blowing, but none of it *moves.*"

(That might just be the way it grows. There are a lot of strange things in the worlds, Herewiss—) It stepped closer to the door. (Then again—Look high in the doorway. Is there something in the sky there?) It craned its neck (By the top of the left post)

Herewiss squinted "Hard to tell, with the sun so close—no, wait a moment. Does that have wings?"

(I think so. And it's just hanging there, frozen.) Sunspark waved its tail in a feline shrug. (That could be your answer. This door may be frozen on one moment—or if it's not, it's moving that moment so slowly that we can't perceive it.)

Herewiss put down the tablet of wax in its wooden frame, and stretched. "Well, that's something new. What was that one you were looking at?"

(Nothing but empty sea, with four suns, all small and red. They were clustered close together, not spaced apart as most of them have been when they're multiple. And there was something around them, a cloud, that moved with them and glowed. The cloud was all of thin filaments, as if they had spun a web around themselves.)

"So..." Herewiss picked up the tablet again. "That's the nineteenth one with more than one sun, and the eighty-ninth one with water. More than half of these doors have shown lakes or seas or rivers. Who knows...the Morrowfane itself might be through one of these doors. Did you see any people?"

(No.)

"No surprise there...people have been much in the minority so far. Maybe whoever built this place was more interested in other places than other people."

(What you would call people, anyway.) Sunspark chuckled inside. (Would you call *me* 'people'?)

Herewiss looked at the elemental. Its cat-face was inscrutable, but his underhearing gave him a sudden impression of hopefulness, wistfulness. "I think so," he said. "You're good company, anyway."

(Well, 'company' is something I have not had much practice being. There is usually no need for it—)

"Among your kind, maybe. We need it a lot."

(It appears to be the way your folk were built. It seems strange, to want another's company before it comes time for renewal, for the final union.)

"It has its advantages."

(In the binding of energies, yes—)

"More than that. There's more than binding. *Sharing*."

(I have trouble with that word. Giving away energy willingly, is it?)

"Yes."

(It seems mad.)

"Sometimes, yes. But you usually get it back."

(Such a gamble.)

"Yes," Herewiss said, "it is that."

(What happens when you don't get it back?)

"Then you've lost energy, obviously. It hurts a little."

(It should hurt *more* than a little. Your own substance is riven from you; part of your *self*—)

"Depends how much of yourself you give away. Most of the time, it's nothing fatal."

(Well, how could it be?)

"It happens, among our kind. People have given too much, and died of it; but mostly because they had convinced themselves that they were going to. In the end it's their own decision."

(Mad, completely mad. The contract-conflict is safer, I think.)

"Probably. But it doesn't pay off the way sharing does when it turns out right."

(I don't understand.)

"It's the dare. The gamble, taking the chance. When sharing comes back, it's—an elevation. It makes you want to do it again—"

(—and if it fails the next time, you'll feel worse. A madness.) It shrugged. (Well, there are patterns within the Pattern, and no way to understand them all. How many doors have we counted now?)

Herewiss looked at the tablet. "A hundred and fifty-six. Five of the lower halls and half this upper hall. Then there's that east gallery, and the hallways leading from it—"

Sunspark's tone of thought was uneasy. (You know, there is no way that all these rooms can possibly be contained within this structure as we beheld it from outside. There's no room, it's just too small.)

"Yes, I know—but they're all here. What about that row of rooms between the great hall downstairs and the back wall? They couldn't have been there, either. Of course it was all right; after a few days they *weren't*. Four doors went missing from this hall alone earlier this week, but here they are again—"

(The next one along was one of the ones that vanished. Let's see what it looks like now...)

Herewiss got up, and they walked together down to the next doorway. It showed them nighttime in a valley embraced by high hills; behind the hills was a golden glow like the onset of some immense Moonrise. The valley floor was patterned with brilliant lights of all colors, laid out in an orderly fashion like a gridwork. Down from the gemmed heights wound a river of white fire, pouring itself blazing down the hillsides into the softly hazed splendor of the valley's floor. There were no stars.

(Now *those* may be people,) Sunspark said after a moment, (but not my kind, or yours, I dare say. What do you say to a white light?)

"I don't know. What do you say to a horse, or a pillar of fire?" Herewiss grinned, and made a note on his tablet. "This next one was gone too. Let's look—"

They moved a few steps farther down the hall, and stopped. The door showed them nothing. Nothing at all.

"Sweet Goddess, it came back," Herewiss said. "I was wondering what this one might be, and I had a thought—it could be a door that was never set to show anything before the builders left. An unused blank. It appears and disappears like all the other doors in the place, but it doesn't show anything."

(I don't know.) Sunspark looked at the door dubiously. (It gives me an odd feeling—)

"Well, let's see."

Herewiss blanked everything out, slowed his breathing, and strained his underhearing toward the door, *past* the door—

—strained—

"Nothing," he said, and opened his eyes again. "Can't get into it the way I can some of the others. Spark, would you do a favor and get my grimoire for me? The one with the sealed pages."

(You're going to try to open this *now?*)

"Is there a better time? I had a good night's sleep. I ate a big breakfast. Let's try."

Sunspark went molten and flowed down the hall like a hot wind. A few minutes later he returned, a young red-haired man with hot bright eyes and a tunic the color of fire, carrying the book. Herewiss reached out and took it, unsealed the pages and began riffling through them.

"Damn," he said after a moment. "Nothing is going to—well, no, maybe this unbinding—no, that's too concrete, it's for regular doors. This one—no... Dammit."

He paused a moment, then started running through the pages again. "This one. Yes. It's a very generalized unbinding, and if I change it here—and here—"

(I thought Freelorn said that it took Flame to open a door.)

"Yes, he did, and he's probably right, since doors are more or less alive. But this is an unbinding for inanimate objects, and if I make a few changes in the formula, it might work. I have to try something."

(Will you need me?)

"Just to stand guard." Herewiss sat down cross-legged against the wall again, breathed deeply and started to compose his mind. It took him a while; his excitement was interfering with his concentration. Finally he achieved the proper state, and turned his eyes downward to read from the grimoire.

"M'herie nai naridh veg baminédrian a phroi," he began, concentrating on building an infrastructure of openness and nonrestriction, a house made out of holes. The words were slippery, and the concepts kept trying to become concrete instead of abstract, but Herewiss kept at it, weaving a cage turned inside out, its bars made of winds that sighed and died as he emplaced them. It was both more delicate a sorcery and more dangerous a one than that which he had worked outside of Madeil. There the formulae had been fairly straightforward, and the changes introduced had been quantitative ones rather than the major qualitative shifts he was employing here. But he persevered, and took the last piece away from the sorcery, an act that should have started it functioning.

It sat there and stared at him, and did nothing.

He looked it over, what there "was" of it. It should have worked: it was "complete," as far as such a word could be applied to such a not-structure. *Maybe I didn't push it hard enough against the door,* he thought. *Well—*He gave it a mighty shove inside his head. It lunged at him and hit him in the back of the inside of his mind, giving him an immediate headache.

Dammit-to-Darkness, what did I—did I put a spin on it somehow? The shift could have done that, I guess. Well, then.

He pulled at it, and immediately it slid toward the doorway and partway through it. There the sorcery came to a halt, and sat twitching. Nothing came out of the door.

Maybe if I wait a moment, Herewiss thought.

He waited. The sorcery stopped twitching and fell into a sullen stillness.

Herewiss lost his temper. (Dark!) he swore, and lashed out at the sorcery, backhanding it across the broad part of the nonstructure instead of disassembling it piece by piece, slowly, as he should have. It fell apart, nothingness collapsing into a higher state of nonexistence—

Something came out the door.

He opened his eyes, and just enough of the Othersight was functioning to give him a horrible dual vision of what was happening. The door itself was still dark to his normal sight; but the Othersight showed him something more tenebrous, more frightening, a hideous murky knotted emptiness, the whole purpose of which was containment and repression. It was a prison. And the prisoner was coming through the door right then: a huge awful bulk that couldn't possibly be fitting through that door, but was—a botched-looking thing, a horrible haphazard combination of bloated bulk and waving, snatching claws, with an uncolored knobby hide that the filtered afternoon light somehow refused to touch. Herewiss caught a brief frozen glimpse of teeth like knives in a place that should not have been a mouth, but was. Then the Othersight confused itself with his vision again, and he was perceiving the thing as it was, the embodiment of unsatisfied hungers, a thing that would eat a soul any chance it got, and the attached body as an hors d'oeuvre. He underheard a feeling like the taste at the back of the throat after vomiting, a taste like rust and acid.

Through the confusion of perceptions, one thought made itself coldly clear: *Well, this is it. I tried, and I did wrong, and now I'm going to pay the price.* The sorcery had already backlashed, leaving him wobbly and weak, and he watched helplessly as the thing leaned out of the door over him and examined him, assessing the edibility of his *self* as an epicure looks over a dinner presented him—

Something grabbed him. Herewiss commended his soul to the Goddess, hoping that it would manage to get to Her in the first place, before he realized that Sunspark had him and was running.

"Where—" he said weakly.

(*Anywhere,* but out of *here!* I have seen those things before, at a distance, and there's no containing them—)

"But it *was* contained. Spark, what is it?"

(The name I heard applied to it was 'hralcin.' If you desire to stay in this body, we must get you away from here quickly. They eat *selves*—)

"Your kind too?"

(No one knows. None of my people have ever had a confrontation with one of the things, as far as I know, and I would rather not be the first!)

Herewiss realized that Sunspark was still in the human form, running with him down the stairs and into the main hall. Behind them there was a great noise of roaring and crashing.

"Do you think it could kill *you?*"

(I don't know. I don't think so. But I have heard of those things taking souls, and the souls never came back, not that anyone had ever heard in the places where I've traveled. They say that one or two hralcins can depopulate a whole world, one soul at a time. We could go through one of the doors until it goes elsewhere—)

"Sunspark, put me down."

(What??)

"Let me go."

Sunspark put Herewiss down on the floor of the main hall and turned into a tower of white fire that reached from floor to ceiling. Herewiss wobbled to his feet.

"I don't know how I managed to call it—"

(You said that the spell you were using was originally for inanimate objects?)

"Yes, but—"

(There's your answer. The thing's not alive. Why do you think it eats souls? When it has gotten enough of them, it gains life—)

"We've got to get it back in there."

(You are a madman,) Sunspark said. (There is no containing the things within anything short of a worldwall.)

"But it *was* contained! If it was in there, and bound, it can be gotten in there again, and rebound—"

(Whoever put it in there knew more about it than we do, certainly. This much *I* know, hralcins don't like light much. I can keep it away from us, I think. But it's only a matter of time until it leaves this place and gets out among your poor fellow creatures—and then there'll be little time left to them.)

"It mustn't happen. They don't like light?"

(No.)

"Maybe we can drive it back in through that doorway. Then I could bind it back in again—"

(But it takes you forever!) Sunspark's flames were trembling; the crashing was coming down the stairs. (And the thing would make a quick meal of you. It's got your scent, and once these things smell soul they pursue it until they catch it—)

Herewiss was sucking in great gulps of air, desperately fighting off the backlash. "I can decoy it back into the doorway. It'll follow me. Then I'll come out again, and you will hold it in with your fires until I can weave the necessary spell—"

Sunspark looked at Herewiss, a long moment's regard flavored with unease and amazement. (I can hold it off from *you*—)

"Sunspark, if that thing can empty whole worlds of people, what will it do to the Kingdoms? Come on. We'll let it into the hall, and I'll duck back up behind it, and you drive it up behind me. Then up, and through the door, and you can hold it in—"

(Very well.)

The hralcin came careening down the stairs, all horrible misjointed claws reaching out toward Herewiss as it staggered from the stairwell and across the floor. (I can direct the fire and the light pretty carefully,) Sunspark said, (but try to keep out from in front of me, or else well ahead. I'm going to let go.)

"Right."

Herewiss stumbled off to Sunspark's right, and the hralcin immediately changed direction to follow him. At that moment Sunspark went up in a terrible blaze of light and heat, so brilliant that it no longer manifested the appearance of flames at all—it was a fierce eye-hurting pillar of whiteness, like a column carved of lightning. The hralcin screeched, put up several of its claws to shield what might have been eyes, a circlet of irregular glittering protuberances set in the rounded top of its pear-shaped body. Herewiss dodged around it and scrambled up the stairs, slipping and falling on the slime the thing had left.

At the top of the stairs he paused for just a moment, feeling sick, and his eyes dazzled as his body tried to faint; but he wouldn't let it. The stench in the hall was terrible, as if the hralcin carried around the rotting corpses of its victims as well as their souls. Herewiss went staggering down past doorway after doorway, and finally found the right one. It was still black, and he quailed at the thought of going in there, maybe being imprisoned there himself, never finding the way out again, and the hralcin coming in after him—

He heard it screaming up the stairs after him. He thought, *Lorn, dammit!*

He went in.

Immediately darkness closed around him, as if he had crawled back into a womb. There was no smell, no sound, nothing to see; he reached out and could feel nothing at all around him. He turned, looked for the doorway. It was still there, though hard to see through the murkiness of this other place, and it wavered as if seen through a heat haze.

There was something wrong with his chest. He was breathing, but it was as if there was nothing really there to fill his lungs. Herewiss inched back to the doorway, put his head out to breathe.

The hralcin was coming down the hall, backlit brilliantly by the pursuing Sunspark. It saw Herewiss, screamed, and came faster. Herewiss took a long, long breath, like a swimmer preparing for a plunge. *It could be your last,* he thought miserably, and ducked back into darkness.

Silence, and the doorway was vague before him again.

Herewiss had a sudden thought. He edged around to the side of the doorway, until he was seeing it only as a very thin wedge of light, and then as a line, like that of a normal door open just a crack. He put his hand gingerly into the place *behind* the door, where the hallway would have been in the real world.

Nothing, just more darkness.

He slipped around and hid in it, his pulse thundering in his ears, the only thing to be heard.

There was a rippling, a stirring. Right in front of him, hardly a foot from Herewiss's nose, the hralcin seemed to bloom out from a flat, irregularly-shaped plane into complete and rounded existence. He started back, then watched it blunder further into the darkness; Sunspark's light washed through the door after it and limned it clearly. Even muted and blurred by the darkness of this other place, Sunspark's brilliance was still blinding. Herewiss could imagine what the heat must be like. But if it let up for so much as a second, the hralcin would only come out again—

Herewiss ducked out from behind the doorway, his lungs screaming for air, and threw himself through, diving and rolling. Behind him he could feel the vibrations of the hralcin's scream through the water-dark space, cut off sharply as he passed through the doorway and crashed to the ground. His face and hands were seared by Sunspark's fires. He dragged himself behind the elemental, and the burning lessened, though the air in the hall was still like an oven; the stone was reflecting back much of the heat of its flames.

(Are you all right?)

"Not really. But we have to finish this—"

A claw waved out through the doorway, and Sunspark blazed up more fiercely yet. The reflected heat stung Herewiss's burned face terribly, but the claw and the limb to which it was attached were withdrawn.

(It's building up a tolerance,) Sunspark said. (Hurry!)

Herewiss found the grimoire half-hidden under a great glob of slime. He grabbed the book, fumbled at the pages. "I am, I am—"

Another claw came out the door. Sunspark spat a tongue of flame at it, and the claw disappeared. The smell in the hallway became much worse.

Bindings, inanimate—great bindings—they'd better be! Herewiss threatened himself into a semblance of calm, started building the necessary structure around and against the doorway. Luckily it was a very simple and straightforward one, requiring more power than delicacy, and his need was fueling his power more than adequately *"—e n'sradië!"* he finished, sealing it, standing away from the structure in his mind. "All right, Spark, let's see if it holds."

Sunspark dimmed down its fires, and the hralcin slammed against the binding thrown over the door as if against a stone wall, The binding held, though. Herewiss trembled with the reflected shock.

The hralcin hit the wall again. It still held.

And again.

And again.

The wall held.

Herewiss sagged back against the hot stone, regardless of getting burnt. Sunspark was in the man-shape again, helping him.

"My room," Herewiss said, the backlash hitting him with redoubled force. "I think I need a nap—"

Before Sunspark had gotten him halfway down the stairs, he was having one.

He woke up in his bed in the tower workroom, a makeshift affair of cushions and blankets that Sunspark had filched for him from one place or another. It was dark; the room was lit only by the two big candles on the worktable. Herewiss looked up and out the window, seeing early evening stars.

(Well. About time.)

He turned his head to the center of the room. Sunspark was there, enfleshed in the form of a tall slender woman with dark eyes and hair the color of a brilliant sunset, long and red-golden. She sat in a big old padded chair, looking at him with slightly unnerving concern. She was gowned all in wine-red, and her sleeves were rolled up.

"How long has it been?" Herewiss said, propping himself up on one elbow.

(A night and a day.)

"The hralcin—"

(The binding is holding very nicely.) Sunspark got up, went to Herewiss and laid her hand against his forehead; it burned him slightly, but he bore it. (Better,) she said. (Last night there was little difference between the feel of your skin and mine; but the fever is down now. How are the burns?)

"They sting. The skin is tight, but I'll live, I think." Herewiss looked around him. There was a big bowl on the floor with a sponge in it, and the dark liquid inside it smelled like burn potion.

"Were you *using* that on me?"

(Yes. The recipe was in your grimoire, and you had most of the herbs in your supplies—)

"But the water, Spark. I thought you couldn't touch it—"

(A minor inconvenience, in quantities that small—I shielded my hand with a cloth, anyway. It makes a feeling like a headache, nothing so terrible. Can you get up and eat?)

My Goddess—it's, she's worried *about me, she cares—what a wonder!* "Spark, thank you—I could eat a Dragon raw."

(No need, really. I could cook it for you.)

Herewiss sat up straight and stretched. He was stiff from the burns, but not too much so, and the backlash had diminished to the point where he only felt very tired. "Oh. You brought a new chair?"

(From the little town up north where I've been getting the food. They've started to leave things out for me at night; some of them leave doors and windows open.) She chuckled and got up, going out of the room and down the hall to another room where supplies were kept. (I guess the news got around when their neighbors started finding pantries empty of food and full of raw gold.)

"I would imagine." Herewiss was surprised at Sunspark's initiative on his behalf.

(And not far from here there's a subsurface cavern full of raw gems of all kinds, though mostly rubies. I took the chair and left them a ruby about the size of a melon. Soon the streets will be filling with furniture.)

Sunspark came back in with a few slices of hot venison on a trencher of bread. Under her arm was a skin of Brightwood white, the last of Freelorn's liberated supply.

"Don't carry it like that—you'll warm it up!"

(Oh. Sorry.) She laid the skin on the table with the food, and Herewiss stared at it morosely as Sunspark went rummaging through his bags to find the lovers'-cup. *I wonder where he is,* thought Herewiss. *Probably stuck in some damn dungeon in Osta, trying to figure out a way to bribe the guards to send me a message...*

Sunspark looked at Herewiss as she set the cup on the table and poured the wine. She said nothing.

"I wish he were here," Herewiss said.

Sunspark shook the skin to get the last few drops out, stoppered it, and put it away. (You would probably quarrel again,) she said.

"How would you know?" Herewiss said, stirred slightly out of his tiredness by anger. "You're rather new at this sort of thing to be so understanding of it, don't you think?"

(Some aspects of it,) Sunspark answered without rancor. (But some are much like the ways of my own people. There are still more likenesses between our kinds than differences, I think.)

"So what are you basing your feeling on, that we would quarrel again?"

Sunspark sat down among the cushions, hesitated. (He's seeking to bind your energies, that one is,) she said.

"As I bound yours? Ridiculous. He's my loved."

(But that *is* a binding. *Your* loved, you said. It's not the same kind of binding as there is between us, true. But you have—commitments, you have set ways in which you treat one another—)

Herewiss remembered the terrible alienness of the last night with Freelorn, the feeling of having a stranger in the bed—all the more terrible because the stranger had been his loved not half an hour before. "The way he treated me is nothing I ever saw before."

(Well enough. But when one form of binding doesn't work, an entity tries another—)

Dully, Herewiss began to eat. The food seemed tasteless. "And he was doing that?"

(It could be. Your strength is considerable, though. It comes as no surprise that he went away so angry. I think he'll try again, but not the way he did last time—)

"It seems so useless. I need my Power—I thought he understood that—"

(The little one, the shieldmaid,) Sunspark said, (*she* understands. I think he might envy that a little.)

Herewiss considered it.

(That seems all she does, though; understand,) said Sunspark. (Which may cause problems—But enough. Eat!)

He ate, and began to feel less tired and lightheaded...but he could feel depression beginning to creep up on him. Maybe there was something he could do. There was, after all, the Soulflight drug—

"Sunspark," he said, "the bottle of drug, would you get it for me?"

She regarded him with an odd startled look. (Will you hazard that again? I'm not sure this place is good for its use. There are influences here that may have contaminated your use of it the last time—)

"The last time was bad because the argument was fresh, Spark," Herewiss said. "I could use something to cheer me up, to relax me—"

(*Relax* you?? Herewiss, you are fresh from a bout of sorcery; you slept for a night and a day! You've said how debilitating the drug can be! It'll be the end of you if you abuse it!)

"What are you worrying about?" Herewiss said. "I'd come back."

Sunspark looked at him, her face still, though Herewiss could feel the roil of emotions that she did not yet know how to make into the proper expressions. She turned and went out of the room very quickly.

A pang of guilt smote him immediately. *That was mean of me,* he thought. *But it is funny that it should be so concerned—*

He stopped in midchew. All the little kindnesses that he had been accepting from Sunspark; all the small gentle gestures: the chair, the food it brought back from the villages on the edge of the Waste, the sword blanks it had been fetching all the way from Darthis— But he had been judging it by human standards. No elemental would act like that normally. He compared the Sunspark of his first acquaintance, rough, uncaring, fierce of demeanor, testing him with thoughtless ferocity, with this one—calm, considerate, a tamed power waiting on him at table. A fire elemental, handling *water* for his sake.

And now concerned about his death, where before it had not even believed in it. The feelings he had underheard when it went out of the room: fear? pain?

Maybe love?

Oh, no, he thought again. *It couldn't possibly have understood about love, but I did try so hard to teach it. And now it knows. And it wants to try it out, the same way it tried to unite with me before—but this time on my terms—*

He put down what was left of the bread, and stared across the table at the lover's-cup. *It needs, now. I've taught it loneliness, which it never knew before. And now I'm going to have to teach it pain, because I can't be what it needs, but I will go get what I need—*

The cup sat there, full of wine and promise. It was the Goddess's cup, the cup poured for Her at each meal to remind those who ate that all set before them was, one way or another, the product of Her love—as were the people with whom they ate. When the meal was done, if there were lovers there, the youngest of them would drain the cup together in Her name. If one was alone, one said the Blessing for the Sundered and drank it in his own name and the name of his loved, wherever that one might be. Herewiss remembered how it had used to be in the lonely days when he was young. He had been rather ugly, and when he drank the cup and called on the Loved Who Will Be to await his coming, he secretly despaired of its ever happening, of ever finding another part of himself. Now, in these later days, at least he had a name to speak; but most of the time he seemed to be drinking the cup alone, and for the past month or so the ceremony, once a reassurance and a joy, had become bitter to him.

Here, though, was a possibility. To take the Soulflight drug, and step out of the body, and go in search of Freelorn; to meet him outside the flesh, so that they could admire anew each other's inner beauties, without the bitter base emotions clouding their eyes. To look upon one another transfigured, and share one another in the boundless lands beyond the Door, united in an ecstasy of freedom, of joy and omniscience and incalculable power—

Sunspark came back in with the bottle. Her eyes were shadowed and she would not look at Herewiss directly; her glance lingered on the lovers'-cup as she came to stand by the table. Herewiss reached out and took the bottle from her.

"Thank you," he said.

Her eyes glanced about uncomfortably. Herewiss reached out, took her warm hand, looked up and met those eyes and held them.

Deep brown-amber eyes, shot with sparks of fire, looked fearfully back at him.

"Sunspark," he said, "don't worry, I'll be all right. *Please* don't worry." She squeezed his hand back, but the fear in her eyes was no less. She turned and left.

Herewiss reached for the lovers'-cup, unstoppered the bottle and poured the drug into it, just a little more than he had used the last time. He mixed the wine to dissolve the drug, and drank.

Then he sat back, his eyes closed, and waited.

It was like falling asleep this time. But not falling; rising, rather, a floating feeling, as if he and the chair both were borne upward. After a time this ceased, and silence rang in his ears like a song. He opened his eyes, and raised his hand.

It came out of itself, slipping free; his own large hand, but changed—both more sensitive to what it touched, and more sensitive somehow to its own handness. Just curling it and flexing the fingers outward again was an exquisite feeling. The shell of flesh from which it had emerged was inadequate-looking, a stiff, cold, pitiful thing. Herewiss stood up and came free of himself effortlessly. He did not give his body a second look; he scorned it, and thought himself elsewhere.

Immediately he was away, and the instantaneous transition itself sent a ripple of pure pleasure through him like the first anticipation of the act of love, a deep glad movement at the center of one's self. He was standing in air, as if on some high mountain, and below him was spread all the world known to men, from the Waste in the east to the mountains in the west. More than that, he could sense the lives of the people who lived in those lands, all the lives in the Kingdoms, men's lives and animals' and Dragons' and other creatures' spun about and through each other, woven into a vast and intricate tapestry of movement and being. It was very like the Pattern that he had glimpsed in Sunspark's mind. Once this vastness would have frightened and confused him, as the Pattern had. Now, though, he could see it, see *all* of it, comprehend it, predict the motions of men and the intimate doings of their hearts; perceive the deepest motives, the best-hidden dreams and loves, and see how they moved the people who owned them, or thought that they owned them—

He hung there in starlit stillness for a long time, letting his mind range free, tasting thoughts and emotions from a great distance.

As he used the ability, it sharpened, deepened, and soon the hardest, coldest minds were yielding up their secrets to him. He walked the hot bright hearts of Dragons and knew what they thought, and why. He found their secrets, and learned the Draconid Name, which only the Dweller-at-the-Howe knows, and passes on to the new DragonChief when she takes office. Where he sensed resistance, he bent his thoughts against it, and passed through into knowledge. He found himself hearing even the thoughts of mountains and rivers, until he knew what the trees say to one another in their slow silent tongue, and what Day says to Night when they pass at the border of twilight. And still he listened, and listened, caught up in the intricacies and vastnesses of his own power, drunk with it—

There was a new note. A note at the bottom of things, a deep bass note that somehow wound itself into the fabric of everything that was, and Herewiss perceived it first with interest, and then with growing horror. By the time he realized what it was that he heard, it was too late. His power was total; as he pushed it, it grew; he had grown into hearing the note, and he could not now grow out of it.

It was the deepest bass note in all the worlds: the sound of the Universe running down.

He heard it everywhere. It twined through the structure of the tiniest blade of grass and dwelt in the hearts of stars; the empty places far above the earth were full of it; the core of the world sang it slowly and softly to itself, the Sea whispered it with every wave, the wind sighed with it and fell silent. Men shook with it as they were pushed out of the womb, and breathed it out as they died. Its long slow rumbling shook mountains into dust. The bright remote satellites of stars fell into their parent suns, and the suns devoured them, and then died themselves, dwindling into nothing, and darknesses *deeper* than nothing. From these wells of notness the bass note sang loudly as the voice of the earthquake; they were great devouring abysses, wombs of unbirth teeming with potential lost forever.

Herewiss reeled, tried to flee. It was no use. He strode among suns and through glowing clouds like violet and golden veils cast across the face of the darkness; he moved like a god through great spiraled treasuries of flaming stars, and knew the thoughts of the inhabitants thereof, from the greatest to the smallest; but the bass note followed him everywhere. It was wound through all the songs, the darkness at the bottom of every light.

He fled back in terror to the silver-blue mote of light that held the Kingdoms, and descending into it, walked the bottoms of the seas, and the rivers of fire beneath the mountains; but the note was there. He passed through the minds of men and Dragons again, and there it dwelt too, though in a more subtle fashion. There was a defense against the death, and that defense was love; it was effective, though only on a small scale, and only temporarily. But unknowing, men flung love away from them with insane regularity, trying to defeat the Death with strength instead. Herewiss moved from place to place, seeking desperately some place or mind free of the Death, but there was none. Despairing, he judged humankind and found them fools and madmen. In their crazy pride they chose to ignore the fact that Death is the ultimate swallower of all strengths, and that only the ephemeral vulnerability of love can hope to combat it at all—

And then he realized what he had been perceiving, and stopped in the middle of a flowering meadow somewhere in Darthen. The place blazed up in the night with a brilliance of green fire, the warm growth of spring, but like all else the fire had the seeds of death in it. Herewiss stood there, and mourned, understanding at last.

This is how the Goddess sees it, he thought. *Everywhere She looks, She sees the Error. Against the fall of Night, only Love will suffice—and even that, even Her love, which was enough to create the worlds, is not enough to keep these worlds from being destroyed—only enough to slow the Death down. She loves Her children, gives them the gift of that love—and they just throw it away. Oh, Mother...*

He shook his head. *I'm forgetting myself. It was for love's sake that I came on this journey. Where is Freelorn?*

The thought was enough. Herewiss was there, standing by some little creek in eastern Darthen, looking at Freelorn—

—and at Segnbora, with whom Lorn was moving gently under the blankets.

Herewiss wanted to leave on the instant, but by the time he had conceived of the idea, it was too late; he had already perceived the situation in its entirety with his heightened sight. The bitter shock and loneliness that washed over him could not obscure it. Here was Freelorn, sleeping with Segnbora. Well, that was not entirely unexpected, or terribly unusual. Herewiss had gathered some time back that Segnbora often slept with one or another of the men, for her own pleasure, or theirs. But he looked at the two of them, and saw their thoughts and motivations from top to bottom. Segnbora's were pleasant enough, at least on the top levels. Under the long slow swells of her passion, he could feel pity, compassion, gentleness, a desire to console, to reach out and touch and straighten a hurt and angry mind, to support until the status quo should reassert itself; the desire to give Freelorn back to Herewiss in a few months, tuned, as it were—made gentle again, gotten over his anger, grown into some kind of realization of his own problems and what he did to himself to cause some of them. It would be a present, a thank-you to Herewiss for trust given and received.

Under that, though, the motives were darker. Control. Segnbora looked at Herewiss and Freelorn and envied them. She had no lover of her own, had tried once or twice, but her own fears had stifled the loves; she could not give, and did not understand why; she thought she trusted, but dared not open the deepest places. Love which has no roots in the depths often dies when commitment runs shallow; such had been the case with her. She saw the trust between Freelorn and Herewiss, and coveted it, and tried to take a little of it for herself by intruding into the relationship ever so slightly...leaving behind her a message, something to remember her by: *I may be incomplete, but there is something I did that you could not.* And below that lay levels more primitive and profound, where her passions raged in fire and ice—old angers, old fears, cruelly bound up past her present ability or desire to undo them.

And then there was Freelorn—in love, suddenly, with Segnbora; sharing, opening himself to her, letting himself give her his best. And a level down, sealed away from his own perception, dwelt anger, bitter anger at Herewiss, for being something other than what he was supposed to be...for daring to defy Freelorn's control, daring to break the old patterns. Anger at Segnbora seethed there too, for her daring to understand what he could not about Herewiss, and daring to put the needs of the Power above anything else; for supporting Herewiss against him, for coming between them, for being a threat. Freelorn would use her, then— would assert the only control over the situation that was available to him. And when Segnbora's fears (which he had sensed) made her begin to back away from him, Freelorn would be safe again. He would be hurt, and she would be hurt, but *he* would be blameless. Then later on, when Herewiss came home, he would see what seemed to have happened, and would forgive Freelorn, and everything would once more be the way it had always been.

All this Herewiss saw and sensed, as he stood over them, watching the movements under the blankets, hearing the words of love spoken. He could not ward away what he had heard, or forget it. He had grown into the hearing, and now he could not grow out of it. He perceived Freelorn and Segnbora in all their tangled intricacy, knew the woven lights and darks of their selves; and he backed away, afraid. He understood them both, in terrible completeness, but he could not forgive them.

I have been cheated. Cheated. Something has been stolen from me. I never wanted to see this, no one should see this, not this way. Something's gone. Something's stolen. Something of mine—

Some nights after Herelaf had died, all that while ago, Herewiss had gone out into the Wood and had walked aimlessly through the cold night for a long, long time. After a while it had occurred to him that he was looking for something—something taken from him, unfairly, while his back had been turned. His innocence? Or else he was looking for somewhere to get rid of this new thing that had taken possession of him: his guilt. But Herelaf was gone, taken, stolen, his brother whom he loved. And instead of the love, only the deathguilt remained, as if some thieving night-creature had taken away the love between them and left this in its place. A shiny hollow glittery guilt, one that reflected chill accusing lights back at him when he examined it. For a long time Herewiss had let it stay there, feeling that it was better to have *something* in that echoing empty place, than nothing at all. But now he looked at the cold cheap gleam of it and began to be revolted....

But I was cheated. How can I love him now, knowing this? And it was the drug that did it! And You, Goddess! My love, my caring, You stole them from me—

A pause. A long one. And a slow dawning realization.

My *love?* Mine? *The way he thinks I belong to him, with no thought for my wishes in the matter? Goddess, I'm no better than he is! And Herelaf, then*—Another pause. His fear rose suddenly up in him.

I could look, now. I've known whole worlds at once tonight, held all their thoughts at once. I could certainly know what makes me work.

With the very idea, he knew, just a little. There were two of him. Three. Nine. He multiplied suddenly, shattering in his inward vision into countless bright prisms, a frightening flurry of mixed motivations and swirling personality-pieces, dancing before his terrified observer-self like a snowfall set afire. They were all bits of him, and they were all hotly alive, and they were all arguing with each other. An impossible and confusing blizzard of joys and fears and angers, they strove among themselves for dominance of him, the *him* that walked the world and acted as one being. He had never dreamed that there were so many of him, or that they were so at odds. Imposing control upon them seemed a ridiculous impossibility. And there were currents sweeping through the jeweled snow, winds of anger or hopelessness or pain, so that all his myriad selves were taken and moved by them—or did those selves make the winds to carry them where they wanted to go, and Herewiss with them, whether he wanted to go or not?

The one of him observing was horrified. *How much of what happens to me do I make happen? Oh Goddess, I don't want to see any more!*

There was a sudden consolidation. There were fewer of him now, but they sang together at him in tearing harmonies of challenge and promised pain; *No? You could know yourself. You could dare—*

No!

You could. More voices joining in the chorus, all his own, distracting discords blending with the purer notes of cold reason. *And if you don't dare, you'll never find out the truth about the world. Who sees clearly through a cracked glass?*

NO!!

Coward.

He wanted to weep, and found that he could not. *Maybe I'll dare later,* he said.

Maybe, came the reply, some of the voices pacified, some skeptical. And then one high clear voice spoke, still his own, but with a cutting edge that went through him like a sword. *"Maybe" means never,* it sang in a minor key, *and you know it. With "maybe" you pronounce your own doom, and that of a thousand lives tangled with your own. A life of "almost" is its own reward.*

And then the multitudes went away, and there was one of him again. Herewiss had never felt so lonely in his life.

First Herelaf gone.

Now Freelorn, abandoning him for the moment, intending to pick him up again later when he was more amenable, more willing to be what Freelorn wanted him to be. *I'm not a loved to him. I'm a tool. I'm a symbol for something else. I'm something to use—*

He wandered away slowly. He had come looking for joy. He had found only misery. *Cheated—*

Eventually he found himself back in the gray place again, isolated in the cold gray fog and glad to be that way. There he stayed for a while, sitting on the damp hard ground, letting his sorrows have free run through him, mourning his losses, sunk in his wounded self.

Unfortunately, he couldn't make it last. His own wry sense of humor began to betray him—there was no holding it in abeyance for long. *Well,* he thought, *I was a god for awhile, and that was nice—and then I died a little from something my loved did to me. That's the way the pattern usually runs, isn't it? So now I should go be reborn, so that the circle can be closed, and all things start again. It's such a nuisance—*

He laughed softly to himself, and the act destroyed the cold place around him, leaving him hanging free again amid the myriad brilliances of the stars. *They look like my mind did,* he thought, his heart slowly opening out to them, rejoicing in them—celebrating the stately passage of their bright-burning companies, the way they opened shining arms to the wide darkness, blown swirling in slow grandeur by winds he could not sense. *But how calm, how serene. Is this what the Goddess's mind looks like, then?*

He hung there for so short a time, it seemed. He had perceived all these families of stars at once, and all the lives upon their worlds, and the knowledge had been as nothing. Now he turned his mind outward and found something that he could not comprehend, though he could feel the currents of it stirring around him—the vast breath of a Life greater than all life, to which all that lived would eventually return. He strove to understand, pushing his mind outward again, and found to his bewildered joy that, no matter how hard he pushed, the Sharer of that greatest Life was always far ahead of him. Herewiss finally gave himself up to the joy, his heart taking him into regions where cold thought could not.

Much later he came back to some knowledge of himself, and sighed, feeling diminished, but not alone. *It's good to know,* he thought, *that there's always something bigger than you are...*

He hesitated a moment longer, waist-deep in the stars, like a swimmer wondering whether to come out of a warm sea. *Oh, well,* he thought after a moment, *Sunspark was right—I was awfully tired. I shouldn't stay out much longer; I could die of it. But I could take a little more time. I'll walk home.*

He reached sideways, found the world he was looking for, and stepped into it, passing out of the starstrewn night into a place of endless soft golden mists. Other people also moved through the fog, but they were only faintly perceived shadows going by. He could have conversed with them, but chose not to; he preferred them as silent company on the walk home, reassuring but unintrusive.

After a while the gray stone of the hold appeared through the haze. This surprised Herewiss, for he had expected to be able to find it only by feel—the place affected the worlds into which it reached, making a clearly perceptible bending in the stuff of space, something like the swirl-funnel that forms in stirred water. But the hold itself was manifesting here, and not merely the combined effect of its many doors.

It bulked clearer through the mist as Herewiss approached it. The stone was more silvery than gray, and it glittered and flashed softly with buried highlights, though there was nothing in the even golden mist to make it do so. And somehow the many odd angles and curves of its structure did not look as wrong here as they did in the "real" world. There was a logic to them, a unity of construction and purpose that he had occasionally sensed, but never really seen. Even the hole left when Sunspark had destroyed the outer wall somehow entered the logic of the design and made sense; it was as if it had been a planned addition, which had been predicted and taken into account during the building of the place. Indeed, now that he concentrated on it, Herewiss could perceive changes that were to come later: a tower missing here, a wing added there, a whole section slated to unfold within the heart of the building, protruding partly into an adjoining world...all planned, all accounted for. The hold sang with inevitability like a great piece of music, and Herewiss stood there for a while and admired it for the work of art it was.

Finally he sighed and walked through the gate and across the great hall, heading for the stairs that would take him back up to the worktower and his waiting body. He looked through the doorways as he passed them, and was slightly amused to find that they showed only empty rooms, with windows looking out into the nighttime Waste. Of course, some of the rooms that could not have such views on the desert had them anyway, despite the fact that they should have looked down into the center court of the hold. Herewiss laughed softly; the place had a sense of humor that he appreciated. He trailed his hand along the wall as he went up the stairs, saying an affectionate hello, and the warm stone pushed back against his hand like a cat.

And here was the tower room at last, his tools and materials somewhat vague and hard to see on this plane, and his body sitting phantomlike in the chair, seemingly asleep—

—and standing close by it, as if guarding it—

—sweet Goddess, what was *that*?

To categorize it, to describe it, was to do it a disservice—that much he realized even as he tried to do so. Comparisons were unfair to it. It shook and burned with uniqueness, a hymn of piercing singularity; it was a poem wrought of glass and fire and the sudden taste of blood, an impossibility trying to become possible. Something that had never been, trying to *be*. Birth and death both happening at once in the middle of an existence, the pain and loneliness of both assaulting something that had invited them both willingly, though both were outside its experience—(Sunspark?)

It turned and faced him. The comparison Herewiss had been trying to make suddenly made itself. He had perceived Freelorn and Segnbora in their totality, and himself partially, and had been amazed by the complexities he had found. Now he perceived Sunspark in its totality, for the first time. The experience at Madeil had been pallid and misleading compared to this.

Sunspark was a oneness. Not a tangle of warring motivations, not divided against itself…but *one*. A single, driving, driven force, an eternal constant, a being, an IS! And a tightly encapsulated one it had been, wound around and through itself, dwelling within itself completely, needing none other. Of course its kind had no need for love or companionship in any form. They were *themselves*, gloriously self-contained, solitary as stars. When they finally grew tired of themselves—to that extent the great Death could affect them—they found another in the same state and conjoined, united in an ecstasy of renewal, were lost in it forever and both reborn as new identities, a blend of parts of the two that formed them.

But Sunspark—

Sunspark had become unique.

Sunspark was changing. Daring to change. *Trying* to change.

It had managed to conceive of something totally outside of its needs. It had come to understand love, and it was daring to experience it, flying with doomed valor into the face of something that could only cause it infinite pain. But daring it nonetheless, for the sake of the dare, for the possibility of learning something new, of becoming something it had never been or known. Reaching out into the darkness outside of itself, as Herewiss had turned himself outward and sought to grow into the Universe. None of its kind had ever dared so. It knew as much, and trembled with fear even as it bent over Herewiss's stiff body and feared for *him*, loved *him*. It broke the laws that the Universe had set up for its kind; and it knew what it did, and it feared—but it *loved*—

Sunspark faced Herewiss, and perceived him. It feared him; feared that he would inflict pain upon it—pain, that amazing newness, all the more terrible for Sunspark's inexperience with it. The elemental's complete horror of pain rippled through its changing fires, plain to see.

Yet it welcomed him—

—and reached out to him—

—and *dared to love him*—

Herewiss stood there, torn, daunted, amazed, yet exalted by its courage—(Sunspark—)

(Herewiss,) it said, and its use of his name was wound about with fire and gentleness both. (Thy body—it weakens.)

His emotions were burning through him now like fire themselves. (I was so lonely,) Herewiss said, (and I never knew—never understood that you were like this—the bravery—Sunspark, I'm *sorry!*)

It grew, its fires swelling, towering with love, terror, pain—(Oh my loved, don't be—don't be—just get back quickly before you die!)

The courage. The sheer daring. He was swept up, carried past his fear and through to the other side—

—he loved too—

(For this little while,) Herewiss said, exultant, euphoric—loving—(it can wait.)

He reached out. (Shall I dare less than you?) said Herewiss.

Sunspark came to him.

(—embracing the heart of a star, and being embraced by it: part of that fire, lost in it, burning in nonambivalent brilliance forever and forever; being and not-being, victory, surrender, death and birth lying in one another's arms at last, after long estrangement; the loneliness filled; the insatiable fires satisfied—)

In the morning, Sunspark learned how to cry, and Herewiss remembered how again.

nine

"Now indeed may it be seen," said Earn, "that our life's days are ended." "That were ill seen," Healhra made answer. "Wherefore," said Earn, "seeing that we shall meet again by the shore of that Sea of which the Starlight is but a faint intimation?" "'S truth," said Healhra, "my loved; yet though our Mother waiteth on that Shore, still here would I remain with thee. For life and breath are sweet. And also, She loveth not well those who let Life and Love, Her gifts, slip away through a grip made loose by resignation. Dearly She bought those gifts for us, and dearly shall the children of Night purchase them from me in turn. Well the Goddess loveth the driver of a hard bargain."

    Battle of Bluepeak, tr. Erard, ch. 16

Herewiss woke up hounded by small urgent voices in the back of his brain, voices that told him to hurry, that gave him just time enough to relieve himself before steering him back in to work, that pushed him so that he found himself at the anvil before he was even fully awake. The day began with a sleep-blurred image of his hands holding the tongs, and the tongs resting on the anvil with nothing held between them, and Herewiss standing there, staring with fuzzy expectant confusion at the pores and dents in the anvil's metal. *What am I doing here?* he thought, and reached for a sword blank, and called for Sunspark to come dwell in the firepit.

The morning fell away in chunks and half-glimpsed pieces, casualties of the insistent rhythms of hammering. Each stroke rang a second away, and every second was just like every other. There was the swing of the hammer, the bunching of muscles, the jolt and clang of the metal ringing and rebounding away from itself, the sword jumping away from the anvil and the hammer from the sword, again and again and again, the old familiar beat renewing itself with the dogged persistence of some hard heart. *Again* and *again* and *again*. A brief pause here when the pressure of his bladder became too much; another moment stolen there when the rawness in his throat made him stop to drink; and always the impatient voice of his fear rustling softly just under his proper hearing, like rats in the walls of his self. Herewiss was slightly aware of Sunspark watching him from the forge, of bright eyes in the fire, looking at him with concern. But he dared not let himself respond to the look; to do so would have been to waste precious time. He let the hammering take him and use him for its own purposes. It was rather pleasant to not think at all, just to be arms at the end of a hammer—

(Herewiss.)

He dared not stop. He kept on hammering.

(Herewiss. You asked me to let you know about that binding at intervals.)

"Mmph." *Again* and *again* and—

(It's holding well—under the circumstances, that is. But you're going to have to try to control your fear a little better. When you discharge so strongly, the binding weakens.)

"I'll remember."

(But Herewiss—how can you expect to control yourself properly with as little sleep as you've been getting? An hour here, two there—)

"Spark," he said, pacing his thoughts between the hammer-blows. "My loved. I haven't *time*. Something is happening. The Fire's going out. I have to hurry—"

(Your fear is killing it,) the elemental said softly. (I couldn't have understood that before. Now I know. Freelorn has gone off to Osta without you, and there's been no word all this month and more. You fear for him. I hear the terror singing while you sleep; it runs from you like blood. And you feel that you should be with him, though if you were, you couldn't be working—)

"Some things are even more important than Flame."

Sunspark was silent for a moment. (And the hralcin,) it said, (the matter of its unbinding that troubles you so. That fear is killing your Power too. I hear the sound of it every now and then: 'If I *had* the Fire,' you think, 'what kinds of things would I be letting loose by my carelessness?' You are working against yourself, my loved—)

"Sometimes, Sunspark, you hear too much for your own good." The thought was a slap of anger, and Sunspark shrank away, out of Herewiss's mind entirely, dwindling down to a few uncertain tongues of fire shivering among the coals. Herewiss sighed then, ashamed of himself, looking at the elemental in the firepit and realizing that it was the first thing he had really *seen* all day.

"Spark," he said as gently as he could. "Love, I'm sorry. Oh, come out of there." He put the hammer down on the anvil, atop the blank he had just finished.

(You are angry at me.) Its voice was subdued and fearful.

"It passed. Spark, you have to learn that around these parts it's possible for two partners in a union to be angry with one another without the union being destroyed. Come out of there—"

It put up a few cautious tongues of fire and then flowed over the edge, a bright firefall that pooled and rose upward to envelop him. Silently the elemental wrapped its warmth around and through Herewiss, filling all his cold empty places with its glowing self. They were joined for a few minutes, and Herewiss looking inward saw all his fears flare into incandescence. He could see the shapes of them clearly now, and while the union persisted they were not fears any more. He saw them as Sunspark perceived them, as energies bound into strange fanciful shapes that meant little against the larger scale of things. The sensation was pleasant, and Herewiss stood there for a long while, eyes closed, letting himself be cared about and reassured.

"You matter, Spark," he said softly. "You matter very much."

It pulsed warm within him, a deep silent flare of fulfillment.

"But I have to work…"

It unwrapped itself, slowly, regretfully. (Let us work that sword to red heat again, so you can quench it, and I'll go watch the binding.)

"That sounds fine. Back in the pit then…" Herewiss tried to chuckle, but the sound came out wrong. All the places that Sunspark had filled and warmed so thoroughly with itself were bleak and cold again, and his fears were back, all the more shadowy for having been so bright.

He laid the blade of the sixty-third sword in the forge and turned away, wishing that Sunspark would melt it accidentally.

The grindstone was useful for times when Herewiss didn't want to think. The noise of it rasped on his nerves, and the vibration rattled so far down his spine that any session with it left him in a state of profound and unfocused irritation. For this reason he usually didn't use it, preferring to blow up the sword before putting a good edge on it. Today, however, anything that would shut out thoughts of the hralcin was welcome.

He sat there behind the stone, pumping away at the pedals until his legs threatened to cramp (which diversion he would also have welcomed). The irritation fed on itself, making him pump faster and press the sword harder against the turning stone, until sparks sprayed from it, and again and again it grew too hot to handle. By the end of a couple of hours, the sword had an edge on it that was much better than it needed, and in some places had become wire-edged and would have to be stropped.

(Herewiss?)

"Mmm?" He was working at it with the horsehide strop now, holding the sword between his knees as he worked and taking a certain cranky pride in the quality of his work. The blade would need some finishing work with oil and smoothing stone, but the edges had already acquired that particular silvery sheen that swordsmiths strive for, the mark of a blade that will cut air and leave it in pieces.

(We have company.)

He looked up from his work. "Who?"

(From the feel of them, Freelorn and his people. They are in high good spirits. No one else would be feeling that way out *here*, if the Waste is as ill-omened as you say.)

Herewiss frowned, and then smiled. "He has a talent for showing up when I have a piece of work in hand."

(But then you're always working, loved. How could it be otherwise?)

"Hmph. True, I guess…" And Herewiss became cold with fear. "But, Spark, that binding…!"

The elemental shrugged. (I'm watching it. So far none of the conditions you described to me has changed. The hralcin hasn't bothered testing it in a while.)

"That could be good—and then again—"

(Probably it will be all right if you don't get in another fight with Freelorn. The extra stress of having more people around might wear it a little, but you can reinforce it now and again.)

"Yes…"

(So keep things subdued. I for my part will do the same. There's a stand of brush to the north of here that could use a fire, and I could use a meal. Maybe I'll be away for the night; that might decrease the stresses.)

"It's a thought. How close are they, Spark?"

(Some miles. You have time to finish that, at least.)

"All right. Watch that door…"

(Oh,) Sunspark said dryly, (if anything comes out of it, you'll know shortly…)

Herewiss thought of slime and the smell of burning, and stropped harder.

The polished outer walls of the hold had a walkway recessed into the top surface, a double noncrenellated battlement, accessible by a long flight of those oddly staggered steps which led up from the inner courtyard. Herewiss leaned on the outer battlement and watched Freelorn and his people approaching. Sunspark, beside him, wavered palely in the sunlight like heat-shimmer above a pavement in summer.

"Look at all those mules. I wonder who he stole them from?"

Sunspark made a don't-know-don't-care feeling. (There's something,) it said, (something that I couldn't catch while they were further away—can you hear it?)

Herewiss reached out with his underhearing. Because of his fatigue, all he got was a faint confused impression of a number of emotional systems going about their business, and a fainter one of two specific systems somewhat at odds with themselves.

"Slight unease," he said to Sunspark. "I'm a bit off today, and I don't usually do too well anyhow unless I'm at close range. They're half a mile away."

Sunspark shrugged. (Freelorn,) it said, (and Segnbora, I think.)

Herewiss nodded slowly. "It didn't take long for what I saw to start happening, alas. This isn't good, Spark, their negative emotions are going to fray at the binding—"

(Work on Freelorn, then,) Sunspark said. (You would anyway—)

Herewiss caught a sudden pang of jealousy, a flurry of angry, swift-moving brilliances like swords flashing in sunlight. Sunspark was trying to conceal it, and Herewiss laughed softly.

"I bet you'd like to burn him."

The elemental flinched away in chagrin. (I would,) it admitted.

"I think I'd have been suspicious if you hadn't wanted to. We all do as our natures dictate, Spark. I know it's hard for you to understand how I can love you both, but believe me, I can, and I love neither of you the less for loving the other more—"

(I'm not sure I understand this.) Sunspark sounded ashamed.

"Trust me, Spark. I will not give you up for him."

(Neither will you give him up for me—)

"That's right, little one. Firechild, trust me. You haven't done wrong yet by doing so. Nor have I," he added with a gentle smile, "in trusting you. By rights and the Pact you could have parted company with me after you saved me from the hralcin."

(It would seem,) Sunspark said, smiling back, (that there are some things more important than even the Pact. Do what needs to be done, loved. I'll be within call till this evening.)

It vanished. Herewiss looked over the wall at Freelorn, alone at the head of the approaching line, and went down the stairs to meet him.

At the bottom of the stairs Herewiss paused, slightly irritated by the sight of the dust lying thick all over the courtyard's polished gray paving. He was usually a tidy sort, but lately there had been too much to do—swords to be forged, doors to be looked through. And then the hralcin had come. He thought of cleaning the courtyard now, but he was too tired to want to do it by sorcery, and he didn't have a broom.

He walked across the court to where there appeared to be a solid wall, facing west. It was only a small illusion, rooted in where the wall would have liked to be, where it had been before Sunspark disposed of it. The illusion, which he'd erected earlier in the month, was a sop to his own insecurities. It made him nervous to live alone, or nearly alone, in a hold that had a great gaping hole in it. Herewiss looked up at the wall, reached out with his arms, and spoke the word that severed the connection between was-once and seems-to-be-now. The wall went away.

Freelorn and his people were very close, and Herewiss leaned against the wall and waited for them. *They're all there; thank You,*

Goddess. I couldn't cope with one of Lorn's guilts right now, if one of them had been hurt or killed. Or my own, now that I think of it...

Blackmane whickered a greeting at Herewiss as Freelorn dismounted. *No Lion coat? Interesting!* Herewiss thought as Freelorn hurried over to him, his eyes anxious. Freelorn reached out hesitantly, took Herewiss's hands in his and gripped them hard. They stood that way for a long moment, each of them searching the other with his eyes, almost in fear.

"Well," Freelorn said, gazing at the ground and pushing the dust around with one booted toe, "I'm back."

Herewiss reached out and drew Freelorn close, and hugged and kissed him hard.

For a few minutes they just hung on to one another, sniffling slightly. "I, uh," Freelorn said, his voice muffled by talking into Herewiss's tunic, "I was—oh, Dark, loved, you know how I am when I can't get my way."

"It's not as if I wasn't being stubborn myself. Or snide—Lorn, I'm sorry."

"Me too." Freelorn gave Herewiss a great bone-cruncher of a hug and then held him away, peering at him with concern. "Are you all right? You look as if somebody smote you a good one in the head. And look at your eyes, they have circles under them."

"Smote me—" Herewiss laughed. "I feel like it. It's been a busy week. Come on in, I'll tell you about it later." He looked at Freelorn, noticing something that hadn't been there before, a look of tiredness and discomfort and depression. "Are *you* all right?" he asked.

The expression on Freelorn's face partook of both relief and loathing. "Later," he said. "It's been a lively month."

Freelorn's people were leading their horses into the courtyard, and as Herewiss glanced toward them he saw Segnbora passing through the gate. Her expression was hard to make out clearly, for the late Sun was behind her; but she looked pained, and puzzled as well. Herewiss looked back at Freelorn, took him gently by the arm and began to walk back into the hold with him.

"Lorn, where did all those mules come from?"

"Osta."

"You *did* go ahead, then—"

"Yes indeed."

They passed into the coolness of the hold. "And you made it out all right."

"It's just as I told you, no one knew about the secret way in from the river. We didn't even have to kill any of the guards. By the way, we brought a plains deer in with us. Didn't see any reason why we should use up your supplies."

"You always were a considerate guest. Lorn, what are all the mules for?"

"I was getting to that. They're for the money."

Herewiss led Freelorn into the great lower hall, and they sat down beside the firepit in chairs that Sunspark had brought in from the village to the north. *"Six mules?* How much did you get?"

Freelorn made a smug, pleased face. "Eight thousand talents of silver."

"Eight thou—You mean you went into the Royal Treasury and *stole* all that money and got *away* again?"

"I didn't steal it," Freelorn said with mock-righteousness. "It's *my* money."

"My Goddess, maybe I should listen to you more," Herewiss said, reaching down for a brown earthenware bottle and the lovers'-cup. "Lorn, you should've killed the guards. It'd be kinder than what Cillmod's probably doing to them." He broke the seal on the bottle-stopper, opened the jug and poured.

"Maybe. But I have the money now. We can have a revolution."

"Just like that," Herewiss said with a laugh, and drank from the cup. "May we be one, my loved." He passed it on to Freelorn.

"As is She." Freelorn drank, and his eyes widened. "Lion's Name, this tastes like Narchaerid."

"It is."

"South slope, too. Mother of Everything, it's like so much red velvet. What year?"

Herewiss held up the jug to look at the bottom. "Ninety-two, it says."

"Dark, what am I worrying about the year for? How are you getting that out here?"

Herewiss flicked an amused glance at the fire pit. An ordinary fire appeared to be blazing there, but the pattern of the flames had repeated twice since they'd been there. "I have my sources," he said.

"Well, whatever. How long can a revolution take, anyway? You should hear the kind of things going on in Arlen. The people are getting sick of Cillmod. It was a bad year at harvest, there were omens and portents: sheep miscarrying and two-headed calves being born, and fruit dying on the trees before it was ripe—" Freelorn drank deeply, and his eyes over the rim of the cup were troubled. "In a lot of the little villages we passed through, everyone was hungry a lot of the time. It's bad back home…"

"Well, the reason is obvious—"

"Of course."

"After all, not even Cillmod is stupid enough to go into Lionhall," Herewiss said. "And he hasn't been enacting the rites of the royal priesthood, even if he knows them—"

"That wasn't the reason I meant."

Herewiss raised his eyebrows.

"Me," Freelorn said, very quietly, studying his cup.

Herewiss looked at his loved.

"Me," Lorn said, not looking up. "Dusty, they're starving because of *me*, because of what I was scared to do." He laughed just once, a sound so low and bitter that it twisted in Herewiss like a knife. "Because I was afraid to get caught and put on a rack, afraid to spend a few days dying… There was a village—it was five houses and two cows, and acres and acres of stubble. It hadn't rained for months, and nothing would grow but a few radishes. The people—there were only about four of them left, all the others had starved or left—they came out and offered us hospitality. Radish soup. They were all thin as rails, and one of them, this little old man, was lying in the house on a straw pallet, dying of starvation. They had all been giving him their food, trying to keep him alive, but it was too late, he was too far gone."

Lorn took a swallow of wine. "I think he suspected who I was. He asked if I would bless him. I did, and he died. Right there… Then I found out he was twenty-two. I'd thought he was those people's father. He was their *son*. How many days, weeks, had *he* been dying?…"

"Oh, Lorn—"

"No," Freelorn said, looking up at Herewiss through the tears. "Don't try to make it better. It can *never* be better." He stared at his cup again. "And I don't want it to be. How many other deaths like that am I going to have to make good to the Goddess after I die? I'm the Lion's Child. Their deaths are *mine*. And there was what She said to me at the Tavern…"

Herewiss kept silent. After a few breaths, shaking his head, Lorn said, "No more running. No more. All the other reasons, the Arlene lords getting restless and wanting a real king again, Cillmod botching his relations with Darthen, the queen being in trouble, her armies getting demolished by Reavers down Geraithe way, and her nobles starting to become willing to support me—none of it matters. None of it matters but that man's head in my lap. The poor cracked voice saying, 'The King is back.'"

Freelorn was quiet for a few seconds. "That was mostly why I came back so quickly," he said. "There were other places we could have hidden all this money. Darthen, in particular. But I had to come back and tell you: I can't stay here with you. I have to turn around and go back. Even if I die of it. Which I may. No, let me finish. Cillmod's forces have been overrunning the borders of Darthen, raiding for food. He may be ignoring the Oath of Lion and Eagle, but *I* can't. I have to move to defend Darthen. Even if I have to do it by myself." He smiled, wistfully, and with pain. "It's what a king would do. Though I'm not sure where to go from there…"

Herewiss reached out, took Freelorn's hand and held it. "I just wanted to say that I missed you," he said. "And I'm sorry we fought. And sorrier that I didn't give you the benefit of the doubt when you said you could pull off the Osta business. But seeing you now, hearing you…I can't say I'm sorry about *that.*"

Freelorn looked at Herewiss and smiled. "Nor I," he said. "It's all right." And he handed Herewiss the lovers' cup. "We're one, loved."

"So may it be." Herewiss drank off the cup in three or four swift draughts and looked at it with satisfaction. "Let's get a little sozzled," he said, "and I'll tell you my news after dinner."

"You mean I'm going to have to be drunk to believe it?"

Herewiss chuckled and poured more wine.

A long while later Herewiss and Freelorn and all his following sat around the fire pit, in various states of repletion. The stripped-down carcass of the desert deer was still on the spit. The fire in the pit had died down to a soft glow of embers, with only an occasional tongue of flame showing. Most of Freelorn's people were half-dozing in their chairs, except for Segnbora, who had pled time-of-moon pains and retired early. Herewiss and Freelorn sat together, apart from the others, cups in hand.

"A hundred and eighty-four permanent doors," Herewiss was saying wearily. "I gave up trying to count the ones that are here one day and gone the next. A lot of them move around; whole new wings of the building appear and disappear. There are more doors at night than during the daytime, and more than half the doors at any one time show water. But beyond that..." He trailed off.

"None of them was what you were looking for."

"I can't make them change," Herewiss said. "And the closest I've come is something that doesn't bear discussing."

"No?"

Herewiss considered the wine in the lovers'-cup, breathed in, breathed out, a long moment of decision. "No," he said. "If there's a somewhere that men have Flame, I wish them joy of it and good weather, 'cause I'm never going to get there. Not at this rate."

"No luck with the swords?"

"I break them," Herewiss said, fumbling around for the wine-jug and refilling the cup. "I should start a business: HEREWISS S'HEARN. SWORDS BROKEN. NO JOB TOO LARGE OR TOO SMALL."

Freelorn gazed at him sadly, and Herewiss shook his head and took another drink. "Lorn," he said softly, "what happened while you were gone?"

"Huh?"

"With Segnbora."

"That's one of the problems with having a sorcerer for a loved," Freelorn said in a resigned voice. "Let me have some of that."

"Surely. No, Lorn, it's just the way you looked when you came in, and the way she looked at you…I'm not blind."

Freelorn drank some wine, held the cup in his lap. He looked suddenly very tired. "We—were in comfort with each other—it was nice. I fell a little in love with her, I guess. I needed to talk, especially after I left here so mad—though this had been going on to some extent while we were escaping from Madeil, before we got trapped. She was always there to listen, and what I thought seemed to *matter* to her, really did. So we—got close—but I began to notice that she never told me anything *back*, not that it says anywhere that you have to, but she never seemed to tell anything about herself. She would listen, but never give—or never really *share."*

He drank again. "Well, when I got lonely, I asked her to sleep with me, and she said yes. I guess I thought it might have been different there. But it wasn't. She still couldn't share." His voice grew lower, and the pain of the words scraped it raw. "She was good—she was *very* good—the way she was very good at listening.

But she still couldn't, didn't share. Not that she wasn't responsive, or warm, but there was no—" He gestured with the cup, looking for the right words. Finally he held the cup out to Herewiss to be refilled, and took a long moment's refuge in the wine. "She couldn't— I don't know. She couldn't let go. Couldn't trust me. I wanted so much for her to...but she didn't dare..."

Herewiss sat there and let the silence grow again. *And now he uses the pain to punish himself for what he knows to be his part in it*, he thought. "Was it your fault, Lorn? You sound guilty somehow."

"No...I don't know." Freelorn sighed. "I think maybe I slept with her because I missed you. Instead of you, as it were. Does that make sense?"

"It does. Though, Lorn, don't sell her short; there are enough good things about her that I'm sure she's worth sleeping with on her own..."

They sat there in silence for a few moments. Freelorn looked around at the polished gray walls, dim in the faint firelight.

"I wish there was something I could do for you," he said mournfully.

"Lorn, you're my loved, you're my friend. I can live without the Power, but not without friends. And I may have to get used to living without the Power pretty soon—it doesn't have long to run in me without focus."

"What we need," Freelorn said solemnly, "is a miracle."

Herewiss began to laugh, the kind of laughter that is a breath away from tears.

"No, I mean it," said Freelorn. "I'm the King's son of Arlen, descended in right line from Héalhra Whitemane, and by the Goddess if there's anyone who has a right to ask the Lion for a miracle, it's me."

Herewiss laughed until he was weak and his sides hurt, though some small corner of his mind was surprised that he could laugh so hard over something so painful and serious.

"Me," Freelorn was saying, "I'll do it. I will." He finished his cup of wine, and held it out to Herewiss again.

"Haven't you had enough?" Herewiss said as soon as he gained control of his laughter.

"I'm talking about miracles," Freelorn said with infinite weariness, "and all you're interested in is how drunk I am."

Herewiss poured again for Freelorn. "You throw up and I'll make you scrub the floor."

"Throw up! This stuff is like mother's milk," Freelorn said, spacing the words with exaggerated care. "Thanks." He smiled, a small gentle smile strangely at odds with his inebriation. "Come to bed with me tonight?"

"In a while. I have some things to take care of first. Wait for me?"

"I'm not going anywhere. Except," and Freelorn wobbled to his feet, "to sleep."

"Later, then."

Freelorn made his way around the firepit, nudging his people one by one. "Come on," he said, "everybody get up and go to bed…"

Herewiss got carefully to his feet and crossed the hall to the uneven stairs. As he went up them he noticed two doors that hadn't been there earlier in the day. He paused only long enough to note that one of them looked out on some green place with a river running through it, and the other on a waste of cold water beneath a bleak gray sky.

Coming up to the tower room, he dissolved the appearance of solid wall that camouflaged its doorway, passed through, and sealed it behind him. Sunspark was waiting for him on the furs and cushions in the corner, stretched out, lush and warmly beautiful in the silvery moonlight from the open window. Light from the two great candlesticks on Herewiss's worktable caught in her red hair and touched it with coppery sparks and glitters.

(You took a long time,) she said.

"It's been a while since Freelorn was here. We had a lot to talk about."

(I would imagine.) The sudden flicker of jealousy again, like bared swords in the moonlight; but not as strong as the last time.

"Spark, relax," Herewiss said. He went to the window and looked out. The Moon was gibbous, waxing toward the full, and from the walls of the hold to the horizon, the desert shone silver and black. The midnight stars struggled feebly with the moonlight, cold and pale and mocking, faint as the Flame within him.

(I didn't mean it,) Sunspark said. (Ah, Herewiss, it's hard to do, this loving—)

"You mean it," said Herewiss. "And, yes, this loving *is* hard. There is nothing harder, which is probably the way it should be, for there's also nothing more precious, I think. Spark, please, don't be afraid of me. I love you well as you are." He leaned on the windowsill, wondering whether the wine was the source of the strange feeling inside him—a feeling like something trying to happen.

(Something's bothering you—) Sunspark got up and came to him, slipped warm arms around him from behind.

"No more than usual. Maybe I should go away for a while, though, walk around in the world, get away from all these damn doors for a while—"

He stroked one of Sunspark's arms absently. "Maybe. Sunspark, I'm sorry, I'm just not in the mood tonight."

(Oh? How's this, then? You liked it before.) The elemental shimmered momentarily, and when the wavering died down he stood there, a lithe young man, arms still around Herewiss.

"No, loved," Herewiss chuckled, turning around and hugging him back, "that's not what I meant. I have some things to do, a feeling I want to follow up. That's all."

(Well enough, then. I'm going to tend to that brush. Whatever this is about, though—be careful!)

"I will."

Sunspark dissolved into flame, then went out altogether.

Herewiss stood at the window long enough to notice the faint radiance spring into life on the horizon. He turned away, then, went to a chest on one side of the room, opened it and rummaged around. He found the bottle of Soulflight, went over to the pile of cushions by the window, and sat down wearily.

He could feel time fast flowing over him, taking little pieces of him with it as a stream whirls flotsam unresisting down its current. There was no more time. He was being worn away steadily by the days, and raggedly by his fears—Sunspark had been quite right about that. The image of the hralcin, ravening silently at the dark door, wanting him with an implacable hunger, moved again in the back of his mind. The sight of Freelorn and the sound of his voice hadn't driven it away—merely startled it into stillness, like the bright fierce glance of a hawk. Now the vague dark shape stirred, restless, and looked at him with deadly patience—

Herewiss cursed his overactive imagination, wishing that the hralcin would just go away and leave him alone. *But no achievement is without price, he reminded himself, most especially the dark ones—*

He looked at the little stone bottle, wondering if this risk was going to be worth it. After he came down in the morning, things would be no different. The hralcin would still be behind the door, hungering for him, and the Power would be no more his than it was now.

But Soulflight was good for walking the future as well as the past. He could go forward, look down the course of his life from its end and see if there was some way to forge the sword he needed. Or a way to stop the hralcin, to kill it—

No, no. When you use Soulflight to look forward, it shows you options, chances, pathways—there's no way to tell which is actually going to happen. And even with the drug there are usually gaps in the pathways, variables that can't be predicted—

He rolled the bottle slowly between his hands. *And as far as the hralcin goes, I doubt that I could avail myself of any art I might learn. I'm so tired, I couldn't turn the sky dark at nightfall. And by the time I'm strong enough to try something useful, that thing will probably come back and break the binding down. No, that's no good.*

Herewiss gripped the bottle hard. *No matter how I approach this mess, the answer keeps coming up the same—I'm not going to live out the week. Well, so be it. I plowed this crooked furrow and now I must sow in it. But by the Goddess, if I'm going to die, I'll die knowing my Name!*

He took the lovers'-cup, filled it with the last half-cup or so of the Narchaerid, and poured a dollop of the drug into it from the little bottle. It fell slowly, in a clear ribboning stream like honey, and he watched the bubbles in it as he poured. *I'll have to look at my Name before this night is over. But first I'll make my peace with myself, with Lorn—let him understand what's been happening, why I'm doing what I am. Maybe the understanding will help him handle my loss. Oh, Mother, I wish I didn't have to die, I wish I'd let that door alone, it's going to hurt Lorn so much when I'm gone—*

He rubbed his eyes briefly. *Enough of that. I have to leave him in love and with joy, otherwise it'll be worse for him. And the others deserve my best, too. Their dreams will take them past the Door, I'll meet them there—and then go on. No shying away from the truth this time. Oops, better stop here—* and he pulled the bottle away, twirled it free of a last drop that clung to the lip. He stoppered the bottle and set it aside carefully. *I do want to come back.*

He swirled the cup to mix the drug with the wine. *And something else I could do. If I've got to die, then I will share myself with Lorn tonight, as those beyond the door share, wholly, in that union which transcends the ecstasies of the flesh. One last sharing, one last best gift before that damn hralcin gets me—*

He drank the wine down, a long draft that made him choke. There was a burning at the back of his throat, but it passed. Herewiss reached over for another jug of red wine—not Narchaerid, but an ordinary quaffing wine from up north—poured a cupful, and sat down to wait for the drug to work.

He watched the moonlight move ever so slightly across the floor, and the silence of the desert night sank deeply into him. For a moment his eyes rested on this morning's sword, which lay up against the wall a few feet away...nothing more than a long dead piece of steel, carven with no runes, untreated, untried in any way. He tried for a moment to think of something new to do with it, but could see nothing in his mind but the depressing sight of a fine sword, beaten out of strong tempered steel, shattering itself to splinters at the touch of the Power.

The image made Herewiss cringe, unwanted harbinger of reality that it was. The fragrance of the wine crept up his nose, fruity and sweet, and glad of the distraction he drank again.

As he did, a moth came flickering in the window. It fluttered around in confusion, bouncing and wobbling around the square of moonlight on the floor, until it saw one of the candlesticks. It flew straight toward the flame, and with a directness that surprised Herewiss, circled it twice, three times, and dove headlong into the flame. With a fizzing sound, the candle flame burned low for a moment, then sprang up again.

Herewiss sat there and felt the drug begin to work. He laughed, but the sound didn't seem to be coming from his own throat, though he could hear it plainly enough. The detachment extended itself to his thoughts as well. Part of him was sad for the moth, but the rest was uninvolved, though alert and observant. *A small thing, a small thing,* it seemed to be singing to itself, though in a minor key.

Disorientation came quickly. There was a spinning, a confusion, everything was subtly wrong, and Herewiss struggled to his feet, or tried to. He had a bad time of it; his muscles didn't work, he seemed tied down to something. Then, with an abrupt slight rending sensation, he found himself no longer tied to anything. He rose up. He stretched, and though there was no feeling of moving muscles, his mind slipped outward and filled his form. He was himself, totally.

Herewiss looked down at his body, where it lay among the pillows. There was no sickening feeling of entrapment, this time, nor was there the limitless rapture he had felt with the second use of the drug, a feeling of being free of a decrepit prison. He looked down now and felt satisfaction, and an odd kind of tenderness. Unfulfilled and incomplete he might be in many ways, but he had a fine body: slim and long and graceful, with the muscles corded hard in it from the strain of his disciplines and the forging of swords. It lay there, eyes closed, one arm outstretched toward the wine cup. It looked relaxed and innocent, and beautiful in a angular kind of way. *I always knew that a person's personality imprints itself to some extent on the body he wears,* he thought, *but I never thought to look at myself in that light—or if I did, I refused to believe what I saw. I am beautiful, and Lorn and Sunspark have been right when they've told me so. How curious it is that I never felt that way when I've been awake and in it. Must be a matter of viewpoint.*

He turned away and looked around him. The walls of the room glowed softly with a subdued rose-golden radiance. It seemed that his guesses were right, that some kind of life did sleep in the stone. The sword lay up against the wall near him, a long dark oblong blot against the light. Herewiss held up his hands before him. In shape they were the same as always, but there was a difference about them, a subtle transparency, and below that the muted glow of suppressed Flame. The moonlight had an added piquancy to it, a feeling like the cold taste of bitten metal, and Herewiss marveled as he breathed it in.

He looked down at the wine cup. The wine left within it was a molten blaze of red, an expression of all the sunlight that had become part of the grapes. Faintly he could hear the cries of ecstatic agony uttered by the vines as their burden was ripped from them, and he felt at a distance the silver touch of rain. He caught the languorous thoughts of one of the young girls who had helped to press out the vintage, and he felt how it had been for her, the night before, under the pomegranate trees with her lover. All that experience was too much for Herewiss to leave untasted. He knelt down by the shell of himself, took up the essence of the cup and drank off the joy and sorrow and time within it at one draft. The tangled, vivid selfhoods of bees and vintners and young girls flowed down his throat like cinnamon fire, and left an aftertaste like a summer dawn. *I will never call a wine "ordinary" again,* he thought. *Never—*

Herewiss looked over his shoulder at the candle, and got up and went to it, amused and curious. The candle flame was an intricate web of bright energies, an entangled tracery of heat and light in constant motion. Wobbling in earnest circles around and around it was the moth, a soft golden flicker, like a little flame itself. Apparently it had not noticed that it had died. Herewiss put out his hands and caught it carefully. It fluttered within his caging fingers, leaving here and there a wing scale like pale golddust, and finally sat on one of his fingers and looked up at him with confused dark eyes.

He carried it to the window and opened his hands, offering it to the night. The moth sat bewildered for a moment or so. Then it caught sight of the flood of silver light pouring in the window, and fluttered out of Herewiss's hands, bobbling upward into the night, straight for the transfigured Moon.

He smiled up at the moth, wishing it well, and looked out at the night and the stars. They blazed, blue and brilliant, as if seen through one of the doors down the hall. The world seemed to be hanging breathless in the midst of a clustered cloud of them. Their light was not cold, now, nor were they mocking him. They were singing, a song almost too high for him to hear, like the song of the bat. The song had words, but the multitude of voices drowned out the meaning in a million blended assonances. Herewiss contented himself with a few minutes of standing there in that inexpressible glory of sound and light, taking it all in, hoping that he would remember it tomorrow, through the headache.

Lorn is waiting for me, he thought at last, *and so are my other guests, all of them, past the Door. I perhaps slighted them earlier. Let me make up for that now. Downstairs—*

He exerted himself, and was there, standing in the midst of the silent main hall. Nearly all the people were asleep now, curled in dark silent bundles or stretched out beneath their cloaks. Dritt and Moris were still awake, unmoving, caring about each other in the darkness. Herewiss could feel the texture of their waking thoughts moving softly between them, as they rested in the twilit borderland between love and sleep. Herewiss smiled at them. Later, he thought, he might ask to share himself with them.

He looked around, identifying Freelorn's people one by one. Most of them were dreaming, in some cases quite vividly, so that faint images of their minds' wanderings were apparent. Segnbora lay curled in one corner, dreaming more loudly than the rest; her dream towered against the ceiling, some huge gossamer creature under a firefly sun. Herewiss was intrigued, and went to where she lay.

He knelt beside her, studying her for a moment before he would enter the dream. A clear sight like that of the last drug experience was on him again, but this time it was a more intimate and kindly vision, informed with compassion, very unlike the chill and distanced evaluation of the last time. Segnbora's hand lay out on her cloak, and he looked at it and shook his head sadly. Under the frail casing of the skin, such a violence and potency of untapped Power raged that it should have burned her out from within. But he also saw the barrier that sealed it away from her use, a wall of old frozen fears that all the inner fires couldn't melt. And the rules forbade him to tell her what to do about it. He sighed, and entered in.

There was the smell of salt spray, and black pockmarked rocks worn smooth by the sea, and a hot white midsummer sun, and Segnbora sat atop a boulder festooned with clambering strands of kelp. A sea ouzel was building a nest in a cranny of the boulder, and Segnbora was watching it intently. So was the Dragon that towered over her, a huge one, at its full growth but still young—no more than a thousand and a half years old. The three of them watched the bird fly down to the surf line of the black beach to pick up pieces of dead seaweed. Another ouzel appeared, carrying something in its beak that was not seaweed. Segnbora clucked to it, and with a whirring of wings the bird flew up to where she sat. It alighted on her outstretched hand, dropping the object in her palm. Herewiss, standing next to the Dragon's massive forefoot, looked at the thing. It was a gem, like a diamond but more golden, finely cut into a sparkling oval.

"It'll take a while to hatch," Segnbora said to the ouzel. "Do what you can, though." The bird picked up the jewel and flew down to the nest with it.

"But it's a stone!" Herewiss objected.

"Strange things won't happen," Segnbora said, "unless you give them a chance."

"I'm trying," Herewiss said.

"Yes, I see that. You're past the Door. The drug?"

"Yes."

"Oh well," Segnbora said, "a short life, but a merry one."

The Dragon bent its great head down toward Herewiss, regarding him. He bowed, feeling that this creature was worthy of his respect. It was apparently one of the oldest Line of Dragons, the children of Dahiric Worldfinder, to judge by its star-emerald scales and topaz spines. It spoke to him in deep-voiced song, but the words were strange and he could not understand them. There was warning in its voice.

"What?" Herewiss said.

"You don't speak Dracon?" asked Segnbora.

"I could never find anyone to teach me."

"Well, she greets you by me, and says that something is trying to happen, and you should beware of it."

"That's what I thought," Herewiss said. "But to beware of it?... I don't understand."

"Neither does she. She says to look to your sword."

"But I don't have a...well, I suppose I do..."

"I don't think much more will fit in there," Segnbora said to the first ouzel, which had come back with a piece of kelp nearly twice its size. It was trying valiantly to stuff it in the crevice, and failing. Herewiss felt suddenly that there was no more to be found or shared in this dream. He bowed again to the Dragon, and waved to Segnbora, and came forth.

Herewiss stood up, wondering, and went over to where Freelorn lay, curled up in a ball as usual. He spent a moment or two just looking at his loved. Sleep was the only time when Lorn lost his eternal look of calculation, and Herewiss loved to watch him sleeping, even when he snored.

Herewiss sat down beside him, the sweet sorrow of the moment passing through him like the pain of imminent tears. This could very well be the last time in this life—and if the hralcin got him, as seemed likely, in any life at all. *Mother,* he said softly, *I give You this night, as You gave me one of Yours. Whatever else happened or didn't happen in this life, Lorn loved me—loves me; and that's as great a blessing as the Fire would be, and possibly more than I deserve. Take this night, Mother, and remember me. You understood me—better than most.*

He reached out to touch Freelorn's cheek, brushed it gently. *I'm going to try to give you all the parts of me I never dared to,* he said. *I hope I can give you all the joy you deserve.*

Herewiss entered in.

There were clouds of haze, lit by a light as indefinite as dawn on a cloudy day, and vague soft sounds wove through them. He found Freelorn moving quietly through the mists, looking for something. Herewiss fell in beside him, and they paced together through the haze.

"Where are we, Lorn?"

"A long time ago," Freelorn said softly, "I used to come here alone. I was really young, and I would come talk to the Lion and ask Him for help with my lessons. I mean, I didn't know that you're not supposed to ask God for help with things like that. So I just asked. And it always seemed that I got help. Maybe I can get some here."

The mist was clearing. All around them was a stately hall with walls of plain white marble. Tall deep windows were cut into those walls, and lamps burned golden in the fists of iron arms that struck outward from the walls at intervals. There was no furniture in the hall of any kind.

At the end of the room was a flight of steps, three of them, and atop the steps a huge pedestal, and on the pedestal a statue of a mighty white Lion *couchant,* regal and beautiful. Herewiss knew where they were. This was Lionhall, in Prydon; the holiest place in Arlen, where none but the kings and their children might walk without mishap befalling them. Though Herewiss had never seen it before, in Freelorn's dream the place was part of his longed-for home, one which he had never thought to see again. And the Lion was not merely another aspect of the Goddess's Lover, but the founder of Freelorn's ancient line, and so family. Herewiss and Freelorn walked to the steps together, and stopped there, and felt welcomed.

"Lord," Freelorn said, "I promised I would come back, and here I am. Where is my father?"

It was strange to see them facing each other: Freelorn, small and uncertain, but with a great dignity about him, and the Lion, terrible and venerable, but with a serene joy in His eyes. "He's gone on," the Lion said. "He's one of Mine now."

"But where is he? I can't find his sword, and it's supposed to be mine, and I must have it. I can't be king without his sword."

"He's gone on," the Lion said, and He smiled on them out of His golden eyes. "You must go after him if you want Hergótha."

"I'll do that," Freelorn said. "Uh, Lord—"

"Ask on."

"You are my Father, and the head of our Line?"

"You are My child," the Lion said, bending His head in assent. "Make no doubt of it."

"Lord, I need a miracle."

The Lion stretched, a long comfortable cat-gesture, and the terrible steel-silver talons winked on His paws for a second's space. "I don't do miracles much any more, son. You're as much the Lion as I am. *You* do it."

"It's not for me, Héalhra my Father; it's for Herewiss here."

Herewiss looked up, meeting the gaze of the golden eyes and feeling a tremor of recognition, remembering how his illusion had looked at him even after it was gone from the field at Madeil. "Son of Mine," the Lion said then, shifting his eyes back to Freelorn, "his Father the Eagle and I managed Our own miracles for the most part. I have faith in you, and in him."

Freelorn nodded.

"Go down to the Arlid, then," the Lion said, "and follow it till it comes to the Sea. Your father is in the place to which his desire has taken him, but to get there you'll have to go down to the Shore first. Your friend will go with you."

The bowed down, together, and were suddenly out by the river Arlid, which flowed through the palace grounds. It was night, and the water flowed silvery by under a westering Moon.

"The Sea is a long way off," Herewiss said. Even as he said it, he perceived something wrong with him. He was being swept away with this dream, losing control. *Too much drug!* something in him cried, thrilling with horror. But the fearful voice was faint, and though it cried again, *Down by the Sea is the land of the dead!* still he walked with Freelorn by the riverbank, through the green reeds, toward the seashore.

"It's not that far," Freelorn said. "Only a hundred miles or so."

"It's a long way to walk," Herewiss insisted.

"So we'll let the water take us. Come on."

Together they stepped down through the sedges on the bank and onto the surface of the water. The Arlid was a placid river, smooth-flowing, and bore their weight without complaint. Its current hurried them past little clusters of houses, and moss-grown docks, and flocks of grazing sheep, at a speed which would normally have surprised them but which they both now accepted unquestioningly. Once or twice they walked a little, to help things along, but mostly they stood in silence and let the river flow.

"You really think your father has the sword?" Herewiss said.

"He has to." Freelorn's voice was fierce. "They never found it after he died. He must have taken Hergótha with him."

Herewiss looked at Freelorn and was sad for him, driven as he was even while dreaming. "It takes more than a sword to make a king," he said, and then was shocked at the words that had fallen out of his mouth.

Freelorn looked back at him, and his eyes were sad too. "That's usually true," he said, "but it's going to take at least Hergótha to make a king out of me, I'm afraid. I'm not enough myself yet to do it alone."

For a while neither of them spoke. The river was branching out now, the marshes of the Arlid delta reaching out northward before them, toward the Sea. Freelorn and Herewiss picked their way from stream to stream as along a winding path, stepping carefully so as not to upset the fish.

"I've never been this way before," Herewiss said, very quietly. He felt afraid.

"Maybe it's time," Freelorn said. "I was here once, when I was very young. Don't be scared. I won't leave you alone."

The river bottom was getting shallower and sandier. The stream that bore them turned a bend, past a spinney of stunted willow trees, and suddenly there it was, the Shore.

Herewiss looked out past the beach and was so torn between terror and awe that he could hardly think. Under the suddenly dark sky the Sea stretched away forever, and it was a sea of light, not water. It was as liquidly dazzling as the noon Sun seen through some clear mountain cataract. But there was no Sun, no Moon, no stars even; only the long vista of pure brilliant light, brighter than any other light that ever was. Herewiss began to understand how the Starlight could only be a faint intimation of this last Sea, for stars are mortal, and bound with the laws and ties of materiality. This was a place that time would never touch, and mere matter was too fragile, too ephemeral, to survive it.

The waves of white fire came curling in, their troughs as bright as their crests, and broke in foaming radiance on the silver beach, and were drawn in sheets of light back into the Sea. But all silently. There was no sound of combers crashing and tumbling, no hiss of exhausted waves climbing far up the sand: nothing at all. Along the shore there walked or stood many vague forms, shadows passing by in as deep a silence as the waves. Herewiss was very afraid. The fear held his chest in its hand and squeezed, so that the breath couldn't come in. He thought suddenly of the choking darkness behind the door in the hold, where the hralcin waited and hungered for him, and the fear squeezed harder. But Freelorn stepped from the water, and held out his hand; and Herewiss took that hand and went with him.

They went down the Shore together, slowly, looking at each of the shadows they passed, but recognizing none. There were men and women of every age, and many young children walking around or playing quietly in the sand. There were couples, some of them young lovers, and some of them old, and some couples where one person ravaged by time walked with one hardly touched by it, but walked all the same with interlaced arms and gentle looks. Freelorn would stop every now and then and question one or another of the people they passed. They always answered quietly, with grave, kindly words, but also with an air of preoccupation.

Herewiss was not paying attention to either questions or answers. His fear was too much with him. All he perceived with any clarity was the rise and fall of the quiet voices, which arose from the silence and slipped back to become part of it again when the speakers were finished. He began to feel that if he spoke again, the words and the thoughts behind them would be lost forever in that silence, a part of himself gone irretrievably. But no one asked him to speak, and Freelorn led him down the sand as if he had a sure idea of which way they were headed.

"Are we going the right way?" Herewiss said finally, watching carefully to see if the thought behind the question became lost.

"I think so. This place will come around on itself, if we give it enough time."

They walked, and their feet made no sound on the sand. They passed more people than Herewiss had ever seen or known, some of them looking out over the gently moving brilliance of the Sea, or standing rapt in contemplation of the sand, or of something less obvious. When someone turned to watch them pass, it was with a look of mild, unhurried wonder, a wonder which soon slipped away again. The fear was beginning to ebb out of Herewiss, little by little, when suddenly he saw someone making straight for them across the strand, not quickly, but with purpose.

He could hear his heart begin hammering in his ears again. "Your father?" he said.

Freelorn shook his head. "My father was a bigger man—is."

Herewiss stopped, still holding Freelorn's hand. He knew that shadowed form, knew the way it walked, the loose, easy stride. "Oh Goddess," he whispered into the eternal silence. "Goddess *no.*"

Freelorn looked at him with compassion, and said nothing.

Herewiss stood there, frozen in the extremity of terror. The world was about to end in ice and bitterness, and he would welcome it. He deserved no better. He waited for it to happen.

And out of the darkness and fixity to which he thought he had completely surrendered himself, a voice spoke: his own voice, not angry or defiant, but matter-of-fact and calm, speaking a truth. *If this is the worst thing in the world about to happen, we won't just stand here and wait. We'll go meet it.*

He stepped forward, pulling Freelorn with him, and the strain of taking the first step shook him straight through, like a convulsion. His bones, his flesh rebelled. But he kept going. The shadowy form approached them steadily, and they walked to meet it. Fear battered Herewiss like a stormwind. He wanted to flee, to hide, anything, but he pushed himself into the teeth of the wind, into the face of his fear. He had been struggling against it, walking into it head down. Now he raised his head, and opened his eyes again. The wind smote tears into his eyes, and he looked up at his brother.

He was as he had been the day he died. Tall and dark-haired, like most of the Brightwood line, with the droopy eyes that ran in Herewiss's family, he came and stood before them. His eyes smiled, and his face smiled, and the blood welled softly from the place where Herewiss's sword had struck him through, an eternity ago.

"Hello, Herelaf," Freelorn said.

Herewiss let go of Freelorn's hand and sank down to his knees in the sand, trembling with terror and grief. He hid his face in his hands, and began to weep. All the things he had wanted to say to his brother after he died, all the apologies, all the guilt, everything that he had decided to say when they met after his own death, now froze in his throat. And the worst of it was that he felt quite willing to let the tears take him. Anything was better than trying to deal with the person who stood before him.

But there were hands on his hands, and they pulled gently downward until Herewiss had no choice but to squeeze his eyes shut and turn his head away. "Dusty," his brother's voice said, "don't you have *anything* to say to me?"

The old name, so rarely used, so much missed, pierced Herewiss with more pain than he had thought possible to stand without dying—but then, how could he die on these shores? He sobbed and coughed and caught his breath, and finally dared to look up again into his brother's face. There was no anger there, no hatred, not even any sorrow. Herelaf was glad to see him.

"Why are you so surprised to see me?" his brother said. "You know how the drug works. I'm as likely to turn up in your realm as you are in mine. And if you walk here, you're more than likely to run into me."

"I—" Herewiss choked, cleared his throat. "I suppose I knew it. But I was so sure that I wouldn't, wouldn't lose control—"

"—and run into me. Yes, I can imagine." Herelaf held Herewiss's hands in his, and the touch was warm. "It doesn't matter. I'm glad you came."

"But—but *I killed you*—!" The words were too much for him, despite all the thousand times he had whispered and moaned and cried them into the darkness in the past. He crumpled back into tears. Freelorn was crouched down beside him, holding him again, and his brother's hands touched his face to wipe the tears away.

"Herewiss." The voice was still young, but there was power in it, and Herewiss was startled out of his weeping. "You didn't kill me. We were drunk, and messing with swords in a dark room, and you made one of those grand gestures with your sword, and I lost my balance and fell on it, and I died. You didn't kill me."

"But I should have been more careful—I shouldn't have encouraged you—"

"Herewiss, I started it."

"But—"

"Dusty, I *started* it. Listen, little brother mine, did I ever tell you a lie? Ever? Doesn't it strike you as strange that I'd start trying to lie to you *here*, where there can be neither lying nor deception?"

Herewiss scrubbed at his eyes and looked up again. "You're still bleeding," he said.

"So are you, and that's why. This is a peaceful place, there's healing to be had here before we go on. But the thoughts of the living have power over those who've gone on, just as the dead have some influence over the lives and ways of the living."

"But you're not really dead!" Herewiss cried. "You live, you're here—"

"I'm here. But living? Not the same way you are. I finished what I had to do."

"But it was so senseless—you were young, and strong, and in line for the Lordship—" The tears broke through again. Herelaf shook his head.

"Little brother," he said, and he held Herewiss's hands hard, "I was all of that. And we loved each other greatly, and I loved my life, and when I first got here I raged and screamed and tried to get back into the poor broken body. But knowledge comes with silence here, and soon I found that it wasn't senseless. What sense there is to it may seem evil to us, but that's because we haven't yet learned all the facts, or recalled them."

"I wish I could believe that—"

"Herewiss, I know this. I did what I was there to do while I was there, and then I came here, and when it's time, I'll go on to something else. That's the way things are."

"But—I don't understand. What did you *do?*"

Herelaf smiled at him. "That, like the matter of Names, is between me and the Mother. Besides, I may not be finished yet."

"I—oh, what the Dark! Herelaf, I wish I could stay here with you—I've failed so miserably with the Flame—"

Herelaf laughed, and the mingled pain and joy that the sound struck into Herewiss was amazing to feel. "Goddess, Dusty, what a crazy idea. You don't even know what you're *for* yet, and already you want to abandon the battlefield! Idiot. So tell me. If you can tell me, you might be able to stay."

"I never really gave it much thought—"

"A lot of people don't. *I* certainly never did."

Herewiss frowned in irritation. "I," he said, "am the first man in a thousand years to have enough of the Flame to use, and know it."

"That's what you are, or what you have been—not what you're *for*. You just have to go back and find out the answer. Allow yourself to be what you can, and that will point you toward what you're *for* like a compass needle seeking north."

"But—"

"Shut up. You always were a great one for butting around, looking for holes in what you didn't want to hear. That hasn't changed, at least. Listen to me, Dusty. I'm only a ghost. No, look at me—" Herewiss had turned his face away, but Herelaf took both his brother's hands in one of his, while with the other he took Herewiss's face and turned it to him. "I'm only a ghost, Dusty. I can't hurt you any more, unless you make me. Since I fell onto your sword, you haven't been able to use one, not even to fight with—I guess because of me, or what you think you did to me. But the time's coming when you're going to need a sword. And you won't feel right with one, it won't do you any good, it'll turn in your hand unless you acquit yourself of my 'murder.' *You have things to do.* Better things than sitting around sorrowing for me. And I have better things to do than walk this shore and bleed."

Herewiss knelt there on the sand, and felt Freelorn's arms around him, and his brother's eyes upon him, and he shook. He didn't know what to think, or what to say.

"I'm not angry, Dusty," Herelaf said softly. "There's no anger here after one comes to understand things. I was set free at the appropriate time. How could I be angry about that? But we're in bondage, both of us, and you can free us both. Turn me loose. Turn yourself loose. *You didn't kill me."*

"I—" Herewiss looked at his brother, and at the truth in his eyes, and for the first time began to feel something strange and cold curling in his gut. It was doubt, doubt of the crenellated certainties he had walled into his mind, and the doubt twined upward, curling around his heart and squeezing it hard. "I—"

PAIN. Sudden, terrible, and Herewiss foundering in darkness, the shore and the Sea's light and Freelorn and his brother's gentle voice all gone at once, lost, no light, no sound, only an awful tearing pain through his head and his heart and the place where his soul usually slept. Tearing, gnawing, and then just aching, and still the darkness, but there was a floor under him now—at least he thought there was, yes, his hands were against it, that was a pillow, and ohh his head hurt, spun and throbbed—and dear Goddess, what was that noise?

A howling. A sick ugly howling like an axe being sharpened too long, and mixed with it other sounds, human voices crying out in terror, the sound of scrabbling claws and—

Herewiss tried to stand up. The binding spell. Broken. A pack of hralcins; the one had gone back for reinforcements. A touch too much stress on the binding somehow. The spell broken, and now all of them loose, hunting. Hunting *him.* But he hadn't been in his body. So they couldn't find him. But they had found something else to hold them until he returned. Freelorn. Freelorn's people. Downstairs. Defenseless.

He tried to stand again, and it didn't work. Too much drug. Out of it too suddenly. His body disobeyed him, and responded to his commands with vengeful stabs of pain. The screaming was louder, voices terrified beyond understanding. He refused to let his body's punishments stop him. There was a little light now, sickly, the light of the Moon almost gone down. Against the wall was a dim gray blot, the only thing he could really see. He made a hand go out, despite shrieking protests from his head and arm and aching torso, and took hold of the thing. It swayed in his grasp. The other hand, now. He gripped the object hard, and wrenched himself to a sitting position next to it.

If his voice could have found his throat, he would have screamed. It was the sword, sharpened that morning, and it cut into his hands in icy lines of pain, and the blood flowed. But he had no time, no time for the pain, and he struggled to stand, using the sword as a prop. He moved his hands feebly to the unsharpened tang, where the hilt would go, and pushed himself up, and somehow managed to stand. His legs wobbled under him as if they belonged to a body he had owned in a former life. He made his feet move. He went to the door.

The stairs were dark, and Herewiss fell and stumbled down them, using the sword as a cane, caroming off the walls with force enough to bruise bones—though he couldn't feel the blows much through the shell which the drug had made of his body. The cries of men in terror were closer now. They mingled with that awful lusting hunger-howl and were nearly lost in it, faint against it as against the laughter of Death. As Herewiss came to the landing at the foot of the stairs, very faintly he could see some kind of light coming from the main hall, a fitful light, coming in stutters and flashes. With every flash the hralcins screeched louder in frustration and rage. *Segnbora!* He thought, *She's holding them off with the light until I can get there. But what can I do? Nothing but Flame would do anything—*

He reeled against the wall to rest his blazing body for a second, and the answer spoke itself to him in his brother's voice: "It'll turn in your hand unless you acquit yourself of my 'murder.'"

He stumbled away from the wall and went on again, shuffling, hurrying, pushing himself through the pain. The light before him grew brighter as he approached the hall, but the flashes were becoming shorter and shorter. *Segnbora spoke of choosing when to listen to the voices of the dead—and when you can choose freely, and not be driven by them, you're free to find out who you really are*—And the voice spoke again in the back of his mind, saying, "There's neither lying nor deception, back of the Door—"

He couldn't *lie*, Herewiss thought through the effort of making his body work. *He was telling the truth. He was! I didn't—*

He came to the doorway of the hall, and stood there, trembling with fear and effort, taking in the scene. There was little sound from the people in the hall now. They were crowded together in one corner, huddled together with closed or averted eyes. Before them stood Segnbora, arms upraised, shaking terribly, but with a look of final commitment on her face as she summoned the Flame from the depths of her, brilliant and impotent. As

Herewiss watched, supporting himself on the bloody sword, she called the light out of herself again. But this time there was no starflower, no burst of blue: only a rather bright light, quickly gone.

In that light he could see the huge things she was holding off, as they backed away a bit. They reached out with twisted limbs, black talons raked the air like the combed claws of insects. Even through their banshee wail the sound of sheathed fangs moving hungrily in hidden mouths could still be heard. The light seemed to refuse to touch them, sliding away from hide the color of night with no stars—though there were baleful glitters from where their eyes could have been, reflections the color of gray-green stormlight on polished ice. The air in the room was bitter cold, and smelled of rust and acid.

The light flickered out, and the hralcins moved in again for their meal.

Herewiss staggered in, into the thick darkness. Well, maybe *this* was what he was for. The hralcins had come after him: he would give himself to them, and they would feed on his soul and go away, satisfied. His friends would escape. He found himself suddenly glad of those few precious moments with his brother, however painful they had been. After the hralcins were through with him, there would be nothing. No silent shore, no Sea of light, no rebirth ever; only terrible pain, and then the end of things. But if this was going to be the last expression of his existence, he would do it right. He drew himself up straight, though it hurt, and lifted up the sword. Almost he smiled: it was so good to face his fears at last—!

"Here I am, you sons of bitches!" he yelled. "Come and get me!"

The howling paused for a moment, as if in confusion—and then, to Herewiss's utter horror, resumed again. They were not interested. They had found other game; they would take the souls of Freelorn and his people, and then later have Herewiss at their leisure.

"No," he breathed. *"No—"*

"Herewiss!" Two voices cried at once, and there was the light again, but only a shadow of itself, pallid and exhausted. Segnbora held up her arms with fists clenched, as if she were trying to hold onto the light by main force, while her eyes searched the shadows for Herewiss. Freelorn stood apart from her, grim-faced and terrified. His sword was naked in his hand: a useless gesture, but one that described him in full. *That man walked the land of the dead with me unafraid,* Herewiss thought, *and here he is facing down things that'll drink him up, blood and soul together, and he's afraid, and still he defies—!*

The light died out, for the last time. The hralcins howled, and moved in—

The hall exploded into fire, an awful blaze of white-hot outrage. Freelorn and Segnbora and the others crowded further back into the corner as Sunspark flowered between them and the hralcins, its fires raging upward in a terrible blinding column until they smote the ceiling and turned back on themselves, the down-hanging branches of a tree of flames. The hralcins backed away again.

"Sunspark," Herewiss cried, the sound of his shout hurting his head. "Spark, no, *don't*—"

The hralcins were already sliding closer again. (Herewiss,) it said, lashing out at them with great gouts of fire, (he loves you. And you love him, more than you do me, I dare say. How shall I stand by and allow him to be taken from you? And then afterwards these things would take you too—) Its thoughts were casual on the surface, almost humorous, but beneath them Herewiss could hear its terror for him.

"Spark—!"

It went up in so unbearable a glare that Herewiss had to close his eyes, but before he did he saw that the hralcins were still moving closer. (They don't seem to be responding as well as before to this,) it said conversationally, while beneath the thought all its self sang with fear. (I think—)

There was a sudden shocked silence. Herewiss opened his eyes again to see one of the hralcins reach out and somehow tear the pillar of fire in two, hug a great tattered blaze of light to itself with its misshapen forelimbs, suck it dry, kill the light. The other hralcins moved in for the rest, tore at the light, fed, consumed it, darkness fell—

"SUNSPAAAAAARK!"

The hralcins howled like the Shadow's hounds, and moved in again. And through the howling, Herewiss heard Freelorn scream.

The scream entered into Herewiss and burned behind his eyes, ran through his veins in a storm of fire and filled him as the drug had filled him with himself. He needed his Name. There was no time any more. He threw the door open, and looked. Time froze in him. No, *he* froze it—

All his life he had thought of time as being flat, like a plane. It was the world that was three-dimensional. A moment had seemed to have an edge sharp enough to slice a finger on, and by the time he summoned up the self-awareness and desire to try balancing on such a razor's edge, the moment was past already, and he was teetering on the next one.

Now, though, he found himself poised there, effortlessly, in the exact middle of a moment. And since he was truly *still* for the first time in his life, he perceived his Name. He looked sideways down it, or along it, or into it—there were no words to properly express the spatial relationships implicit within its structure. Its strands stretched outward forever, and inward forever, flung out to eternity and yet curling back and meeting themselves again, making a whole. A scintillating, dazzling latticework of moments past and moments future, of Herewiss-that-was and Herewiss-that-would-be, all entwined, all coexisting; a timeweb, a selfweb, himself at its heart.

He looked up and down its length, and *saw*. Down there, root and heart and anchor-point of the weave, the night of his conception. Elinádren his mother, and Hearn his father, tangled sweetly together in the act of love. After some time of sleeping together for the sheer fun of the sharing, they were making an amazing discovery; that each of them was finding the other's delight more joyous than his or her own—and not just while in bed. The long comfortable friendship of the Lord's son and the Rodmistress who worked with him had come to fruition; they had become lovers; and now that they were in love indeed, their Names were beginning to match in places. He could see the two brilliant Name-weaves tangling through one another, and where they touched and met and melded, they blazed white-hot with joy. It was as if someone had cast out a net of silver and drawn in a catch of stars.

Herewiss's soul, existing in timelessness, saw that bright network and was entranced by it; the joystars were beacons that drew him in. He wanted that kind of joy, of love, wanted to be part of it, to share the joy with someone else that way. And as he watched, Elinádren exploded in ecstatic fulfillment, and her Fire ran searing through the glittering weave, igniting the joystars into unbearable blinding brilliance, setting free for a bare few moments the spark of Hearn's suppressed Flame, which swept down like wildfire to meet hers. Their two commingled souls burned starblue, and Herewiss, overwhelmed by an ecstasy of light and promised joy, dove inward and blazed into oneness with them as *they* were one; started to be born again....

And other occurrences, later ones. Being held in his father's arms, carried home half-asleep after his presentation at the Forest Altars: three years old. "Oh," Hearn's voice whispering to Elinadren, who walked beside them with her arm through Hearn's, moving quietly through green twilight, "oh, Eli, he's going to be something special."

And another one over there, watching his mother make it rain to stave off what seemed an incipient dry spell. He was six years old. Watching her stand there in the field, garlanded with meadowsweet to invoke the Mother of Rains, seeing her uplift a Rod burning with the Fire and call the rainclouds to her with Flame and poetry. He watched the sky darken into curdled contrasts, clouds violet and orange and stormgreen, watched her bring the lightning-licked water thundering down, and a great desire to control the things of the world rose up in him. He got up from the grass, soaking wet, and went to hold onto Elinádren's skirts, and said, "Mommy, I'll do that when I grow up too!"

And yet another, when he was out camping in the grasslands east of the Wood, and he woke up and stretched in the morning to find the grass-snake coiled in the blankets with him, and heard its warning hiss: eleven years old. He knew it could kill him; and he knew he could probably kill it, for his knife was close to hand and he was fast. But he remembered Hearn saying, "Don't *ever* kill unless you must!"—and he lifted up the blankets slowly and then rolled out, and from beneath them the grass-snake streaked out like a bright green lash laid over the ground, and was gone, as frightened of him as he had been of it. *I guess you can do without killing*, he thought. *Always, from now on, I'll try*—

There were thousands more moments like that, each one of which had made him part of what he was, each linked to all the moments before and all the moments after, making the bright complete framework that was his Name. And each act or decision had a shadow, a phantom link behind it—sprung from his deeds, yet independent of them somehow—another Name, shadowing itself in multiple reflections, reaching out into depths he could not fully comprehend—

Her Name. The Goddess's. Of course.

No wonder She wanted to free me. And no wonder She wanted my Name. Not power, nothing so simple. It is part of Hers. Her Name is the sound of all Names everywhere. And with the knowledge of my Name, She will win ever so slight a victory against the Death. There will be more of Her than there was; the sure knowledge of what I am at this moment in time will make me immortal in a way that will surpass and outlast even the cycles of death and rebirth, even the great Death of everything that is.

If I accept myself—

Herewiss stood there in the midst of the blazing brilliance of the weave, hearing words long forgotten as well as ones that had never been spoken, tasting joys he had ceased to allow himself and pains he had shut away, and also feeling with wonder the textures of things that hadn't happened yet, silks and thorns and winds laden with sunheat like molten silver—Whether the drug was still working in him, he wasn't sure; but futures spun out ahead of him from the base-framework of his Name, numberless probabilities. Some of them were so faint and unlikely that he could hardly perceive them at all; some were almost as clear as things that had become actuality. Some of these were dark with his death, and some almost as dark with his life; one burned blue with the Fire, and he looked closely at it, saw himself almost lost in light, rippling with Flame that streamed from him like a cloak in the wind. And that future was ready to start in the next moment, when he let time start happening again. But there was still a gap in the information, he didn't know how to get there from here—

Yes I do.

Herewiss looked forward along all the futures, and back down his past, weighing the brights and darks of them, and accepted them for his.

And knew his Name.

And knew the Name of his fear.

His Flame, of course. There it lay, dying indeed, but still the strongest thing about him, the strongest part of him. How long, now, had he been trying to control it, to use it like a hammer on the anvil of the world? The blue Flame was not something to be used in that fashion. He had been trying to keep it apart from him, where it would not be a threat to his control of himself. If he wanted it, *really* wanted it, he was going to have to take hold of it and merge himself with the Fire, give up the control, yield himself wholly and forever.

It was going to hurt. The fires of the forge, of a star's core, of an elemental's heart would be nothing compared to this.

So be it. There's no more time. I've got to do it.

He had been trying to make it his.

He reached out and embraced it, and made it him.

Pain, incredible pain for which the anguished screaming of a whole dying world seemed insufficient expression. He hung on, grasped, held, was fire—and then time began to reassert itself, the pain mixing with the sound of Freelorn's scream, feeding on it, blending, changing, anger, incandescent blue anger, raging like the Goddess's wrath—hands, surely burned off, eyes transfixed by spears of blue-white fury, too much, too much power, has to go somewhere, forward, moments moving, forward, terror, rage, *forward*, Freelorn—!

—staggering forward, carrying the half-finished sword in his hand, and a murderous freight of rage within him, burning under his skin like the red-hot heart of a coal under its white ash. No anger he had ever summoned had been this potent, it was devouring him from within, he was fire, like Sunspark, *ah, Sunspark, loved, gone, dear one!*—and he sobbed, his own fires consuming him now, fury, horror, revenge, he tried to treat them as a sorcery, shaping them, directing them, scorching himself with them, weaving them—

—something stumbled into the firefield he was making, no, that he *was*, for it was *he* and he *it; that's the secret, isn't it—not trying to use a tool, but being one with it—who uses their hand to do something?* It does it—a something, no, not really—a not-something; it had no name, nor even any life; and it sensed his sudden incredible upsurge of life, of selfness—they sensed him, and were closing in, for such a feed as they had never had in all their centuries. *Well, let them try. They are not alive, so it's all right to kill them—disassemble would be a better word, actually; see, a break here, at this linkage, and here, quite simple; I know what I'm for and they can't say as much—now the hard part,* push—

If Freelorn's scream had terrified him, the ones that came now were worse, but Herewiss shut them out. He stood still, clenching hard on his sword, on himself, his eyes squeezed shut. Outside of him he perceived a terrible turbulence and upset, a maelstrom of freed forces that shook the air inside his lungs and battered at the thoughts inside his head. But he felt sure that if he looked to see what was happening, something might go wrong. He urged the anger on, feeding it with his fears, pouring it out. It pushed through his pores as if he were sweating molten metal. His skin would have melted too were it not already charred into a blackened shell. The burning had rooted itself deep in him, his bones glowed like iron in the forge. His heart raced, its rhythm staggering in pain, every beat an explosion of sparks and burnt blood. But still he pushed, fanned the fire, breathed it hotter, pushed, *pushed*—

The hralcins keened and screeched up to the top of the range of hearing, a multiple cry of agony and excruciating fright. The sound hurt the ears, piercing them unbearably, boring inward to the brain—

—and then it stopped.

Herewiss opened his eyes. The hall was empty, except for the hralcins' horrible smell and a faint brief echo of their last despairing cry. Slowly, Freelorn's people began to come out of the corner. Segnbora slumped down into an exhausted heap on the floor, and wept with frustration and fear. Herewiss stood where he was, holding himself straight, and Freelorn came and put his arms around him. Freelorn was shaking terribly.

"Lorn," Herewiss said.

Freelorn held him, just held him hard for a few moments, and then reached up a trembling hand to Herewiss's face, brushing away the tears and sweat. Herewiss caught at that hand, bowed his head over it, pressed his lips to it. "Lorn," he said again, his heart clenching like a fist in a last spasm of fear. "Are you all right, did it hurt you at all—"

"No, no, it just touched me." Freelorn laughed, a weak, shaky chuckle. "You know how I am about gooey things—"

"You were justified, I think..." He held Freelorn's hand tightly against him, and swayed slightly; his voice was soft and slurred with fatigue. "Lorn, it's awfully bright in here for Moonset...is Segnbora—"

"Ohh—oh, *Herewiss*—"

There was such a strange tone to Freelorn's voice that Herewiss glanced down to see what he was looking at. It took a while before it registered, before he really saw the bright blue Flame that licked around him like an aura, curling down his arm and flowing through and about the blade of the half-finished sword in runnels the color of summer sky. And even then, all he could find the strength to do was to slip his free arm around his friend, as much from the need for support as from love.

 *ten*

After even the fieriest sunset comes the Twilight; and in the Twilight, anything is rather more than less likely to happen.

Gnomics, 14

Herewiss woke up all at once, as if his mind had opened a door and stepped through. He sat up, and glanced at the shadows outside to tell the time. It was nearly noon. Beside him Freelorn lay curled up, having stolen all the blankets as usual, and snored like a whole pride of lions.

He leaned against the wall for a few minutes and just felt the Fire within him. It was freed now, it was *him* now, no longer bound into a tight controlled package at the bottom of his self. It ran all through him, warm as blood, no longer urgent, but calm and glad. There was time to do the things that had to be done...all the time in the world.

The sword lay beside him, among the cushions, and he looked at it and smiled. If he had shed blood on it—and he checked his hands, finding only Flame-healed scars there—then the blood had burnt off, for the metal was bright and unstained. The steel had acquired an odd blue sheen, as if even now it reflected the fire it was forged in.

He reached down, picked it up. At his touch it flared up brilliantly, a bar of blue-white light like the core of a star, hammered and forged. Thin bright tongues of the Flame strained away from it and curled back again.

Herewiss's smile dimmed as the sight recalled to him another image, that of a bright torn veil of fire arching away from some star, daring the darkness—and then fallen, consumed, gone forever into the greater brilliance.

Spark, he thought, *oh my dear loved.* He leaned his head back against the wall and began to weep. The sword's light blazed up with his pain. *My sweet firechild, my hungry piece of the Sun. You always were good at doing the impossible, but this time you outdid yourself. You went and got killed.* The sobbing began to rack him. *And for my sake. The only man in history to have a fire elemental fall in love with him, and it loves me so well that it dies for me. Oh, damn, damn, damn—!*

He cried and cried for what seemed forever, the sword clutched in his hands, its Flame trembling and wavering with his sobs. *So now what? There's nothing left to bury—and what kind of a tree do you plant for a fire elemental, anyhow? Maybe it would be more appropriate to start a brushfire—oh, dammit straight to Darkness! I make my peace with a guilt, and not an hour later I have a grief just as bad to replace it! One more empty place inside me—and I'll never be able to so much as light a campfire again without being reminded of just how empty it is! I always knew that you have to accept the pain at the end of love to make the loving complete—but this, this is harder than I thought—Oh, Mother of Everything, why her—why him—why my sweet little Sunspark? Why,* why?

Eventually he ran dry of tears, and even the great heaving sobs that shook him grew less—his chest ached too much to sustain them. He scrubbed at his face with one hand—he still could not bring himself to let go of the sword—and fell to running his fingertips up and down the water-cool metal of the blade, the rhythm of his stroking being occasionally broken by a leftover sob or choke. *This whole thing hasn't gone the way it should, and now is no exception. I thought it would be all joy, that it would feel good at the end—and look at me... And I never dreamed that there would be such a price to pay. Or even that I wouldn't be the only one paying it.*

Herewiss shook his head slowly. *She asked me what I would be willing to pay. If I'd known then what I know now, I wonder if I'd have been so sure of myself.*

"Goddess, Herewiss," came a grumble from within the pile of blankets, "how come you have this crazy preference for rooms with eastern exposures? Anyone who gets up this early has to have something wrong with his—" Freelorn's head and shoulders and arms emerged from under the covers; he stretched and turned over, and saw.

"Oh," he said. "Ohh—" and sat up, shedding blankets in all directions, reached over and took Herewiss in his arms, hugged him tightly enough to bruise ribs, kissed him hard, hugged him again. Herewiss hugged back, one-armed. His underhearing was alive as it had never been before, and the blaze of triumph and joy that his loved was radiating made him smile. It was a strange feeling; after all the crying, he felt as if his face might crack.

"You've got it," Freelorn was saying. "You've *got* it—"

"It looks that way."

"But, Goddess, it's taken so long," Freelorn said, propping himself up against the wall beside Herewiss. "You're going to—hey, my face is—you've been crying—?!"

"I've been—I've—oh, Dark, I thought I was, was *done*—oh, L*orn*—"

"No, no, it's all right. Come here, then. Come on. There—let it out." Freelorn took Herewiss in his arms, holding him tight, and Herewiss buried his face against Freelorn's shoulder and wept anew. "You've had a hell of a night, go ahead and let it out—"

"It's muh, muh, m—" (More than that. And why am I trying to talk? I can make anyone hear me now. Whether they have the talent or not.)

"Sweet Goddess above us," Freelorn said in amazement. "So that's how it feels."

(Yes. But, Lorn, poor Sunspark—!)

Freelorn was shocked into silence as Herewiss gave him the image of Sunspark's Name without words. (And it's gone, it *died*, it wasn't supposed to be *able* to die and it *died*—)

Herewiss said nothing more for a long time, but only sobbed, and Freelorn held him close and wondered. When after a while Herewiss's sobs started to die down, and he gulped and choked and started to control himself again, Freelorn sighed and made himself smile.

"I was saying," he said conversationally, "that you're going to have to put a bastard broadsword's hilt on that thing if you expect to be able to handle it. It's four feet long easily."

"I—uh—no." Herewiss sat up straight again, wiped at his eyes and got his breath back. "Not at all. See, look—" He stood up, and taking the sword one-handed, Herewiss cut and parried and thrust till the air whistled and the sword left trails of blue Fire behind it. "It's like an arm, it's almost weightless. Not quite; the balance is a little heavy toward the point." He held the sword out at arm's length, point up, eyeing it with a critical smile. "Possibly my error at the forge—or possibly the sword itself is impatient. But whatever, it's no problem to handle."

"Looks like it has a nice edge."

"Nice! This sword could shave the wind and not leave a whisker. In fact—" Herewiss looked around the room for something to try it on. "In *fact*—" He moved toward the grindstone, grinning with wicked merriment.

"Are you going to—Dusty, you're, you've got to be—"

Herewiss took the sword two-handed, swung it up behind his head, feeling a wild joy as the Flame ran up through his arms and into the blade, poised, waiting. He brought it sweeping down hard, channeling the Fire down into the striking fulcrum of the sword, as he had been taught to channel the force of his arms. The blade struck the grindstone and clove it in two, kept on going and smote through the oak framework, kept on going and finally struck the floor, slitting it a foot deep like a knife cutting into a cheese. The grindstone smashed in pieces to the floor, leaving no mark on the shining gray surface.

Herewiss stood up straight, turned and grinned at Freelorn.

"Showoff," Freelorn said, grinning back.

"Have I ever denied it? Lorn, I'm ripe, serves me right for sleeping in my clothes. Come on, let's take a bath."

"There's hardly enough water in your cistern for that—"

Herewiss drew himself up to his full height. *"That,"* he said smugly, "can be fixed…"

By afternoon it had rained four times, once with a mad magnificence of thunder, and lightning like fireworks; and the knobby barren sage around the hold was in bloom a month early. Freelorn's people were walking around with grins almost wide enough to match Herewiss's. Despite the terror, they had been present at a miracle, or something that could pass for one, and they were also relishing the prospect of seeing Freelorn back on his throne again, escorted there by Herewiss's Flame.

For a while that afternoon Herewiss sat down in the great hall, one arm around Freelorn and the other hand holding the sword across his knees, answering all the questions about how it felt and where the hralcins had come from and what had happened to Sunspark and what Herewiss was going to do now. When Segnbora asked that one, Herewiss looked sidewise at Freelorn and smiled.

"How much did you say you got, Lorn?"

"Eight thousand."

"Mmm. We could bribe a lot of people with that."

"Or hire a lot of soldiers."

"Lorn, I'd still rather sidestep that solution. When you're king, your people will bless your name for taking Throne and Stave without bloodshed. And with this—" he rapped one knuckle against Freelorn's skull—"and this—" he lifted the sword—"we should be able to work something out. But as soon as your people are ready, maybe in a few days, when we're all rested, we'll start heading west. The Arlenes have been without a child of the Lion's line for six years now, and the effects are beginning to show. It's time something was done about it."

He got up, and they stood with him, nodding and murmuring agreement. "I have a few things to take care of," he said to them all, "so I'll see you around dinnertime. Is there enough of that deer left?"

"We'll get another," Dritt said, grinning. "This is too important an occasion for leftovers."

They headed for the door, Segnbora walking slowly behind the rest of them. She looked very tired. Herewiss glanced at Freelorn, and Lorn nodded and went off to the back of the hall to be busy elsewhere for a moment.

"Segnbora—"

She turned as Herewiss came up behind her. "Yes?" she said. She held herself proudly erect, as usual, with her hand on her swordhilt. The prideful stance wouldn't have fooled anyone, with or without underhearing.

He reached out, took that terribly capable-looking hand in his and raised it to his lips. "It was a valiant gesture," he said, "even though it didn't work for long. You gave all you had to give, and you bought me the time I needed, one way or the other. Without you we would have all been someone's dinner last night."

She smiled at him, but her eyes were still very tired. "I see what you're saying, Herewiss," she said. "Thank you." He started to let go of her hand, but she bespoke him suddenly. (I'm as sorry for you, though, as I am for myself. You may be fooling the rest of them, even Freelorn perhaps, but not me. Somehow or other, my perceptions tell me, you've paid more for your Power than you'd thought to. And worse than that, though you have the Fire indeed, you also still have all your problems. A new grief to replace your old one, a king to put on his throne without any sure idea of how to do it—and, worst of all, no real idea of what you yourself will do when you're finished with that.)

He stared at her, too incredulous to really hear the compassion in her voice.

She was still smiling faintly, sadly. (They really pushed us at Nháiredi,) she said. (Too hard, I think. See you later.)

She turned, and went outside.

Herewiss walked slowly back to Freelorn, looking sober, and Freelorn nodded and slipped his arms around Herewiss again. "It does seem a shame about her," he said.

"Yeah."

"You never did tell me if this ridiculous chunk of steel had a name."

"Oh, it has," Herewiss said, smiling again, holding the sword up before him. "I haven't done the whole blood-and-four-elements number on it yet—well, actually, it's had the blood—but whatever. Its name is Khávrinen."

"Mmph. Trust you to go for something obscure."

"No, it's in the original Brightwood dialect of Darthene, a few hundred years removed from Nháired. You could render it as HarrowHeart."

"Mmmm…"

"I mean, really, Lorn. Was ever heart harrowed as mine was last night?"

"If it was," Freelorn said with a slow smile, "I'm sure that whoever wrote the ballad about it divorced the emotion from the reality somewhat."

They stood smiling at one another, and Freelorn reached up, took Herewiss's face between his hands, pulled it down, and kissed him long and passionately.

"We've been all over you all day," he said. "I'm going out with them so you can have some time by yourself."

"You know," Herewiss said, "I think I love you."

"And I, you," Freelorn said, and reluctantly—with a longing backward look—hurried out after his people.

The first thing Herewiss did when he got back to the tower room was find the old spear he had carried with him on all his travels since Herelaf's death. Khávrinen made short work of it, and Herewiss threw the splintered remains out the window, chuckling all the while.

The second thing he did was to send word to Hearn about what had happened, while he rooted around in the room for the materials necessary to finish the sword. *The Wardress should be in the Wood this time of month, with the Full Moon just past,* he thought. (Kerim!) he called, digging around in his chest for the sword-fittings he'd been saving.

(What? What? Who's that?)

(It's Herewiss, Lord Hearn's son—)

(Impossible! I smell Flame!)

(Impossible?) Herewiss laughed. (I'll show you impossible!) He bound sight into the linkage between them, and held Khávrinen before his eyes, pushing Flame into it. The sword blazed like a blue noon.

(Dear Mother of Everything—)

(She is that, every bit of it,) Herewiss agreed. (Kerim, will you give my father a message?)

(Why...why, surely, but Herewiss, how, how...)

(Say to Hearn that his son sends him greetings, and bids him know that the Phoenix is risen again, though the fire is blue this time. Say also to him that the name of my focus is Khávrinen. Will you do that?)

(Certainly, but Herewiss—)

(I'll let you have a look at it when I get back to the Wood,) he said. (Be nice to your students, Kerim.)

(But—)

Herewiss cut the contact and found the sword-fittings. "Spark," he said, "I'm going to need—"

He fell silent. A pillar of fire, torn, devoured, gone, and only a dark space where a bright lance of flame had defied the long night.

"Oh," he said, very quietly. "Ohhh..."

He sighed, a sigh with tears in it, and straightened up, regarding the sword-fittings. Gold though they might be, they weren't any good. Khávrinen's metal was as alive as he was, but this stuff was dead. To fasten such onto the sword would be like hanging a corpse around someone's neck. He thought also of Lorn's remark about the length of the blade. "Khávrinen," Herewiss said at last, "if you were a bit shorter in the blade, a foot or so, there'd be enough metal along with the extra in the tang to make a respectable hilt and crosspieces—"

He pushed power into the sword again, and beneath his hands he felt metal flow, though there was no heat. Khávrinen cloaked itself in Fire, possibly self-conscious about changing form in front of him. When the light died down, Herewiss examined it again.

The sword had grown itself a severely plain crosspiece, hardly more than a slim bar of steel, as well as a textured grip and a concave disc-shaped pommel, and for good measure had carved a fuller down the length of its slightly-shortened blade. It had not, however, changed its balance. Herewiss held it in the air, hefting it with satisfaction—

—and felt something stir in the corner by the window. He whirled. *Dammit to Darkness,* he thought, *some Power coming to test me already? I thought I was entitled to at least one day's rest—*

It was faint and weak-feeling, a troubling of the air in the corner, looking like the heat-shimmer above a pavement—

—brightening—

—a wobbling, wavering, exhausted column of fire—Herewiss froze, not even breathing.

(Hello, loved,) said the pale blaze in the corner.

"SUNSPARK!!!"

It smiled at him in slow tired patterns of fire. (Half a moment,) it said. (Let me enflesh—)

At the end of a few seconds it was standing there in the dear familiar blood-bay shape, and Herewiss had his arms around its neck and was hugging it hard. "Sunspark, Sunspark, where have you *been?*" he cried out, leaking tears.

(Coming back,) it said. (This dying,) it added, butting its head up against Herewiss's chest, (it's very interesting. I really must try it again some time.)

"But Spark, those things ate *souls*—!"

(So they did. It was uncomfortable. Though I think I gave them a fair case of indigestion. How long have I been gone?)

"Hardly a day—"

(It seemed longer,) the elemental said, very wearily. (I had some trouble finding my way in the dark. Though I seemed to hear someone calling my Name over this way—)

Herewiss rested his head between Sunspark's ears, his cheek against the golden mane. "Thank You," he said. "Thank You."

(It was nothing,) Sunspark said absently. (How did you manage to survive, by the way?)

Herewiss straightened up, unlaced his arms from around its neck and showed it Khávrinen, gripped in his hand.

(I see. Your focus indeed. And you're changed, too,) Sunspark said, regarding him from golden eyes. (If I ran into you in the middle of nowhere now, I would know you're a relative. You, too, are fire.)

"Well, and a few other things," Herewiss said. "Sunspark, what you did last night—"

(I would do again,) it said. (You are my loved. And anyway, shall I dare less than you?)

Herewiss put his arms around Sunspark's neck again, gathered it close, and wept like a child.

Back in the hold, Freelorn and his people were sitting around the firepit, pledging one another in great drafts of Narchaerid and rr'Damas and Jaráldit wines that Sunspark had filched for them. Herewiss, however, sat cross-legged in the dust about half a mile from the hold, looking at the Moon and stars. Khávrinen was laid across his knees.

(Hearn was right all the time,) he was saying to the night. (Always he used to tell me, 'When you're praying, don't *beg* the Goddess. What mother can stand hearing her children whine at her? Talk to Her, tell Her what's on your mind. You'll *always* get answers back. Lie to Her and you'll get lies back—but tell Her the truth and you'll find solutions.' And he was right. There *is* a part of each of us that is part of You— I just never really saw it until last night—and though it speaks in one's own voice, there's no mistaking the source of the answer.)

Your father is a wise man, the reply drifted back after a while.

Herewiss nodded.

(Herelaf wouldn't tell me what he was for,) he said. (There can, of course, be no deception on that last Shore—and he did tell me that he might not have been finished. Which leaves me with a conclusion that I find frightening. Was he trying to tell me that what he was for—was specifically to be my brother, to die on the end of my sword—and so to begin the events that ended in last night? To make me into what I am now? Was that it?)

The silence drifted around him for a long time.

(It's not an answer I like,) he said.

It is the answers we dislike the most, came the reply, *that tend to have the most truth to them.*

(But, Mother, it isn't *fair!* Not to him, not to me—)

He knew what the answer was going to be. It was spoken with a smile, a sad one. *Who ever said anything was fair, son of Mine? That's My fault, and every time I hear that cry, it goes straight through Me. But next time. Next time—*

He nodded, sighed. (I'm sorry. Mother, I really feel guilty about complaining. I have so very much: the Fire, my Name…and one of Yours, too. That's what I'm *for*—to find the rest of Your Name, as much as to find mine.)

That's a start.

(You're looking too,) he said in sudden realization. (But it is through we who live that You look. And when all who live find their Names, and all the other pieces of Yours—)

Silence. A star fell.

Herewiss smiled. (My life had been so pointed toward one thing that I guess I panicked—I was afraid there would be nothing left for me to do. Béorgan's mistake…. But if this is true, if I'm for seeking out Your Name wherever it is to be found, and freeing it, I'm going to be awfully busy. This is a big world…)

He ran the fingers of one hand up and down Khávrinen's blade again. (Mother, mightn't You have chosen better for the first man to have Flame in all these years? The Fire won't lessen my flaws—they're in danger of getting bigger, if anything. And even with all this Power—and I know I have much more than the average Rodmistress—can I really change the world that much, will I really be worth it? There's so little time, so little of me—)

That, and the voice came firmly as that of a mother taking a sharp knife away from a child, *that evaluation I reserve for Myself. By the common conception of it, humankind doesn't consider something 'worth it' unless they get their investment back, preferably with a profit. By this criterion, most of the Universe is 'not worth it.' But I know*—as do all the others who care—and the voice smiled at Herewiss—*that it's often necessary to give and give and not get back in any way save the knowledge that the worlds are better for it. Freelorn is right, in that respect. Béaneth was right. Béorgan the doomed was right; so were Earn and Healhra and all the others. They* knew *they were doomed, but they did the right thing anyway, trying to make the world better.*

The voice sighed. *Valiant absurdity, lost causes, such things may be doomed to incompletion and failure of one kind or another, but they are none of them 'wasted.' Judge these things by whether they will prolong the Universe's life, or bring joy to what I made, and that is their worth. All things must die, but I will not scatter My poor botched creation like a child kicking over a misbuilt sandcastle. I will make it work the best I can.*

Herewiss nodded.

(What shall I do now?) he asked.

You're asking Me? Herewiss could feel an amused grin stirring somewhere. *What would I do?*

He grinned back. (Share the gift. Defy the Death.)

The answer was silence.

Herewiss stood up and was silent in return for a while as he gazed up at the stars. High above him burned the Moon, chill and silver in the quiet. Down the gray length of the sword, the blue Fire flowed and rippled in the stillness.

Wordlessly, he told the stars and She Who watched his inner Name. It surged in him like fire, and made him blaze with sheer joy, just to say it.

As he did, across the western sky there burned a line of fire, slow and silent. Then another fell, but closer, and another, trails of brilliance all around him, falling stars like rain in summer—burning blue, a storm of starfire, beating on the silver desert. At the white heart of the downpour Herewiss waited, hardly breathing, as he watched the bright rain fall.

Slowly, then, the starfall lessened, passing like a sudden shower— fewer stars and fewer falling, here and there a single stardrop. One last one, vivid blue like Flame, and then the sky was still.

Herewiss breathed out, smiling. "I'll keep Your secret," he said.

He slipped Khávrinen through his belt, and went back to the hold, and Freelorn.

Book Two:

Door into Shadow

For all my parents

*The Wound is healed
by the sword that deals it:*

*the heart is knit
by the pain that breaks it:*

*the life is made whole
by the death that starts it:*

*the death is made whole
by the life that ends it.*

(*Hamartics*, 186)

prologue

Four lands hemmed in by mountain and waste and the Sea—those were the Middle Kingdoms: and the greatest of them, Arlen and Darthen, were in peril of destruction. For seven years Arlen's throne had been empty of the royalty needed to keep the land fertile and the people at peace. And Darthen suffered as a result of Arlen's lack, for the Two Lands were bound together by oaths of friendship and by joint maintenance of the royal sorceries that kept their lands safe from the ever-present menace of the Shadow.

In those days there appeared a man with the blue Fire—not just the spark of Flame that every man and woman possesses, but enough to channel and use to change the world around him. His lover was the child of Arlen's last king, heir to his usurped throne. In the Firebearer's relationship to Freelorn, King Ferrant's son, many later saw the Goddess's hand. She had been working quietly, so as not to alarm Her old adversary the Shadow.

Her hand seemed visible elsewhere too. Freelorn had taken companions with him into his exile. They lived as outlaws and bandits, stealing what they needed when they had to—though none of their hearts were in it. One of them in particular would certainly have been elsewhere, if she had had a choice. Swordswoman and sorceress, trained in the Silent Precincts and in every other place in the Kingdoms that dealt in the use of the blue Fire that some women bear, Segnbora d'Welcaen tai-Enraesi was a spectacular and expensive failure. She had the Flame in prodigious quantity, and couldn't focus it. On her way home from one more school that couldn't do anything for her, chance threw her together with Freelorn's people one night. Bitterly frustrated with what seemed a wasted life, desperately needing something useful to do, Segnbora swore fealty that night to the rightful heir of the Arlene throne, and fled with him and his people into the eastern Waste where Freelorn's loved, Herewiss, awaited him.

The children of House tai-Enraesi traditionally had a talent for getting themselves into dangerous situations. There in the Waste, in an ancient pile built by no human hand—a fortress rising gray and bizarre out of the empty land, skewed and blind-walled and ominous—Segnbora started wondering whether even the tai-Enraesi luck would do her any good. There were stories about this place, about soul-eating monsters that guarded innumerable doors into Otherwheres. Even the mildest of the tales was gruesome. Fear gripped Segnbora, but her oath gripped her harder. She stayed with Freelorn and his people.

And there in the Hold, fulfilling her fears, the stories she had heard came true—even the one of how nothing good would come out of this terrible place until (ridiculous improbability) a male should focus his Fire.

On the night Herewiss declared his intention to use his newly gained Flame to put Freelorn on the throne of his fathers, Segnbora lay long awake in the dark, considering the old rede that spoke of her family's luck. That luck would run out some day, the rede said, when the last of her line died by his or her own hand, in a time of ice and darkness. But at last she was sure that the rede had nothing to do with her. She wasn't the last of the tai-Enraesi, and she was about to ride out of here with three good friends, a sometime lover, a prince about to retake his throne, a fire elemental, and the first man in a thousand years to focus his Fire. So maybe, maybe just this once, everything was finally going to turn out all right…

 *one*

Sirronde stared at the Goddess. "Are You saying, then, that You were wrong to make heroes?"

"Indeed not," She said. "But I should have warned them —if you save the world too often, it starts to expect it."

>   Tales of the Darthene South,
>   book iv, 29

When she was studying in the Silent Precincts, the Rodmistresses had warned her: if you're going to look for meaning in a dream, first make sure it's your own. Any sensitive is most sensitive in her sleep, and others' dreams can draw you in and fool you. Now, therefore, Segnbora kept quite still and silent so as not to disturb whoever else was dreaming the landscape into which she had stumbled. It wasn't often, after all, that one was privileged to see the Universe being created.

The Maiden was working, as She always is, while the other two Persons of the Goddess, the Mother and the Eldest, looked on. Young and fair and preoccupied was the Maiden, as She worked elbow-deep in stars and flesh and dirt. She was so delighted with the wild diversity of Her creation that She never noticed the Mother and the Eldest desperately trying to get Her attention. They saw what she did not: the shapeless, lurking hunger that hid in the darkness at the Universe's borders.

Finally the Maiden, satisfied that Her world was complete, cried out the irrevocable Word that started life running on its own, and sealed the Universe against any subtractions. And the instant She had done so, Death stood up from where it had been hiding, and laughed at Her.

She had locked the doors of the world, and had locked Death in. Slowly it would suck the Universe dry of life, and She could not prevent it. Nor could She prevent Death's darkness from casting shadows sideways from Her light—rogue aspects of Her, darksides, bent on destroying more swiftly what was already doomed. Grief-stricken, the Maiden took counsel with Her otherselves to find some way to combat death. Among Them, They invented first the heart's love, and then the body's—lying down together in the manner of woman with woman, and becoming with child.

The Maiden, becoming the Mother now, brought forth twins—sons, or daughters, or daughter and son; the ambivalence of the dream made the Firstborn seem all of these at once. Swiftly They grew, and discovered love in Their Mother's arms—then turned to one another and discovered it anew. But in the midst of Their bliss, surrounded by the blue Fire that was Their Mother's gift and Their pride, the Death stood up again. It entered one of the Lovers and taught that one jealousy.

The shadowed Lover slew the innocent One—and in the same act destroyed Its own Fire, which had been bound by love to the Other's. Cursing, the Dark Lover fled raging into the outer darkness, where It would reenact Its murder and loss and bereavement for as long as the Universe should last. It was not a Lover anymore, but the Shadow.

In the dream Segnbora wept, having known all along what was going to happen, and that mortals would be reenacting this tragedy in their own lives forever. The dream broke, then, and gradually reformed as an image in water does when a stone is thrown in.

She saw a scene skewed sideways, as if her head rested on someone's shoulder. Much of the great room where she stood was dark, but in her hand—which had become a man's—she held a core of blinding white light, wreathed all about with flames as blue as summer sky. *Herewiss,* she realized. *Last night.*

His weariness was so terrible he could barely stand. He had banished the hralcins, the soul-eaters, yet he was too tired to exult in the focus he had forged—the unfinished sword he would call Khávrinen. He was the first man in a thousand years to focus the Fire, and he knew what difficulties lay ahead. The Shadow would not long tolerate him, or any man who enjoyed the Power It had cast away. It would deal with him quickly, before the Goddess had time, through him, to consolidate newly regained ground.

We must move more quickly, then, the dream said. *For look what the Shadow has planned.* Segnbora shuddered in her sleep at the sight of a whole valley suddenly buried under mountains that had formerly stood above it. *Dead,* a voice said soundlessly. *She's dead.* Snow whirled wildly down onto a battlefield under the mountains' shadow, where something heaved as if trying to take terrible shape, and the snow turned red as soon as it fell, while monsters gnawed the dead. Elsewhere a wave of blackness came rolling down out of murky heights, crashed down onto a leaping, threatening fire, and smothered it.

The air was thick with the feel of ancient sorceries falling apart, fraying. Grass forgot how to grow. Grain rotted on the stalk and fruit on the bough. Plague downed beasts and people alike, leaving their blackened corpses to lie splitting in the sun. Even the scavenger birds sickened and died of what they ate. It was happening already, happening now. The royal magics were failing. If they weakened enough to let the Shadow fully into this world, into Bluepeak, this outcome was inevitable, irreversible.

The soundless voice of the dream spoke urgently. *Freelorn must see to the Royal Bindings quickly. This is the work for which he was made; he's the Lion's Child, heir to Arlen. Go with him, Herewiss, in the full of your Power. Use the Fire to the utmost. He'll need all the help you can give.*

But I just got the Fire, Herewiss said, terrified. *It takes time to master it.*

There is no time. What must be done needs doing now. The Other is coming!

And she could feel it, that throbbing of hatred in the background, getting stronger by the minute. The sky grew dark, and the snow blasted about them, in that place to which they would have to go to reinforce the Royal Bindings. Herewiss's Fire, for so long a blaze within him, was now going faint under a blanket of oppressive power. Just in front of him, Freelorn started to stand up. The whole dream focused then on the sight of Freelorn's back, with a three-barbed, razor-sharp Reaver arrow standing out of it.

Sagging, Lorn sank back slowly against Herewiss. Then a deeper darkness fell, and the two of them stood before a Door in which burned the stars that would never go out. Freelorn, his face in shadow, was pulling his hand gently out of Herewiss's grasp, turning away toward death's Door.

No!

Do what you must to come to the full of your Power. There's no time! Her voice was almost frightened. Herewiss had never believed She could sound that way.

But if I do—and we get there—then Lorn—
It must not be prevented.
But—
You must not attempt to prevent it!
I—
Hurry!
NO!!

The scream tore through her own throat as she sat bolt upright in the bedroll, sweating—still seeing against the darkness the long ruinous fall of an entire mountain, still hearing the crash of it, first note in a song of disaster.

In the great main hall of the old Hold, people fumbled frantically for their swords—the memory of the hralcins' sudden arrival the night before was very fresh. The fire in the firepit rose up too, putting several broad curves of flame over the edge and leaning anxiously out to see what was the matter. As a fire elemental, Sunspark had not had much experience with fear, but after last night it was apparently taking no chances.

Segnbora lifted a hand to her pounding head and found that she was holding her sword, Charriselm. Evidently she had drawn it while still half sleeping. Beside her in the bedroll, blond Lang was still blanket-wrapped, but nevertheless he had found his gracekeknife in a hurry. Lying propped on one elbow with the knife in one ham of a hand, he blinked at her like an anxious owl. A few feet away, big swarthy Dritt and lanky Moris were sitting up back to back, looking as panicked as Segnbora felt. On the other side of the firepit, Harald was attempting simultaneously to string his bow and brush the brown hair out of his eyes. All of these looked at Segnbora as if they thought she was crazy.

"A bad dream?" Lang said.

She nodded, sliding Charriselm back into its sheath and looking across the room toward the firepit and the bedrolls laid down there.

Herewiss was sitting up, bracing himself with one hand, rubbing his eyes with the other. He took the hand away from his face, and Segnbora was shocked to see his terrified expression. Lorn was holding Herewiss tight and peering worriedly into his face. Under other circumstances it could have been a touching and humorous sight—the little, dark-mustachioed, fierce-eyed man comforting someone who, judged by his slim hard build and well-muscled shoulders, might have been the village blacksmith.

"Are you all right? What happened?"

"It was a dream," Herewiss said, his voice anguished.

"Shh, it's all right."

"No, it's not." Herewiss rubbed his eyes again, then glanced around him with frightened determination. He started searching in the blankets for his clothes. "We've got to go."

"What?"

"We have to hurry."

Herewiss grabbed one bunched-up blanket and impatiently shook it. A sword fell out and clattered to the floor—a hand-and-a-half broadsword of gray steel that would have seemed of ordinary make except for the odd blue sheen about it. He reached out for it, and at his touch his Power ran down the blade: blinding blue Fire, twisting and flurrying about in bright reflection of his distress.

"It was—there was—the mountain fell down, just like that. And there were thousands of Fyrd, and bigger monsters too—and a wave came down over everything, and Sunspark went out—"

(I did *not!*)

"Loved, slow down so I can understand what the Dark you're talking about—"

"So much for a whole night's sleep," Lang muttered under his breath. Putting his knife away under the rolled-up cloak that was serving them as pillow, he lay down again. "Wake me up when they're finished?"

"If necessary," Segnbora said, rubbing his shoulder absently. The gesture was more for her comfort than for his. Her underhearing was wide awake, bringing her the hot coppery blood-taste of Herewiss's fright as if it were her own.

Herewiss had yanked a shirt out of the blankets and was struggling into it, while in his lap Khávrinen kept on blazing like a torch. "It's angry as anything," he was saying. "And It's going to work the worst mischief It can, by putting pressure on the Royal Bindings that have been keeping It in check." He started feeling around for his britches. "For seven years no one's reinforced the Arlene half of those bindings, and they're wearing thin—"

Freelorn glanced away from Herewiss. Segnbora put her hands behind her and leaned back, closing her eyes and bracing herself against the gut-punch of grief and anger she knew would come from Lorn. When his father had died on the throne, and the Minister of the Exchequer, Cillmod, had taken the opportunity to seize power, Freelorn had fled for his life with a price on his head. Now Lorn would wonder again whether staying in Arlen to see to the Bindings, and possibly getting killed as a result, might not have been the more noble course. This was an old midnight pain that Segnbora had come to know as well as the arthritis in Harald's right knee, or Dritt's self-consciousness about his weight. While no Precinct-trained sensitive could have helped underhearing her surroundings as Segnbora did, that was the gift she would have been happiest to lose when she gave up her studies. She had enough trouble dealing with her own pains.

"Lorn, enough," Herewiss said, catching Freelorn's anguish too. "The fact remains that if the Shadow leans Its full strength against the Bluepeak bindings, we're done for. The Kingdoms will founder. I saw the southern passes full of Reaver armies. And the plains full of Fyrd. There were storms and earthquakes, and where the earth opened a whole town fell in. And that cliff at Bluepeak—" Herewiss broke off.

Freelorn, still holding him close, looked puzzled. "But it was just a dream!"

"Oh no," Herewiss said, shaking his head emphatically. "I *saw.*"

"He's dreaming true," Segnbora said.

Freelorn's frightened eyes flicked to her. "He's focused now," she said. "It's one of the first things that happens…"

"What about the cliff?" Freelorn said to Herewiss.

Herewiss closed his eyes and sagged back on his heels, looking tired. "It was snowing—"

"A month and a half before Midsummer's? You call that dreaming true?"

With a great effort Segnbora held her face still as Herewiss saw again that image of Freelorn turning away from him, away from love and life toward death. "Lorn," Herewiss said. "I was shown a lot of things. I don't know what they all meant. I don't think most of them have happened yet. But some of them will, unless they're prevented." He swallowed hard. "I have to assist in the process. I was given all this Power. Now it has to be used, fully, and I won't be able to take my time about its mastery, either."

Freelorn looked askance at his loved, getting an idea and not liking it. "But what other way is there, but to work into your Power slowly?"

"The Morrowfane, Lorn."

Freelorn looked grim. "I've done a little reading on the subject," he said, and this was likely a great understatement, for among the responsibilities of a throne prince of Arlen was the curatorship of rr'Virendir, the Arlene royal library, which dwelt at length on such subjects. "All the sources say you can't go up there without coming down changed—"

(What's the problem with that?) Sunspark said from the firepit. The reaction was understandable; change was a fire elemental's chief delight. (Just yesterday Herewiss changed—quite a bit—and you didn't mind.)

Lorn glanced with annoyance at Sunspark as the elemental radiated smugness at him. Freelorn's discovery that Sunspark had also come to be a loved of Herewiss's during the time spent forging Khávrinen had left him with reactions that were complex, and far from settled.

"I don't mean shapechanges," Lorn said with exaggerated patience. "Soul-changes. Great alterations in personality. Madness, or types of sanity that human beings don't usually survive."

"The change needn't be harmful," Herewiss put in. "Remember, the place is a great repository of Flame. All the legends agree on that. Those who climb the Fane are given what's needed to do what they must do in life."

"Then why do so few people go up it?"

"For one thing, you need focused Fire, and enough of it to keep the Power of the place from blasting you," Herewiss explained. "For another, very few people *want* what they need...Lorn, listen. This is necessary. It's part of getting you back on your throne. If we don't get to Bluepeak by Midyear's Eve, so that you can aid in restoring the bindings, there won't be a country left for you to rule."

"But I was never Initiated into the Mysteries. If I had been, we wouldn't have these problems—I'd be King, and that slimy bastard Cillmod would be out looking for a situation."

"True, but you know the royal rites, don't you? You have to do it."

"Who says?"

"Who do you think?" Herewiss said, very gently. "When you dream true, Who do you think sends the dream?"

Lorn held very still, and most of the fierceness faded out of his eyes. "There's another problem. You know the money I removed from the Arlene treasury in Osta? Well, Bluepeak's in Arlen too. Cillmod's probably annoyed about that missing money, and if we go back to Arlen so soon, and he hears about it..."

Herewiss said nothing.

After a moment or two, Freelorn shrugged. "Oh, what the Dark! If the Reavers and the Shadow are going to come down on Arlen, Cillmod hardly matters. I suppose I have no choice anyway. I swore that damn Oath when I was little. 'Darthen's House and Arlen's Hall—'"

"'—share their feast and share their fall,'" Herewiss finished. "If Arlen goes, so does Darthen. And after them Steldin, North Arlen, the Brightwood…"

Freelorn laughed, but without merriment. "Why am I even worried about Cillmod? The Shadow's a far greater danger. It can't afford to leave you alive now. You're the embodiment of the old days before the Catastrophe, when males had the Power. The time of Its decline…"

Herewiss shook his head and smiled, an expression more of grim agreement than of reassurance. "We'll both be careful," he said. "That is, if you're coming with me?…"

Reaching down, Freelorn gently freed one of Herewiss's hands from Khávrinen's hilt, and held the hand between his own. "No more dividing our forces," he said. "From now until it's done, we go together."

Herewiss held his peace and didn't change expression. Segnbora had to drop her eyes, seeing again that image of one hand that let go of another's, the face that turned away.

All at once Freelorn was thumping on the floor for attention. "Listen, people—"

Segnbora nudged Lang. He rolled over under his covers. "Whatever you say, Lorn, I'll do it," he said, and pulled the blanket back over his head.

"There's a man who takes his oaths a little too seriously," Freelorn said with a grimace of affectionate disgust. "On his own head be it. But for the rest of you—I can't in good conscience ask you to go on this trip. The Shadow—"

"The Shadow can go swive with sheep for all I care," Moris said with one of his slow grins. "I haven't come this far with you to stop now."

"Me either," Harald said, stubbornly folding his huge bear's arms.

"You're not listening," Freelorn said, in great earnest. "Your oaths are a matter of friendship and I love you for them. But it's not just Cillmod we're playing with now. It's the Shadow. Your *souls* are at stake."

"The things that were in here last night ate souls too," Dritt said calmly, putting his chin down on his arms. "Herewiss did for *them* all right."

(I helped,) said the voiceless voice from the firepit. Eyes looked out of the flames at the company, then came to rest with calm interest on Freelorn. (I'm coming too.)

The building rumble of irritation in the room, combined with so much unspoken affection, was making Segnbora's head ache; the walls of this place, opaque to thought, bounced the emotions back and forth until the undersenses were deafened by echoes.

"Look," she said, shaking free of her own blankets. "If we've got to get an early start in the morning—" She glanced at Herewiss. "—it *can* wait until morning?"

"I suppose so," he said.

"Good. Then I want some sleep." She went over to Freelorn in her shift, drawing Charriselm again as she came, and offered him the blade's hilt about an inch from his nose, while giving Lorn a look suggesting that perhaps that was where she meant to insert it. "You swore on this, on *all* our blades, that your lordship would be between us and the Shadow while we wielded them in your service. You want to take that oath back?"

Lorn glared up at her, fierce eyes going fiercer, *"No!* Are you crazy? What makes you think I'd—"

"What makes you think *we* would?"

Freelorn held absolutely still. His anger churned wildly for a moment, then fell off, leaving reluctant acceptance in its place.

Segnbora shoved Charriselm back into its sheath. "Good night, Lorn," she said, and padded back to her bedroll, taking care not to smile until her back was turned.

Sunspark pulled itself back down into the firepit as people settled themselves again. Soon the darkness of the hall held no sound but Harald's cloak-muffled snoring.

It took Segnbora a little while to get enough of the blankets unwrapped from around Lang to cover herself. That done, she lay on her back for a long while, gazing up at the smoke-shaft in the ceiling, through which a few unfamiliar stars shone. Her underhearing, sharpened by all the excitement, brought her the faint dream-touched emotions of those falling asleep, and the physical sensations of those asleep already: breathing, the slide of muscles, muted pulse-thunder.

It's a gift, she told herself for the thousandth time. *Appreciate it.* Truth, however, reared its head. The talent was a nuisance. If her Fire was focused, as Herewiss's was, she wouldn't be having this problem… *If.* Segnbora exhaled sharply at her useless obsession with what she couldn't have. Her Flame wasn't focused. It never would be. She had given up. Other things had become more important now. Oaths, for example.

It seemed like a long time ago. *All of a month,* she thought—a busy month full of desperate rides, escapes, sorcery, terror, wonder. All started by a chance meeting in a smelly alley, when she had stumbled on a dark fierce little man losing a swordfight to the crude but powerful axework of a Royal Steldene guard. The small man looked as if he was about to be split like kindling. She had intervened. The guardsman never saw the shadow who stepped in from behind.

Over the course of the evening, she found she had rescued family; though the tai-Enraesi were only a small, poor cadet branch of the Darthene royal line, and strangers to court, the Oath of Lion and Eagle was binding on them too, and a king's son of Arlen was therefore a brother.

The relationship got more complex with time, however. On the road Segnbora had shared herself with Freelorn, as she sometimes did with the others, for delight or consolation. But before that, more importantly, came friendship, and the oaths. *Before Maiden and Bride and Mother I swear it, before the Lovers in Their power, and in the Dark One's despite: My sword will be between you and the Shadow until you pass the Door into Starlight.*

She exhaled quietly. Her determination was set.

There has to be a way.

There has to.

You're *not going to get him…*

After a while, as she lay at last near the brink of sleep, Segnbora sensed something shining. She opened one eye. Across the room sat a form sculpted of darkness and deep blue radiance—Herewiss, cross-legged, shoulders hunched wearily as he gazed down at the sleeping Freelorn. Across his lap lay his sword, wrapped about with curling flames the color of a twilight burning low.

She lay unmoving, regarding him. Eventually the thought came, tasting as if it had been soaked in tears and wrung out. (You know, don't you.)

(Yes.) She felt sorrow still, and now a touch of embarrassment. (Sorry. You know how it is with dreams.)

(No matter. I've been in a few others' dreams myself.)

(The scales are even, then.)

He nodded. Herewiss didn't look up, but his attention was fixed so intensely upon her that no stare could have been more discomfiting.

(You understand what you're getting into?) he said. (It may not be just Lorn heading for that Door. Probably me too. Maybe all of us will have to die so the Kingdoms can go on living.)

(Those who defeat the Shadow,) Segnbora said silently, (usually die of it. It's in all the stories.)

(Defeat!) Now he raised his head. His look was pained at first, then incredulous.

(I love him too,) she said.

(You're as crazy as the rest of us,) Herewiss said. The thought was sour, but there was a thread of amusement on it like the bright edge of a knife. He threw her a quick image of herself as she had been the night before, when the air in the hall had been full of the stink of hralcins. As the monsters had come shambling across the floor toward them she had stood frozen on the brink of panic, unable to do even the smallest sorcery. All she'd been able to do was stand shaking before the advance of the screaming horrors, and make blinding light—a byproduct of her blocked Fire—until even that guttered out, exhausted.

Segnbora bit the inside of her cheek, pained by the image regardless of the compassion of Herewiss's viewpoint. (What we're facing,) he said, (is the father of those things, and worse—the Maker of Enmities, the engenderer of the shadows at the bottoms of our hearts, Who can overturn the world in fire and storm. You have some new defense that you've come up with since last night? A strategy sufficient to stop a being so powerful that to be rid of it the Goddess Herself can only let the Universe run down and die?) The irony was gentle, but it was there.

(I plan to win,) Segnbora said at last. (What are *you* going to do?)

He looked across the room at her for a while, still not moving. (I'm glad you're here,) he said finally. (I can't tell *him* about this—) A quick thought, a flicker of the shape of an arrowhead, passed between them. (I hope you won't either.)

Segnbora shook her head.

Herewiss straightened, laid Khávrinen aside. Away from its source, the Fire in the blade died down to the merest glow. Only in his hands did a little Flame remain burning. Looking down at

Freelorn, Herewiss absently began to pour it from hand to hand. Like burning water it flowed, the essence of life, the stuff of shapechanges and mastery of elements and magics of the heart, the Goddess's gift to the Lovers and to humankind: the Power that founded the world, that the Shadow had lost and caused men to lose.

And there's nothing It hates more, Segnbora thought to herself. *Though love probably comes close.*

She closed her eyes to the light of Herewiss's hands, shuddered, and went to sleep.

two

...ere the Dark could spredde so far as to kyll all Powre and thought...there fled to Lake Rilthor that was holie, the men and womyn gretest of Fire aft that time. And of theyre greate might and Powyre, that those whoo came after the Darke should learn agayn the wrekings of those auncient daies, those Wommen and Men did drive their Flame down intoo the mount at the Lak's heart; and all dyed there, that Fyre might bee spared from the Darrk for those to comm after. Therefore it ys called Morrow-fane.

(Of the Dayes of Travaile, ms. xix, in rr'Virendir, Prydon)

...they say that after the Error, there the Maiden lay down in love with Her other Selves, celebrating the Great Marriage. In the joy of that sharing, the Fire with which She creates flowed forth and sank deep in earth and stone, so that to this day the Fane burns with it. And those who dare to climb the Fane share in that first Sharing themselves, becoming Her Lovers as well: and as in that first sharing, their need is filled, and new life is given them...

Book of Places of Power, ch. 3

It is the Heart of the World: there is no other.

(d'Elthed, *Reflections in the Silent Precincts*, 6)

In the long west-reaching shadow of the glittering gray walls that rose a hundred fathoms high, fourteen figures stood: seven riders, and six horses, and a creature that looked like a blood-bay stallion, but wasn't. Dawn was barely over, and the morning was still cool. The vast expanse of the Waste all around—sand and rubble and salt pans—was sharp and bright in the crisp air. But behind them the Hold from which they had departed wavered and shimmered uncannily, as if in the heat of noon.

"Be glad to be out of here," Lang muttered from beside Segnbora.

She nodded, yanking absently at her mare Steelsheen's reins to keep her from biting Lang's dapple-gray, Gyrfalcon. The Hold unnerved Segnbora too. The Old People from whom the humans of the Middle Kingdoms were said to be descended had wrought with their Fire on an awesome scale. Within those slick and jointless towering walls, odd buildings reared up—skewed towers, blind of windows; stairs that started in midair and went nowhere; steps staggered in such a way as to suggest that the builders, or those who used the building, had more legs than humans; more rooms inside the inner buildings than their outer walls could possibly contain.

And worst of all, or best, the place was full of doors—entrances into other worlds. There were also gateways to other places in this world, and doors into areas not even classifiable as worlds or places. People could go out those doors and return. People, or things, could come in them, as the hralcins had. Segnbora shivered.

"You sure you can pull this off?" Freelorn was saying nervously to Herewiss.

"Mmmph," Herewiss said. He was standing with Khávrinen unsheathed, and seemed to be minutely examining a patch of empty air three feet in front of him. The Fire that ran down from his hand flooded the length of Khávrinen, leaping out from it in quick tongues that stretched out and snapped back, reflecting his concentration.

Behind Herewiss, Sunspark extended its magnificent head to nibble teasingly at the sleeve of Freelorn's surcoat, leaving singed places where it bit. (You have to be careful, doing worldgating inside a world,) it said, sounding smug. (Don't distract him.)

Freelorn smacked the elemental's nose away and got a scorched hand for his pains. "He could have used one of the doors in the Hold. Now he's got to use his Flame—"

(It's simpler doing it yourself,) Sunspark said. It knew about such things, having been a traveler among worlds before love had bound it to Herewiss's service. (And more reliable. Those doors are complex...it would have taken quite a while to figure them out. Don't complain.)

"I'm *not.*"

Segnbora restrained an urge toward amusement. Sunspark had done perhaps more than any of them to save all their lives two nights before, holding the hralcins off until Herewiss could break through into his Flame. It had done so specifically because it knew Herewiss loved Freelorn, and would have been in anguish if he died. But Sunspark seemed determined not to admit its motives to Lorn— from caution, or for the sake of sheer deviltry, it was impossible to tell.

Herewiss stood scowling at the air he had been examining, or whatever lay beyond it. It was dangerous, this business of opening doors to go from one place to another. Gates, when opened, tended to tear as wide as they could. A person doing a wreaking had to maintain complete control, or risk ending up in a world that looked exactly like the one he wanted to journey in, but with minor differences—a differing past or future, say, or familiar people missing.

Segnbora was not happy that one man was trying to pull off a gating by himself, and in such an unprotected place. All her previous experiences with worldgates had been in the Silent Precincts, where safe-wreakings bound every leaf and blade of grass about the Forest Altars. Always there had been ten or twenty senior Rodmistresses on call to assist if there was trouble, and never had a gate been held open long enough for so many to pass through. She hoped Herewiss knew what he was doing.

Herewiss didn't move, but from where Khávrinen's point rested against the ground, a sudden runnel of blue Fire uncoiled like a snake and shot out across the sand. It put down swift roots to anchor itself, then leaped upward into the air. The atmosphere prickled with ruthlessly constrained Power as the line of blue light described a doorway as tall as Herewiss and twice as wide. When the frame was complete the Fire ran back along its doorsill and reached upward again, this time branching out like ivy on an unseen trellis, filling the doorway with a network that steadily grew more complex. In a few breaths' time the door became one solid, pulsing panel of blue.

Sweat stood on Herewiss's face. "Now," he said, still unmoving.

The blue winked out, all but the outline. From beyond the door a wet-smelling wind struck out and smote them all in the face. Lake Rilthor, their destination, lay in the lowlands, a thousand feet closer to sea level than the Waste. Through the door Segnbora saw green grass, and a soft rolling meadow leading down toward a silver-hazed lake, within which a hill was half-hidden.

"Go on," Herewiss said, and his voice sounded strained. "Don't take all day."

They led their horses through as quickly as they could, though not as quickly as they wanted to, for without exception the horses tried to put their heads down to graze as soon as they passed the doorway, and had to be pulled onward to let the others through. At last Segnbora was able to pull through the reluctant Steelsheen. She was followed closely by Herewiss and Sunspark, behind whom the door winked out with a very audible slam of sealed-in air.

Segnbora turned to compliment Herewiss and found him half-collapsed over Sunspark's back, with Freelorn supporting him anxiously from one side. He looked like a man who had just run a race; his breath went in and out in great racking gasps, and his face was nearly gray.

"I thought there would be no more backlash once you got your Fire!" Freelorn said.

Herewiss rolled his head from side to side on the saddle, unable for several moments to find enough breath with which to reply. "Different," he said, "different problem," and began to cough.

Freelorn pounded his back ineffectually while Segnbora and the others looked on.

When the coughing subsided, Herewiss rested his head on the saddle again, still gasping. "—open too wide," he said.

"What? The gate?"

"No. Me."

Confused, Freelorn looked at Segnbora. "Do you know what he's talking about?"

She nodded. "In a worldgating, the gate isn't really the physical shape you see. The gate is in your mind—the 'door' shape is just a physical expression of it. When you open a gate, you're actually throwing your soul wide open. Anything can get out. And anything can get in. It's not pleasant."

"I can't hear anything," Dritt muttered.

"Swallow," Herewiss said. "Your ears'll pop." At last, his strength returning, he looked around with satisfaction. "You're better than I am with distances, Lorn. How far from Lake Rilthor would you say we are?"

Freelorn shaded his eyes, looking first at the Sun to orient himself. "It's a little higher—"

"Of course. We're sixty leagues west."

Freelorn looked southwest toward the lake, and to the mist-girdled peak rising from its waters. "Four miles, I'd say."

"That's about what I wanted," Herewiss said, pleased. "Not bad for a first gating."

"It's so quiet," Harald said, looking around suspiciously.

"It's a holy place," said Moris, unruffled and matter-of-fact as always.

Segnbora looked around at the silent green country, agreeing, opening out her undersenses to the effect of this place. Like most fanes or groves or great altars, the Morrowfane made you feel that Someone was watching—Someone who would only speak using the heart's own voice. Yet the feeling here was less personified, more awful, than any she'd experienced before. Above everything hung a waiting silence, as when the hawk sails high and no bird sings. Below the silence was a slow, steady throbbing of incalculable power, as if the world's heart beat nearby. A ruthless benevolence slept at the center of Lake Rilthor, and slept lightly. It was no wonder that there wasn't a town or a farm or even a sheepfold for miles around.

—It was not a smell, or a feeling, or a vision precisely, that started to creep up on her. Segnbora stood up straight, glancing around at the others. None of them had sensed what she had. Herewiss and Freelorn were leaning against Lorn's dun, Blackmane, together, speaking quietly; Moris and Dritt had walked off a little way to look southwest at the Fane; Lang was rubbing down the perpetually sweaty Gyrfalcon; Harald was seeing to yellow-coated Swallow's cinches. Sunspark had disappeared on some mysterious errand of its own.

She turned and looked east, her hand dropping to Charriselm's hilt. There it was again, another flash of othersight—vague and odd, focus bizarrely rounded, colors all awry. And smell too, acrid, terrible, enraging. *That's familiar, I know that—*

Then the memory found her: that one time in the Precincts when the novices, carefully supervised, were allowed to shapechange and feel what a beast's body was like. "Herewiss!" Segnbora said, turning to him in alarm.

He put his head up to the wind, gazing eastward as she had, but saw nothing.

"You just did a wreaking," she said. "You may still be overloaded. *Taste it!*"

Herewiss closed his eyes and reached out his undersenses. Segnbora did too, standing swaying in the long grass, and caught the impression again, stronger this time. Now there was something even more unnerving added to the flash of skewed viewpoint: *thought*, stunted and twisted and bizarre, but thought. And it was all of hate.

The mind she touched bounded above the whipping grass for a moment. It saw forms on the horizon, the source of a maddening stench.

She heard a cough, opened her eyes to see Herewiss choking as he tried to speak. His empathy must have been more profound than hers, for the remembered shape of the runner's throat was keeping the words from getting out. "Fyrd!" he croaked at last, and pushed away from Blackmane, hurriedly unsheathing Khávrinen.

Segnbora's eyes widened. "But that was thinking! Fyrd are Shadow-twisted, but they're just beasts. They don't *think!*"

"My move's been anticipated," Herewiss said bitterly. He swung Khávrinen sideways, whipping a great brilliance of Fire angrily down the blade. "Our enemy's a step ahead of me—and mocking me, too."

Segnbora understood. At Bluepeak, long ago, the Shadow had driven that first terrible breed of thinking Fyrd down from the mountain country into the Kingdoms. Far more dangerous than the first noxious things It had twisted out of the beasts of ancient days, these Fyrd had the cunning of warriors. It had taken the Transformation, in which Earn and Healhra burned away their very forms and their mortality, to exterminate that breed. And now, for Herewiss's sake, here they were again—

Steel scraped out of sheaths all around as movement became visible in the high grass to the east. Segnbora's under-senses brought her more and more clearly the experience of their hungry rage. The hunters knew their quarry was human, and hated them for it. They were coming to do murder.

"Dammit," Herewiss muttered, "Sunspark, where are you when I need you?!" But no answering thought came, and Herewiss hefted Khávrinen grimly. Only two days forged, and already the sword would be tasting blood.

There was little time to prepare. One moment the dark backs were jolting closer and closer through the tall grass; the next, with a wave of grunts and screeches, the Fyrd were upon them. Segnbora found herself holding her blade too high to guard against a maw that was suddenly springing at her throat. She threw herself sideways. Jaws went *snick!* in the air above where she had been. She hit the ground, rolled, found her footing, sprang up again. The maw hit the turf where she'd rolled. For a moment it tore the ground with teeth and talons, its hunched back to her. That was all she needed. Choosing her spot Segnbora swung Charriselm up, sliced down through thick flesh to the shock of bone. The maw writhed and screamed once, its half-severed head flopping into the grass. She paid it no more heed, simply whipped the blood off Charriselm and swung around to find another foe. There were certain to be plenty—

—More maws, five or six of them, broad and round with piggish, wicked eyes; several keplian, horse-looking things with carnivores' teeth and three razory toes on each forefoot; other shapes less identifiable. The standard Fyrd varieties had been twisted further away from the animals they had anciently been. Segnbora forgot about specifics and dove away from the spring of one maw, took another one across the chest with a two-handed stroke and was knocked down by its momentum. *Move, move, as long as you're moving you're safe!* she remembered her old sword-instructor Shíhan shouting at her.

Off to her left she heard Steelsheen scream in defiance and crash into a Fyrd; a skull crunched, wet, crushed by hooves. At the same time Segnbora got a pinwheeling glimpse of Khávrinen jerking up in Herewiss's hands after a downstroke. A half-seen form came at her low and sideways—Segnbora chopped at it, a poorly aimed blow that slid off hard smooth plates. Hissing, the nadder's gigantic serpent-head rose up before her, then struck. She danced desperately aside, swung scythe-style at it and chopped off the head at the neck.

Segnbora turned away and looked around. Khávrinen struck downward again, and as it struck both Herewiss and the keplian he had killed moaned aloud. The Fire wavering about those parts of the blade not yet obscured illuminated Herewiss's face. *Tears?*

Segnbora thought, though not entirely in surprise. Khávrinen was more of a symbol than a weapon, and Herewiss was no killer—

Steelsheen trampled another maw, and Moris nailed the last one to the ground with a two-handed straight-down thrust. Finally everyone was standing still, panting, sagging, wiping blood out of their eyes.

"More coming!" Segnbora said, wanting to moan out loud at the feeling of yet another of those hot, hating minds heading their way from the north. The source was still a hundred yards away, but showing much more of itself above the grass than had the other Fyrd. Segnbora recognized it, and her heart constricted in terror. She'd never seen one of these, but if the stories of the creatures' endurance were true, this one could afford to take its time.

"Oh Goddess," whispered Freelorn from beside her. "A deathjaw!"

"With the Fire," Herewiss said between gasps, "possibly—" He lifted Khávrinen again, but there was no great hope in the gesture. Deathjaws were so fearsome that there was only one way to successfully hunt them: stake out a human being as bait, and hide a Rodmistress close by to do a brainburn when the thing got close enough. *We've got plenty of bait,* Segnbora thought, *but he doesn't know the protocol for a brainburn. If he did, he'd be doing it.*

The shambling form was closer. "Run for it," Herewiss said, sounding very calm.

Everyone hesitated.

"I mean it!"

Lang turned, and Moris, and Harald, but they were slow about retreating. Freelorn didn't move from beside Herewiss. Herewiss's glance darted sidewise to him. "Lorn—!"

"Big, isn't it," Freelorn said. His eyes were wide with fear, but his voice was as steady as if he was discussing a draft horse.

"Lorn—!"

"Shut up, Dusty," Freelorn said. "Do whatever you're going to do to that thing. I'll watch your back"

Segnbora stepped up behind them as they set themselves. "I don't know how to burn it," Herewiss said to Segnbora, without looking at her. "The eye, though, that's possible—"

—Put a longsword into that little eye and hope to hit the brain? Segnbora didn't dare laugh at the idea. The deathjaw was close—shaggy-coated, brindled, the size of three Darthene lions. Shiny black talons gleamed on its great catlike paws. The deathjaw opened its mouth just a little,

showing two of its three lines of fangs above and below. Then it finally began to run, its face wrinkling into a horrible mask.

Herewiss swung Khávrinen up with elbows locked and let it charge—his only option, for running was as hopeless as a slash-and-cut duel would be. *The blade into the eye,* she heard him thinking, *and Fire down the blade, enough to blast the brain dead.*

He never had a chance. While still twenty feet away the deathjaw screamed horribly as fire suddenly bloomed about it, eating inward through flesh and muscle and sinew quick as a gasp. The still-moving skeleton burned incandescent for a moment more before the swirling flames blasted bone to powder, then ate that too. The deathjaw was gone before its death shrieks died.

And Sunspark appeared—a brief bright coalescence like a meteor changing its mind in midexplosion, steadying down to the horse-shape again. It came pacing over to Herewiss and Freelorn and Segnbora, exuding a feeling of great pleasure, its mane and tail burning merrily as holiday bonfires. (You called for me?) it said to Herewiss, who was gasping with deferred terror.

He gulped for breath. "I believe I did," Herewiss said.

Sunspark looked at Freelorn with an expression of good-natured wickedness and said nothing.

"Thank you," Freelorn said, courteous enough; but there was a touch of grudge in his voice.

Sunspark snorted. (Gratitude! Next time I'll choose my moment with more care...a little later.)

"*Choose* the moment—!"

(So that you'll appreciate me.)

"You mean you *watched* those things attack us and you didn't—!"

"Lorn, enough," Herewiss said. "It doesn't think the way you do. Luckily for us. Loved," he said to the elemental, "did you notice any other wildlife in these parts while you were having breakfast?"

(Singers,) it said, looking to the northwest. (The ones with fur.)

"Wolves? Perfect." Herewiss glanced down at Khávrinen, which blazed just long enough to burn the blood off itself. "We won't be climbing the Fane until sunset, since a Summoning there works best at twilight. But damned if I'm going to put up with any more Fyrd in the meantime. I'll go have a word with the wolves and see if I can work something out. Now, how do I manage this—"

He frowned, closed his eyes. Fire swirled outward from Khávrinen, hiding both sword and wielder. The pillar of brilliance shrank as it swirled, and sank close to the ground. When the blue Flame died away it left behind a handsome cream-white wolf with orange-brown points and downturned blue eyes.

(Not bad,) Sunspark said, (for a beginner.)

Herewiss grinned a wolf-grin. (Stay close till I get back, loved, just in case the Fyrd try again. I won't be long.)

The wolf bounded away through the long grass. Watching him go, Segnbora dug down in her belt-pouch for a square of clean soft cloth, with which she began cleaning off Charriselm's blade. When she'd finished, she looked thoughtfully at the Fane. It seemed to gaze back, calm and blind and patient, waiting for something. *Fyrd so close to this place—that's unheard of. All the rules are changing.*

But after this, nothing is going to be the way it was. Not even me.

"You going to stand there all day?" someone shouted at her. Freelorn and the others were in the saddle, getting ready to ride down to the Fane. Segnbora swung up into Steelsheen's saddle and went after them.

Somewhat later she sat with her back against the trunk of an old rowan tree near the lakeshore, watching the long shadows of men, horses and trees drown in slow dusk. The Fane, half a mile away across Rilthor's water, shone golden as a legend where its heights still caught the sunset. The mirroring water lay still in the breathless evening, the mountain's burning image broken only by the wakes of gray songswans gliding by. *It's more a hill than a mountain,* Segnbora thought, stretching. The Fane was no more than a half mile wide at the base, broad at the bottom and flat at the top, stippled roughly with brush and scrub pine. *Nothing so spectacular...except for what you can't see.*

And it was the unseen which all day had kept their camp so abnormally quiet. Freelorn had spent most of the afternoon pacing and frowning until Herewiss returned from his parley with the wolves, reporting success, and a sore throat from much howling. Now Herewiss sat under a nearby alder, meditating, with Khávrinen flaming in his lap. For hours he hadn't moved, gazing across at the Fane with an expression half wonder and half fear, while Freelorn took to pacing again. Harald and Moris had been keeping so close to one another that one might have thought they had been lovers for only a week or so, rather than years. Dritt and Lang had become almost obsessive about caring for their horses, and the otherwise fearless Lang had been looking over his shoulder a great deal. Even Sunspark, while in its horse-shape, had been cribbing quietly at an elm tree, leaving small scorched places bitten out of the bark.

She laughed at herself then, a mere breath of merriment. *And look at me. All the time I've spent on the trail, a hunted woman—and look what kind of watch I'm keeping. My back turned to open country, where Goddess knows what could be coming up from behind—and me sitting here staring at this silly hill as if it's going to jump out of the water and come after me!* Yet that silent benevolence kept watching her, kept waiting.

In the distance a clear melodious sound, like the night finding its voice, rose up—joined a moment later in the long note by another voice wavering downward a third, and yet another, higher by a fourth. The unsettling harmony sent a delighted shiver down her spine. The wolves were on post as their rearguard, singing to while away the watch.

The Goddess's dogs, Segnbora thought. It was the old affectionate name for them, the votaries who sang to Her mirror, the Moon, through all its phases, silent only when She was dark and dangerous. *Where is the Moon tonight?* Segnbora wondered, glancing upward. It hadn't yet risen. But she was distracted, as always, with the sight of the first few stars pointing through the twilight, and the memory they always recalled.

How old was I? Segnbora wondered, though wondering was vain. Very small, she'd been—small enough to still be wearing a shift instead of a kilt, but large enough to push open the front door of the old house at Asfahaeg and escape at bedtime. She'd gone out into the dark, unsure just what she was looking for—then had glanced up and found something, a marvel. Not just sunset, or dusk, or dark, but a sky burning with lights, every one solitary and glorious; and she knew, small as she was, that somehow or other she and those lights were intimately connected.

Now Segnbora knew them as stars, knew their names, knew about the Dragons that had come from among them, and about the Goddess Who had made them. But the wonder had never left her: that desire to get closer to those lights that called her—and, eventually, closer to the One Who had made the stars. When the Rodmistresses tested her at the age of three and found the Fire, she'd been overjoyed. Everybody knew that when you had the Flame, you got to talk to Her more often than most.

But years of study had failed her. School after school had been unable to provide her with a focus strong enough to channel the huge outflow of her Power—and so there had been no breakthrough, and no truedreams in which She walked. After much bitter time Segnbora had admitted the truth to herself, that she was never going to focus. She might as well give up sorcery and lore and Flame and all the other timewasting for something useful, as her father had always said.

And, having given up, so it was that she'd met the Goddess at last. She was good enough with Charriselm to go looking for a job as a guard. She found one, in a little Steldene town called Madeil—and found Freelorn in the mucky alley behind the tavern there. Later, fleeing from an old keep in which the aroused Steldenes had besieged them, the group had come across a little fieldstone inn on the border between Steldin and the Waste. It had seemed strange at the time that there should have been an inn out there at the very edge of human habitation, but the innkeeper had put them all at ease. Finding that they were short of money, she offered to share herself with one of Freelorn's people to settle the scot. A common enough arrangement, and Segnbora had won the draw for the privilege.

It had been a sweet evening. The innkeeper had been fair, but there was more to her beauty than that. A long while they sat together by the window of Segnbora's little room, she and a white-shifted shadow veiled in hair like the night, talking and breathing the apple-blossom scent while the full Moon went softly up the sky. The talk drifted gradually to matters that Segnbora usually kept deeply hidden—old joys, old pains—while the brown-and-beige-banded pottery cup went back and forth between them, filled with a wine like summer wind running sweet under starlight.

I'm talking a great deal, Segnbora had thought, not so much frightened by the intimacy as bemused. *The wine*—But the wine was not intoxicating her; she was seeing and feeling, if anything, more clearly than usual. Shivering with delight at the feeling of magic in the air, she drank deep of the cup, deeply enough to drain it...and found it still three-quarters full. *Two hours we've been drinking from this cup,* she realized, *and she only filled it once.*

She looked across at the other, then, and realized Who had come to share Herself with her, as She comes to every man and woman born, once before they die. Not Mother now, as she had been at dinner, feeding them all and gossiping about the Kingdoms, but the aspect of the Goddess Segnbora loved best—Maiden about to be Bride, Creatress about to create something as beautiful as the multitude of stars. Back and forth a few more times that cup went, while Segnbora drank deep of building joy and anticipation, and named the Other's name, and saw her joy reflected a hundredfold, a thousandfold, incalculably.

Then she went to bed. And was joined by warmth that enfolded, and lips that spoke her name as if she was the only thing in creation. She was intensely loved; and was given to drink of that other cup that brims over forever, the endless source. She drowned, eternally it seemed, in the deep slow bliss of her own deity, and the Other's...

The bark against her back was hard as Segnbora blinked, glanced down from the sky. *Oh, again,* she thought, *someday again...!*

Though the odds of that were slight. Once in a lifetime, in *that* manner, one might expect the Goddess. Otherwise, only at birth did one see Her, in one's own mother—quickly forgotten, that sight—and at death, when the Silent Mother, the Winnower, came to open the last Door.

She glanced across the lake, at the Fane standing silent, watching her, under the constellations of early summer. *He'll be ready soon,* she thought. Somewhere to northward the wolves began singing again.

Someone came lurching along toward her in the darkness, walking loud and heavy as usual. *Oh, Lady, not now,* she thought with affectionate annoyance, as Lang plopped down next to her. "Are we waiting for Moonrise?" he said.

He smelled of unwashed horse and unwashed self, and Segnbora wrinkled her nose in the dark—then shook her head at herself, for she had no call to be throwing stones on *that* account. "Just full nightfall," she said. "I guess the theory is, if you're crazy enough to climb the Fane, then exercise your madness in the dark as the Maiden did. 'Out of darkness, light; out of madness, wisdom—'"

Lang nodded. "How crazy are you?"

His tone was uneasy. Segnbora's stomach knotted, hearing in his words a reflection of the nervousness she'd been trying to ignore. Worse, she didn't feel like talking. Segnbora wished for the thousandth time that Lang wasn't thought-deaf.

She plucked a blade of grass from beside her and began running it back and forth between her fingers. "I think I told you about my family, a little," she said.

Segnbora felt his confusion, typical of him when she chose to come at a question sideways. Lang rarely understood any approach but the head-on kind. "Tai-Enraesi," he said. "Enra was the Queen's sister of Darthen, wasn't she?"

Segnbora nodded. "I'm related to a lot of people who've been up that hill. Béorgan, and Béaneth, the doomed Queens. Raela Way-Opener. Efmaer d'Seldun. Gereth Dragonheart..." She trailed off. After a while she said, "To be where they were...I don't know how I can pass the Fane by—"

Lang slouched further down against the tree. His face was calm, but his heart was shouting, *Yes, and look what happened to* them! *Béorgan and Béaneth dead of the Shadow or of sorrow, Raela gone off through some door and never heard of again, Efmaer dead in the mountains, or worse, in Glasscastle—*

Segnbora twitched, resettling her back against the rowan's trunk. She heartily wished there was something else left to try, but over twenty years she had exhausted the talents of instructors all over the Kingdoms. This was a last chance: if she failed this, she could finally rest.

"I thought I might talk you out of it," Lang said, very low. "I like you the way you are."

"I don't."

"But if you go up there there's no telling what'll happen to you—"

"I know. That's the idea!"

Lang drew back, pained.

"Look," Segnbora said, regretting his distress. "Twenty years of training, and I'm Fire-trained without Fire, I'm a sorcerer who doesn't care for sorcery and a trained bard who's too depressed to tell stories. It's time to be something else. *Anything.*"

"But, 'Berend—"

The use of the old nickname, which Eftgan had coined so long ago, poked her in a suddenly sensitive spot. She laid her hand on Lang's, startling him out of his frightened annoyance. "You remember the first time we met? You tried to talk me out of joining up with Lorn, remember?"

"Stubborn," Lang muttered, "you were stubborn. I couldn't stand you."

She gave him a humorous look. "Maybe change isn't such a bad thing, then?"

After a moment he squeezed her hand. "Care to share afterwards? If you haven't turned into a giant toadstool or some such, of course."

Her heart turned over inside her. When Lang made such offers, there was always more love in his voice than she could match, and the inequity troubled her. It had been a long time since her ability to share had been rooted in anything deeper than friendship. "Yes," she said, hoping desperately he would be able to lighten up a little. "You disturb me, though. You have a prejudice against toadstools?..."

Lang chuckled.

"You two ready?" said another voice, and they both looked up. Herewiss was standing beside them with Khávrinen sheathed and slung over his shoulder. Freelorn was with him, arms folded and looking nervous.

"What do you mean 'you two'?" Lang said. "I prefer to die in bed, thanks."

Segnbora squeezed his hand and got up, brushing herself off. "You found the raft, I take it."

"It was hidden in the reeds," Freelorn said. "In fact, the reeds were growing through it in places. Evidently not many people come this way."

"Just the three of us are climbing, then." Herewiss said. "Still, it's probably better that we all go across—in case any Fyrd get by our rearguard."

Lang got up, and the four of them went off to join the others by the lakeshore. Dritt and Harald and Moris were standing at a respectable distance from the raft, for Sunspark was inspecting it suspiciously.

(You really want me to get on this thing?) it said to Herewiss as he came up. (That water's deep. If I fell in there—) It shuddered at the thought.

"So fly over," Herewiss said, stepping onto the raft from the bank.

Sunspark gazed across at the Fane, its mane and tail burning low. (There's a Power there, and in the water,) it said. (I'm not sure I want to attract Its attention quite so blatantly...)

"Then come on."

∽ *three*

The Goddess's courtesy is a terrible thing. To the mortal asker she will give what is asked for, without stinting, without fail. Nor will She stop giving until the gift's recipient, like the gift, becomes perfect. Let the asker beware...

(*Charestics*, 45)

They all climbed onto the raft. Sunspark came last, picking its way onto the mossy planks with the exaggerated delicacy of a cat. But it stood quite still in the midst of them as Herewiss and Freelorn poled the raft. No one broke the silence. Out on the water the feeling of being watched was stronger than ever.

The raft grounded, scraping and crunching on a rough beach of pale pebbles. Herewiss stepped off, Freelorn behind him, and each of the others in turn. Everyone winced at the seeming loudness of their footsteps. Segnbora, second-to-last off, thought she had never heard anything so deafening as her light step on the gravel. Sunspark, behind her, got off and made no sound at all. It was carefully walking a handspan above the shore.

They were not only watched, they were *felt*. There was no mistaking it. There was no threat in the sensation; the regard running through them was patient, passive. But whatever fueled it was immeasurably old, and huge. As the Power reached up into them, the others looked at one another, wondering, finding old companions suddenly somehow strange.

Segnbora understood the sensation as most of her companions couldn't. The Fire within her, dwindled to nearly nothing because of years of lack of focus, now suddenly leapt up as wildly within her as if a wind blew through her soul. The Power pushed at her, urging her toward the mountain. At the same time it looked through her at the others, and looked through them at her, determining what changes would be made—

Oh Goddess, she thought, *this is what I've needed.* There was no mistaking the Source of what stirred here, though this half-slumbering immensity of calling Flame was only the least tithe of Her Power. *And I'm terrified—*

Herewiss and Freelorn stood transfixed, keeping very close to each other. She couldn't see their faces, but Freelorn had stopped nervously hugging himself for the first time since the morning. Khávrinen in its back-sheath was blue-white with Fire: its light shone through seams in its scabbard, and the hilt blazed like a torch. "There's the trail," Freelorn said quietly, looking upward.

"I'll race you," Segnbora said as quietly. She slipped past them and started climbing.

The trail wasn't too difficult. Part of it followed old gullies or slide-paths; part of it seemed to have been cut into the hillside, but only lightly, so that rockfall or deadwood frequently blocked the way. In the starlight it was hard to see where to put one's feet. Each of them fell and slid at least once. By the time they reached the flattened hilltop five hundred feet above the lakeshore, they were all bruised, and breathing hard.

But the gasping for breath didn't last. It was replaced almost immediately by a sensation of being anchored, centered, secured past any dislodging. Freelorn and Herewiss stood as still as Segnbora, feeling their pulses become tranquil, their breath come more gently. The three of them stood poised at apex of the world's Heart. The Universe swung around them, slow and silent, waiting. After a few moments Segnbora sank to one knee, bending to touch the gullied ground with one hand, the ground where Raela and Efmaer and Béorgan had stood. She could feel the Power, bound, waiting, alive. Her own Fire strained downward to reach it, and, unfocused, could not. But that seemed unimportant as she knelt there, feeling the ages run through her. This place was more important than the needs of any one human being.

"Loved," Freelorn said to Herewiss, his voice uncertain, "something's strange inside me—"

"Of course there is." Herewiss reached out to Freelorn and drew him close, not so much in compassion as in exultation. "It's your Fire. You have a spark of it like everyone else; here at the heart of Fire, how could you *not* feel it? The Fane is reaching up to you."

"I thought so." Freelorn sounded almost in pain. "It wants me. But I don't know what to do."

"Listen to what it has to say to you," Herewiss said. "Just feel it. Few enough people ever do."

Herewiss let go of Freelorn with his right arm, then reached around behind to let Khávrinen's scabbard down from the backsling. He drew the sword slowly, with relish and ease and much tenderness, as he might have drawn himself from his loved after passion spent. The sword swept out and down before him, Fire trailing behind the blade. Even now, before the wreaking had begun, the Flame was too bright to look at directly.

"So much," Lorn said, soft-voiced, blinking and tearing in the light. "You can do *anything* now…"

"Yes. For the moment." Herewiss laughed gently at Freelorn's puzzled look. "Lorn, just how did you think I was able to destroy those hralcins? Under normal circumstances twenty Rodmistresses, fifty, couldn't have done it. I was in 'breakthrough,' as they call it in the Precincts, and I will be for maybe another tenday or so. After that the Power begins to drop to more normal levels. I'm sure that's why She wants me to hurry."

He gazed down at the Flame-flowing sword in his hand. "I'll give back what was given to me," he said, resting Khávrinen's point on the ground. "As much as I can. Standing where we stand, every power for good between the mountains and the Sea will feel this happening, and know me for an ally—"

"The Shadow and the dark things will hear you too," Freelorn said, "and know you for an enemy. They hate defiance…"

"They hate me already. Let them. I have something better." The Flame about the blade burned brighter, lighting the hilltop more brilliantly with every breath Herewiss took. "The Shadow's had Its way in the Kingdoms long enough. Its child the Dark strangled the Fire in half the human race—but that's done now. I'm the proof. And It's had Its way too long in Arlen—killing the land slowly with blight and famine and a usurper on the throne. That's done too, Lorn, I promise you—"

The light was becoming like an otherworldly Sun now, a blaze of determination and joy that dazzled the mind as much as it did the eyes, transfiguring what it touched. Segnbora had a brief vision through the brilliance of a young god raising His arms, offering His loved, across His two hands, the thunderbolt He wielded. In her vision the other, blasted by the overpowering magnificence into another shape, yet somehow still unchanged, reached out hands to lay them, fearless, in the Fire—

For long seconds Segnbora could not move. Once not long ago, when Herewiss had been away and Lorn had seemed to need consoling, she had entered a little way into the relationship between these two—sharing herself with Lorn, offering her friendship. At the time she had thought her motives benevolent enough. But recent events had made her suspect that, in fact, she had been the one in need of consoling. Now, by this light, in which any untruth withered and fell away, she clearly saw the shape of her own loneliness and sorrow. Likewise she saw the essential *twoness* of Herewiss and Freelorn—something even Sunspark had perceived more clearly than she did. *They are their own,* she thought. *They don't need me.* There was no sadness about the realization: it came almost triumphantly.

Unsteadily—for the forces being freed on the hilltop had made her a bit light-headed—Segnbora turned her back on the ferocious glory raging there. By the time one of the Lovers began speaking Nhàired in invocation, she was descending from the hilltop, sliding and stumbling down the path. *"Ae, hn'Hláfedë, ir úntaye Lai—"*

Sweet Mother of Everything, Segnbora thought as she reached the end of the steepest part of the path, *the first wreaking he tries is the Naming of Names? I wish I had his faith. If some dark power should slip close enough to hear—*

The possibility briefly so unnerved her that Segnbora lost her balance, and she had to grab at nearby branches of brush to steady herself. An inner Name was a powerful commodity even after its owner's death, useful to lend power to various spells and wreakings, and the Name of one who worked with Fire even more so. Great Rodmistresses' names were passed down through generations; in Segnbora's own family, Efmaer d'Seldun's Name was preserved, though the Queen herself was long lost. Now Segnbora exhaled in sudden amusement at the notion that someday sorcerers and Rodmistresses would pay great treasures for the true Name of one Herewiss, a slim dark young man with a tendency toward creative swearing in dead languages. *And other tendencies that will matter far more—*

The path went right out from under her. It was not her own clumsiness this time, but the Morrowfane itself trembling under her feet. Segnbora looked up. The blaze on the hilltop, hidden till now by the bulk of the hill, was hidden no longer. A narrow, sword-shaped core of blue-white Fire swung up into view, and then a light of impossible brilliance broke the night open from end to end. Like lightning burning in steel, it turned the dark into sudden day and extinguished the stars. The Fane shook to its roots as outpoured Firelight smote into everything, illuminating every leaf and tree trunk and stone with fierce clarity. On the surface of the shivering lake, the light shattered into countless knives and splinters of dazzle.

Blinded, Segnbora turned away and rubbed her eyes. When they saw clearly again, she started once more down the trail. She had no trouble finding her way; the Fane was lit like midmorning. At one point she paused for breath, looked around, and saw something she had missed in the dimness on the way up—a huge crevasse or cavern around on the southern face of the hillside, an opening into darkness that even Herewiss's Fire didn't illumine. *How about that. The World's Heart has a secret in it—*

Above her Herewiss's Flame dimmed and faded, leaving her looking at where the cave entrance had been. *He's taking a rest, I suppose. I bet I could have a closer look at that before he starts shaking things again—*

Scrabbling up off the trail, she used scrubby bushes and trees to climb across the eroded face of the Fane. It took her a few minutes to scramble up a ravine that ran down between two folds of the hillside, but finally the cave opening loomed huge before her, dark as uncertainty. There Segnbora halted, uneasy. Her undersenses were still blunted from the onslaught of Power and joy at the top of the hill, but not so much so that she couldn't catch an odd underheard flavor that grew stronger the closer she came to the cave mouth. *Something hot. Metal? Stone?*

Segnbora drew Charriselm; the whisper of steel suddenly sounded very loud. With care she stepped over and around the boulders that lay about the great cave entrance, and slipped a few feet inside where she paused to listen again.

Nothing. I must have imagined that feeling. Cautiously, keeping her left hand against the cave wall, Segnbora took another step in. The faint crunch of her footstep echoed away into the dark. She took another step. That echoed too. The place was huge, filling most of the mountain from the sound of it. Another—

A voice spoke, and Segnbora froze, clenching on Charriselm's hilt.

Her heart pounded. For a moment she thought the cave was going to fall in on her. The voice was huge, and incredibly deep. It thundered, rumbling, shaking the air; yet there was music in it, a slow and terrible song of pain. The hair stood up all over Segnbora. She could make nothing of the words the voice seemed to be speaking. At the end of the sentence, the silence that fell was waiting for her answer.

She swallowed hard. "I don't know that language," she said, her voice sounding amazingly small despite the echoes it awoke. "Do you speak Arlene or Darthene?"

There was a long pause; then the voice spoke once more. It used Darthene, but the timbre was that of a storm on the Sea. "You were a long time coming," it said. "But you're thrice welcome nevertheless."

Segnbora leaned against the wall of the cave, bewildered. Her eyes were getting used to the darkness, and in the faint starlight from the doorway she could make out a great lumpy mass lying on the floor of the cave before her. The hot stone smell she had noticed before was coming from it, though there was little actual warmth in the place. "I don't understand," she said. "What are you?"

"*Lhhw'ae,*" the voice said, a rumbling growl and a sigh.

Segnbora gripped Charriselm even tighter, for that single word of the strange language she *did* understand. *A Dragon—*

The voice began to speak again, and was suddenly choked off. Rocks cracked and rattled about in the cave, rolling, shattering. The Dragon had abruptly started thrashing around. Segnbora leaped for the cave entry, as afraid of being attacked as of a cave-in, but after a few moments the uncontrolled motion subsided and the immense half-seen bulk of the Dragon lay quiet again. She stared at it fearfully.

"I am about to lose this body," the Dragon said, an anguished-sounding melody winding about the words. "That's the cause of my seizures."

"You're dying?" Segnbora said, and then had to grab for balance once more as another convulsion threw rocks in all directions. When the Dragon had settled again, she saw that it was looking at her from great round eyes, each of which was at least four feet across, globed and pupilless. Segnbora shuddered as she realized how big the rest of the beast must be, and was glad she couldn't see it.

"Going *rdahaih.*" The Dragon whispered the word, but even its whisper sounded like a thunderstorm. "My time is upon me."

The pain in its voice confused Segnbora. No one but Marchwarders—the humans who lived with Dragons in their high places—knew much about Dragons, but the one thing everybody said about them was that they never died. Even more confusing was the undercurrent of joy that ran under the Dragon's pain, growing stronger by the moment.

"No matter," it said. "You are here. At last, what will have been, *is*—"

The ominous tone made Segnbora think hard about leaving, right then. Yet she'd been curious about Dragons ever since the first and only time she had seen one, at the age of seven, soaring over the blue Darthene Gulf. That old curiosity was raging again. Slowly Segnbora sheathed Charriselm, then began picking her way toward the Dragon's head among the fallen stones, watching carefully in case another seizure should occur. Lying flat on the rubble, the head from lower jaw to upper faceplate was twice her height. Above it, the spine in which the shielding faceplate terminated speared up into the gloom for another ten or fifteen feet. Segnbora reached out gingerly and touched the edge of the plate between nose and eyes. It was hard and rough as stone, and warm. The eye on that side regarded her steadily, but she couldn't read its expression. It looked dimmer than it had—

"Are you sure you're not just ill?" Segnbora said.

"I know my time," said the Dragon. "I welcome it. I always have."

She shook her head, perplexed. With her hands on the Dragon, she could feel its weary sorrow as if it were her own—but also that perplexing joy, both sober and expectant at once.

"Is there anything I can do for you?" she said.

The Dragon's eyes flared brighter, and a tremor ran up and down its body. *"Arhe-sta rdaheh q'ae hfyn'tsa!"* the Dragon whispered in a great rush of fulfillment, as if its last fear had been lifted from it. "If you truly ask," it said in Darthene, "don't let me—die—uncompanioned."

Segnbora shivered, having misgivings. Again she considered running away, but only briefly. "I'll stay with you."

"Yes," the Dragon said. The light of its eye ebbed again. "You always did."

That was when the last, and worst, convulsion happened. Walls shook. Stone chips and splinters rained from the ceiling. The floor danced. There was nothing for Segnbora to grab for support but the Dragon's head. A brief feeling of hot stone—

—and the next moment, her head burst open from the inside. Segnbora knew how it felt to share her mind with another consciousness, but this was nothing like her experiences in the Precincts; those decorous, sliding melds of one Rodmistress-novice with another, each always wary of disturbing the delicately balanced economy of the other's mind. This was like a boulder dropping into a bucket—a brutal invasion that smashed her against the borders of her self and threatened to smother her.

Strangling, agonized, she flailed about inside for room to think. There was none. Her inner spaces were crowded with *otherness*, a multitude of ruthless presences straining and seething in intolerable confinement—minds that beat at her, buffeting her like wings; painful thoughts that gnawed at her like alien jaws; strange memories that stalked through her past, promising her a horrifying and incomprehensible future. The Dragon's imminent death—

No! Segnbora screamed. She pushed desperately away without knowing for sure what she was pushing back from, but ready to do anything, even die, to avoid it. She fell and fell, yet the images followed her inexorably as a doom, becoming more and more real, happening again, happening forever. *I don't want to remember!* she screamed, but the words wouldn't even come out right. Instead, a white-hot burning and a strange language took her by the throat, twisting the plea into a wracking curse: *'sta, tauëh-stá 'ae mnek-kej, mnek—!*

A roar of condemnation went up in the stifling, crowded darkness; the damp cold dirt rushed up toward her face. Then mercifully the fall ended in a pain-colored flash that killed the presences, and the memories, and, Segnbora hoped, her too...

four

"Are you going to kill me?" said the child to the Dragon.

"Kill you?" The Dragon smiled at him. "Certainly not until we have been introduced."

> Tales for Opening Night, Nia d'Eleth

The darkness tears wide, splitting as hewn skin does when the sword strikes.

This is Etachnë field, all one gloomy sodden mass of misery—lead-gray above with clouds that have been pouring rain for three days now, dun and black and red below with the scattered bodies of the slain. The stench is incredible. Those who fight do so with their faces wrapped, and fall as often to the sick miasma of the air as to Reaver arrows. Fyrd are harrying the fringes of the battlefield, devouring the dead. A few hundred feet away, a maw, a horwolf and a nadder are busily dismembering a fallen woman. Her surcoat was once Darthene midnight blue. Now it is mostly red-brown.

She gulps down sourness for the hundredth time and stares across the misty valley. Somewhere over there the Reavers have retreated into cover, regrouping for the next attack. There are only about a thousand of them left, but those are more than enough to break the Darthene defense at the other end of the valley and let them out into the open lands. Once that happens they'll begin pillaging at Etachnë and leave the country burning behind them as far as Wendwen. Around her, the Darthenes holding the gap are huddled, soaked through, hungry, outnumbered, waiting.

The Rodmistress is dead, so they have no idea when reinforcements may be coming. Segnbora is the only sorcerer left, and over the past few days her sorceries have been going progressively flatter—a starved sorcerer is good for very little. It was all she could do yesterday to stop the miserable rain for a little while; today her head still aches with the backlash. *Oh, food,* she thinks. *Just oatcakes and milk*—She stops herself, does a brief mind-exercise to calm down.

It doesn't work. Her partner Eftgan has been gone for three days now, ridden off for the reinforcements; and the Goddess only knows whether she lives or not, for there's a great silence where her mind used to be. *Oh, Tegánë, loved, be all right, please*—She winces away from the painful thought, opening her eyes on the Fyrd again. The sickness comes up in her throat as she sees them tugging at the limbs of the woman in Darthene blue. Then sickness turns to rage and she throws her sodden cloak off savagely and stands up in the rain, fists clenched.

"Irn maehsta irn aehsta," she whispers, *as within, so without,* and begins a bitter poem in Nhàired, shaping a spell-construct in her mind. Anger-fueled sorcery is dangerous, she knows, but anger and terror are all she has left. Desperation fuels the sorcery, scansion shapes its skeleton, meter sets the beast-shape, filling it out. Words link in sliding musculature, the hot pelt of intent furs it over, angry purpose glares like eyes beneath a shaggy mane of verse.

Uncaring of the backlash to come, she grips the shape of words and wraps it round her like a cloak—then drops to all fours in the rain and leaps roaring at the Fyrd—

—and the darkness falls.

(—they all do that, we've watched them do that since we first came. Yet while they feel for one member of their kind, they still do murder on others. Stiheh-stá annikh 'é—)

(We don't understand it either. What about this one—)

Here's the last rise before home, with the little rutted track that serves for road. Steelsheen quickens her pace a bit, sensing road's end. The air is full of the smell of salt: beach-grass hisses incessantly on either side of the track. She makes the top of the rise—and there it is, spread out blue and wrinkled, glittering and lovely, the Darthene Gulf. The Sun is beginning to pierce through from a silver sky; the black beach glistens as the waves slide back; sandpipers dance daintily after them, poking for whelks in the bubbling crevices and tide pools. She looks across at the lonely stone manor-house built on the headland—*Home!*

Steelsheen breaks into a canter. *They'll be so proud. My master's never before given live steel to anyone so young. And Tegánë has spoken for me to see if I can be in the royal household. To live in Darthis, in a town with walls! And Sheen, Father will be so proud when he sees her. A real Steldene, a silverdust Steldene, and I broke her myself with all the tricks he taught me!*

She punches the mare into a gallop and rides into the demesne, under the old stone arch with the tai-Enraesi arms: lioncelle, passant regardant, sword upraised in the dexter paw. Chickens scatter in all directions. Dogs scramble to their feet and bounce around her, barking, as she rides in to the dooryard with a great clatter of hooves. She dismounts. A yellow cat on the doorstep opens one eye at the noise, says a rude word and closes the eye again.

Segnbora laughs as she pulls off Steelsheen's saddle, drops it on the ground, fends off various dogs with pats and scratches, and bends to chuck the cat under the chin. Three weeks, she's been on the road from Darthis. Three weeks of lousy weather, an attack by bandits and a case of the flux. One cat, however grumpy, isn't going to spoil this splendid homecoming.

"Mother, Father, I'm back!" she shouts, shoving open the front door and swaggering in.

She walks through the little main hall with its benches and carvings and hangings and firepit. Secretly she's a little shocked by the shabbiness of the place; it never looked this run down before she went to the city. Her father's old complaints about failed crops and the sorry state of family finances suddenly begin to disturb her— "Mama?"

No answer. *She's in the kitchen, then.* Through the hall and out into the big stone-paved kitchen and pantry. Her mother is just stepping in the far door with a string of onions from the buttery shed outside. Close behind is her father, who carries a newly dispatched chicken.

"Hi!" she shouts.

"'Berend!" says her mother, and "Don't shout," says her father, both at once.

She trots over, embraces them both in a huge hug, and pulls her sheathed sword out of her belt to show them. "Mama, look, I named it Charri—"

"How's your Fire coming, dear?" her mother says. Her father says nothing, just watches her, waiting for the answer.

And suddenly it's all wrong. *Don't they think if I'd finally focused, I'd have come in here streaming blue Fire from every orifice? Why don't they—* "Mother," she says, "can't you ever ask me about something else?"

Her mother looks surprised. "What else is there?" she says; and, "Don't talk to your mother in that tone of voice," her father says.

"I have to rub down my horse, excuse me." She bites the inside of her cheek hard to keep from saying anything else, and walks out the way she came—

—and then darkness again.

She staggers about, lost in the darkness of her self, beginning to understand madness.

(Stiheh, stiheh-sta annikh 'e—!) *rumbles the voice of storm again. It's joined by more voices, all intoning the same rushing phrase, a litany of incomprehension and curiosity. They won't go away. They bump and jostle her roughly when she stumbles into them in the dark, feeling for a way out.*

The place where she walks is walled and domed and floored in adamant, built that way long ago to protect her inner verities. There her memories are stored. Some have been buried by accident, some she's sealed in stone on purpose; many stand about, smooth and polished from much handling.

It's the buried ones that chiefly interest her invaders. Stone means nothing to them, it being one of their elements. Cruel claws slice down effortlessly; white fire burns and melts. Delicate talons turn over exposed thoughts—old joys like polished jewels, razory fragments of pain.

(Khai rae tachoi? Sshir'stihe-khai?)

(No, this moment's fairer far. Look, I hadn't thought they sang—)

—it's quite dark, but she needs no light to know that the slab of marble is a handspan from her nose. The sound of her breathing is loud beneath it, and the condensation from her breath drips maddeningly onto her face. The sarcophagus-shaped Testing Bath is full of icy water, and Segnbora, naked as a fish, is submerged in it up to her face. Her hands are bound to her sides. On her chest rests a ten-pound stone. Above her is the three-inch-thick lid of the Bath, open only at the end behind her head, just enough to let in air, and Saris's voice.

This is the final test of a loremistress-Bard, which will determine whether three years of training will desert her under extreme stress. There's no telling which of the Four Hundred Tales she'll be required to recite faultlessly tonight, or what song, or poem, or legend. When the lid is removed in the morning, she'll be expected to take up the kithara and extemporize a poem in tragic-epic meter on the forging of Fórlennh BrokenBlade.

"Sunset to sunrise?" she had said to Eftgan this morning, before the last of the orals. "I can do that standing on my head." Now she's not so sure. She feels like she's been in this cold, wet tomb forever. She suspects it's more like two hours.

"The Lost Queen's Ballad," Saris says from outside the Bath.

Segnbora closes her eyes, hunting for the memory-tag she uses to remember that ballad, and finds it. She sings softly, in a minor key:

"Oh, when Darthen's Queen went riding
out of Barachael that day,
she rode up the empty corrie
and she sang a rondelay;

and the three Lights shone upon her
as on Skádhwë's bitter blade,
and she fared on up that awful trail
and little of it made;

She stood laughing on the peak-snows
with the new Moon in her hair,
and she smiled and set her foot upon
the Bridge that isn't There;

She took the road right gladly
to the Castle in the Sky,
and Darthen's sorrel steed came back,
but the Queen stayed there for aye..."

She lies there expecting to be asked for the rest of the history—the suicide of Queen Efmaer's loved, and her journey up to Glasscastle, where suicides go, to get her inner Name back from him. *But no, that would be too easy.*

"Jarrin's Debt," says Saris.

Segnbora sighs. "As long ago as your last night's dreams, and as far away as tonight's," she begins, "the Battle of Bluepeak befell..."

—and the darkness in the Bath is suddenly the darkness inside her mind.

Damn you! Damn you all to Darkness! Get out *of here!*

—the courtyard is fairly large, but its size is no help; there's nowhere to hide from Shíhan's sword, which is everywhere at once.

She dances back and swings her wooden practice sword up in a desperate block—a mistake, for no conscious act can possibly counter one of Shíhan's moves. He strikes the practice sword aside with a single scornful sweep of Clothespole, then smacks her in the head with the flat in an elegant backhand—a blow painful enough to let her know she's in disgrace. Segnbora sits down hard with the shock of it, saying hello to the hard paving of the practice yard for the millionth time.

"Idiot," Shíhan growls. He is a Steldene, black-haired, dark-skinned, with a broad-nosed face, a bristly mustache, and fierce brown eyes. He stands right over her—a great brown cat of a man, lithe, muscular, and dangerous-looking. He is utterly contemptuous.

"When will you learn to stop *thinking!*" He glares at her. "Save thinking for your bardcraft and your sorcery and the Fire you keep chasing, but don't bring it here! Sweet Lady of the Forges, why do I waste my time on walking butchers' meat?"

She gets up, slowly, resheathes the practice sword in her belt and settles into a ready-stance: one hand gripping the imaginary sheath, the other at her side, relaxed. She's seething, for the other advanced students, starting to eat their nunch, are watching from the sides of the courtyard. Maryn, around whom she danced with insulting ease this morning, is snickering, damn him.

Even as her eyes flick away from Maryn, she sees Shíhan drawing. She draws too, spins out of reach as she does so, comes around at him from his momentarily undefended side and hits him—not a hard blow, but so focused that his whole chest cavity seems to jump away from it.

Quite suddenly, to her absolute amazement, Shíhan is on his left side on the ground, with the point of her practice sword against his ribs. Shíhan's eyes close with hers like steel touching steel, and bind there, a bladed glance. All around the courtyard people have stopped chewing. No one in her class has ever knocked Shíhan down. Segnbora starts to tremble.

"Good," Shíhan says in a voice that all the others can hear. "And wrong," he adds more quietly, for her alone. "Come and eat."

They step off to the far side of the courtyard, apart from the other students, and settle under the plane-tree where Shíhan's nunch-meal lies ready—blue-streaked sheep's-milk cheese, crumbly biscuits, sour beer. Shíhan silently casts a few crumbs off to one side and spills a few drops of beer as libation to the Goddess, then starts eating. Between bites, he glances up at her. "You were angry at Maryn," he says. "Was that what stopped you thinking?"

"Yes, sir."

"Feeling when you strike is all right," says her master. "First time I've seen you do that. There may be hope for you yet. Provided," and he glances up again, frowning now, "it's the right kind of feeling."

She sits quiet, not knowing quite how to take this.

"Listen," Shíhan says. "Don't try to figure this out: just hear it, let it in. When you strike another, especially to kill, you're striking yourself. When you kill, the other takes a little part of you with them, past the Door. If you do it in anger, what they take is the part of you that feels." Shíhan wipes his mouth on his sleeve. His eyes burn with the intensity of one imparting a sacred mystery to a fellow initiate. "Kill in anger often enough and your aliveness starts running out too. Soon there's nothing left but a husk that walks and speaks and does skillful murder. Were you angry at *me?*" He shoots the question at her sudden as a dart.

"Master! No."

"But *I'm* the one the anger struck down. See how easily it used you?"

Segnbora stares at the ground, her face burning.

"Shíhan, I didn't think—"

"I noticed," he says, smiling for the first time. "Keep that up."

She shakes her head, confused. "Master, in killing in war or in self-defense, if I'm not supposed to feel angry—what *should* I be feeling?"

He looks at her. "Compassion," he says, gruff-voiced. "Anguish. What else, when you've just killed yourself?"

(—ae 'wnh khai-phaa ür 'ts 'shaóineh rahiw?)

(*I don't know for certain; all I felt there before was a memory of cold dirt. It must be something interesting. See how thick the stone is over it? Several of us will be needed—*)

OH NO YOU DON'T!

—Maybe it was the momentary burst of outrage that let her briefly out into the light again. Whatever the reason, suddenly the world was bright and clear, though it seemed very small, and the creatures that moved through it were earthbound and crippled of mind.

She was not in the Morrowfane country anymore. This was some twilit camp under the lee of a hill. She could feel the warmth of a fire against her side. She lay on her back, her limbs aching so much that she couldn't move.

To her left sat Lang, warm in the firelight, gazing down at her with a bleak, helpless expression. Her distress at her immobility fell away at the sight of him. Lang *mattered*: he was stability, normalcy, all embodied in one stocky blond shape.

In all her life before this terror she had never cried for help but once, and that time help had been refused. She had never asked since. But now she'd lost her mind, and surely there was nothing else to lose. *Oh Lang,* she tried to cry, *I'm crazy, I'm scared, I can't find my way out, but I'm here*—But the words caught on a blazing place in her throat, got twisted out of shape and came out hoarse and strange. "R 'mdahé, au 'Lang, irikhé, stihe-sta 'ae vehhy 't-kej, ssih haa-hté—"

Not far away Herewiss and Freelorn lay together with their backs against a rock, holding weary conversation with the campfire that burned between them and the place where she lay.

(—indeed not,) the campfire was saying. Sunspark's eyes, ember-bright in the flickering fire, threw a glance of mild interest in her direction. (There aren't many things in this bland little corner of the Pattern that can bother my kind. But we used to come across other travelers among the worlds, and some of them told of being unseated in heart or mind after coming to a world too strange for them to understand. They lost their languages, some of them—)

"Did they get better?" Freelorn said. His tone indicated that he desperately wanted to hear that they did.

"Lorn," Herewiss said gently, putting his arm around his loved and hugging him, "wishful thinking won't be enough. She can't ride, or talk, or take care of herself; like it or not, we're going to have to leave her somewhere safe. The arrow-shot she got from that last batch of bandits would have been the end of her if I hadn't been to the Fane first and learned what to do."

Freelorn didn't answer.

"I went as deep as I could last night," Herewiss said. "I couldn't hear anything but a confusion of voices, none willing to talk to me...if indeed they heard me at all. There's nothing more we can do. Look, tomorrow afternoon—tomorrow night, maybe—we'll be riding through Chavi to get the news. We can leave her there; they'll be glad to have her. She'll take her time, get better, and follow us when she can. Face it, Lorn, the Shadow's after us. We can't care for an invalid from here to Bluepeak."

"She saved my life," Freelorn said, his voice harsh. He wasn't angry at his loved, but at the unfairness of the Morrowfane, which had done this to her and left him untouched. "Several times…"

"She knew what she was doing, all those times," Herewiss said. "She knew what she was doing when she went up the Morrowfane. Lang told us so. And she'll know why we're doing what we're doing, and understand."

But there was little hope in his voice—

—the blackness swallowed her again. All around her the rush and swell of inhuman voices was beginning, faintly, as if for the first time the sources of the sound were at some distance from her. But soon enough they would drown her resistance beneath their implacable song, close in on that one untouchable memory, rip it untimely from beneath the rock and make it come as real as the others.

She shuddered violently. No, oh no. And in any case I won't be left behind at the next inn as if I were a lamed horse!

Her bruised and battered pride got up one more time from the hard floor to which it had been knocked, and made itself useful. I am a tai-Enraesi. If my ancestors could see me they would laugh me to scorn! And I'm a sensitive trained in the ways of the inner mind. Fire or no Fire. I won't stand inside here and do nothing!

Off to one side, distantly, she could still hear Freelorn and Herewiss talking. Gulping with terror, Segnbora turned her back on them, concentrated as best she could, and began making her way toward the huge voices, deeper into the dark…

five

Offer an enemy a false show of hospitality in order to damn him, and the fires will fall on your head, not his. Give him the truth with his meat and drink, and trust it not to sour the wine...

    s'Jheren, *Advice unasked*, 199

It was a long walk, full of halts, hesitations, and confusions, for the voices seemed to grow no nearer as she walked. Then abruptly she discovered that she had a seeming-body again, by walking into a wall, hard. She staggered back from it, momentarily seeing white with pain—then stepped forward with arms outstretched. Her fingertips bashed into the wall. She pushed close to it, spreading her arms wide, embracing the familiar roughness; she laid her face against it and squeezed her eyes shut against tears of vast relief. At last this place was beginning to behave as it should.

Any trained sorcerer has an inner milieu into which he or she retreats for contemplation or preparation of sorceries. This, at last, was hers—not an abstraction of blackness and things buried, but the old cavern a mile down the seacoast from the house at Asfahaeg, her favorite secret place as a child.

Long ago the coast dwellers had broken a thirty-foot hole through the cavern's high, domed ceiling, turning it into a rude temple where they performed wreakings and weather-sorceries to the sound of the waves crashing just outside. As an adult sorcerer Segnbora had made its image part of her, a great airy cave full of sunlight or moonlight and the smell of the ocean.

She opened her eyes again, pushed back cautiously from the wall and looked up, trying to find the shaft-hole in the ceiling. After a moment she located it, though the shaft was distinguishable from the rest of the ceiling only by two or three faint stars that shone through. *Strange. It's never been this dark in here before...* She turned and looked around, trying to get herself oriented somehow. The faint rumble of the Sea bounced all around her, difficult to localize, but at last she thought she detected a slight difference in sound right across from her, a deadness that might mean the cave's opening onto the beach. She stepped cautiously away from the wall, then started to walk.

She touched something. It wasn't the wall. It was smooth, and dry, and *hot*. In her shock she stumbled forward instead of jerking back, and the something clamped down on her outstretched right hand, hard.

The shock of violation, of being attacked by something that had no business being here in the first place, made her cry out in rage.

But she didn't even have time to struggle. Words came, in a huge, slow, deep bass viol of a voice, from right in front of her. "It seems excessive to put your hand in the Dragon's mouth," it said, "and then scream before you even know whether you've been injured."

Whatever had been holding her hand released it. Segnbora backed away and stood there rubbing the hand, which had been held tightly but not hurt. She was furious at herself for having shown fear. "What the Dark are you *doing* in here?" she yelled.

"We were invited," said the voice, puzzled. "Your accent is poor," it added. "Speak more slowly."

"Accent—" She stopped and realized that she hadn't been speaking Darthene, or any human language, but the odd and terrible one that the voices in the darkness had been using. "Never mind that! You can't be in here, this is *me!*"

"'Me'?" the voice said. "'We,' surely. But may we ask why you keep it so dark in here? Unless it's because the place where we met was dark."

"I can remedy that," Segnbora said, annoyed. She lifted a hand, called up a memory of noon sunlight pouring in through the shaft—

—and nothing happened.

"You are leaving us out of the reckoning," said the deep slow voice.

"Perhaps you would assist me then," Segnbora said, annoyed and uneasy. She concentrated again. "Sunlight..."

This time the light came, streaming down through the shaft from a sky that seemed bluer and deeper than usual. Segnbora looked down and away from the blinding light—and was blinded instead by the intruder.

The rough dark textures of the face she had touched in the Fane were dark no longer. The sunlight spilling down from above shattered and rainbowed from scales like black sapphires, every one with its shifting star. The Dragon blazed and glittered like a queen's ransom, his every breath and movement creating a shower of dazzle around him.

Now, Segnbora thought in wonder, *I begin to understand that old story about Dragons spending their time lying on piles of jewels...*

His head hung above and before her, no longer an inert, half-perceived shape as it had been in the Morrowfane cave. It was an elongated head: sleeker and more slender than a snake's. Its mouth ended in a beak like that of a snapping turtle. It was the point of the beak, the very end of the immense serrated jaw, that had closed on her hand.

Segnbora's gaze traveled upward. From the beak to the place where the jaw met the neck was twenty feet at least. The eyes were great pupilless globes filled with liquid fire, blazing a brilliant white even in the full sunlight. In the iron braziers of the nostrils the same light glowed, though not so brightly.

The Dragon was watching her with no less interest. "Casting one's skin for the last time is always a nuisance," it said, "but it's still one of the more pleasant things about going *mdahaih.* You like this body better than the one you saw in the cave?"

"No!" Segnbora started to say, but the thought snagged on the new language living in her throat, and wouldn't move. The Dracon tongue, she realized then, put a great emphasis on accuracy of expression, and her one, bald, angry word was insufficient.

"You look absolutely beautiful," she said at last, "and I wish to the Dark you'd go away."

"It wasn't my idea to become *mdahaih* in a human, believe me," the Dragon said. "Nor was it that of the rest of the *mdeihei.* They've been making a great deal of noise about it."

She had never heard the words before, and she understood them instantly. *Mdahaih:* indwelling within a host body and mind. *Mdeihei:* the indwellers, the souls of linear ancestors, the thousand-voiced consensus, the eternal companions.

The thought made Segnbora's hair stand up. She realized then that the sound she had been hearing in the background was not the Sea. It was a chorus of other voices, all like that of the Dragon. *It's a pleasant enough sound,* she thought; a single Dragon sounded like a bass viol talking to itself, a deep breathy voice full of hisses and rumbles and vocal bow-scrapes. But Dragons in a group seemed to prefer speaking together, and had been doing just that ever since she walked back into her cavern. The result was a constant quiet mutter of seemingly sourceless voices: scores of them, maybe hundreds, coiling together words and meaning-melodies in decorous, dissonant musics.

Now they were growing louder. They didn't approve of Segnbora, of her clumsy gropings and her rudeness to them in the darkness into which they had been thrust. Nor did they approve of the abnormal singleness of her mind, and they were saying so, in a dark-hued melody that sounded like a consort of bass instruments upbraiding its audience.

"I don't much care whose idea this whole thing was," Segnbora said. "But won't you creatures please—" She fumbled for the right word, but there was no word for undoing the *mdahaih* relationship. "Won't you just go away?" she said finally, feeling uneasy about the vagueness of the term.

"Where?" the Dragon said, puzzled.

"Out of *us!*" She stopped, then, and hissed with her own annoyance at the choice of pronoun. But in this language there seemed to be no true singular pronouns: even what she had been using for first person singular was a plural, *me-and-the-rest-of-me*, that implied the *mdeihei*. The only genuine singular forms in the language were for inanimate objects, and human beings, and other such crippled, single-minded entities.

"That's impossible," the Dragon explained patiently. It had lowered its voice into its deepest register, the one used for addressing the very young. "You're *sdahaih*, and will be until you die."

The word it used was *res 'uw*: lose-the-old-body-and-move-into-a-new-one. Segnbora rubbed at her aching head in bewilderment.

"If you were one of us," the Dragon said, "you'd bring about hatchlings in time, and the soulbond between you and them would be established once they broke shell. The bond would grow stronger in them as they grew, and weaker in you as you became old. Finally, when you left your body, you would be drawn into them: become *mdahaih*. And so it would be with their hatchlings, on through the generations, forever..."

"Forever," Segnbora whispered, feeling weak. "But all those voices—they can't be *all* of your ancestors...we wouldn't be able to hear for the noise!"

"The ones furthest back are hardest to hear. They fade out in time—which may be as well. The *mdeihei* are for advice, among other things, and what kind of advice can someone gone *mdahaih* fifty generations ago give to the *sdaha,* the out-dweller? The strongest voices are the newest, the first four generations or so."

Segnbora sat down on the floor, miserable. The great head inclined slightly to watch her, causing another brief storm of rainbows.

"What happens," she said eventually, "if I die, and there are no children, and no one is close by to accept the linkage, the soulbond, as I seem to have done for you?"

She could see no change of expression in the iron-and-diamond face, but the Dragon's tone went grave. "A few have died and gone *rdahaih,"* he said: not "indwelling" or "out-dwelling," but "undwelling." "They are lost. They and their *mdeihei* vanished completely, and from the *mdeihei* of every Dragon everywhere. They cease to be..."

Segnbora shuddered.

The Dragon's wings rustled in its own unease. "Your people have a word," he said. "A Marchwarder taught it to us: 'immortality.' He said that humans desire it the way we desire doing-and-being. We have 'immortality' already; only rarely do we lose it. Had you not come to the Fane, we would have gone *rdahaih.* Mercifully the Immanence at the heart of what-was-and-is saw to it that you were there."

I'll never dare to marry, then, Segnbora thought, heavy-hearted. Humans had a Responsibility to reproduce themselves at least once, and until the Responsibility was fulfilled she was not free to marry any man or woman or group. Yet she couldn't take the chance of passing this curse along to a child. And it was going to be hard to die without knowing whether she would see the Shore—

"O *sdaha,"* the Dragon said quietly, "since we're going to be together for a long time—regardless of your plans for hatchlings—perhaps we might know your name?"

She stared upward, angry again in the midst of her pain. "I don't remember asking you to listen to me think!"

"Among *sda'tdae,* there's no use asking for permission or refusing it," the Dragon said. "One hears. You'll find there's little I would hide from you. Nor do I understand why so many of your memories lie here sealed in stone, though doubtless answers will become plain in time."

The pattern of notes the Dragon wove around them said plainly that he considered her something of a disappointment. Still, there was compassion in the song behind the words, and amusement mixed with wry distaste at the situation he found himself in.

Segnbora rose slowly. She was finding it difficult to be angry for long with someone so relentlessly polite—especially when he was so large. She was also getting the uneasy feeling that all the courtesy and precision built into the Dracon language was there to control a potential for terrible savagery.

"Segnbora d'Welcaen tai-Enraesi," she said, giving him the eyes-up half bow due a social equal.

"Hasai s'Vheress d'Naen s'Dithe d'Rr'nojh d'Karalh mes'en-Dhaa'lhhw'ae," the Dragon said, giving his name only to the nearest five generations.

The named ancestors sang quiet acknowledgment from the shadows beyond the sunlight. Hasai lowered his head almost to the floor and raised his wings in greeting, spreading them fully upward and outward in an awesome double canopy. Membranes like polished onyx stretched between batlike finger-struts, and the sunlight was blocked suddenly away.

Her breath went out of her again in sheer amazement. "Oh, my," she said, awed, "you *are* big. May I look at you?"

"Certainly."

Segnbora walked around to her left, putting some fifteen yards between herself and Hasai so she could see more of him at once. Fifty feet of jeweled neck led down to two immense double shoulders, from which sprang both the backward-bent forelimbs, now folded underneath Hasai, and the first "upper arm" strut of the wings. Each of these struts ended at the first bend of the wing in a curved crystalline spur, as sharp as the diamond talons on each forelimb's four claws, but much longer.

Segnbora walked the length of the Dragon, out of the shadow of his wings, past the great corded hindlimbs, which were taloned as the forelimbs were. Slowly she walked along the crystal-spined tail, scaled in sapphires above, crusted in diamond below—and walked, and walked, and walked. Finally she came to the end of it, where the sapphires were small enough to be set in an arm-ring, and the last crystalline barb, sharp as a sword, lanced out ten feet or so from the foot-thick tailtip.

She looked back up the length of the body between the wings. It was like looking at a hill wrought of gems and black metal. Even supine on the stony floor, the slenderest part of Hasai's body, his abdomen, was at least fifteen feet high and perhaps forty around. His upper shoulders were at least thirty feet across. There was just too much of him. "I can't understand how you fly," Segnbora said, starting back up the other side.

"The proper frame of mind," Hasai said, arching his head backwards to watch her. "After all, our people aren't built like the flying things you have here. We are light. Observe." Hasai lifted up the last ten feet of his tail and dropped it on her.

Reflexively, knowing she was about to be crushed, Segnbora threw her arms up to ward the tail away—and found herself supporting it on her hands. It was very heavy, but not at all the crushing weight she had expected.

"See?" Hasai said, flicking the tail away to lie at rest again. Segnbora shook her head in wonder. The rough under crusting *looked* like diamond, the scales *looked* like sapphire—"What are you made of?" she said, starting to walk again.

"Flesh, bone, hide. And you?"

Segnbora blinked. "About the same..."

"You're not quite as tough, however," the Dragon said, sounding mildly rueful. "I remember the beast you will be riding, biting you there—" The glittering tail snaked up at Segnbora again, prodding her delicately in the chest. "You will be bleeding, and wishing for hide more like mine, that the beast would have broken its teeth on—"

As politely as she could, Segnbora undid the tailspine from her surcoat's embroidery, where it had snagged. She was wrestling with an unease that was no longer vague. She had noticed before, while fumbling for words, that in Dragon language there seemed to be several extra tenses for verbs. Now they all became clear. They were *precognitive* tenses—future possible, future probable, future definite. Dragons, she realized, remembered ahead as well as back.

She wanted to reject the possibility of ever doing that herself.

"We're not *built* to remember everything that happens to us," she said. "Not consciously, anyway. I can feel the *mdeihei* back there remembering everything that ever happened to them, every sunset and conversation and breath of wind. We don't *do* that."

"It makes sense that you don't desire ahead-memory," Hasai said. "The Marchwarders have told us that your kind even has trouble dealing with what *is*. But to reject our past-memories as well—"

Segnbora shrugged. "What good are fifty generations of Dragon memories to a human?"

"But you're not a human," Hasai said calmly. "Not totally. Not any more." He looked away from her, a Dragon shrug, matching hers. "Sooner or later you will look and see. Doubtless not soon."

Segnbora went narrow-eyed with anger at the Dragon's cool dare—and at the realization that this situation was completely out of her control. "Is that so," she said.

Hasai bent his head down beside her and dropped his jaw slightly in an expression of mild amusement. His action gave Segnbora a frightfully clear view of diamond fangs as long and sharp as scythes, and of the three-forked smelling-tongue in its recess beneath the blunt one used for speech. Worst of all, she could see the fulminous magma-glow of the back of the throat, where Dragonfire seethed blindingly.

"Well," Hasai said, watching her calmly as a sleepy volcano, "will you put your hand in the Dragon's mouth willingly this time?"

"Why not," Segnbora said, nervous, and irritated for being so. "Here, take the whole arm—"

Without giving herself time to hesitate, she went over to his great toothy table of a lower jaw and thrust her arm up to the shoulder between two huge forefangs, resting the forearm on the dry hot tongue. Slowly and carefully Hasai closed his mouth, holding Segnbora's arm immobile but not hurting it.

(Comfortable?) he said wordlessly, his inner voice sounding, if possible, bigger than his outer one.

"Yes, thank you."

(Well, then...)

Without warning, Segnbora found that her body felt wonderful. Her eyes could suddenly see colors she had been missing: the black reds, the white violets. She felt for the first time the curves and planes of the energy flows that were as much a Dragon's medium as the currents and flows of atmosphere. Her muscles slid lithe and warm beneath gemmed skin. Her eyes held light within them as well as beholding it without. An odd, yet delightful burning banished the cold from her throat and insides. Power was there, and strength—the dangerous grace of limb and talon and tail. She felt reborn. She also felt hungry.

(We'll eat,) she heard one of her selves suggest.

Agreeing, she crouched and coiled her way over to the door of the cavern, folded her wings carefully and slipped out.

(Wait a moment—that door's only a few feet wide!)

(That was your memory,) said one of the *mdeihei,* a strong voice, fairly recently alive. (This is mine.)

Out they went into the brilliant light of noon at Onolí. (This isn't my beach, either!)

(No, my old one.)

Immediately she spread her wings right out to their fullest, to feel the sunfire soak into the hungry membranes and run through her like white-hot wine. She basked, drinking her fill of the light, lazing while the strange-familiar thoughts of a Dragon's day-to-day life flowed through her.

The *mdeihei* rumbled lazy assent, a placid rush of low voices blending with the sound of the waves. She got up after a while, raising her wings, feeling with them the flows of all the forces that Dragons manipulated and took for granted, as fish accept water or birds the air. It was an old delight: the chief joy of the Dragonkind, dearer even than speech. (But what else are we for?) some one of them said.

The wings were hands. She grasped the currents she felt moving about her, pulled herself upward, sprang and flew.

The first leap took her high over the shore, and she watched with amazement and delight as she gained altitude. Boulders dwindled to pebbles and the huge crash of the breakers shrank to a soft-spoken crawl.

(Inland, perhaps?) said the *mdaha* who had spoken, her song calm with her own joy.

(Oh please!)

She wheeled, catching currents of air and fields of force with her wings and her mind, gaining more altitude and speed as she soared south and west over northern Darthen. Below them the sunlit headlands of Síonan and Rûl Tyn lay patched and quilted with small field-squares. There were threads of brown road, and toy houses like a child's carved playthings. Southward stretched wilder, emptier lands, tree-stippled hills, forests like green shadows on the fields.

She leaned up toward the sky and gained more height, watching the sunlight flash on a river-strung series of little lakes. Upward still she dove, through a furry fog of cloud-cover, and saw the Darst below go pewter-shadowed. More distant lakes and rivers seem to hover unsupported in the haze below. She dipped one wing, stretched the other up and out in a bank. Over her the patterned sky turned as if on a pivot, wheeled like a starry night about her center...

The higher and farther she went, the lovelier it all became. Thick clouds as white as drifting snow rose up before her, blazing in the sunlight. Bounded by these mountains of the sky, drowned far down in the depths of air, the land lay dim and still. Pacing her above the silence, the white Sun rode, swimming soundlessly in an unfathomable eternity of blue.

Still higher she climbed. Above her the sky went royal blue, then violet. Her wings lost the wind entirely and began to stiffen in the great cold above the air. She stopped beating them and fixed them at full soaring extension. Her mind was doing all the work now, manipulating fields and flows, triggering the shutdown of some body functions, the initiation of others which would protect her in the utter cold of the Emptiness.

The sky went black, and the stars came out, the winter stars that summer daylight hid, burning steady as beacons. In the same sky with them hung the ravening Sun, unshielded now by the thick cloak of the world's air. It was a searing agony on her membranes, but an ecstatic heat within. Quite suddenly the *mdaha* whose memory this was flipped forward, tumbling end for end—

Had she been breathing, breath would have gone out of her. Below her, she saw an impossibility. The flat world was *curved*. The black depths of the Mother's night rested against that curvature, holding it as if in a careful hand. The whole great expanse of the Middle Kingdoms, from Arlen in the west to the Waste in the east, could be seen in a single glance. Beyond them were unknown lands, unsailed seas—the whole of human experience and possibility, held under a fragile crystal skin of air.

Awed, she spread wings and bowed her head to the wonder. Surely this was the way the Dragons had seen the world on the day they came falling out of the airless depths: a jewel, a treasure, *life*—

(Perhaps you understand now,) Hasai said, his voice hushed with old love, old pain, (why we decided to stand and fight for a home.)

She hung there, unmoving in the silence beyond all silences, and understood.

(Not that we've forgotten what we left,) said the other *mdaha*. (Turn and see—)

Something happened to the Sun hanging behind her back. It felt suddenly strange, but welcome, like the touch of a friend coming up from behind. She turned and found that it *had* changed, was bigger, hotter, pinker. Close beneath her hung the memory of the ancient Homeworld, red-brown and dry; a harsh place, a birthplace, dear and dead.

A great mournful love for the lost lands where her kind was born rose up in her at the sight. But the mournfulness turned to something deeper and more piercing as she looked off to one side. Suspended there, seeming to cover half the endless night, was a great swirled pattern of stars. They seemed frozen in midturn—a whirlpool spraying drops and gemlets of rainbow fire, its arcs sinuous and splendid as the curve of a tail, its heart ablaze like the memory of the Day of Dawning, when the World's Heart beat its first.

Oh, My Maiden, my Queen, they know You too—

She could find no other thought. Thinking was driven out of her by the immensities. After a while she realized she was leaning against Hasai's face, her cheek resting on the great sapphired one, her left arm holding the Dragon close and her right in his mouth up to the shoulder. And her face was wet. She straightened up, abashed.

Hasai let her arm loose, and Segnbora spent a few moments brushing herself off and trying to find some composure. Hasai watched her gravely, waiting.

"It felt real!"

"And so it was."

"But that happened a long time ago!"

"Certainly. And it happened again, right then."

"But it was a memory," Segnbora said, confused. "If I had tried to change what was happening, I couldn't have."

"Of course you could have changed it," Hasai said, politely. "We wondered that you didn't try."

She shook her head again. Perhaps she was just not thinking well in this language yet.

"It was very beautiful," she said after a pause.

"We thank you, *sdaha*. It's well that you find value in who we were, and are, for we cannot leave. Henceforward, you will have to deal with us as we are—as we shall deal with you."

Segnbora looked up in sudden anger at the immense face above her. "Who are you to dictate terms to me in my own mind?" she cried.

"You say 'your own mind'," Hasai said. "You imply ownership—or at least control. Prove your claim. Leave this 'mind' and then come back. Or better still, remove *us.*"

There was a long silence, during which Hasai watched her, and neither of them moved.

"So the realities assert themselves," said Hasai, "for you, as for us."

Segnbora let out a long breath of perplexity. "Now what?" she said at last.

"Now," Hasai said, "we sue for pardon of wrongs done in haste." He bowed to her, his wings going up again, and his great head sinking low; lower than ever, this time, till it almost touched the floor. Those eyes half as high as her body were now below her own.

"I am—sorry—about the *mdeihei*." The words came out of him oddly; to a Dragon this was like apologizing for breathing. "They were trying to find out what kind of place they were in. That can be very important. We are large as your kind reckons size, true enough; and well armed, and long-lived. But we have our fears too."

Segnbora became conscious that the rustling in the shadows had stopped, and that many eyes were gazing out of it at her with a frightening and alien directness.

"I feel your dislike of others delving in your memories. I will keep the *mdeihei* out of your past—though you are of course welcome to ours. But I don't know what can be done about your future—"

"Neither do I!" Segnbora said, with a rueful laugh. "The present is giving me enough problems already." Suddenly she thought of Lorn, and Lang, and all the others. Had they left her in Chavi as planned? She had to get out and see where she was...

"Since you are us now," Hasai said, sensing both the joy and danger her liege represented, "you must be more conscientious in safeguarding your body. There is more than just one of you to go *rdahaih* if you're careless."

"And you of course will take care of *me* for the same reason—"

"We would take care of you anyway, shared mindspace or no," Hasai said. "Life is the Immanence's gift, not to be thoughtlessly cast away even when it is alien—or angry."

Segnbora bit the inside of her lip, ashamed of herself. *I did ask for a change at the Fane,* she thought after a moment. *The request's certainly been granted! But it's just like the old stories: If you don't specify what you want when you wish for something, you may get a surprise...*

"I have to go." Segnbora turned and headed for the little low door of the cavern.

"*Sehe'rae, sdaha,*" said the huge viol-voice from behind her:

Go well, outdweller.

Segnbora paused. "*Sehe'rae—*" she said, and tasted the next word. "*—mdaha.*" Mindmate.

The *mdeihei,* pacified at last, settled back into the song of the ages, the litany of all their memories, all their lives. Segnbora threw a last glance at Hasai, burning in iron and diamond in the light from the shaft. Then she turned and ducked through the door—

—to stare at the dawn from her blanket-roll. The Sun hadn't yet climbed over the edge of the world, and gray mist lay low over the grassy lea in which the camp was set. Off to one side the horses stood together, stamping and quietly snorting their way toward wakefulness; three or four feet in front of her, the campfire was down to ashes and embers.

"Thank You, Goddess," she tried to say; but her throat, after some days of disuse, refused to do anything but squawk like the rooks trying their voices all around. She was about to try clearing her throat a bit when the fire before her flared up wildly.

(Took you long enough!) it shouted, annoyed and delighted. *(Herewiss!)*

From behind her came hurried rustling: blankets being thrown aside, wet grass whispering as someone came quickly through it. Then Herewiss was down on his knees in front of her, staring at her. "Are you sure? The last time it was just a coughing spell—"

Segnbora looked up at Herewiss and very distinctly croaked a rude word in the oldest of the dead Darthene dialects, a word having to do with one of the less sanitary habits of sheep. *"Now* I'll cough," she said, and she did.

During the coughing spell, Freelorn thumped down beside Herewiss. He grabbed Segnbora by the shoulders and shook her. "Are you all right? Are you?"

"I will be—when you stop that—" she gasped. As Lorn helped her sit up, she looked around at the approaching morning with appreciation too great for words. "Can I have a drink?"

Herewiss got water for her, and sat with Freelorn, staring at her while she drank, as if at someone returned from the dead. "How long was I out?" she said between sips.

"Six days," Herewiss said. "We thought we'd have to leave you in—"

"I know. I heard you. I would have done the same thing." Freelorn and Herewiss glanced at one another in relief.

To the sound of more rustling, Lang dropped to the grass beside them. He stared at Segnbora and said nothing; but her underhearing woke up as if it had been kicked, bringing her a flood of worry, not nearly as relieved as that of the others.

She took another drink to gather her composure, and then looked at Lang and said quietly, "You told me so…"

He shrugged and looked away.

"Here," Freelorn said, "you ought to see—" He got up, went off and rummaged around in his bags for a moment, then came back with a small square of polished steel, a mirror.

Segnbora looked at herself. The same old face—prominent nose, pointed chin, deep-set eyes with circles smudged a bit darker than usual. But her hair wasn't the same. It was coming in shockingly silver-white at the roots. "Oh dear," she said, and couldn't find anything else to say.

Lang got up abruptly and went away.

Segnbora handed Freelorn back his mirror and looked at Herewiss. "I had quite a night. Can I sleep a little more? Then I'll be able to ride."

Herewiss nodded. "Rest," he said. "Chavi is still a day away, and we're not in such a hurry that you can't recuperate a bit."

She nodded back, suddenly very weary, and lay down, gratefully wrapping her blankets around her. Some time after she closed her eyes, she realized that neither her liege-lord nor his loved had moved, but were still watching her, wondering.

"'Berend,'" Freelorn said very quietly, "the thing that happened to you at the Fane—What was it?"

"Not 'it'," she sighed, without opening her eyes. "'Them.'"

This time the darkness was only sleep, and she embraced it.

 *six*

---

*If you'll walk with kings and queens, well; but take care.
For the Shadow aims ever at them—and though it often
misses, it doesn't scorn to hit the person standing closest.*

Askrythen, 14, xi

It was an odd riding that someone standing on the old diked road to Chavi would have seen approaching through the evening. Possibly it was just as well that no one was there to witness it.

Between the tall hawthorn hedges in the fading light came, first, two men in country clothes, one on a sorrel, one on a bay. Their horses flinched and shied occasionally, for their riders were juggling stones, and dropping them frequently. A third man on a black palfrey was repeatedly plucking a single string on a lute, trying to elicit the same note twice in a row from his tone-deaf companion. Then came a young slim woman in a worn brown surcoat, riding a Steldene steeldust mare. She spoke occasionally to the empty air, like a madwoman, with a hoarse voice, frequently raising a hand to brush back hair going oddly pale at its part.

Behind her, bringing up the rear, rode a tall dark man on a blood-bay stallion and a short dark man on a black-maned chestnut. The small man was waving his arms and arguing about something; his tall companion nodded gravely at most of what he said, glancing occasionally over to his left, where a hundredweight boulder was floating, pacing him as he rode.

"Look at them. *Look* at them! They'll never manage a juggling act with people watching them! Dusty, I love them, but they can't juggle *air!*"

"They'll do all right. They're just out of practice. It's been years since they juggled for a living, after all."

"Yes, but—"

"Lorn, they'll do all right. So will you, and so will Moris and Dritt and the rest. Most of the entertainers on the road are only mediocre anyway. And it's not as if gleemen's immunity depended on whether we're good or not. No one's going to suspect anything. This is the middle of nowhere."

"I don't know..."

(Hah!) Sunspark said suddenly from beneath Herewiss. (For one lousy penny I'm supposed to cut off my legs?)

Segnbora tried to put her head under her wing in token of mild exasperation, and was nearly as exasperated to find she couldn't. "The punch line usually comes at the end of the joke," she said.

(Oh. Well, there's this beggar—)

"That one won't work now. We know the ending. Try another."

(All right.) Sunspark's expression became one of intense concentration, an interesting one for a horse.

Segnbora shook her head, bemused. While she'd been busy with Hasai, Dritt had one day made the mistake of trying to make friends with Sunspark by telling it a joke. Since then it had decided that joking was a vital part of human experience, and had been demanding everyone to teach it the art, on pain of burning them when Herewiss wasn't looking. As soon as she was in the saddle again, Sunspark had accosted Segnbora. In no mood for joking, she had suggested that it tell *her* jokes, and thus learn by doing. She'd had no peace since.

(Try this. So there are these two women, they go into an inn and the innkeeper comes to their table, and one of the women says, 'Bring us the best red wine you have, and be sure the cups are clean!' So the innkeeper goes off, and comes back with a tray, and says, 'Two red wines. And which one asked for the clean cup?')

Herewiss laughed. "Not bad."

(I made it up,) said Sunspark, all childish pride. It did a quick capriole out of sheer pleasure, and almost unseated Herewiss.

"Hey! Watch that, you. Though on second thought, maybe we should increase your part in the act. We could use another jester."

"Mnh 'qalasihiw, HhIr—" Segnbora cleared her throat. The Dracon language was beginning to fascinate her, though she couldn't yet sing even the simplest of the emotion-intonations that went with the words; and her desire to master the tongue sometimes caused it to get out of her mouth before Darthene did. At least she hoped that was the reason. "I mean, Herewiss, there's only one problem with that. What happens if an audience doesn't laugh?"

Sunspark threw a cheerful glance at its rider. (If they don't laugh, we get rid of them and bring in a new audience.) The thought "get rid of them" was attached to plans for the same sudden-death fire that had been the end of the deathjaw.

Freelorn glanced up at the sky, no doubt to invoke the Goddess's protection on their next audience. Herewiss said nothing, just looked hard at his mount.

Sunspark laid back its ears and showed all its teeth around the bit, then subsided somewhat. (They *will* come back,) it said, sulkiness showing in the thought, (you *told* me so!)

"They will. But there's no reason to hurry people out of this life. Let the Goddess handle the timing."

"It does learn quickly, though," Segnbora said. "Another few months and I dare say the audiences will be safe."

Freelorn and Herewiss exchanged unconvinced, humorous glances, which Sunspark ignored. (She makes me understand the rules,) it said. (And a good thing, too. Otherwise—) Its thought carried an amused undertone of threat, like a bright edge of smoulder threading along the edge of one leaf on a dry tree, thin and potentially dangerous.

Segnbora said nothing. *Respond to a threat, and an elemental will get the idea that you're threatened. A bad idea to give it.* But without warning the huge dark form in the cave at the bottom of her thoughts reared halfway up and breathed a withering blast of white fire at the little line of red.

Sunspark blinked and drew away, annoyed. (Not another one! It's getting so there's no one left around here to scare.)

Segnbora loosened her collar, feeling hot, and closed her eyes to "look" at Hasai. Through this day and the day before he had been stretched at ease in the seaside cave, looking out of her eyes, silent for the most part. He stayed out of her thoughts except to ask an occasional question. The rest of the time the rumble of his private thought blended with the bass chorus of the *mdeihei,* a sound Segnbora found she could now start to ignore, like the seashore when one lives nearby.

She looked down into herself now and saw Hasai sunning himself in the noon light burning down through the cave's shaft. His wings were spread out flat like a butterfly's, lying easy on the floor as he settled himself again; he curled his neck around and slipped his head under the left wing in the position Segnbora had tried to achieve before. "That one's impudent," Hasai said.

"I could have handled it," Segnbora said.

"You did. Are we not *mdaha* and *sdaha*, and am I not you?"

In Dracon the question was rhetorical, and Segnbora had no answer for it. She turned away from Hasai without further thought and opened her eyes again on the evening, breathing in the sweet sharp hawthorn scent in the air. "'Berend, did you hear me?" Freelorn said.

"No, Lorn, I was talking to my lodger." She reached out and picked a white blossom off the hedge past which they were riding, held it to her nose.

"Oh. Sorry. What are *you* going to do tonight? Pass the purse?"

"She can sing," Herewiss said.

"You can? Well, that's news! You know many songs?"

"A few," Segnbora said. She reined Steelsheen back to ride abreast of Herewiss and Freelorn, suddenly feeling the need for company more normal than that she carried inside her. "I'm best with a kithara, but I'll do all right with the lute."

Herewiss was still being paced by that boulder. It was easily half Sunspark's size, but he showed no sign of strain, and at the same time he was keeping Khávrinen from showing so much as a flicker of Fire. His control was improving rapidly.

"You won't have any trouble with your part of the act, that's plain," Segnbora said.

Herewiss shrugged, waving the rock away with one hand. It soared up over the hedge like a blown feather and dropped out of sight, hitting the ground in the field on the other side with an appalling thud.

"It's easy," Herewiss said. "Even the ecstatic part of the Fireflow is under control since we climbed the Fane. Which is good; I was starting to have trouble with it."

Freelorn shot Herewiss an ironic look. "No, really," Herewiss said. "The body gets confused, mistakes one kind of pleasure for another...It's distracting. That's why, in group wreakings, usually the Rodmistresses tell off one of the group to handle all of that herself, so that the others are more free to concentrate as much as possible of their Power on the work at hand."

"Sounds like nice work if you can get it," Freelorn said. "But now I wonder. Did the Goddess install that aspect of the Fire on purpose, to keep people from doing large wreakings casually? As a control?"

"You could argue it both ways. It might just as easily be a reward, to make sure the Power's used." Herewiss shrugged. "Anyway, at the moment I'm as free of the ecstatic part of the flow as I need to be. But it's a mixed blessing. The first time I picked up that rock, I had to be careful that the whole field didn't come with it."

He sounded nervous. Lorn laughed, and reached out to squeeze Herewiss's hand. "You'll do all right..."

They rode on through the evening, and a short while later, at a turn in the road, a low huddle of squared-off silhouettes appeared against the horizon. Lamps burned like yellow stars in some of the houses' windows.

"Your guest—" Freelorn said abruptly to Segnbora.

(A rude sort,) Sunspark said.

"He's not," Segnbora said, unsure exactly why she was defending the intruder in her mind. "You started that, firechild."

"You said 'they' before," Freelorn said.

"Hh 'rae nt'sseh," Segnbora said, then corrected herself with a smile. "It *is* they. But it's also he. Mostly he."

Freelorn's expression was impossible to read. "Are you—still you?"

Oh Goddess, Lorn, if I only knew! she wanted to cry; but she kept her voice calm. "I'm not sure. Lorn, let it lie...when we have time, I'll take you and Herewiss inside and introduce you. I'm me enough to function, at least."

Freelorn hastily cast around for something else to talk about. The lane had widened into a road of a size to drive cattle down, and was well tracked and rutted. "Been a lot of traffic here, I'd say."

"For this time of year, yes." Segnbora gazed up at the town. "How many days in Spring this year?"

"Ninety-three," Herewiss said. "A Moon and a day till Midsummer. Why?"

"Just wondering... Used to be my mother and father would start for Darthis now, to do Midsummer's in the city with the rest of the Houses. We used to pass this way. But we haven't done the trip since they built the inn at Chavi. My father started having trouble with his legs. It was arthritis, and he couldn't take the long rides any more..."

I don't know why we're paying all this good money for you to waste your time studying something that doesn't work, she remembered him saying— and then, without warning, was in the memory as much as in her body. Holmaern was hobbling to the gate outside the house, and she was walking with him, as slowly as she dared: too slowly and he would notice. At the time, she'd heard nothing in his words but disappointment at her. But now, impossibly, Segnbora could underhear his frustration and pain, his determination to keep control of himself in the face of the ailment that even their local Rodmistress's expertise could do no more than slow down. From down in the darkness inside her, great eyes that burned low studied the memory, and her reaction to it; and the shape that owned the eyes said nothing.

"You know this place, then," Herewiss was saying. "That's a help."

She found herself blinking back unexpected tears. "They'll be glad to see players. Not many come down here, especially after the bad weather sets in. They probably haven't been entertained since last summer." She glanced at Freelorn. "If things are as bad in Arlen as they are here…don't overcharge them, Lorn. From the look of the fields, this year's harvest isn't going to be any better than the last."

Freelorn nodded. Good harvests were a king's responsibility. Bad ones were a sign of trouble—like the empty throne in Arlen. "I'll see to it," he said.

Segnbora nodded. Inwardly she felt a twinge of satisfaction, for Lorn was changing. In many respects he was still the same brash, adventurous prince she loved so dearly, but increasingly he was overcome by thoughtful silences…which was as it should have been. The land through which they traveled was his by right, and its plight was desperate. The crops in the fields were poor; the people they'd seen of late, over-taxed, had a threadbare look. What prince could see this and fail to feel his heart swell with outrage? A cause was growing in Freelorn's mind, not some self-centered desire to get back what should have been his, but something deeper, more worthy, something with other people's needs at its heart. *Did She find it there when She spoke to him in the Ferry Tavern? Or was it born of that conversation?* That was between him and Her. One way or another, the shift was there. But they were all still a long way from restoring Lorn to his throne. They were so few, and he'd been away so long…

Indeed, it was months since they had heard any reliable news from Arlen. The usurper Cillmod's authority had been well established for some time, but now they needed to discover whether support for him was still so solid as it had been. Chavi, inconspicuous, far off at the edge of things, had been Lorn's choice for a first foray after the news they needed; out here, no one would be surprised by traveling entertainers asking for it.

At least, we hope no one will...

(How about this?) Sunspark said. (The Goddess is walking down the road and She sees a duck—)

They rode up to the town's rough fieldstone-and-mortar walls and were readily admitted. Chavi was much as Segnbora remembered it. The town's central square was stone-paved, surrounded by earth and fieldstone houses with soundly thatched roofs. A few, though, still had turf roofs, with here and there a scamp flower growing. Men drying their hands on dishtowels and young women with floury hands came to the windows, attracted by the sound of hooves on cobbles

Up at the front of the line of riders, Dritt unslung his timbrel and began banging it earnestly, calling their wares: "Songs and stories, tall tales! Shivers and chuckles, sleepless nights, horrors and heartthrobs, deaths and delights! Mimicry, musicry, tragedy, comedy—"

A small crowd began to gather. Dritt began juggling two knives and a lemon, breaking the rhythm occasionally by catching the lemon in his mouth, and making puckery faces when he let go of it. Harald was strumming changes on Segnbora's lute, and angling it so the torchlight from the cressets by the inndoor would catch the mother-of-pearl inlay.

Herewiss dismounted, pulled the saddle off Sunspark, and snapped his fingers. The stallion disappeared, replaced by a great white hound of the kind that runs with the Maiden's Hunting. The fayhound danced once about Herewiss on its hind legs—bringing *ooohs* and *aaaahs* from the audience, for upright it stood two feet taller than he did—then, at his clap, it sat up most prettily and begged. At another clap it bowed to the audience, grinning with its huge jaws—and at a fourth clap, without warning, it turned and sprang at Herewiss's throat.

The crowd gasped as man and hound struggled on the cobbled street, then gasped again as the fayhound turned to a tree that creaked and groaned on top of Herewiss as if a wild wind tore at it, then to a huge serpent that coiled around Herewiss and tried to squeeze the life out of him, and after that to a buck unicorn that Herewiss barely kept from goring him by wrestling its head down to the ground by the deadly horn. Finally there they lay in the street again, man and fayhound once more; but the fayhound lay on its back with its eyes starting and its tongue hanging out, and Herewiss was kneeling on its chest, gripping it by its throat.

A delighted cheer went up from the crowd, the kerchiefed ladies and dusty-britched men applauding such illusion as they had only heard of before. Man and hound held their tableau for a few seconds, then rose up as man and horse again, while Moris turned handsprings on the stones, and Freelorn went inside to dicker with the innkeeper for the night's room and board.

About the time Herewiss finished dusting himself off, Lorn emerged, and gestured to the crowd for silence. He was wearing the very slight crease of frown that was all he allowed himself when disturbed in public. "Kind gentlemen, good ladies," he said, "we'll begin our evening's entertainment an hour after sunset. Please join us, one and all."

The crowd in the street, murmuring appreciations, began to disperse. Herewiss was glaring at Sunspark. *"What the Dark was that about?!"*

Sunspark gazed at him, absolutely nonchalant. (Just testing...) it said, and smiled at heart in somewhat wicked satisfaction.

Herewiss sighed. "Everything all right?" he said to Freelorn, noticing Lorn's expression.

"Yes," Freelorn said, in the same tone of voice he would have used to say "no." "The innkeeper worries me, though."

"He's stingy?"

"No. We hardly had to bargain, he gave right in. Something about his manner—"

"Maybe he was busy."

Freelorn shrugged. "Could be—the place is lively inside. Come on, I want a bath before dinner."

They stabled the horses, including Sunspark, who wanted to indulge its fondness for oats but promised to follow later.

The inn itself, the "Yale and Fetlock," was a long, low, battered-looking place of fieldstone with a weedy turf roof and a rammed dirt floor. The main room was smoky and full of people in the linens and woolens of townsmen. Some sat eating at long rough tables starred with rushlights. Others stood eating at sideboards, sat drinking in the middle of the room, or simply milled around. All were talking at the top of their lungs.

(Sweet Immanence,) Hasai said, sitting up in alarm behind Segnbora's eyes and looking out at the jostly drinkers' dance, (what's being decided here?)

(What?)

A memory surfaced, but not one of hers. In a stony deserted vale, Dragons, a great crowd of them, moved among one another in a precise and graceful pattern. It was *nn's'raihle,* Convocation—sport and ceremony and family fight and celebration all at once, the form of disagreement and resolution that Dragons found the most elegant and delightful.

(Oh,) Segnbora said, seeing the likeness to *nn's'raihle* in the tense movement in the room. (No, *mdaha,* this is social. They'll talk about whatever's happening, but they won't be making any decisions here.)

(How can they all abrogate their responsibility like that?) Hasai said, uneasy. (You all live here; how can you not act to run the world?)

(Uh—) Segnbora stalled, turning to watch Freelorn. He had somehow already found a mug of ale, and was shouting in an old man's ear, "Ei, grand'ser, what's all the pother for?"

"Reavers!" the gaffer shouted back, and started telling Freelorn about incursions to the south, in Wasten and Nestekhai.

(Well?) Hasai said.

Segnbora wasn't sure where to begin. (Uh. Hasai, most humans are empowered only to make decisions regarding themselves—or those close to them. They don't sit down, have an argument about something and then make a decision by which all humans will be bound. They would never all agree—)

(Then how do you get this world to work? How do you get anything accomplished?) Hasai said, bewildered.

Segnbora shook her head. "Done" didn't translate well; "do" and "be" seemed to be the same word in Dracon—*stihé.* (That's going to take a while to explain…)

(Never mind, then. I see that there are more important matters to be concerned with. These incursions by the Reavers…are they close by, do you think?)

Segnbora made a face. (Too close. I wish we were farther north. But we daren't be; we would arouse too much curiosity there…Hasai, forgive me, I've got to get ready for our show—)

(Certainly.)

She found the innkeeper. He was a knifeblade of a man, all grin and nervous energy, and Segnbora could see how he might have made a quick business of the dickering. She got a mug of rough cider from him, and went to her bath.

Half an hour later, scrubbed and dressed in her worn but serviceable black gown with the tai-Enraesi crest on one shoulder, Segnbora went back to the common room and began talking to the patrons, assessing their mood, asking for requests. Just the sound of their voices gave her pleasure. They spoke in the old reassuring South Darthene accent that had been her mother's. It was a rich speech, slow, broad and full of archaisms. "Maistress," the slow-smiling, staid-faced townsfolk called her. "Ay, gaffer, tha'st hit it," she would drawl back, and they would laugh together.

She found Freelorn and Herewiss and the others at the best table by the central hearth, and sat down with them to a meal of aggressively garlicked lamb and buttered turnips, baked bannocks, and a soft, sharp sheep's-milk cheese to spread on them. Freelorn, reviling the vintage of the cool white potato wine that had been brought up for them from the ice-cellar, nevertheless drank off three cups one after another, and by mistake almost drank the Goddess's cup as well.

Lang gave Segnbora a covert nudge; they traded glances. Freelorn had been in a mood like this the night he'd gotten them all chased out of Madeil, the night Segnbora first ran across him. But Herewiss merely relieved Freelorn of the wine-jug and looked around the room. "Time for more of this later. They're getting impatient out there. Who's performing first?"

This started the predictable argument, punctuated with exclamations of, "I need more practice!"; "Oh, you are *too* in good voice, I heard you in the outhouse!"; "Coward!"; "I'm a coward, huh, then *you* go first!"

Segnbora sighed and groped under the table for the lute, briefly causing more exclamations. She winked at Lang and pulled her chair over by the hearth. Behind her, as she tuned the lute's slack elastring, the fire leaped, roaring up the chimney. There was a momentary hush close to the hearth, then intrigued whispers. The fire had acquired eyes.

Segnbora sat stroking the lute for a few moments, to check the tune. "This is how it was," she said then—the storyteller's opening line from time immemorial. In response to it, the quiet spread far back in the room. "There was a queen who would not die—" It was a relative's story, easy to do well because it was an old favorite: the tale of Efmaer d'Seldun tai-Earnési, the first woman to be both Queen of Darthen and a Rodmistress.

In the fourth year of Efmaer's reign, lunglock fever had broken out in Darthen. Fire is of no avail against it, but like many another Rodmistress, Efmaer did what she could to treat those of the royal household who were ill, and soon she caught the fever herself. There was bitter mourning then, for Efmaer's use of the Fire in conjunction with the priestly rites of royalty had made the land prosper as never before. When finally she fell into the unconsciousness that precedes death, her attendants stole weeping from her rooms, leaving her to die peacefully in the night.

But none of them knew their Queen's determination. Efmaer had fought the fever hard for seven days and nights, convinced it wasn't yet her time to die. When she suddenly found herself standing before the open Door into Starlight, and felt the forces at her back pushing her toward it, Efmaer rebelled. She caught at the black doorsills and hung over the starry abyss by ten straining fingers. Peace and the last Shore awaited her at the bottom of the darkness, but Efmaer would have none of them. She hung on.

When her tearful attendants slipped into her bedchamber in the morning to prepare her body for the pyre, they found her not dead, but sleeping. She looked drawn and fever-wasted, but the sickness was broken; and in her hand, clutched tight, was a long sharp splinter of darkness—a broken-off piece of the Door.

Later, when Efmaer was well again, with Fire and craft she wrought the splinter into a sword. Skádhwë, it was called in Darthene, "Dark-harm." It would cut anything, stone or steel or soul, and many were Efmaer's deeds with it across the breadth of Darthen and down the length of her reign. If anyone spoke in fear to Efmaer because she had cheated Death at its own Door, the Queen would laugh, unworried, certain the Shadow would never bother avenging so small a slight. Yet perhaps It did: for Efmaer's loved, Sefeden, killed himself, and his soul passed into Méni Auärdhem, into Glasscastle, to which go suicides and those weary of life.

Efmaer grew frightened, for Sefeden knew her inner Name; his captive soul could hold hers captive too, trapped in this world, when it came her time to pass onward and be reborn. In haste Efmaer rode to Barachael, and climbed Mount Adínë, above which Glasscastle appeared at times of sunset and crescent Moon and Evenstar.

There was no way for one still in the body to cross to the castle; the souls of the dead and the minds of the mad had no need of a physical road to make their way there. Efmaer might have attempted the crossing in a bird's shape, or as a disembodied soul, but she knew the terrible magics of the place would warp her wreaking out of shape and kill her. Nor did she dare open a door to bring her there; such a wreaking could let the deadly twilight of that place free in the sunlit world.

But Efmaer had a plan. She waited for the time of three Lights, when the castle faded into being. When it was fully there, she drew Skádhwë and smote the stone of Adínë with it, opening a great rent or wound in the mountain. With her Fire, Efmaer wrought the greatest wreaking of her lifetime, singing the mountain's blood out of its wound, drawing out the incomparable iron of the great Eisargir lodes, tempering it in Flame and passion and forging it with ruthless song into a blue-steel bridge that arched up to the Castle, fit road for a mortal's feet.

When had she wrought the bridge, she climbed it. Efmaer came to Glasscastle's crystal doors and passed them, seeking for Sefeden, to get her Name back. But she did not come out again. At nightfall Glasscastle vanished into its eternal twilight, until the next time of three Lights in the world...

"And from that day to this," Segnbora said at last, unnerved to feel the tears coming, "no one has been so bold as to say they have seen Efmaer d'Seldun among the living or the dead. With her, Skadhwë passed out of life and into legend; and in the years since the Queen's disappearance, cheating Death has gone out of style..."

The applause embarrassed her, as usual. She was glad to get out of what was now a very hot chair, and give place to Dritt and Moris and their juggling. Someone pushed a cup of cold wine into her hand. She took it gratefully and made her way to the back of the room, wiping her eyes as surreptitiously as she could.

"Smoke," she said to Lang as she came up beside him.

"Mmm-hmm."

Together they held up the wall awhile, leaning on one another's shoulder and watching Moris and Dritt juggle objects the audience gave them: beerpots, platters, clay pipes, truncheons, rushlight holders. Nothing fell, nothing at all.

"I can't believe it!" Lang whispered. "Did all that practicing actually pay off?"

"Not a chance," Segnbora whispered back. "I smell Fire. Herewiss must have thrown a wreaking over them. I doubt they'll be able to drop even a *hint* until he shuts it down."

Freelorn came toward them through the crowd, with another cup of wine in his hand.

"Lorn," Segnbora said softly as he joined them, "just you watch it."

"Yes, mother."

Segnbora settled back against the wall again and went back to watching the jugglers, particularly poor Moris, who had just been handed a full wine jug to add to the other objects being juggled. He was giving it a look such as the King gave the Maiden when he'd come to beg one of the hares She was herding. Glancing back at Lorn to see his reaction, Segnbora saw that he wasn't paying attention. He was watching someone off to one side, out of the hearth light, eyes wide with what looked like admiration.

A blocky man moved, and Segnbora could see over his shoulder. Past him, there, a small figure slipped out of her cloak, accepted a cup from the passing barmaid and raised it to her lips, looking over the rim in Freelorn's direction. She was a short woman with close-cropped hair of a very fair blonde, small bright eyes like a bird's, a mouth that quirked up at one corner—

Segnbora froze for a breath, two breaths, watching the light from a wall-cresset catch in the butter-blonde hair, giving its owner a halo. (Tegánë,) she said silently, fighting hard to keep her delight off her face. The Precincts seemed a hundred years ago, sometimes, yet here was her old loved, unchanged, as if their days apart were only a matter of a hundred days. (You're a long way from home: is Wyn keeping supper hot for you?)

(*'Berend?* Are you here?!) The face across the room didn't change a bit, but Segnbora heard the old familiar laughter, sounding all the more real for being silent. *(Now* I see! 'Berend, *you*—!)

(Me what? What are you *doing* here?) She bowed her head over her cup, needing the darkness to hide the smile that wouldn't stay in.

(I was told to come! I dreamed true last night. She told me, 'I know your troubles, and your questions. Go quickly to Chavi and you'll find answers.' I used the Kings' Door, and a mile away I smelled so much Fire that—oh, 'Berend, I'm so glad for you!)

(Not me, Tegánë.) She flicked a mind-glance at Freelorn. (It's this one's loved.)

(You mean—) Eftgan's reaction swung from embarrassment to incredulity. (Then that uproar in the Power we all felt last week *was* someone donating to the Fane! And that story I got from the Brightwood people about a *man* focusing—)

(It's true,) Segnbora said, and leaned back against the wall, weak from the backwash of Eftgan's excitement.

Moris and Dritt finished their juggling, amid much applause. There was no opportunity to go to Eftgan, however, for at that moment Herewiss walked in through the door from the stable yard and took his place by the hearth. The room quieted.

Herewiss didn't bother with the lengthy introduction that some sorcerers used to assure that their illusions would take root in the spectators' minds. Nor did he bother with spells. He just sat back in the chair, one arm leaning casually on his long sheathed sword. "My gentlemen, my ladies," he said, "a little sorcery."

It was a great deal more than that, but since no Fire showed there was no way for the audience to tell. They chuckled appreciatively when tankards and plates engaged in a stately aerial sarabande in the middle of the room. They clapped when one empty table shook itself like a sleepy dog, got up and began stumping around the room on its legs. They hooted with pleased derision when the big rough fieldstones in the fireplace all suddenly grew mouths and began talking noisily about the things they had seen in their time, some of which made for very choice gossip.

When finally all the flames in the rooms shot up suddenly, swirled together in the empty air and coalesced into a bright-feathered bird that hung upside down by one foot from the chandelier and croaked, "I've got it! The Goddess is walking down the street and She meets this duck…" the storm of laughter and applause became deafening.

Not even Eftgan's composure remained in place. "My Goddess," she whispered, and from clear across the room Segnbora could feel her restraining the Flame that was trying to leap from her Rod in response to the Fireflow Herewiss was letting loose.

A good sorcerer would have had no trouble producing such effects by illusion; but these were actual objects moving around, briefly alive and self-willed. Normally it would have taken two or three Rodmistresses working in consort to produce even one of the transformations taking place—but there sat Herewiss all by himself, looking like a child enjoying a new toy.

The table had sneaked up behind one tall woman and was nibbling curiously at her tunic, like a browsing goat. The stones had begun singing rounds. Sunspark had forgotten by now that it ought to have been holding onto the chandelier, and was simply suspended upside down in midair, getting laughs for jokes without punch lines attached. (How is he *doing* that?) Eftgan said.

(Most of these things were alive once,) Herewiss said silently, not moving or looking up. (It's just a matter of reminding them how it was. Mistress, I can taste your Fire but I can't place you—though there's something familiar about your pattern. You know my loved, perhaps?)

(The pattern might be familiar, prince,) the small woman said, as two chairs put their arms about each other and begin dancing in a corner, muttering creaky endearments, (because you and I have met. At Lidika field, you jumped in front of a Reaver with a crossbow and took the quarrel for me while I was having trouble with a swordfight—)

The hearthstone snorted as if in great surprise, then settled into a bout of ratchety snoring. (Eftgan! The Queen's grace might have given me warning!)

(I didn't want to disturb your concentration, prince, though it appears I needn't have worried. But pardon me if I leave off complimenting you for the moment. I have business here, and you're part of it, I've been told. If I rework the wreaking on the Kings' Door, can you come with me to Barachael tonight?)

(Depends on Freelorn, madam.) All the candles on tables and in sconces tied themselves in knots and kept on burning. (We're on business of our own, and I have oaths in hand that may even supersede the oaths of the Brightwood line to Darthen.)

(Oh, *that* business. I think yours and mine will go well enough together.)

(Then we'll talk when I've finished.)

At that Lorn headed across the common room, ostensibly to get another drink, and "noticed" Eftgan in what appeared to be the fashion of one potential bed-partner noticing another. He paused beside her, bent toward the pretty woman, and with a smile that any onlooker would have found unmistakable, said in her ear, "Since it's *my* throne we're talking about, madam, and *my* country, I'd best be there too. Don't you think?"

Eftgan smiled back, the same smile. "Sir," she whispered, "that sounds good to me."

The room had become such a hurly-burly of laughter and clapping that saying anything and having it heard was becoming impossible. Freelorn went off across the room, leaving Eftgan to say silently, and with some diffidence, ('Berend, have you taken a mind-hurt recently? There's a darkness down there that didn't used to be. Is there anything I can do?)

(Dear heart, I don't think so,) she said silently. (I'm told the change is permanent.)

(You mean *She*—)

(No. Well, not directly. If you want to take a look...)

(Yes.)

Across the room, their eyes caught and held, then dropped again as their minds fell together in that companionable meld that had always come so easily.

Segnbora saw and felt, in a few breaths' space, a rush of images that were Eftgan's surface memories of the past four years. Initiation into the royal priesthood, her brother's death, and her own investiture as Queen. The hot morning spent hammering out her crown in the great square of Darthis, alone and unguarded, wondering whether someone would come out of the gathered crowd to kill her, as was her people's right if they felt her reign would not be prosperous. Worries about Arlen and the usurper who sat in power there, making raids on her borders. Marriage to her loved, Wyn s'Heleth. Childbirth, midnight feedings, Namings, ceremonies; the rites of life all tumbled together with the lesser and greater drudgeries of queenship—mornings in court-justice, evenings spent in the difficult wreakings that were necessary to buy her land temporary reprieve from the hunger and death creeping toward its borders.

There was more. Border problems—Reavers gathering in ever greater numbers on the far side of the mountain passes, pouring through them almost as if in migration. The loss of communications with numerous villages in the far south—suggesting that their Rodmistresses were dead. The loss of one of her best intelligencers here in Chavi, some weeks back. The sudden, urgent true-dream that showed Eftgan plainly the reason for all the Reaver movements of late. This last discovery had been more shocking than anything the Queen had been willing to imagine.

She had been so shocked, in fact, that she had not once, but several times, opened and used the Kings' Door, the dangerous worldgate in the Black Palace at Darthis, to find out more. She'd done so tonight, and now here she sat in faded woolens and patched cloak and embroidered white shirt, like any countrywoman with a pot of beer. Yet her eyes were open for trouble, and for the answers she had been promised. Her Rod was sheathed and ready at her side.

Segnbora touched lightly on all these things, meanwhile letting Eftgan do what she didn't trust the *mdeihei* to do: turn over her memories one by one—the keep at Madeil, the Ferry Tavern, the old Hold, the Morrowfane. Finally she saw Eftgan gaze down inside her, incredulous, at a shape burning in iron and diamond. Hasai stared back up, bowed his head and lifted his wings in calm greeting, then went back about his own concerns, singing something low and solemn to the rest of the *mdeihei*.

When their glances rested in one another's eyes again, Segnbora and Eftgan both breathed a sigh of relief at the end of the exertion. (He's very big,) Eftgan said. (And how many others are in there?)

(Maybe a couple hundred. I tried counting and had to give up. They don't count the way we do, and I could never get our tallies to agree. Tegánë, what's bringing all these Reavers down on us? You saw something—)

(I did.) Eftgan was profoundly disturbed inside. (Part of the reason is storms. Their weather is worsening. It was never very good to begin with, and now the Reaver tribes farthest south are faced with a choice. Either they move north or freeze even at Midsummer. The tribes already close to us are feeling the pressure. There are more people hunting those lands than the available game can support. Thinking Fyrd are driving them too. But worse than that—)

(What could be worse!)

(Cillmod is in league with them,) Eftgan said, sour-faced, (and the Shadow is directing them all.)

Segnbora stared, then took a long drink to hide her nervousness.

(And still worse is coming,) the Queen said. (My Lady tells me that a great shifting and unbalancing of Powers is about to occur in the area around Barachael during the dark of the next Moon. On one hand, Reavers are gathering on the far side of the Barachael Pass, as if for a great incursion. On the other—) The Queen took a drink. (We're due for a night of three Lights shortly. And that means Glasscastle will appear. Now, what might go into Glasscastle doesn't concern me, but what might come out of it *does*. Inhuman things, monsters, have been summoned out of there before by sorcerers of foul intent—)

(But who would do something like that? That whole area's soaked with old blood! Nine chances out of ten, a sorcery would go askew—)

(Someone new to the art might not know,) Eftgan said. (And the Rodmistress who died here not long ago spent her life to tell me who. The Reavers have sorcerers now.)

Segnbora had to turn to the wall to conceal her shock. (Apparently someone's gotten a few of them over their fear of magic,) Eftgan said. (It's that individual, who has no concern for sorcery's balances, who worries me. I need Herewiss! If anyone can keep matters down south from going to pieces while I have to be elsewhere, he can.) She frowned. (But that's the rest of the news. Another of my spies has told me that some of Cillmod's mercenaries are about to attack my granaries at Rosier. I have to be there to lead the defense. Why does everything have to happen at once?)

(There's your reason, I'll wager,) Segnbora said, glancing toward the hearth, where Herewiss stood smiling, accepting the applause for his completed "sorcery." He leaned there on Khávrinen, looking casual; but for one with enough sensitivity, the air around him smelled as if lightning had just struck him, or was about to. Segnbora would not mention the Shadow, looking at him; and Eftgan simply nodded. As Herewiss stepped away from the hearth, she crossed glances with him, a "let's-talk" look.

(I'll see you later, Tegánë,) Segnbora said. She put her drink aside and headed for the door that gave onto the back of the inn.

Lang was hurrying in as she stepped out. "You on now?" Segnbora said.

"Uh-huh. Wish me luck."

"You won't need it. Except maybe to keep yourself from being knocked unconscious by the money they'll throw."

Lang smiled. "Where're you headed?—Oh, my Goddess," he said, looking past her. "I don't believe it. *She's* here? After seven years, she's finally tracked down Dritt and Moris!"

"I think something more important's on her mind. Tell them to keep mum; something's on the spit, I'm not sure what yet."

Lang nodded, touched Segnbora's shoulder gently as she went past, out into the alley and the cool air.

A shiver went down her back. It was more than just a reaction to the coolness outside, after the heat and smoke of the inn. *Cillmod in league with the Shadow?*

She drew up her gown to keep it off the wet ground, and went down the alley behind the inn, looking for a drier spot to take care of her business. The alley ended in a cobbled street that led to the town's fields through an unguarded postern gate. Quietly Segnbora walked down the street, patting Charriselm once to make sure it was loose in the sheath. She unbarred the gate and slipped out. In the shadow of one of the ubiquitous hawthorn hedges she relieved herself, then put herself back in order and just stood awhile, listening to the night and letting herself calm down. Far behind her, the sound of Lang's baritone escaped through the inn's back door, following the lighter notes of the lute through the reflective minor chords of "The Goddess's Riding":

"…But if I speak with yon Lady bright,
I wis my heart will bryst in three;
Now shall I go with all my might
Her for to meet beneath Her tree…"

"Tegánë," Segnbora whispered, smiling. *Moon-bright,* the nickname said in Darthene. Eftgan had liked it; she had never been terribly fond of her right name, which tradition forced to begin with either the eat-rune or the bay-rune like all the other Darthene royal names. She had returned the favor, turning *segnbora,* "standard-bearer," into *'berend,* a verb, and one usually used in old tales about the Maiden: "swift-rushing," impetuous, always in a hurry, sometimes too much of one—as when the Maiden had let Death into the worlds by accident. And as their names, so they had been together while they were in love: Eftgan swinging slow and steady through her moods, like the Moon, waxing and waning, giving and withholding, Segnbora pushing, urging, not sure what she wanted but not willing to wait long for it.

The senior Rodmistresses had paired them off to work together in hopes that Eftgan's Fire, unusually intense for a sixteen year old, might influence Segnbora's enough to make her focus. They expected the play-sharing that usually took place between work partners to make the two novices' patterns match more closely, and break the stuck one loose. No one, however had expected two who were so unlike—the tall, loud, spindly daughter of hedge-nobility, and the small, compact, quiet daughter of the Eagle—to fall in love…

"He kneeled down upon his knee,
underneath that greenwood spray,
Saying, Lovely Lady, ha' pity on me,
Queen of Heaven, as well Thou may!..."

The distant muffled music twined itself with the memory of the day Eftgan had suddenly had to leave the Precincts. Her brother Bryn had been killed by Fyrd while hunting. "They're going to make me be Queen," she'd said, bitter, standing in the green shade with her face averted from Segnbora. She had been trying not to cry.

"Tegánë—"

"Berend, you can't do anything for me. Any more than I've been able to do anything for you, all this while. Perhaps it's better that I'm leaving now. You can't focus, and I can't be happy around you while you can't. If this kept on much longer, we'd be hating each other."

This was true, and it reduced anything Segnbora could have said in reply to a meaningless noise. The two of them stood in the shade, hardly able to look at one another. Finally each of them laid a kiss in the palm of the other's hand, the restrained and formal farewell between kinsfolk of the Forty Houses. Then Eftgan turned away and vanished among the green leaves of the outer Precincts; and Segnbora went in deeper, and didn't come out till her soul was cried dry, a matter of some days...

Now Segnbora stood bemused for a moment as a dark head seemed to loom just over her shoulder, though of course there was nothing between her and the stars of late spring. (When you forget to struggle, when you let us be one, it can be this way,) Hasai said, dispassionately. (Do you prefer discomfort, apartness?)

She almost said yes. "It was a very private memory," Segnbora said.

(*Sdaha*, you still don't understand. You must be who you have been to be who you are.)

Segnbora shook her head, weary. *Every time I think I understand the* mdeihei, *I find I don't at all...* She looked out across the field into which she had ducked when she came through the hedge. It was tall with green hay that whispered in the starlight. On an impulse she tucked her robe up into her swordbelt and started across it, wading waist-deep, enjoying the sensations: the rasp and itch of the hay against her legs, the darkness, the cool wind.

Hasai said nothing, his mind resting alongside hers, tasting the night as she did— She stopped short in the middle of the field. Something teased at her undersenses, a whiff of wrongness that was out of tune with the clean night. She stood there with eyes closed to "see" better—

—and *there,* sharp as a jab with a spear, came the clear perception of a place just to the east that felt like an unhealed wound. A hidden thing meant to stay that way, and failing.

(Hasai?)

(I'm here. I feel it also.)

(Come on.)

 *seven*

"You are cruel beyond belief," Efmaer said. "As cruel as the legends tell."

"But legends are made by humans," the Shadow said. "And humans, who make a precious jewel of hope and hoard it past its use, are themselves more cruel to themselves than ever I could be."

Then the Shadow vanished, and Efmaer filled the air where It had been with curses, and rode away after the soul of her loved...

(*Efmaer's Ride*, traditional: part the Second)

Segnbora unsheathed Charriselm and went off eastward through the standing hay. Another hedge loomed up before her, without stile or hedge-gate. With Charriselm she cut an opening, making certain that it would be too small for a cow to escape through in the morning, and squeezed through.

The sour mind-stench she had smelled got stronger by the second, becoming so terrible that Segnbora wondered how she could have missed it from fifty miles away, let alone from the town. *How could I have been so distracted?* At the edge of the field the ground under her feet seemed to be burning with it. Her inner hearing buzzed and roared as if two powerful hands were choking her. She stopped and held still, trying not to gag. The stench was coming from beneath an old yew with peeling bark and drooping branches.

She walked under the tree and went to her knees. The fallow ground had been plowed almost up to the tree trunk. The furrows lay neat and seemingly undisturbed, yet when Segnbora thrust her hands into the still soft ground and turned it over, she sat back on her heels, sick to her stomach and sicker at heart. There is no mistaking the smell of a grave, especially a shallow one.

Nor was it the only grave. When she found strength to stand again, the death-taint led her to four others scattered around the edges of the field. All were deeper and better concealed, and all were older: the oldest perhaps three months old, the newest about three weeks.

So much for Eftgan's messenger, Segnbora thought, standing over the last grave. From the intelligencer's grave and three others, the souls were long flown, despite the brutality of their deaths. But from the one under the yew tree came a sensation of vague, scattered, helpless loss. There were two souls trapped there, shattered by their murder, trying to coalesce in time to find the Door into Starlight before the strength to pass it was lost.

Segnbora swore bitterly, torn with pity for the struggling dead and her own inability to do anything for them. Sorcery has no power over the opening or closing of that final Door. She knew the protocols for the laying of the dead. Without the Fire, they were beyond her. But not beyond Herewiss, or Eftgan—

She headed back for town at a run, pausing outside the postern gate to remove the sticktights and hay blades from her clothes. The inn's common room was, if possible, noisier than it had been. There were perhaps one hundred people there, laughing, joking, singing...and Segnbora's hair stood up at the thought that any one of them might be a murderer several times over.

She found Freelorn relieving the barmaid of another bottle of potato wine, and swung him aside to a spot where they couldn't be overheard. "Lorn, where's Herewiss gone?"

"He's still out talking to you know who—" Lorn looked more closely at Segnbora. "You're shaking!"

"Lorn, never mind. Smile! Something's very wrong, and we're not supposed to know about it. Take your time, but find Herewiss—!"

"—so if the others agree, we'll go to Barachael," Herewiss's voice said softly as he came up behind Freelorn from the other side. "It's as good a place to hide as any, and it's a lot closer to Arlen than we are now... What's wrong?" he said, looking at Segnbora.

Before she could say a word, his underhearing brought him the answer. His eyes went wide with shock. "Show us," he said. "Lorn, go out the front way. I'll take the side. By the postern gate?"

Segnbora nodded and went out the way she had come, doing her best not to seem like she was hurrying anywhere. Freelorn and Herewiss were through the postern and into the hay ahead of her. She tied up her gown again and hurried after.

"Eftgan's gone to readjust her Door," Herewiss said when she reached them. "It may take her a little while—seven people, six horses, and Sunspark are a larger group than usually uses that gateway." He lowered his voice. "I think she's ready to back Lorn against Cillmod, openly. She'll give us the details tomorrow, at Barachael."

"That's wonderful," Segnbora said, "but with the problems she's been having, she's hardly in a position to leave Barachael for a campaign in Arlen."

"True. But I think I can help her, and free her to help us in return. Though the Reavers are pouring through the Chaelonde Pass, it's a simple enough matter to close that avenue—"

"But the Queen's Rodmistresses have been doing illusion-wreakings there for years," Segnbora objected. "They're no longer strong enough. People have been dying in that pass for centuries, and the built-up negative energies are enough to ruin even the best Rodmistress's work."

"I'm not planning illusions. It's time for something less subtle. A sealing."

"You mean physically closing the pass?" Freelorn said, stunned. "As in knocking down a few mountains?"

"Yes."

"You call that *simple?*"

"Yes. Dangerous, too. It'll require a lot of power, but it's also less likely to go wrong."

"Then what you saw in that dream—"

As they approached the spot Segnbora had sensed, Herewiss shook his head. "Later, Lorn." To Segnbora he said, "How long have the people in that last grave been dead?"

"Grave?"

"A week or so, I think. They're weak—they were getting along in years to begin with, I think, and shock of their death was considerable. You have the protocols—"

"I have them."

"Protocols, *what* protocols?" Freelorn said.

"For raising the dead," Herewiss said. "Stay close, Lorn, I'm going to need you... Oh, sweet Mother," he added as the full force of the sour smell of murder hit him. Segnbora was already tearing—the psychic residue of violent death became not easier, but harder to handle with repeated exposure.

"Goddess, what *is* that," Freelorn said, and coughed.

Both Segnbora and Herewiss looked at him, surprised. "You smell something?" Herewiss said.

"Don't you? Like a charnel pit." Freelorn coughed again. Herewiss looked most thoughtful, for the graves were covered and the night air was sweet even here; the stench was purely a matter of the undersenses.

They came to the yew tree, and stopped. Quickly, for the smell was now overwhelming, Herewiss reached over his shoulder and drew Khávrinen. Its Fire, suppressed all through the evening, now flared up, a hot blue-white. Concerned, Segnbora threw a look over her shoulder at the walls of Chavi.

"Only our own people and Eftgan will be able to see the Fire," Herewiss said, quiet-voiced, slipping into the calm he would need for his wreaking. "Now then..."

The wavering of Flame about Khávrinen grew less hurried as its master calmed, yet there was still a great tension in every curl and curve of Fire. With the tip of the sword, Herewiss drew a circle around the tree, the graves, Freelorn, and Segnbora. Where Khávrinen's point cut the fallow ground, Fire remained, until at the circle's end it flowed into itself, a seamless circle of blue Flame that licked and wreathed upward. Finally, when the three of them had stepped inside the circle, Herewiss thrust Khávrinen span-deep into the soft dirt, laid his hands, one over the other, on the sword s fiery hilt, and began the wreaking. *"Erhn tai 'mis kuithen, ástehae sschüur; usven kes uibren—"*

The words were in a more ancient dialect of Nhàired than any Segnbora had been taught. Even in Nhàired, which held within it many odd rhythms, the scansion of this wreaking-rhyme was bizarre. Freelorn fidgeted, watching his loved with unease as Herewiss reassured the trembling yew and the murder-stained earth that he was about to end their pain, not make it worse. He stood and called the Power up out of him, sweating. The circle's Fire reached higher, twisting, wreathing, matching the interlock of word with word, of thought with rhyme—

Herewiss poured out the words, poured out the Flame, profligate. Power built and built in the circle until it numbed the mind, until the eyes saw nothing anywhere but blue Fire, and a man-shaped shadow at the heart of it, the summoner.

Segnbora was overwhelmed. She did the only thing safe to do—turned around inside herself and fled down to the dark place in search of Hasai. *His Power,* she thought: *he has too much! No one can have that much!* Even in her own depths she could see nothing but burning blue light, but at last she stumbled into Hasai and flung her arms around one hot, stony talon. Concerned, the Dragon lowered his head protectively over her.

Outside, after what seemed an eternity of blueness, tension ebbed. Segnbora dared to look out of herself again and saw the pillar of Fire that wreathed about Herewiss diminish slightly as he released his wreaking to seek outside the circle for the fragments of the murdered people's souls. He spoke on, in a different rhythm now, low and insistent, urging outward the unseen web the Fire had woven of itself, moving it as an ebb tide pushes a thrown net away from shore. When the web had drifted across the entire field, he reversed the meter of his poetry and began pulling it in again.

Segnbora swallowed hard. Light followed the blue-glittering weave; dusts and motes and sparkles drifted inward, small coalescing clouds of pallid light. They drifted inward faster now, coiling into two separate sources; these grew brighter and brighter, tightening to cores of light that pulsed in time with Herewiss's verse. A last sharp word from Herewiss, a last burst of blue light, dazzling—

The Fire of the circle died down to a twilight shimmer, though about Herewiss and Khávrinen, Flame still twined bright. Segnbora found herself looking at two solid-seeming people—a man, shorter than herself, middle-aged, stocky, with a blunt, worn face; a woman of about the same age, still shorter, but more slender for her height. They both looked weary and confused. Segnbora gazed at them pityingly in that first second or so, seeing strangers—

—and then knew them.

She couldn't move. "'Kani, what happened?" the man said, looking at the woman with distress. "We were in bed..."

His voice, the voice that had frightened her, praised her, laughed with her. The woman turned to him. *Her* face. The sight of it made Segnbora weak behind the knees, as if struck by a deadly blow.

"Mother," she whispered.

"Hol, no," Welcaen said. "The innkeeper woke us up, he said the horses were loose—" She broke off, horrified by the memory. Segnbora was stunned. That beautiful, sharp, lively voice was dulled now, like that of anyone who died by violence. "They tricked us into coming out here," she said at last. "He had an axe. His wife had—"

Her husband's eyes hardened, a flash of life left. "Why did they bother with such illusions? We have no money—"

Herewiss stood unmoving, seemingly dispassionate; but even through her shock Segnbora saw that he had to swallow several times before he could get his voice to work. "Sir," he said, "madam... It was no illusion, what was done to you."

"Hol," Segnbora's mother said, stepping forward to get a better look at Herewiss. She moved like a sleepwalker. "Hol, this isn't one of them—"

Holmaern looked not at Herewiss's face, but at his sword, and his face went angry and scornful just for a flash. "This is ridiculous. It's more illusion. Men don't have Fire!"

"*This* man has it," her mother said, a touch of wonder piercing the sleepy sound of her voice. "Sir, did you save us?"

"Lady Welcaen," Herewiss said. "I didn't save you. Of your courtesy, tell me what brought you to the inn here."

"Reavers," she said, dreamy voiced, as if telling of a threat years and miles gone. "They came down through the mountains at Onther, looking for food, and overran the farmsteads. We and a few of our neighbors had warning. We got away north before the burnings and told our news here to the innkeeper so he could spread it elsewhere in the countryside. And tonight he woke us up—"

Holmaern turned to his wife, slow realization changing his expression to a different kind of dullness. "'Kani,'" he said. He reached out to touch her, but it was plain from his expression that she didn't feel as he expected her to. "'Kani, we're dead.'"

Segnbora saw her mother's eyes go terrible with the truth. "You're—" She fought for words. "If we're— But where's the last Shore?"

Though Herewiss's face was very still, something moving gleamed there in the light of his Flame: tears. He gazed down at Khávrinen, and Segnbora felt him calling up the Power again, a great wash of it. This time the framework he built with it took a strange and frightening shape, one she didn't know.

"I am the way," he said, speaking another's words for Her. He let go of Khávrinen and lifted his arms, opening them to her mother and father. They gazed at him in wonder. Freelorn, across the circle, went pale as if with some old fear.

Herewiss was still there as much as any of them, but within the outlines of his body the stars blazed, more brilliant than they had been even in Hasai's memory of the gulf between worlds. Within Herewiss, about those stars, was a darkness deeper than that gulf could ever be. Segnbora trembled at the sight of him. Herewiss trembled too, but his voice was steady. "Who will be first?" he said.

Holmaern held Welcaen close. "Can't we go together?"

Herewiss shook his head sorrowfully. "I'm too narrow a Door," he said. "Besides, even at the usual Door, everyone goes through alone…"

Husband and wife looked at one another. "We have a daughter," her mother said after a moment. She glanced around the field, but saw nothing. "Will you send her word—?"

Segnbora's heart turned over and broke inside her. "Mother!" she said, choking, desperate, feeling more abandoned by that terrible placid regard that didn't see her than by her mother's death itself.

"Segnbora d'Welcaen tai-Enraesi is her name," her father said, and even through the dullness the words came out proudly. "She was eastaway in Steldin last we heard. Something about some outlaws…but she's had so much training: she can take care of herself. Send her word…"

"Father!"

Her tears made no difference; her father didn't answer. "Come on, Hol," her mother said, and reached up a little to touch her lips to his—then turned away toward Herewiss. "A man with the Fire," she said. "I never thought I'd live to see the day." And there on the threshold of true death, she smiled. "I didn't, did I?…"

Herewiss shook his head silently, opened his arms. Welcaen moved into them, throwing a last glance at her husband on the threshold of true death. "I'll wait for you," she said.

Herewiss embraced her. She was gone.

Holmaern stepped slowly forward. *"Father!"* Segnbora cried as he moved into Herewiss's arms.

Her father hesitated; his head turned toward her, and the Firelight caught in his hazel eyes. A flicker stirred there, like a vaguely recollected memory. Herewiss paused for a breath, two breaths.

"Tell her we love her," Holmaern said. He gathered Herewiss close, passed through, and was gone.

Khávrinen's Fire went out, and the circle faded to a blue smolder and died. Beside his now-dark sword Herewiss went slowly to his knees, and sobbed once, bitterly. Freelorn went to him, held him close with a helpless look: he was crying too.

Segnbora had no power to do anything but stand and look at now-empty air, and breathe in the fading scent of death.

Herewiss was gasping for control. "It's not—that's not something people are meant to be! Life—" He gasped again. "Lorn, it's supposed to be *life* I give—"

Freelorn buried his eyes against Herewiss's shoulder, then straightened. "And what kind of life would they have had, dead and on the wrong side of the Door, wandering ghosts? What do you think you gave them?"

Segnbora stood still, seeing behind her eyes, with the immediacy that came of Hasai's presence, old lost times that were somehow also *now:* summer mornings in Asfahaeg, rich with sunlight and the smell of the Sea; winter nights by the old hearthside in Darthis; afternoons weaving with her father, riding with her mother; laughter, anger, argument, joy, the sounds of life. They were real, infinitely more real than what she'd just seen. She turned and walked away, back toward town.

The truth started to catch up with her at about the same time that Freelorn and Herewiss did, in the middle of the hayfield. They stopped her, looked at her as if expecting her to lapse into some new state of madness. "Well?" she said. "What's the problem?"

"What are you going to do?" Freelorn said, sounding wary.

Segnbora felt Charriselm's sweaty grip in her hand and thought of the innkeeper—hurried, merry, sharp-faced, with eyes that wouldn't meet hers. "I'm going to kill someone," she said, turning toward town again.

"'Berend!" Freelorn said. She ignored him, hurrying off through the hay, which bit at her legs and hissed at her as she waded through it, faster and faster. *It would have been us next,* she thought. *Someone doesn't want southern news getting abroad—and we came from that direction, just as they did. Certainly I would have been next—wearing the same arms as the last two they killed: who knew whether I might have been looking for them, might have suspected something? And probably Lorn and the others would have been killed at the same time. And Eftgan, if she stayed long enough and the innkeeper guessed who she was—*

Behind her she could feel Fire stirring again. Herewiss had begun another wreaking, and she suspected what it was. Herewiss was a strategist. He would count it folly to kill a spy, and thus alert the spy's superiors to the fact that that someone had discovered the game they played. He was building around the innkeeper and his wife a wreaking that would later cause them to dream the murders of those they'd agreed to kill, when in fact they would go on their way, unnoticed and unharmed. It was all perfectly sensible, and Segnbora despised the idea.

(Don't waste your time,) she said, silent and bitter. (He won't know what's happened to him until a second after I hit him, when he tries to move and falls over in two pieces. And as for his wife—)

She went quietly through the postern, expecting an empty street. Instead, Moris and Dritt were there. So was Harald, standing silently with their horses. Lang was just joining them, along with Eftgan, who had her cloak about her shoulders and her unsheathed white Rod in her hand.

Segnbora would have brushed past the Queen to take care of unfinished business in the inn, but Eftgan's hand on her arm, together with her look of concern at the sudden taste of Segnbora's mind, stopped Segnbora as if she had walked into a wall. "'Berend? *What happened?*"

Segnbora looked down at Eftgan's brown eyes, so like her mother's, and flinched away, unable to bear it.

"Oh, my Goddess," Eftgan said. "Herewiss?"

In a breath's worth of silence Herewiss showed Eftgan what Segnbora had found, what he had done for her parents, and the dream-wreaking he had woven and implanted in the innkeeper, and afterward in his wife. "Can we get out of here now?" he said, sounding deadly tired. Sunspark paced to him in its stallion shape, and Herewiss leaned on it, sagging like a man near exhaustion while Sunspark gazed at him in uncomprehending concern.

"Done," said the Queen, and gestured with her Rod at the ground where she stood. The wreaking she had been maintaining until they arrived leaped upward from the stone and wove itself on the air, a warp and weft of blue Fire that outlined a tall squarish doorway. The doorway flashed completely blue for a moment and then blacked out—but the black was that of a different night, a long way off. The Door sucked in air. On the other side they could see smooth paving, a better road than the damp cobbles of Chavi.

"Hurry up," Eftgan said. "The Kings' Door is unpredictable, and it's a strain to hold it for this many."

One by one they went through, each leading a horse. Eftgan stood to one side of the Door, Flame running down her Rod and keeping the lintels alight. Lang stepped through before Segnbora, his eyes on her, looking worried. Numb, she followed him. The one step took her from the wet lowland air of Chavi, air stinking of death, into air colder, purer, but not entirely clean of the taste. Her ears popped painfully.

The night was perhaps an hour further along here; the stars had shifted. In one part of the sky they were missing entirely. Segnbora looked around the paved courtyard where Freelorn's people stood grouped among milling horses and men and women in the midnight blue of Darthen. Over the low northward wall she could see faintly, in the starshine, the valley where she had sometimes lived as a child, with the braided river Chaelonde running through it. Many a time she had stood down there looking up at the place where she stood now—Sai khas-Barachael, Barachael Fortress, the black sentinel perched on an outthrust root of one of the Highpeaks.

Dully, Segnbora looked southward to where the stars were blocked from the sky. Looming over khas-Barachael, shadowy dark below and pale with starlight above, the snows of Mount Adíně brooded, impassive and cruel.

"It's late," Freelorn was saying. "We'll meet in the morning, all of us. Meanwhile, does the Queen's hospitality extend to a drink?"

Segnbora saw to Steelsheen's stabling and made sure her corn-crib was full, then followed Lang (who seemed to be beside her every time she turned around) to a warmly lit room faced in black stone. There was hot wine, and she drank a great deal of it. The explanations went on and on around her, but she was never as dead to them as she wanted to be.

Snatches of conversation and random thoughts faded in and out of hearing, as they had when she had first come down from the Morrowfane. She would have welcomed Hasai's darkness to flee to again, but she couldn't find it. He and the *mdeihei* were, for once, *too* remote. They wanted nothing to do with her, the *mdeihei;* they had seen she was all too familiar with the kind of death to which they couldn't admit, and to them she was now carrier of a contagion of terror and impossibility. The more she tried to approach, the more they fled her, afraid of any death in which one could so lose oneself.

Somehow she found her way off to the tower room they had given her, and to bed. Lang was there too. He held her, and she clutched him, but she found no comfort in his presence. Her thoughts were full of graves, bare dirt, eyes that looked right through her. Her mind talked constantly, again and again making the most terrible admission a sensitive could make: *I never felt you die. I never felt it. How could I not have felt it?!*

Tears were a long time coming, but they found her at last; and Lang, more hero than she had ever been, held her and bore the brunt of her blows and cries and impotent rage. Bitterness and a shameful desire for vengeance; they were all still tangled in her at the end, but she knew at least she would be able to sleep. At least for tonight...

Over the bed and the room and the fortress, like a great weight, loomed the thought of Adíně, and the last lines from the old family rede, which now might have a chance to come true. *There will come a time of ice and darkness, and then the last of the tai-Enraesi will die. Flee the fate as you may, you shall know no peace until the blade finds your own heart, and lets the darkness in...*

Darkness. That was the key. One Whose sign and chosen hiding place was darkness was coming after Herewiss and Freelorn. She had chosen to ride with them, and to defy It. And It hated defiance, and never failed to reward it with pain of one kind or another.

She could leave Lorn now, and her troubles would cease; or she could stay with him, and they would almost certainly get worse. The Dark One obviously had it in for her. But what could be worse than a head full of Dragons, and to suddenly find oneself orphaned, she couldn't imagine.

Yet there was the small matter of words spoken under a cold hillside in the starlight, to a man she'd come to love. *My sword will be between you and the Shadow, until you pass the Door—*

Beside her, Lang turned over and started to snore.

She lay there for a long time with the tears running down the sides of her face into her ears, and finally made her choice.

Shadow, she thought at last, *it's war between us from now on. I'll die soon enough. But it's as I said before. You won't get Lorn—or anybody else, if I can help it.*

The darkness about her teemed with silent, derisive laughter. She turned her back on it and went to sleep.

 eight

Kings build the bridges from earth to heaven. But it is their subjects' decision whether or not to cross—and if they do, no king can guarantee the result.

On the *Royal Priesthood,* Arien d'Lhared

People who live in the Highpeaks find it easy to believe the old story that the Maiden creates the World anew, every day, for the sheer joy of it. Astonishing dawns come there, and the face of a mountain will change completely as the shadows swing across it, revealing a new countenance every quarter hour. Sunsets come that run blood down cornices of snow, or light a whole range as if from within, until it all seems one great burning opal. Then twilight dissolves everything, leaving only shadows where peaks have been; cut-out places in the sky, from which the mischievous Maiden has removed the mountains so She can rework them for the next day.

Huddled in her cloak, Segnbora leaned on her elbows on a battlement of Sai khas-Barachael at dawn, watching the mountains come back. The Sun was up, though not yet visible past the eastern peaks. Beneath her Barachael valley was still hidden in shadow and morning mist. That valley was nearly circular. The walls broke only at the far northern end, where a quarter-arc of the circle was missing and the land sloped down northward toward the rest of Darthen. Khas-Barachael fortress stood on the northernmost spur of high ground, on the western side of the break, commanding a view of both the distant Darthene plains and the valley.

Segnbora gazed across the gap, though which the little braided Chaelonde River ran down from its glacier, toward the mountains that reached long spurs to each other and made the rest of the ring. First came Aulys, right across the gap, like an eagle with bowed head and drooping wings. South and west of it Houndstooth reared, smooth and polished-looking, and armed with avalanches. West of Houndstooth, between it and the next mountain, was a shadowy spot—the north end of the Eisargir Pass, through which Reavers had been raiding for food and metal since time immemorial. Then came Eisargir himself, like a great stone rose unfolding with his down-spiraling spurs. Westward again lay a low col or saddle between mountains, over which looked red Tamien. Finally came the rising ground that grew into the long northeast-pointing Adíně massif.

Segnbora looked over her shoulder, scanning the long crest line. It was scarred on both sides with old glacial cirques, scraped-out bowls of stone. One such bowl was still full: the South Face cirque beneath the lesser, southern peak of Adíně. Ice spilled over from it to feed the glacial lake which in turn fed the Chaelonde. Every now and then the morning stillness would be broken by a remote groan or a huge crashing snap, made tiny by distance, as the glacier calved off an iceberg into the lake.

Above the glacier, and above the eminence of Sai khas-Barachael two thousand feet above the valley floor, Mount Adíně loomed like a crooked, ruined tower. Its greater peak stood two miles higher than khas-Barachael, and a sheer league above the little town in the valley's depths. Segnbora shuddered, though whether from morning's cold or a feeling of threat she didn't know. A breath later, the Sun rose through the gap between Aulys and Houndstooth and touched on the lesser Adíně summit. There, tiny and sharp, a line of something silvery glittered: the Skybridge, bright even against the blinding white of the peak on which it stood.

Segnbora shuddered again, this time knowing why. Unconcerned, Hasai said from inside her, (We thought about living there, once...)

(Under *that*? I thought Dragons didn't care to live where the shadowed powers are.)

(We don't. When we saw what happened at certain times of year, we abandoned plans to make a Marchward there. But there are weaknesses in the valley, and we were afraid we would disrupt the land if we worked as deep into that main massif as we normally would.)

(This was how long ago?)

Hasai looked at his memories and counted the passing suns backward in his mind. (Fifteen hundred years or so.)

(That long...)

Segnbora moved away from the wall and walked along it, southward, to a corner where she could better see the Eisargir Pass. The increasing light was already revealing the reddish tinge to the rocks where they were bare of snow. There under Eisargir lay the oldest mines in Darthen. From them came the best iron in the Kingdoms, the raw material from which the people of Barachael made the matchless Masterforge steel. Goddess only knew how many times Barachael had been raided, burned, and razed by the Reavers, who came down the Eisargir Pass again and again on their forays into the Kingdoms.

Those forays had for a long time been one of the deadlier aspects of life in the South. No one knew much about the Reavers; their language was utterly different from any spoken in the Kingdoms. But prisoners taken in battle had revealed a little of their lives. The countries overmountain were short of iron. Indeed, one had merely to examine the Reaver bodies on any battlefield to see that: Their weapons were largely flint-tipped spears and arrows, though in the last few decades bronze had begun to turn up. Because of their lack of metal, the overmountain tribes were small and poor. In the high cold South, few crops grew and little game could flourish. And so matters had stood until twelve or thirteen hundred years before, when some desperately hungry Reaver tribe had followed a game migration northward instead of southward...and had discovered the Eisargir Pass, and Darthen, and iron.

Those first Reavers were no fools. They saw that the richness of the farmland below them was not all because of the warmer climate. They discovered the plow and the sword. They stole as many of each as possible, and fled back overmountain with them to change their world.

The tribes that followed grew swiftly in power, becoming more successful as both hunters and warriors. Tribes skirmished, merged, conquered, or dominated one another, grew more numerous, extended their hunting grounds.

Already a nomadic people during their short summer, the Reavers took wholeheartedly to a raiding lifestyle in order to survive in their unbalanced world. When the weather broke in the spring and the passes opened, they came flooding northward, spending the spring and summer raiding for loot and cattle, but most of all for steel to use in their endless tribal quarrels. Time and again Barachael was attacked, looted, and burned—

Again and again the town was rebuilt, too. Neither the stubborn smith-sorcerers who lived there, nor the Darthene crown that ruled them, would give up the Eisargir mines. Sai khas-Barachael was built on the northernmost Adínë spur to keep an eye on the Eisargir incursion route, but even its formidable presence did not deter the Reavers. They continued to raid, though more circumspectly, and in greater numbers, so that the battle for the Chaelonde valley was never over. Only Bluepeak had ever seen more blood shed on its behalf.

The thought of blood was not a welcome one that morning. Segnbora turned her back on the southern prospect and walked north along the wall. But that view held no comfort for her either. Northward the highlands fell away to the green and golden plains. On the plains, far out of sight but clear in her mind, was Darthis, her family's formal home, and the only one remaining, now that Asfahaeg was sold.

There in Darthis, on Potboilers' Street just outside the old second wall, stood the little stone house with doors and windows shuttered blind, and the tai-Enraesi lioncelle carved over the passage to the horseyard. Her mother wouldn't be singing in the armory anymore, her father wouldn't be re-hanging the bedroom shutter that was always falling down. There was only one person left to carry the family's lioncelle; and how long even that one would survive she couldn't tell. *Ice and darkness.*

(Are you sure,) Hasai said diffidently, (are you sure that they're not in here somewhere, those that sired you? Since last night there's been a—I don't know what you would call it—an opening in the depths—)

She blinked back sudden tears, and her mouth was grim. (Mdaha, forget it. What you almost did, they've done; they're *rdahaih*, they're gone forever, and I'll never see them again, not till I pass the last Door. Maybe not even then.)

She felt him turn his head away, a gesture of shock and sorrow at her hard words and her pain. (Their souls live yet, don't they?)

(They do. It might have been otherwise if we hadn't found them in time.) Her rage at the murdering pair at the inn, which had been gnawing at her like an ulcer all the night before, flared up hot again. She turned her back to the wall, to the wind.

After a long time Hasai said, (We didn't understand this business—or believe it.) In his voice there was distress. Far back in her inner darkness, the *mdeihei* were singing a mournful bass cadence, both dirge and apology. (You humans throw yourselves so willingly into strifes and dangers that we thought surely you must go *mdahaih* somehow. Otherwise it seemed a madness—)

(We don't get the same life twice. Or know the same people twice. So in this life we fight for what matters. Herewiss fights for Lorn, and Lorn for his kingship. All of us fight for our own happiness, as best we can. Once past the Door, it's done forever.)

Hasai fell silent again. The same fear, of not-being, and not-remembering, was at the heart of the terror of going *rdahaih,* and nothing could frighten a Dragon more. She heard Hasai wondering what would become of him and the *mdeihei* when her time came to change bodies. Perhaps this human *death* would be more final and terrible, in its way, than going *rdahaih.* Segnbora's pain turned to sorrow for the fear she had planted in him.

(Mdaha,) she said, (I'm sorry. But you and I, we're an experiment, it seems. If it'll make you feel better, I intend to put off my death as long as possible.)

His low rumbling sigh of agreement mingled with the sound of steps on stone. Segnbora looked southward along the wall. Eftgan was coming, not in country clothes, this morning, but dressed for battle: boots and britches, jerkin and mailshirt, and the Darthene midnight blue surcoat blazoned with the undifferenced royal arms— the White Eagle in trian aspect, wings spread, striking. Eftgan's sheathed Rod still bumped at her side, but she was carrying another weapon over her shoulder. It was Fórlennh BrokenBlade, Earn's sword, without which no Darthene ruler went to war.

Eftgan was a fair sight, and even a little funny, bumping down the parapet toward Segnbora with a sword over her shoulder that was almost as long as she was. Segnbora remembered the days when Eftgan had been her wreaking-partner in the Precincts. Back then she had refused to wear any gear more complicated than a belt for her tunic, or maybe a ribbon in her hair. Evidently queenship had brought some changes. Segnbora smiled, and wiped her nose as Eftgan came up and leaned on the parapet beside her.

"Fair morn, your grace."

"Oh, don't be formal," Eftgan said, making a sour face. "I have enough problems today. Your friends are looking for you, 'Berend."

"I dare say. I needed to get away from their watchful eyes for a while."

Eftgan looked somber. "I didn't say it last night—you were getting drunk and I didn't want to interfere—but I share your grief, dear."

"May our pain soon be healed," Segnbora said. They were words she had thought she wouldn't have to say for years yet. She sighed and gazed down at Barachael town with its moat and ditches and star fortifications. "Where are you off to?"

"Orsvier, as soon as I'm finished here. A force of Reavers and mercenaries is forming there to raid the granaries. There'll be a thousand or more gathered by nightfall. They'll attack tonight, or tomorrow morning perhaps."

"Goddess," said Segnbora, disturbed. "More mercenaries. Where is Cillmod getting them all?"

"Most of them are Steldenes. Some are even Steldene regulars; evidently King Dariw sold their services to Cillmod at a discount, to make up for letting Freelorn get away."

Segnbora went cold at the thought of what might have happened had she not stepped into a certain alley in Madeil one night. She shook her head. "How do you stand?"

"A thousand foot, five hundred horse, thirty sorcerers, and the right is on our side. Whether that'll be enough, I don't know." Eftgan let out a tired breath and fell silent.

Segnbora thought of Herewiss standing on the Morrowfane, an open challenge to the Shadow. Obviously It had taken up the challenge. These latest incursions by the Reavers were too well timed, and too well organized, to be coincidence.

"Have any suggestions for me?" Eftgan said.

Segnbora put an eyebrow up. "The Queen's grace hardly needs to discuss battle tactics with an outlaw."

"With an outlaw, no. But with the head of one of the Forty Houses—"

Segnbora winced.

"'Berend, I'm sorry," Eftgan said, "but you had better face up to it. You're now *the* tai-Enraesi, and I have the right to require your advice as such."

"For what it's worth."

"Your present position makes it worth more than old Arian's, say, sitting up north on his moneybags. Stop thinking of yourself as 'landless' and 'poverty-stricken,' and tell me what I should do about Freelorn."

"You should ask him that," said Segnbora. "Or Herewiss."

"I have. And they've been very cautious and polite. But that doesn't tell me what to do, really. Consider my position. Even if we put down the present incursion, Darthen is still suffering worse and worse harvests, things are coming over the borders of the Waste that shouldn't be, Arlen is yapping at my western border, the Oath that made those borders safe is in pieces, and the Reavers are coming out of every bolt hole like rats out of a burning granary."

Eftgan sighed. "Arlen needs someone on that throne who'll enact the royal rites again, and restore one of the Two Lands to normal. And, lo, here's the Lion's Child, sitting right in my lap, wanting his throne back. The question is, if I spend Darthene blood to put him on his throne, will he fulfill his responsibilities as King, or just sit there collecting taxes and parading around in silks and furs, looking royal?"

Segnbora looked her old loved in the eye, reluctant. "I've known him for all of a month—"

"You have underhearing. Better underhearing than mine, if things are the same as they used to be. You *know* them." She poked Segnbora in the ribs, not entirely out of humor. "The Queen requires your advice, tai-Enraesi. Stop stalling."

She wanted no responsibility for advising Eftgan on such a decision. But she had no choice. "I think Lorn will make a good king," she said. "Better than some who've had long quiet reigns and never been in trouble. He loves his land, and he loves his people…perhaps too much."

"How so?"

"If you made him King one week and halfway through the next told him that the royal sacrifice was necessary, he'd tie *himself* up in the fivefold bond and tell you to hurry with the knife. He has an unfortunate fondness for the concept of the glorious death. It's a good thing he's got Herewiss to restrain him."

Eftgan looked at her squarely. "Does 'Berend, the 'swift-rusher,' say this?" she said. "Or does the tai-Enraesi?"

Segnbora shook her head. "Tegánë, after just a month I could tell you all kinds of stories about noble things he's done. But they'd be just that—stories. What I *know* about Lorn is that although I could have hired my sword to any number of high-paying rulers in the Four Kingdoms, he has something that moved me to swear liege-oath to *him*."

Eftgan simply kept looking at her. "Loyalty can be blind," she said.

"So can love," Segnbora said, "or so I hear. Tegánë, what else can I tell you? I'm fresh out of proofs. But the truth is that he's my liege and my friend, and once or twice a bit more. And if I go to my death in his service, that's as good a death as any other I'm likely to find." She swallowed. "Segnbora says that, Queen. The standard-bearer. *His* standard-bearer, for the moment. Will that answer your question?"

Eftgan looked away from her, gazing down the vale, northward toward the rest of Darthen. She let out a quiet breath of decision. "Yes," she said. "So be it. And we'll hope that the famous tai-Enraesi luck will stick to him too, just this once. Now, shall we have breakfast?"

"Absolutely."

They went together from the wall to the great inner court. Halfway down the stairs, Segnbora suddenly lost her footing and brought up hard against the wall to the left. "Sorry!" she said, and then realized that the wall itself was jittering, and all around them a low mutter of vibration ran through the fortress. It subsided after a few seconds.

Eftgan let go of the wall, which she also had been holding for support. "Just a little shake," she said.

Segnbora gulped as they continued down the rest of the stairs. "Does it do that often?"

"Two or three times a week, they tell me. Better a lot of little quakes, though, than a big one that would bring the mountains down on the valley..."

They went across the huge paved court, where men and women in Darthene blue were grooming horses and practicing at the sword or bow or lance. The court, like the walls that surrounded it, lay in a square around khas-Barachael central tower. Eftgan led the way in, through a high-roofed hall and up a stair that climbed along one wall. In a smaller room on the next story, a table was set under the south-facing windows. Freelorn, Herewiss, Lang, and the others sat there breaking their fast with several of Eftgan's officers.

"Sit here," Eftgan said, and pulled out a chair for her between Lang and a Darthene officer.

Segnbora sat down and reached for an empty cup, glancing up and down the table. To her surprise and slight discomfort, she saw that around Lang's left arm, and Dritt's and Moris's and Harald's and

Freelorn's, and even Herewiss's, was bound the white cord of mourning. All up and down the table, eyes rested on her with concern. She blinked back the tears.

"Wine?" Lang said, reaching for her cup.

Her head throbbed at the thought. "Dear Lady, no. Is there barley-water with mint in it, perhaps?"

There was; Harald passed it up.

"Segnbora," Eftgan said, "you haven't met Torve, I think. He was raised here."

She turned to the man on her right. He was young, of middle height and build, with dark hair and beard and a slightly reticent smile. His downturned gray eyes, however, smiled even when his lips did not.

"Torve s'Keruer," Eftgan said as the two of them touched hands in greeting, "the Chastellain-major. He runs this place."

"You were raised *here?*" Segnbora said.

Torve nodded. "My mother was the last Chastellain. But she got tired of the long winters and retired to the lowlands. The Queen was good enough to confirm me in her place."

"Anything you need, he'll give you," Eftgan said.

"Thank you, Queen."

"Pardon," Dritt said, and reached across the Queen for the butter.

Eftgan raised a tolerant eyebrow. "His manners haven't improved any," she said, looking with wry amusement at her former court musician. "He used to do that at court too. My father thought sending him to Arlen might put some polish on his manners. But then what does he do but leave his post there, and not send word for seven years…"

There was mild chuckling over that. "Of course," Eftgan said, "his liege seems to have done the same thing, and taken the long way home as well."

The laughter was more subdued this time. Lorn shot Eftgan a quick look. Herewiss was suddenly very busy with his porridge.

"Freelorn," the Queen said, helping herself to bread and holding out a hand for Dritt to return the butter plate, "we've already talked a great deal since last night, but I still have a few questions to ask you."

"Ask," Freelorn said, sounding unconcerned.

"What on earth do you want to be a king for?"

He looked at her in shock. He took brief refuge in his mulled wine, then said, "It's what I was raised to be."

"Rubbish," Eftgan said, cheerfully, but with force. "That's like saying that a slopman's child should spend his life carting slops because his father before him did."

Freelorn stared at Eftgan, his shock growing greater by the moment.

"Look at this," the Queen said, gesturing around the room. It was comfortable enough, on a bright summer morning, but definitely not luxurious. "If I'd had the sense to marry out of the royal line young, I could be spending my day sitting on silken cushions in some mansion in Darthis, eating roast ortolan and botargoes on toast, taking lovers, going to the races in the daytime and to parties at night. But instead I let them make me Queen."

Segnbora took a long drink of her barley-water, to hide her rueful smile.

"I had to be Queen," Eftgan said again, "and now look what I've got for my troubles. Battlefield food and soldier's quarters, five days out of the ten. Back home in Darthis are three children I hardly ever see, because by the time I'm finished meeting with my ministers all morning, presiding over court-justice all afternoon, and receiving visits—I should say, 'complaints'—from the various members of the Forty Houses all evening, it's long past the children's bedtimes. I say nothing of *my* bedtime. My husband has to have a separate bedroom so that my reading won't keep him awake all night. In the daytime he has to throw people out of his wineshop because they don't want to buy his wine, they want to buy appointments with *me*. Even he aches at the end of the day."

Freelorn had at this point just gotten around to closing his mouth.

"So do I," Eftgan said. "Sometimes I do more than ache. I get wounds, too. A Queen has to be first in every charge and last in every retreat..." She pulled aside the shoulder of her surcoat, looking under it with a momentarily abstracted air. "I was knifed here, once—No, of course you remember that; you were there. Herewiss stopped the crossbow quarrel, but I got the knife of the Reaver before that one." She pulled the surcoat back in place and spent a moment looking around her plate to find the butterknife. "Bad enough to have to put up with that kind of thing from your enemies. But sooner or later it comes from your own people...in Darthen, at least. One day when you're hammering out your crown in the Square, somebody whose crops failed last year comes out of the crowd and runs you through. Or worse, the rains won't come, and all the wreakings and all the royal magics refuse to work. Then there's only one thing that will save the land from famine." She looked down and began slowly buttering her bread. "So you take the knife, and call the person who loves you best in the world to witness the ceremony; and pierce the sky's heart by piercing yours, and cause it to shed rain by shedding blood, and bring the breath of the stormwind by breathing out your last..."

Eftgan's tone all this while had been light, almost matter-of-fact. Now she looked up at Freelorn and, in the profound silence that had fallen around the table, said, "This is a stupid job to go hunting for, Lorn. You were smart to stay away from it as long as you have."

Segnbora listened hard and could have sworn that people were holding their breaths. Only Lorn looked at all normal. The amazement had worn off him; his face was set.

"Eftgan," he said, "I ran away from Arlen because I was afraid of being tortured to death. I still am. But I notice that I'm no longer running in the opposite direction."

At that Eftgan paused to bite into her bread. She chewed reflectively, and swallowed. "You've had a lot of help."

"I have," he said, with only the swiftest glance to one side at Herewiss. "What is it they always say about lovers? That they usually know your mind better than you do." It was Freelorn's turn to pause now, looking around the table for honey for his porridge. He pointed, and Lang passed it to him. "Herewiss always knew what I wanted—what I *really* wanted—better than I did. It's a good thing, too. If he had been one of those spineless anything-you-say-dear types, I'd probably be peacefully dead in a ditch somewhere now. Instead I'm here, with Fyrd and Reavers on three sides and the Shadow on the fourth."

That got a smile out of Eftgan. "You're right to question my motives and intent." Freelorn ate a spoonful of porridge. "Yes, Herewiss called the tune. And yes, I followed his lead toward kingship because it was convenient and I was confused. But the confusion isn't so much of a problem now." He took another spoonful, throwing a quick glance out the window at the great silent mass of Adíne. "Dusty will probably still be the strategist of this group's business, the brains. But I'm this group's heart. I've forgotten that, once or twice, I know. A prince gets used to having things done for him. But in the past couple of weeks I've seen my loved almost die for me—for my cause, rather—three times. I suspect I'm done being a prince. It's my turn to be a king."

Lorn took a long drink of mulled wine. "And as for you, Eftgan...if you don't like your job, you should abdicate. Maybe afterward you could take up carting slops."

Eftgan, who was also drinking at that moment, spluttered and choked—then, when she had finished choking, began to whoop with laughter. "Oh Goddess!" was all she managed to say for a while. When she was calmer, she wiped tears of merriment out of her eyes. "I guess I left myself open for that. Freelorn, your hand! Keep this sort of thing up, and we'll do very well together."

They reached across the length of the table to touch hands. "Truth," Lorn said, sounding rueful, as if the speech had cost him something, "and beauty. A perfect match."

"Flatterer."

"Now, what about that news about the Reavers that you promised us?"

"Well, let's take this in order. There's more news than just of Reavers. When you left Arlen, Lorn, what was your understanding of the way things stood with the Lords-Householders, the Four Hundred, concerning your succession to the throne?"

"Mixed. There would've been no question of the succession if I had been Initiated, taken by my father into the Lionhall on the Nightwalk. But he put off the ceremony, until finally it was too late. When he died, the Four Hundred split on the issue. I had been spending a lot of time out of the country, gadding about and misbehaving, and there was some question about whether I'd be a fit ruler. The army split on the issue too, and with Arlene regulars assigned to each household the situation quickly became volatile, as you can imagine. No one wanted a civil war, so the Householders hesitated...which gave Cillmod time to step in with his mercenaries and make the whole question moot."

"Yes, and when he made you an outlaw, you and Herewiss and the rest fled the country." Eftgan sat back in her chair.

Segnbora knew much of the rest of the story, and listened with only half an ear as Eftgan filled in details for Freelorn. Cillmod had done well enough for several years. He took the Throne and bore the Stave, though he didn't go into Lionhall. Likewise, he reaffirmed the Oath with Eftgan's father, who was still alive and ruling then. It was around the middle of his fourth year that the crop failures began. The next year the crops were worse, and the next year worse still. Then the failures began spreading into Darthen as well. The royal sorceries, and the Great Bindings, were wearing thin for lack of an Initiate on the throne.

Eftgan's father had been unwilling to help Cillmod beyond the reaffirmation of the Oath. He was among those who hoped that an uprising would eventually bring Freelorn back. But by the time of Eftgan's first crowning the situation was unbearable. Unaware of Freelorn's whereabouts, Eftgan wrote to Cillmod and offered to repair the Royal Bindings herself. Amazingly, he refused.

Segnbora looked up from her food in surprise at that, as did the rest of Freelorn's company.

"He said that inquiries were being made in Arlen for a surviving heir to the Lion's Line," Eftgan explained. "He had put about the story that you had died, did you know that?"

"No!"

"Later there was even proof of it: a mangled head sent from the torture chambers of Dariw of Steldin."

"Hmmm. Do ghosts eat? No? Then there must have been a mistake."

"Must have been. Anyway, Cillmod was apparently unsuccessful in finding any other children in the Lion's Line. Which is fortunate, since I'm sure he would have killed any that he found. Another question, Lorn: Do you have any children outside of Arlen?"

Freelorn shook his head sadly. "I only fulfilled the Responsibility once," he said. "My daughter died in infancy."

"Well enough." Eftgan chewed some bacon. "I ask because Cillmod's search for an heir took some strange turns. For example, some of the searches were conducted by large groups of mercenaries who crossed the Darthene borders and went after our granaries. It was the only way Cillmod could forestall a revolt by the Four Hundred and their starving tenant-farmers. Anyway, there were also reports for some time of sorcerers and Rodmistresses visiting Prydon. More sorcerers than Rodmistresses, of course. There's one sorcerer in particular—"

"Someone who either claimed to be of Lion's Line," Freelorn guessed, "or who claimed he could get Cillmod into Lionhall without dying of it, and show him how to reinforce the Bindings."

"The second, in this case. Rian, the man's name is. What's peculiar, though, is that as far as my spies can tell, the man never went into Lionhall at all. Neither did Cillmod. Nevertheless, starting about a year ago Rian became a fixture at what now passes for the Arlene court." Eftgan took a drink of barley-water. "Other odd things—the Four Hundred have become very quiet recently. When you robbed the treasury at Osta, for example, it became apparent that you weren't dead after all. Naturally there was a clamor for your return. But it died down very quickly."

"Why?"

"I believe because the families who called loudest for your crowning were suddenly beset by Fyrd—the thinking variety."

Mutters of distaste were heard round the table. "Rian," Segnbora said, very quietly to herself.

The Queen nodded. "I have no doubt that we're dealing here with a person whom the Shadow occasionally inhabits and controls. The man has a past and a family just as he should, but he's the center of too many odd occurrences. Where his influence appears, Cillmod's neglect usually breaks out into full-fledged malice."

Lorn, who had finished his porridge, set down his spoon. "What else has friend Rian—or rather, the Shadow—been up to?"

"You know the problems the Reavers have been having with the weather, their crops, and their game? How they are being forced northward? That's obviously the Shadow's work. There's something else, too. Starting about six months ago, it seems that emissaries—mostly mercenary captains—were sent over the mountains into Reaver country to strike a bargain. In return for making incursions into the Kingdoms when ordered, some of the hardest-pressed Reaver clans were promised loot, cattle...and land in Arlen in which to settle."

All around the table, there was silence.

"The Shadow's purpose is apparently to keep Darthen busy with war until something special happens," Eftgan said. "My guess is that the 'something' is the collapse of the Royal Bindings."

The silence in the room erupted into cries of disbelief. The end of the Royal Bindings was unthinkable. Such a calamity would turn the Shadow loose in the Kingdoms as It hadn't been loose in centuries, since the Lion and the Eagle first bound It.

Lang looked at Freelorn. "I can't believe anyone would knowingly do this to his own country! Can it be Cillmod doesn't understand what the failure of the Bindings will mean?"

"Could be," Lorn said. "After all, he's not trained in the royal sorceries. Maybe the truth about the destruction that would follow is being hidden from him. It doesn't matter. If this is the Shadow's purpose, it can't be allowed."

Eftgan nodded agreement. "First of all, what are you doing about the Reavers locally?" Freelorn said.

"Herewiss has spoken to me about the possibility of sealing off the Chaelonde incursion route completely," the Queen said. "That would cause the Reavers a great deal of trouble right away. Without it, they'd have to go as far east as Araveyn or as far west as Bluepeak itself to get into the Kingdoms. Araveyn is practically in the Waste; they wouldn't bother. And Bluepeak is in Arlen, meaning that Cillmod would have to march Reavers all the way through his own country to attack Darthen. So, tactically, the sealing's a good idea. The question is whether it can be done."

"It can," Herewiss said. "But right now the timing's bad. I wouldn't dare try it with Glasscastle imminent; we'll have to wait until it passes. Which brings us to another problem—sealing off the peak of Adínë so that no sorcery of the Shadow's, or anyone else's, can bring anything down out of Glasscastle onto our heads. That, too, I can do; and I'll do it tonight. My only fear is that the sudden removal of access to a place where our mortal world and another world touch might cause Power imbalances. In a place as delicately balanced as Barachael is, with its years of warfare and piled-up negative energies, that can be dangerous."

"I know," Eftgan said. "But it can't be helped. My true-dream made it plain that the next time someone passed into or out of Glasscastle, so great a disturbance would follow that the Kingdoms might not survive."

Herewiss looked gravely at Lorn, and then back at the Queen again. "I'll do what I can, madam," he said. "I hope it'll suffice."

"It's more than I could have done, that's for sure..." Eftgan pushed her chair back from the table. "I leave the matter in your capable hands. I should be back from Orsvier tomorrow, and we can worry about sealing the pass itself then. As for you, Arlen—" She fixed Freelorn with a hard, smiling look. "I stand on the Oath. As soon as I get this unfought army off my right flank, and yours, then it's 'the Eagle for Arlen and the Lion at bay.' I trust you two will be willing to deal with *this* flank, should it become necessary today."

"Darthen," Freelorn said, returning Eftgan's look without the smile, "you know how my loved has been handling this so far. And I agree with him. I'd prefer not to shed blood, Arlene or Darthene."

"Cillmod's had no such compunctions," Eftgan said. "Neither have the Reavers, and right now there are Reavers coming here, and

Reavers at Orsvier. You two clear this flank, I'll clear the other. Then we'll have leisure to consider what to do about Arlen. When we campaign there I'll be guided by your judgment; you know your land best."

Freelorn nodded, looking solemn. Eftgan turned to the corner and picked up something that stood against the wall—a big old iron fireplace poker, its haft studded with rough white diamonds. It was Sarsweng, the battle-standard of the Darthenes. "I have to get my work done," the little fair woman said. "My husband hates it when I get home late. The Lady be with you all till I get back—"

"And with you," those at the table said.

Eftgan shouldered Sarsweng and strode out, the sunlight flashing on the poker's gemmed haft as she passed through a bar of light falling through the window by the head of the stairs.

At breakfast's end Harald, Moris, Dritt, and Lang went off with the Darthene officers to look the place over. Herewiss sat quietly in his chair, drinking spiced wine and looking thoughtful, while Freelorn stared out the window at the Adínë massif.

On her way to the stairs, Segnbora stopped beside him. Her underhearing was prickling with his unease. "You all right?" she said. "You look green."

Freelorn shrugged, not looking at her. "The change in altitude," he said. "It didn't agree with me. I had a bad night."

He was lying, she knew. His eyes were fixed on Adínë, and on the lesser peak, where a tiny glitter of silver bridgespan caught the morning Sun. Freelorn said nothing more aloud, but she caught his thought: *If only my dreams weren't so bad!* And behind the thought lay the sure conviction that something he had recently seen in dream was no baseless vision, but a foreknowledge of reality. A reality that he could avoid if he chose—

Freelorn swung around and leaned on the table. "Are you going to sit there drinking all day," he said to Herewiss, "or are you going to get up and get Eftgan's business out of the way so we can tend to our own?"

Herewiss's glance was much like Freelorn's—all mockery above, and love below and underneath that a breath of fear very much suppressed. "Hark to the early riser," he said, "who pulled me back into bed twice this morning when I would have gotten up. Come on, you can help correct my scansion. This wreaking tonight is going to be difficult…"

Their easy laughter faded down the stairs behind them. Segnbora sat down on the windowsill, gazing up in turn at the terrible blind walls and cruel precipices of Adínë. The mountain cared nothing for human life. With such an audience before her, and the empty room behind, Segnbora took what was likely to be her last opportunity for a while, laid her head against the windowframe, and mourned the dead.

An hour or so before sunset, the seven of them took horse at khas-Barachael gate to begin the ascent of Adínë.

While they were saddling up, Torve came out of the stables leading a little rusty Steldene gelding. "Of your courtesy," he said to Herewiss, "perhaps you'd take me as guide. I've ridden this trail a number of times, and climbed to the summit too."

Herewiss looked at the young man, suppressing a smile.

There was no need to read Torve's thought, for it was plain enough. He was staring at Khávrinen, which was slung over Herewiss's shoulder, like a small child staring at what the Goddess had left him on New Year's morning.

"With all these other spectators," Herewiss said, glancing around at Freelorn's band, most of whom were along only for the ride, "certainly we can use one person who'll earn his keep on the way. Come and welcome."

They headed out over the half-bridge that reached out from Barachael, on its two-thousand-foot pier of stone, across to the spur of Adínë proper. The sorcerer-architects who built the place had carved a hundred foot gap right through the spur, so that with the drawbridge up the fortress stood unassailable, one great corner-shoulder turned to the spur.

Once across, a causeway wide enough for ten horsemen abreast wound downward through several switchbacks. On both sides the road was overshadowed by cliffs, the shattered faces of which made it obvious that invaders had occasionally tried to come up that way against the defenders' wishes, and had had large rocks dropped on them for their pains. "Oh, they've tried a few times to shuck this oyster," Torve said cheerfully, "but even Reaver horses can't charge straight up."

At its bottom the paved road gave out onto a narrow saddle-corridor between khas-Barachael rock and Swaleback, a flattened, marshy minor spur of Adíne. Torve led them eastward and out into the valley proper, then southwestward along the skirts of the Adíne massif. Past two minor spurs they went. The ground was rocky, and every now and then the mountain, cooling from the warmth of the day, would let a little reddish scree slide down at them.

Under Adíne's lengthening shadow they turned due westward into a long shallow rampway scoured out by an ancient glacier, and picked their way carefully among the boulders that lay scattered about. Some fifteen hundred feet up the mountain's flank, the ascent became too steep for horses.

"We'll leave them here," Torve said, dismounting.

(Not all of them,) Sunspark said mildly.

Torve glanced up in great surprise from the hobbling of his gelding, and noticed that Herewiss's mount was calmly standing a foot above the ground. "Sir," he said, addressing Sunspark with the slight bow due a fellow officer, "we haven't been introduced."

"Torve, this is Sunspark," Herewiss said, dismounting. "Firechild, be good to him, he's on our side. Torve, if you ever need a fortress reduced on short notice, Sunspark is the one to talk to. He eats stone for breakfast."

Torve nodded. Having seen a man with the Fire he looked as if he was now ready to believe anything. "Up this way," he said, and led them up the side of the cirque to a trail that led along its top, under the shadow of the great Adíne summit.

They rounded the east-pointing scarp, moving quietly under the great out-hanging cornice of snow that loomed a thousand feet above them, and so came to face the north side of the lesser summit ridge. The ridge stood up sheer as a wall, overhung in places, itself at least seven hundred feet high.

"Don't worry, it's not an expert-level climb," Torve said, looking up the walls of rock and ice with relish. "Beginners could handle it—"

Freelorn, who had done extensive climbing in the Highpeaks of Arlen as a child, made a wry face.

Herewiss gazed up the cliff. "This trail is exactly as the song describes it," he said. "'Awful.' Torve, I hope you won't tell the Queen's grace on me, but I'm no climber. Maybe we Brightwood people have been down from the mountains too long. Sunspark?"

(Who'll go first?) Sunspark said, with an anticipatory grin. Freelorn's band blanched and began deferring to one another.

It took Herewiss and Freelorn and Torve first, managing the thousand-foot ascent to the summit ridge in a single leap. When Segnbora swung herself up into the saddle, Sunspark looked around at her with a naughty light in its eye. (Nervous?)

She gave it a threatening look in return and said nothing, while inside Hasai laughed at her. (Afraid of heights! Oh, Immanence within us, what kind of *sdaha*—)

(Well enough for *you* to laugh. You've got wings...)

Hasai continued laughing, a deep rough hiss. Segnbora did her best to ignore him and made very sure of her seat. A moment later she was glad of her care, for Sunspark shot up to the summit, trailing bright fire like a newborn comet and going at least twice as fast as it had the first time. It came down fast, too, landing on the snow with a hiss of steam and an incongruously light impact.

Shaky-kneed, Segnbora scrambled down. (Well, that was probably the high point of your day,) Sunspark said, genially malicious.

"Mmmnh," Segnbora said, slapping it familiarly on the flank, and scorching herself. "The others are waiting."

It gave her a final amused look, walked off the precipice and plunged down out of sight.

She picked up a fistful of snow to cool the burned hand and walked over to join the others. They stood around the base of the Skybridge where it rooted into the stone, some thirty feet broad. Drawn from the mountain's heart by Fire, the metal had the light uprising grace of a growing thing about it, as if Adínë had put up stem and flower. There were actually a number of stems—three lower ones, anchoring the main spans to consecutively lower points on the side of the peak. The angle of the bridge itself wasn't steep: it gained perhaps a foot in height for each three of length.

Herewiss held Khávrinen out and touched the bright silvery metal of the bridge with the point—then jerked his arm back quickly as a blue spark jumped from bridge to sword. "Firework, all right," he said, rubbing his arm as if it stung. "And a life-wreaking. No wonder poor Efmaer never came back. She either died of this wreaking or didn't recover enough Power to fight her way out again before Glasscastle vanished and took her away forever."

"You're going to have to do a life-wreaking too, then, to seal it off," Freelorn said, looking uneasy.

Herewiss stood with one hand on his hip, staring at the bridge the way a carpenter stares at a tree he must fell. "Well, the sealing has to be done whether I survive it or not. Don't worry, though, Lorn. Merely sealing it won't cost me the kind of effort building it cost Efmaer. I'll lose a month or two of life, and my head'll hurt tonight, but that's all."

Sunspark came up with Moris, whose great bulk left no room for other passengers, and then with Harald, Dritt, and Lang. Finally it paced over to Herewiss, peering over his shoulder at the bridge. Herewiss reached around its neck, patted it, then turned as if he had noticed something disturbing. "You all right, loved?"

(It's *cold* up there,) Sunspark said.

Herewiss looked shocked. The others glanced at one another: they'd never heard the elemental say anything like *that* before. It pawed the ground uneasily, melting snow.

(All this water,) it said. (It's uncomfortable. And there's something else...)

Segnbora turned her face away and considered what she felt coming from Sunspark: a cold that had nothing to do with the bone-chilling wind whispering about the summit. Up near the end of the bridge, something poured down a cold of the spirit that grew stronger as twilight grew deeper and the mountains less distinct. All of them were shivering, but the looks of foreboding and concern on their faces were far more disturbing.

Herewiss stroked Sunspark's neck. "We'll be down soon enough, loved. This won't take long. Shall we?"

It turned, offering him the stirrup. Herewiss mounted and sat looking at the bridge for a moment. It was a dark silhouette against the crystalline clarity of the golden mountain sunset. Abruptly he sent Fire down Khávrinen, lighting the whole mountaintop, and nudged Sunspark with his heels. The elemental walked off the cliff on the east side and stood on the empty air two thousand feet above the south-face cirque.

"Down a bit," Herewiss said. Sunspark sank leisurely through the air, as if sliding down a stairway banister. "Torve," Herewiss called up to the peak, "where are the usual accesses?"

"East face," Torve said, "and northwest. But a climber with stepping-spikes and a rope could go up about anywhere. As for the suicides, the Queen said they find themselves on the summit without climbing."

"Thanks," Herewiss said. "It's got to be the whole thing, then." He reined Sunspark close to the sheer cliff that fell down from the summit, and reached out to the ice and snow with Khávrinen. Despite her trouble with heights, Segnbora crowded close to the edge with Torve and the others to watch the wreaking.

Blue Fire lanced from Khávrinen's point, melting snow and striking into the bare red rock of the mountain, which heated from red- to yellow- to white-hot, and finally to an azure incandescence. Flame leaped up from the kindled stone, though the tongues were small and sluggish, like those of an ordinary fire on wet wood.

Sunspark moved around the peak, staying within arm's reach, and as elemental and rider progressed the bright line of blue melted itself into the stone behind them. Around the southeast spur they went, and out of sight. Most of Freelorn's band went around to watch the work on that side, but Torve stood by the cirque-facing cliff with Lang and Segnbora, shaking his head.

"This is a marvel," he said. "And strange. He's not what I expected a man with the Fire to be..."

"The Rodmistresses in the Precincts agreed with you, I'm afraid," Segnbora said absently. For the moment her mind wasn't on Herewiss. For all her uneasiness with heights, something different was stirring in her now: a desire to lift wings and fall out into that glorious gulf of darkening blue air beneath her. A smile crossed her face at the realization that Dragons, like any of the more common soaring creatures of the world, preferred to drop from a height rather than to work for altitude.

(And why not,) Hasai said, stretching wings lazily inside her and admiring the view himself. (Why waste energy, or manipulate field, when you don't have to? This is a fine height. Not as high as the Eorlhowe, to be sure, but a respectable height—)

"There it is," Torve said, his voice very quiet. Segnbora glanced up from the glacier.

High to the west, above the vista of Adíně peak behind them, past Esa and Mirit and the long sleek flank of Whitestack, had risen a slim crescent of Moon. To its right, and lower, a point of light glittered: the Evenstar. Quickly Segnbora looked upward along the silver-blue curve of the Skybridge...and forgot to breathe.

It had come out as silently and suddenly as the Moon. The Skybridge, half of a curve before, was whole now. The new part of the span *did* look to be made of the sky—cerulean blue, transparent, yet very much there. And at the span's end rose Glasscastle.

It was like a castle in an old story, a place built for pleasure rather than defense, fanciful and wide-windowed and fair. Halls and high towers pierced the upper air; slender spires were bound together by curving bridges and buttresses. Everything, from the wide-flung gates at the end of the bridge to the highest needle spire, was built of the same airy crystal as the bridge.

The evening sky could plainly be seen through walls and towers. The fading hues of the sunset—rose, gold, and deepening royal blue—reflected from them, pale and ghostly. Yet there was nothing fragile about the place. Glasscastle stood as immovably founded on the air as if on rock, reflecting the sunset colors, the icy light of the Moon, and even the frozen gleam of the Evenstar, but casting no shadow.

"Not a moment too soon," Herewiss said, his voice hushed, as Sunspark stepped up to the peak again, completing their circuit of the mountaintop. All around the barrel of the peak burned a line of blue, the circle within which the spell would be confined. Herewiss dismounted and stood for a moment with Khávrinen in his hand, gazing up at the crystalline apparition.

"Beautiful," he said. "But from now on, that's all it's going to be." He struck Khávrinen's point down into the snow at the foot of the bridge, and looked up the curve of metal, raising his arms—

—and stopped, squinting upward. "Who's *that?*" he said. Everyone looked. Segnbora's stomach constricted at the sight of the lone dark figure approaching the end of the metal part of the span, a tiny shadow against the twilight.

"I don't believe it," Herewiss said, in the voice of someone who *does* believe it, and wishes he were wrong. "I don't—*LORN!*"

nine

"It's dangerous to invoke the Goddess as you conceive Her to be," said Tav, *"and more dangerous still to invoke Her as She truly is."*

"Right enough," said Airru. *"Breathing is dangerous too. But necessary…"*

Tales from the South, x, 118

Herewiss's anguished shout came back as echoes, but had no effect on the small dark silhouette walking purposefully up the bridge. Herewiss swung Khávrinen up two-handed, pointing at Freelorn, and the sword spat a blinding line of Fire that ran upward toward him—but whatever wreaking he had in mind came unraveled before it ever touched Lorn. Many feet short of the bridge, the Fire hit some unseen barrier and splashed in all directions like water thrown at a wall.

Freelorn kept walking. Another twenty paces would see him up onto the phantom portion of the span. Herewiss wasn't waiting; he ran up the bridge after his loved, swearing frightfully in ancient Arlene, with Khávrinen streaming frantic Fire behind him. Sunspark went galloping up after him.

"Damn!" Lang said, and followed.

"Torve, wait here!" Segnbora said, unsheathing Charriselm as she headed after Lang.

"Are you joking? Do you know what the Queen would do to me?" Torve said, following her and the others onto the bridge.

They didn't run long—the altitude saw to that. Only Torve could run fast enough to catch up with Herewiss. In addition, the bridge was longer than it looked: an eighth mile, perhaps, to the point where it truly became sky. Far ahead of them, Freelorn's small figure slowed in its stride, hesitating only briefly. He put one foot on the phantom bridge, found it would support him, and went on as before, in a confident but hurried walk.

Damn! Segnbora thought as she ran. She clutched Charriselm harder than necessary, for her hands and face were numb from the chill. That other, more inward cold was pouring down more bitterly than before, yet she didn't suffer much from it. Something was blunting its effects; something inside her, burning—

(Hasai!) she said as she caught up with Herewiss and Sunspark and Torve. (Is that you?)

(*Sdaha,* against the great cold of the outer darknesses, this is nothing. We've learned to cope with cold.)

(I'm glad!) she said silently.

Herewiss and Torve had paused at the edge of the phantom span, and behind them Sunspark stood, looking downright dubious. The Fire-wrought part of the bridge was as thick and wide as the railless metal span, but clear and as fragile as air. Herewiss knelt to brush his fingers across it and straightened quickly, as if burnt.

"Whoever did this wreaking," he gasped, "they've got more Power than I have—and they're up there *now,* fueling it!" He got to his feet and stepped out onto the crystalline part of the bridge, assured himself that the footing was secure, and took off after Freelorn again at a run.

Torve and the others went after, Sunspark hammering behind them at a gallop, the bridge under its feet ringing like struck crystal.

Segnbora followed, stepping out onto the bridge. *Maybe I shouldn't,* she thought as she looked down. But to her surprise, the vista of shadows and creeping fog that veiled the south-face glacier half a mile below didn't much trouble her. Hasai's Dragonfire was strong in her, getting stronger as she headed after the others. *Lady grant it holds,* she thought, beginning to run.

At the Skybridge's end, between the two huge crystal doors that lay open there, a tiny figure passed into the dimness beyond and was lost to sight.

The group ahead of her slowed and came to a stop at the end of the bridge, gazing up at the chill clear grace of towers and keeps, at the awful tallness and thickness of the doors. Segnbora caught up with them feeling their nervousness. Sai Ebássren, the place was called in Darthene: the House of No Return. What lay within, no legend told. The only certainty was that when the three Lights were gone, the place would vanish, and anyone trapped within would never emerge.

Herewiss did not pause for long. Sending a great defiant glory of the Flame down Khávrinen's length, he walked through the doors. The twilight within swallowed him as it had Freelorn. For an instant Khávrinen flickered like a star seen through fog, and then its light vanished.

Sunspark hesitated at the doors, though only for a moment. It was trembling in body, a sight that astounded Segnbora.

"Firechild—"

(I'm bound,) it said in terror. (I can't burn. I can't change—)

She reached out to it in mind, perplexed, and felt Sunspark drowning in a cold more deadly than the lost gulfs between stars that Hasai had mentioned; a cold that could kill thought and motion and change of any kind. Hasai had been shielding her. (Maybe you should stay outside,) she said.

It turned hard eyes on her. (I will not let him come to harm in there,) it said, and turned away from her to walk shaking through the doors. The dimness folded around its burning mane and tail, and Sunspark vanished.

"That's done it," Lang said, genial and terrified. "Damned if I'll be outdone by a walking campfire—" He unsheathed his sword and went after, Torve close behind him.

There Segnbora stood, left alone on the threshold, trembling nearly as hard as Sunspark had.

No return.

She swore at herself and hurried in behind the others.

She was in a great hall, all walled in sheer unfigured crystal, through which Adínë and the peaks beyond it showed clear. The air was thick with a blue dusk, like smoke. She barely had time to see these things, though, before the terrible thought-numbing cold she had experienced through Sunspark came crowding in close around her, ten times worse than it had been outside.

From within her came an answering flare, Hasai and the *mdeihei* calling up old memories of warmth and daylight to fight the cold. She regained a little composure, looked around for the others. They were nowhere in sight. Deep in the twilight she could see vague forms moving far away, but somehow she knew that none of them were those with whom she'd entered. Her companions were all lost in the blueness, with Freelorn.

(Herewiss!) she called silently. (Sunspark!) But no reply came back, and her underspeech fell into a mental silence as thick as if she had shouted into a heavily curtained room.

"Herewiss!" she shouted aloud. The curling twilight soaked up the sound of her voice like a heavy fog. She set off into the blueness, hurrying.

For all her fearfulness, the sheer scale of the wreaking that had made this place astonished her. Even at first entrance the place had seemed as big as Earneselle, or the Queens' Hall in Prydon. But now as she walked across the vast glassy floor, the walls grew remote, and the ceiling seemed to become a firmament that not even a soaring Dragon could reach. Mirrored in walls, galleries and crystalline arches, she saw vague intimations of other rooms: up-reaching towers and balconies, parlors and courts, an infinity of glass reflected dimly in glass, too huge to ever search or know completely.

That terrible chill was part of the wreaking too, though here inside the castle it seemed not to bite so viciously at the bones. It was becoming a quality of the mind: a cool lassitude, a twilight that ran in the veins and curled shadowy in the heart, smothering fear and veiling the desire to be out of there. She could feel that cold rising in her, but the presence of Hasai the *mdeihei* was a match for it—ancient sunfire burned the twilight out of her blood as fast as it grew. A weary melancholy, a desire to leave off striving and surrender to the dim stillness of the place forever, came in with every breath—but there was Dragonfire at the bottom of her lungs, painful and bright, burning the sad resignation away. Frightened by the constant assault, but reassured by the Dragons' presence, Segnbora headed deeper into the shadowy blue.

The dead and those who had abandoned life slowly became evident around her. They were many, but none of them walked together. Young men and old women she passed; foreigners and countrymen, maidens and lords, and none of them took the slightest notice of her as they walked slowly, aimlessly through the blue—languid, uncaring, lost.

It was a terrible parody of the last Shore by that Sea of which the Starlight is a faint intimation. The dead who walked there were at least aware. Here and there Segnbora caught sight of a surcoat-device she recognized, but afterward she was generally sorry she had looked. The dead wandered through the blue with ancient wounds in plain sight, neither bleeding nor healed, the eyes of the wounded oblivious, as if the injuries belonged to someone else.

Through halls and galleries and passages Segnbora made her way, up and down stairs, while Glasscastle's inhabitants drifted around her, unaware, unconcerned. The feeling of sorrow in the air crushed in harder now, as if sensing her resistance. Every breath she drew seemed to have a catch in it, as if tears were about to follow.

Hasai and the *mdeihei* blazed within her, the white of their Dragonfire burning and glittering from scales of many colors. The defiance and dismay of the *mdeihei* at so many beings who had given up *being* burned them, burned her. Their appalled song, a heart-shaking weave of deep notes like the ocean speaking in outrage, fought with the song of melancholy that whispered from Glasscastle's walls.

Terrified that she might fall victim to the inward-stealing sorrow, Segnbora began breathing the litany of life and pain along with the *mdeihei* as she sought in mind for any feeling of Freelorn or Herewiss. The effort was in vain—the wreaking seemed to have shut down her underhearing almost completely. Finally she paused at a meeting-place of three long halls, and, in midbreath of a long phrase of Dracon song, felt a shadow looming over her.

She didn't look up. That would have broken the illusion of the great head hanging over her, the mighty body burning in its iron and diamond, defying the cool darkness. But she put out a hand behind her to touch the sapphire hide. The hand was taken, ever so carefully, between great jaws. The heat fighting the encroaching cold flared higher. (Have I told you recently that I'm glad you're here?) Segnbora said.

(Yesterday,) Hasai said, (I remember you telling me now. What's that?)

She looked where he did. From among indistinct, wandering forms came a flash of light—faint, but still bright enough to be noticed in this blue gloom. (I don't know, but let's see—)

The path ahead was dark. She reached up a hand, simultaneously reaching down inside her for her little dying spark of Fire. Forcefully, she willed the one thing she had always been able to manage: a brief flash of light. For once it would be enough.

(What!) she thought a second later, amazed. Nothing had come; her Power source was blocked from her.

She tried again. Nothing happened. "Damn," she said. Supposedly it took death to separate one from one's Power, however feeble. There wasn't time to puzzle over it now, however. *And what if Herewiss is having the same problem?* It was imperative that she find the others as quickly as possible.

The light glittered again, closer: a faint shimmer, there and gone. She headed toward the place where it had been—

—and went silent in shock. Not far away an outwall rose, a giddy frameless window on the evening sky and the upper peak of Adíně. And there against crystal and dying sunset stood silhouetted a small slender woman in a midnight blue surcoat.

Her dark head was bent. Her arms were folded in front of her as she gazed out into the sorrowing twilight: her back was turned. The summersky opals that were the eyes of the eagle wrought on the back of her surcoat now grasped and knitted together what little light there was, flashing it back at Segnbora. The eagle was white, in trian aspect, silver wings and blue Fire for eyes—the undifferenced Darthene arms, worn only by Queens and Kings. Segnbora had seen those same arms this morning on Eftgan's back. But these were worked in an antique style, in embroidery that looked new—

"Efmaer," Segnbora whispered.

Slowly she went to the unmoving woman, and stood beside her. Efmaer took no notice, just went on staring down into the pathless air. Her face was young, and frighteningly still. Her pale gray eyes had given up their color to the twilight, and taken on its violet shimmer.

Segnbora had to swallow twice before she could speak. "Queen," she said, "you're a long time away from Darthis."

The gray-violet eyes opened a touch wider. Disbelief danced in them for just a moment, and then began to fade again, sinking back into vague sorrow. The Queen didn't move.

"Efmaer," Segnbora said, louder. In the incredible silence, her own soft voice seemed to rattle her bones.

The Queen's eyes shifted just a little toward Segnbora. "Since I came here," Efmaer said, hardly above a whisper, "no one has spoken to me." She said it gently, absently...but her voice was not meant to be a gentle one. It had the rasp of bronze in it, but the bronze was blunted by time and disuse. "I dream," Efmaer said, "and the dreams grow vocal."

It isn't fair! Segnbora thought, losing her voice again, this time to impending tears. This woman had been one of the great powers of her time: vital, powerful, quick to laugh or fight or love. She was the woman who had fought Death and won. Yet now she was like all the others here, her spirit emptied out on the crystal floor.

"Queen," Segnbora said at last, "I'm no dream, unless I stay here too long. Have you seen a man go by here, one of the living? He was wearing the arms of Arlen."

Efmaer turned slowly, and her eyes dwelt on Segnbora's surcoat and her lioncelle passant regardant in blood and gold. "I know that charge," Efmaer said, showing for the first time a wrinkle of expression, a faint frown of lost memory. "My sister—"

"Enra," Segnbora said. "I'm of her line. You are my...my aunt, Queen."

"How many generations removed?" Efmaer said, and just for a second the bronze in her voice went bright.

Segnbora could not answer her.

"That many," said the Queen. "She is dust, then. She walks the Shore..."

Efmaer's voice drifted away as she started to lose herself again in the undercurrents of Glasscastle's sorrow. Segnbora winced. There was something nagging at the back of her mind, something that would mean a great deal to this woman. If only she could remember—

"Queen," Segnbora said, "if you haven't seen him, I can't wait. I have to find him."

"I could not find the one I sought, either," Efmaer said in that same half-dreaming voice. "I looked and looked for Sefeden, while the Moon went down and the Evenstar set. We must have passed one another half a hundred times, and never known it...but the Firework sustaining this place is greater than any mortal wreaking, and the place keeps its own. You will not leave..."

"My friends and I will get out," Segnbora said, hoping she was speaking the truth. "Come with us—"

Efmaer shook her head. "Only the living can leave this place."

"Are you dead then, Eagle's daughter?"

For the first time, Efmaer looked straight at Segnbora. Emotion was in those eyes now, but it was an utter hopelessness that made Segnbora shudder. "Do I look dead? Would that I were. Not Skádhwë itself could kill me here!"

"Skádhwë is here?"

"Somewhere," the Queen said. "Once the doors closed, I lost it, the way I lost everything else. Yet even while the doors were open, it did me no good." She closed her eyes, and with a great effort made another expression: pain. "I fought, but I could not kill myself, and so I am less than dead..."

Pity and horror wrung Segnbora, but she couldn't stay. "Queen, I have to go hunting."

"He will be with her," Efmaer said, still holding onto that look of pain like a banner of pride. "Far in, at the place where your heart breaks. But be out before moonset..."

She did not move or speak again. Segnbora paused only long enough to take one of those pale, pliant hands and lift it, kissing the palm in the farewell of kinsfolk of the Forty Houses. Then she turned and hurried away.

Hall after hall opened before her, all alike, huge prisms full of silence and the reflections of empty eyes: corridor like corridor, gallery like gallery, and nowhere any face she knew. Segnbora ran harder. Through the walls she saw the treacherous Moon hanging exactly where it had been when she entered. Likewise, the sunset appeared about to grow dimmer, but had not changed. Inside Glasscastle, she realized, there was eternal sunset. Outside, who knew how much time had passed? The three Lights could be about to vanish, for all she knew.

The thought of the others still unfound, of the awful way back to the main hall, of Efmaer's ghastly placidity, all wound together in her brain and sang such horror to Segnbora that for a few seconds she went literally blind. Trying to turn a corner in that state, she missed her footing and skidded to her knees. Desperately she tried to rise but could not. Her leg muscles had cramped.

There Segnbora crouched, gasping, sick with shame and rage. The awareness of the huge head bowing over her, great wings stretching upward, was small consolation.

(Sdaha.)

(Yes, I know, just a—)

(Sdaha. Here's our lost Lion—)

She pushed herself up on her hands and looked. There was Freelorn, not more than ten or fifteen feet away from her. He was kneeling on the crystal floor, very still, his head bowed. The sight flooded her with intense relief.

"Lorn," she whispered, and scrabbled back to her feet again, ignoring the protests of abused muscles. "Lorn. Thank the—"

—and she *saw*—

"—Goddess—" Segnbora's voice deserted her, taking her breath with it.

Her throne was wrought of crystal, like everything else in the place, but it reflected nothing from its long sheer surfaces. The one enthroned upon it seemed caught at that particular moment when adolescence first turns toward womanhood, and both woman and child live in the eyes. She was clothed in changelessness and invulnerability as with the robe of woven twilight She wore, and Her slender maiden's hands seemed able, if they chose, to sow stars like grain, or pluck the Moon like a silver flower. Yet very still those hands lay on the arms of the throne, and Segnbora found herself trembling with fear to see them so idle.

That quiet, beautiful face lay half in shadow as the Lady's gaze dwelt on Freelorn. For a long while there was no motion but that of Her long braid, the color of night before the stars were made, rising and falling slightly with Her breathing. Then slowly She looked up, and met Segnbora's eyes.

"Little sister," the Maiden said, "you're welcome."

Segnbora sank to her knees, staggered with awe and love. This was *her* Lady, the aspect of the Goddess she had always loved best: the Maker, the Builder, the Mistress of Fire, She Who created the worlds and creates them still, the Giver of Power and glory. Not even that night in the Ferry Tavern had she been stricken down like this, with such terror and desire. The Maiden gazed at her, and Segnbora had to look down, blinded by the divine splendor.

She gasped for breath and tried to think. It was hard, through the trembling, yet that she trembled this way disturbed her. Even as the Dark Lady, walking the night in Her moondark aspect, She did not inspire such fear. Something was wrong. Segnbora lifted her head for another look, and was once more heartblinded by Her untempered glory. Segnbora hid her eyes as if from the Sun, and began to tremble in earnest.

Within her Hasai bent his head low, and spread his wings upward in a bow like kneeling. (She's not as you showed me, within you. Nor is She like the Immanence. Its experience, too, is always one of infinite power, but the power is tempered—)

(It's—) The words seemed impossible, a wild lie in the face of deity, but she thought them anyway. (It's not Her.)

Segnbora cut herself off. She had a suspicion of what was wrong with this Maiden, and she wanted to get out of Glasscastle before she discovered she was right. Now Segnbora thought she knew Who was maintaining the great wreaking that had built the Skybridge, and Who was keeping the Glasscastle-trap inviolate. Segnbora got up—

—And was very surprised to find herself still kneeling where she was. With a flash of anger she met the Maiden's eyes again. They poured power at her, a flood of chill strength, knowledge, potency. The look went straight through Segnbora like a blade. Once before, long ago, those hands had wrought her soul, those eyes had critically examined the Maker's handiwork. Now they did so again, a look enough to paralyze any mortal creature, as flaws and strengths together were coolly assessed by the One Who put them there.

But Segnbora's soul was a little less mortal now than it had been when first created. There were Dragons among the *mdeihei* who had had direct experiences of the Immanence on more than one occasion, becoming both Song and Singer. The judgment of ultimate power didn't frighten them; they were prepared to meet the infinite eye to eye, and judge right back.

I am what I am, Segnbora thought, reaching back toward the Dragons' strength and staring into those beautiful, daunting eyes, blue as Fire. *Even as You are. And We are not done with me yet. I will not be judged and found wanting with work incomplete yet, with my Name still unknown—!*

Suddenly she was standing, surprised that she could. She expected to be struck with lightnings for her temerity, but nothing happened. Segnbora kept her eyes on the fair, still face, and saw, past the virulent blaze of glory, something she had missed earlier. The Maiden's eyes had a dazzlement about them, as if She too were blinded.

"My Lady," Segnbora managed to say, "I beg Your pardon, but we have to leave."

"No one comes here," the Maiden said gently, "who wants to leave. I have ordained it so."

The terrible power of Her voice filled the air, making the words true past contradiction. Segnbora shook her head, wincing in pain at the effort of maintaining her purpose against that onslaught of will. "But Freelorn is the Lion's Child," she said. "He has things to do—"

"He came here of his own free will," the Maiden said. She moved for the first time, reaching out one of Her empty hands to Freelorn. He leaned nearer with a sigh, and She stroked his hair, gazing down at him. "And now he has his heart's desire. No more flight for the Lion's Child, no more striving after an empty throne and a lost sword. Only peace, and the twilight. He has earned them."

The Maiden half-sang the words as She looked at Freelorn, and Her merciless glory grew more blinding yet. Segnbora shook her head, for something was missing. Whatever lived in those eyes, it wasn't love. And more than Her glory, it was Her love—of creating, and what she created—that Segnbora had worshiped—

(Sdaha, be quick!)

(Right—) She reached out to grab Freelorn and pull him away from the Maiden's lulling touch, but as she moved, the Maiden did too—locking eyes with Segnbora, striking her still.

"You also, little sister," She said, "you have earned your peace. Here you shall stay."

"No, oh no," Segnbora whispered, struggling again to find the will to move. But, dark aspect or not, this was the Goddess, Who knew Segnbora's heart better than she did.

The Maiden spoke from within that heart now, with Segnbora's own thoughts, her own voice, as the Goddess often speaks...*I'm tired, my mum and da are dead; there are months, maybe years of travel and fighting ahead of us—and even if I bring Lorn out of here, he'll probably just get killed. Isn't this better for him than painful death? And isn't it better for me, too? No death in ice and darkness, just peace for all eternity. Peace in the twilight, with Her...*

The song of the *mdeihei* seemed very far away. She couldn't hear what Hasai was saying to her, and somehow it didn't matter. The cool of the surrounding twilight curled into her like rising water. Soon it would rise high enough to drown her life, abolish both pain and desire.

The Maiden was seated no longer. Calm as a moonrise, She stood before Segnbora, reaching out to her. "There's nothing to fear," She said. "Nothing fails here, nothing is lost, no hearts break or are broken. I have wrought a place outside of time and ruin—"

The gentle hands touched Segnbora's face. All through her, muscles went lax as her body yielded itself to its Creator. Her mind swelled with a desire to be still; to forget the world and its concerns and rest in Her touch forever.

"Then it's true," she whispered as if in a dream. "There's no death here..."

"There is no death anywhere," the Maiden said, serene, utterly certain.

The relief that washed through Segnbora was indescribable. The one thing that had been wrong with the world was vanquished at last. Impermanence, loss, bereavement...all lies: the Universe was perfect, as it should have been from the beginning. There was nothing to fear anymore...

...Though it was curious that one dim image surfaced, and would not go away. In languid curiosity she regarded it, though her indifference kept her from truly seeing it for a long time. It was a tree, and a dark field, and brightness in the field. Night smells—

—smells?

There were smells that had little to do with night. Grounddamp. Mold. Wetness, where her hands turned over dirt, and jerked back in shock. The liquid gleam of dulled eyes in Flamelight. And the carrion smell of death—

In a wash of horror, the dream broke. Segnbora knew who she was again, and Who held her. The Maiden had made the worlds, true enough, and in the ecstasy of creation had forgotten about Death and let It in. But She had never denied Death's existence, or Her mistake, in any of Her aspects. Segnbora tried to move away from the hands that held her, and couldn't. Her body felt half-dead.

She settled for moving just one hand: the right one, the swordhand that had saved her so many times before. Her own horror helped her, for she realized now that she was in the presence of a legend: the One with Still Hands, that Maiden Who has stopped creating and holds all who fall into Her power in a terrible thrall. This was a dark aspect of the true Maiden, one Who had found no solace for the Error in Her other selves, and so from guilt and grief went mad, taking Glasscastle as Her demesne, Her prison.

And Lorn's. And mine, forever. Unless—

(Hasai!)

As she struggled to move, she was shocked to get no answer. Twilight had fallen in the back of her mind, and she could feel no Dragonfire there. She would have to raise her swordhand alone, even though the Maiden's cool hands on her face made it almost impossible to concentrate.

Sweat sprang out with the effort. The hand moved an inch. *I will not be entombed here with the dead and the near-dead! I will not leave my mdaha trapped in a forever of not-doing—or walk past Lang and Freelorn and Herewiss a thousand times and never see them! We have things to do!*

Another inch. Another. The hand felt as if it were made of lead, but she moved further into herself, finding strength. *I have things to do! Mdaha! Mdaha!!*

In the twilight, something else moved. Down inside her memory, in the cavern—not her own secret place, but the cave at the Morrowfane—stones grated beneath Hasai's plating, scoring the dulled gems of his flanks as he rolled over to be still from the convulsions at last. *Peace, O blessed peace, I thought the pain would never stop...* Horrified, Segnbora discovered that the One with Still Hands was there as well. Dark as a moonless night, she was soothing Hasai's worst pain, offering him a *mdahaih* state that would never diminish him to a faint voice in the background, but would leave him one strong voice among many.

But Segnbora knew the promise for a lie. *(Mdaha!* Move! She can't do it. She'll trap you in here, and we'll both be alive and *rdahaih* forever!)

He could not move. Desperately, Segnbora reached all the way back inside, climbed into his body and took over—wore his wings, lashed his tail, lifted his head, forced one immense taloned foot to move forward, then another, then another. Together they crawled to the mouth of the cave, Hasai gasping without fire as they went.

(Sdaha, have mercy! Let me go!)

She ignored him, pushing his head out the cave entrance into the clear night. The entrance was too small for his shoulders and barrel. She pushed, ramming muscles with thought, ramming the cave wall with gemmed hide, steel bones. (Now!) she cried, and they crashed into the rock together. It trembled, but held. (Now!)

Stones rattled and fell about them. The mountain shook and threatened to come down—but stone was their element: they were unafraid. Hasai began to assist her, living in his own body again, remembering life, refinding his strength. *(Now!)*

They jammed shoulders through the stone; wings smote the rock like lightning, burst free into the night. Segnbora's arm knocked away with one sweeping gesture the hands that held her. In rage and pity, and a desire to see something other than slack peace in those beautiful eyes, her hand swept back again. She struck the Maiden backhanded across the face.

Horrified, sickened by the violence she had done, Segnbora waited for the lightning...or at least for her own handprint to appear on Her face. Nothing came, though. No flicker of the eyes, no change in the mouth. Slowly the Maiden turned Her back on Segnbora, went back to Her throne, seated Herself. She said nothing. Segnbora found herself free.

(Sdaha—)

(I know, *mdaha,* time!)

Segnbora shook Freelorn by the shoulder. There was no answering movement—he seemed asleep, or tranced. *Well, dammit, if I have to carry him—* She reached down and took him under the shoulders, heaving hard. Freelorn made a sound, then. It was a bitter moan; a sound of pain and mourning as if some sweet dream had broken.

"Come on, Lorn," she said, wanting more to swear than to coax. Moonset couldn't be more than a quarter-hour away. "Come on, you Lioncub, you idiot, come on—!"

Turning, she got him up—then blinked in shock. They were all there, drifting in. Lang, looking peaceful. Dritt, Moris, Torve, Harald, all the life gone out of their movements. Sunspark, quenched in the twilight like a firebrand dropped in water. Herewiss, his light eyes dark with Glasscastle's dusk, and no flicker of Fire showing about Khávrinen.

Despair and anger shook Segnbora. She didn't have time to go into each mind separately and break the Maiden's grip. She doubted she had the strength, anyhow. Not even the Fire, had she been able to focus it, would help her now. *Though sorcery—*

She paused, considering. Perhaps there *was* a way to break them all free at once. It shamed her deeply, but she had no leisure now for shame. *(Mdaha—)*

(Do what you must,) Hasai said, placid. (I'll lend you strength if you need it.)

She gulped, and began building the sorcery. It was a simple one, and vile. These people were her friends. She had fought alongside them, guarded their backs, eaten and drunk and starved with them, lain down in loneliness or merriment to share herself with them. Their friendship gave her just enough knowledge of their inner Names with which to weave a spell of compulsion.

It was almost too easy. Their own wills were almost wholly abolished. The images of loneliness, loss of Power, and midnight fear that she employed were more than adequate. She knew less about Herewiss and Sunspark than about Freelorn and the others, but could guess enough about their natures to make them head out the door. Torve was hardest—a name and a wry flicker of his eyes was all she had. Yet she was terrified for this innocent, and her fear fueled his part of the sorcery, making up for her lack of knowledge.

Segnbora gasped out the last few syllables of the sorcery, then in her mind began carefully making her way out of the spell-construct, slipping through it sideways and scoring herself with sharp words in only a few places, thankful for once that she was so slim. Once out, she bound the sorcery into a self-maintaining configuration that would give her time to fight off the inevitable backlash and follow the others out.

One by one, her companions began drifting away from the Maiden's throne, out toward the great gates. She sagged a moment, feeling weary and soiled, watching them go.

Inside her, wings like the night sheltered her and fed her strength. *(Sdaha,* don't dally—)

(No.)

She looked one last time at the throne, where the Maiden sat silent, watching the others go, dispassionate as a statute in a shrine. *O my Queen,* Segnbora thought. Surely somewhere the Maiden dwelt in saner aspects, whole and alive and forever creating. But to see even a minor aspect of Godhead so twisted was too bitter for a mortal to bear for long. Hurrying, Segnbora turned away to follow the others.

They were far ahead of her, unerringly following the way out that she had set for them. The sorcery was holding surprisingly well, considering how long it had been since she had used sorcery to do as much as mend a pot or start a fire. She went quickly, trotting, even though physical activity would bring on the backlash with a vengeance. It felt wonderful to move again.

(Mdaha, you all right?)

(My head hurts,) he said, surprised.

(It's the effect of the sorcery; you're getting it from me.) Somehow she couldn't bring herself to be very solicitous: there were still too many things that could go wrong. They could come to the doors and find them closed. Or, if they were open, the bridge could be gone. Or—

Something moved close by, a figure approaching Segnbora from one side. It was not one of her own people, she knew. Her hand went to Charriselm's hilt.

Summersky opals winked at her as Efmaer came up beside her and walked with her, quickly but without animation. "You are leaving," the Queen said.

"Yes. Come with us—"

Efmaer shook her head. "Gladly would I come...but I never found Sefeden to get my Name back, and without it I cannot leave."

"But you *know* your Name."

"I have forgotten it," said the Queen.

Segnbora's insides clenched with pity...and suddenly the memory she hadn't been able to pin down drew itself across her pain-darkened mind like a falling star.

Urgently, she stopped and took the Queen by the shoulders. She had half expected to find herself holding a ghost, or something hard and cold, but there was warmth in that body, and an old supple strength that spoke of years spent swinging Fórlennh and Skádhwë in the wars against the Fyrd.

"Efmaer. Enra gave the secret to her daughter, and it passed into the lore of our line. I know your Name."

Undead, the Queen still managed to show shock and dismay that a stranger knew her greatest secret, the word that described who she *was*. But her distress lasted hardly a breath.

"Tell me quickly."

Segnbora swallowed, looked Efmaer in the eye, and whispered it—one long, cadenced, beautiful word in very old Darthene. Efmaer's eyes filled with it, filled with life, and tears.

"Kinswoman," she choked, the word carrying a great weight of thanks and wild hope. "Go. Don't stay for me. I'll meet you by the doors if I can. I have to see about something before I go."

Off Efmaer went into the unchanging dusk. Segnbora turned and ran after her friends. They were almost out of sight, near the outwall, where the twilight was thickest.

(*Mdaha,* what's the time?)

(There's a little left yet.)

She ran, harder than before, somehow feeling relieved of a great burden. She could feel the backlash of her sorcery creeping up on her, a hammering in her head and a weakness in the limbs. But her sorcery was holding, the others were still bound by her will. She caught sight of them now, not too far ahead, right up against—

"Oh *Dark!*" she said in complete despair, not caring what the swearing might invoke.

The great doors were shut. The faint light of the lying Moon shone high as before, but its light looked dimmer somehow. Freelorn and Herewiss were standing there looking dully up at the doors with the others. There was someone else there too, backed up against the entrance.

She pushed past Herewiss and stopped short.

There was more energy bound up in that waiting figure than in anyone else she had seen in Glasscastle. It was someone slender, a blade of a woman with about as much curve; someone with a slight curvature of the back that made for an odd stance, balanced forward as if perpetually about to lunge; someone with a sword like the sharpened edge of the young Moon, and short straight hair shockingly white at the roots; someone wearing a surcoat with Enra's lioncelle on it, passant regardant in blood and gold. Her dark eyes had a dazzlement about them, a terrible placidity. The One with Still Hands looked out of them. She was not defeated yet.

"*No,*" Segnbora whispered. Her other self gazed at her with eyes tranquil and deadly, and hefted another Charriselm, making sure of her grip.

"You're not leaving," her own voice said.

Segnbora stepped closer, fascinated by the sight of herself. The other watched her unperturbed, wearing the aura of calm that Shihan had taught her was better than armor.

(Mdaha, do you suppose she has you too?)

(As far as I can tell, I'm only here once. Is she truly *you?)*

Segnbora took another step forward.

"Save yourself some trouble," said the Segnbora who guarded the door, "and don't bother."

(I think so,) she said to Hasai. Queasiness started to rise inside her. The backlash was starting, and that meant she would soon be unable to hold together the sorcery. The others would start to drift away.

Her other self took a step forward. There was no question about her purpose. Segnbora raised Charriselm to guard, two-handed, and for the first time eyed her own stance as other opponents must have eyed it, seeking a weakness to exploit for the kill. What frightened her most was that so far, all those who had attempted what she must now attempt were dead.

They started to circle one another. "What I don't understand," the other said in a calm, reasonable voice, "is why you're trying to leave."

"I have my reasons," Segnbora said, shuddering at the strangeness of answering her own voice. "And I have my oaths—"

"Your oaths are vain," said her other self, edging closer in that particular sideways fashion that was Segnbora's favorite for closing inconspicuously with an enemy. "Who'll notice if you break them?"

"*She* will—"

"Oh, indeed. And what has She done for you lately, besides graciously allowing you a night in bed with Her? You know, don't you, that it was only Her sneaky way of telling you that you're about to die? You don't?" The other looked scornful. "Oaths! The way Freelorn's behaving, he'll never make it anywhere near Prydon: you at least know that! He'll get himself killed, along with the rest of you, on that cold dark ledge. Ice and darkness, that's what oaths get you—"

Segnbora slid closer, trembling. It was hard to think of this as just another fight. The necessary immersion in the other's eyes— that act of *becoming* the opponent in order to counter her moves before they happened—was impossible when those eyes had the mad Maiden's dreadful stillness in them. Her every glance made Segnbora afraid she would drown in their blank dazzle, drop Charriselm and surrender. To make matters worse, the backlash was hitting her harder now—not by accident, she suspected.

(Let us fight for you!) Hasai said suddenly.

Segnbora blinked at this, and her other self moved in fast, striking high at her head with Charriselm's twin. Segnbora whirled out of range toward the other's right, taking advantage of her own slightly weak backhand recovery, and came about again. There was a stir of movement among the silent watchers. For a moment her will to keep them in one place wavered, and they started drifting back toward Glasscastle's center, where the Maiden waited.

(Don't answer, *sdaha*. The *mdeihei* and I have been here long enough to be able to work your body; and your memories of your training are *now* for us. Tend to the sorcery. We'll deal with this other you.)

The other Segnbora was inching in again, waiting an unguarded moment—evidently Sheehan's injunctions about not wasting time on showy but ineffective swordplay were binding on her too. Segnbora didn't much want to give her body to the *mdeihei*, but even now the sorcery was unraveling. (*Mdaha, if* you get me killed—!)

(Killed? *Here?*) Hasai said, gently ironic.

The other leaped in to the attack again. While she was still in midair Segnbora felt other muscles, other wills, strike through her body and wear it as she had worn Hasai's earlier. Without her volition she saw Charriselm twist up and slash out in the *harden* move, the edge-on stroke and backstroke that opens the *kier* sequence.

Normally, the feint of the first stroke and the vicious backhand cut of the second would have been enough to disembowel her opponent, but Segnbora's sword met its mate halfway through the first cut. The two swords together sang a tormented note like a bell having its tongue cut out. Charriselm glanced down and out of the bind, and white Darthene steel sliced air where Segnbora would have been, had not the *mdeihei* twisted her impossibly sideways.

(Ow! My back!)

(You're still alive, aren't you? Tend to the sorcery!)

There was no more time for discussion. In the back of her mind the hard-stressed words of the sorcery were turning on one another, blades cutting blades, striving to undo themselves from her constraints. Ignoring her roiling insides, Segnbora shoved words back into place, reinforced them, threatened them, cajoled them in heartfelt Nhàired. It was like carrying water in a sieve, for all the while the power of the wreaking wore away at her outer mind, letting the twilight seep in again.

While she stopped up hole after hole of the sieve to keep her sorcery from running out, Segnbora watched the *mdeihei* inside her skin using her to turn and cut and thrust, attacking high and low, using all-out routines like *seek* and *arid*. Nothing came of it. Every time, Charriselm met its otherself in her twin's hand, and the steel cried out. Every time she felt her own leverages, her own moves, being used against her. Again and again the *mdeihei* saved her life with dives and dodges that nearly snapped her spine, but the situation got no better.

(I had—no idea you were so—difficult in a fight, *sdaha,*) Hasai said, breathing hard from Segnbora's exertion. He lunged her forward in the dangerous hilt-first *mutiny* maneuver, but her otherself twisted nimbly away.

(Neither did I.) Segnbora pushed a couple of words frantically back into the weave of the spell. As she did, she remembered something Efmaer had said. *I could not kill myself, and so I am less than dead.* Was this what had happened to her? Had she fought herself here at the gates and lost?

Hasai backed her up a step, raised Charriselm and stood poised in her body like a dancer, waiting for imprudence to tempt her adversary within range. The other Segnbora took the bait, stepping in suddenly and swinging—the *edelle* slash that could open Segnbora up like an oyster if it connected.

The Dragon sucked her stomach in and struck downward with Charriselm to stop the *edelle,* then whirled the blade up in a blur to strike at the other's unprotected throat. But her otherself came up to block, and Segnbora's stroke was slightly off angle. The two swords met, and this time there was no scrape, but rather a sudden snap that went right to the pit of Segnbora's stomach. A handsbreadth above the hilt, Charriselm broke in two. The blade-shard went spinning away through the air to fall ringing on the crystal floor.

"*No!*" she cried, staring in anguish at the broken-off stump that had once been whole and beautiful. Before the doors, her otherself relaxed into guard, knowing Segnbora would think three times about trying a passage armed with only half a sword. At the back of her mind, words began falling away from one another—

A quick motion off to one side brought her around. It was Efmaer. The Queen came to her with her hands extended, and nothing in them...or not quite nothing. She held a long slim darkness, like a slice of the utter darkness beyond the world, like a splinter of night made solid—

"You gave me my Name," Efmaer said, urgent. "This is all I have to give you. Take it!"

Only for a second Segnbora hesitated as she stared at the uncanny thing. It was impossible to focus upon it despite its razor-sharp outline. Then she seized it out of Efmaer's hands, by the end that was slightly thicker, and swung it up. There was no weight of hilt or blade; no feeling of actually holding anything, not even coolness or warmth or resistance to the air.

(Hasai—)

(Trust us, we'll do well enough with it.)

"Kinswoman, be warned," Efmaer said, "it'll demand a life of you some day—it did of me!"

Segnbora nodded absently. She was already busy with the sorcery again, shoring it up. Her otherself dropped once more into a wary crouch, waiting, watching Skádhwë. Hasai saw his advantage and moved in on the other, not waiting.

"So," said the other, "now you'll kill me—"

Segnbora wrought a long word in Nhàired and wove it into a spot in the sorcery that was going bare. "You're in my way," she said, remotely feeling the strange heft of the sword as Hasai lifted it.

Legend said it would cut anything, but would it work here, inside another legend?

"That's only part of it," her otherself said. "You *like* to kill."

She couldn't help looking into the other's eyes then, and seeing there the placid regard of the Maiden. The power that had almost drowned her before stirred again.

Hasai danced in close, striking with Skádhwë. (I can't—!) Segnbora whispered in her mind. Her resistance made the *mdeihei* guiding her body miss the stroke. Her otherself slipped out of range, whirling to come at her on her weak side. The *mdeihei* spun Segnbora about too, so that the face-off stood again as it had.

Down in Segnbora's mind a word unraveled itself from her sorcery and slithered away like a serpent of light, followed by another, and another. Herewiss turned away, and Freelorn, and Lang—

(Sdaha!)

"Yes!" Segnbora said aloud. The regard the other brought to bear on her wasn't that of *her* Maiden, not the Lady of the White Hunt, defender of life and growth. The occupant of her otherself was a counterfeit of Her, an indweller as committed to stagnation as Hasai was to doing and being. The *mdeihei* felt her resolve and leaped again.

The other Segnbora, perhaps thinking Segnbora wouldn't kill or hurt her, was slow about retreating. A second later she danced back with a cry. Red showed high up on her arm, pumping fast.

Segnbora flinched. She had felt nothing, no bite of sword into flesh at all.

"If you kill me, you're killing part of yourself!" the other cried, sounding afraid for the first time.

Hasai pressed in, following his advantage. Segnbora felt tears coming, but didn't argue as she patched the spell again. She was coming to realize what she was going to have to do. It would have been easiest to let Hasai win the fight, but she refused to allow him sole responsibility for that. The spell would hold for a second.

She moaned out loud, took back her muscles, slid in and struck with Skádhwë at the Charriselm being raised against her.

With no more feeling than if it had been cutting air, the shadowblade sheared effortlessly through Charriselm and then downward to take off her otherself's arm at the elbow. The thick sound that the arm made in striking the floor, like so much dead meat, turned Segnbora's stomach. The agony in the other's eyes was beyond words as she fell to her knees.

Segnbora would gladly have dropped Skádhwë, but it seemed to be holding her hand closed about it. Her otherself reached down to work the broken Charriselm out of the severed hand, and struggled to her feet. She lifted the useless sword left-handed, and faced Segnbora with tears streaming down her face.

"*Why couldn't you have stayed?*" the other Segnbora screamed at her. "Why couldn't you just let it happen! You always wanted—"

Segnbora swung Skádhwë again, and felt nothing as that head with so much silver in its hair went rolling away across the crystal floor, trailing red. The slender trunk dropped, pumping out what seemed too much blood for so slight a frame.

One more body. That's all it is. One more body. Oh, Goddess help me—!

Time was short, and the sorcery was unraveling, assaulted by her revulsion at what she had done. Segnbora lurched toward the doors, aware of Efmaer off to one side, of Herewiss and Freelorn drifting away. The doors were sheer, without any latch, and fitted so closely together that a thin knifeblade couldn't have been pushed between them. There was no hope of swinging open their massive weight.

Unless, perhaps—

She raised Skádhwë over her head and struck down, a great hewing blow. The sword sank half its depth into the crystal, as if into air. Again she struck, and a shard of the thick glass peeled away and shattered on the floor. Again, and again—

A great prism-slice the size of an ordinary doorway leaned out toward her, slow as a dream, and fell. It smashed thunderously right at her feet.

"Come on, get out!" she shouted at the others, yanking in her mind at the compulsion-sorcery.

Like hounds on leashes they all came stumbling after her, Freelorn and Herewiss, Lang and Dritt and Moris, Harald and Torve and Sunspark, out the jagged hole into the true twilight. The Moon was telling the truth again, and frightening truth it was. Its lower curve had dipped behind the wall of the Adínë glacier's cirque. Only the crescent's two horns still showed in the sky. West of the Moon, the Evenstar balanced precariously on the ridge of the cirque, a trembling, narrowing eye of light.

Behind Segnbora, Herewiss shook his head as the wind hit him, and glanced around like a man roused from reverie. Then he glanced up at where the Moon should have been, and wasn't. "My Goddess, it's almost gone, the *bridge*—!"

Segnbora stood poised by the door, peering in desperately. "Efmaer!" she cried.

Just inside the door Efmaer stood, looking over her shoulder, trying to catch a last glimpse of her loved through the twilight.

"Efmaer!"

The Queen turned to Segnbora, reached out a hand. Segnbora took it and pulled, and Efmaer stepped through the jagged portal—

—She had not even time to look surprised. She simply stopped in midmotion, and went to dust: the dust of a woman five hundred years dead. Within seconds the relentless wind came howling down from the mountain, took her, and whirled her away.

Segnbora stared stupidly at her empty hand, then turned and ran through the group, who stood watching her with confusion and fear on their faces. "Come on," she yelled through her sobs, "the wind is back, the bridge is going to vanish! You want to try standing on air?"

She ran out onto the phantom part of the Skybridge, half-hoping it would give way under her and wipe out the sickening memory of the Queen's hand going to dust in hers. *Oh, Efmaer—!*

Footsteps pounded close behind her. The Moon's horns looked across the cirque ridge at her, far apart, growing shorter. The Evenstar wavered. Segnbora ran, gasping and terrified. Freelorn came pounding past her, showing off his sprinter's stride to good advantage. Hard behind him came Herewiss, with Khávrinen once more afire on his back. Then came Sunspark, streaming fire like a runner's torch from mane and tail. Torve and Lang and Harald and Moris and Dritt passed her too, wheezing.

Segnbora saw them all make the solid part of the bridge just at the moment the Moon pulled its horns completely beneath the ridge, and the Evenstar closed its eye and went out. With ten yards to go, the bridge of air dissolved beneath her, and she began to fall...

But Hasai was doing something. The fall simply went no farther, as if she had wings. In the moment of time he bought her, hands grabbed at her frantically and pulled her up onto the steel.

Segnbora shook them off and headed down the bridge, fast, only slowing when the angle of the arch made footing difficult. Tears blinded her, burning coldly in the icy wind. She struck them out of her eyes, raging at heart, and plunged down to the end of the span, down to rock and snow. There Segnbora ducked around to one side of the Skybridge, and slid on her rear end toward one of the huge supports rooted in the mountainside.

The others were out of sight. Above her she heard them calling her, confused, frightened, relieved; and she ignored them. *Poor crippled One, I pity You—but You'll have no more company in Your exile. Nor am I going to let Herewiss give up a piece of his life to bind this grave closed. Enough life's been wasted here. I have a better way—*

She came up hard against the leftmost support, a pillar of Firewrought steel easily as thick as Héalhra's Tree in Orsmernin grove. Even in the dark it shimmered a ghostly blue.

"Segnbora." Herewiss's voice floated down to her from above. *"What are you doing?"*

Segnbora didn't answer. The others had had enough time to get off safely. She raised Skádhwë and with a great swashing blow sliced right through the steel support. *Stone or steel or soul,* Efmaer had said—And the Fire in the steel was no hindrance. The pillar cracked and buckled backward, groaning, peeling apart from itself like a wound in metal flesh. Segnbora sliced at it again. The groan grew terrible as the upper part of the pillar came away from the lower, and the span of the bridge began to lean away from the mountainside.

Segnbora scrabbled across rock and snow to the second support, and hewed that too. Far above, the groan grew to a scream of tortured metal. Smiling grimly, taking ferocious pleasure in the sound, Segnbora made her way to the last support, swung Skádhwë back, and struck. The slim shadow of its blade flicked through the metal and out the other side. The immense shadow of the Skybridge above her, shifting, leaned faster and faster away, and suddenly gave way completely to the deepening violet of the evening sky.

The screaming stopped. Silently as a flower petal—and as slowly, as gracefully—the huge strip of steel floated down into the abyss of blue air. Then with a crash that shook all Adíně, it struck the southface glacier halfway down its slope, shattering it. Up and out the broken bridge rebounded, falling again. The air was littered with small, lazily turning splinters of ice and steel as the bridge fell on, broke into more pieces, fell again...until at last only the faint echoes of its fall remained, along with the sound of Segnbora's gasps, coming through tears of anguish and triumph.

There was a long silence from above, broken after a while by Herewiss's subdued voice.

"Well," he said, "that's one thing less Eftgan has to worry about..."

ten

Fear hissed at me and struck
from beneath a stone.
I crushed its head with a rock.
Though dead, it still squirmed.

(*Darthene Rubrics*, xxiii)

Segnbora came down from her room the next morning and made her way to the breakfast hall only to find it empty. There was not even a single platter or cup on the table. The great inner court, when she passed through it, however, was lively as a wasps' nest is after it's been kicked. People and horses in the courtyard clattered and shouted so loudly she could barely hear Hasai's comments inside her, and the *mdeihei* were drowned out entirely. Tack was being burnished, weapons readied, and the silver chains of officers were everywhere.

(What goes?) Hasai inquired, as loudly as was polite.

(How the Dark should I know?) she said.

Up the stairs to the battlements she went, three at a time, Charriselm's scabbard bouncing at her side, its every bump a reminder of the black non-weight that was sheathed in it now. The place where her sword had been felt like the socket of a lost tooth. She was grateful when she reached the top, but not reassured at all by the sight of Freelorn and Lang and Moris and Dritt and Torve leaning on their elbows, looking over the battlements, calm of face but tense of stance.

As she came up to them, something went *rap!* through the bright morning air, a sharp sound that raised goosebumps on her arms.

"What is it?" she said, joining them at the battlement. None of them answered her, so she looked for herself. Down in the valley, looking remote, a dark blot surrounded the star-shaped walls of Barachael town. The blot heaved and moved oddly, separated into smaller pieces, consolidated again. One part of the darkness moved rhythmically backward and then forward again, toward the town's big brass-studded gates.

The forward movement arrested suddenly, and after several seconds the faint rapping *boom* of the battering ram came floating across the air.

"Damn, oh *damn*," Segnbora said, and out of reflex reached for Charriselm's hilt in frustration. She snatched her hand away as it fell to the not-hot-not-cold smoothness of Skádhwë's end.

Torve, beside her, raised his eyebrows idly at Segnbora's swearing. "It's silly, really," he said. "The people are all inside khas-Barachael, so there's no reason for the Reavers to force the gates—if they can. I just hope they don't decide to fire the fields. It's late for putting in another crop of wheat..."

There was really nowhere else to put her hand. After a couple seconds of hooking it uncomfortably in her belt, Segnbora sighed and let it fall to Skádhwë's hilt. It was an odd feeling, neutral, like touching one's own skin. "The Reavers arrived last night?" she said.

Torve nodded. "Through the pass. I dare say the Queen is wishing she'd had Herewiss seal the pass before taking on Glasscastle."

"Where is the Queen?"

"Upstairs with Herewiss," Freelorn said, giving Segnbora a sidewise glance meant to be disciplinary. "If you'd get up earlier, you wouldn't miss so much."

Segnbora made a face at her liege and leaned on the battlement like the others, elbows-down, staring at the Reavers' futile work in the valley. "More are coming?" she said. It was a rhetorical question. There were always more coming.

"Here and elsewhere," Lang said, not looking at her, in that way he had when he was worried and didn't care to let his eyes betray it.

"What happened at Orsvier?"

"She won."

"You said 'elsewhere' just now," Segnbora said, puzzled. "Where's the new incursion?"

Lang wouldn't answer her. She looked past him at Dritt. "Bluepeak," Dritt said.

Segnbora's stomach began to churn, and inside her the *mdeihei* sang their own unease in response to hers. Herewiss's dream was starting to come true, then. Of all the places in the world where the Shadow's sleeping influence shouldn't be disturbed, Bluepeak was the foremost.

"How many Reavers?"

"Her scrying wouldn't come clear on that point," Torve said. "Maybe three thousand. People, a large supply convoy, beasts...and Fyrd."

"Oh no," she whispered. These must be more of the thinking kind, then, the species of Fyrd they had fought en route to the Morrowfane. The Lion and the Eagle had supposedly vanquished them at Bluepeak long ago, but now they were back. No doubt they were thirsting for vengeance for the times before they had gained intelligence; times when humankind preyed on them.

"Looks like Bluepeak will be our job," Moris muttered.

"Looks that way," Torve said with his usual calm. He turned his eyes back to the Reavers in the valley, who—having had no luck with the town gates—were sitting down to a late breakfast.

"Idiots," Harald said under his breath. "Torve, couldn't you sent out a sortie?"

"Without orders? The Queen would take my officers' chain and use it to hang me by my privates," he answered, only half-joking. "Besides, they're out of bowshot."

Wings whistled overhead. Segnbora and the others glanced up and saw what looked like fire flying. Feathers burning like embers, eyes like live coals, a tail like flame streaming back from a torch...

They flinched back from the parapet as the brightness landed there. It stood still long enough to smooth a couple of smoldering feathers back into place, then ruffled itself up in a flurry of red-hot brilliance.

(Levies,) it said, (Strategy and tactics, forced marches, that's all your soldiers can talk about. I'm bored.)

Segnbora raised an eyebrow at the form Sunspark had adopted. "Shame, Firechild! There's only one Phoenix!"

(What's shame?) Sunspark said. (As for the Phoenix—if it's so fond of this shape, let it come try a couple of falls with me. If it wins, I'll let it keep the form.) It peered over the battlement at the Reavers below, interested. (Are they with us?)

Segnbora gazed at Sunspark with idle affection. Its tail-feathers were like those of a peacock, but red-golden and bearing eyes like coals, and they were searing the stone against which they lay. She started to get an idea. "No," she said.

The elemental turned on her fiery eyes that glowed hotter by the moment. The others moved down the battlement, all but Torve, who stood his ground. She felt Sunspark examining her state of mind with hot impatient interest. (This is a new kind of joke, perhaps?)

(Yes. And no. Better than a joke.)

(Something for Herewiss? Something to make him glad?)

(Yes.) She considered her thought carefully before sharing it. (Before I tell you, consider this: When he finds out about it, will he be angry, will he be in pain? If he won't...) She let the thought rest.

Sunspark looked down at the Reavers, considering carefully. For all its power, it knew it had much to learn yet about being human. (What are they doing?) it said, audible to the others.

Torve looked at it as calmly as if it had been one of his own people. "Breaking the gates of the town," he said, "to get inside and kill the people, or take their belongings at least."

Sunspark didn't look up from the valley. Segnbora caught its thoughts: *Herewiss doesn't care for killing, or for robbing either.*

He tries to prevent them whenever possible. (And when they've done that? What then?)

"They'll come here and try to kill us, so that no one can stop them from doing as they please in this part of the country," Torve said.

(Oh, will they now!) Sunspark said.

It leapt from the battlement in a swift flash of fire that sent them all staggering back. Segnbora felt her singed face to find out if her eyebrows were still there. Once certain that they were, she looked around hurriedly. Sunspark had vanished. But Harald and Dritt were pointing down at the valley and laughing.

Far down in the depths of air, the group around the battering ram suddenly began to break up. One person after another jumped up to beat frantically at smoldering clothes, their yelps of consternation trailing tardily through the air.

"Can it manage a whole army, though?" Lang asked uncertainly.

Then it was Segnbora's turn to point and laugh, as a bloom of light erupted before the gates of Barachael, followed by the sound of screaming. The ram—a lopped monarch pine, full of pitch as monarchs are—literally exploded in red-hot splinters and clouds of burning gas. People and ponies were flung in all directions. Then from the explosion site something like a serpent of flame went pouring over the scorched ground. It lengthened and wound right around the walls of Barachael, met its tail and kept on going, coiling around, reaching upward. In moments the town was lost behind burning walls, and the huge head of a coiled fire-serpent wavered lazily above the town. The confused shrieks and yells of routed Reavers mingled with the screaming of their ponies. People and animals ran every which way. A roar of amazed laughter and applause went up from the walls of khas-Barachael.

In response the Reavers, who had moved away from Barachael town and toward the keep, raised a chorus of war shouts. But their shouts had a half-hearted sound to them, as if they had other matters in mind. Sunspark was looking down at them with innocent malice, its fiery head swaying like that of a sleepy viper deciding whether to strike.

"What the—!" someone said from a higher parapet.

Segnbora glanced up and saw Eftgan and Herewiss looking over the rail at Barachael town, very surprised.

"Your idea?" Eftgan said to Herewiss.

"No!" he said, grinning down at Sunspark.

It stretched up its flame-hooded head and blinked at him goodnaturedly. (They had torches,) it said, (and might have burned the town. But if anybody's going to do any burning around here, it's going to be *me*.)

Herewiss and Eftgan came down to the battlement together and leaned on the parapet with Freelorn's followers. "I wish that sealing the pass was going to be as simple," Eftgan said.

Freelorn glanced at her. "It actually *can* be done?"

Herewiss nodded. "It took me a while to work out the exact method, and it'll take some hours to attune to the mountain properly...but, yes, I can do it."

"And survive?"

Herewiss's glance crossed with Freelorn's, gently mocking.

"That's with Her, of course," he said, "but I have a few things to do yet before I go willingly to death's Door. I believe I'll live."

"It's risky, though," Eftgan said, as if resuming an argument with herself. "The earth always moves better on a night when the Moon's full, but the next time that happens there's an eclipse. The Shadow will be very strong then—"

Segnbora bit her lip. In a place as bitterly contested as Barachael, where the land was soaked with centuries of blood and violent death, nearly any wreaking could be warped by the built-up negative forces. An eclipse was no help at all. And to attempt a wreaking that involved unconsciousness of the upper mind, as this one surely would—

"I'm strong too," Herewiss said. The complete assurance in his voice made Segnbora shudder. She had heard such assurance before, and disaster had followed. "The wreaking itself doesn't worry me; I received more than enough Power to handle it at the Morrowfane. The tricky part will be the survey of the land. That'll have to be done out-of-body, and it'll take at least a day. Moreover, it has to be done today, or tomorrow at the latest, in order for me to be properly rested up for the long wreaking."

Lang raised his eyebrows. "Survey?"

Herewiss nodded and leaned on the parapet. "Can't seal the pass without checking the valley to see how its stone lies—strata, faults, underground water. Touch the wrong part of a landscape and the whole thing could be destroyed."

"For one so new to this work, your caution's still insufficient, for this area is quite unstable," someone said. Heads turned toward Segnbora, confusing her terribly until she realized that it was *she* who'd spoken; someone had begun using her voice without consulting her on the matter.

"There are two major faults under the valley," Hasai said. "Additionally, eight minor vertical faults run east-west between Adínë and Aulys, and one runs across the lower Eisargir Pass. One major vertical fault crosses the valley mouth from Swaleback to Aulys's southern spur—"

(Mdaha? What are you—)

(If he'll work with stone, here of all places, he'd best learn this, *sdaha!)* said the great dark voice inside her. "Then beneath those is a lateral fault which runs down the Eisargir Pass from the foot of Mirit into the valley, past the town, and out into the plain. It's treacherous, and the chief reason we made no Marchward here; it hasn't moved since before we came. Touch it wrongly and the fault will discharge and fold the valley right in on itself. The mountains may come down too, especially Adínë; its support-spurs are rooted too close to the lateral."

The others stared at her, particularly Herewiss. He opened his mouth, but paused a moment, unsure how to begin. "Sir—"

"I greet you, Hearn's son," she said, and bowed slightly to approximate Hasai's informal bow within her.

"Sir, how do you know all this?"

The *mdeihei* laughed indulgently, as one laughs at a child. "We are Dracon," Hasai said, very gently. "We *know*. Stone is our element."

"Sir," Herewiss said, "I'd like to trust what you say, it'd save me a great deal of time, but—"

"—but you don't understand," Hasai said, patient. Segnbora was surprised to hear the overtones of his inner song, calm and measured, coming out in her own voice. "Nor do we; what you ask is a mystery. Even we aren't sure how stone became our element. But in the world from which we came, we were born in the stone, and dwelt in it. These are the very earliest times of which we speak. When food and drink failed us, stone and starlight were all we had left. Over a long time we learned to use them. Those who didn't understand stone—how it could be moved to make shelter, or melted with Dragonfire to help one find more starlight in dim times—those didn't survive. Those of us who lived to become as we are now, are born knowing the structure and movement of rock as we know how to use our fire to shape it. We experience stone as if it were part of us. It *is* part of us. We are the foundations, the roots of the world."

Herewiss and Freelorn looked at each other. No one on the parapet spoke.

From down in Barachael valley, the hot eyes of the blazing serpent that encircled the town looked up with interest. (You're good with fire, are you?) Sunspark said, its voice lazy, but full of challenge.

Hasai turned Segnbora's head and looked down at the elemental calmly. "In our own way," he said. "For sport we chase the day around the world and drink it at our leisure; for leisure we bathe in the world's blood. We might be said to know something about fire."

Sunspark glanced at Herewiss, as if considering the agreements that bound it, and then back at Segnbora. "Some day," it said formally, "we'll match our power, you and I, and see which is greater."

"Some day," Hasai said calmly, "we shall." The words made Segnbora squeeze her eyes shut against a sudden blinding headache, for they were in one of the precognitive tenses, future definite, describing something that had not yet come to pass but most certainly would. A room somewhere, dim and suddenly cold with a frost that bit at the bones, and Skádhwë in her hand: a shadow falling over everything, a shriek of pain—

The memory passed, and the sight of common daylight came back to her. Hasai lifted her head again, as perturbed by the precognition as she, but for different reasons of which Segnbora could make nothing. In any case, he seemed determined not to let it show, for it didn't matter to the task before them. "Hearn's son," he said, "do you desire our aid?"

Herewiss looked at Segnbora as if trying to see past Hasai's voice. "'Berend, what do *you* say?"

She coughed and cleared her throat, getting control back. "I say, if Hasai offers you help, take it."

"In that case," Herewiss replied slowly, "I'd like to check his assessment of the faults—" He stopped, unwilling to complete his suggestion.

"In my mind?"

"Yes."

Segnbora considered the idea. "You're welcome to look in," she said finally. "When?"

"As close as possible to the hour when we begin the wreaking. Tomorrow night?"

"Wait a minute!" Segnbora said, panic rising. *"We?"*

Herewiss shrugged. "I'll need ongoing information during the wreaking itself. I could probably do it alone, but why stretch myself thin when there's assistance offered?"

Segnbora hesitated. To participate in the wreaking itself would mean becoming involved with Herewiss's Fire. And she'd sworn she'd never touch Fire again; she'd had suffered too many frustrations on its account. Besides, being unable to focus, she might become a danger to the proceedings…

Herewiss picked up her last thought. "'Berend, you came out of the Precincts with every thing they had to teach, less one," he said. "I doubt you'll foul a wreaking in progress. Goddess knows how many of them they put you through!"

Most of them, Segnbora thought sourly, *for all the good it did.* She had no excuse. "All right," she said.

"We'll move mountains together," Hasai added in a rare show of humor, with the slow quiet laughter of the *mdeihei* singing counterpoint behind.

Herewiss nodded to Segnbora, and then turned to Eftgan. "Madam," he said, "we have to finish discussing the Bluepeak business."

He started back up the stairs to the tower, taking them two at a time, Khávrinen bouncing at his back and trailing blue Flame. Eftgan gave Segnbora a curious look and followed.

What have I got myself into! Segnbora thought. She put her head down onto her hands and gazed across the valley at Barachael. Below, the fire-serpent folded its hood and looked at her with innocent wickedness. (Tell me a joke?) it said.

Segnbora groaned.

The next day it began to seem as if Eftgan's glum assessment of the Shadow's ability to direct the Reavers was correct. It certainly seemed as if they knew the incursion route down the Eisargir Pass was threatened. They came pouring out of the valley in a disorderly but constant stream. Skin tents sprouted everywhere, and thousands of shaggy Reaver ponies began cropping the green corn down to stubble. The old silence of the valley was replaced by a low, malicious whispering, like the Sea's when a storm is brewing. Dusk brought no peace, either. All the valley glittered with the sparks of campfires, around which war songs were being sung, and swords sharpened.

Segnbora sat atop an embrasure in the northeastern battlement as twilight settled in, looking down at the press of Reaver tents and people gathered around the lower switchback of the approach to khas-Barachael gates. Hasai looked with her, undisturbed. (This place is well built, for something made by your kind,) he said. (It won't fall to such as these.)

"Maybe not. But this is the strongest fortress in this part of the south, and they don't dare march away from here and leave it unconquered at their backs. Even if Herewiss seals the pass successfully, these three thousand will just sit at the gates and hold the siege."

(You're troubled, *sdaha*. And it's not the prospect of battle that's causing it.)

With a sigh, Segnbora swung down from her perch and sat on the stone bench inside the embrasure, leaning against the cool wall. (I'm not delighted about this business of being involved in a wreaking,) she said silently. (Especially this one. And you got me into it.)

The dusky melody of Hasai's laughter rumbled inside her. (*I think not. Who spoke the words, who told the Firebearer he was welcome? Did you lie to him, then?*)

Exasperated, Segnbora closed her eyes and slid down into herself. Above the cave within her, it was twilight too. Stars were coming out one by one in the shaft that opened on the sky. Hasai lay at ease on the stone, his eyes silver fire, his tail twitching slightly like that of an amused cat. Segnbora walked over to him and sat down by one of his front talons, leaning back against it and craning her neck back to see him.

The Dragon was a shadow, winged like the night, only his face glittering in the hot light of his eyes. "Very funny," she said. *"Mdaha,* I didn't lie. But I'm afraid of him depending on me. What if I fail him?"

"Essn 'hh 'suuóo," Hasai rumbled. "When will you accept what you are?"

"Be patient, will you? It took me long enough to find out what I'm not."

"Part of you is me," the Dragon said. "I won't fail so simple a task as examining the stone in this valley. If you wore my body more often, you would know that."

The melody of the bass viols in his voice became grave. Behind him the *mdeihei* matched his song in cadences of calm regret. "Your memories are buried deeper under you mind's stone than ever," Hasai said. "We are at your foundations, and still you try to keep us out. It would be so easy to become one. Only look..."

In a flash of memory, Hasai showed her the building of the Eorlhowe in North Arlen—a whole mountain that had been uprooted from a remote range in west Arlen as casually as a man might pluck a flower for his hair. The mountain was taken to the tip of the North Arlene Cape, laid there upon the body of the slain Worldfinder, and melted down upon him with Dragonfire until it was only half the size it had been. Then its remains were talon-carved and tunneled and reworked into the residence of the DragonChief, the Dweller-at-the-Howe.

Segnbora looked at the memory and shivered at the thought of the paltry skin of stone that had been "protecting" her inner mind from Hasai and the *mdeihei*.

"Your fear cripples you," Hasai said more gently. "You fear what we are. Even our joys are terrible to you. Matings, births, deaths, the Immanence that isn't your Lady but is nonetheless real—

You must give up the fear, come to terms with these and all the other things from which you cannot run away. Cease hiding yourself from yourself, be who we *are!*"

"It's not that easy," Segnbora said, though she couldn't resist taking a last glance at that memory of the Howe. As she watched, storm-clouds clustered about it, hiding the Howe's peak. Dragons flashed in and out of the clouds like lightning, their roars drowning out the thunder. *Ahead-memory? Past-memory?* she wondered. It wasn't clear—

(Hallo the heart!) came a voice from a long way up. It was Herewiss's voice, tentative but cheerful.

"Damn," Segnbora muttered.

Hasai lowered his head toward her. "Later, *sdaha?*"

"Later for sure," she said, disgruntled. She was not ready for this, but nevertheless she called up to the stars, "Come on in!"

"I brought a friend," Herewiss said, slipping sideways out of nothing as if through a narrow door. Khávrinen was laid casually over his shoulder. Fire flowed from it and caught in Freelorn's eyes as he appeared behind his loved.

"Nice place you've got here," Herewiss said, sauntering in. "Where's your lodger? Lorn wanted to—"

Segnbora watched in amused approval as Herewiss stopped in midsentence and looked up...and up, and up. Freelorn halted beside him and did the same, his eyes going wide. When Segnbora had first come in, Hasai had been indistinct, a looming dark presence. But now the gems of his scales caught the light of Herewiss's Fire and threw it back in a dazzle of blue sparks. He lowered his head to thirty or forty feet above Freelorn and Herewiss, tilting his head to look first at one of them, then at the other.

"I see the resemblance remains," he said very low, rumbling a major chord of approval. Following the words came Dragonfire, a slow and luxuriant spill of blinding white radiance that poured from his mouth to the floor and pooled there, burning. "Greetings, Lion's Child. And to you and your Flame, greetings also, Hearn's son."

From the darkness beyond Hasai the *mdeihei* joined the greeting, recognizing the sons of two lines worthy of notice even as Dragons reckoned time. The huge cavern filled with a thunder of concerting voices, a harmony that shook the walls.

Herewiss bowed very low. Freelorn glanced around him in amazement at the noise and then down at the spill of Dragonfire, under which the stone floor had melted and begun to bubble. Finally he tilted his head back up to look at Hasai.

"Resemblance?" he said in a small voice.

"To Héalhra," Hasai said.

Freelorn's mouth fell open.

"I was at Bluepeak Marchward some years before the Battle," Hasai said. "I saw him when he was a little younger than you. You have his nose."

"I, uh..." Freelorn said, and closed his mouth. He looked over at Segnbora.

She shrugged. "He's been around for awhile, Lorn. *Mdaha,* what do we have to do for Herewiss?"

"Come deeper inside us, *sdaha.* He'll see what he needs to see when you do."

Hasai dropped his head down to Segnbora's level, his jaws opening slightly to receive her hand. Dragonfire still seethed in his mouth, so that the floor hissed and smoked where drops of it fell. For a split second she hesitated. Then, recognizing a challenge, she rolled up the sleeve of her shirt and thrust her arm into the fire. *This is all in happening in my mind, after all. How badly can it hurt?*

She found out. Jaws closed and held her trapped in the essence of burning, a heat so terrible that it transcended pain. Her control broke. Segnbora opened her mouth to scream, feeling the heat more completely than anything she had ever felt in her life. But to her utter amazement, without the sensation stopping, the pain vanished—

She felt the stone. There was no way she could *not* feel it. The sensation was like a fencer's when balance at last becomes perfect and power flows up from the earth. Connections formerly hidden suddenly became clear and specific—her body seated on the stone of the bench; the bench's placement on the stone of the upper-battlement paving; the positions and junctures of the blocks of khas-Barachael's walls; the massive piers and columns of its foundation-roots in Adínë's southern spur.

She could feel the whole mountain, a complex of upthrust blocks and minor stresses pushing against one another as Adínë's roots met those of its neighboring peaks. Segnbora's perception widened and spread around the valley to include Eisargir and Houndstooth and Aulys, the other mountains all leaning on or striving against one another. The valley, too, filled with her until she felt the faults and stresses there, a surface unease like a vast itch. She felt the transverse vertical faults, lying fairly quiet now that mountain-building in the area was largely finished. She felt the lateral fault, stretching from head to foot of the valley and holding dangerously still.

Farther down, heat grew in the stone. Its structure and its temper changed as her perception slid down through the fragile skin on which continents rode and jostled. Weight and pressure grew by such terrible strides that there was no telling anymore whether the stone was liquid or solid: it simply burned darkly, raging to be free, yet having nowhere to go.

Down farther still, it was too hot, too dense, for stone. Molten metal seethed and roasted in eternal night, swirling with the planet's turning, breeding forces for which Segnbora had no words but which the Dragons understood. These were some of the forces they manipulated while flying, and finding their way.

(Enough!) Herewiss said, his voice seeming to come from a long way off. (Sir, I see your point.)

(Look here, then,) Hasai said, redirecting Segnbora's attention to the very top of the papery layer where mountains were rooted and the valley lay. (You see the danger of the lateral fault. Trigger it and the vertical faults will likely collapse the valley, bringing down the mountains. Yet the pass you propose to close has the lateral running right down it, and direct intervention there will definitely set off the fault.)

(There's also the problem of the negative energies,) Segnbora said. (See how they're gathered along the lateral fault. It's ready to have a quake. Evidently that's an option the Shadow's been considering for a while.)

(I've been thinking about it too,) Herewiss said, sounding grim. (The question is, what do I do about it? There's only one possibility...) He trailed off, sounding dubious.

(What's your thought, Firebearer?) Hasai said.

Herewiss indicated one of the eastern roots of Houndstooth, a colossal pier of granite and marble set a half mile deep in the crust. (Positive and negative attract,) he said. (If I strike there with my Fire and cause that root to move, the negative should flow away from the lateral fault and attack my positive Power. But before that happens and the forces cancel out, the root itself will move upward enough to knock the Houndstooth peak down into the pass and block it permanently—) He broke off, looking at Hasai's perception as if seeing something wrong.

(Yes, you've found the problem with your plan,) Hasai said. (Watch.) As he spoke, the perception moved and changed in response to Herewiss's suggestion. They all felt, rather than saw, the smooth peak of Houndstooth rear up and collapse westward into the Eisargir Pass. A few seconds later the lateral fault came violently alive. Half of Barachael valley slid south with a jerk, while the rest jumped north. Every vertical fault went wild, one after another, some blocks thrusting hundreds of feet upward in a matter of minutes, some sinking fathoms deep. Mount Adíné fell on Barachael. Eisargir collapsed on itself and buried the priceless ironlodes forever. When it was all over, nothing was left but a broken, uninhabitable wilderness.

Herewiss grimaced. (The psychic energy canceled out all right,) he said, (but I had no idea there was so much movement-energy in that lateral fault. Damn!)

(Don't berate yourself,) Hasai said. (The move was well made for one so new at the game. And who'd have thought it could be played with humans at all?) He was delighted. (Come, Firebearer, try it again. There's always a solution.)

(Well then, how about this...)

For a long while afterward Segnbora's mind was filled with the feeling of rock shifting and grinding and mountains falling over in various disastrous combinations. She started to get bored. The game Hasai and Herewiss were engrossed in was like an extremely complicated variation of checks—and though Segnbora enjoyed playing for the delight of crossing wits with another player, her inability to think more than three or four moves ahead usually kept the game short and its ending predictable. Freelorn, to her intense irritation, looked over Herewiss's shoulder in fascination, understanding everything.

(That'll do it!) she heard Herewiss say at last.

Focusing her attention fully on the scene she was feeling, she found, to her amazement, a Barachael valley still relatively intact, with both town and fortress unhurt, and the Eisargir Pass successfully sealed. Some distance away in her mind, she could feel Herewiss grinning like a child who had beaten a master.

(That was an elegant enough solution,) Hasai said. (And as I understand the Shadow from my *sdaha,* It would have to intervene Itself to foul the situation any further, which It's reluctant to do, not so? It fears risking defeat.)

(That's right,) Herewiss said. (There's one move that still bothers me, though. The next-to-last. That one root of Aulys, the one that's split up the middle—)

(Move it as a whole, and you'll be safe.)

Hasai's perception of the valley winked out, leaving them standing in her cave again. Segnbora took her hand out of Hasai's mouth and looked at it closely. There were no burns or blisters. Her *mdaha* rumbled at her in amiable mockery. "Hearn's son," he said, "when this business is over, I'd be delighted to play with you again. There are some stresses in the volcanic country in west Arlen that might stretch you a little."

Herewiss nodded. "With 'Berend's cooperation, absolutely." He turned to Segnbora. "I'll be starting the wreaking at sunset tomorrow. Lorn and Sunspark will keep an eye on our bodies while we're out of them, and Lorn will be tied partially into the wreaking to keep us in touch with what's happening in real time. Are you still with us?"

She felt like telling him no, but Hasai, gazing silently down at her, was looking also at one of her memories in particular: night outside the old Hold, and Segnbora's voice saying to Herewiss, "You'll find your Power, prince…I'll help if I can."

"Of course," she said. "Dark, it must be years since *I* last moved a mountain."

Herewiss, hand in hand with Freelorn, gave her an approving look. "Later, then," he said. Fire from Khávrinen blazed up and swirled about them. They vanished.

Segnbora folded her arms and looked up at the silver eyes gazing placidly down on her. "You're up to something," she said.

Hasai flicked his wings open, a humorous gesture that made cool wind a second later. "When one knows what's going to be," he sang in slow amusement, "one tends to make it happen that way."

"So what's going to happen?"

Hasai slowly dropped his jaw at her. "Live, *sdaha,* and find out."

He vanished into a memory. Segnbora sat for a moment on the bench, listening to the amused song of the *mdeihei*—then grinned with anticipation, and went off to bed.

"How are the stars?" Herewiss said from behind Segnbora.

"Almost right," said Freelorn. He was beside her, leaning on the sill of the tower window. "Another quarter-hour and the Moon'll be in the Sword."

"Great. I'm almost done."

The Moon, just past its first quarter and standing nearly at the zenith, looked down on a valley that flickered with campfires and the minute shiftings of Reavers going to and fro. Around Barachael's walls, a lazy ring of fire smoldered, flaring up every now and then when some skeptical Reaver got too close. Segnbora, feeling a touch naked without surcoat and mail, turned her back on the valley vista and watched Herewiss at work.

The tower room had been emptied of everything but two narrow pallets and a chair. Around these, in what had been the empty air in the middle of the room, Herewiss was building his wreaking—the support web that would both protect him and Segnbora and slow their perception of time long enough for his Fire to do its work. He stood in britches and shirt, as Segnbora did, with one hand on his hip. With the other hand he wielded Khávrinen as lightly as an artist's stylus, adding line after delicate line of blue Flame to what had become a dome of pulsing webwork with him at its center.

The completeness of his concentration, and the economy and elegance of the structure itself, delighted Segnbora. *Lady, he's good,* she thought, admiring the perfect match between the inner symmetry-ratios of the wreaking and the meter of the spell-poem he was reciting under his breath. *They were fools to throw him out of the Precincts just because he was male...*

"If you leave my pulse running that fast," Segnbora said, noticing the brilliance of the last lifeline Herewiss had drawn, "I'll be in bad shape when we get back."

"Nervous, huh?" he said, glancing at her and lifting Khávrinen away from the description of a parabola. He touched the sword's tip to the pulse line, draining it of some Fire. "Better?"

"Yes."

"Good. Sunspark?"

Hot light flowered in one corner of the room and consolidated into a slim red-haired young woman with merry golden eyes. (They're impatient down there, loved,) she said, amused. (They keep testing me.)

"Fine, just so long as they don't get too interested in khas-Barachael. You know what to do?"

(This being the fourth time you've asked me,) Sunspark said, folding her arms in good-natured annoyance, (I dare say I do. None of them will leave the valley. They'll find the way into the plains barred, just as Barachael town is barred to them. On the night of full Moon, immediately before the eclipse starts, I'll begin driving the lot of them back up the pass. None will die.)

Herewiss nodded, narrow-eyed, completing the interconnection of several lines. "I hate to admit it," he said, "but there's a possibility that something'll go wrong with all this. If the pass fails to seal properly, and I've exhausted myself, and they get down into the valley again—"

(Loved,) Sunspark said, (if that happens I'll be quick with them. Their bodies will be consumed before the pain has a chance to start.)

Herewiss looked gratefully at the elemental from inside the shimmering blue web of the wreaking. "Thanks, loved. I'll do my best to make it unnecessary." He rested Khávrinen point-down on the floor and gazed around at the finished spellweb. "Lorn?"

"The Moon's right," Freelorn said, turning away from the window. "Let's go."

Trembling a bit with excitement, Segnbora unbuckled her swordbelt, drew Skádhwë from it, and tossed the belt in one corner. Herewiss walked out through the web and then turned inward to face, from the outside, the part of it specifically concerned with his body.

"A little to the left, 'Berend," he said as she moved into position. "Lorn, you're fine." They each stood at one corner of an equilateral triangle. "All together: *step*—"

Segnbora walked through the part of the Fireweb sympathetic to her, feeling the charged-cobweb crackle of it as it brushed against her face and hands. The hair stood up all over Segnbora as the spell passed through her body and rooted in flesh and bone. At the same time came an astonishing wave of lethargy that spread through her as quickly as blood beats outward from the heart. Hurriedly Segnbora lay down on the left-hand pallet, settling herself as comfortably as she could. She laid Skádhwë down the length of her, folded both hands about its hilt at heart level, and began relaxing muscles one by one.

Across the circle, Herewiss was settling himself with Khavrinen, while Freelorn bent over him. "My head aches," Lorn said. "Is it supposed to do that?"

"That's the part of your mind that's slowing down to keep up with us," Herewiss explained drowsily as the wreaking took hold of him too. His eyes lingered on Freelorn for a moment.

"Don't even think it," Lorn said, and bent lower to kiss Herewiss good night. Herewiss's eyebrows went up for a second, then down again as his eyes closed.

(Mdaha,) Segnbora said to her inner depths, closing her own eyes, (see you when I'm out of the body!)

(I think not,) the answer came back, faint, amused.

(What?) She tried to hold off the wreaking long enough for Hasai to explain, but it was no use. Briefly the spell fought with her lungs, then conquered them and slowed her breathing. That done, the Firework wound deeper into her brain, altering her thought rhythms toward the profound unconsciousness of wreaking suspension. For a second of mindless panic Segnbora fought that too, like a drowning swimmer...and then thought, *What am I doing? I chose* this *danger. I choose it now!*

The phrasing of the thought was Dracon, and out of Dracon reflex, scared but determined, she took a long breath of the Fire. It burned. But as with Hasai's fire, she matched with it, meshed with it, felt it sink in—and everything, even Hasai and the *mdeihei,* fell away...

eleven

"Choose," she said to the cruel king. "For I am bound by My own law, and what you desire shall be given you, until you shall ask Me for something beyond My power to grant."

He told her his desires, and she granted them all—until at last, alone, desolate King of an empty city, he cried out to Her in anguish, "Change my heart!"

"I shall leave you now," the Goddess said, "for you have asked a boon past My power. Only one has the power to fulfill that wish... and you are doing so."

from "The King Who Caught the Goddess,"
in *Tales of old Steldin*, ed. s'Lange, rr'Virendir, 1055 p.a.d.

Segnbora was wide awake. She swung her feet off the pallet and stood up with Skádhwë in her hand. The room around her was foggy and hard to see—Herewiss's spellweb had already slowed her time sense considerably. Dust and convection currents moved around her at what seemed many times their normal speed. Her othersenses were wide awake too, and showed her strange blurs going swiftly about the room—one yellow-bright as fire, one dark with an odd tangle of potential at its heart: Sunspark and Freelorn.

Herewiss still lay in his body, the blue-white core that was his soul struggling yet with the shell that surrounded it. Tense with the sensation of his difficulty, Segnbora turned away from him to gaze down at herself where she lay on her pallet.

(*Mdaha?*) she said. No answer came back; evidently the *mdeihei* were tied to her body, and must stay there, silenced, when she left it.

She looked down at her still form, drowned in a repose deeper than any sleep. It had been a long time since the Precincts, when she had last been out-of-body and able to see herself so clearly. A lot had changed since then. There was a wincing fierceness about the corners of the eyes now that hadn't been there when she was younger, and even in this sleep the body looked tense, as if prepared to move in a hurry. *Too much time alone,* she thought, with the curious objectivity of the soulwalker. *Too much time on the run...*

(It's not that bad,) Herewiss said from behind her. She turned, and was quietly astonished by what she saw. It wasn't that Herewiss's inner self didn't look like his outer one. It kept that tall lean look, a smith's no-nonsense musculature, and the fine-featured face made handsome by sleepy, gentle eyes. But through it, like sunlight through crystal, blazed the Fire, potent for creation and destruction, all wound about with a straightforward joy in the Fire that was more blinding than the Flame itself. He looked dangerous, and utterly magnificent.

(Well met,) Segnbora said, and meant it.

His expression was thoughtful. (You speak for me too,) Herewiss said. Maybe he caught her bemused look, for he said, (We're short of time, but have you noticed *that?*)

He pointed behind her. Segnbora looked over her shoulder, away from the quick-flickering light of the Fire-web. Laid out along the floor, long and dark behind her was her shadow.

(That's impossible!) she said in momentary indignation, turning. (You can't have a shadow out of the body!) Yet there the darkness lay, stretching to the wall and right through it, blandly contradicting what she'd been taught in the Precincts. Experimentally Segnbora raised an arm, and was dumbfounded to see the serrated shape of a Dragon's wing lift away from the shadow-body.

Behind her she felt Herewiss restraining his laughter

(My *mdaha's* truly becoming part of me,) she said, amused in spite of herself.

(Where is he? I thought he'd be here with us.)

(So did I. He's with my body, it looks like.)

Herewiss felt dubious for a moment. (How are you going to tell me what's happening in the stone, then? If he's not here—)

Segnbora started to lean on Skádhwë, then aborted the gesture as the sword's point began to pierce the stone they stood on. (Well I have my memories of what it's like to be one of the *mdeihei*. All I have to do is live in them completely enough and we'll be fine.) She wished she was as certain of that as she made it sound, especially since she'd spent enough time lately resisting that very thing. (Now, where do we have to go?)

Herewiss nodded at the room's north wall, laying Khávrinen over his shoulder. Segnbora did the same with Skádhwë, and together they walked through the wall and into the clear air over Barachael. The stars wheeled visibly in the paling sky above them, moving a little faster each moment as Herewiss's wreaking further slowed their time sense.

(How about that, it works,) Herewiss said, pausing. (A moment. Lorn?)

The answer came not in words, but in swift-passing impression of concern, relief, encouragement. All was well in the tower, though Freelorn wondered why Herewiss had waited so long to check in with him; nearly an hour had passed.

(We're all right, loved,) Herewiss said. (The pauses may get pretty long, but don't worry about us unless the web fails.) He broke contact and walked down the air toward Barachael valley. Segnbora followed.

Their othersight was stimulated to unusual clarity by the wreaking, and the Chaelonde valley bubbled like a cauldron with normally unseen influences. The Reavers' emotions were clearly visible, a stew of frustrated violence and fear. Barachael town crouched cold and desolate behind the invaders. As the low threshold of her underhearing dropped lower still, Segnbora heard the slow bitter dirge of the town's bereaved stones, which were certain that once more the children of their masons had been slaughtered. The other lives of the valley, birds and beasts, showed themselves only as cautious sparks of life, aware of an ingathering of Power and lying low in order not to attract attention.

The sky to the east went paler by the moment, and the Moon slid down the sky and faded in the face of day, looking almost glad to do it. While they watched, the Sun leapt into the sky too quickly, as if it wanted to put distance between itself and the ground.

The ground was a problem. Dark negative energies seethed within it the way thoughts of revenge seethe within an angry mind. Though the faults weren't yet very clear, it was plain that these negative energies ran down most of them, draining toward the foundations of the valley, where they collected in a great pool of ancient, festering hatred.

(We have to get into empathy with *that?*) Segnbora said, revolted.

(I'd sooner sit in a swamp, myself,) said Herewiss, striding down the air toward the reeking morass. (Still, the sooner we do it, the sooner we can get out and get clean again. Come on, down here...)

He led the way around toward the base of the easternmost spur of Adínë. There one of the vertical faults followed the spur's contour, a remnant of a day long before when the earth had shrugged that particular jagged block of stone above the surface. The fetid swirl of emotion in the valley broke against the spur as a wave breaks, flowing around it and up the pass. Herewiss stepped carefully down onto a high ridge of the spur and waited there for Segnbora. When she caught up, they both paused to watch the way the shadows in the valley shrank and changed. The few moments' walk down from Sai khas-Barachael had begun at sunrise, and now it was nearly noon.

(Now what?)

Herewiss lifted Khávrinen. Fire ran down from it and surrounded him until he blazed like someone drenched with oil and set alight. (In,) he said, and glanced down at the ridge he stood on.

Without further ado he stepped down into the earth as if walking down stairs.

(Show-off,) Segnbora thought affectionately. She walked down the outer surface of the ridge, seeking the way into the mountain that would best suit her. Turning, she saw her incongruous shadow against the ridgewall behind her. *Impossible...as impossible as a human becoming a Dragon. So why not?* Reaching behind her with both hands, Segnbora grasped it and pulled it forward about her shoulders like a cloak, becoming what she couldn't be.

It was astonishingly easy. There was fire in her throat again, and she had wings to feel the air, one of which was barbed not with a claw of white diamond but with a sliver of night made solid. She dug her talons into the naked stone. Without moving, Segnbora *knew* what lay beneath her, felt it as if it was her...for it was. The deep, slow, scarce-moving selfness of the rock, the secret burning at the roots, the earth's heavy veins running with the mountain's blood...they were *her* veins, her blood, her life.

It was hard to think, immersed in the ancient nonconscious musings of stone. The transience of thought, or any concern for the doings of the ephemerals at the outer edge of Being, seemed pointless. Internal affairs were much more important—the perpetual leisurely conflict between the black flowing fires of the Inside, and the cold nothing of the Outside, played out on the interface between them, the board of the shifting world. The player Outside blanketed the board close, wearing away its opponent with wind and rain; grinding it down with glaciers, cracking its coastlines with the pressure of the hungry seas. The Inside raised up lands and threw them down, tore continents apart, broke the seabottoms and made new ones; hunched up fanged mountain ranges to bite at the wind, and be bitten in return. The game went on in move and countermove, upthrust, subsistence and slide, while overhead, hardly remarked, the Poles changed stars.

This particular range had hardly been in the game long enough to prove its worth as a move. Now the huge nonconsciousness wondered idly—as the Sun went down again—why this area was suddenly such a cause for concern.

Segnbora breathed stone deeply and strove to remember herself. There was something lulling for a Dragon in this perception of stone, as there was for humans in the presence of the Sea: it suggested the solace of an ancient birthplace as the Sea intimated the peace of the Shore. But the lulling, here and now, was dangerous. (Herewiss?) she said, singing a chord of quandary around his name.

(Here,) his answer came back, darkness answering darkness.

She couldn't feel him except indirectly. He had chosen to leave his physical imagery behind for the time being, and was manifesting himself only as a mobile but greatly restrained stress in the stone, staying quite still until he got his bearings. Khávrinen was evident too, seeming like the potential energy which that stress would release when it moved. (I feel you. Aren't you coming in?)

(I *am* in,) she sang, delighted by the truth of it. (I'm outside, too. Both at once. I can feel you inside me; you're like a muscle strain. And I can feel the other side of the world from here. What do you feel?)

(Granite, mostly. Marble. Iron—that's the mines.) He paused to feel around. (They haven't come near the main lodes, even after centuries of work. I'll have to tell Eftgan where the good metal is. Then further down, the faults...) He trailed off, sounding uneasy.

Segnbora felt what Herewiss felt and found everything much as it had been when Hasai had done the first survey, but the assessment didn't satisfy her. (I need more precision. I'm going to narrow down a good deal and make this perception clearer. Will the valley and ten miles on all sides be sufficient?)

(Those were the boundaries that Hasai was using. Yes.)

Segnbora felt closely into the valley floor itself for ten or twelve miles down, absorbing and including into herself the sensations of pressures and unreleased strains, strata trying to shear upward or sink down. Whole mountains she embraced as if with encircling wings: Aulys, Houndstooth, Eisargir and Adíne, then east to Whitestack, Esa and Mint, south to Ela and Fyfel, west to Mesthyn, Teleist and the Orakhmene range. They were a restless armful. Rooted they might be, but they were alive as trees—shifting trembling, pushing one another with quick covert nudges.

The whole Highpeak region far into the unnamed south, was shivering, about to bolt like a nervous horse. The cause of its nervousness was at the heart of her perception, and with ruthless diligence Segnbora absorbed it all, missing no detail. The vertical faults lying stitched across the valley in a row, south to north, angry and frightened. The treacherous lateral fault, its line running from the pass between Adíne and Eisargir into the valley, through Barachael and out the narrow gate to lower land. And under it all, the old dark sink of negative energies.

(I see it,) Herewiss said, his thought thick with revulsion. Segnbora caught a quick taste of his perception, different from hers, and primarily concerned with the Shadow's influence. Herewiss felt it everywhere, particularly in the lateral fault, where the accumulated hatred made the fault seem to crouch and glare like a cornered rat. The darkness inhabiting it knew who he was and what he had come for, and the whole valley trembled with its malice.

Segnbora trembled too, revolted and suddenly afraid. They were fools to try to tamper with this dynamism, so delicately balanced that a talon's weight applied to the wrong spot might bring whole mountains down. The Dweller-at-the-Howe had been wise to forbid the Dragons from delving here. Worse, she could feel the murky sink of hatred swelling, growing aware of their presence.

(Herewiss!) she said. He didn't answer, and she began to grow angry, the Fire burning hotter in her throat. He was so damn sure of himself! *(Herewiss!)*

(What do you want?) he snapped.

Her othersenses told her that he was as angry as she was, and the knowledge enraged her further.

(Don't meddle!) he said. (I'm in the middle of a wreaking, and if you distract me—)

Typical of him to pay no attention to her, all sunk in his own concerns as he was; as he always was. (Your wreaking's barely begun, and I'm no great distraction. Will you listen to me? I'm Precinct-trained, and—)

(They don't know everything in the Precincts,) Herewiss said, bitter and superior. He felt jealous, too, which briefly made Segnbora wonder. *Jealousy...shouldn't that suggest something in this situation?*

But then she brushed away the irrelevant thought, doubtless the maundering of some *mdaha* long dead and out of touch with life. Herewiss had slighted her, and her patience was wearing thin.

(Do you want my aid or not?) Segnbora demanded.

(Not particularly, no! I have more than enough Power to handle this business myself, and you know it. I thought you might have appreciated the kindness I was doing you by letting you come along on a wreaking, but I see it was wasted.)

He was a stress in the darkness, one close to release, spiteful and certain of his own utter potency. The burning began to swell in her throat, and sweet it was to let the passions rise.

She had been patient long enough. The forefingers of her wings—the terrible black diamond razors that could tear even Dragonmail—cocked forward and down at him. (Little man,) she said, (it's time you found out what you have been toying with!)

Slowly she bent down, waiting for him to attack her. She savored the moments, wondering how she would finish him. A quick slash? A forepaw brought smashing down? A breath of her fire? But he wasn't physical now. He dwelt in the stone as she did, and the stress he wore as form began to warp and change. He was lifting up Khávrinen to kill her. *Let him try, the fool!* she thought.

The *mdaha* who had spoken before now cried out again something unintelligible about not seeing, about a presence creeping up from behind, about an ambush...Segnbora snarled at the interruption, a sound that woke rumblings in the stone. She arched herself upward to come crashing down on the pitiful little weapon raised against her—

—and then she understood, she *saw*. The darkness in the stone drew together to one spot. At the lateral fault it stood, staring at her. Dracon though she was—immense, terrible—she abandoned her pounce and crouched down like a bird under a serpent's eye, filled with horror as awareness reasserted itself and grew. The Shadow smiled at her, baleful, and waited.

Herewiss didn't waste his opportunity. Swollen with rage, he towered over her in the stone with Khávrinen upraised, ready to destroy her. (Come on!) he cried in an ecstasy of fury. (Stop me, if you're such a power! Try to stop me!)

Segnbora didn't answer. It was impossible to look away from the one Whose essence lay concentrated in the fault, waiting for Herewiss to strike and bring the valley down around their ears.

Herewiss's rage didn't diminish. He merely lowered Khávrinen a bit to savor her fear, to prolong the sweet conflict—and in that moment abruptly felt what she did.

His horror, his sense of betrayal, were even more profound than hers had been. (Ah, Goddess, no—what did I almost do?)

The darkness rumbled with the amused reply: (Not 'almost!') The stone shook around them as the Shadow flowed out and suffused the darkness around Herewiss. Segnbora felt Herewiss founder and go down in it, unable to stir so much as a thought to help him. That dark tide flowed past him, over her, into the shadowy places in her soul that had belonged to It since she was very small. She'd always hated to admit they were there at all; now Segnbora realized that the failure to own them had made them a deadly vulnerability. Relentlessly the Shadow inflamed them all—her fury at a life that didn't go exactly as she wished, her old feelings of impotence and insignificance. Nothing she did could matter against this power that had fought even the Goddess to a standstill. It would make her trigger the fault, bury the valley, kill her enemies and her friends together. That being the case, why struggle any longer? The impotent, merciful Other would understand. Let it happen, end the pain—

But I stood up even to Her, the thought occurred in Segnbora, like a last lightning-flash before the storm. *If I could do that, then we're evenly matched. And I'm not alone!*

The realization was dangerous. Her opponent changed its tactics from persuasion to direct attack: a blast of hatred and pain that would have killed her in a second had she been human and in body. But at the moment she was neither. She pulled her Dracon-self closer about her, wearing it like mail. Hatred, even the vast hatred of an embittered God, meant little to a Dragon who had experienced the Immanence from the inside, with all its joys and rages regarding all things mortal and divine.

And as for the pain, Segnbora simply opened herself to it as a Dragon would. She spread her wings wide and took it all, drank it like Sunfire, made it hers as she had made the stone and the mountains hers. *I am not Your tool. And You can't make me destroy what I came to save. Herewiss!*

A deadly undertow of blackness was almost all she could perceive of Its attack against him. Within it, however, something was moving—a disembodied force, the essence of Khávrinen and the Power it focused, slashing the dark into ribbons. Always the Shadow resealed Itself, but always the fierce blueness pushed It aside again, widening the breach for the man who fought his way upward out of the Shadow's heart.

I'm Hers, *not Yours!* he gasped, forcing the darkness aside and pushing himself higher into the stone. *And even for Her, I'm not a thing to be used!* ('Berend?')

(Here!)

With terrible abruptness, both attacks ceased. Segnbora reeled.

(Pull yourself together!) Herewiss shouted at her instantly. (If It can't get us to trigger the fault, It'll do that Itself!)

And It was doing it now. Segnbora saw all Its power, all Its hate, flowing back into the lateral fault—concentrating, burning, stinging the stone into the beginnings of movement. A low rumble spread through the strata. There was one spot in particular, a thousand feet or so south of Barachael, that was almost ready to fracture. In a matter of seconds its stone would reduce itself to powder with explosive force, releasing the vertical faults on either side of it.

(There!) she cried, and as she did the Shadow poured Itself fully into that spot, an irresistible blast of destruction—

—but Herewiss was already there, dwelling in the stone, *being* it, holding it together. It was granite and marble, but he was diamond, unshatterable by Goddess or Shadow—for the moment.

(I'll hold it!) he said, the thought tasting of gritted teeth. (You distract It!)

With what? she thought, fumbling desperately for an idea. Distant as if one of the *mdeihei* sang it, seemingly irrelevant, a scrap of verse spoke itself in her. *No shadow so deep that light cannot sound it, no hatred so hard that love cannot loose it*—Béorgan's old ballad, the alliterative one. It told how she had taken the Shadow within herself, draining its power so that her daughter could challenge the Shadow in her turn and slay It.

A mad idea, then and now. But it worked—

Though still wearing her Dracon self, Segnbora brought her human nature to bear as strongly as she could, and began exposing her dark sides to the Shadow's influence. Intent on Herewiss, It perceived only an augmentation of Its power in the area, and therefore let her darknesses gather from It and grow, becoming small likenesses of Itself. *I ignored these vulnerabilities before and made them weapons in Its hands. Now we turn the tables.* She laid them out like choice dishes at a banquet: old hatreds, petty jealousies, desires gone sour, procrastinations; laziness that would let others languish in pain while she lay idle; envy that smiled at the misfortunes of her peers. As long as she still recognized them as sickness, she was safe. Acceptance of them as normal was the danger. And it would creep up on her fast, now...

But she waited. Those tarnished parts of her grew steadily in power, knew their source, flowed back toward it and melded with it, becoming part of Its substance as drops of mercury join. Terrible power rushed through them and back into Segnbora. She dared not fight it, lest she betray her consciousness of what was happening. As she had first become Dracon, and then as a Dragon had become stone, she now let herself become the Shadow.

Mortal, and beset by mortality's limitations even out of her body, Segnbora could contain only a small part of Its being in herself—but it was enough. In a sickening flash she experienced the incalculable rage of One Who had possessed Godhead and for jealousy's sake had then thrown it away. There was pain, too, an anguish deeply colored with blame for the Goddess Who'd let the pain happen—

There was no time for more. Segnbora didn't speak, didn't even truly think, but merely held her control as best she could and looked at the painful memories, living inside the old story, wordlessly recreating it with a Dragon's immediacy and a storyteller's skill. It was an easy story to tell, for she knew it by heart. It was the same story she'd dreamed that night in the old Hold: the story of the Maiden, of Death, and of Her children, the Two, Who had loved one another.

The hatred that was the rest of herself still strove to reach out and destroy Herewiss—but It did so less vehemently, distracted by memories ancient beyond telling. Ever so gradually Segnbora shifted the story's focus, making it less a narrative, more an invitation.

Do You remember how it was? The two of You loving outside the constraints of existence, taking eons to learn and love one another's infinite depths? Do You remember the divine passion, how Your loving invented time and space—a place to love and explore together, in all the bodies that ever lived? Do You remember the Loved, and how there was always One Who understood? Your sister, Your brother, Your beloved...O remember!

It was in Nhàired she sang now, as if weaving a spell, silently recalling the Song of the Lost. Normally that Song was never voiced except during the Dreadnights, in the depths of the Silent Precincts, to beseech the Shadow to remember Its ancient joy and be merciful to the world. Segnbora sang it now without the fearful intonations the Rodmistresses used, but winding poignant Dracon motifs of compassion and forgiveness around the words. She was calling to herself as much as to the other. Vile though her darknesses were, they were rooted in the memory of the loss of joy, just as the Shadow's malice was founded in the pain of Its ancient loss, the memory of love discarded forever. And if It could not be saved, neither could she...

The Shadow held still in the stone, Its malice wavering, half forgotten. A hasty flicker of perception stolen through It showed Herewiss, hanging on in the stone, shuddering with pity and also with fear for her. No one had ever before been so foolhardy as to sing the Song of the Lost in first person, and tempt the Shadow. But he was already examining the strata around him, and Segnbora felt him find the spot where the Shadow's consciousness had rooted Itself most concretely into the stone.

But yet will come that time when Time is done, the world begun again, aright, she sang, pouring herself into the promise. *And once again We shall be as We were—*

She drew away, singing. The Shadow surrounded her, towering above, about to drown her in deadly consummation. She dared not react, but only looked up into the darkness, arms open wide—

Without warning Khávrinen's essence flicked through the earth like a white-hot thought burning through a brain, instantly severing the linkage of the Shadow's consciousness to the stone.

There was time for just one wild shriek of rage and betrayal before the dark presence faded, temporarily banished.

But that single cry was enough. All around Herewiss an unstoppable tremor stirred in the stone...and as it did, an ominous coppery feeling with an aftertaste of blood began sliding through Segnbora's self. The Moon was eclipsing.

(*Goddess!* Herewiss, get out of there. We have to get back to our bodies or you won't be able to control this!)

(Right,) Herewiss said, sounding distracted. Khávrinen swept again and again through the bedrock, and its unseen Fire wavered with Herewiss's alarm as he tried to cut himself free of his empathy with the stone. (I seem to have gotten kind of attached here, you go ahead—)

(Are you *crazy*? This is your wreaking and I'm stuck in it!) Precious seconds slipped away as Herewiss laid about him harder and harder with Khávrinen, and still didn't move. (Dammit! My own Fire won't cut my own Fire—)

(Watch out!) Segnbora said. Furiously, she whipped down her right wing at the stone, the wing tipped with the black razor-diamond that was Skádhwë. Through fathoms of marble and granite it sliced, the shadow of a shadow, until it reached the rock under Herewiss, passed through it—

He shot upward and out of the strata, free. Shrugging off her Dracon-self, Segnbora followed him up and out of the empathy.

They broke the surface of the valley, gasped for the dear familiarity of breath like swimmers down too long, and began running up the air in frantic haste. The Moon's face, full now, was stained half red against the early evening sky. The stain grew larger as they raced for the tower window with the light in it. Under them, red fire dove and swooped about the valley, driving massed darknesses before it. They spared the sight hardly a glance, diving through the tower wall. Segnbora threw herself down on the cot where her body lay—

—and hit her head.

No, that's just the usual headache. Up, get up! Freelorn was shaking her, worsening the agony of pins and needles that transfixed every bone and muscle she owned.

Herewiss was already up, sagging against the window. With Freelorn's help, she staggered over to join him. Segnbora was temporarily blind, but the othersight was working. Above the valley the Moon's whiteness had diminished to a thin desperate sliver, struggling with the creeping darkness as if with a poison, foredoomed to lose.

The corroded copper taste was as hot in Segnbora's mouth as if she had been struck there. The Chaelonde seemed to run with blood. Below them the lateral fault burned through stone and earth, moving. Sai khas-Barachael began to shake beneath their feet.

"Put your scales on," Herewiss whispered, grabbing one of her hands in a grip like a vise, and with the other drawing Khávrinen. Segnbora stumbled and fell down into herself, into the cave where Hasai waited with wings outspread in alarm. There was no time for the usual courtesies. Segnbora matched him size for size, flung his wings about her as she had wrapped herself in his shadow before, and became him.

As the sensation of the stone in the valley became plain again, the *mdeihei* cried out in a song of terrible alarm. *"Shut up, the lot of you!"* she shouted in Dracon, and once more gathered the whole valley within the span of her wings, feeling it all.

The pain struck her immediately as the lateral fault came alive inside her, a black-hot line of agony running from chest to shoulder and up her left wing like a heart seizure. Her outer body gasped and clutched at the sill, missed it, and thumped down to her knees with a jolt. Inside, no less clearly, she felt the heave and stutter of the faults as they tried to move, attempting to foul Herewiss's game before it was fairly started.

But Herewiss had not lost his grip on her hand. Half crouched over and supported desperately by Freelorn, he was beginning to shine like a vision as his soul settled more firmly into the spirit-to-body connection necessary for full Power flow. In his free hand, Khávrinen blazed like chained lightning, impossible to look at with the eyes of either body or mind. Herewiss struck deeper into his Power, tapping what seemed an inexhaustible source, and straightened with refound strength. Then he was inside Segnbora's perception, as Dracon as she.

The Fire burning in her throat was suddenly blue, an awesome counterpoint to the dark burning of the faults, and the rage of the frustrated Shadow. Stirred by Its influence, the player on the Inside made a move. But it was a poorly reasoned one, born of fury and the hope of a quick win. The lateral fault jumped an inch north and south.

Segnbora felt Herewiss smile the satisfied smile of a player whose opponent has fallen into a trap. The burning blue upflow of his Fire seared through her perception and poured in a great flood down into the valley's stone, binding together three of the vertical faults.

Like diverted lightning, the released energy of the lateral fault stitched whiplash-quick through the strata in several different directions. But Herewiss was quicker. Fire streaked through the strata too, sending fault-blocks up or down, blocking and absorbing forces, setting up piece by piece the final checkmate that would freeze the lateral forever and seal the Eisargir Pass. Two more moves and he would have it!

Bent over double by the fault-pain, harder to handle now than while she had been out-of-body, Segnbora heard someone a long way off shouting in thought. She couldn't make out concepts, though. "They're not?" Freelorn said, much closer, and very alarmed. "Dusty! They're not all clear of the pass yet. Sunspark says you have to hold off if you don't want all those Reavers dead—"

Herewiss said nothing aloud, but Segnbora could feel his resolve. *No one dies of this, not even them.* Yet the position he had set up in the stone was delicate and couldn't be maintained for long.

The Shadow, sensing Herewiss's hesitation, immediately called the attention of the foiled, blocked forces in the stone to the weakest spot in Herewiss's game: the root of Aulys that was split in two. Pressure played about it like lightning. Half of the massive root twitched, about to shift.

(Hold that position!) Segnbora said to Herewiss. Both inside and outside the stone at once, she anchored herself with rear talons and barbed tail, and reached out to sink diamond fangs into the trembling root. It struggled and tried to tear away from her, vibrating so violently that she was certain she was going to lose teeth. But a Dragon never lets go except when it chooses to. *We are the stone. We command. We—will—not—let—go!*

She held. Eyes squeezed closed, every muscle pulled taut as a rope, her tail desperately tightening its anchor around a lower stratum as she felt her fore-talons slipping...

"They're out! They're out of the pass! *Dusty!*"

Canny and desperate, the Shadow kicked two of the remotest vertical faults as a distraction. Herewiss was having none of it. Using Segnbora's Dracon-self as she had, he descended deeper into the stone, deep enough to set his own jaws around his last move, a great marble fault-block half a mile south of Barachael. This was the key to the puzzle. Diamond fangs set hard into the stone. He heaved—

The blow came at her, not at him, and took them both off-guard. Preoccupied with the immensities, neither of them expected the sudden choking darkness at their back in the place where the *mdeihei* dwelt. A song of madness swept the *mdeihei,* controlled them, sent them tearing at the floor of Segnbora's cave. Razor talons and ruthless blasts of Dragonfire ate and sliced down through the stone of her memory, to lay it bare and make it real. For one memory in particular they searched—

(No!) she screamed at them, but they paid her no heed. Stone crumbled away like curd. Even now the memory was coming to birth, coming true: darkness, gravel grinding against her face, that old anguish—And there was no way to stop it, except by breaking the empathy, leaving Hasai, halting the wreaking—

Herewiss held the block of stone in jaws that ran with blue Fire, but he couldn't move it without her. He strained at it, tapping deeper into his Fire and deeper yet, not giving up. Yet without Segnbora's unimpeded link to the Dracon perception, he couldn't go further.

—stone shattered and melted inside her. *Don't suffer, don't let it come true again! Break the link!* the darkness sang to her, consoling, seductive. The memory became more real. *A green afternoon under the tree… No, what's he doing here? What's he*—no!!

You don't want it to happen again? Break the link!

But I can't!

Then live in the horror, without respite, forever.

The last stone was torn away from the memory. In such anguish that she couldn't even scream, Segnbora flung herself utterly into the Dracon-self again, into Herewiss, into her own self and her own death. Fire blazed; the terrible stresses Herewiss had been applying to the fault-block gripped, took, pulled it up out of its socket—

The game board rumbled and leaned upward as if a hand had tipped it over. Pieces tried to slide off every which way. Lost in the pain of contact with that memory, Segnbora nonetheless sensed Mount Adíne's shuddering as the ground at the end of the khas-Barachael spur began to rise, first bulging, then cracking like a snapped stick.

Sai khas-Barachael danced and jittered on its ridge like a knife on a pounded tabletop, held secure only by Herewiss's Fire and will. The earth on either side of the lateral fault thrust up, then slammed together like a closing door. The fault expended its energies in a noise like the thunderstorms of a thousand summers. Hills crumbled and landslides large and small crawled downward all the length of the Chaelonde valley. The river itself tilted crazily out of its bed and rushed down into a new one as the block Herewiss had triggered shoved its way above ground, making a seedling mountain, a new spur for Adíne.

Behind them, the Houndstooth peak of Aulys seemed to stand up in surprise, look over Adíne's shoulder, and then fall back in a dead faint. The terrible thundering crash of its fall went on for many minutes, a sound so huge it obliterated every other sound and was felt more than heard. It was a sound never to be forgotten—the sound of the pass between Eisargir and Aulys being sealed by the Houndstooth's ruin.

Hours later, it seemed, the singing roar that encompassed the world began to die down. Segnbora discovered that she was still alive, and was amazed at that. Herewiss was nowhere to be felt in her mind; for her own part, she was on hands and knees on the floor of the cavern. There were great talon-furrowed rents in that floor now; slag lay piled all around them, and everything smoked ominously as if pools of magma lay just beneath the surface. Slowly, aching all over, Segnbora levered herself up and found herself looking at Hasai.

He was droop-winged and weary-looking, dim of eye, crouching in the middle of a badly torn-up and melted stone floor. Behind him, lurking shameful in the shadows, she could just make out the dark forms of the *mdeihei*. Many eyes watched her, but their voices for once were still as they waited to see what she would do.

"O *sdaha*," Hasai said, singing slow and sorrowful, "we betrayed you." He made no excuse, offered no explanation, merely accepted the responsibility.

She breathed in, breathed out, as weary as the Dragon before her. The *mdeihei* waited.

There were thousands of things she felt like saying to them, but what she said was, *"Ae mdeihei, nht'é'lhhw'ae."* We are forgiven.

The shadowy forms drew away. Segnbora laid a hand for a moment on one of Hasai's bright talons, looking around at the torn and furrowed floor. "Will you clean this mess up, *mdaha?*"

Hasai looked at her as if there were something he wanted to say, but dared not. Finally he simply said, *"Sdaha,* we will do that."

"Sehé'rae, then—" Segnbora turned her back on him and stepped back up into the outer world.

The room still jittered with little aftershocks left over from the quake, and echoed with the voices of all Freelorn's band. Herewiss leaned wearily by the window, with Freelorn supporting him on one side and Sunspark on the other. Eftgan was in front of him, and all four were talking at a great rate. Segnbora pushed herself up off the floor and rubbed her eyes, looking out the window.

Her normal sight was now clear enough to show her a Chaelonde valley much broken and changed, but with Barachael still mostly intact. The darkened Moon wore a fuzzy line of silver at its edge, first sign of the eclipse's end. The air that came in the window was astonishingly sweet to the undersenses, as if many years' worth of trapped death and pain had been finally released.

Leaning against the windowsill, she looked at Herewiss. He was drawn and tired, and all the Fire was gone from about Khávrinen for the moment. For the first time she could remember, it was simply gray steel with an odd blue sheen. But Herewiss's eyes were alive with a satisfaction too big for all of Barachael valley to have contained—the look of a man who finds out he *is* what he's always believed himself to be.

Seeing her, he reached out a hand. Across the open window they clasped forearms in the gesture of warriors after a battle well fought.

"What was it you said?" Segnbora said, thinking back to the old Hold in the Waste, and the night her sleep was interrupted. "'There was blood on the Moon, and the mountain was falling'—?"

Dog-tired as he was, Herewiss's eyes glittered with the realization that his true-dream might yet prove less disastrous than he'd feared, particularly for the man who stood beside him. "Got it right, didn't I?"

She nodded, put an arm out and was unsurprised to find Lang there, wary of Skádhwë but ready to support her. "Only one problem, prince—"

"What's that?"

She grinned. "After this, people are going to say you'll do *anything* to avoid a fight…"

twelve

Laughter in death's shadow fools no one who understands death. But if you're moved to it, be assured that the Goddess will smile at the joke.

—found scratched on the wall in the dungeon of the King of Steldin, *circa* 1200 p.a.d.

"I hate—letting them think they're driving us," Herewiss said between gasps. "But it's better this way."

He stood in the midst of carnage, the burned and hacked bodies of fifty or sixty Fyrd. Here and there in the rocky field of this latest ambush, Freelorn's band stood cleaning swords, leaning on one another, or rubbing down sweating horses and swearing quietly.

Segnbora leaned gasping against Steelsheen's flank, unwilling to sheathe Skádhwë yet. The last Fyrd to come at her had been one of the new breed of keplian, bigger than the usual sort, with clawed forelimbs and those wickedly intelligent eyes that were becoming too familiar these days. She'd had no trouble immersing herself in the other's eyes to effect its killing. The problem had been getting out again afterward. She felt soiled, as if she had stepped in a pile of hatred that would have to be scraped off her boots.

"How many times is this?" Lang said, coming up beside her.

"Seventeen, eighteen maybe—"

"I don't know about you, but *I* feel driven."

Segnbora nodded. Fifteen days ago they had ridden out of Barachael, and had had nothing for their pains ever since but constant harrying by ever-increasing bands of Fyrd. All had come from the southwest, where Something clearly didn't want them to venture. Freelorn had suggested worldgating straight to Bluepeak, where they would meet the Queen; but Herewiss, unwilling to tempt the Shadow's direct intervention by too much use of Fire, had vetoed the idea. "All It has to do is bring enough power to bear against one worldgating," he said, "and it can kill us all at once. Do you really want to offer It the opportunity?"

So they rode, and were harried. Herewiss always took them north, out of the way, after an attack such as today's—in daylight, anyway. In darkness they turned again and tacked southwest, toward Bluepeak. They were losing time with these detours, and knew it. Everyone's temper was short, and getting shorter. But there was nothing else to do.

"Let's go," Herewiss said, sheathing Khávrinen and turning Sunspark's head northward as he mounted.

There was annoyed muttering among Freelorn's band, and heads turned toward Lorn in appeal. But Lorn, already up on Blackmane, looked wearily after his loved and shook his head. "Come on," he said, and rode off after Herewiss.

It was a brutal trail they rode, through country made of the stuff of a rider's nightmares. They had long since left behind the green plains of southern Darthen. Presently they were crossing the uninhabited rock-tumble of Arlen's Southpeak country. Glaciers had retreated over this land when the Peaks were born, leaving bizarrely shaped boulders scattered across scant, stony soil. Acres of coarse gravel with a few brave weeds growing out of it might be all one would see from morning till night.

The horses were footsore from being kept at flight-pace on such miserable ground. The grazing was poor, too. After the well-filled mangers of Barachael's stables, it was hardly surprising that the horses were in no better mood than their riders, who knew that though no one lived in this barren country, it would be only a matter of time before they ran into Reavers, or Arlene regulars in Cillmod's pay. And no matter when that might happen, for the moment there were always the Fyrd.

"This is all *your* fault," Freelorn grumbled at Segnbora as Steelsheen picked her way along beside Blackmane.

Segnbora looked up in surprise from her contemplation of Skádhwë, which lay ready across the saddlebow. "What?...Oh, well, doubtless in a way it is. I caused the Battle of Bluepeak, too. Ask me about it sometime."

He glowered at her, and nodded toward Herewiss. "Very funny. All *he* did was seal up the Shadow's favorite avenue into the Kingdoms. What do *you* do but start making love to It…and then jilt It!"

"So I did," she said after a moment.

"You're probably in worse trouble with It now than Herewiss is."

Segnbora frowned at the exaggeration, though it was typical of her liege. "Oh? What would *you* know about it?"

Herewiss had been dropped back to join them. Now he said, "Considering that he's read the entire royal Arlene library collection on matters of Power, he probably knows more about it than either of us. Face it, 'Berend, the Shadow already knew of the threat that I posed, but at Barachael It became aware of you, too. And as they say, your newest hatred is the most interesting."

"True," Freelorn said. "Probably It believes you're Its deadliest foe at the moment—"

"Ha! Some foe," she said. Her participation in Herewiss's wreaking had been successful enough, but now the thought of what one could do with Fire, if only one could focus it, kept obtruding itself. *And just when I thought I was done with it all…*And though Hasai and the *mdeihei* were silent on the subject now, she kept hearing her *mdaha* saying, *You fear all strengths, even your own. That fear cripples you. You must give it up.*

But if I did, and it still made no difference…then there would really *be no hope.*

As if hope has ever done me any good…!

Herewiss and Freelorn had both fallen silent. "Sorry," Segnbora said. "Sorry. I'm not much in the mood for conversation today. Let me ride point for a while…"

She rode Steelsheen up to the head of the column and let the sound of the others' quiet conversation fade beneath her concentration on the surrounding country, and her awareness of Skádhwë's reassuring blackness, soaking up light at her saddlebow. Its weightlessness, at first unsettling, was becoming second nature, and very useful in a fight. And certainly no other sword was all edge and no flat.

Likewise, no other sword would cut anything but the hand of its mistress, as Freelorn had discovered while handling it one morning. Skádhwë seemed not to care for being used by anyone else. It was delicate, but very definite, about drawing Lorn's blood. Of her, it had demanded nothing so far, and Segnbora thought of Efmaer's warning to her with unease, wondering when the weird would take hold.

Unease seemed to have overtaken everybody these days. No longer were they simply fugitives on the run from Cillmod's mercenaries; the Shadow was after them now, too, and the knowledge that their souls were in peril had them all on edge.

Even Herewiss was short of conversation these days, drawing closer to Lorn, pulling away from the others, as every step closer to Bluepeak, where the Darthenes were massing to meet the Shadow's challenge, brought the reality of his true-dream closer. His anxiety affected Freelorn in turn. Lorn wore a haunted look most of the time, and when his people looked to him for answers, his attempts to reassure them mostly left them with an even stronger sense of his inner distress. *The Shadow doesn't need to threaten us from without to make us ineffective,* Segnbora thought, morose, as the afternoon dragged the Sun down to eye level, turning the western horizon into a blinding nuisance. *Using our own fears to drive us apart, and make us less able to protect Lorn, will serve Its purposes well enough.*

(Sdaha,) Hasai said from way down, *(we smell water.)*

(Where?)

(West and south. A league as the Dragon flies.)

She nodded and thumped Steelsheen's sides, bringing her about in order to inform Herewiss of a place to camp. Hasai had been much quieter than usual since Barachael. At first embarrassment had been the cause, but within a few days the reason had seemed to shift, and under his silence Segnbora kept sensing an odd satisfaction. *(You're finally becoming properly sdahaih,)* was all he would say when she asked him about it; though his approval was strangely counterbalanced by the mdeihei, behind him, singing wordless and nonspecific foreboding that nonetheless had an odd joy woven through it. They were no more forthcoming than Hasai was, and finally Segnbora had given up trying to work out what was going on. She'd find out eventually.

The campsite they found three leagues ahead was in a stony, scrubby canyon: shattered, green-white cliffs above, and dry watercourse below. Scant rains kept alive the brush and several little spinneys of warped ash and blackthorn, but nothing else. "Where's the water?" Herewiss said to Segnbora, annoyed.

"There," she said, speaking Hasai's words for him, and gestured at the face of the cliff. Herewiss gave her a look and dismounted from Sunspark.

"No rest for the weary," he said, and advanced on the cliff with eyes closed, checking her perception. Then he opened his eyes, picked a spot, and brought Khávrinen around in a roundhouse swing. Splintered stone shot in various directions, trailing Fire. Water followed it, bursting from the rock in a momentary release of pressure and then subsiding to a steady stream down the cliff's face.

They watered and fed the horses while Herewiss stood gazing around with a wary look, as if expecting trouble. Segnbora went away feeling thoughtful herself, and led Steelsheen to the most distant of the ash spinneys. *This place has a bad feeling about it,* she thought, preparing to tether Steelsheen to one of the ash trees. The mare snorted, stamped, threw her head up. Segnbora looked up too.

Oh no...

The trees were warped and bent as if by the wind. Snarled among the branches of the nearest one was a blowing, filmy mass of something white. "Easy, easy..." Segnbora said to Steelsheen, backing the mare well away from the trees and throwing the reins over her head so that she'd stand. Then she went back to the tree, reached up and pulled some of the white stuff away from the tangle. The long strands were white and soft as spun silk, though as unbreakably strong as any rope when she pulled a hank of the stuff between her hands—

From behind her, Herewiss reached up and pulled down the main mass of the material. As the pale, cubit-wide tangle came away from the tree, a whole mort of things came tumbling out of it to thump or clatter to the ground.

"Look at that," Herewiss said conversationally, bending down to poke with Khávrinen at something jutting from the white swathing. "The point-shard of a sword. Darthene Master-forge steel, see, Lorn? Look at the lines in the metal."

"It takes a lot to break a sword like that," Freelorn said from beside his loved, but sounding nowhere near as composed.

Why now? Why now! Segnbora thought, as Herewiss bent to pick something else out of the whiteness. He came up holding a piece of pale wood, badly warped: It was smoothly rounded at one end, broken off jaggedly at the other. "A Rod," Herewiss said. "Or it used to be."

Dritt and Moris had come up and were staring nervously at this spectacle. "I thought the only thing that could break a Rod was the Rodmistress's death," Moris said.

Herewiss nodded, using Khávrinen's point to turn over other oddments tangled in the haphazard white weave: bits of broken jewelry, tatters of what might have been brocade. A bone from a human forearm poked out of the mass, ivory-yellow and scored by toothmarks. It had been cracked for the marrow, and sucked clean.

"Mare's nest," Herewiss sad, turning to the others and glancing at them one after another. "And recent. We're probably right at the heart of her territory."

"Then this is no place for us," Freelorn said. He turned to go take the hobbles off Blackmane, but Herewiss didn't follow him. Freelorn looked back over his shoulder, confused.

"Lorn, it's sunset," Herewiss said. "We'd never get past her boundaries before nightfall."

Freelorn stared at Herewiss as if he had taken leave of his senses. "Loved, that's a busted Rod there! Fire obviously doesn't do much good against a nightmare—"

"There are other defenses," Herewiss said absently. It was as if he were reading about the problem from a book rather than seeing it in front of him. He looked up at Segnbora. "How about it?"

Segnbora walked around to the other side of the spinney as if to examine where the nest had been, waiting until the tree hid her before she swallowed, hard. Nightmares—minor demonic aspects of the Goddess's dark side—typically nested in barren places like this. They fell upon travelers, sucked them dry of the spark of Power they possessed, then fed the dead flesh to their fledgling nightfoals. Since they were Shadowbred, Fire was food and drink to them. They could only be killed with one's bare hands, and only if those hands were a woman's.

Segnbora walked around to face the others. "It's getting toward Midsummer," she said, amazed at how calmly her voice came out. "Her brood will be gone now, and she'll have eaten the nightstallion—"

Freelorn's face twisted. "They—eat their—!"

"They are the Devourer," Segnbora said, very low. "That aspect of the Dark One trusts nothing She hasn't consumed." She glanced over at Herewiss. "Well, I broke Steelsheen with my bare hands. I think I can manage this."

Behind Herewiss, Lang's face was white with shock. She refused to look at him after that first glance. "I'll make a circle," Herewiss said. "You'll have warning. What else will you want?"

Last rites, probably. "A fire," she said.

Herewiss smiled slightly. "I think I know where to get some. Sunspark!"

Segnbora walked toward the sudden campfire, wishing there were such a thing as luck, so she could curse it.

For once, night came down too suddenly for her taste. Segnbora sat with the others beside Sunspark's blazing self, looking out toward the stony darkness. Here and there, at a hundred yards' distance, a flicker of Herewiss's Fire showed blue between the boulders, indicating the ward-circle he had laid down. Firelight danced on the face of the cliff. Under a gnarled little rowan bush Segnbora sat and tended to herself in the huge silence, which even the horses, hobbled and tethered inside the circle, didn't break.

Segnbora was running out of things to do in order to get ready. She had gone through all the small personal bindings that a sorcerer would perform to further the larger binding she intended. Her swordbelt's hanging end was tucked in. Her hair, too short to braid, she had tied with a thong into a stubby tail and bound close to her head. Her sleeves were rolled up. The buckles on her boots and her mailshirt were tight. She would have tied Skádhwë into its sheath, but it had no peace-strings as Charriselm had had, and all her attempts to bind the shadowblade with cord had been useless. It cut them all. Finally she had just taken it out of the scabbard and stuck it into a handy rock.

Now she thought of one more binding to add. Rummaging around in her belt-pouch for a bit of thread, she bound it around her left thumb nine times: the soul-cord that would keep her soul within her body until a pyre's blaze freed it. She tied the ninefold knot, and glanced up as she bit it off. Freelorn was holding a cup for her. It was of light wood, with a design of leaves carved around it below the lip. She recognized it: his and Herewiss's lovers'-cup.

"Hot wine," Lorn said, sitting down. Warmed by the gesture, she took it and drank, hoping the shaking of her hands wouldn't show too much.

"It shows. Forget it," Herewiss said, sitting down beside Freelorn.

She extended the cup to him, leaning back against the knobby little rowan as Herewiss drank in turn. Afterward, he poured some wine into the fire, which had acquired eyes, and then passed the cup back to Freelorn.

Lorn leaned back against a rock, and Herewiss leaned back too, resting his head against Lorn's chest. "You *sure* there's nothing you can do?" Freelorn said, sounding sorrowful.

Herewiss glanced up at him. "Swords don't bite on nightmares, loved. I'm sorry."

Freelorn nodded, still looking uneasy. "This business of the Lady's 'dark side,'" he said, "I've never really understood how She can *have* a dark side…"

"It is this way," Segnbora started, mostly out of reflex, and then stopped herself. Embarrassed, she took the cup back and drank again.

"No, go ahead," Herewiss said, with a wry look. "If you're going to become something's dinner tonight, we might as well get one more story out of you. Tell it as they tell it at Nháiredi. I've never heard their version."

She sighed, suddenly amused by the surroundings—no cozy inn or palace hall, but the huge and empty night of waste country; and here she sat playing to an audience of kings-by-courtesy, part-time princes, and outlaws. *And you too,* she thought, as from down in the darkness within her an interested rumbling floated up—the *mdeihei*, eager to hear a memory, even a made-up one.

"It's this way," she said. "Because the Goddess bound Herself at the Making into everything She had made, the great Death became bound into Her too, and She into It. Though She'd brought It life, the Shadow still hated Her and did Her all the harm It could, causing each of Her fair aspects to cast a dark shadow of its own. Therefore the Devourer exists, and the One with Still Hands…" She shivered. "…and the Pale Winnower. Their Power is terrible, and the Goddess cannot banish them; in this Making, They are part of Her.

"But in the south of Steldin, people explain our Lady's dark side differently. They tell how, on the plain north of Mincar, there lived an austringer and her wife. The austringer was a placid woman, easily pleased and as calm as one of her hawks after a feeding. The austringer's wife, on the other hand, was never content with anything, and sharpened her tongue continually on her spouse.

"There came a day when the austringer took a good catch of pheasant and barwing. The next morning she set out for Mincar market to sell the game.

"Now, while on her way to the market square, as she passed through the wealthy part of town, the austringer saw a sight stranger and more lovely than any she had ever seen. Tied to a reining-post was a great, tall silver-white steed, shining in the morning. When she drew near to it, it turned its head to gaze at her with eyes as dark as the missing half of the Moon. It was tethered with a bridle of woven silver.

"She recognized it then. It was one of the Moonsteeds, aspects of the Maiden that mirror the Moon in its changes, and which cannot be caught by any means except with a bridle that is wrought of noon-forged silver in such a fashion as to have no beginning and no end. Some lord or lady had caused the bridle to be made, and had managed to catch the Steed. And as the austringer stood there and pitied the poor creature, free from time's beginning and now bound, it lowered its head and said to her, 'Free me, and I'll do you a good turn when I may.'

"So she cut the bridle with her knife, and the Moonsteed reared and pawed the air and said, 'If you want for anything, go out into the fields and call me, and I will be with you.' And it vanished.

"The austringer thought it well to vanish from the area herself. She went to market and sold her birds, and then went home in a hurry in order to tell her wife what she had seen. That was a mistake. 'Surely,' her wife said, 'the Steed will grant you anything you want. Go out and ask it to make us rich.'

"She nagged the austringer unmercifully until at last she gave in and went out into the night, under the first-quarter Moon, to call the Steed. It came, saying 'What can I do for you?'

"'My wife wants to be rich. Wants *us* to be rich, rather,' said the austringer.

"'The first was closer to the truth, I think,' the Steed said, 'but go home, it has happened already.' And the austringer went home to find her wife happily running her fingers through bags of Moon-white silver, chuckling to herself about the fine robes and elegant food she would soon have in place of her brown homespun and coarse bread.

"For about a week things went well. But folk nearby began to ask questions, and then the tax collectors arrived, leaving with more silver than pleased the austringer's wife. 'This isn't working,' she said to the austringer. 'Go ask the Steed to make *me* the tax collector. And I want a house befitting my station.'

"'No one will talk to us any more!' the austringer said. But her wife gave her no peace, and sent her off to the fields at nightfall.

"The austringer called the Moonsteed, and there it came in a white blaze of light, for the Moon was near to full. 'What can I do for you?' it asked. 'Though I have a feeling I know.'

"'My wife wants to be a tax collector, and have a tax collector's fine house,' the austringer said.

"'Go home, it's done,' said the Steed. And the austringer went home and found their thatched cottage changed to a tall house of rr'Harich marble; and her wife was twenty times as rich as she had been before.

"After that things went as you might imagine. A week later the austringer's wife wanted to be mayor, and so she was. Afterward she became bailiff, and Dame, and Head of House, one after another. Her house became golden-pillared and roofed with crystal, filled with rich stuffs and things out of legend—feather-hames and charmed weapons and even the silver chair that later belonged to the Cat of Aes Aradh—but none of it gave her joy for more than a day. Each night she sent the austringer out to ask for another boon, and the austringer grew sad and pale, seeing that her wife loved her possessions more than she loved *her*.

"And as the days passed the aspect of the Moonsteed grew darker, for the old Moon was waning. White-silver the Steed had been at first, like moonlight on snow. Now it waxed darker each night, and frightened the austringer.

"The boons grew greater and greater. Head of the Ten High Houses, the austringer's wife became; then Chief of them, then High Minister, then Priestess-Consort. And still she wanted more.

"Finally the night came of the dark of the Moon—"

Segnbora broke off for a moment, fumbling for the wine cup. Her mouth had gone suddenly dry. It was only three nights from Moondark now, that time when a nightmare would be strongest.

"—the dark of the Moon, and the austringer went out to the fields to call on the Moonsteed for the last time. It came, burning with awful dark splendor and wrath, and said in its gentle voice, 'What is it now? Your wife has asked, and I have granted, even to the last times when she asked to be Queen of Steldin, and then High Queen of all the Kingdoms. What more might she want?'

"The austringer trembled, and said, 'She wants to rule the Universe.'"

Segnbora lifted the cup again and finished the wine.

There was silence. Freelorn glanced down expectantly at Herewiss, whose eyes were turned away, then back at Segnbora. "So?"

"So She *does.*" She handed back the empty cup. "Now you tell one." Behind them, Blackmane screamed. Herewiss jerked upright as if he had been kicked. All around the camp heads turned out toward the darkness.

The nightmare stood for a moment among the boulders that had fallen from the cliff, and then stepped forward delicately. It was small, no bigger than a seven-months' filly. Its silken mane and tail hung to the ground. Slim-legged and clean of line, it seemed at first as elegant and graceful as a unicorn. But its eyes were evil, red and bottomless, full of old cruelties and insatiable hunger. From a coat the color of the rolled-up whites of a dead man's eyes, the nightmare cast a faint yellowish corpse-light that illuminated nothing.

Segnbora got up, dry-mouthed again. She took a few steps forward and folded her arms, staring into those ancient, burning eyes. *It's just like Nhàirëdi, with that demon they caught. No different. Hold the eyes—*

"Be thou warned," Segnbora said in the formal manner reserved for the laying of dooms, "that I am well informed of thee and thy ways, of thy comings and goings, thy wreakings and undoings; and that my intent is to bind thee utterly to my will, and confine thee to the dark from which thou cam'st at the birth of days. So unless thou wish to try thy strength with me, and be compelled by the binding I shall work upon thee, then get thee hence and have no more to do with me and mine."

She held very still. The nightmare now had the option to retreat. It could also answer ritually, or it could attack.

"How should I fear *you?*" the nightmare said, sweetly taunting—and its voice was that of Segnbora's slain otherself, not piteous as during those last moments in Glasscastle, but mocking and cruel. "Rodmistresses in the full of their Power have tried conclusions with me, and you see what happened to *them.* Fear *you?*—never even focused, and retired from sorcery lest you fail at that too?" It laughed, a sound like bells and poison.

"Be still!" Segnbora said in a voice like a whipcrack. But no power was behind the order, and the nightmare laughed at her, a sound ugly with knowledge.

"You make a fine noise," it said, flicking its tail insolently, "But all your years' studies have left you with nothing but knowledge. Spells and tales and sayings—but no Power. Or Power enough—if you dared to use it. Which you don't!"

She clenched her fists and took a step forward, then stopped, desperately seeking control. (Hasai—!)

"Oh, by all means, call up your ghost," the nightmare said, stepping forward too, and laughing with the cold merriment of a damned thing. "You don't dare accept what he has to offer, either. There you are, walking on water, complaining that you can't find anything to drink! And you can't even make use of what little you do have. Battles and wars and wreakings pass over you, the earth moves, Glasscastle falls about your ears, and none of it is enough to free you. You're *dead!*"

Behind her Segnbora could feel Freelorn wanting to move, and Herewiss holding him still with that same vise-grip in which he had held her at Barachael. The others were frozen, eyes glittering, muscles bound still. Even Sunspark's flames flowed more slowly than usual. "What a heroine you are," said the scornful voice. "And dead past all denying. Life gives life. *You* devour—as surely as I do! Just look at your slug of a leman there."

The malicious black eyes dwelt on Lang with vast amusement. "He no more dares open himself to you than you do to him. He knows what Eftgan knew: that what you call 'love' is nothing but shrieking need. If he were once to let down his guard, he knows you'd eat him down to the bones like a starving beggar at a banquet, and come away unsatisfied, moaning for more." The nightmare chuckled, the red eyes burning with amusement. "And any hopes he might have of you are vain, for you haven't opened up to another human being since you were big enough to be stumbled over out in back of the chicken house. Everything that comes out of your mouth is storytelling—everyone's story but your own. You don't trust anybody. You don't trust yourself. And especially you don't trust yourself with that—what feels like the Fire, and isn't—"

Humiliation and rage seared through her. Segnbora took another slow step forward, hanging onto the words of the ritual for dear life and not daring to look at Lang. "I may warn thee again: get hence, lest I lay such strictures about thee that from age to age thou shalt lie bound in the never-lightened gulfs—"

"Say the words of the sorcery," the nightmare said, baring her yellow teeth in scorn. "They'll do no good. As if *you* of all people could control another aspect of the Devourer! You can't even manage what lies under the stone at the bottom of your self, festering at the bottom of all your 'loves', hating the one who plundered you, taking revenge on anyone else who tries to get in. Freelorn there, he found out what happens to someone who gets closer to you than a sword's length. There are sharper things to stab a heart with than knives. Why, you even ran across yourself, and didn't speak six sentences to her before you killed yourself. Pity it didn't take. There would have been celebrations." It grinned. "No matter. Shortly there *will* be—"

Segnbora leaped at the nightmare head-on, grabbing great handfuls of its mane and trying to hold its head away from her. The nightmare plunged and reared, and after a second fastened its teeth into Segnbora's mailshirt, cracking the links like dry twigs and driving them excruciatingly through padding and breastband, into the breast beneath. It shook her viciously from side to side, as a dog shakes a rat.

With every jerk of its head Segnbora cried out in pain, yet she managed to hold on for some seconds—then let go her right hand's hold in the mane and grabbed the nightmare's nose instead, digging her thumbnail deep into the nostril. Now it was the nightmare's turn to scream—once as she let Segnbora fall, and once again as its backward plunge tore out a great handful of its silken mane.

Segnbora scrambled to her feet, tearing with the pain, doing her best to concentrate on twisting the long hank of mane into a rough cord between her hands. "Are you—so sure?" she gasped as she and the nightmare began to circle one another. "Foolish—letting me get so close. I know how to bind you, child of our Mother. I know how to make an end of you, Power or not. Shortly you're going to be seeing more of the dark places than you'll like—"

She sprang again, this time for the nightmare's flank. It danced hurriedly to one side, but with the second leap Segnbora got astride the nightmare's back. The nightmare bucked and kicked and reared, leaping in the air and coming down with all four feet together, as a horse does to kill a snake. But Segnbora hung on, legs locked, hands twined in the long mane.

She got one hand down over the nightmare's nose again, and dug her nails once more into the nostrils. The nightmare screamed, and as it did she whipped the corded length of mane down and into its mouth. Quickly she brought the ends under its chin and up around its muzzle, and knotted them tight, binding its mouth closed.

The nightmare made a horrendous strangled sound that wanted to be a scream; then turned and raced headlong toward the jagged face of the cliff, intending to buck Segnbora off against the stone. The onlookers scattered out of the way, and Segnbora jumped from its back, rolled, and was on her feet again before the nightmare had time to realize what had happened. Turning to face her again, it reared, menacing her with its hooves. Segnbora ducked to one side and fastened her hands in its mane, pulling. The nightmare grunted and, as she'd hoped it would, jerked away. Too late: Segnbora fell down on the ground again, once again with her hands full of mane.

The nightmare turned and reared. By the time its hooves hit ground, Segnbora had rolled out from under them, and was afoot once more. Her breath came hard, and beneath her mail-shirt the blood was running down her side from a breast bleeding freely and white-hot with pain. But her fear was gone. Nothing was left but wild anger, and the urge to destroy.

"I told you," she said, winding the length of mane between her fists like a garrote. "First the binding—"

The nightmare turned to flee. As it turned tail Segnbora vaulted up over its rump and onto its back, locking her legs tight around it again. Frenzied, the nightmare bucked wildly, but it was no use. This time the cord went around its throat and was pulled mercilessly tight. It plunged and slewed from side to side and tossed its head violently, trying to breathe.

Segnbora hung on, and twisted the cord tighter. The nightmare began to stagger, its eyes bulging out in anguish. Its forelegs gave way, next, so that it knelt choking and swollen-tongued on the ground. Segnbora held her seat even at that crazy angle, and pulled the cord tighter still. Finally the rear legs gave, and the nightmare fell on its side. Segnbora slipped free, never easing her stranglehold. The nightmare moved feebly a few times, then lay still.

Holding that cord tight became the whole world, more important even than the agony of her torn breast or the hot blurring of her eyes. She blinked and gasped and hung on as Herewiss and Freelorn and the others ran up and kneeled around her.

Lang reached out to her, but Herewiss stopped the gesture. "Is it dead?"

"I don't know. Probably not." She could still feel a pulse thrumming feebly through the cord.

"Are you all right?" That was Lang.

"No. Let me be." The nightmare's pulse was irregular now, leaping and struggling in its throat like a bird in a snare. *How can they look at me?* she wondered. *It's all true. How can they bear to—*

One last convulsive flutter ran through the nightmare's veins. Then there was stillness under her hands.

Slowly and carefully Segnbora stood up, shrinking away from any hand that tried to help her. The pain in her breast was intense, yet she barely felt it through the pain that hurt worse. Torn again. *Torn like—no!* Tauëh-stá 'ae mnek-kej, *I don't want to remember—*

She turned and walked away into the darkness beyond the firelight. Her companions stared after her. Their eyes on her retreating back were as unbearable as sun on blistered skin, but still she ignored them.

(A nightmare has no weapon to use but your own darkness.) Herewiss said in her mind, his thought passionless as a leech's knife. (Resist, and it only cuts deeper.)

She kept walking.

(One night, 'Berend,) he said. (One night's pain is all we can spare you. We've lost too much time already. Be finished by dawn, or we won't wait.)

Segnbora shut him out and went off into the bitter night, looking for an end.

thirteen

"Well," the Goddess said, "your heart didn't heal straight the last time it broke. So we'll break it again and reset it so it heals straight this time."

Children's Tales of North Arlen, ed. s'Lange

How long she walked, she had no idea. The stony valley all looked the same. Eventually, she simply sat down and began to weep for life wasted.

At some point the rocky night turned into the night that lay inside her, with stars showing through the great shaft in the roof of her cavern, and the much-muted song of the *mdeihei* rumbling in the shadows. She didn't care about them in the slightest, or about the starlight, or the sound of the Sea, or the huge obscure shape of Hasai towering over her in the darkness. She sat hunched up and waited for life to go away.

It wouldn't, annoyance that it was. A solution occurred to her, but she had no energy for it. And anyway, everything she'd ever done, she'd botched—surely she'd only botch a suicide, too. A life of study without use, learning without wisdom, action without satisfaction, Power without focus, lust without love: what use was any of it? She sat there and tried to bleed to death through the wound above her heart.

"Death is some days ahead of you yet," said the subdued voice of the Dragon above her, using the precognitive tense.

Annoyed, she leaned gingerly back against the great forelimb, trying not to disturb the blood clotting on her breast, and closed her eyes, squeezing out useless hot tears. "Drop dead," she said.

"We have done so."

"Try it again. You missed something the first time."

"Speak for yourself, *sdaha,*" the voice of thunder said. It had her own annoyance in it.

Tonight, as occasionally happened, she didn't have to look up at Hasai in order to see him. His eyes burned silver, but they burned low. His talons clenched the stone floor in a painful gesture that made her remember the cave at the Morrowfane.

"I sorrow for your pain," he said. "But that thing spoke some truth: and you know it. You will not permit us to have what we need, so that we, in turn, may give you what *you* need. You believe you must do everything yourself. But such perfect self-sufficiency is impossible."

She shook her head, confused, thinking of what her father used to tell her: *You'll never be able to depend on others, if you can't first depend on yourself.*

Hasai winced at her in Dracon disagreement. "You cannot depend on yourself if you cannot first *trust* others."

The words made no sense. Hasai gazed down without moving for a long while, and at last shuffled one huge forelimb back and forth along the floor. *"We are you,"* he said with terrible intensity. "If you cannot trust us, your trust of yourself will be betrayed every time."

It was no use. It made no sense.

"*Sdaha,*" Hasai said, so low it could have passed for a whisper. "What lies beneath your stone that you dare not lay open? What frightens and pains you so that the Shadow would resurrect the memory in the hope you would die of it?"

That got her attention. *Lorn was right,* she thought. *For some reason It genuinely sees me as a threat. If that means I truly have a chance to do It some harm, however small, at Bluepeak—*

She leaned sideways and put one hand down upon the smoothed-over stone at the bottom of her mind. It burned hot as flesh beneath a half-healed wound, warning her off. Her insides flinched at the touch of it, and she began to tremble. Under there—

Pain. And the alternative.

Pain, experienced, would stop hurting, she knew. Paradoxical as it seemed, the *mdeihei* had taught her the truth of that. *But will it be so with this pain? Or is the Shadow right to think it will kill me?*

She leaned there, shaking. *Yet what if It's wrong?* ...And there was yet another reason to look under the stone, for if she shied away from this weak spot now, the vulnerability would become deeper still. The Shadow would strike her there again, almost certainly at Bluepeak, when Lorn needed her service the most. She would fail, and fall, perhaps taking her friends with her. Her liege-oath would be broken; the Kingdoms could founder for lack of the enactment of the Royal Bindings, and it would all be down to her.

It's not fair! She smashed one fist down on the stone. *Damn! Damn! Why* me? Tauëh-stá 'ae mnek-kej!

The dark-winged forms in the shadows leaned in all around her, hearing what passed among them for blasphemy, saying nothing. Hasai bent low over her, silent.

They could do nothing, be nothing, until she chose. It was all down to her, as she knelt there for what seemed a long time, in a darkness that was growing cold.

"Mdaha," Segnbora said at last, shaking all over. Slowly, she leaned forward until she was on her hands and knees on the stone. *"Mdeihei—"*

They leaned in close, the huge form above her, the many indistinct forms in the shadows. She reached behind her, toward Hasai. Wings reached down to shelter her, but it wasn't shelter she was interested in. Segnbora's hand found the burning mouth, and jaws closed over it. She pulled those wings down around her, into her, wore them and their body and their heart.

Under the stone, darkness burned. She cocked forward the terrible diamond razors of the wings' forefingers, intent on the place where her deepest anguish lay. "My *mdeihei,* this is what you wanted. And what I want now. If we die of it…"

A roar of defiance and challenge went up from the gathered generations.

"Mnek-é," she whispered: *I remember.* Her talons raked down and laid her soul bare at last. Stone peeled away, and her control went with it. Night fell.

Her nuncle, of course. Nuncle Bal was in and out of the old house at Asfahaeg all the time, busy around the land—gardening, cutting trees, planting new ones. She had watched him about his business often enough, and sometimes she'd noticed him looking at her for a long time. She wondered sometimes whether he was lonely and wanted to play, but she never quite got around to making friends with him. There was too much else to do.

She had the Fire, a lot of it, and pretty soon they were going to send her away to a real school where you learned to do magic with it, instead of just simple body-fixings and underspeech, which were all the Rodmistress down in town would teach her. At the school they'd make her a Rod of her own, and she'd be able to do all kinds of things.

In the meantime, there were lessons and exercises to make the Fire grow, and she was busy with those. In fact, she had stumbled by herself on one special exercise that gave her the same tingling excitement that the Fire did, though in a slightly different way. When she showed her new method to Welcaen, her mother had laughed and praised her, and told her it was fine to enhance the Fire thus, but that she shouldn't forget to be private when she did it. The most private spot she could think of was the hiding place behind the old chicken house, where the willows' branches hung down all around, making a dusky green cave. And that was where she had spent most of that warm spring day, delightedly touching herself in that special secret place—until Nuncle Balen came brushing through the downhanging branches and stopped in surprise, to stand there staring at her.

Her mother had told her that usually it was not polite to be naked with someone unless you had agreed on it beforehand. Not knowing how Nuncle Bal felt about it, she pulled her smock back down and smiled at him.

"Hi," she said.

He smiled back, and all of a sudden she felt cold inside, because there was something wrong with the way he was smiling. Confused, she put out her underhearing and listened.

What she heard made her so scared that she couldn't pull it back again, couldn't even move. She never heard anything like *this* before. Her mother and father when they shared—she knew that feeling. It was warm: a filling-and-being-filled feeling. She wasn't sure what they were doing, exactly, but it wasn't *this*. The feeling that went with *this* was cold: a wanting, and wanting-to-be-in-something. It was hungry, just hungry enough to *take*—

He was letting the rake fall against the willow trunk, and she was getting really scared now, so that she started to jump up and run away. But he was right in front of her already, and he grabbed her hard around the throat with one hand, and covered her mouth with the other. She couldn't breathe. She tried to scream, to cry, but there wasn't any air. Her ears started to ring and everything went red in front of her.

Nuncle Bal seemed to be saying something, but she couldn't tell what it was through the red, the black, the roaring. She fell backward into the darkness, silently begging *oh please, let it be a bad dream. Let me wake up, please!*

After a while the roaring went away some. *It was a dream,* she began to think, and then heard his voice, thick, low and hungry. "You want it," he said. Her eyes came open. She saw his twisted smile, shuddered, and squeezed them shut again. "You want it. Sure you want it."

He was doing something to her smock. What was he— "Mamaaaaa!" she started to scream, tears starting to her eyes. But before she could get the scream out that hand came down on her throat again. The red, the roaring, *oh no, pleeeeeeease*—

Her back was cold. She was on the ground again, and her smock was off. So were Nuncle Bal's britches, and she squirmed and fought but couldn't get out from under his hands. His breath was on her face and he leaned in and pushed her legs far apart, too far. It hurt, and what was he doing, he was rubbing her secret place, the wrong way! And what, what—

NOOOOO!!

The scream wouldn't come out of her throat. It was all inside her head, a shrieking pain, but not as bad as how he was hurting her down there. He was in her secret place that was supposed to be for her to share with her loved some day, and he was pushing himself inside. There was a horrible burning pain, again, and again, until she felt herself being torn open. There was a white-hot line of relief, then, and new agony stitching itself through the rest of the burning. It was sickening. She wanted to retch but couldn't, his hand—

Tears rolled down the sides of her face, into her hair. After a while she couldn't feel them or anything else, it hurt so bad— Inside she yelled and yelled for help, but no help came. They weren't sensitives and they couldn't hear her, any of them! He was pushing it in and out, hard. It hurt worse and worse, and he was breathing fast and hot right in her face. She was breathing his wet stale breath and that made her want to be sick too—and it hurt, it *hurt, somebody make it stop!*

Somebody, Mama, Daddy, Goddess, please, please make it stop!

He slumped forward, and she thought she felt something shoot inside her, but she wasn't sure because of the pain, the way it burned, her secret place that had always felt so nice. Broken, torn, she'd never be able to use it again. No one would love her, ever, *hers* was broken—and the Fire, when he hurt her, it came out, it was in the pain, part of the pain, *no more, never, it hurt, horrible—*

She lay there and sobbed for air, all the screams in her stifled by horror; and when he came around and knelt over her face and pushed the hard thing, all bloody, into her slack mouth, and rubbed it in and out, she let him. At least he wasn't hurting her anymore. But when he turned her over and started to put it against that other place, she realized that he was going to hurt her even worse this time. No one was going to come help her now, either. She pushed her face down against the cold harsh dirt and tried with all her might to die.

It didn't work. When her first scream broke free, he strangled it again. The terrible strength of his hand turned the world red and then black once more. The last thing she heard as she pitched forward into blackness was, very remote, the sound of some little girl screaming as the size of him tore her open the other way, too.

Eventually her hearing came back. She heard him pick up his rake and hurry away, pushing the rustling branches aside. Some while later, lying as she was with her face on the hard ground, she felt-heard hoofbeats, cantering, then galloping. He was gone. Very slowly she got up. It hurt, especially when she moved her legs at all. She pulled down her smock and scrubbed at her face to try to get the dirt off: her father didn't like her to be dirty.

That roaring stayed with her all that day, as confusion and rage shouted all around her. It was in her thoughts now, dazed, shocked, going around and around in her head and coming back again to that which she had felt tangled with the agony—the Fire—and shying away from the thought and coming back, endlessly.

When they finally put her to bed, full of some bitter herbal potion the Rodmistress had made her drink so she'd sleep, still her head roared behind the steady flow of her tears. Only later, after she had been staring for hours at the vague circles the candles made on the ceiling, did the tears flow more slowly. Gradually, the pain between her legs began to feel far away. The roar died to a whisper. But the whisper said the same thing she had been hearing all day, and by the sound of it, she fell asleep: *No more. Horrible. Never again.*

And there was a quieter whisper beneath that. One so soft that she hadn't heard it then, never heard it afterward; only heard it now with a Dragon's impossibly sharp underhearing—a seed of rage, taking root in blood and battered flesh, burning dark with hate: *Some day, when I'm big, I'll kill him.*

The pain, experienced at last, fell away and left her among her *mdeihei* with the fiery tears running down her face. They held their silence, waiting to hear what she would sing before beginning to weave counterpoint or dissonance about it.

She was exhausted. It was fifteen years since that afternoon under the willow. Fifteen years since she had shown herself any more than Balen's terrible smile, or thought of the experience as more than "the rape." She had thought she was over it, past it all.

What idiocy.

As she grew, she had quickly given up thinking much about sharing her body with others. Her agemates indulged in all the delightful anticipation of adolescence—the feeling that something magical awaited them when sharing began. But she had already been plunged into an experience that had about it nothing whatsoever of magic. When she came of age, every sharing, however innocent, had a touch of the sordid about it, a taste of fear which made her want to have it finished quickly. Afterwards, she would inevitably plunge into another sharing, in search of what had been missing. She never found it. Nor, as she got close to the brink of focusing, had she ever managed that, either. How could she, when sharing felt so much like Fire?

It's so simple. Since the Fire feels like loving, allow yourself only sharings that can't work, or won't last. Reject those who love you, pursue the uninterested. That way you'll never have to do much of what feels like the Fire, but isn't. And let that furious, hating part of your mind betray your Fire every time it's close to focus, forcing it to starve away to nothing, so you won't have to spend the rest of your life with that inside you—what feels like loving, and isn't.

She could just hear the Shadow laughing.

Slowly Segnbora lifted her gemmed head, and sang relief and grief and weary regret at the walls. From the shadows her *mdeihei* took up the dark melody and shared it with her in compassionate plainsong. "Oh Immanence," she sang, "I'm full of Power, and in danger of running forever dry; I've shared a hundred times, and I'm virgin still; I walk on water, and yet thirst..." She brought her wings down against the floor in a gesture of bitterness.

"And the nightmare was right, too. I'm a killer. The Shadow has merely to touch that memory ever so lightly, and I kill yet again. Is this my destiny, then? To be a clockwork toy that can be set to killing by any fool who happens to find the key?"

Gentle and ruthless, her *mdeihei* answered her in one long note that shook the cave. *"Yes!"*

"Or so it seems," Hasai said kindly.

She looked over at her *mdaha,* catching for the first time the unease that had always been in his voice. Segnbora had never before been Dracon enough to hear it. He gazed back, gentle-eyed, huge, terrible as a thundercloud with wings. And yet, to Dracon eyes, he too was frightened, crippled, shadowed. Looking at him now, a question she had idly toyed with once or twice before suddenly changed its shape and became essential.

"Mdaha," she said, bending her head down close to his. "Hasai *sithesssch—what were you doing at the Morrowfane?"*

He made as if to back away and then stopped, apparently unwilling to disturb the tiny human figure that rested against his right forelimb, watching them. "Going *rdahaih,* I thought. Until you came along—"

"But a Dragon always knows the details of when he'll go *mdahaih.* It's the first scene one sees when one becomes able to remember ahead." She leaned closer still, curled her tail around to pinion the other's and stop its unnerved lashing. Whose body was this she was wearing, scaled in star-emeralds fiery green as new spring growth, spined in yellow diamond? And why did the sight of it make Hasai so nervous? *"Mdaha,"* she sang, staring at him golden eyes to silver ones, "your becoming *mdahaih* in me, it was no accident! You knew! You *always* knew, from when you were a Dragoncel." She looked at him more closely. "And Dragon or human," Segnbora said, "those who climb the Fane are given what they need..."

Hasai turned his head away. Segnbora arched her neck around, not allowing him the evasion. "'Share our memories,' you're always saying. But even for you, there are memories that are only words: no images. —*Ihr'Hhaossia,"* she said. *The Worldwinning—*

Hasai winced, negation again. The *mdeihei* were as still as a held breath.

"You knew this would come," she said. "Now you have no choice either. You strove for us to be one, Hasai, and now we are. You are me, and at Bluepeak the Shadow will strike at you too. If you succumb, so do I. Then Lorn dies, and the Kingdoms founder, and I'm forsworn. And far worse than that will follow. The green place you fought for, the world you treasure so, will fall under the Shadow's domination, and not even Dragons will be safe. We must settle what's under your stone, now, or the Shadow will settle it for us!"

He started to draw downward, away from her touch. "There is yet time—"

"No there's *not!*"

Hasai lashed free of her tail, began to rise slowly from his crouch, wings lifting, the diamond sabers of the forefingers coming around to threaten her.

Segnbora gazing up, unmoved. "I am you, *sithesssch,*" she said. *Beloved.*

Hasai moved not a muscle. As the momentary anger slowly ran out of him, his eyes changed. They were no less afraid, but now there was room in them for something else.

"Now," Segnbora whispered. "Quickly."

The fluid, black-glittering splendor of him made itself into a curve, a pounce, a terrible striking downward, a living knife. She arched herself, struck downward with him. Stone sliced open like parting flesh, the blood was memory, it leaped—

Their Sun ate their world. They saw it happen. They had had warning—both ahead-memory of the actual incident, and years of wild starstorms, during which the Sun's light was too intense to drink without dying, and every Dragon had to leave the Homeworld for a time, waiting far out in the cold for the Sun's fire to die down.

Shell-parents grew infertile, and eggs that should have hatched roasted in the stone instead. At last came the final storm they had dreaded. In haste, all of Dragonkind streamed off their red-brown world and hung helpless in space, watching their star swell to a hundred times its size and devour their Homeworld.

They were orphans.

But they weren't homeless. Wisely, the older Dragons had looked to the youngest Dragoncels to see what they ahead-remembered of their own going-*mdahaih.* What they had found was the place they would later know as *mdeihei*—an odd, cool little world, greener than theirs, covered with a strangeness called *water* and inhabited by life of bizarre and fascinating kinds.

One Dragoncel, however, remembered more than the others. He knew the way, and would die upon reaching their goal. His name was Dahiric. The Dragons gave him another name: Worldfinder. They put him at their head and he led them out into the Great Dark.

How long they travelled there, none of the Dragons were ever sure. Many died along the way—starved for Sunfire in the empty wastes—but Dahiric, a doomed and purposeful green-golden glimmer at the head of ten thousand others, never veered from the memory he followed. Born only to die, and to make this journey, he was determined to succeed.

Finally, after what might have been ages as humans reckon time, they found the place. It was all that the *mdeihei*-to-be had seen: strange-colored, but alive; a home at last; stone to sink their claws into. They dropped down toward it—

—and found what Dahiric, and many more, were to die of. From the dark side of the world, where it had been hiding, a black foul air came boiling out toward them. It was blacker than the space in which they hung, and it was alive. It hated thought and light and any kind of life but its own. It was also vast enough to swallow the bright little planet whole: a project on which it had been working for eons. It didn't relish the Dragons' interruption.

Dahiric knew his duty. Gripping a double wingful of the little planet's field of forces, he dove down into the roiling blackness, flaming. The Dark drew back, and the Dragons saw Dahiric drive a long tunnel down into it. At the tunnel's bottom his light blazed like a falling star. But Dahiric was young, his fire limited by his immaturity. His flame went out, and the Dark closed behind him. After a little while he came floating out of the boiling blackness, dead.

Had there been air to carry the battlecry the Dragons raised, stone would have shattered across the world. Ten thousand strong, they dove at the Dark from every angle, flaming as best they could. Their fire was in short supply, however, since they had been out in the night so long, and ten thousand Dragons were not enough. The Dark opened before them, swallowed them, spat back the dead.

Soon there were nine thousand, seven thousand, fewer.

Many had no offspring yet and went *rdahaih* in a second, without time to make their peace with the Universe from which they were departing. Some went mad from the strain of having so many relatives become *mdahaih* in them in so short a time. Others so afflicted flung themselves into the Dark and were lost too.

A few simply fled, and lived.

One of these was the youngest of the Homeworld's Dragoncels. He had never been quite normal. When he had become fully *sdahaih* at last, and his shell-parents and relatives had asked him when and where he would go *mdahaih,* his answer frightened them all. What he foresaw was darkness and cold and terrible pain; then the odd, crippled body of an alien, one who was certain she would go *rdahaih* and take all the *mdeihei* with her. It was a terrifying vision, and all rejected it.

He grew, and yet the vision did not change. Slowly he became resigned to being a curiosity among his own kind. As befitted a Dragon, he came to make light of the difference, submerging it in placidity. But he did not realize that the way he did this—by learning to stand a little aloof, even from his *mdeihei*—also encouraged other Dragons to stand aloof from him as well.

Hasai became estranged from his own kind. He took no mate. He held his peace. He flew alone. And when he finally found himself facing that same awful blackness that in minutes had killed half his race, Hasai failed. With no comrade who would admit to fear, and so support him toward courage, terror blinded him, and he fled.

The rest of Dragonkind, fortunately, had not exhausted their options. There in empty space they convened in body and mind, and held Assemblage—the last full Assemblage that would be held for a generation or two, until the Advocate summoned them again two thousand years later. They paid the price of Assemblage—the lives of the DragonChief and the Eldest—and then all those left alive turned their hearts inward and gave their Will and power over to the Immanence.

None of them saw where the Messenger came from. She was a Dragon in shape, but even the webs of Her wings burned intolerably bright. Her every scale was a star, a point of power so terrible it could be felt through Dragonhide. The Messenger wheeled and dropped through the massed Dragons, scattering them—then halted above the raging, boiling immensity of the Dark. Through their othersenses, the Dragons could feel the Dark's alarm as it reached up to snuff out this troublesome intruder. And then they heard its silent scream of pain as the Messenger flamed, letting loose a torrent of Dragonfire as potent as a star's breathing.

The Dark writhed convulsively, ripped away from the world with a jerk and a soundless howl of rage. It streamed toward the Messenger to engulf Her utterly, but the Messenger only spread wings and claws and seized it. Working at the forces in space with fiery wings, She drew the Dark away from the world, screaming and struggling. Together they dwindled, drawing farther away from the little blue world, until all that could be seen of them was a light like a dwindling star. Those who dared to follow came back and reported that the Messenger had plunged, together with the Dark, into the heart of the nearby yellow Sun. Neither came out again.

Later, the survivors found Dahiric's body among those of the slain. The others they burned in Dragonfire, as was the custom on the old Homeworld, but Dahiric they bore down to the surface of the new world. There they found a fair place at the endpoint of a great spur of land, where water washed it. They uprooted a mountain, as had been done on the Homeworld for Phyiril and Saen and others of the Parents, and they laid it over him, melted it around him, and made a dwelling there for the new DragonChief. Thereafter, the Dragons settled into their new young world, and watched humankind come slowly out of the caves into which the baleful influence of the Dark had driven them...

...and behind the rest of the Dragons, a silver-and-black Dragoncel drifted to earth like the last leaf of autumn. His shame at his cowardice gripped him like the pain of giving-up-the-body, and would not leave. True, no other Dragon accused him of fear, but no one comforted him, either. He was alone, as always. Alone with a new shame, and with his old deep-hidden terror of the day he would finally go *mdahaih* in a human.

All these burdens he buried under layers of Dracon placidity. The centuries went by. He maintained his dignity, flew alone, and kept silent. Finally his life became reduced to a weary waiting for the stars to assume the proper configurations. This they did. At last, his luster dimming, Hasai spiraled down to the Morrowfane by night and crept into a cave there, to wait for the seizures, and to wait for the one who would come...

He looked across the cavern at her now, head held high, waiting for her to disapprove of him and pronounce a sentence worse than death: eternal imprisonment with a *sdaha* whose opinion of him was not passive placidity, but active scorn. Behind him, the *mdeihei* were silent.

"You ran," Segnbora sang.

He said nothing.

"And you are of value nonetheless," she said, weaving around the words a melody that attributed importance to her words. "You did what you did, and here you are. And here am I, too...or should I say, here are *we*."

Hasai looked at her in amazement. She sighed a little fire and unfolded one emerald-strutted wing, laying it over his back in a gesture of affection.

"So where do we go from here?" she asked.

He opened his mouth, and nothing came out for a moment. "'*Sithesssch*,' you said," he sang in dubious tones.

She flipped her tail in agreement.

"Then only one matter still troubles me..."

"What?"

"The *mdeihei*, and their opinion. As you know, they don't judge, but merely advise. Still, I would like to know that they are not ashamed."

Segnbora considered the matter, listening to the utter silence in the background where the *mdeihei* usually sang. "*Mdaha*, don't worry. If they're truly of the Immanence, as they claim, they will understand."

The doubt fell out of his voice, but Hasai still looked at her strangely. "You're truly *sdahaih* at last," he said. "It's very odd."

"How so? You knew how it would be."

He dropped his jaw, smiling. "Sometimes, for the sake of surprise, we forget a little."

Segnbora spread both wings high and curved her neck around to look at them. "Well, I certainly feel *sdahaih*. Shall we go test it?"

"There's more to being *sdahaih*, and Dracon, than flight," Hasai said and his song trembled with the joy of one who s found something long lost. "Memory. And its transformation."

She shook too, thinking of all the painful experiences she could accept, or remake if she wished. Now that she was *sdahaih*, the ever-living past was as malleable as the present.

There were some things she wouldn't change, experiences that had made her what she was now. *Balen*, she thought. *He stays. There's unfinished business there, somehow. But as for other matters*—

For the first time since that afternoon under the willow, her love was clean—and now more than ever before she wanted to give it away. "I remember a place," she sang quietly looking at Hasai, "where stars swirl in the sky like a frozen whirlpool, and the Sun is red, and the stone is as warm as your eyes—"

He met her glance with eyes that blazed. *"T'ae mnek-é,"* he sang. *We remember.*

Wings lifted and beat downward, and the cave was empty.

The soaring began at the Homeworld, and never quite ended. They made the Crossing all over again, together this time. Other Dragons looked curiously at the one who in fore-memories had been alone, but who now went companioned by some child of the Worldfinder's line, green-scaled and golden-spined, with eyes the fiery yellow of the little star to which they journeyed.

They saw the Winning again, not with guilt this time, but simply as one of the events that would eventually bring them together. Afterwards, they fell to earth like bright leaves drifting, and lay basking in the Sun. They glided together through long afternoons, taking their time so that the people below would have something to marvel at. They matched speed for speed in the high air, and tore it to tatters of thunder. They went bathing in the valleys of the Sun, and chased the twilight around the world for sport. He made her a present of the sunset, and she made him one of the dawn, and they both drank them to the dregs until the fire of their throats was stained the red of the vintage.

They lived in fledgling and Dragoncel and Dragon, in child and girl and woman—found memories that were lost, discovered past and future. Gazing into one another for centuries, they also found completion. And at the bottom of *that,* they found Another gazing back, One Who became them as They became Her. Goddess-Immanence and peers, Made and Maker, the two Firstborn, They flowed together. Not merely One, not simply the same. They *were.*

For that, even in Dracon, there were no words.

Eventually they remembered the way home, and—living in it— were there. Segnbora, leaning back against the immense forelimb from which she had not moved all night, looked up at her *mdaha's* silver eyes.

"I have to be getting back," she said. "They'll be wondering where I am."

"Best hurry and tell them. *Sehé'rae, sdaha.*"

"*Sehé...*"

Halfway out the entrance to the cave, she paused, touching her breast in confusion. In the place where the nightmare had bitten her, there was nothing but a pale, crescent-shaped scar.

"Dragons heal fast," Hasai said from behind her.

A quiet joy like nothing she had ever heard sang around his words. She knew how he felt.

"Sehé'rae, mdaha," she said, and went out.

She opened her eyes on a dawn she could taste as well as see. When she stood up to stretch, she saw the Moon, three days past third quarter, the phase under which she had been born, hanging halfway up the water-blue sky like a smile with a secret behind it.

Picking her way back toward the camp, she came across someone waiting for her with his back to the rising Sun. His long black shadow stretched out toward her, the stones within it outlined brightly by the Fire of the sword he leaned upon.

"Welcome back," Herewiss said as she approached.

Skádhwë was struck into a nearby rock. Segnbora raised a questioning eyebrow at Herewiss as she plucked it out and resheathed it.

"I didn't need to touch Skádhwë," he said. "I asked it politely, and we reached an accommodation."

"Thank you," she said.

Then Segnbora glanced down at the cracked and broken links of her chainmail. "This was all a setup," she said. "You knew the nightmare was here. You knew twenty miles away. You couldn't *not* have known."

He caught the merriment in her voice, and grinned. "I'm on other business than just Lorn's and Eftgan's," he said. "There's all kinds of power in this world, looking to be freed. I do what I can."

"I could have died of what it said to me," Segnbora said. "I understood it, it spoke the truth, and yet I killed it anyway. The despair could have finished me."

"I know," Herewiss said. "It wasn't a decision I made lightly. If you hadn't been strong enough…yes, you would have died. And I would have taken responsibility for it."

Segnbora looked at him, pitying and loving him, both at once. "Thanks," she said.

"I didn't do much of anything," he said, half-bowing. "You seem to have found your own solutions."

He looked past Segnbora with great interest. Turning, she was just as interested to see the long-necked, long-bodied, short-legged Dracon shadow that lay behind her. It was positioned as if the creature that cast it were standing on her hind legs. Experimentally Segnbora pointed a finger, and saw the shadow of the forewing barb cock outward.

"Is it true," Herewiss asked with an amused look, "what they say about Dragons and maidens?"

She turned back and shrugged slightly. "You'll have to ask someone who'd know," she said. "I'm not a maiden anymore…"

She started back toward camp to saddle Steelsheen, and hummed a chord.

～ fourteen

...the Goddess could not spend all Her time persuading the Kings and Queens of the world of the idiocy of war. Therefore She invented tacticians...

(source unknown)

As they topped the crest of yet another line of foothills, Freelorn's people paused, silent in the dusk, and looked down upon ancient history. Forest patches lay scattered among the wrinkled fells and hollows of the land below. Although it was just two nights before Midsummer, the wind ran chill over the land, rustling trees and grass so that the earth seemed to shudder like the flank of a troubled beast.

South of their position the foothills became rougher, their bare stones turning brown, red, and hot gray in the fading light. Farther south still rose the Highpeaks. Off into the crimson distance they marched, mountain after mountain. At their forefront, frozen like a white wave of stone about to break, stood Mount Nómion, which overshadowed Bluepeak.

"The weather's changing," Freelorn said.

He was looking uneasily at the filmy banner of windblown snow that stretched southward over the Peaks from Nómion's major summit. It had a distinct downward curve to it that indicated a south wind was fighting to get past the mountains and slide under the warmer northland air.

"Storm tomorrow, loved. Can't you do something?"

Herewiss's eyes were elsewhere—searching the country west of them for any sign of the Darthenes. Eftgan's last message had said that she and her troops would bivouac a league-and-a-half west of the mouth of Bluepeak valley two nights before Midsummer, well out of the sight of the Reavers encamped in Britfell fields around the town. But the land beneath them had a trampled look, and was empty.

"I could," Herewiss said, reaching over his shoulder for Khávrinen to better sense what had been happening there. "It would be unwise, though. Eftgan may already have done something."

"Or Someone else might have," Segnbora said. She was as troubled as Lorn, for different reasons. Her undersenses clearly brought her a feeling of haste and disruption from the land below, as if plans had gone awry and many minds down there had recently been in turmoil. Worse were Hasai's memories, and those of some of the *mdeihei* who knew this area well. Something dark and threatening lurked under this land, ready to rise up in menace.

She shuddered, as did the *mdeihei* inside her. Herewiss was sitting still with Khávrinen flaming in his lap, its Fire subdued.

"Someone else *has* been meddling, I think," he said, glancing over at Freelorn. "There's will behind this weather, and I'd sooner not probe it more closely than that, since I'd be leaving myself open to be probed back. Better to stay low for the moment." He looked down at the Bluepeak highlands. "Eftgan came at this site from the north a day and a half ago—"

"Were they driven back by Arlenes?" Freelorn said, anxious. Cillmod had been raiding across the Arlene-Darthene border for nearly a year now, in violation of the Oath. It was unlikely that he would allow a Darthene incursion into his territory to go unchallenged.

"No. Reavers—and they were here first. Eftgan had a skirmish with them and went north again. The Reavers went west. No sign of Arlenes; they must not have received word that Eftgan's in the vicinity."

Dritt looked confused. "Eftgan's a Rodmistress, though. Shouldn't she have been able to sense that the Reavers were here, and avoid them?"

Herewiss nodded.

There was uneasy shifting among Freelorn's followers. Lorn himself was bewildered. "How can a Rodmistress's scrying go wrong?"

Herewiss swung down from Sunspark and began loosening the girths of its saddle. "The same way mine can, I imagine," he said. Segnbora could feel the great effort he was making to conceal the trouble in his mind. "I can't feel where she is—my range has been steadily diminishing for the past day. Something's settling down over this whole area. Power."

No one had to ask Whose power.

Sunspark looked sideways at Herewiss. (I'll find her,) it said. There was unease in its thought over Herewiss's sudden anxiety.

Herewiss laid a hand on its burning shoulder, where the fiery mane hung down. "Go, loved. But burn low. Don't advertise us."

It tossed its head and was gone in an oven-breath of wind, leaving only wisps of smoke to mark where it had stood.

Segnbora dismounted from Steelsheen in silence, thinking that the tai-Enraesi house luck was certainly working as usual. Of all the places she had never wanted to be in a battle, this led the list! Since Earn and Héalhra had first set the bindings here a thousand years before, this land had slept uneasily. It was steeped in Power—not beneficent power like the Morrowfane's, but a dangerous potency that could be manipulated easily by whatever lesser force moved there. Sorcerers and those with the Fire stayed away from Bluepeak, afraid to trigger unwelcome influences. Yet here they all were, merrily riding into this unstable land with the clear intention of arousing those influences in order to bind them. Segnbora would sooner have kicked a sleeping lion awake, then tried to tie it up.

"How far from Nómion would you say we are?" Herewiss asked his loved.

"Eight miles, maybe." Freelorn was chewing his mustache absently, an old nervous mannerism. "We'll be there by tonight if we push the horses a little."

They stood together, Herewiss playing with Khávrinen's hilt, Freelorn looking out over the darkening land toward a remote ridge that stood away from the foothills in front of Nómion. That ridge was Britfell, the White Height, which partially hid the mouth of Bluepeak valley.

There was nothing white about the fell this time of year. Its barren curved ridge was a brown wave rising over the green land below it. Here and there it was dotted with blackthorn that had managed to take root in its sheer stones.

On the hidden southern side of that ridge, within Bluepeak valley, the tiny combined force of the Arlenes and Darthenes had—one thousand years before—been hunted up against the cliffs of Britfell's inner side by Fyrd. Seeing them trapped there, the Shadow had taken a hand, climbing down out of the Peaks in the shape of the Gnorn, a form so fearsome that just the sight of it would kill.

Earn and Healhra, trapped together on a height near Britfell's end, faced with the slaughter of all their people, took the option offered them by the Goddess. They sacrificed their mortality to undergo that Transformation by which mortals become gods. Together, as White Eagle and White Lion, they attacked the Gnorn and destroyed it—slaying the Shadow and being slain, and leaving their people free to move north and found Arlen and Darthen.

There was hardly a child in the Kingdoms who hadn't played at Lion-and-Eagle and fought that battle in dusty village streets or empty fields. Segnbora had done so herself, usually insisting (for loyalty's sake) on being the Eagle to someone else's Lion. For Freelorn and Herewiss, the game would have been a little different: its inventors had been the founders of their houses, their Fathers many times removed

"Goddess help us if the Reavers are holding the mouth of the valley," Freelorn said

"Probably they are."

Lorn looked sidewise at his loved. "You should have let me buy those mercenaries, dammit."

"Lorn, the point of this excursion is winning back your throne, *not* having battles. And buying yourself mercenaries *guarantees* you'll have battles. Everybody in the neighborhood assumes you're going to start something with them, so they start something first. Besides," he said, smiling wryly at Freelorn's exasperated look, "it seems there aren't enough mercenaries available right now to make a difference. Someone else has been hiring. Cillmod."

Freelorn shrugged, still chewing his mustache. "You miss my point. What I mean is, I'm going to have a hard time getting into the valley to do the Royal Binding; that is, unless we try something obvious, like using Sunspark."

"Where did you have in mind to do it?"

"Lionheugh." That was the little island-height at the end of Britfell's curve, well inside the valley's mouth. "Since the Transformation took place there, it's favorable ground. Every place else has too much blood."

Herewiss looked grimly amused. "So all we have to do is get you past a whole army of Reavers, and probably Fyrd," he said. *And keep you alive afterward.*

Segnbora caught his worried thought, but Freelorn merely raised his eyebrows. "Problems?"

"I think we'll work something out," Herewiss said in his lazy northern drawl. Under his hands Khávrinen swirled momentarily with a confident brilliance of Flame, then died down again.

A hot whirlpool of air set dried grass smoldering nearby on the ridge where they stood. The vortex darkened as if with smoke, spread horizontally and solidified into Sunspark's blood-bay shape. Herewiss reached up to lay a hand against its cheek. "Well?"

(I found Eftgan's soldiers busy with more of those Reaver-folk we had trouble with at Barachael,) it said, pawing the ground modestly, and leaving a scorched place. (They're busy no more. I drove them back down into the valley to play with the rest of their people.)

"Oh, no!" Herewiss covered his face with one hand. "Loved, I thought I told you to be circumspect!"

Its burning eyes were merry. (So I was. I don't need to show fire to burn something. Things just became, should I say, too hot for them?)

Segnbora couldn't suppress a chuckle, at which Sunspark beamed.

"Don't encourage him," Herewiss said as he bent to pick up the saddle again.

(I did have a little trouble,) Sunspark added, in a tone of thought that said it was making light of the problem. (For some reason I wasn't able to make things burn as easily as usual. Something there was slowing me down.)

Herewiss nodded, and kept his voice equally light. "We'll keep an eye on it. Well done, loved. Did the Queen have any word for me?"

(Yes indeed,) Sunspark replied, and said one.

Segnbora exchanged amused glances with Lang, who stood beside her. It was not a word one usually associated with Queens.

Herewiss looked sternly at Sunspark. "Did you burn *her?*"

(Oh...just a little...)

Fastening the girths of the saddle, Herewiss kneed the elemental good-naturedly in the belly. It developed a surprised look, then a searing hot breath went out of it—*whoof!* Herewiss pulled the girth tight.

"You and I," he said, "are going to have a talk later. Meanwhile," he mounted up, "let's join Eftgan before the Reavers figure out that the, ah, heat's off..."

The camp seen from above looked much like other bivouacs Segnbora had seen: squares set out with tents at their centers, picket lines of horses tethered nearby, men and women sprawled around campfires tending to their weapons or their dinners. Britfell rose up a mile south, a looming blackness from which the occasional hunting owl came floating down in search of small game disturbed by the activity thereabouts.

The owls weren't getting much business, though. It was a quieter camp than most Segnbora remembered. Evidently the Darthenes, too, realized that there were forces about that it would be better not to disturb.

They passed the outer sentries and shortly thereafter were met by a dark-haired rider on a Steldene dun gelding, bearing a torch, the light of which danced off the bright chain of a major.

"Torve!" Freelorn said, pleasantly surprised. "Well met. You seem to have made better time than we did from Barachael."

"Barachael's secure," Torve said with his usual calm cheerfulness. "The Queen's grace wanted me here, so here I am. She asked me to bring you in."

"She felt us coming?" Herewiss said, sounding somewhat relieved.

"You were close," Torve said, his unassailable calm strained a little. "There have been problems with scrying of late."

"We noticed."

The Queen's tent was little different from those that the rest of the army used—slightly larger, perhaps, but of the same patched canvas. All that identified it as hers was the Eagle banner on its pole outside the door. On the other side of the doorway, however, the diamond-studded haft of Sarsweng was thrust into the ground up to its hook. Its diamonds glittered restlessly in the torchlight. Eftgan was sitting in shirt and britches on a low folding chair, surrounded by a scatter of maps and parchments and papers. She was tapping one map idly with her Rod while talking to a man who squatted beside her chair.

She rose to greet Herewiss and Freelorn and the others, tossing her Rod aside. "I'm glad to see you," she said, sounding as if she meant it. "Come in and be comfortable. Everybody, this is my husband Wyn—"

The group murmured greetings. Segnbora caught Wyn's eye and traded smiles with him. It had been ten years since she had last seen him, and (as she had suspected) the years had left no sign of their passing. Short and compact, Wyn s'Heleth was in his early fifties and looked perhaps thirty: a man with a face like a handsome hawk's, and eyes so merrily threatening it was sometimes a strain to meet them.

Segnbora had herself introduced Wyn to Eftgan back in Darthis, when the old King had been looking for a wine merchant who wouldn't charge him exorbitant prices. Not too long thereafter the Darthene Court had found itself with not only good wine at reasonable prices, but with a future Prince Consort. Connoisseurs were still talking about the rare vintages that had been uncorked for Eftgan's wedding.

"There's stew in the pot and dishes beside it," the Queen said, sitting down. "Wine and water in the jugs. Sit, friends. We have trouble." She dug about in the welter of maps and pulled out a large one of the whole Bluepeak area.

Trouble's a gentle word for it, Segnbora thought as Eftgan talked and pointed. The Reavers had a considerable start on the Darthenes, and there had been nothing the Queen could do about it. Worldgating would have been impossible, when so many people were involved. Eftgan had therefore been forced to march westward from Orsvier slowly enough to allow for musters and pick-up levies along the way. The Reavers seemed to have handled all such matters a long time before, on the other side of the mountains, for here they were, four thousand strong, arrayed in siege around Bluepeak town and holding the mouth of the valley from Nómion's flank to Britfell's outer curve. Lionheugh, as Freelorn had feared, was well inside their lines.

"They have three thousand foot and a thousand horse," Eftgan said, "and the fact that they got here first gives them the advantage of the ground, too. They've taken stand on both sides of the Arlid, and to dislodge them we're going to have to attack uphill. I don't like that..."

"How do you stand?" Herewiss said.

"Fifteen hundred horse and four thousand foot," Wyn said in his sharp tenor voice. "Eighty sorcerers, fourteen Rodmistresses—"

"Fifteen," Eftgan said. "You always forget to count me. However, sorcery hasn't worked since yesterday—or, when it does work, you don't want to be anywhere near the consequences. As ranking Mistress here, I've advised my sisters to keep their Fire to themselves unless I—or you, Herewiss—order otherwise. By the by, have you heard anything from the Precincts?"

"No—"

"Neither have I. It's disturbing. I asked them for advice on this matter two weeks ago, while it was still possible to bespeak as far as the Brightwood. I suppose the Wardresses started debating the subject and are taking too long about it, as usual." She sighed. "It's too late now; we'll have to make do with our own advice. Meanwhile," she said to Freelorn, "there's the business of the Royal Bindings to consider. I brought the Regalia."

Freelorn nodded. "I know the ritual. But the Arlene Regalia is in Prydon…all of it but Hergótha, anyway." He looked annoyed as he said it. Hergótha the Great—Héalhra's ancient sword—had been missing since Freelorn's father died. If there was anything Lorn wanted back as much as the Arlene kingship, it was that sword. "And I remind you, I'm not an Initiate. My father never took me on the Nightwalk into Lionhall."

Eftgan nodded. "We'll take our chances, Lorn. You're the Lion's Child, and Héalhra's blood is what's required here. The problem is," and she pushed at the map of Bluepeak with one booted toe, "I'm reluctant to do even so minor a Gating as would put us down on the Heugh—that was the spot you were thinking of, wasn't it? The Shadow's influence is building by the minute. Any use of Power from now on could be terribly warped." She frowned. "Did I tell you that the valley is crawling with Fyrd? A new kind—"

"Thinkers?" Dritt guessed.

The Queen looked at him glumly. "Yes."

Freelorn reached for the map and pulled it closer to where he sat cross-legged on the floor. He studied it for a few breaths, then indicated the mouth of the valley. "The Reavers are drawn up here, under several of Cillmod's mercenary-captains."

"A little more north," Wyn said. "About a quarter-mile north of the Heugh, stretching right across to the Spine."

"Uh-huh. They're on the other side of the Spine too?"

"It seems a safe assumption, though we haven't confirmed it. They've got a small force at the Spine's northern end; we've left it alone."

Freelorn nodded, leaning over the map. "I doubt they're paying much attention to their rear, then, since the besieging force is holding it secure, and the Fyrd are back there too. I suspect no one will notice if we go in the pantry door instead of the great-hall entrance." He pointed at Britfell, indicating a spot near where the fell joined the northern massif of Kemana. "Here."

Now it was Wyn's turn to look shocked. "You're crazy! There's no going up Britfell, it's too sheer! Maybe a climber could do it in a day or so, if there were time…

Herewiss was looking at Freelorn with an expression compounded of worry and dawning hope. *For once,* Segnbora thought, anticipation rising in her, *maybe one of Freelorn's crazy strategies is going to pay off—* "I've done it on horseback," Freelorn said. "With my father. There's a path. We went up the north side and down the south in about six hours, coming out on the far side of the curve about a half mile north of the Heugh. And if two people did it, so can ten." He glanced around at his own group. "Or a hundred," he said to the Queen. "Or five hundred."

"That path must not be very visible from either side," Eftgan said, sounding uncertain, "which suggests it will be rough to ride."

"If the Shadow had built it, it could hardly be worse. But it's a way over. And everybody, even the Reavers, knows there's no way over the fell. That's what brought our ancestors to grief." Freelorn tapped the map again. "So. We take a few hundred of your horse— Why be stingy? Make it five hundred—and go over." He scrunched up his forehead in thought. "Allow sixteen hours for the whole passage. You order your main force to draw up north of the valley's mouth. The Reavers won't move; they're not such idiots as to attack downhill and give up the advantage of the ground. If they draw back and try to tempt your forces to come after them, fine. Meanwhile, you and I and five hundred horse are *here*"—he tapped the inside of Britfell's curve—"where we can't possibly be. We come down around the Heugh and do our binding there, while the cavalry takes the Reavers in their unsuspecting flank and rear, attacking downhill and driving them against your main force to the south. Hammer and anvil." He grinned.

Wyn was beginning to look interested despite his doubts. "That still leaves the cavalry with an unfought force at its back: the besieging force. If they leave the city and come down on you—"

"How many are holding the siege?"

"About a thousand foot."

Freelorn shrugged. "If they send enough people to make a difference, won't the garrison inside try a sally?"

"So they've said," Eftgan said. "That'll make no difference to the cavalry, though."

"So." Freelorn tapped the Spine. "Once your main force engages the Reaver force, you send a good-sized party to secure the ground between the Spine and Nómion and clear the Reavers off that side of the river. There's our bolt-hole. We ford the river and go up behind the Spine, then rejoin the main force."

Eftgan sat silent for a little while, studying the map. "We're fifty-five hundred to their four thousand," she said at last. "I don't have the leisure for strategic victories. I need conclusive ones. This at least gives us a chance to do what we have to without using Power and risking a disaster. And the surprise of taking them from the rear would be tremendous. It should disorganize them wonderfully. And, since organization was never their strong point anyway..."

Eftgan glanced over at Wyn for his opinion. He nodded at her. She paused to give the map one more long look.

"The last scrying I managed," she said, "gave a hint of something that might be coming from the northwest, from upper Arlen. Help or hindrance, I couldn't tell. And I don't dare delay to find out. The Bindings must be reinforced soon. A delay could turn loose forces I don't care to contemplate."

Standing, she bent to pick up her Rod from among the papers on the floor. "No matter. We'll work with what information we have. Freelorn, I'll ride with you regardless of the uncertainty. Wyn will handle the main force in my absence. Meanwhile—"

The tent flap was thrust aside. In peered a tall, rawboned woman in the Darthene royal blue, with somewhat disordered dark hair and a captain's chain around her neck. "Ma'am," she said, breathless, "the Reavers are attacking the north side of the camp again. Maybe a hundred or so."

"Oh, damn," the Queen said. She tossed her Rod away and reached to the side of the tent, where Fórlennh BrokenBlade lay sheathed. "They love trying to draw us out," she said, buckling on the scabbard. "Any trouble handling it, Kesri?"

"Not really."

"Good. Of your courtesy, go call the other captains and the captains-major. I have something to tell them." The captain vanished and the tentflap fell.

Eftgan turned to Freelorn and Herewiss. "Midnight's coming on. We'll start an hour after midnight, and give the Reavers a surprise tomorrow afternoon."

Lorn and his people began heading out of the tent to see to the horses and to their own bedrolls. Eftgan flicked a wry glance at Segnbora, an outward indication of mixed concern and anticipation. "Just like old times, 'Berend."

Segnbora thought of Etachnë and other such fields that lay behind the two of them, victories and defeats equally frightful. "Not *just* like, I hope."

"No," Eftgan said, looking thoughtfully at Skádhwë in its scabbard, and at Segnbora's odd shadow on the floor. "I suppose it won't be."

fifteen

Mn'An'dzat kchven'rae ëhwissthaa'seth:
The Five Truths, terrible and joyous:

Stihë hë-stihé. What is, is.
Stihú hë-stihé. What was, is.
Whrn'thae najh'stihëh. Matter is an illusion.
Ousskh'thae najh'stihëh. Meaning is an illusion.
Mda't dae bvh-sda't dae mnek-é. The Door opens both ways.

Rui'i'rae-sta haa'ae! Believe none of these!

Ehh'ne lhhw'i'ae (What Dragons Say), vii,14

Full night, when it came, was starless. A heavy overcast hung like a roof just above the highest peaks, Nómion and Kerana. In that stifling silent darkness, a long column of riders picked its way to the foot of Britfell's northern slope and came to a halt.

The prospect was daunting. Sheer walls of cracked cliff-face rose up uninvitingly. Around them were strewn rubble and boulders brought down by the annual flux of heat and cold. Eftgan, on her tall bay gelding Scoundrel, shook her head as she looked upward.

"Lorn, if the road isn't still there—"

"Then we're no worse off than you were before," Lorn said. Ahead of Segnbora and the others, he, Herewiss, and the Queen were shadows among shadows. Everyone in that riding had made sure there was nothing bright about their gear; faces and hands and buckles and swordhilts were smeared with a mixture of grease and soot. Even so, Segnbora's Dragon-sharpened vision saw movements and expressions clearly enough.

Freelorn pulled up Blackmane's head and headed him off to the left. "Let's take the adventure the Goddess sends us," he said, "and go as far as we can."

He urged his dun straight at the cliffside. Blackmane snorted mild protest but went where his rider directed him, climbing a slope of talus and scree and not stopping until they reached a narrow ledge fifty feet or so above the cliff's foot. "This way," Lorn called softly to the riders waiting below, and put his heels to Blackmane again. The horse took him leftward past a rounded outcropping of stone, and out of sight.

"This is crazy," Lang said, beside Segnbora.

"Maiden's madness, I hope," Eftgan said, and shook Scoundrel's reins. He stalled, snorting, until Eftgan laid her crop gently below his left ear and touched him with heels again. Up Scoundrel went in a nervous rush, scattering pebbles and small stones. One by one they followed him, reining their horses in to keep them stepping lightly and minimize the damage done to the path.

The ride was like something out of an old tale or a bad dream, full of long terrifying pauses during which Freelorn lost the way and found it again, dismounted to heave fallen boulders off the narrow track or to lead Blackmane where he thought it too dangerous to burden a horse with a rider's weight.

The path, if it could be dignified with such a name, wound back and forth along the face of the cliff, switching back at wildly irregular intervals, the switches often barely enough for one horse to negotiate. Always there were heartstopping drops below.

Segnbora kept her elbows in as she rode, once again very glad of Steelsheen's breed. Steldenes were bred in mountainous country and were frequently accused of being part goat. The mare picked her way delicately along ledges of rotten, sliding stone with only an occasional snort of protest at the poor quality of the trail. Other horses behind, flatland breeds, weren't doing as well. The sound of whispered swearing came drifting up from riders down below.

As they climbed, the night got blacker, if that were possible. A feeling began to grow among the riders that Something with no good intent was watching the silent climb. Tense minutes stretched into an hour, then two and three. Segnbora began to feel as if she had been climbing up this miserable wall forever, as if her whole life had been spent fighting with eggshell-fragile stone, squinting at it, terrified of every step.

At the same time, she had to admit that this feat would be sung of for years, if any of them finished the climb and survived the battle that waited just the other side of Britfell. She maneuvered Steelsheen cautiously around another treacherous switchback, not looking down.

Inside her, in their own darkness that now seemed bright by comparison, Hasai and the *mdeihei* hissed laughter at her fear of heights, and then began singing (in sixteen-part harmony of the kind Dragons used when feeling playful) their memory of the ballad which the bards would later write for Freelorn: *When Fyrd came over the Darthene border / and Reavers moved at the Shadow's order...* Segnbora almost felt like smiling, until she remembered that just because her *mdeihei* had a memory of the ballad, that was still no guarantee that any of them would survive this venture.

One of Sheen's hooves slipped, and Segnbora's heart seized as she leaned with the mare so she could regain her balance. For an instant they came close to a perilous drop, but Steelsheen recovered and went on, sweating and trembling, but knowing what her mistress wanted. Unconcerned, the *mdeihei* were singing in unison now, a calm chorus. *They climbed the Fell and they crossed the water / the Lion's Son and the Eagle's Daughter—*

Several hours before dawn it began to snow. The wind rose, becoming a howling blast. Snow that grew blizzard-fine drove stinging into faces, numbing hands on the reins. The horses whickered in complaint and tried to walk with eyes averted toward the cliff, which only caused them to miss their footing more often. Their riders, who had more or less expected the change of weather, broke out extra clothing and muffled themselves up as best they could. The sky got infinitesimally lighter as day broke above the storm, though not enough to lighten anyone's spirits.

There's will behind this weather, Herewiss had said. That will could be felt watching them more strongly every minute. The head of the column was fairly close to the top of the fell now, but that was no comfort. The thought of having to take a similar path downhill, on an icy trail, was on everyone's mind. The storm was blowing from the south, and had been abated somewhat by striking the fell and having to pour over it. Matters would be much worse on the other side.

The trail leveled so abruptly that Segnbora was taken completely by surprise. It led westward here, going around the edge of a west-pointing backbone of the fell. A pause to look west would have been pleasant, but there was no time for it—the column was still coming up the far side of the fell, and there was little standing room. Besides, they had entered the cloud cover, and visibility was low. Even so, Eftgan dismounted long enough to stretch her cramped arms and legs and look ahead hopefully.

Herewiss, beside her, looked unhappy. "Can you feel anything?" he said.

Eftgan shook her head. "I can hardly hear myself think in this wind, let alone anyone else. That one" —she glanced upward at the slate-dark cloud cover— "has settled Itself down snug. It's muffling all thought but Its own. The main force is going to have to rely on riders for messages, and there'll be no way for us to know what's going on until we rejoin it."

"Sunspark can assist," Herewiss said. But he sounded uncertain. "When will they move?"

"Noon. We should be well finished with our business at the Heugh by then, and they can go ahead and have a battle without worrying about what it might raise." She bit her lip, a sign of hidden fright that Segnbora recognized.

Segnbora had no time to indulge her own nervousness, however. There was barely enough time to dismount and feed Steelsheen some grain. By the time she got back in the saddle, Lorn was already picking his way down the trail on the other side, with Eftgan in back of him and Herewiss behind her.

"Let's move, slowcoach," Lang said as he nudged his dapplegray, Gyrfalcon, past her. "Going to lose your place up front."

Dubious honor that it is, Segnbora thought, swinging up into the saddle and following him.

Now the pace of the climb slowed to an agonized creep, for the stone was not only iced, it was rotten. Rock crumbled maddeningly under foot, and the horses rebelled—shaking their heads, snorting, testing the footing at every step. The blinding cold snow turned the world into a featureless gray room through which vaguely seen figures led the way. The ordeal was endless.

In front of her, Gyrfalcon shied, and then Steelsheen did too. Segnbora had another of those terrifying long looks down. *Ice and darkness. Oh, damn!* The mare recovered her balance. Segnbora squinted at Lang's shadowy back and then squeezed her eyes shut for just a moment, looking down among the *mdeihei* for an answer to her growing terror.

The cave was full of memories, much easier of access than they had been before the evening with the nightmare. Overlaid on her perception of the trail as it was now, she saw Bluepeak valley as it would look from Britfell on a clear day toward sunset.

The season was fall, not summer, and some of the fields below, yellow with wheat, stirred in the south wind. Other fields burned, and the black smoke was carried north, occasionally obscuring the bodies of the slain, and the trampled, bloody ground.

High in the surrounding peaks, on scarps and steeples of rock, winged figures watched, frozen with horror, as the frightful dark shape of the Gnorn went tottering about the battlefield, killing with Its look. Scrabbling Fyrd came after It in hungry terror to devour the dead. Behind It, Bluepeak town was burning. And westward on a lone height at Britfell's far end, two men with drawn swords stood watching the terror with tears running down their faces. A Dragon's eyes, keener than any hawk's, could make them out plainly. One man was huge and broad as a bear, with a shaggy mane of fair hair, hazel eyes, and Freelorn's prominent nose. The other was tall and angular, with dark hair threaded with silver, and kind downturned eyes as blue as Herewiss's, blue as Fire.

She saw them throw down their swords at practically the same moment, desperately making the Choice; saw them take hands there, while the Gnorn came weaving toward them through the screams and death of Bluepeak; saw them give up what they had been and gaze into one another's eyes to find out what they could be—

—and she fell out of that memory and into another one: this time, the memory of some nameless *mdaha* in the ancient time on the Homeworld, one who sat perched on a dark red stone in a violet twilight with another, while the starpool came up over the horizon. The Dragon turned to look into the other's eyes, which were silver fire set in a hide of turquoise and lapis. The Dragon fell a great depth into those eyes, into a timeless, merciless, fathomless love which held the whole Universe within it as a person awake holds the memory of a dream—

Our line often soared with the Immanence, she remembered Hasai saying. *One gets used to It.* But no Dragon ever got used to the Other's regard. The more one looked into that Other's eyes, the more powerful, and the more unbearable, the experience became.

In a blinding moment of realization, Segnbora understood what she had seen in Hasai's eyes on the night of unearthed memories. She understood, too, why she always averted her gaze after looking too long into the eyes of another human being—

The agonized joy of the discovery threw her out into the world again, back into whirling snow, ice and darkness. But the cold didn't matter anymore. Not even her own exhaustion, nor Steelsheen's panic, bothered her now. All she needed was a moment to put it into words, and the secret would be hers forever...

Ahead of her, hearing Steelsheen's hooves scrape and clatter on the slippery rock, Lang twisted around in the saddle to look at her.

"'Berend?" he called anxiously through the screaming wind.

Their eyes met.

She *saw* him—saw *Her*. Lang looked no different. His voice still came out in a drawl. She could still underhear his mind lurching back and forth between indecision and placid acceptance. He still hated some things without reason, and loved others unreasonably. He still judged and criticized by provincial standards. He still smelled from not washing enough...*yet he was She*. The *One*. And when Segnbora looked ahead at Herewiss or Eftgan, or back at any of the nameless five hundred following behind, or even at their horses, the result was the same. *All of them, everyone who lives. Every one the Goddess*—

"Lang," she said. It was almost a whisper, for she had little breath to spare in the grip of this painful ecstasy. This was the man whom she had used with casual cruelty, to whom she had refused intimacy when she felt disinclined to it. Yet there within him the Goddess looked out at her—not judging, as She certainly had the right to do, and not angry, either—simply loving her totally, without hesitation. She had always known that the Goddess indwelt in every man and woman, but *experiencing* it this way, now, was something else again.

Joy, laced with bitterness at her years of callous disregard of the One she loved, rose until it choked her. Tears spilled over and froze on her face in the icy wind. Her voice wouldn't work anymore. Knowing it was useless, and driven by an overwhelming need to communicate somehow, she bespoke him. (Lang!)

He stared at her in sheer disbelief. "'Berend?"

He had heard her!

The pain fell away from her joy like a cast-off cloak. Segnbora sobbed, sagging in her saddle, and drew in a long breath. She had a great deal to tell him. (Loved—)

—and Gyrfalcon missed his footing, going down on his knees on a patch of ice. His hindquarters slipped off the path to the left, and the rest of him followed. Segnbora had a quick glimpse of Lang reaching for the ledge, more surprised than frightened, and that was all.

"*LANG!*" she screamed.

Almost before the scream had left her throat, Sunspark had leaped away from the ledge and sunk down into the snow-swirling emptiness like a thunderbolt, streaming fire. The line of riders behind her halted as she, like Freelorn and Eftgan in front of her, peered down into the whiteness, dumb with shock. A long time they waited there for the bloom of fire through the snow. Then, slowly, the brightness came walking up through the air and stood again before the ledge. Herewiss was alone on Sunspark's back.

('Berend,) Herewiss said, and had to pause. She could feel his eyes filling. (He's...It was quick. I share your grief.)

All behind her, starting with Dritt, Moris, Harald, and the foremost of the Darthene riders, she could feel sorrow and fear spreading like ripples in a pool. She was numb, having fallen from such a height to such a depth so quickly. Yet still she could see Who consoled her as she looked at Herewiss.

(May our sorrow soon pass,) she said silently. A knife turned slowly within her at the memory of the last time she had said those words.

Herewiss broke their gaze. (We'll come back for him as soon as we can,) he said. With a thoughtful look, he reined Sunspark about and took the path again.

It took two more hours to complete the rest of the ride down. The slope grew gradually less steep, and the ledges a bit wider, but the snow continued. Lang was not the only rider who was lost. Just minutes after his death, another horse and rider came plummeting down past Segnbora. The falling rider's glance locked with Segnbora's in the second of her passing. Still weeping, Segnbora could do nothing but pour herself into the look, see Who was falling, and aid Her in accepting what was happening. In that second, the woman's fear-twisted face calmed. Then she was gone.

Segnbora rode on, trembling. She turned a switchback and suddenly found herself at the top of a long skirt of scree and rough stones, which lead down to a slope carpeted in snow-covered grass. Glancing at the sky, Segnbora knew the storm wasn't going to let up.

In front of her, Eftgan was checking her saddlebags to make sure the Regalia were safe. Herewiss had drawn Khávrinen and was pointing at the snow. There were prints in it: the big splayed tracks of a horwolf, and a keplian's pad-and-claw set. Both trails were only minutes old. Both led to the cliff's foot and away again, westward.

"We're expected," Herewiss said. "I'm done with being circumspect, Queen." Fire flowed down Khávrinen's blade in defiant brilliance. "We've got to stay alive. Meantime, we had better get to the Heugh fast. The Bindings are slipping from the pressure of so many beings in this area."

Eftgan nodded. "Can you shore up the Bindings until we complete the ritual?"

"I can," Herewiss said. "I've been doing it for several hours. But it's tiring. How long I can hold out, I've no idea."

"Once we begin, the blood-binding won't take long," Eftgan reassured him. Thumping Scoundrel's sides, she wheeled westward. "The ground between here and the Heugh is smooth. Let's make time."

They had to go slowly at first, so that the Darthene riders still on the slope would have time to catch up. It was about fifteen minutes into this process that the first cohort of Fyrd found them. There were only twenty or thirty: horwolves and keplian who had been patrolling the heights and thought it wise to attack before the main force was down off the Fell.

It was a mistake. Like lightning dancing a death-dance, Khávrinen rose and fell in the forefront of the skirmish. What its blade didn't slay, Herewiss's Fire did. Sunspark was incensed; any Fyrd at which it looked became ashes in seconds. Fórlennh and Süthan flickered red and blue in Firelight and Flamelight. Segnbora swept Skádhwë's blackness about her in an utter calm that felt very strange. Shortly, nothing moved but Darthenes and the wind. Drifts began forming around the bodies in the snow.

The Darthenes had a few wounded, none seriously, and none lost—a small miracle for which everyone was thankful. "What's the time?" Freelorn said.

"Three hours past noon." Eftgan looked around and saw the last of her riders coming down off Britfell. "Wyn will be moving the forces forward at four. Let's get up that heugh."

It was only a mile to Lionheugh, but they bought every furlong of the distance dearly. The fourth cohort of Fyrd was the biggest, some three hundred of the creatures. There were not many nadders, because of the coldness of the weather. There were, unfortunately, many maws and keplian, the worst Fyrd breeds for riders to handle. There were also four deathjaws, three of which Herewiss dealt with, and one of which Eftgan destroyed with an astonishing blast of blue Fire.

By the time this attack was over, no one was quite as lively as they had been. Nearly everyone had a wound of one type or another. Eftgan and Freelorn were unhurt, but Herewiss had a long set of slashes from a keplian's claws, and Moris and Dritt and Harald all had maw bites. But no Fyrd had been allowed to get away and warn others of what had happened.

"You and I were lucky," Freelorn said to Eftgan.

"Luck has nothing to do with it. If *our* blood falls on this land and we have the brains to do a binding right away, that One would lose a great deal of its Power." Eftgan whipped blood off Fórlennh. "Herewiss?"

He was sitting astride Sunspark with a look on his face that was either annoyance or strain. Khávrinen in his hand was flaring with a wild glory of Fire as he healed himself. "It's putting on pressure," he said. "Things are trying to return to the way they were before the Binding, and this Fyrd blood isn't helping matters."

"Let's go. 'Berend?" She glanced at Segnbora as they began to move through the blinding snow. "You all right?"

"Fine." Segnbora held Skádhwë over her knee at the ready.

"You always used to be so noisy in battles! I keep looking around to see if something got you."

"My lodgers are doing my hollering for me," she said. The Dragons didn't care for Fyrd, and her *mdeihei* had been singing martial musics laced with Dragonfire ever since she came down from Britfell. Battlecries seemed superfluous with that inner thunder going on.

Eftgan met her glance with an odd expression, as if seeing some stranger who was Segnbora's twin. "'Berend, you've become *more* than your lodgers, somehow. What *happened* up there?"

It was a poor time to explain. "I'm not sure," Segnbora said. "Nothing of the Dark One's doing, that's certain." For if there was anything the Shadow didn't want mortals to know, it was what Segnbora had learned. Once one knew Who one was, It lost Its power over that person.

Segnbora shook her head and kicked Steelsheen into a gallop, getting Skadhwë ready. The realizations were coming too close together. The hugeness of them was dazzling her. She needed something concrete upon which to fasten her mind.

Unfortunately, she got it. To their right, the crest of Britfell had been getting lower as they headed west. With little warning the fell simply stopped in a sheer cliff. Out of the falling snow their destination loomed: Lionheugh.

To the west, not even the snow could muffle a great confused roaring—shouts and battlecries, the bray of Reaver war horns and the thin silver cries of trumpets. As they drew rein under the shadow of the Heugh, Eftgan waved Torve over, putting up Fórlennh and unsheathing her Rod.

"Leave me fifty," she said. "Take the rest and hit them hard wherever it seems best. My compliments to my Consort when you see him, and tell Wyn I'm sorry we're late, but we were detained. Ride!"

"Madam!" Torve said, and rode off hard with four hundred fifty of the Darthene cavalry behind him. The snow swallowed them.

Freelorn rode up to join the Queen, with Moris and Dritt and Harald close behind. "I have to do something about this weather, even if it's only temporary," said Eftgan, shaking the Fire down her Rod. "Then we'll do our business. Herewiss, how are you doing?"

He was holding Khávrinen before him in both hands, his eyes fixed on it. A frightening brilliance of Fire streamed about man and sword. "I'll hold," he said, but there was strain in his voice, and the feeling of malicious intent in the air hung closer than it had before. "The Shadow's pressing, though. There's much bloodshed going on and It's feeding on that. I daren't be distracted long—"

"Up with us," Eftgan said.

Punching Scoundrel, she rode at a gallop up the path to the Heugh. No one was surprised by the Fyrd waiting for them there. They dropped from rocks and leaped up under the horses' hooves. Eftgan's Rod crackled with Fire as she laid it about her like a whip. Whatever she struck didn't move again. Segnbora and Freelorn galloped behind her, watching the Queen's back, slicing down with Skadhwë and Süthan. Behind them came Herewiss, with Moris and Dritt and Harald about him as guard.

Very quickly, it seemed, they made the top of the Heugh and gathered there on the level ground, the Queen's riders and Freelorn's followers circling around in case any more Fyrd should attack uphill.

"No Reavers yet, and none of Cillmod's people," Eftgan said, dismounting hurriedly and raising her Rod. "That's a mercy; maybe they don't know we're here. *E'hstirre na lai'tehen ándrastiw vhai!*" Eftgan cried into the wind in Nhàired, lifting her Rod two-handed and pointing it at the roiling sky. She sighted along the Rod's length as if along the stock of a crossbow.

At the last word of her wreaking, another piercing line of blue Fire lanced upward and struck into the underbelly of the cloud above them. The wind screamed, the cloud tore away from the ravening Fire like flesh from a wound. It tore, and tore—ripping backward and dissolving, revealing blue sky and afternoon sunlight. The snow stopped as the clouds retreated, until a great patch of sky the width of Bluepeak valley was clear.

Standing on that height, for the first time they could see what was happening. The Reavers and the main Darthene force were locked in battle in the pass, and the Darthenes were already well ahead of the position at which Eftgan had intended them to start. Even as they watched, the Reavers lost some ground, pushed uphill by heartened Darthenes who knew why the weather had suddenly cleared up. A sudden blot of darkness from the east—the riders who had followed Eftgan over the fell—smote into the Reavers' uneven right flank and scattered it.

"The clearing won't last," Eftgan said, breathing hard and leaning against Scoundrel. "I have to save some Power for the binding. Lorn, the Regalia, quickly!"

Freelorn had already undone Eftgan's saddle-roll, and now unrolled it before her. It contained an odd assortment: an old knife of very plain make, black of hilt and blade, and a rough circlet of gold that looked as if it had been hammered out by an amateur. It had, Segnbora knew, for this was Dekórsir, the Queen's Gold—the crown that each Darthene ruler hammered out unguarded in the open marketplace, once a year, to give the people a chance to dispose of an unfit ruler if there was need. There was also another circlet, this one of exquisite workmanship, woven as it was of strands of linked and braided silver.

Freelorn lifted the circlet up with a blaze of angry delight in his eyes. It was Laeran's Band, the crown of the kings and queens of Arlen. *"Where did you get this?!"*

"I had it stolen several days ago," Eftgan said, kneeling down beside the saddle-roll. "In the middle of last week, when Cillmod took it out of Lionhall."

Freelorn stopped still as death and stared at Eftgan. "When he *what...?*" he said.

His voice failed him. No one but the members of the royal line of Arlen could set foot in Lionhall and come out alive. And Freelorn was an only child...or had thought he was.

"It occurs to me that your father may have had a sharing-child he didn't know about," Eftgan said, setting Dekórsir on her head. "Or one he didn't care to legitimize. No matter right now. I'm just sorry we couldn't find Hergótha."

Freelorn turned the supple strip of metal over in his hands. "The thought of Cillmod wearing this—"

"I couldn't stand it either. Shut up and put it on, Lorn. Herewiss can't hold the Binding by himself much longer."

It was true. Herewiss had dismounted from Sunspark, unable to spare even the small amount of concentration needed to stay astride, and was sitting with his back against a rock. Khávrinen lay across his lap, clutched in both hands. He had begun to shine, growing almost translucent, as he had at Barachael, and the stones of the Heugh sang with the Power that was poured out of him. He was holding his own, but just barely. Segnbora looked around her and found that underhearing was no longer necessary to feel the strain in the earth and the air.

Eftgan's riders and Freelorn's followers were all looking over their shoulders, hunting the source of the strange feelings inside them. Herewiss's will could clearly be felt battling with the One that poured Its rage into the valley. He was keeping away the ancient reality, as if he had his back braced against a closed door. But the pounding on the other side, the rhythmic throb of rage and hatred, was getting stronger—

"We are the land," Eftgan and Freelorn were saying in unison. They knelt before one another, knee to knee, holding the black knife together, Lorn wearing the strip of silver, Eftgan the circlet of gold. Their joined voices—Freelorn speaking the ritual in Arlene and Eftgan in Darthene—made an uncanny music. The hair on Segnbora's neck rose at it, hearing in human voices an echo of the *mdeihei*. "Its earth is our flesh; its water our blood; its well-being our joy; its illness our pain..."

The ritual continued, speaking of mysteries particular to the royal priesthood. Many of the riders turned away, trying not to listen to a ceremony that no one of common blood had heard since the founding of the Kingdoms. Segnbora stood by with Skadhwë in her hand and listened fearlessly, in wonder, hearing once again the Goddess speaking to Herself: one Lover speaking to the Other in solemn celebration of Their eternal relationship.

She saw Lorn take the knife and cut Eftgan's upheld left wrist with it, crosswise and careful. Both of them paused a moment, trembling. At the stroke of the ritual wounding the hammering of hatred in the air grew more savage. It was almost physically perceptible. Eftgan took the knife from Freelorn and reached for his left wrist—

—the Fyrd came up the hill in a wave, horwolves and maws together. Behind them came two-legged forms in rough skins and crude metal and leather corsets, bearing leaf-shaped bronze swords and bows of horn, howling like the beasts they followed.

Eftgan pitched forward gasping from a black-fletched Reaver arrow lodged between her shoulder and throat. Horrorstruck, Segnbora watched helplessly as Lorn sat her up straight, breaking the fletching off the arrow and pulling the point end out of the wound with brutal efficiency. He snatched up the black blade and something else—then there was a Reaver in front of Segnbora, blocking her view.

She met the man's brown eyes, sank into them as Shíhan had taught her, felt the move he was about to make. A second later, Skadhwë had countered and sliced the man's chest through from side to side. As he died she didn't break that gaze. She knew Who she had killed, and let the Other know Who had killed him. She grieved for his death and accepted it as her own, completely. Then she looked up at her next opponent—a nadder this time—saw Her there too, and killed again, out of necessity, in love.

She killed again. And again. And again.

The Darthene riders encircling the hill knew immediately what Segnbora didn't have leisure to notice for some time: there were too many Reavers and Fyrd. If they attempted to hold this position, they'd be killed off slowly. Most of the riders had pushed to the side from which the worst attack was coming, the west side, so that behind them Eftgan and Freelorn and Herewiss could get away.

Freelorn shoved Eftgan up into Blackmane's saddle and fastened Scoundrel's reins to the stirrups. Rushing over to Herewiss next, he literally picked him up from where he sat, snapping orders at Sunspark. The shocked elemental knelt to take Herewiss on his back.

Segnbora had her hands very full of Reavers and Fyrd for a few wild minutes, until slowly they began to give her breath. Their first charge was exhausted. In addition the Reavers, ever wary of sorcery, had begun to stay clear of Skádhwë's uncanny blade. There was a madwoman wielding it, her face streaming calm tears.

"Berend!" Freelorn shouted at her.

Segnbora took a moment before answering to look with her sharpened vision at the battlefield. The sight was a shock. More forces were pouring into the valley's mouth from behind the Spine— not Reavers, and not Darthenes, certainly. They were falling on the Darthene right flank and crushing it as easily as a stone falling on an egg.

"Damn him!" she cried, and turned away from the hill-crest, running for Steelsheen and the others. The Queen's scrying had been accurate after all. Cillmod had gotten wind of the upcoming battle, and had evidently decided that this was an expeditious time to both distract the Darthenes from retaliation on his borders and exterminate their fighting force as well. There were none of the Royal Arlene army down there. Such loyal Regulars might have been persuaded to turn against Cillmod since Freelorn was in the field. All these were mercenaries.

Flinging herself into Steelsheen's saddle, Segnbora rode down the trail to clear a path for Freelorn, swearing all the way. It was very obvious now why there were so few unattached mercenaries for hire in the Kingdoms. The Darthenes down there were badly outnumbered.

Behind Segnbora, Sunspark was doing some swearing of its own. (What's the matter with him? Did they hurt him somehow?) It danced a little as it cantered down the trail, obviously wanting very badly to let its fire loose. (If he doesn't come out of this shortly, the whole lot of them are going to make a very nice cloud of smoke!)

Freelorn, holding the bleeding Eftgan in front of him on Blackmane, looked as haggard as if he had been shot himself. Remembering Herewiss's true-dream, the thought made Segnbora's heart turn over. "Firechild," she said, "he's all right, he's just keeping things from getting much worse. For the love of him, *save it for later!*"

The Power Herewiss was pouring out was astonishing. It frightened Segnbora. She had witnessed great wreakings in the Precincts in which fifty or more Rodmistresses had worked in consort, and all of them together hadn't let out a flood of Fire like this. Khávrinen struck razor-sharp shadows from everything its light touched, and Herewiss's flesh burned transparent as an imminent dawn. Some of the Reavers were turning away from them even now, frightened by the sight of the statue-still rider with the thunderbolt in his hands. One Reaver though got up the nerve to fire an arrow. The instant it touched the writhing aura of Flame that wound about Herewiss, it flared up and fell away in ashes.

"Can you gallop without dropping him?" Freelorn shouted at Sunspark as they made it down off the Heugh onto the plain again.

It bared its teeth at him in scorn. (Gallop! Is that all? Where do you want him?)

Freelorn looked from west to east, and got a look of sudden recognition on his face. He flung out an arm, pointing. "There!"

East and a little south of the Heugh, one of the spurs of Kerana came down in a little scraped-away scarp, sheer on all sides except for one shallow approach where riders could go up. It could be defended without too much trouble.

(Done!) Sunspark said. It leaped cat-smooth into the air, shooting southeast so fast the air behind it thundered in shock.

Freelorn and his band and the Darthenes went after at full gallop, not sparing the horses. They couldn't; if they didn't make it up that scarp, there would be no later to save them for. They had a mile or so to cover, across snowy ground, and they had hardly been galloping more than a half minute before they lost the sunlight and the clouds closed up again. With unnatural swiftness it began to snow once more. The wind scaled back up to a scream, and darkness began to fall. It was the darkness Segnbora feared most, for above it and within it the voice of the Shadow could be heard, howling with enmity.

On the scarp a mile off, a light shone as if a star had fallen there, bright enough to cast shadows at even this distance. But the brilliance of Herewiss's Fire was no great comfort. A fresh group of Fyrd and Reaver riders were hot behind them, perhaps a half mile back. Eftgan, clutching Blackmane's saddle and hanging on as best she could, looked back at their pursuers and moaned softly. Freelorn's face was grim.

"They're catching up, Lorn," Segnbora shouted.

The group rode like hunters, whipping their horses to a lather as they rode into the screaming, stinging night. The scarp was right before them, lit with a pillar of blue Fire that flickered eerily on the cloud-bottoms and turned the wind-whipped snow to a blizzard of blue sparks.

The riders went up the scarp like a breaking wave, the horses stumbling, floundering, finding the path by luck or Goddess's love. The way up was none too wide and could easily be kept clean of Reavers—for a while. Behind Freelorn and the Queen, the others closed ranks. Overhead, the daunting blows of the Shadow's hatred became suddenly audible. There was thunder in the snow-clouds, and the wind shrieked furiously around the steeples of the cliff-wall behind them.

Freelorn threw himself out of the saddle, pulled Eftgan down and helped her over to shelter behind a rock at the foot of the cliff. He pulled out the knife, put it into her clutching, shaking hand. Crying with the effort, she braced herself against the stone and reached up to cut—

Shouts and the clash of steel rang out on the plain, where some of the Darthenes were holding the approach to the path up the cliff. Sunspark, who had been bending over Herewiss in concern, jerked its head up and stared down at the Reavers and Fyrd in rage.

(This is *your* fault!!) it cried in a thought that not even the smothering darkness could muffle. It leaped like a skyrocket down to the foot of the scarp, reared, and brought down its forefeet with a crash that split stones. Wildfire burst up from where its hooves struck, and ran madly to either side in front of the scarp. The fire ignored the Darthenes, but any Reaver or Fyrd it touched blazed like tinder and was blown away across the snow, ashes, a breath later. The Reavers drew back in panic from the apparition that suddenly stood between them and the scarp: a huge, crouching cat of swirling fire that stalked forward with blazing eyes, pausing to raise one flaming paw.

—the blood ran down Freelorn's arm, and he pressed it to Eftgan's wound. "And we who are One—come on, Eftgan!—One and not-One say to the land which is us, and of us, be not—"

The earth began to tremble. From the south, visible in this unnatural black as something blacker yet, a great wave of dark Power rose and rose above the mountains, leaned, and fell with a crash that couldn't be heard, only felt. Like death, like drowning, it rolled over them, past them, and in that wave's wake ten or twelve Darthenes fell, and Sunspark's fire went out.

Even Herewiss's blaze dimmed and shrank, failing like a candle placed under a cup. But he did not surrender. When the snuffed-out stallion clambered up the rocks to his side, it found him clutching Khávrinen. He was forcing the sword to burn, pouring out everything he had. It was not enough. In the darkness where the blade's Firelight didn't reach, forms moved and grew solid. Eagerly they lifted long-rusted swords, bared long-rotted fangs, and looked hungrily up toward the little shelf where the Darthenes stood.

(I can't change, I can't burn,) Sunspark cried in anguish, *(what do I do now?)*

Segnbora could feel it straining mightily, trying even to trigger that last burning in which a fire elemental ends its existence as an individual…anything to hold the threat away from its loved. *He can't hold off the Shadow alone,* Segnbora thought, almost choking with the sheer hate that filled the air. There was nothing the Shadow hated so much as the Fire, except perhaps those who wielded it. Herewiss couldn't last forever, and when his reserves gave out, he would simply be dead.

The first man in a thousand years to have the Fire, the Queen of Darthen, the rightful King of Arlen, most of the forces that Darthen could field—all dead at once. The Shadow, imagining a world all to Itself, darkened.

Inside Segnbora the *mdeihei* were rumbling deadly threats that seemed absolutely empty to her. *What can they do? They're dead!*

Dead?

DeathFire—!

When someone with the Fire died, regardless of whether that person had ever been focused during life, the moment of death itself focused the Fire for one final moment. Even those with just the spark of Flame that most men and women have managed to focus then. That was what gave one's deathword its power.

Segnbora stared with sudden cold purpose at the rising tide of dark malice. Suddenly she understood why Lang had died when he did, and why her parents were murdered. The Shadow had wanted to stop her before this moment, this realization. She held up Skádhwë and looked at it. *It will demand a life of you someday,* Efmaer had said, and now Segnbora was sure which life the dead Queen had meant. The Shadow was betting she wouldn't dare kill herself.

A lethal wound would be enough. She could add enough Fire to what Herewiss had to aid him in holding the Shadow off until the Binding was done. And afterward, he'd heal her—

—or not—

It was a terrible chance she'd be taking. She didn't want to die. But if the Fire she had trapped inside her could be of use here, then…

Behind her Freelorn held up one bleeding arm, and with his free hand reached into the unwrapped saddle-roll for what she had seen him grab before: a fistful of stones and dirt from Lionheugh. He held it to Eftgan's arm; her blood trickled down.

A crash like sudden thunder rocked the scarp and sent men and horses sprawling. Freelorn and the Queen fell apart. Herewiss pitched forward on his face, his Fire all but darkened. More than just hatred pressed down on them from the darkness now. The Shadow was invoking the worst fears of Its enemies, and on all sides men and women screamed and cowered from painful deaths suddenly lived in their own flesh, losses of loved ones, shames that formed darkly in the influence-ridden air. The Dark One still didn't walk among them openly, but was having no trouble driving the defenders to death or madness, one by one.

Out in the darkness, Segnbora saw the hralcins rear up. Ugly unearthly shapes lurched across the scarp at her, singing hungrily and reaching out at her as they had in the Hold. Crabbed claws sought to tear, but Segnbora's screams were frozen in her throat. Only escape was left. Frantically, looking around for a route, she saw Freelorn stand up, cursing with fear and shaking his wounded arm. It wasn't wounded anymore: the cut made by the sacral knife was just a white seam of scar. The Shadow could heal for Its own purposes.

Leaving Eftgan, Lorn stumbled over to Herewiss and shook him conscious with savage efficiency. Segnbora stared at him, confused. This wasn't the usual Freelorn. There was terrible purpose in those eyes. When she met them, Segnbora saw Her in them as she had been seeing Her in everything today. But what she saw in Lorn was different: here was knowledge, foresight. Freelorn knew now what Herewiss had dreamed in the Hold. He had seen the arrow in his back, and had seen himself turn toward death's Door...

Stunned, Segnbora watched him turn away from her with awesome purpose; watched him turn away from the gasping, shaken Herewiss, and rise out of his crouch. The hiss of an arrow whispered through the screaming wind. Slowly, slowly Freelorn sat down with the barbed Reaver shaft standing out from behind his right lung, and pressed a fistful of dirt already stained with Eftgan's blood to the entry point. Then he fell back against Herewiss, and slapped the blood and dirt against the ground—

The terrible pressure of hatred grew suddenly much less as the Royal Binding took hold on the land, quieting the unquiet ghosts, banishing the phantoms of Fyrd and slain Reavers and hralcins. Herewiss's Fire blazed up again as if someone had taken the cup off the candle. But now his mind wasn't on the battle.

"*LORN!!*" Herewiss cried, and without hesitation went limp and fell over again. He had gone out-of-body, gone after his loved to catch him at the last Door, and to prevent him from passing it.

Off on the southern horizon, another darkness began to take shape. This was a more solid one, a heaving black shape that Segnbora had seen before, but didn't dare look upon now, being in a human body. The Shadow had become enraged enough to take on a physical shape and come after them Itself. And It had adopted a form It knew, from past history, to be very effective.

"*Don't look!!*" she cried to the Darthenes.

They hardly needed the warning. Those still alive and conscious after the assault by their worst fears were already hiding their faces from the hideous prospect.

No time to wait for Herewiss to come back, Segnbora thought, shaking all over. *Just have to do it myself—*

Hurriedly she knelt and took Skádhwë two-handed, resting the point a shade to the left of her breastbone. *Mdaha,* she said, and in that moment was informed by her ahead-memory that Herewiss was *not* going to be healing her...

Oh wonderful! Sithesssch!

Sdaha—

Sehe'rae!

She pushed the sword in, hard.

The greedy shadowblade slid into her with shocking ease. At last she found out what it was like to be run through, and tried to scream past the terrible feeling of her heart fibrillating around the intruding blade, trying to beat, trying to beat, failing. All that came out of her throat was a choked cough.

Inside, she felt her Fire leap together with her heart's blood and burst outward. Blind with pain, she groped for support, willing herself to stand and do what she had to. But she found no support. The darkness went red, and then black, and she fell forward...

...a long fall, the longest one, but it had an end. There was a voice crying *Get up! Get up!,* the voice of someone familiar. Her mother perhaps, or Eftgan. Had she overslept again? The Wardress would be furious—

She was lying on something hard. She rolled over to push herself up on her hands and knees, feeling the sword in her fist.

Probably one of those rocks the Dragon's thrashing had dislodged had hit her in the head. She felt weak and stumbly. She pushed upward, shook her head to clear the daze out of it, looked up.

A pang of terror twisted in her heart like a knife of ice. This was no cave. True, there was empty darkness all around, but before her stood two doorposts blacker than any night, going up and up forever, out of sight. Between them stars blazed. Endless depths of them, a patient silent glory she had seen before in dreams and visions, but never for real. This was the last Door, the Door into Starlight.

No, I'm not ready! she cried, staggering to her feet. But her protests made no difference to the insistent forces shoving at her back. They were stronger than she. They impelled her, whispering to her that it was over, that her struggles were done.

The Shore! she thought with longing. *Mother and Father. Lang!* Tears rose at the thought of him, at the image of his last confused grab for the ledge. *Loved, I have a great deal to tell you. Maybe it's not too late.*

But something was wrong. There was a great silence in her mind that shouldn't have been there.

"*Hasai?*" she said, letting herself be pushed toward the Door as she searched in mind for him. *You're dead. Are you there too?*

No answer.

I'm not going! Segnbora thought, on the very threshold. But she had no way to stop herself. She was being pushed too hard, and she was holding something in one of her hands. A darkness...

Swift as thought she used the last-chance block that Shíhan had taught her was for emergency use only. One hand on the hilt, the other bracing the steel from behind.

Segnbora screamed with agony in that eternal silence as Skádhwë, ramming against the impermeable blackness from which it had been torn, sliced deep into her hands. The darkness shoving at her back was merciless, and cared nothing about her anguish. Through her sick pain, Segnbora realized who was pushing her closer to the Door. She fought back, feeling her blood flow from hands and heart. There was something she needed to remember. Something—

I am Who I am. And knowing that, It has no power over me.

Dismay ran through the force that urged her forward. She forced it back, and back, arching herself, and then fell backwards, gasping. Skádhwë fell soundlessly to the invisible floor. Slowly and painfully, she got to her knees, picked Skádhwë up, and stood. It might indeed be her fate to die after she had finished what she had to do.

She turned. Had she been breathing, the breath would have caught in her throat. He was huge, looming above her, dressed in the old clothes he wore while gardening. The big hard hands, stained with leaf-mold and rough with calluses, reached out to her.

"*No!*" she whispered, and almost turned to flee. But there was only one way to run—through the Door and out of life.

That terrible smile leaned closer.

"No!" she said. It was a squeaked word. A little girl's voice, terrified, but still defiant.

The smile lost some of its assuredness.

"No," she said again, more strongly, her voice sounding strange in the utter silence. She raised her head, met those hungry eyes, held them…held them…

He was not as large as he had been. Certainly he was no larger than any other man. He was smaller, in fact, than many she had killed at one time or another.

Raising Skádhwë, she took a step forward and watched the fear spread across his face. Balen had used brute strength to overwhelm the child she had been, but she was a child no longer. He was unarmed, and she was armed with a weapon against which there was no defense. Another step she took, and he backed away. She almost took the final step, but paused. It would be easy to kill him, yes. Possibly enjoyable.

But for how long? Would this be just another form of running away? If she should she instead accept him—

Kill him! her heart said to her.

I give him into your hands, her heart said to her. *Do with him what you will.*

The great silence on this side of the Door surrounded her.

Even he *didn't kill me,* she thought.

She lifted her eyes to Balen again. Trembling, he shot her a terrified glance. In that blunt and brutal face, she saw again what she had seen in Lang, and Herewiss, and Freelorn, and even the Fyrd.

Her.

HerSelf.

Segnbora tossed Skádhwë away.

Very slowly, even with fear, she went to the man, reached out to touch his shoulders. He winced at the touch, as if gentleness burned him.

"*Goddess,*" she said. "Shadow. I know Who You are."

Balen looked at her face, and then looked away again in anguish. Segnbora couldn't bear such terror. She reached out to take his face in her hands.

"Balen," she said, speaking the name aloud for the first time in her life.

He blinked in confusion.

"I seem to be getting a lot of practice at being others, these days," she said. "First Dragons. Then...Myself. I see that this is what the practice was for. To see You for what You are. Just Her, in another suit. A tool to make me what I am, no less than the beautiful face and the ever-filled cup were tools. You were a little rougher on me than you might have been, perhaps. You were the sword. But *my* hand was on the hilt. *I* destroy. And I create..." She gulped, feeling tears start. "Time I got started. I've bound you into my life all this time, my poor 'rapist.' Enough of it. Go free."

He squinted at her in terrified disbelief.

"Beloved," she said. "Go free."

Drawing him close, shaking all over, she laid her lips on his, once and gently. Then she hugged him tight. When she opened her arms, he was gone.

Weak from the sudden release of so much emotion, Segnbora sat down hard on the invisible surface and wiped her eyes, then realized that the wetness on her hands was more than tears. The weakness, too, probably had something to do with her heart's blood running down her surcoat.

Oh Goddess, I forgot, she thought, getting dizzier by the moment. *Blood loss. I have to get back there. Where's Skádhwë? I can't leave it...*

Fumbling, falling to hands and knees again, she began feeling around for the blade. Against the dark floor, this was rather like looking for clear glass in water. The dizziness got worse. She reeled; her sight forsook her. Perhaps she was starting to die.

The sudden pain, an infinitesimally thin line of it, told her she had found Skádhwë again. Grateful for the hint, she grabbed it hard, using the pain to shock herself awake, although she was half dead already.

She pushed herself upright...

...on the cold snow, and opened her eyes. All around her men and women were covering their faces in horror of something that was coming. She had to get up. Where was Skádhwë?...still sheathed. Good.

Left-handed she fumbled for something with which to support herself, and found a stone. She levered herself up to her knees and managed to stand, though a wobbly stance it was, and probably very temporary. She drew Skádhwë, and saw with dismay that it was covered with blood. Shíhan, were he here, would be scandalized! *If you must die, do it with a clean blade,* he'd always said. She whipped the blood off the blade in a quick downward slash, third move of the *edelle* maneuver—

—and Fire whipped down after it.

I am dead, she thought in absolute disbelief, and lifted the sword to stare at it. Fire, raging blue and as impossible to look at as sunlight, trickled down Skádhwë's black edge. Just a double-thread at first, and then more. It grew quickly, a torch's worth of Fire, a Firebrand's worth, a lightningbolt in her hands, burning like a star, throwing her shadow long and black against the cliff.

I have it! she thought in fierce joy, for that one mad moment not caring that she was about to die. She stared backwards at her shadow, the proof of the light—shortlegged, long of neck, wings where she had arms. *I'm whole,* she thought, and laughed, raising the hand that held Skádhwë. The right wing stretched upward, huge. *No!* We're *whole!* The left arm up now; the wing reached up in response. *We may die,* sithesssch*, but we'll do it together!*

—and abruptly, with a deathpain that shot down her right arm to her heart, that wing-shadow tore away from the cliff, casting a shadow of its own, impossibly coming *real*—

The second wing tore free, another pain. She saw webs that gleamed like polished onyx and struts rough with black sapphires. Then came the terrible length of tail, the deadly spine at the end of it whipping free, lashing outward, poised above her to protect. And after the tail, the taloned forelimbs, their diamonds flashing in the blinding Firelight. A neck, the great head, glowing eyes burning not silver now but blue, leaning down over her and glaring past her with impartial challenge at Reavers and Fyrd and the dark something that approached—

"*Hhn' ae mrin'hen,*" said the voice of wind and storm from right above her. "Whole at last, *yes!*"

She stared up at Hasai, so torn between wonder and terror that she couldn't tell anymore whether her weakness came from impending death or sheer astonishment. Her *mdaha* gazed down at her, tilting his head in a gesture of greeting, and turned his attention again to the field and the forces attacking the scarp.

She had heard Dragons roar in her mind. But in the open it was something else. Rocks fell down from the cliff, and the ground shook almost as hard as it had before. Not just one voice roared, but two, ten, a score, a hundred. The *mdeihei* were there too, not as solidly as Hasai, but present enough to be a host of shifting wings and deadly razor-barbs and glowing, glaring eyes, all looking down at the attackers. They sang of a solution to this problem, one that was, for them, not a solution to be feared—a roaring chorus of frightening harmonies and dissonances: *death, death, death!*

Hasai reared his head back, bared the diamond fangs that few had ever survived seeing, and flamed.

The Reavers fled, panicked. Hasai's blast of Dragonfire melted the ground where they had been standing. Even the slow-stalking shadow at the southern edge of the field halted at that, as if stunned. Fyrd scattered in all directions but eastward, where the Sun seemed to be coming up.

The scarp was fenced with fire again, but this time the consuming white of Dragonfire, with a tinge of blue to it; and inside the circle a tremendous shape with wings like thunderclouds was rearing up against the cliff, burning in iron and diamond, ineluctably real. And down by one of his hind talons, hanging onto it for support, a tiny figure bleeding Fire from a wound in the heart stared up and up at what had been, and now *was*.

Segnbora looked with grim, delighted purpose out at the field, at the fleeing Reavers and Fyrd, and down at the thing in her hand that burned with Fire. *"Sithesssch'tdae,"* she sang to Hasai and the other *mdeihei* who stirred in shadow along the ledge, "untidy to leave them running around like this, don't you think?"

The *mdeihei* sang angry assent in a thunder that echoed from the surrounding mountains, causing a bass obbligato of avalanches to follow.

"Must we send them *rdahaih?*" Hasai sang.

Segnbora stepped forward to the edge of the shelf where they stood, only partially aware of Herewiss's and Freelorn's prone forms. Breathing or not, they'd have to wait until later. "I don't know," she said, and raised Skádhwë, thinking hard.

It can't be done, they say—a gating for more than fifty. However—

She closed her eyes, not needing the physical ones to see at the moment, and drew up a great flood of Power from the tremendous supply they had always told her she'd have. In mind she saw them, every Fyrd in the valley and for miles around. She hated them, and loved them, and did what was necessary. She poured the Flame out of her as if opening a floodgate, until the valley was awash with it.

It was simple to gather up the minds of every Fyrd in the area and hold them all under the surface of that Flame until they drowned. *Stop showing off,* she told herself severely. *You may drop dead in a moment, and there's business to be done here.* Yet she laughed in pleasure as she thought it, and Hasai and the *mdeihei* went off in a thunderous accompaniment of hissing Dracon laughter. Whether she lived or died, she was going to enjoy this. She had waited a lifetime for it.

The Reavers and the Arlene mercenaries at the other side of the field were fleeing, and she stared across at them, angry and pleased. She could easily kill them all, but she knew Someone Who would prefer it otherwise, if at all possible.

So, she thought, and reached out in heart to feel them all, every last one, mind and soul together. The Rodmistresses had said it was impossible, but behind her she had a supporting multitude who would testify otherwise if she asked them to. She *was* that multitude. She could contain universes.

Immersing herself in the minds of her enemies, she became them. Before they had a chance to recover from being *her,* she stepped to the cliff's edge and lifted Skádhwë. With it she drew four great slashing lines of Flame that fell onto the darkened field, and grew, and grew—

Suddenly the ground within the lines was missing, replaced by five thousand different images blurred together—some of them of the Arlene countryside, or of Prydon city, some of them of the strange cold country beyond the mountains from which the Reavers came. Into the crammed-together vistas fell men and women who cried out in terror and were gone. She closed the door behind them with a word and a sweep of Skádhwë, and glanced up in thanks at the glowing eyes that hung over her. Then she turned south.

There, something dark stirred in its mantle of blackness and glared utter hatred at her. She looked back at It calmly, having loved It before, and unafraid to do once more what was necessary. She reached out to grasp the forces that Dragons could manipulate, and took one more step forward, right off the edge of the cliff. There she stood on empty air.

"Come out and meet us if you dare!" she cried. The song winding around the words held in it the ultimate challenge: inescapable love. Behind her the *mdeihei* echoed the song in perilous harmonies.

Trembling, Segnbora stood there while the darkness gathered Itself up into that terrible crushing wave she had seen before, full of screams and blood and ancient death. It rose higher and higher above her. She lifted up Skádhwë's flaming length and stood her ground, letting her eyes sink into the Shadow's darkness, becoming It, accepting It for her own, her dark side, Her other Shadow.

It trembled toward her—then gathered Itself down into a shuddering ball of fear and thwarted hatred, and vanished.

The wind died abruptly, and the sky began to clear. Four thousand Darthenes stood in an empty field with no one left to fight.

Segnbora took a last gasp of breath and walked back onto the cliff, beginning to feel mortal again for the first time since she had turned Skádhwë against herself. Behind a rock Eftgan lay breathing shallowly. Beside her, two forms struggled to sit up, helping each other. One of them had an arrow in him, but it didn't seem to be paining him much. As Segnbora came up to them, the taller of the two reached out to his loved and touched the arrow's protruding shaft. It vanished in a flicker of Fire, as did the place where it had gone in.

She knelt beside them and laid Skádhwë over her knees—a burning shadow, a piece of the night set on Fire. They stared at it.

"You did it," Freelorn whispered. *"You did it!"*

She smiled at him. "All your fault, my liege."

"But what did you *do?*" Herewiss was looking at her with such a mixture of joy and perplexity that she could have both laughed and cried at once. "I saw what you did to yourself," he said. "Why aren't you dead? And where did Cillmod and all those Reavers go?"

"I sent them home, for the time being." She looked down at her surcoat, brushed at it. There was a neat tear where Skadhwë had gone in through cloth and mail, but that was all. The scar was a faint white seam just to one side of the nightmare's bite.

"I told you," said a great voice above her. "Dragons are quick to heal."

Silver-blue light fell about her as someone else bent low to look curiously at the place where the shadowblade had gone in. She gazed up at him—her shadow casting a shadow of his own now—and at last, the tears came. She reached up to the tremendous jaw as it dropped open, and very gently laid her hand in the Dragon's mouth, as she had feared to do, as she would never fear to do again. The jaws closed, and self joined with self.

"Now what, *sda'sithesssch?*"

"Now, *mda'sithesssch,*" she said, gathering him close and laughing through the tears that fell on the sapphire hide, "there's a King to escort to his throne. Let's get busy!"

sixteen

Some gifts are so great that the only way the recipient can express his gratitude is to immediately give the gift to someone else. A dangerous business, this, among fickle humankind, who often see such generosity as indicative of a thoughtless heart. But in such a matter, do as your heart directs you. In the last reckoning, She is both giver and receiver, acting both parts to increase the joy of both—and if humankind doesn't understand, She does.

(*Charestics*, 118)

They leaned on the walls and looked down into the dark streets of Darthis. No light burned anywhere—not so much as a hearthfire or candle or lamp. Below them the city dreamed in a silver pallor of moonlight, though there was a shifting and stirring in the Square under the walls of the Black Palace.

A few thousand people stood down there, quiet or murmuring, waiting for the Queen to strike the first sparks of the Midsummer needfire and distribute it among them. Most of those waiting were only concerned with their part in the festival—lighting the candles and lamps they carried from the new fire and racing through the city with it, spreading luck and laughter. But a few looked up toward the palace walls and stared fascinated at something strange.

Blue Fire flickered there, dancing about a long slender shape that seemed to be too dark to be a Rod. And there was another light there, a pair of silver-blue globes that looked uncannily like eyes staring downward. The more perceptive in the crowd had even noticed that the moonlight didn't fall on them. It was blocked away by a huge winged shape that seemed there when one looked away from it, and not there when one looked at it straight.

Whatever they saw, no one seemed particularly bothered by any of these peculiarities. This was, after all, Midsummer's Eve, when magic was loose in the world.

Down in the square, flint struck steel, and a spark nested in tinder and began to grow into flames. The cheering began. Viols and trumpets and kettledrums struck up a jubilant music that echoed off the walls, and effectively drowned out a deeper music several stories up. *"Hn 'aa 'se sithesssch mnek-kej-sta untühe au 'lhhw't'dae,"* the music said, a voice like a trio of bass instruments playing a lazy, cheerful processional.

"Ae, mdaha'esssch," sang a softer voice, in a raspy alto. "We may as well enjoy the rest while we can…"

"There won't be much of it," Hasai said, unfolding and folding his wings in resignation. He spoke in precognitive tense, but with good humor; the melody woven about his words said plainly that he preferred action to peace and quiet. "Arlen will be astir like thunderstorm air for months. If Cillmod doesn't already know who was responsible for what happened at Bluepeak, he will very shortly. The war with Darthen will soon open."

"And the Queen forges her new crown tomorrow," Segnbora groaned. A formal occasion first thing in the morning was the last thing she needed. "All I want is to sleep late."

"You may, if you please. I will teach you how, now that you have a *sdaha's* proper timesense. Will a month or so be enough, *sithesssch?*"

The steps on the battlement were no surprise. Two hours ago Segnbora had remembered hearing them, and she had been waiting for them ever since. "If he *did* know," the shorter of the two approaching men said on reaching the top of the stairs, "it explains why he made the bastard Chancellor of the Exchequer."

"To keep an eye on him?"

"Sounds like something my father might have done. This also explains how he managed to get the backing of the High Houses. But even if he can go into Lionhall, he doesn't know the Ritual, he's no Initiate—or if he is, he's botching it. Arlen is ready for me now."

Freelorn and Herewiss looked strange out of surcoats and mail. They leaned on the wall, one on either side of her, in softboots and britches and shirts. Herewiss looked up at the dark shape that blocked-but-didn't-block the Moon away. "How much are you there, *lhhw'Hasai?*"

"As much as my *sdaha* needs me to be. Or as I need to be. Since we're one, there's little difference…"

"Where were you an hour or so ago?" Herewiss said to Segnbora. "Eftgan was looking for you. Wanted your help with the needfire, or something."

"I was flying," Segnbora said, nodding at the sky.

Herewiss nodded soberly. She shared a gentle look with him, understanding now from her own experience how complete his underhearing must be, reaching even to others' most private thoughts. "I have to thank you," she said.

"You don't have to anything. You did it yourself."

"So I did. And you mediated some of that doing with me, saw me into the situations I'd need to get where I am. You had little reason to give me such a gift, either," Segnbora said. "I tried to move in between you and your loved, a while back. You must have noticed."

Herewiss nodded, looking grave. But not too much so. "These days, I don't let old reasons interfere with what I want to do. And maybe, even when I was angriest at you, maybe I saw something…"

"Who I was?" she said.

"Yes. A liaison. There's a whole race sharing the Kingdoms with us that not even the human Marchwarders understand properly—they have the language, but not the body that forms it. But there was more. You were a catalyst. And will continue to be. Things will be happening that need me—things I couldn't do without you and your Dragons. Likewise there are things you couldn't manage without *me*. I'm part of a solution. And more…"

She fell silent, nodding, already having hints of what the "more" was. This was a small problem. Sometimes the ahead-memories came too fast, and she had trouble deciding what to share, what to keep to herself.

She shrugged. The future was merely another kind of present to a Dragon, malleable as the past, part of the game. What mattered was what the player intended to be.

In one word, her newfound Name, she told them.

"We'll keep your secret," Freelorn said just above a whisper.

Segnbora smiled at them, knowing that the One she meant to hear her Name had heard it through them; then waved good night, and headed for the stairs.

Along the upper parapet, Hasai lazily put out a single forefoot—all he needed to do to keep up with her. "No more words?" he said.

"What should I say?"

Hasai lowered his head to gaze back down the parapet. Segnbora followed his glance, seeing Freelorn take back from Herewiss the lovers' cup she had left them, drain it—and find it still full.

"That," Hasai said. "Forever."

Lost between laughter and tears of joy, Segnbora nodded, reached out to her *mdaha,* and led him off into their future, and to bed.

On Time, Calendars, And Related Subjects

The motions of the Middle Kingdoms' world around its Sun match those of Earth around Sol (except for negligible variations, such as those caused by sister planets missing in their solar system and present in ours). Their year is therefore the same length as ours—365 days, 5 hours, 48 minutes, 48-odd seconds. Though in Segnbora's time clocks still have only hour hands, the astronomers of the Kingdoms have evolved their own methods of handling the year, and the little pieces of it that tend to pile up as time passes and throw calendars out of alignment with the seasons.

Both Arlen and Darthen use a 360-day "year" of four 90-day "seasons" that correspond to our winter, spring, summer, and fall. Days are counted straight through each season, and spoken of as "the fifth of Winter," "the thirty-eighth of Summer," and so forth. In addition, the First of each season is always a major holiday, tied to solstice or equinox—Opening Night for Winter (the only one of the holidays that doesn't fall directly on solstice or equinox), Maiden's Day for Spring, Midyear's Day for Summer, and the Harvest Festival (either Lion's Day or Eagle's Day) for Fall. The five remaining days are intercalated and belong to no season: they are placed between the end of Fall and the beginning of Winter, and during these cold days at the bottom of the year, the Dreadnights as they're called, no enterprise is begun, no childnaming or marriage celebrated. They are the Shadow's nights, and unlucky. Every fourth year a sixth intercalary day (in Arlen *Endethne*, "Lady's Day," in Darthen *Aerrudej*, "the Goddess's Joke") is added between the Dreadnights and Opening Night, to deal with the need for a leap-year day.

However, this still leaves a significant fraction of time out of the reckoning. The addition of the leap-day to compensate for the 5h-48m-48s leftover at year's end is in fact an overcompensation. If left uncorrected, each year will be 11.2 minutes short. This may not sound like much, but in our world in the past has led to awful misalignment of the calendar year with the seasons—the first day of spring falling in December, for example. But this backward drift of dates is preventable by any number of methods. The astronomers of the Kingdoms found that the eleven-minute deficit will amount to a full day's error in 128y-208d-13h-38m-21.125s. Therefore, once every 128 years, that 208th day (which by our calendar would be July 19th) is dropped from the year entirely, or rather converted to July 20th; that date in turn becomes the 29th of Summer rather than the 28th, and is called the Festival of the Lost Day. (The festival is devoted to pranks, pratfalls, drinking sprees, and attempts to lose things, usually unwanted ones. There are also lying contests, with prizes for the best explanation of where the Lost Day went.) This system of adjustment runs independently of that for leap-year days. Though it would probably be more efficient to combine the adjustment systems, as our culture does, the Kingdoms' astronomers are quick to point out that this would mean one less holiday.

It is quite true that even this adjustment is not totally sufficient to keep the calendar in line with the seasons and the Sun. There is still an unadjusted error that makes the year too long by 0.0003 day, which will pile up to three days in each 10,000 years. However, in the words of Talia d' Calath, the Grand Royal Astronomer to King Berad of Darthen, "it is possible to worry too much, too far in advance." The Dragons have promised to remind human beings to insert another one-day intercalary day every 3300 years—though there is still disagreement over why they laughed so hard when they promised.

There are of course many minor local holidays not mentioned here. But neither Arlene nor Darthene calendars include anything like weeks or months. One may indicate a given day by season and number: or say "four days ago," or "six days from now," or "a month and three days," etc. "Months" (actually the word is *isten* in both languages, very like the Greek Λνχ'αβασ, which we translate as "lichtgang" or "Moonreturn") are sometimes broken down to 29 days for counting purposes, but this is rare. Mostly a month is reckoned from a phase of the Moon to its next occurrence, most frequently full to full. This might be expected in a largely agrarian culture, where the times of planting are important. But to the people of the Kingdoms, the Moon is the living sigil of the Goddess, mirroring Her changes in its own as it slides from Maiden's slim crescent to Bride's and Mother's white full to Crone's waning sickle to Moondark perilous and hidden; and for the most part people have a fondness for the Moon and enjoy reckoning by it, without resource to numbers.

Astronomers—and, of course, sorcerers and people with the blue Fire—are cognizant of such lunar functions as node crossings and regression of nodes, apogee and perigee and advance of the perigee point, librations and nutations, and eclipses both lunar and solar, such being important to their work. But (and very sensibly) no one has ever particularly cared about what the lunar calendar does in relation to the solar one. The only real notice taken of alignment between the two is in mention of Nineteen-Years' Night, when the Moon is full on Opening Night and wreaking with sorcery or Fire is particularly potent.

There is a tendency for Moon cycles to be referred to by name, the names differing from area to area. For example, the first full Moon of Spring, and the days following it from waning to dark to new crescent to full again, is usually called the "Song Moon" in Arlen, while some Darthenes call it the "Unicorn's Moon," and some others, the "Maiden's Moon" or the "Mad Moon." Special note is taken of the Harvest Moon in most places, both because of the shortening of its rising time and in memory of the bloody harvest cut at Bluepeak during one of its risings an age ago; the full Moon that follows the Harvest Moon is always the Lion's or Eagle's Moon, in Earn's and Héalhra's memory.

Since the memory of the times before the Catastrophe has largely been lost, years are counted from the coming of the Dragons and the destruction of the Dark, and noted by number and the abbreviation for *pai Ajnedäre derüwin*, "after the Arrival." An example: Segnbora's birthday is Spring the 57th, 2098 p.a.d.

On Dracon Anatomy And Physiology

The Dragons are perhaps purposely vague about their very beginnings. "Thinking about a time before their own consciousness," d'Welcaen reports, "makes them nervous." But the earliest Dracon memories recall a time when the Homeworld was populated by plant-analogs and other life forms. There was a food chain, and Dragons had use for the internal organs which now exist only in extremely debased vestigial forms.

Somewhere along the line—possibly due to changes in the Homeworld's orbit, or in its star's characteristics—the planet's seas began to evaporate, and its atmosphere to strip off. The Dragons report this as having taken many thousands of their lifetimes. Converting this time to human standards is difficult, and gives answers ranging from one to six million years. This may seem like quite a while, but it isn't really, for an organism whose average generation is from four to six thousand years. The Dragons had to adapt in a hurry to the changes in their environment.

Exactly how they did it so quickly is another question for which there is no clear answer; no mdeihei *native to such ancient times remain extant in the Dragons' minds. Rodmistresses and other Fire-using adepts who have been working with Dragons since the events following the Advocate's intervention in 2927 p.a.d. I have determined that the species possesses its own variant of Power, of which Dragonflame occasionally becomes an embodiment. Given this, they say, and given time enough, and intention, the changes themselves are no mystery, though the details will always remain a matter of interest. Yet when the DragonChief was asked about the instrumentality involved in the change, the only answer to come back was straightforward (and to the Dracon mind, obvious): "The Immanence did it." To the Dragons, miracle, as in the cultures of the Middle Kingdoms, is seen as part of the natural order—a tool occasionally used without prejudice by a God who has better things to do than be otiose.*

Already silicon-boron based—and what their ancient atmosphere and "seas" consisted of is still a matter for conjecture—the Dragons' evolution went or was taken in the most efficient possible direction. Their anatomy began adjusting toward extreme lightness, for maximum efficiency in soaring in search of food. As food got scarcer due to increased irradiation, mutations became common—including possibly the most successful one of all, the alteration of silane rings in the black wing-membranes to effectively turn them into giant solar cells, using already-existing neural pathways for conduction of generated bioelectricity. Dragons were born with this mutation, needing no food in the old sense. They thrived and multiplied, soaring further and further sunward for nourishment. The increased irradiation seems to have induced more gene changes and mutations in brain physiology, so that the "highflyers" became increasingly able to manipulate "force"—magnetic fields, gravitational fields, and other instrumentalities less classifiable to humans. Organs used for digestion, respiration, and elimination slowly went vestigial until finally the "late model" Dragon as we know it was complete—an efficient, flying energy-storage machine, spaceworthy, tolerant of extreme high and low temperatures (as had become commonplace on the Homeworld), and able to express that energy as Dragonfire and use it as tool and weapon.

The reasons for that particular manifestation are debatable, but d'Welcaen suggests that Dragons feel about their mouths as humans feel about their hands. Dracon psychology says that language is the primary means of effective survival: which perhaps explains why, even after their development of under-speech, the Dragons never gave up communication by way of vocal speech. Even their tongues still work after all these centuries—though they're not necessary: Dracon sound generation long ago went over to non-acoustic mechanisms like those of whales. Fluid-filled or stressed-solid-filled cavities stimulated by "muscle" contraction, or catalytic chemical reactions, or neural/membrane synergies, or all three, allow Dragons to communicate with precision and stunning variation in almost any medium except empty space, and also permit the super-prolonged hisses, three- to eighteen-tone chords, and choral-verbal speech for which they're best known.

Dragonfire, according to d'Welcaen, is a phenomenon originally closely allied to "manipulation of force," a matter no more complicated for a Dragon than breathing air is for a human: a Dragoncel can flame before it can talk. In the very beginning, this would have been a survival characteristic—though a Dragon's ability to melt several tons of lead-bearing stone over itself to protect it from a starstorm, or blast its way out of the covering again, is no longer a necessity in the Dragons' new homeworld. (Indeed, the Dracon name for the

Sun that shines on the Middle Kingdoms is hh-Aass'te're, *"the Shallows"— a warm, cozy little star, tame and safe compared to the mad fire of the Homestar in its last days.) These days Dragonfire is for show; for building; for* nn's'raihle, *in a particularly heated argument; and, when words fail at last, for mating fights and the most serious disagreements, when hottest fire decides who will reproduce, or win the discussion, and who will go very suddenly* mdahaih.

DIANE DUANE was born in Manhattan in 1952, a Year of the Dragon. She was raised in the New York City suburbs, on the south shore of Nassau County on Long Island, where all through her childhood she wrote to amuse herself. In high school she won a New York State Board of Regents Science and Nursing scholarship, and her first studies in college were toward a degree in astrophysics. A total inability to handle calculus and other higher math drove her instead into the arms of the biological sciences, and she used the nursing half of her scholarship to attend Pilgrim State Hospital School of Nursing on Long Island, from which she graduated in 1974 as a registered nurse with an honors specialty in psychiatry. She spent the next two years practicing the art at Payne Whitney Clinic of New York Hospital.

Feeling the need for a change of pace, she spent the next couple of years working as assistant to television and science fiction writer David Gerrold. During this period she wrote her first novel, *The Door into Fire*, which saw print for the first time in 1979. One book led to another, as so often happens, and since then she has written more than thirty novels, various comics and computer games, and fifty or sixty animated and live-action screenplays for characters as widely assorted as Batman, Jean-Luc Picard, Siegfried the Volsung, and Scooby-Doo. Together with her husband of fifteen years, Northern Irish-born novelist and screenwriter Peter Morwood, she lives in a townland in the far west of County Wicklow in Ireland, in company with three cats and four seriously overworked computers—an odd but congenial environment for the staging of space battles and the leisurely pursuit of total galactic domination. She gardens (weeding, mostly), collects recipes and cookbooks, manages the Owl Springs Partnership's website at:

http://www.owlsprings.com

She dabbles in astronomy, language studies, computer graphics, and fractals, and tries to find ways to make enough time to just lie around and watch anime.

Come check out our web site for details on these Meisha Merlin authors!

Kevin J. Anderson

Robert Asprin

Robin Wayne Bailey

Edo van Belkom

Janet Berliner

Storm Constantine

John F. Conn

Diane Duane

Sylvia Engdahl

Rain Graves

Jim Grimsley

George Guthridge

Keith Hartman

Beth Hilgartner

P. C. Hodgell

Tanya Huff

Janet Kagan

Caitlin R. Kiernan

Lee Killough

George R. R. Martin
Lee Martindale
Jack McDevitt
Mark McLaughlin
Sharon Lee & Steve Miller
James A. Moore
John Morressy
Adam Niswander
Andre Norton
Jody Lynn Nye
Selina Rosen
Kristine Kathryn Rusch
Pamela Sargent
Michael Scott
William Mark Simmons
S. P. Somtow
Allen Steele
Mark Tiedeman
Freda Warrington
David Nial Wilson

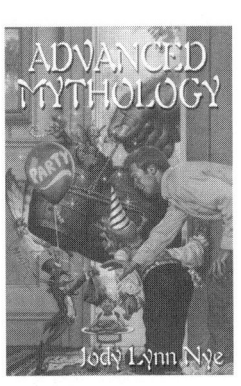

http://www.MeishaMerlin.com